Studies in Short Fiction

Studies in Short Fiction

FIVE SHORT NOVELS AND TWENTY-FIVE STORIES

Edited by

DOUGLAS A. HUGHES

Washington State University

HOLT, RINEHART AND WINSTON, INC.
New York Chicago San Francisco
Atlanta Dallas Montreal Toronto

Library of Congress Catalog Card Number: 70-131287
ISBN: 0-03-084188-7
Printed in the United States of America
2 3 4 5 090 9 8 7 6 5 4

For My Brother Roger

The process of reading is not a
half-sleep, but, in the highest sense, a
gymnast's struggle . . . the reader
is to do something for himself, must
be on the alert, must himself or
herself construct indeed the poem,
argument, history, metaphysical
essay—the text furnishing the hints,
the clue, the start or framework.
Not the book needs so much to be
the complete thing, but the reader
of the book does.

Walt Whitman

Preface

The aim of this book is to introduce college students to short fiction as a particular type of prose narrative and to provide a chronological sampling to indicate the development of short fiction in the last two centuries. As a text for any introductory course in literature the book is flexible enough to permit either a historical or technical approach to fiction.

Studies in Short Fiction is a collection of twenty-five short stories and five novellas divided into three historical periods—nineteenth century, modern, and contemporary fiction. The introduction briefly traces the history of prose fiction from ancient times to the present. It explains the general characteristics of short fiction at various periods of its development and differentiates between the short story and short novel. The appendix includes succinct, clear remarks on narrative techniques by six commentators, including the late E. M. Forster, Percy Lubbock, and Wayne C. Booth.

I have tried to include both the best and most representative short narratives, especially in British and American literature. Anthologizing works by George Moore, Elizabeth Bowen, and Robert Penn Warren, who have contributed measurably to the short story in English, took valuable space away from important European writers. If space had been available, I would like to have included works by Gogol, Turgenev, Verga, Gide, Camus, and Beckett.

I would like to express my thanks to my wife for her assistance on this book and for being a father as well as mother for a number of weeks; to my friend Dick Kappler for his new translation of Chekhov's "The Lady with a Dog"; and to my colleague Don Ross for his critical contributions.

D. A. H.

October 1970
Pullman, Washington

Contents

Introduction

I

Imaginative literature as art may be defined as the controlled objectification of human emotion and will for contemplation and appreciation. What in general distinguishes most modern short fiction from the bulky body of prose stories and tales recited or written between the Ice Age and the nineteenth century is the modern writer's deliberate effort to mold and form his material into art. This statement does not deny that some ancient prose narratives were works of genius, but prose *as art,* something other than formless entertainment or moral didacticism, is decidedly new, at least from a historical point of view. Narrative fiction or story-telling, of course, is as ancient as the species and recorded narrative in the Western world is as old as Homer, but the novel and the short story, as distinct prose works, are rather recent literary developments. The novel was born less than two hundred and fifty years ago and passed out of its adolescence and into maturity in the late nineteenth and early twentieth centuries. The short story and novella, with their filial bonds to and dependence on the early novel, appeared later in the mid-nineteenth century, developed cautiously in the subsequent decades, and then dramatically achieved near-perfection in the first half of the twentieth century, particularly in the United States and Ireland. Thus, it is a curious paradox that although the short prose narrative is the oldest of literary types, it was the last form—after epic, lyric, drama, and the novel—to realize its *artistic* potential.

When we look at the ancient background of narrative prose, we discover that prose—as opposed to poetry—was universally neglected by the creative artists of the time, being employed principally in light entertainment or in moral instruction. The first recorded stories, called legends, fables, parables, or tales, were unsophisticated narratives growing out of an oral tradition that stretched back beyond recorded history. The art-conscious Athenians, those laughing pessimists who invented tragedy and comedy and refined lyric and narrative verse, even they did not develop prose fiction into an art form. In fact, the Greeks did not deign to devote one of the nine muses to prose fiction.

Although in the Middle Ages poetry continued to dominate literature, two significant narrative forms appeared that would later influence the Renaissance tale and eighteenth-century novel. The French developed a variation of the fable called the *fabliau,* an earthy, realistic short narrative in verse. The realism and economy of the *fabliau* made an impression on Renaissance writers, including Geoffrey Chaucer who adapted the form in a number of *The Canterbury Tales.* If the *fabliau,* with its piquant character, may be considered the crude short story of the Middle Ages, the medieval romance may be regarded as a novel-like narrative. A lengthy, artificial story of adventure, courtly love and religious faith, the romance was written almost exclusively for the nobility and embodied the ideals of feudal life. In England many of the romances dealt with the adventures and exploits of King Arthur and his Knights of the Round Table. In the fifteenth century Sir Thomas Malory collected and imaginatively rewrote these as *Le Morte Darthur,* the best medieval romance in English owing to its beauty of form and language.

The Renaissance was man's reawakening to the possibilities of temporal life and a turning away from the medieval notion that life is cruel and dreary and that man ought mainly to prepare himself for life after death. Renaissance man cautiously embraced life, divested himself of the idealism that characterized the Middle Ages, and showed a curiosity and concern for what is real in life. Therefore, narrative of this time in verse and prose became richer in substance, more realistic, and better proportioned. Boccacio in prose and Chaucer in verse broke with the custom of relying on ancient material and depicted contemporary men and situations. Their tales exhibit sharp outlines, minimum background material, and clearly organized plots. But despite the enormous strides taken in the Renaissance toward the polished short story and novel, the time and conditions were not right for the flowering of these prose forms, and it would be centuries before narrative prose would surpass the tales of Boccacio.

While drama and lyric poetry flourished in Renaissance England, narrative prose, for the most part, languished. "The very fact that Shakespeare wrote in English," says Walter Allen in *The English Novel,* "made the novel . . . impossible except as an occasional sport." Not only did Shakespeare and drama in general dominate the Elizabethan period, but no strong prose tradition existed and no large reading audience was ready to support prose works. Most of the tales of the time were crudely designed and without originality. The pastoral romances digested by the aristocracy were overly long, unrealistic works about improbable characters, works so dull to modern tastes that it is difficult to imagine they were once read with pleasure by sophisticated members of society.

The development of fictional prose in England appeared arrested in the seventeenth century and the major accomplishments were recorded in poetry with the refinement of the heroic couplet. T. O. Beachcroft in his recent study of the English short story observes, "The poetic genius of the century for saying something short yet poetically significant, a characteristic that we see in Donne, Herbert, or Marvell, has no counterpart in prose fiction." Nevertheless, a major change in literature was taking place in the seventeeth century throughout Europe as men more and more demanded an objective examination of the world. At a time when rationality and science were blossoming, prose took on a new importance and became increasingly accepted in serious literature. Moreover, by the end of the seventeenth century printing had become relatively inexpensive, making it possible for travel books, journals, and polemical pamphlets to enjoy wide readership. In England periodicals like the *Tatler* and *Spectator* sprang up, and the informal prose essay, the staple of these periodicals, occasionally took the form of a short, moralistic tale, a hesitating step toward the short story as we know it.

Thus, early in the eighteenth century the social and aesthetic conditions were ripe in England and parts of Europe for the rise of the novel, a middle-class genre which deals objectively and realistically with the everyday world. After a seemingly interminable delay, prose fiction was brought to life in the art of Daniel Defoe, Samuel Richardson, and Henry Fielding in England and Pierre de Marivaux and Abbé Prévost in France. Although the novel now began to attract creative imaginations that formerly would have worked in narrative poetry or the drama, few writers explored the realm of short fiction, partly because of its inherent formal restrictions. A century would pass after the emergence of the novel before the art of short fiction would appear in the United States, Russia, and France.

II

In spite of the influence of such seminal figures as Edgar Allan Poe and Nicolai Gogol, the refinement of short fiction in the nineteenth century really depended less on single innovators than on changing cultural conditions. At the close of the eighteenth century the intellectual and emotional climate of the Western world had begun to change, and the dry winds of rationality, realism, and didacticism that had characterized the Age of Reason gradually subsided. By the beginning of the nineteenth century the moist, beautiful haze of romanticism was creeping over Europe and

America and a radically new way of viewing the self and individualism came into being. Romanticism, Wylie Sypher has written, "was essentially a counterattack of the self on the world outside—on the world invented by Descartes and Newton and the scientists who followed them." This solitary self, which has remained alienated and either angry or self-pitying, has provided the modern short story with its most important subject. The late Frank O'Connor observed that the short story has tended from the outset to be romantic insofar as it has been generally indifferent to the community and has been preoccupied with dark, lonely individuals, with what he called the "submerged populations." "Always in the short story," wrote O'Connor, "there is this sense of outlawed figures wandering about the fringes of society, superimposed sometimes on symbolic figures whom they caricature and echo—Christ, Socrates, Moses."

Romanticism ushered in a new and important attitude toward pleasure and the purposes of art, an attitude which would culminate in aestheticism and the notion of art for art's sake in the last decade of the nineteenth century. Wordsworth, speaking for many of his contemporaries, says in the Preface to *Lyrical Ballads* that "the grand elementary principle of pleasure" constitutes "the naked and native dignity of man." This representative statement and all that it implies is a radical departure from the general cultural attitude toward pleasure that existed for centuries in the Western world. Wordsworth, of course, was speaking primarily of the pleasures of the imagination, and at this time the large and growing literate public began demanding new and more intense sensations, revealing an appetite for mysterious and shocking adventures in far off places and for narratives dealing with horror and mysticism. The deadening moralistic cast of literature was being peeled away. Such a dramatic cultural change was highly significant in preparing the way for the appearance of short fiction as an art form, because a tale's emotional effect rather than its ideas or moral posture became of primary importance. Thus, writers more and more became concerned with those devices and techniques which would achieve the most intense impression. An American romantic poet and story writer led the way here in defining this fiction of total effect.

Edgar Allan Poe, often regarded as the father of the short story as an art form, was perhaps the single most important influence in shaping the genre. Poe was not only one of the first great talents to work in the short story but was the first both to proclaim the uniqueness of the form and to articulate the general principles that would characterize the short story for a century. Theorizing on the short story in a review of Hawthorne's *Twice-Told Tales,* he asserted that a successful tale ought to be short enough to be read in one sitting. "The ordinary story," wrote Poe in 1842, "is objectionable from its length. . . . As it cannot be read at one sitting, it deprives itself . . . of the immense force derivable from *totality.*" He went on to say that the short-story writer ought to accommodate his incidents to a preconceived, desired effect, that everything in the story ought to contribute to establishing this effect. "In the whole composition there should be no word written of which the tendency, direct or indirect, is not to be the one preestablished design." Thus, the reader leaves the story with a single, vivid impression which is not attributable to plot, theme, or any other single element but rather to the harmonious blending of all elements into a unified effect. Whatever interferes with this unity, Poe stated, must be rigorously excluded from the work, and therefore the traditional informality, digressiveness, and wordiness of the short narrative would have to be abandoned.

After Poe's formulations and exemplary tales, the short story in the nineteenth century became an aesthetic challenge to skillful writers everywhere much as the sonnet had tested the technical expertise of poets in earlier centuries. For the first time the short story was recognized as a new and distinct literary form, one differentiated from both the old discursive brief tale and the less intense, more far-ranging novella. In one important respect the early masters of the short story did *not* follow Poe's lead. Unlike Poe, who had dealt with the strange and extraordinary, they concerned themselves with dramatizing the *ordinary* in human affairs, with common men in real situations, thus establishing one of the form's conventions.

The artistic story found a ready and convenient vehicle in the newspapers and periodicals that had proliferated throughout Europe and America in the nineteenth century. Designed to satisfy the verbal appetite of the rising bourgeoisie, these publications played a vital role in promoting and sustaining the modern short story. Some of de Maupassant's finest stories appeared in the daily papers of Paris, and the importance of magazines to American short-story writers over the past hundred years could hardly be exaggerated.

Although the short story gained enthusiastic acceptance in America, France, and Russia after the middle of the nineteenth century, it was neglected in England almost until the end of the century. The reasons why England did not take up the short story are many, beginning no doubt with the fact that the country was enjoying the high noon of that great rambling structure called the Victorian novel. Furthermore, as H. E. Bates has pointed out, the short story cannot tolerate "a weight of words," i.e., fancy and inflated language, or moralistic posturing, two characteristics of the popular English novel of the time. In contrast, American writers were immediately attracted to the new form that seemed perfectly suited to the pragmatic, frenetic, swiftly changing quality of American life. And Americans, from Irving and Poe, to Barthelme and Gass, have always been in the vanguard of short-story experimenters.

In general, nineteenth-century short stories are straightforward, realistic narratives wherein action determines meaning and themes are clearly and explicitly stated. While many persons are bewildered by the ambiguity and density of twentieth-century stories, few readers have difficulty understanding nineteenth-century narratives. One reason for this is that the early masters of the story, unlike modern writers, move their narratives forward smoothly with controlled plots to an all-important conclusion. Furthermore, nineteenth-century narrative rarely breaks the pattern of chronological time and generally is presented from an omniscient point of view, suggesting that the narrator is in complete control. There is, in fact, a clarity and orderliness in nineteenth century fiction which is *ostensibly* lacking in the stories and novels of this century.

Twentieth-century fiction—whether long or short—has had the painful and difficult responsibility of telling the truth about modern man's predicament and of rendering a clear image of the complexity of modern life. No longer possessing the naïve confidence that allowed the great nineteenth-century novelists to tackle the big burly questions of life, modern writers have been forced by circumstances to be more modest in their aims; they have hoped to apprehend and dramatize small but significant insights concerning man's experience. In a world in which everything is eddying and in flux, the short story appears particularly well suited to depict and interpret these fragments of experience. In his book *The American Short Story* William Peden has written, "The short story has become the literary mirror for reflecting an age in which the new tends to be obsolete by tomorrow; in which only change seems permanent and ultimate destruction perhaps the only reality; in which old values, old mores, old ideas are reevaluated in terms of next week's headlines."

Reflecting the quality of twentieth-century life, many of the best short stories of the modern period are complex, remarkably subtle, and downright difficult to understand—and many may profitably be read several times. Very much like poets, writers such as Joyce, Anderson, Mansfield, and Hemingway refined the techniques of the short story, making certain that each word and phrase contributed in some way to the story as a whole. Without wholly abandoning realism, these writers infused their narratives with symbols and a suggestive ambiguity that seemed to capture the truth of their experience. By attenuating plot, reducing action, and fracturing chronological time, writers in this century have shifted the focus of the short story from the conclusion to the middle, or a moment before the end. Joyce, and later others, relied on what he called an "epiphany" to illuminate the meaning of his story, an epiphany being a sudden revelation near but not at the end of a story which clarifies the seemingly pointless action and pedestrian thought of the characters. Far from being arbitrary or whimsical, these profound alterations in fiction simply reflect the enormous cultural and scientific changes that have occurred in twentieth-century life. For example, when modern writers radically departed from the traditional methods of characterization to concentrate intensely—even exclusively—on the inner experience of man, they were merely utilizing a new area of knowledge made available by Freud's discoveries, knowledge *not* available in the nineteenth century.

In recent years experimenters with the short story have tended to move beyond psychological analysis to a direct presentation of neurosis or to a totally objective rendering of the non-human world, a world of things in which man is a peripheral creature. In a world thought ultimately meaningless, contemporary experimenters often dramatize the minds of mad or near-mad characters, and although their narratives appear elliptical and disjointed, most readers today find coherence and meaning in their work. The bleak and baffling stories of Samuel Beckett, Alain Robbe-Grillet, Donald Barthelme, William H. Gass, and Jorge Luis Borges objectify frightening truths about man in today's neurotic world.

Although it borrows elements from both the novel and short story, the novella or short novel more closely resembles the story. Loose and even sprawling in organization, the full-scale novel has traditionally been a long, inclusive narrative with a complicated plot and a realistic concern with the depth and breadth of human character. Like the short story, the novella requires economy and tight organization to succeed, and Irving Howe has pointed out that it "is not merely a cut-down novel." Although the novella does not depend on a single incident and may even employ more than one plot, it moves swiftly on one line of action. Like the short story, it never loiters or digresses. A writer often will select the short novel to investigate a single character in depth, though the time span covered will be brief. As the reader will note in the five novellas included in this book, the author of a short novel may feel the form is perfectly designed to dramatize in detail the hidden moral and philosophic conflicts of the self.

Studies in Short Fiction

The Nineteenth Century

Nathaniel Hawthorne

(1804 - 1864)

"The great thing about Nathaniel Hawthorne," wrote his friend Herman Melville, "is that he can say No! in thunder," meaning that he could forcefully question the characteristic optimism of his time concerning the perfectibility of man and the idea of human progress. Much of Hawthorne's fiction focuses on the "power of blackness" and the seemingly ineradicable evil in the world. Although not himself a Calvinist—one may regard him as a skeptical theist—he was a descendant of stern Puritans of Salem, Massachusetts, and his Puritan heritage and the idea of man's predetermined damnation markedly influenced his thought and art. His stories and novels often examine themes we generally associate with Puritanism: the Fall of Man, sin, guilt, and pride. A moralist interested in "the truths of the human heart," Hawthorne sometimes appears curiously modern in his psychological depiction of alienation and the underside of man's nature. The greatest sin for him is the violation of the human heart, of another person's inner being or integrity, regardless of the reason. Concerned with maintaining a balance between reason and emotion, the head and the heart, he often presents allegorical situations in which intelligent, prideful men destroy themselves or others by an excess of reason and a dearth of imagination. Despite the lucidity of his prose, Hawthorne is a writer of ambiguous, sometimes dense stories which are essentially symbolic.

The Birthmark

In the latter part of the last century there lived a man of science, an eminent proficient in every branch of natural philosophy, who not long before our story opens had made experience of a spiritual affinity more attractive than any chemical one. He had left his laboratory to the care of an assistant, cleared his fine countenance from the furnace smoke, washed the stain of acids from his fingers, and persuaded a beautiful woman to become his wife. In those days when the comparatively recent discovery of electricity and other kindred mysteries of Nature seemed to open paths into the region of miracle, it was not unusual for the love of science to rival the love of woman in its depth and absorbing energy. The higher intellect, the imagination, the spirit, and even the heart might all find their congenial aliment in pursuits which, as some of their ardent votaries believed, would ascend from one step of powerful intelligence to another, until the philosopher should lay his hand on the secret of creative force and perhaps make new worlds for himself. We know not whether Aylmer possessed this degree of faith in man's ultimate control over Nature. He had devoted himself, however, too unreservedly to scientific studies ever to be weaned from them by any second passion. His love for his young wife might prove the stronger of the two; but it could only be by intertwining itself with his live of science, and uniting the strength of the latter to his own.

Such a union accordingly took place, and was attended with truly remarkable consequences and a deeply impressive moral. One day, very soon after their marriage, Aylmer sat gazing at his wife with a trouble in his countenance that grew stronger until he spoke.

"Georgiana," said he, "has it never occurred to you that the mark upon your cheek might be removed?"

"No, indeed," said she, smiling; but perceiving the seriousness of his manner, she blushed deeply. "To tell you the truth it has been so often called a charm that I was simple enough to imagine it might be so."

"Ah, upon another face perhaps it might," replied her husband; "but never on yours. No, dearest Georgiana, you came so nearly perfect from the hand of Nature that this slightest possible defect, which we hesitate whether to term a defect or a beauty, shocks me, as being the visible mark of earthly imperfection."

"Shocks you, my husband!" cried Georgiana, deeply hurt; at first reddening with momentary anger, but then bursting into tears. "Then why did you take me from my mother's side? You cannot love what shocks you!"

To explain this conversation it must be mentioned that in the centre of Georgiana's left cheek there was a singular mark, deeply interwoven, as it were, with the texture and substance of her face. In the usual state of her complexion—a healthy though delicate bloom—the mark wore a tint of deeper crimson, which imperfectly defined its shape amid the surrounding rosiness. When she blushed it gradually became more indistinct, and finally vanished amid the triumphant rush of blood that bathed the whole cheek with its brilliant glow. But if any shifting motion caused her to turn pale there was the mark again, a crimson stain upon the snow, in what Aylmer sometimes deemed an almost fearful distinctness. Its shape bore not a little similarity to the human hand, though of the smallest pygmy size. Georgiana's lovers were wont to say that some fairy at her birth hour had laid her tiny hand upon the infant's cheek, and left this impress there in token of the magic endowments that were to give her such sway over all hearts. Many a desperate swain would have risked life for the privilege of pressing his lips to the mysterious hand. It must not be concealed, however, that the impression wrought by this fairy sign manual varied exceedingly, according to the difference of temperment in the beholders. Some fastidious persons—but they were exclusively of her own sex—affirmed that the bloody hand, as they chose to call it, quite destroyed the effect of Georgiana's beauty, and rendered her countenance even hideous. But it would be as reasonable to say that one of those small blue stains which sometimes occur in the purest statuary marble would convert the Eve of Powers to a monster. Masculine observers, if the birthmark did not heighten their admiration, contented themselves with wishing it away, that the world might possess one living specimen of ideal loveliness without the semblance of a flaw. After his marriage,—for he thought little or nothing about the matter before,—Aylmer discovered that this was the case with himself.

Had she been less beautiful,—if Envy's self could have found aught else to sneer at,—he might have felt his affection heightened by the prettiness of this mimic hand, now vaguely portrayed, now lost, now stealing forth again and glimmering to and fro with every pulse of emotion that throbbed within her heart; but seeing her otherwise so perfect, he found this one defect grow more and more intolerable with every moment of their united lives. It was the fatal flaw of humanity which Nature, in one shape or another, stamps ineffaceably on all her productions, either to imply that they are temporary and finite, or that their perfection must be wrought by toil and pain. The crimson hand expressed the ineludible gripe in which mortality clutches the highest and purest of earthly mold, degrading them into kindred with the lowest, and even with the very brutes, like whom their visible frames return to dust. In this manner, selecting it as the symbol of his wife's liability to sin, sorrow, decay, and death, Aylmer's sombre imagination was not long in rendering the birthmark a frightful object, causing him more trouble and horror than ever Georgiana's beauty, whether of soul or sense, had given him delight.

At all the seasons which should have been their happiest, he invariably and without intending it, nay, in spite of a purpose to the contrary, reverted to this one disastrous topic. Trifling as it at first appeared, it so connected itself with innumerable trains of thought and modes of feeling that it became the central point of all. With the morning twilight Aylmer opened his eyes upon his wife's face and recognized the symbol of imperfection; and when they sat together at the evening hearth his eyes wandered stealthily to her cheek, and beheld, flickering with the blaze of the wood fire, the spectral hand that wrote mortality where he would fain have worshipped.

Georgiana soon learned to shudder at his gaze. It needed but a glance with the peculiar expression that his face often wore to change the roses of her cheek into a deathlike paleness, amid which the crimson hand was brought strongly out, like a bas-relief of ruby on the whitest marble.

Late one night when the lights were growing dim, so as hardly to betray the stain on the poor wife's cheek, she herself, for the first time, voluntarily took up the subject.

"Do you remember, my dear Aylmer," said she, with a feeble attempt at a smile, "have you any recollection of a dream last night about this odious hand?"

"None! none whatever!" replied Aylmer, starting; but then he added, in a dry, cold tone, affected for the sake of concealing the real depth of his emotion, "I might well dream of it; for before I fell asleep it had taken a pretty firm hold of my fancy."

"And you did dream of it?" continued Georgiana, hastily; for she dreaded lest a gush of tears should interrupt what she had to say. "A terrible dream! I wonder that you can forget it. Is it possible to forget this one expression?—'It is in her heart now; we must have it out!' Reflect, my husband; for by all means I would have you recall that dream."

The mind is in a sad state when Sleep, the all-involving, cannot confine her spectres within the dim region of her sway, but suffers them to break forth, affrighting this actual life with secrets that perchance belong to a deeper one. Aylmer now remembered his dream. He had fancied himself with his servant Aminadab, attempting an operation for the removal of the birthmark; but the deeper went the knife, the deeper sank the hand, until at length its tiny grasp appeared to have caught hold of Georgiana's heart; whence, however, her husband was inexorably resolved to cut or wrench it away.

When the dream had shaped itself perfectly in his memory, Aylmer sat in his wife's presence with a guilty feeling. Truth often finds its way to the mind close muffled in robes of sleep, and then speaks with uncompromising directness of matters in regard to which we practise an unconscious self-deception during our waking moments. Until now he had not been aware of the tyrannizing influence acquired by one idea over his mind, and of the lengths which he might find in his heart to go for the sake of giving himself peace.

"Aylmer," resumed Georgiana, solemnly, "I know not what may be the cost to both of us to rid me of this fatal birthmark. Perhaps its removal may cause cureless deformity; or it may be the stain goes as deep as life itself. Again: do we know that there is a possibility, on any terms, of unclasping the firm gripe of this little hand which was laid upon me before I came into the world?"

"Dearest Georgiana, I have spent much thought upon the subject," hastily interrupted Aylmer, "I am convinced of the perfect practicability of its removal."

"If there be the remotest possibility of it," continued Georgiana, "let the attempt be made at whatever risk. Danger is nothing to me; for life, while this hateful mark makes me the object of your horror and disgust,—life is a burden which I would fling down with joy. Either remove this dreadful hand, or take my wretched life! You have deep science. All the world bears witness of it. You have achieved great wonders. Cannot you remove this little, little mark, which I cover with the tips of two small fingers? Is this beyond your power, for the sake of your own peace, and to save your poor wife from madness?"

"Noblest, dearest, tenderest wife," cried Aylmer, rapturously, "doubt not my power. I have already given this matter the deepest thought—thought which might almost have enlightened me to create a being less perfect than yourself. Georgiana, you have led me deeper than ever into the heart of science. I feel myself fully competent to render this dear cheek as faultless as its fellow; and then, most beloved, what will be my triumph when I shall have corrected what Nature left imperfect in her fairest work! Even Pygmalion, when his sculptured woman assumed life, felt not greater ecstasy than mine will be."

"It is resolved, then," said Georgiana, faintly smiling. "And, Aylmer, spare me not, though you should find the birthmark take refuge in my heart at last."

Her husband tenderly kissed her cheek—her right cheek—not that which bore the impress of the crimson hand.

The next day Aylmer apprised his wife of a plan that he had formed whereby he might have opportunity for the intense thought and constant watchfulness which the proposed operation would require; while Georgiana, likewise, would enjoy the perfect repose essential to its success. They were to seclude themselves in the extensive apartments occupied by Aylmer as a laboratory, and where, during his toilsome youth, he had made discoveries in the elemental powers of Nature that had roused the admiration of all the learned societies in Europe. Seated calmly in this laboratory, the pale philosopher had investigated the secrets of the highest cloud region and of the profoundest mines; he had satisfied himself of the causes that kindled and kept alive the fires of the volcano; and had explained the mystery of fountains, and how it is that they gush forth, some so bright and pure, and others with such rich medicinal virtues, from the dark bosom of the earth. Here, too, at an earlier period, he had studied the wonders of the human frame, and attempted to fathom the very process by which Nature assimilates all her precious influences from earth and air, and from the spiritual world, to create and foster man, her masterpiece. The latter pursuit, however, Aylmer had long laid aside in unwilling recognition of the truth—against which all seekers sooner or later stumble—that our great creative Mother, while she amuses us with apparently working in the broadest sunshine, is yet severely careful to keep her own secrets, and, in spite of her pretended openness, shows us nothing but results. She permits us, indeed, to mar, but seldom to mend, and, like a jealous patentee, on no account to make. Now, however, Aylmer resumed these half-forgotten investigations; not, of course, with such hopes or wishes as first suggested them; but because they involved much physiological truth and lay in the path of his proposed scheme for the treatment of Georgiana.

As he led her over the threshold of the laboratory, Georgiana was cold and tremulous. Aylmer looked cheerfully into her face, with intent to reassure her, but was so startled with the intense glow of the birthmark upon the whiteness of her cheek that he could not restrain a strong convulsive shudder. His wife fainted.

"Aminadab! Aminadab!" shouted Aylmer, stamping violently on the floor.

Forthwith there issued from an inner apartment a man of low stature, but bulky frame, with shaggy hair hanging about his visage, which was grimed with the vapors of the furnace. This personage had been Aylmer's underworker during his whole scientific career, and was admirably fitted for that office by his great mechanical readiness, and the skill with which, while incapable of comprehending a single principle, he executed all the details of his master's experiments. With his vast strength, his shaggy hair, his smoky aspect, and the indescribable earthiness that incrusted him, he seemed to represent man's physical nature; while Aylmer's slender figure, and pale, intellectual face, were no less apt a type of the spiritual element.

"Throw open the door of the boudoir, Aminadab," said Aylmer, "and burn a pastil."

"Yes, master," answered Aminadab, looking intently at the lifeless form of Georgiana; and then he muttered to himself, "If she were my wife, I'd never part with that birthmark."

When Georgiana recovered consciousness she found herself breathing an atmosphere of penetrating fragrance, the gentle potency of which had recalled her from her deathlike faintness. The scene around her looked like enchantment. Aylmer had converted those smoky, dingy, sombre rooms, where he had spent his brightest years in recondite pursuits, into a series of beautiful apartments not unfit to be the secluded abode of a lovely woman. The walls were hung with gorgeous curtains, which imparted the combination of grandeur and grace that no other species of adornment can achieve; and as they fell from the ceiling to the floor, their rich and ponderous folds, concealing all angles and straight lines, appeared to shut in the scene from infinite space. For aught Georgiana knew, it might be a pavilion among the clouds. And Aylmer, excluding the sunshine, which would have interfered with his chemical processes, had supplied its place with perfumed lamps, emitting flames of various hue, but all uniting in a soft, impurpled radiance. He now knelt by his wife's side, watching her earnestly, but without alarm; for he was confident in his science, and felt that he could draw a magic circle round her within which no evil might intrude.

"Where am I? Ah, I remember," said Georgiana, faintly; and she placed her hand over her cheek to hide the terrible mark from her husband's eyes.

"Fear not, dearest!" exclaimed he. "Do not shrink from me! Believe me, Georgiana, I even rejoice in this single imperfection, since it will be such a rapture to remove it."

"Oh, spare me!" sadly replied his wife, "Pray do not look at it again. I never can forget that convulsive shudder."

In order to soothe Georgiana, and, as it were, to release her mind from the burden of actual things, Aylmer now put in practice some of the light and playful secrets which science had taught him among its profounder lore. Airy figures, absolutely bodiless ideas, and forms of unsubstantial beauty came and danced before her, imprinting their momentary footsteps on beams of light. Though she had some indistinct idea of the method of these optical phenomena, still the illusion was almost perfect enough to warrant the belief that her husband possessed sway over the spiritual world. Then again, when she felt a wish to look forth from her seclusion, immediately, as if her thoughts were answered, the procession of external existence flitted across a screen. The scenery and the figures of actual life were perfectly represented, but with that bewitching, yet indescribable difference which always makes a picture, an image, or a shadow so much more attractive than the original. When wearied of this, Aylmer bade her cast her eyes upon a vessel containing a quantity of earth. She did so, with little interest at first; but was soon startled to perceive the germ of a plant shooting upward from the soil. Then came the slender stalk; the leaves gradually unfolded themselves; and amid them was a perfect and lovely flower.

"It is magical!" cried Georgiana. "I dare not touch it."

"Nay, pluck it," answered Aylmer,—"pluck it, and inhale its brief perfume while you may. The flower will wither in a few moments and leave nothing save its brown seed vessels; but thence may be perpetuated a race as ephemeral as itself."

But Georgiana had no sooner touched the flower than the whole plant suffered a blight, its leaves turning coal-black as if by the agency of fire.

"There was too powerful a stimulus," said Aylmer, thoughtfully.

To make up for this abortive experiment, he proposed to take her portrait by a scientific process of his own invention. It was to be effected by rays of light striking upon a polished plate of metal. Georgiana assented; but, on looking at the result, was affrighted to find the features of the portrait blurred and indefinable; while the minute figure of a hand appeared where the cheek should have been. Aylmer snatched the metallic plate and threw it into a jar of corrosive acid.

Soon, however, he forgot these mortifying failures. In the intervals of study and chemical experiment he came to her flushed and exhausted, but seemed invigorated by her presence, and spoke in glowing language of the resources of his art. He gave a history of the long dynasty of the alchemists, who spent so many ages in quest of the universal solvent by which the golden principle might be elicited from all things vile and base. Aylmer appeared to believe that, by the plainest scientific logic, it was altogether within the limits of possibility to discover this long-sought medium; "but," he added, "a philosopher who should go deep enough to acquire the power would attain too lofty a wisdom to stoop to the exercise of it." Not less singular were his opinions in regard to the elixir vitae. He more than intimated that it was at his option to concoct a liquid that should prolong life for years, perhaps interminably; but that it would produce a discord in Nature which all the world, and chiefly the quaffer of the immortal nostrum, would find cause to curse.

"Aylmer, are you in earnest?" asked Georgiana, looking at him with amazement and fear. "It is terrible to possess such power, or even to dream of possessing it."

"Oh, do not tremble, my love," said her husband. "I would not wrong either you or myself by working such inharmonious effects upon our lives; but I would have you consider how trifling, in comparison, is the skill requisite to remove this little hand."

At the mention of the birthmark, Georgiana, as usual, shrank as if a redhot iron had touched her cheek.

Again Aylmer applied himself to his labors. She could hear his voice in the distant furnace room giving directions to Aminadab, whose harsh, uncouth, misshapen tones were audible in response, more like the grunt or growl of a brute than human speech. After hours of absence, Aylmer reappeared and proposed that she should now examine his cabinet of chemical products and natural treasures of the earth. Among the former he showed her a small vial, in which, he remarked, was contained a gentle yet most powerful fragrance, capable of impregnating all the breezes that blow across the kingdom. They were of inestimable value, the contents of that little vial; and, as he said so, he threw some of the perfume into the air and filled the room with piercing and invigorating delight.

"And what is this?" asked Georgiana, pointing to a small crystal globe containing a gold-colored liquid. "It is so beautiful to the eye that I could imagine it the elixir of life."

"In one sense it is," replied Aylmer; "or, rather, the elixir of immortality. It is the most precious poison that ever was concocted in this world. By its aid I could apportion the lifetime of any mortal at whom you might point your finger. The strength of the dose would determine whether he were to linger out years, or drop dead in the midst of a breath. No king on his guarded throne could keep his life if I, in my private station, should deem that the welfare of millions justified me in depriving him of it."

"Why do you keep such a terrific drug?" inquired Georgiana in horror.

"Do not mistrust me, dearest," said her husband, smiling; "its virtuous potency is yet greater than its harmful one. But see! here is a powerful cosmetic. With a few drops of this in a vase of water, freckles may be washed away as easily as the hands are cleansed. A stronger infusion would take the blood out of the cheek, and leave the rosiest beauty a pale ghost."

"Is it with this lotion that you intend to bathe my cheek?" asked Georgiana, anxiously.

"Oh, no," hastily replied her husband; "this is merely superficial. Your case demands a remedy that shall go deeper."

In his interviews with Georgiana, Aylmer generally made minute inquiries as to her sensations and whether the confinement of the rooms and the temperature of the atmosphere agreed with her. These questions had such a particular drift that Georgiana began to conjecture that she was already subjected to certain physical influences, either breathed in with the fragrant air or taken with her food. She fancied likewise, but it might be altogether fancy, that there was a stirring up of her system—a strange, indefinite sensation creeping through her veins, and tingling, half painfully, half pleasurably, at her heart. Still, whenever she dared to look into the mirror, there she beheld herself pale as a white rose and with the crimson birthmark stamped upon her cheek. Not even Aylmer now hated it so much as she.

To dispel the tedium of the hours which her husband found it necessary to devote to the processes of combination and analysis, Georgiana turned over the volumes of his scientific library. In many dark old tomes she met with chapters full of romance and poetry. They were the works of the philosophers of the middle ages, such as Albertus Magnus, Cornelius Agrippa, Paracelsus, and the famous friar who created the prophetic Brazen Head. All these antique naturalists stood in advance of their centuries, yet were imbued with some of their credulity, and therefore were believed, and perhaps imagined themselves to have acquired from the investigation of Nature a power above Nature, and from physics a sway over the spiritual world. Hardly less curious and imaginative were the early volumes of the Transactions of the Royal Society, in which the members, knowing little of the limits of natural possibility, were continually recording wonders or proposing methods whereby wonders might be wrought.

But to Georgiana the most engrossing volume was a large folio from her husband's own hand, in which he had recorded every experiment of his scientific career, its original aim, the methods adopted for its development, and its final success or failure, with the circumstances to which either event was attributable. The book, in truth, was both the history and emblem of his ardent, ambitious, imaginative, yet practical and laborious life. He handled physical details as if there were nothing beyond them; yet spiritualized them all, and redeemed himself from materialism by his strong and eager aspiration towards the infinite. In his grasp the veriest clod of earth assumed a soul. Georgiana, as she read, reverenced Aylmer and loved him more profoundly than ever, but with a less entire dependence on his judgment than heretofore. Much as he had accomplished, she could not but observe that most splendid successes were almost invariably failures, if compared with the ideal at which he aimed. His brightest diamonds were the merest pebbles, and felt to be so by himself, in comparison with the inestimable gems which lay hidden beyond his reach. The volume, rich with achievements that had won renown for its author, was yet as melancholy a record as ever mortal hand had penned. It was the sad confession and continual exemplification of the shortcomings of the composite man, the spirit burdened with clay and working in matter, and of the despair that assails the higher nature at finding itself so miserably thwarted by the earthly part. Perhaps every man of genius in whatever sphere might recognize the image of his own experience in Aylmer's journal.

So deeply did these reflections affect Georgiana that she laid her face upon the open volume and burst into tears. In this situation she was found by her husband.

"It is dangerous to read in a sorcerer's books," said he with a smile, though his countenance was uneasy and displeased. "Georgiana, there are pages in that volume which I can scarcely glance over and keep my senses. Take heed lest it prove as detrimental to you."

"It has made me worship you more than ever," said she.

"Ah, wait for this one success," rejoined he, "then worship me if you will. I shall deem myself hardly unworthy of it. But come, I have sought you for the luxury of your voice. Sing to me, dearest."

So she poured out the liquid music of her voice to quench the thirst of his spirit. He then took his leave with a boyish exuberance of gaiety, assuring her that her seclusion would endure but a little longer, and that the result was already certain. Scarcely had he departed when Georgiana felt irresistibly impelled to follow him. She had forgotten to inform Aylmer of a symptom which for two or three hours past had begun to excite her attention. It was a sensation in the fatal birthmark, not painful, but which induced a restlessness throughout her system. Hastening after her husband, she intruded for the first time into the laboratory.

The first thing that struck her eye was the furnace, that hot and feverish worker, with the intense glow of its fire, which by the quantities of soot clustered above it seemed to have been burning for ages. There was a distilling apparatus in full operation. Around the room were retorts, tubes, cylinders, crucibles, and other apparatus of chemical research. An electrical machine stood ready for immediate use. The atmosphere felt oppressively close; and was tainted with gaseous odors which had been tormented forth by the processes of science. The severe and homely simplicity of the apartment with its naked walls and brick pavement, looked strange, accustomed as Georgiana had become to the fantastic elegance of her boudoir. But what chiefly, indeed almost solely, drew her attention, was the aspect of Aylmer himself.

He was pale as death, anxious and absorbed, and hung over the furnace as if it depended upon his utmost watchfulness whether the liquid which it was distilling should be the draught of immortal happiness or misery. How different from the sanguine and joyous mien that he had assumed for Georgiana's encouragement!

"Carefully now, Aminadab; carefully, thou human machine; carefully, thou man of clay!" muttered Aylmer, more to himself than his assistant. "Now, if there be a thought too much or too little, it is all over."

"Ho! ho!" mumbled Aminadab. "Look, master! look!"

Aylmer raised his eyes hastily, and at first reddened, then grew paler than ever, on beholding Georgiana. He rushed towards her and seized her arm with a gripe that left the print of his fingers upon it.

"Why do you come hither? Have you no trust in your husband?" cried he, impetuously. "Would you throw the blight of that fatal birthmark over my labors? It is not well done. Go, prying woman, go!"

"Nay, Aylmer," said Georgiana with the firmness of which she possessed no stinted endowment, "it is not you that have a right to complain. You mistrust your wife; you have concealed the anxiety with which you watch the development of this experiment. Think not so unworthily of me, my husband. Tell me all the risk we run, and fear not that I shall shrink; for my share in it is far less than your own."

"No, no, Georgiana!" said Aylmer, impatiently; "it must not be."

"I submit," replied she calmly. "And, Aylmer, I shall quaff whatever draught you bring me; but it will be on the same principle that would induce me to take a dose of poison if offered by your hand."

"My noble wife," said Aylmer, deeply moved; "I knew not the height and depth of your nature until now. Nothing shall be concealed. Know, then, that this crimson hand, superficial as it seems, has clutched its grasp into your being with a strength of which I had no previous conception. I have already administered agents powerful enough to do aught except to change your entire physical system. Only one thing remains to be tried. If that fails us we are ruined."

"Why did you hesitate to tell me this?" asked she.

"Because, Georgiana," said Aylmer, in a low voice, "there is danger."

"Danger? There is but one danger—that this horrible stigma shall be left upon my cheek!" cried Georgiana. "Remove it, remove it, whatever be the cost, or we shall both go mad!"

"Heaven knows your words are too true," said Aylmer, sadly. "And now, dearest, return to your boudoir. In a little while all will be tested."

He conducted her back and took leave of her with a solemn tenderness which spoke far more than his words how much was now at stake. After his departure Georgiana became rapt in musings. She considered the character of Aylmer, and did it completer justice than at any previous moment. Her heart exulted, while it trembled, at his honorable love—so pure and lofty that it would accept nothing less than perfection nor miserably make itself contented with an earthlier nature than he had dreamed of. She felt how much more precious was such a sentiment than that meaner kind which would have borne with the imperfection for her sake, and have been guilty of treason to holy love by degrading its perfect idea to the level of the actual; and with her whole spirit she prayed that, for a single moment, she might satisfy his highest and deepest conception. Longer than one moment she well knew it could not be; for his spirit was ever on the march, ever ascending, and each instant required something that was beyond the scope of the instant before.

The sound of her husband's footsteps aroused her. He bore a crystal goblet containing a liquor colorless as water, but bright enough to be the draught of immortality. Aylmer was pale; but it seemed rather the consequence of a highly-wrought state of mind and tension of spirit than of fear or doubt.

"The concoction of the draught has been perfect," said he, in answer to Georgiana's look. "Unless my science have deceived me, it cannot fail."

"Save on your account, my dearest Aylmer," observed his wife, "I might wish to put off this birthmark of mortality by relinquishing mortality itself in preference to any other mode. Life is but a sad possession to those who have attained precisely the degree of moral advancement at which I stand. Were I weaker and blinder it might be happiness. Were I stronger, it might be endured hopefully. But, being what I find myself, me thinks I am of all mortals the most fit to die."

"You are fit for heaven without tasting death!" replied her husband. "But why do we speak of dying? The draught cannot fail. Behold its effect upon this plant."

On the window seat there stood a geranium diseased with yellow blotches, which had overspread all its leaves. Aylmer poured a small quantity of the liquid upon the soil in which it grew. In a little time, when the roots of the plant had taken up the moisture, the unsightly blotches began to be extinguished in a living verdure.

"There needed no proof," said Georgiana, quietly. "Give me the goblet. I joyfully stake all upon your word."

"Drink, then, thou lofty creature!" exclaimed Aylmer, with fervid admiration. "There is no taint of imperfection on thy spirit. Thy sensible frame, too, shall soon be all perfect."

She quaffed the liquid and returned the goblet to his hand.

"It is grateful," said she with a placid smile. "Methinks it is like water from a heavenly fountain; for it contains I know not what of unobtrusive fragrance and deliciousness. It allays a feverish thirst that had parched me for many days. Now, dearest, let me sleep. My earthly senses are closing over my spirit like the leaves around the heart of a rose at sunset."

She spoke the last words with a gentle reluctance, as if it required almost more energy than she could command to pronounce the faint and lingering syllables. Scarcely had they loitered through her lips ere she was lost in slumber. Aylmer sat by her side, watching her aspect with the emotions proper to a man the whole value of whose existence was involved in the process now to be tested. Mingled with this mood, however, was the philosophic investigation characteristic of the man of science. Not the minutest symptom escaped him. A heightened flush of the cheek, a slight irregularity of breath, a quiver of the eyelid, a hardly perceptible tremor through the frame,—such were the details which, as the moments passed, he wrote down in his folio volume. Intense thought had set its stamp upon every previous page of that volume, but the thoughts of years were all concentrated upon the last.

While thus employed, he failed not to gaze often at the fatal hand, and not without a shudder. Yet once, by a strange and unaccountable impulse, he pressed it with his lips. His spirit recoiled, however, in the very act; and Georgiana, out of the midst of her deep sleep, moved uneasily and murmured as if in remonstrance. Again Aylmer resumed his watch. Nor was it without avail. The crimson hand, which at first had been strongly visible upon the marble paleness of Georgiana's cheek, now grew more faintly outlined. She remained not less pale than ever; but the birthmark, with every breath that came and went, lost somewhat of its former distinctness. Its presence had been awful; its departure was more awful still. Watch the stain of the rainbow fading out of the sky, and you will know how that mysterious symbol passed away.

"By Heaven! it is well-nigh gone!" said Aylmer to himself, in almost irrepressible ecstasy. "I can scarcely trace it now. Success! success! And now it is like the faintest rose color. The lightest flush of blood across her cheek would overcome it. But she is so pale!"

He drew aside the window curtain and suffered the light of natural day to fall into the room and rest upon her cheek. At the same time he heard a gross, hoarse chuckle, which he had long known as his servant Aminadab's expression of delight.

"Ah, clod! ah, earthly mass!" cried Aylmer, laughing a sort of frenzy, "you have served me well! Matter and spirit—earth and heaven—have both done their part in this! Laugh, thing of the senses! You have earned the right to laugh."

These exclamations broke Georgiana's sleep. She slowly unclosed her eyes and gazed into the mirror which her husband had arranged for that purpose. A faint smile flitted over her lips when she recognized how barely perceptible was now that crimson hand which had once blazed forth with such disastrous brilliancy as to scare away all their happiness. But then her eyes sought Aylmer's face with a trouble and anxiety that he could by no means account for.

"My poor Aylmer!" murmured she.

"Poor? Nay, richest, happiest, most favored!" exclaimed he. "My peerless bride, it is successful! You are perfect!"

"My poor Aylmer," she repeated, with a more than human tenderness, "you have aimed loftily; you have done nobly. Do not repent that with so high and pure a feeling, you have rejected the best the earth could offer. Aylmer, dearest Aylmer, I am dying!"

Alas! it was too true! The fatal hand had grappled with the mystery of life, and was the bond by which an angelic spirit kept itself in union with a mortal frame. As the last crimson tint of the birthmark—that sole token of human imperfection—faded from her cheek, the parting breath of the now perfect woman passed into the atmosphere, and her soul, lingering a moment near her husband, took its heavenward flight. Then a hoarse, chuckling laugh was heard again! Thus ever does the gross fatality of earth exult in its invariable triumph over the immortal essence which, in this dim sphere of half development, demands the completeness of a higher state. Yet, had Aylmer reached a profounder wisdom, he need not thus have flung away the happiness which would have woven his mortal life of the selfsame texture with the celestial. The momentary circumstance was too strong for him; he failed to look beyond the shadowy scope of time, and living once for all in eternity, to find the perfect future in the present.

Edgar Allan Poe

(1809 - 1849)

Not only a masterful storyteller and an innovative poet, Edgar Allan Poe was an influential literary critic and the first American to theorize on the short story. Unlike Hawthorne and other American writers who thought art should be at least partially didactic or morally instructive, Poe believed that the purpose of art was simply to create beauty. His ideas on fiction and the example of his own tightly organized tales significantly affected the formal considerations of the modern American and European short story until the 1920's. In a sympathetic review of Hawthorne's *Twice-Told Tales* (1842), Poe declared that a skillful narrative artist accommodates his incidents to a preconceived, unique *effect.* He wrote, "If [the writer's] very initial sentence tend not to the outbringing of this effect, then he has failed in his first step. In the whole composition there should be no word written, of which the tendency, direct or indirect, is not to the one preestablished design." This idea or principle became one of the tenets of a good short story. To achieve this unity of effect Poe emphasized the need for well-constructed plots. Poe's own tales may be divided into those of reason and those of effect or atmosphere. The first group, which includes "The Purloined Letter" and "The Murders in the Rue Morgue," are cleverly plotted tales of suspense and detection. In the second group one may list "The Fall of the House of Usher," "Ligeia," and "William Wilson," stories short on action but long on atmosphere and subtle psychological analysis. Many contemporary readers, living at a time when the self is under severe pressures, are fascinated by Poe's delineation of neurotic characters and by his subjective analysis of the irrational side of the mind. Although it is undoubtedly true, as D. H. Lawrence said, that Poe was "absolutely concerned with the disintegration process of his own psyche," his psychological problems in no way detract from his tales as art. An orphan adopted by a wealthy Virginia merchant, Poe was emotionally starved as a child, and as an adult he suffered many emotional and social conflicts which he could not resolve. In "William Wilson" Poe dramatizes the conflict between conscience and will in an emotionally disturbed man.

William Wilson

What say of it? what say [*of*] *conscience grim,*
That spectre in my path?

Chamberlayne's Pharronida.

Let me call myself, for the present, William Wilson. The fair page now lying before me need not be sullied with my real appellation. This has been already too much an object for the scorn—for the horror—for the detestation of my race. To the uttermost regions of the globe have not the indignant winds bruited its unparalleled infamy? Oh, outcast of all outcasts most abandoned!—to the earth art thou not forever dead? to its honors, to its flowers, to its golden aspirations?—and a cloud, dense, dismal, and limitless, does it not hang eternally between thy hopes and heaven?

I would not, if I could, here or to-day, embody a record of my later years of unspeakable misery, and unpardonable crime. This epoch—these later years—took unto themselves a sudden elevation in turpitude, whose origin alone it is my present purpose to assign. Men usually grow base by degrees. From me, in an instant, all virtue dropped bodily as a mantle. From comparatively trivial wickedness I passed, with the stride of a giant, into more than the enormities of an Elah-Gabalus. What chance—what one event brought this evil thing to pass, bear with me while I relate. Death approaches; and the shadow which foreruns him has thrown a softening influence over my spirit. I long, in passing through the dim valley, for the sympathy—I had nearly said for the pity—of my fellow men. I would fain have them believe that I have been, in some measure, the slave of circumstances beyond human control. I would wish them to seek out for me, in the details I am about to give, some little oasis of *fatality* amid a wilderness of error. I would have them allow—what they cannot refrain from allowing—that, although temptation may have erewhile existed as great, man was never *thus,* at least, tempted before—certainly, never *thus* fell. And is it therefore that he has never thus suffered? Have I not indeed been living in a dream? And am I not now dying a victim to the horror and the mystery of the wildest of all sublunary visions?

I am the descendant of a race whose imaginative and easily excitable temperament has at all times rendered them remarkable; and, in my earliest infancy, I gave evidence of having fully inherited the family character. As I advanced in years it was more strongly developed; becoming, for many reasons, a cause of serious disquietude to my friends, and of positive injury to myself. I grew self-willed, addicted to the wildest caprices, and a prey to the most ungovernable passions. Weak-minded, and beset with constitutional infirmities akin to my own, my parents could do but little to check the evil propensities which distinguished me. Some feeble and ill-directed efforts resulted in complete failure on their part, and, of course, in total triumph on mine. Thenceforward my voice was a household law; and at an age when few children have abandoned their leading-strings, I was left to the guidance of my own will, and became, in all but name, the master of my own actions.

My earliest recollections of a school-life, are connected with a large, rambling, Elizabethan house, in a misty-looking village of England, where were a vast number of gigantic and gnarled trees, and where all the houses were excessively ancient. In truth, it was a dream-like and spirit-soothing place, that venerable old town. At this moment, in fancy, I feel the refreshing chilliness of its deeply-shadowed avenues, inhale the fragrance of its thousand shrubberies, and thrill anew with undefinable delight, at the deep hollow note of the church-bell, breaking, each hour, with sullen and sudden roar, upon the stillness of the dusky atmosphere in which the fretted Gothic steeple lay imbedded and asleep.

It gives me, perhaps, as much of pleasure as I can now in any manner experience, to dwell upon minute recollections of the school and its concerns. Steeped in misery as I am—misery, alas! only too real—I shall be pardoned for seeking relief, however slight and temporary, in the weakness of a few rambling details. These, moreover, utterly trivial, and even ridiculous in themselves, assume, to my fancy, adventitious importance, as connected with a period and a locality when and where I recognise the first ambiguous monitions of the destiny which afterwards so fully overshadowed me. Let me then remember.

The house, I have said, was old and irregular. The grounds were extensive, and a high and solid brick wall, topped with a bed of mortar and broken glass, encompassed the whole. This prison-like rampart formed the limit of our domain; beyond it we saw but thrice a week—once every Saturday afternoon, when, attended by two ushers, we were permitted to take brief walks in a body through some of the neighbouring fields—and twice during Sunday, when we were paraded in the same formal manner to the morning and evening service in the one church of the village. Of this church the principal of our school was pastor. With how deep a spirit of wonder and perplexity was I wont to regard him from our remote pew in the gallery, as, with step solemn and slow, he ascended the pulpit! This reverend man, with countenance so demurely benign, with robes so glossy and so clerically flowing, with wig so minutely powdered, so rigid and so vast,—could this be he who, of late, with sour visage, and in snuffy habiliments, administered, ferule in hand, the Draconian laws of the academy? Oh, gigantic paradox, too utterly monstrous for solution!

At an angle of the ponderous wall frowned a more ponderous gate.

It was riveted and studded with iron bolts, and surmounted with jagged iron spikes. What impressions of deep awe did it inspire! It was never opened save for the three periodical egressions and ingressions already mentioned; then, in every creak of its mighty hinges, we found a plenitude of mystery—a world of matter for solemn remark, or for more solemn meditation.

The extensive enclosure was irregular in form, having many capacious recesses. Of these, three or four of the largest constituted the playground. It was level, and covered with fine hard gravel. I well remember it had no trees, nor benches, nor anything similar within it. Of course it was in the rear of the house. In front lay a small parterre, planted with box and other shrubs; but through this sacred division we passed only upon rare occasions indeed—such as a first advent to school or final departure thence, or perhaps, when a parent or friend having called for us, we joyfully took our way home for the Christmas or Midsummer holy-days.

But the house!—how quaint an old building was this!—to me how veritably a palace of enchantment! There was really no end to its windings—to its incomprehensible subdivisions. It was difficult, at any given time, to say with certainty upon which of its two stories one happened to be. From each room to every other there were sure to be found three or four steps either in ascent or descent. Then the lateral branches were innumerable—inconceivable—and so returning in upon themselves, that our most exact ideas in regard to the whole mansion were not very far different from those with which we pondered upon infinity. During the five years of my residence here, I was never able to ascertain with precision, in what remote locality lay the little sleeping apartment assigned to myself and some eighteen or twenty other scholars.

The school-room was the largest in the house—I could not help thinking, in the world. It was very long, narrow, and dismally low, with pointed Gothic windows and a ceiling of oak. In a remote and terror-inspiring angle was a square enclosure of eight or ten feet, comprising the *sanctum,* "during hours," of our principal, the Reverend Dr. Bransby. It was a solid structure, with massy door, sooner than open which in the absence of the "Dominie," we would all have willingly perished by the *peine forte et dure.* In other angles were two other similar boxes, far less reverenced, indeed, but still greatly matters of awe. One of these was the pulpit of the "classical" usher, one of the "English and mathematical." Interspersed about the room, crossing and recrossing in endless irregularity, were innumerable benches and desks, black, ancient, and time-worn, piled desperately with much-bethumbed books, and so beseamed with initial letters, names at full length, grotesque figures, and other multiplied efforts of the knife, as to have entirely lost what little of original form might have been their portion in days long departed. A huge bucket with water stood at one extremity of the room, and a clock of stupendous dimensions at the other.

Encompassed by the massy walls of this venerable academy, I passed, yet not in tedium or disgust, the years of the third lustrum of my life. The teeming brain of childhood requires no external world of incident to occupy or amuse it; and the apparently dismal monotony of a school was replete with more intense excitement than my riper youth has derived from luxury, or my full manhood from crime. Yet I must believe that my first mental development had in it much of the uncommon—even much of the *outré*. Upon mankind at large the events of very early existence rarely leave in mature age any definite impression. All is gray shadow—a weak and irregular remembrance—an indistinct regathering of feeble pleasures and phantasmagoric pains. With me this is not so. In childhood I must have felt with the energy of a man what I now find stamped upon memory in lines as vivid, as deep, and as durable as the *exergues* of the Carthaginian medals.

Yet in fact—in the fact of the world's view—how little was there to remember! The morning's awakening, the nightly summons to bed; the connings, the recitations; the periodical half-holidays, and perambulations; the play-ground, with its broils, its pastimes, its intrigues;—these, by a mental sorcery long forgotten, were made to involve a wilderness of sensation, a world of rich incident, a universe of varied emotion, of excitement the most passionate and spirit-stirring. *"Oh, le bon temps, que ce siècle de fer!"*

In truth, the ardor, the enthusiasm, and the imperiousness of my disposition, soon rendered me a marked character among my school-mates, and by slow, but natural gradations, gave me an ascendancy over all not greatly older than myself;—over all with a single exception. This exception was found in the person of a scholar, who, although no relation, bore the same Christian and surname as myself;—a circumstance, in fact, little remarkable; for, notwithstanding a noble descent, mine was one of those every-day appellations which seem, by prescriptive right, to have been, time out of mind, the common property of the mob. In this narrative I have therefore designated myself as William Wilson,—a fictitious title not very dissimilar to the real. My namesake alone, of those who in school phraseology constituted "our set," presumed to compete with me in the studies of the class—in the sports and broils of the play-ground—to refuse implicit belief in my assertions, and submission to my will—indeed, to interfere with my arbitrary dictation in any respect whatsoever. If there is on earth a supreme and unqualified despotism, it is the despotism of a master mind in boyhood over the less energetic spirits of its companions.

Wilson's rebellion was to me a source of the greatest embarrassment;—the more so as, in spite of the bravado with which in public I made a point of treating him and his pretensions, I secretly felt that I feared him, and could not help thinking the equality which he maintained so easily with myself, a proof of his true superiority; since not to be overcome cost me a perpetual struggle. Yet this superiority—even this equality—was in truth acknowledged by no one but myself; our associates, by some unaccountable blindness, seemed not even to suspect it. Indeed, his competition, his resistance, and especially his impertinent and dogged interference with my purposes, were not more pointed than private. He appeared to be destitute alike of the ambition which urged, and of the passionate energy of mind which enabled me to excel. In his rivalry he might have been supposed actuated solely by a whimsical desire to thwart, astonish, or mortify myself; although there were times when I could not help observing, with a feeling made up of wonder, abasement, and pique, that he mingled with his injuries, his insults, or his contradictions, a certain most inappropriate, and assuredly most unwelcome *affectionateness* of manner. I could only conceive this singular behavior to arise from a consummate self-conceit assuming the vulgar airs of patronage and protection.

Perhaps it was this latter trait in Wilson's conduct, conjoined with our identity of name, and the mere accident of our having entered the school upon the same day, which set afloat the notion that we were brothers, among the senior classes in the academy. These do not usually inquire with much strictness into affairs of their juniors. I have before said, or should have said, that Wilson was not, in the most remote degree, connected with my family. But assuredly if we *had* been brothers we must have been twins; for, after leaving Dr. Bransby's, I casually learned that my namesake was born on the nineteenth of January, 1813—and this is a somewhat remarkable coincidence; for the day is precisely that of my own nativity.

It may seem strange that in spite of the continual anxiety occasioned me by the rivalry of Wilson, and his intolerable spirit of contradiction, I could not bring myself to hate him altogether. We had, to be sure, nearly every day a quarrel in which, yielding me publicly the palm of victory, he, in some manner, contrived to make me feel that it was he who had deserved it; yet a sense of pride on my part, and a veritable dignity on his own, kept us always upon what are called "speaking terms," while there were many points of strong congeniality in our tempers, operating to awake in me a sentiment which our position alone, perhaps, prevented from ripening into friendship. It is difficult, indeed, to define, or even to describe, my real feelings towards him. They formed a motley and heterogeneous admixture;—some petulant animosity, which was not yet hatred, some esteem, more respect, much fear, with a world of uneasy curiosity. To the moralist it will be unnecessary to say, in addition, that Wilson and myself were the most inseparable of companions.

It was no doubt the anomalous state of affairs existing between us, which turned all my attacks upon him, (and they were many, either open or covert) into the channel of banter or practical joke (giving pain while assuming the aspect of mere fun) rather than into a more serious and determined hostility. But my endeavours on this head were by no means uniformly successful, even when my plans were the most wittily concocted; for my namesake had much about him, in character, of that unassuming and quiet austerity which, while enjoying the poignancy of its own jokes, has no heel of Achilles in itself, and absolutely refuses to be laughed at. I could find, indeed, but one vulnerable point, and that, lying in a personal peculiarity, arising, perhaps, from constitutional disease, would have been spared by any antagonist less at his wit's end than myself;—my rival had a weakness in the faucial or guttural organs, which precluded him from raising his voice at any time *above a very low whisper.* Of this defect I did not fail to take what poor advantage lay in my power.

Wilson's retaliations in kind were many; and there was one form of his practical wit that disturbed me beyond measure. How his sagacity first discovered at all that so petty a thing would vex me, is a question I never could solve; but, having discovered, he habitually practised the annoyance. I had always felt aversion to my uncourtly patronymic, and its very common, if not plebeian prænomen. The words were venom in my ears; and when, upon the day of my arrival, a second William Wilson came also to the academy, I felt angry with him for bearing the name, and doubly disgusted with the name because a stranger bore it, who would be the cause of its twofold repetition, who would be constantly in my presence, and whose concerns, in the ordinary routine of the school business, must inevitably, on account of the detestable coincidence, be often confounded with my own.

The feeling of vexation thus engendered grew stronger with every circumstance tending to show resemblance, moral or physical, between my rival and myself. I had not then discovered the remarkable fact that we were of the same age; but I saw that we were of the same height, and I perceived that we were even singularly alike in general contour of person and outline of feature. I was galled, too, by the rumor touching a relationship, which had grown current in the upper forms. In a word, nothing could more seriously disturb me, (although I scrupulously concealed such disturbance,) than any allusion to a similarity of mind, person, or condition existing between us. But, in truth, I had no reason to believe that (with the exception of the matter of relationship, and in the case of Wilson himself,) this similarity had ever been made a subject of comment, or even observed at all by our schoolfellows. That *he* observed it in all its bearings, and as fixedly as I, was apparent; but that he could discover in such circumstances so fruitful a field of annoyance, can only be attributed, as I said before, to his more than ordinary penetration.

His cue, which was to perfect an imitation of myself, lay both in words and in actions; and most admirably did he play his part. My dress it was an easy matter to copy; my gait and general manner were, without difficulty, appropriated; in spite of his constitutional defect, even my voice did not escape him. My louder tones were, of course, unattempted, but then the key, it was identical; *and his singular whisper, it grew the very echo of my own.*

How greatly this most exquisite portraiture harassed me, (for it could not justly be termed a caricature,) I will not now venture to describe. I had but one consolation—in the fact that the imitation, apparently, was noticed by myself alone, and that I had to endure only the knowing and strangely sarcastic smiles of my namesake himself. Satisfied with having produced in my bosom the intended effect, he seemed to chuckle in secret over the sting he had inflicted, and was characteristically disregardful of the public applause which the success of his witty endeavours might have so easily elicited. That the school, indeed, did not feel his design, perceive its accomplishment, and participate in his sneer, was, for many anxious months, a riddle I could not resolve. Perhaps the *gradation* of his copy rendered it not so readily perceptible; or, more possibly, I owed my security to the masterly air of the copyist, who, disdaining the letter, (which in a painting is all the obtuse can see,) gave but the full spirit of his original for my individual contemplation and chagrin.

I have already more than once spoken of the disgusting air of patronage which he assumed toward me, and of his frequent officious interference with my will. This interference often took the ungracious character of advice; advice not openly given, but hinted or insinuated. I received it with a repugnance which gained strength as I grew in years. Yet, at this distant day, let me do him the simple justice to acknowledge that I can recall no occasion when the suggestions of my rival were on the side of those errors or follies so usual to his immature age and seeming inexperience; that his moral sense, at least, if not his general talents and worldly wisdom, was far keener than my own; and that I might, to-day, have been a better, and thus a happier man, had I less frequently rejected the counsels embodied in those meaning whispers which I then but too cordially hated and too bitterly despised.

As it was, I at length grew restive in the extreme under his distasteful supervision, and daily resented more and more openly what I considered his intolerable arrogance. I have said that, in the first years of our connexion as schoolmates, my feelings in regard to him might have been easily ripened into friendship: but, in the latter months of my residence at the academy, although the intrusion of his ordinary manner had, beyond doubt, in some measure, abated, my sentiments, in nearly similar proportion, partook very much of positive hatred. Upon one occasion he saw this, I think, and afterwards avoided, or made a show of avoiding me.

It was about the same period, if I remember aright, that, in an altercation of violence with him, in which he was more than usually thrown off his guard, and spoke and acted with an openness of demeanor rather foreign to his nature, I discovered, or fancied I discovered, in his accent, his air, and general appearance, a something which first startled, and then deeply interested me, by bringing to mind dim visions of my earliest infancy—wild, confused and thronging memories of a time when memory herself was yet unborn. I cannot better describe the sensation which oppressed me than by saying that I could with difficulty shake off the belief of my having been acquainted with the being who stood before me, at some epoch very long ago—some point of the past even infinitely remote. The delusion, however, faded rapidly as it came; and I mention it at all but to define the day of the last conversation I there held with my singular namesake.

The huge old house, with its countless subdivisions, had several large chambers communicating with each other, where slept the greater number of the students. There were, however, (as must necessarily happen in a building so awkwardly planned,) many little nooks or recesses, the odds and ends of the structure; and these the economic ingenuity of Dr. Bransby had also fitted up as dormitories; although, being the merest closets, they were capable of accommodating but a single individual. One of these small apartments was occupied by Wilson.

One night, about the close of my fifth year at the school, and immediately after the altercation just mentioned, finding every one wrapped in sleep, I arose from bed, and, lamp in hand, stole through a wilderness of narrow passages from my own bedroom to that of my rival. I had long been plotting one of those ill-natured pieces of practical wit at his expense in which I had hitherto been so uniformly unsuccessful. It was my intention, now, to put my scheme in operation, and I resolved to make him feel the whole extent of the malice with which I was imbued. Having reached his closet, I noiselessly entered, leaving the lamp, with a shade over it, on the outside. I advanced a step, and listened to the sound of his tranquil breathing. Assured of his being asleep, I returned, took the light, and with it again approached the bed. Close curtains were around it, which, in the prosecution of my plan, I slowly and quietly withdrew, when the bright rays fell vividly upon the sleeper, and my eyes, at the same moment, upon his countenance. I looked;—and a numbness, an iciness of feeling instantly pervaded my frame. My breast heaved, my knees tottered, my whole spirit became possessed with an objectless yet intolerable horror. Gasping for breath, I lowered the lamp in still nearer proximity to the face. Were these—*these* the lineaments of William Wilson? I saw, indeed, that they were his, but I shook as if with a fit of the ague in fancying they were not. What *was* there about them to confound me in this manner? I gazed;—while my brain reeled with a multitude of incoherent thoughts. Not thus he appeared—assuredly not *thus*—in the vivacity of his waking hours. The same name! the same contour of person! the same day of arrival at the academy! And then his dogged and meaningless imitation of my gait, my voice, my habits, and my manner! Was it, in truth, within the bounds of human possibility, that *what I now saw* was the result, merely, of the habitual practice of this sarcastic imitation? Awe-stricken, and with a creeping shudder, I extinguished the lamp, passed silently from the chamber, and left, at once, the halls of that old academy, never to enter them again.

After a lapse of some months, spent at home in mere idleness, I found myself a student at Eton. The brief interval had been sufficient to enfeeble my remembrance of the events at Dr. Bransby's, or at least to effect a material change in the nature of the feelings with which I remembered them. The truth—the tragedy—of the drama was no more. I could now find room to doubt the evidence of my senses; and seldom called up the subject at all but with wonder at the extent of human credulity, and a smile at the vivid force of the imagination which I hereditarily possessed. Neither was this species of scepticism likely to be diminished by the character of the life I led at Eton. The vortex of thoughtless folly into which I there so immediately and so recklessly plunged, washed away all but the froth of my past hours, engulfed at once every solid or serious impression, and left to memory only the veriest levities of a former existence.

I do not wish, however, to trace the course of my miserable profligacy here—a profligacy which set at defiance the laws, while it eluded the vigilance of the institution. Three years of folly, passed without profit, had but given me rooted habits of vice, and added, in a somewhat unusual degree, to my bodily stature, when, after a week of soulless dissipation, I invited a small party of the most dissolute students to a secret carousal in my chambers. We met at a late hour of the night; for our debaucheries were to be faithfully protracted until morning. The wine flowed freely, and there were not wanting other and perhaps more dangerous seductions; so that the grey dawn had already faintly appeared in the east, while our delirious extravagance was at its height. Madly flushed with cards and intoxication, I was in the act of insisting upon a toast of more than wonted profanity, when my attention was suddenly diverted by the violent, although partial unclosing of the door of the apartment, and by the eager voice of a servant from without. He said that some person, apparently in great haste, demanded to speak with me in the hall.

Wildly excited with wine, the unexpected interruption rather delighted than surprised me. I staggered forward at once, and a few steps brought me to the vestibule of the building. In this low and small room there hung no lamp; and now no light at all was admitted, save that of the exceedingly feeble dawn which made its way through the semi-circular window. As I put my foot over the threshold, I became aware of the figure of a youth about my own height, and habited in a white kerseymere morning frock, cut in the novel fashion of the one I myself wore at the moment. This the faint light enabled me to perceive; but the features of his face I could not distinguish. Upon my entering he stode hurriedly up to me, and, seizing me by the arm with a gesture of petulant impatience, whispered the words "William Wilson!" in my ear.

I grew perfectly sober in an instant.

There was that in the manner of the stranger, and in the tremulous shake of his uplifted finger, as he held it between my eyes and the light, which filled me with unqualified amazement; but it was not this which had so violently moved me. It was the pregnancy of solemn admonition in the singular, low, hissing utterance; and, above all, it was the character, the tone, *the key,* of those few, simple, and familiar, yet *whispered* syllables, which came with a thousand thronging memories of bygone days, and struck upon my soul with the shock of a galvanic battery. Ere I could recover the use of my senses he was gone.

Although this event failed not of a vivid effect upon my disordered imagination, yet was it evanescent as vivid. For some weeks, indeed, I busied myself in earnest inquiry, or was wrapped in a cloud of morbid speculation. I did not pretend to disguise from my perception the identity of the singular individual who thus perseveringly interfered with my affairs, and harassed me with his insinuated counsel. But who and what was this Wilson?—and whence came he?—and what were his purposes? Upon neither of these points could I be satisfied; merely ascertaining in regard to him, that a sudden accident in his family had caused his removal from Dr. Bransby's academy on the afternoon of the day in which I myself had eloped. But in a brief period I ceased to think upon the subject; my attention being all absorbed in a contemplated departure for Oxford. Thither I soon went; the uncalculating vanity of my parents furnishing me with an outfit and annual establishment, which would enable me to indulge at will in the luxury already so dear to my heart,—to vie in profuseness of expenditure with the haughtiest heirs of the wealthiest earldoms in Great Britain.

Excited by such appliances to vice, my constitutional temperament broke forth with redoubled ardor, and I spurned even the common restraints of decency in the mad infatuation of my revels. But it were absurd to pause in the detail of my extravagance. Let it suffice, that among spendthrifts I out-Heroded Herod, and that, giving name to a multitude of novel follies, I added no brief appendix to the long catalogue of vices then usual in the most dissolute university of Europe.

It could hardly be credited, however, that I had, even here, so utterly fallen from the gentlemanly estate, as to seek acquaintance with the vilest arts of the gambler by profession, and, having become an adept in his despicable science, to practise it habitually as a means of increasing my already enormous income at the expense of the weak-minded among my fellow-collegians. Such, nevertheless, was the fact. And the very enormity of this offence against all manly and honourable sentiment proved, beyond doubt, the main if not the sole reason of the impunity with which it was committed. Who, indeed, among my most abandoned associates, would not rather have disputed the clearest evidence of his senses, than have suspected of such courses, the gay, the frank, the generous William Wilson

—the noblest and most liberal commoner at Oxford—him whose follies (said his parasites) were but the follies of youth and unbridled fancy—whose errors but inimitable whim—whose darkest vice but a careless and dashing extravagance?

I had been now two years successfully busied in this way, when there came to the university a young *parvenu* nobleman, Glendinning—rich, said report, as Herodes Atticus—his riches, too, as easily acquired. I soon found him of weak intellect, and, of course, marked him as a fitting subject for my skill. I frequently engaged him in play, and contrived, with the gambler's usual art, to let him win considerable sums, the more effectually to entangle him in my snares. At length, my schemes being ripe, I met him (with the full intention that this meeting should be final and decisive) at the chambers of a fellow-commoner, (Mr. Preston,) equally intimate with both, but who, to do him justice, entertained not even a remote suspicion of my design. To give to this a better coloring, I had contrived to have assembled a party of some eight or ten, and was solicitously careful that the introduction of cards should appear accidental, and originate in the proposal of my contemplated dupe himself. To be brief upon a vile topic, none of the low finesse was omitted, so customary upon similar occasions that it is a just matter for wonder how any are still found so besotted as to fall its victim.

We had protracted our sitting far into the night, and I had at length effected the manœuvre of getting Glendinning as my sole antagonist. The game, too, was my favorite *écarté*. The rest of the company, interested in the extent of our play, had abandoned their own cards, and were standing around us as spectators. The *parvenu*, who had been induced by my artifices in the early part of the evening, to drink deeply, now shuffled, dealt, or played, with a wild nervousness of manner for which his intoxication, I thought, might partially, but could not altogether account. In a very short period he had become my debtor to a large amount, when, having taken a long draught of port, he did precisely what I had been coolly anticipating—he proposed to double our already extravagant stakes. With a well-feigned show of reluctance, and not until after my repeated refusal had seduced him into some angry words which gave a color of *pique* to my compliance, did I finally comply. The result, of course, did but prove how entirely the prey was in my toils; in less than an hour he had quadrupled his debt. For some time his countenance had been losing the florid tinge lent it by the wine; but now, to my astonishment, I perceived that it had grown to a pallor truly fearful. I say to my astonishment. Glendinning had been represented to my eager inquiries as immeasurably wealthy; and the sums which he had as yet lost, although in themselves vast, could not, I supposed, very seriously annoy, much less so violently affect him. That he was overcome by the wine just swallowed, was the idea which most readily presented itself; and, rather with a view to the preservation of my own character in the eyes of my associates, than from any less interested motive, I was about to insist, peremptorily, upon a discontinuance of the play, when some expressions at my elbow from among the company, and an ejaculation evincing utter despair on the part of Glendinning, gave me to understand that I had effected his total ruin under circumstances which, rendering him an object for the pity of all, should have protected him from the ill offices even of a fiend.

What now might have been my conduct it is difficult to say. The pitiable condition of my dupe had thrown an air of embarrassed gloom over all; and, for some moments, a profound silence was maintained, during which I could not help feeling my cheeks tingle with the many burning glances of scorn or reproach cast upon me by the less abandoned of the party. I will even own that an intolerable weight of anxiety was for a brief instant lifted from my bosom by the sudden and extraordinary interruption which ensued. The wide, heavy folding doors of the apartment were all at once thrown open, to their full extent, with a vigorous and rushing impetuosity that extinguished, as if by magic, every candle in the room. Their light, in dying, enabled us just to perceive that a stranger had entered, about my own height, and closely muffled in a cloak. The darkness, however, was now total; and we could only *feel* that he was standing in our midst. Before any one of us could recover from the extreme astonishment into which this rudeness had thrown all, we heard the voice of the intruder.

"Gentlemen," he said, in a low, distinct, and never-to-be-forgotten *whisper* which thrilled to the very marrow of my bones, "Gentlemen, I make no apology for this behaviour, because in thus behaving, I am but fulfilling a duty. You are, beyond doubt, uninformed of the true character of the person who has to-night won at *écarté* a large sum of money from Lord Glendinning. I will therefore put you upon an expeditious and decisive plan of obtaining this very necessary information. Please to examine, at your leisure, the inner linings of the cuff of his left sleeve, and the several little packages which may be found in the somewhat capacious pockets of his embroidered morning wrapper."

While he spoke, so profound was the stillness that one might have heard a pin drop upon the floor. In ceasing, he departed at once, and as abruptly as he had entered. Can I—shall I describe my sensations?—must I say that I felt all the horrors of the damned? Most assuredly I had little time given for reflection. Many hands roughly seized me upon the spot, and lights were immediately reprocured. A search ensued. In the lining of my sleeve were found all the court cards essential in *écarté,* and, in the pockets of my wrapper, a number of packs, facsimiles of those used at our sittings, with the single exception that mine were of the species called, technically, *arrondées;* the honours being slightly convex at the ends, the lower cards slightly convex at the sides. In this disposition, the dupe who cuts, as customary, at the length of the pack, will invariably find that he cuts his antagonist an honor; while the gambler, cutting at the breadth, will, as certainly, cut nothing for his victim which may count in the records of the game.

Any burst of indignation upon this discovery would have affected me less than the silent contempt, or the sarcastic composure, with which it was received.

"Mr. Wilson," said our host, stooping to remove from beneath his feet an exceedingly luxurious cloak of rare furs, "Mr. Wilson, this is your property." (The weather was cold; and, upon quitting my own room, I had thrown a cloak over my dressing wrapper, putting it off upon reaching the scene of play.) "I presume it is supererogatory to seek here (eyeing the folds of the garment with a bitter smile) for any further evidence of your skill. Indeed, we have had enough. You will see the necessity, I hope, of quitting Oxford—at all events, of quitting instantly my chambers."

Abased, humbled to the dust as I then was, it is probable that I should have resented this galling language by immediate personal violence, had not my whole attention been at the moment arrested by a fact of the most startling character. The cloak which I had worn was of a rare description of fur; how rare, how extravagantly costly, I shall not venture to say. Its fashion, too, was of my own fantastic invention; for I was fastidious to an absurd degree of coxcombry, in matters of this frivolous nature. When, therefore, Mr. Preston reached me that which he had picked up upon the floor, and near the folding doors of the apartment, it was with an astonishment nearly bordering upon terror, that I perceived my own already hanging on my arm, (where I had no doubt unwittingly placed it,) and that the one presented me was but its exact counterpart in every, in even the minutest possible particular. The singular being who had so disastrously exposed me, had been muffled, I remembered, in a cloak; and none had been worn at all by any of the members of our party with the exception of myself. Retaining some presence of mind, I took the one offered me by Preston; placed it, unnoticed, over my own; left the apartment with a resolute scowl of defiance; and, next morning ere dawn of day, commenced a hurried journey from Oxford to the continent, in a perfect agony of horror and of shame.

I fled in vain. My evil destiny pursued me as if in exultation, and proved, indeed, that the exercise of its mysterious dominion had as yet only begun. Scarcely had I set foot in Paris ere I had fresh evidence of the detestable interest taken by this Wilson in my concerns. Years flew, while I experienced no relief. Villain!—at Rome, with how untimely, yet with how spectral an officiousness, stepped he in between me and my ambition! At Vienna, too—at Berlin—and at Moscow! Where, in truth, had I *not* bitter cause to curse him within my heart? From his inscrutable tyranny did I at length flee, panic-stricken, as from a pestilence; and to the very ends of the earth *I fled in vain.*

And again, and again, in secret communion with my own spirit, would I demand the questions "Who is he?—whence came he?—and what are his objects?" But no answer was there found. And then I scrutinized, with a minute scrutiny, the forms, and the methods, and the leading traits of his impertinent supervision. But even here there was very little upon which to base a conjecture. It was noticeable, indeed, that, in no one of the multiplied instances in which he had of late crossed my path, had he so crossed it except to frustrate those schemes, or to disturb those actions, which, if fully carried out, might have resulted in bitter mischief. Poor justification this, in truth, for an authority so imperiously assumed! Poor indemnity for natural rights of self-agency so pertinaciously, so insultingly denied!

I had also been forced to notice that my tormentor, for a very long period of time, (while scrupulously and with miraculous dexterity maintaining his whim of an identity of apparel with myself,) had so contrived it, in the execution of his varied interference with my will, that I saw not, at any moment, the features of his face. Be Wilson what he might, *this,* at least, was but the veriest of affectation, or of folly. Could he, for an instant, have supposed that, in my admonisher at Eton—in the destroyer of my honor at Oxford—in him who thwarted my ambition at Rome, my revenge at Paris, my passionate love at Naples, or what he falsely termed my avarice in Egypt,—that in this, my arch-enemy and evil genius, I could fail to recognise the William Wilson of my school-boy days,—the namesake, the companion, the rival,—the hated and dreaded rival at Dr. Bransby's? Impossible!—But let me hasten to the last eventful scene of the drama.

Thus far I had succumbed supinely to this imperious domination. The sentiment of deep awe with which I habitually regarded the elevated character, the majestic wisdom, the apparent omnipresence and omnipotence of Wilson, added to a feeling of even terror, with which certain other traits in his nature and assumptions inspired me, had operated, hitherto, to impress me with an idea of my own utter weakness and helplessness, and to suggest an implicit, although bitterly reluctant submission to his arbitrary will. But, of late days, I had given myself up entirely to wine; and its maddening influence upon my hereditary temper rendered me more and more impatient of control. I began to murmur,—to hesitate,—to resist. And was it only fancy which induced me to believe that, with the increase of my own firmness, that of my tormentor underwent a proportional diminution? Be this as it may, I now began to feel the inspiration of a burning hope, and at length nurtured in my secret thoughts a stern and desperate resolution that I would submit no longer to be enslaved.

It was at Rome, during the Carnival of 18—, that I attended a masquerade in the palazzo of the Neapolitan Duke Di Broglio. I had indulged more freely than usual in the excesses of the wine-table; and now the suffocating atmosphere of the crowded rooms irritated me beyond endurance. The difficulty, too, of forcing my way through the mazes of the company contributed not a little to the ruffling of my temper; for I was anxiously seeking, (let me not say with what unworthy motive) the young, the gay, the beautiful wife of the aged and doting Di Broglio. With a too unscrupulous confidence she had previously communicated to me the secret of the costume in which she would be habited, and now, having caught a glimpse of her person, I was hurrying to make my way into her presence.—At this moment I felt a light hand placed upon my shoulder, and that ever-remembered, low, damnable *whisper* within my ear.

In an absolute frenzy of wrath, I turned at once upon him who had thus interrupted me, and seized him violently by the collar. He was attired, as I had expected, in a costume altogether similar to my own; wearing a Spanish cloak of blue velvet, begirt about the waist with a crimson belt sustaining a rapier. A mask of black silk entirely covered his face.

"Scoundrel!" I said, in a voice husky with rage, while every syllable I uttered seemed as new fuel to my fury, "scoundrel! impostor! accursed villain! you shall not—you *shall not* dog me unto death! Follow me, or I stab you where you stand!"—and I broke my way from the ball-room into a small ante-chamber adjoining—dragging him unresistingly with me as I went.

Upon entering, I thrust him furiously from me. He staggered against the wall, while I closed the door with an oath, and commanded him to draw. He hesitated but for an instant; then, with a slight sigh, drew in silence, and put himself upon his defense.

The contest was brief indeed. I was frantic with every species of wild excitement, and felt within my single arm the energy and power of a multitude. In a few seconds I forced him by sheer strength against the wainscoting, and thus, getting him at mercy, plunged my sword, with brute ferocity, repeatedly through and through his bosom.

At that instant some person tried the latch of the door. I hastened to prevent an intrusion, and then immediately returned to my dying antagonist. But what human language can adequately portray *that* astonishment, *that* horror which possessed me at the spectacle then presented to view? The brief moment in which I averted my eyes had been sufficient to produce, apparently, a material change in the arrangements at the upper or farther end of the room. A large mirror,—so at first it seemed to me in my confusion—now stood where none had been perceptible before; and, as I stepped up to it in extremity of terror, mine own image, but with features all pale and dabbled in blood, advanced to meet me with a feeble and tottering gait.

Thus it appeared, I say, but was not. It was my antagonist—it was Wilson, who then stood before me in the agonies of his dissolution. His mask and cloak lay, where he had thrown them, upon the floor. Not a thread in all his raiment—not a line in all the marked and singular lineaments of his face which was not, even in the most absolute identity, *mine own!*

It was Wilson; but he spoke no longer in a whisper, and I could have fancied that I myself was speaking while he said:

"You have conquered, and I yield. Yet, henceforward art thou also dead—dead to the World, to Heaven and to Hope! In me didst thou exist—and, in my death, see by this image, which is thine own, how utterly thou hast murdered thyself."

Herman Melville

(1819 - 1891)

To the truly honest man "life is, in itself and forever, shipwreck," wrote the twentieth-century Spanish philosopher Jose Ortega Y Gasset. "To be shipwrecked is not to drown. The poor human being, feeling himself sinking into the abyss, moves his arms to keep afloat. This movement of the arms, which is his reaction against his own destruction, is culture—a swimming stroke." The life of Herman Melville was perpetual shipwreck and his own swimming (or saving) stroke was his art. He spent much of his spiritual life bobbing, like the coffin-grasping Ishmael at the end of *Moby Dick,* on a sea of philosophic uncertainities and attendant anxieties. According to two of his biographers, periodic storms threatened to drive him onto the reefs of mental breakdown, and yet his buoyant spirit never went under. Melville's problem was that once he had abandoned his austere childhood religion, he was irretrievably launched onto that sea from which he appears to have deliberately refused all dogmatic lifesavers, religious and philosophic. He simply could not understand or accept the evil in the world, nor could he turn away from the unanswerable questions of life. In his 1856 notebook, Nathaniel Hawthorne wrote of his friend:

> Melville, as he always does, began to reason of Providence and futurity, and of everything that lies beyond human ken, and informed me that he had "pretty much made up his mind to be annihilated.". . . It is strange how he persists—and has persisted ever since I knew him, and probably long before—in wandering to-and-fro over these deserts. . . . He can neither believe, nor be comfortable in his unbelief; and he is too honest and courageous not to try to do one or the other.

This uncertainty, questing and questioning of absolutes and evils, is infused in most of Melville's fiction, especially that great and whalish book, *Moby Dick.* In his own time he was sadly neglected by the critics and reading public and died virtually unappreciated as a literary artist. Possibly because he speaks directly to our time, Melville is now regarded as one of America's greatest, most vigorous writers. "Contradiction and alienation are of the essence in Melville's view of life and in his art," wrote Richard Chase, and he could have been commenting on a contemporary writer. In the powerful short novel *Benito Cereno* Melville dramatizes the belated recognition of evil by an American sea captain, a representative of the New World, who comes to the aid of a man of the Old World. From the first page a sinister atmosphere hangs over the story of revolt of oppressed black slaves.

Benito Cereno

In the year 1799, Captain Amasa Delano, of Duxbury, in Massachusetts, commanding a large sealer and general trader, lay at anchor with a valuable cargo, in the harbor of St. Maria—a small, desert, uninhabited island toward the southern extremity of the long coast of Chili. There he had touched for water.

On the second day, not long after dawn, while lying in his berth, his mate came below, informing him that a strange sail was coming into the bay. Ships were then not so plenty in those waters as now. He rose, dressed, and went on deck.

The morning was one peculiar to that coast. Everything was mute and calm; everything gray. The sea, though undulated into long roods of swells, seemed fixed, and was sleeked at the surface like waved lead that has cooled and set in the smelter's mould. The sky seemed a gray surtout. Flights of troubled gray fowl, kith and kin with flights of troubled gray vapors among which they were mixed, skimmed low and fitfully over the waters, as swallows over meadows before storms. Shadows present, foreshadowing deeper shadows to come.

To Captain Delano's surprise, the stranger, viewed through the glass, showed no colors; though to do so upon entering a haven, however uninhabited in its shores, where but a single other ship might be lying, was the custom among peaceful seamen of all nations. Considering the lawlessness and loneliness of the spot, and the sort of stories, at that day, associated with those seas, Captain Delano's surprise might have deepened into some uneasiness had he not been a person of a singularly undistrustful good nature, not liable, except on extraordinary and repeated incentives, and hardly then, to indulge in personal alarms, any way involving the imputation of malign evil in man. Whether, in view of what humanity is capable, such a trait implies, along with a benevolent heart, more than ordinary quickness and accuracy of intellectual perception, may be left to the wise to determine.

But whatever misgivings might have obtruded on first seeing the stranger, would almost, in any seaman's mind, have been dissipated by observing that, the ship, in navigating into the harbor, was drawing too near the land; a sunken reef making out off her bow. This seemed to prove her a stranger, indeed, not only to the sealer, but the island; consequently, she could be no wonted freebooter on that ocean. With no small interest, Captain Delano continued to watch her—a proceeding not much facilitated by the vapors partly mantling the hull, through which the far matin light from her cabin streamed equivocally enough; much like the sun—by this time hemisphered on the rim of the horizon, and, apparently, in company with the strange ship entering the harbor—which, wimpled by the same low, creeping clouds, showed not unlike a Lima *intriguante's* one sinister eye peering across the Plaza from the Indian loop-hole of her dusk *saya-y-manta.*

It might have been but a deception of the vapors, but, the longer the stranger was watched the more singular appeared her manœuvres. Ere long it seemed hard to decide whether she meant to come in or no—what she wanted, or what she was about. The wind, which had breezed up a little during the night, was now extremely light and baffling, which the more increased the apparent uncertainty of her movements.

Surmising, at last, that it might be a ship in distress, Captain Delano order his whale-boat to be dropped, and much to the wary opposition of his mate, prepared to board her, and, at the least, pilot her in. On the night previous, a fishing-party of the seamen had gone a long distance to some detached rocks out of sight from the sealer, and, an hour or two before day-break, had returned, having met with no small success. Presuming that the stranger might have been long off soundings, the good captain put several baskets of the fish, for presents, into his boat, and so pulled away. From her continuing too near the sunken reef, deeming her in danger, calling to his men, he made all haste to apprise those on board of their situation. But, some time ere the boat came up, the wind, light though it was, having shifted, had headed the vessel off, as well as partly broken the vapors from about her.

Upon gaining a less remote view, the ship, when made signally visible on the verge of the leaden-hued swells, with the shreds of fog here and there raggedly furring her, appeared like a whitewashed monastery after a thunder-storm, seen perched upon some dun cliff among the Pyrenees. But it was no purely fanciful resemblance which now, for a moment, almost led Captain Delano to think that nothing less than a shipload of monks was before him. Peering over the bulwarks were what really seemed, in the hazy distance, throngs of dark cowls; while, fitfully revealed through the open port-holes, other dark moving figures were dimly described, as of Black Friars pacing the cloisters.

Upon a still nigher approach, this appearance was modified, and the true character of the vessel was plain—a Spanish merchantman of the first class, carrying negro slaves, amongst other valuable freight, from one colonial port to another. A very large, and, in its time, a very fine vessel, such as in those days were at intervals encountered along that main; sometimes superseded Acapulco treasure-ships or retired frigates of the Spanish king's navy, which, like superannuated Italian palaces, still, under a decline of masters, preserved signs of former state.

As the whale-boat drew more and more nigh, the cause of the peculiar pipe-clayed aspect of the stranger was seen in the slovenly neglect pervading her. The spars, ropes, and great part of the bulwarks, looked woolly, from long unacquaintance with the scraper, tar, and the brush. Her keel seemed laid, her ribs put together, and she launched, from Ezekiel's Valley of Dry Bones.

In the present business in which she was engaged, the ship's general model and rig appeared to have undergone no material change from their original warlike and Froissart pattern. However, no guns were seen.

The tops were large, and were railed about with what had once been octagonal net-work, all now in sad disrepair. These tops hung overhead like three ruinous aviaries, in one of which was seen perched, on a ratlin, a white noddy, a strange fowl, so called from its lethargic, somnambulistic character, being frequently caught by hand at sea. Battered and mouldy, the castellated forecastle seemed some ancient turret, long ago taken by assault, and then left to decay. Toward the stern, two high-raised quarter galleries—the balustrades here and there covered with dry, tindery sea-moss—opening out from the unoccupied state-cabin, whose dead-lights, for all the mild weather, were hermetically closed and calked—these tenantless balconies hung over the sea as if it were the grand Venetian canal. But the principal relic of faded grandeur was the ample oval of the shield-like stern-piece, intricately carved with the arms of Castile and Leon, medallioned about by groups of mythological or symbolical devices; uppermost and central of which was a dark satyr in a mask, holding his foot on the prostrate neck of a writhing figure, likewise masked.

Whether the ship had a figure-head, or only a plain beak, was not quite certain, owing to canvas wrapped about that part, either to protect it while undergoing a re-furbishing, or else decently to hide its decay. Rudely painted or chalked, as in a sailor freak, along the forward side of a sort of pedestal below the canvas, was the sentence, "*Seguid vuestro jefe,*" (follow your leader); while upon the tarnished headboards, near by, appeared, in stately capitals, once gilt, the ship's name, "SAN DOMINICK," each letter streakingly corroded with tricklings of copper-spike rust; while, like mourning weeds, dark festoons of sea-grass slimily swept to and fro over the name, with every hearse-like roll of the hull.

As, at last, the boat was hooked from the bow along toward the gangway amidship, its keel, while yet some inches separated from the hull, harshly grated as on a sunken coral reef. It proved a huge bunch of conglobated barnacles adhering below the water to the side like a wen—a token of baffling airs and long calms passed somewhere in those seas.

Climbing the side, the visitor was at once surrounded by a clamorous throng of whites and blacks, but the latter outnumbering the former more than could have been expected, negro transportation-ship as the stranger in port was. But, in one language, and as with one voice, all poured out a common tale of suffering; in which the negresses, of whom there were not a few, exceeded the others in their dolorous vehemence. The scurvy, together with the fever, had swept off a great part of their number, more especially the Spaniards. Off Cape Horn they had narrowly escaped shipwreck; then, for days together, they had lain tranced without wind; their provisions were low; their water next to none; their lips that moment were baked.

While Captain Delano was thus made the mark of all eager tongues, his one eager glance took in all faces, with every other object about him.

Always upon first boarding a large and populous ship at sea, especially a foreign one, with a nondescript crew such as Lascars or Manilla men, the impression varies in a peculiar way from that produced by first entering a strange house with strange inmates in a strange land. Both house and ship—the one by its walls and blinds, the other by its high bulwarks like ramparts—hoard from view their interiors till the last moment: but in the case of the ship there is this addition; that the living spectacle it contains, upon its sudden and complete disclosure, has, in contrast with the blank ocean which zones it, something of the effect of enchantment. The ship seems unreal; these strange costumes, gestures, and faces, but a shadowy tableau just emerged from the deep, which directly must receive back what it gave.

Perhaps it was some such influence, as above is attempted to be described, which, in Captain Delano's mind, heightened whatever, upon a staid scrutiny, might have seemed unusual; especially the conspicuous figures of four elderly grizzled negroes, their heads like black, doddered willow tops, who, in venerable contrast to the tumult below them, were couched, sphynx-like, one on the starboard cat-head, another on the larboard, and the remaining pair face to face on the opposite bulwarks above the main-chains. They each had bits of unstranded old junk in their hands, and, with a sort of stoical self-content, were picking the junk into oakum, a small heap of which lay by their sides. They accompanied the task with a continuous, low, monotonous chant; droning and druling away like so many gray-headed bag-pipers playing a funeral march.

The quarter-deck rose into an ample elevated poop, upon the forward verge of which, lifted, like the oakum-pickers, some eight feet above the general throng, sat along in a row, separated by regular spaces, the cross-legged figures of six other blacks; each with a rusty hatchet in his hand, which, with a bit of brick and a rag, he was engaged like a scullion in scouring; while between each two was a small stack of hatchets, their rusted edges turned forward awaiting a like operation. Though occasionally the four oakum-pickers would briefly address some person or persons in the crowd below, yet the six hatchet-polishers neither spoke to others, nor breathed a whisper among themselves, but sat intent upon their task, except at intervals, when, with the peculiar love in negroes of uniting industry with pastime, two and two they sideways clashed their hatchets together, like cymbals, with a barbarous din. All six, unlike the generality, had the raw aspect of unsophisticated Africans.

But that first comprehensive glance which took in those ten figures, with scores less conspicuous, rested but an instant upon them, as, impatient of the hubbub of voices, the visitor turned in quest of whosoever it might be that commanded the ship.

But as if not unwilling to let nature make known her own case among his suffering charge, or else in despair of restraining it for the time, the Spanish captain, a gentlemanly, reserved-looking, and rather young man to a stranger's eye, dressed with singular richness, but bearing plain traces of recent sleepless cares and disquietudes, stood passively by, leaning against the main-mast, at one moment casting a dreary, spiritless look upon his excited people, at the next an unhappy glance toward his visitor. By his side stood a black of small stature, in whose rude face, as occasionally, like a shepherd's dog, he mutely turned it up into the Spaniard's, sorrow and affection were equally blended.

Struggling through the throng, the American advanced to the Spaniard, assuring him of his sympathies, and offering to render whatever assistance might be in his power. To which the Spaniard returned for the present but grave and ceremonious acknowledgments his national formality dusked by the saturnine mood of ill-health.

But losing no time in mere compliments, Captain Delano, returning to the gangway, had his basket of fish brought up; and as the wind still continued light, so that some hours at least must elapse ere the ship could be brought to the anchorage, he bade his men return to the sealer, and fetch back as much water as the whale-boat could carry, with whatever soft bread the steward might have, all the remaining pumpkins on board, with a box of sugar, and a dozen of his private bottles of cider.

Not many minutes after the boat's pushing off, to the vexation of all, the wind entirely died away, and the tide turning, began drifting back the ship helplessly seaward. But trusting this would not long last, Captain Delano sought, with good hopes, to cheer up the strangers, feeling no small satisfaction that, with persons in their condition, he could—thanks to his frequent voyages along the Spanish main—converse with some freedom in their native tongue.

While left alone with them, he was not long in observing some things tending to heighten his first impressions; but surprise was lost in pity, both for the Spaniards and blacks, alike evidently reduced from scarcity of water and provisions; while long-continued suffering seemed to have brought out the less good-natured qualities of the negroes, besides, at the same time, impairing the Spaniard's authority over them. But, under the circumstances, precisely this condition of things was to have been anticipated. In armies, navies, cities, or families, in nature herself, nothing more relaxes good order than misery. Still, Captain Delano was not without the idea, that had Benito Cereno been a man of greater energy, misrule would hardly have come to the present pass. But the debility, constitutional or induced by hardships, bodily and mental, of the Spanish captain, was too obvious to be overlooked. A prey to settled dejection, as if long mocked with hope he would not now indulge it, even when it had ceased to be a mock, the prospect of that day, or evening at furthest, lying at anchor, with plenty of water for his people, and a brother captain to counsel and befriend, seemed in no perceptible degree to encourage him. His mind appeared unstrung, if not still more seriously affected. Shut up in these oaken walls, chained to one dull round of command, whose unconditionality cloyed him, like some hypochondriac abbot he moved slowly about, at times suddenly pausing, starting, or staring, biting his lip, biting his fingernail, flushing, paling, twitching his beard, with other symptoms of an absent or moody mind. This distempered spirit was lodged, as before hinted, in as distempered a frame. He was rather tall, but seemed never to have been robust, and now with nervous suffering was almost worn to a skeleton. A tendency to some pulmonary complaint appeared to have been lately confirmed. His voice was like that of one with lungs half gone—hoarsely suppressed, a husky whisper. No wonder that, as in this state he tottered about, his private servant apprehensively followed him. Sometimes the negro gave his master his arm, or took his handkerchief out of his pocket for him; performing these and similar offices with that affectionate zeal which transmutes into something filial or fraternal acts in themselves but menial; and which has gained for the negro the repute of making the most pleasing body-servant in the world; one, too, whom a master need be on no stiffly superior terms with, but may treat with familiar trust; less a servant than a devoted companion.

Marking the noisy indocility of the blacks in general, as well as what seemed the sullen inefficiency of the whites it was not without humane satisfaction that Captain Delano witnessed the steady good conduct of Babo.

But the good conduct of Babo, hardly more than the ill-behavior of others, seemed to withdraw the half-lunatic Don Benito from his cloudy languor. Not that such precisely was the impression made by the Spaniard on the mind of his visitor. The Spaniard's individual unrest was, for the present, but noted as a conspicuous feature in the ship's general affliction. Still, Captain Delano was not a little concerned at what he could not help taking for the time to be Don Benito's unfriendly indifference towards himself. The Spaniard's manner, too, conveyed a sort of sour and gloomy disdain, which he seemed at no pains to disguise. But this the American in charity ascribed to the harassing effects of sickness, since, in former instances, he had noted that there are peculiar natures on whom prolonged physical suffering seems to cancel every social instinct of kindness; as if, forced to black bread themselves, they deemed it but equity that each person coming nigh them should, indirectly, by some slight or affront, be made to partake of their fare.

But ere long Captain Delano bethought him that, indulgent as he was at the first, in judging the Spaniard, he might not, after all, have exercised charity enough. At bottom it was Don Benito's reserve which displeased him; but the same reserve was shown towards all but his faithful personal attendant. Even the formal reports which, according to sea-usage, were, at stated times, made to him by some petty underling, either a white, mulatto or black, he hardly had patience enough to listen to, without betraying contemptuous aversion. His manner upon such occasions was, in its degree, not unlike that which might be supposed to have been his imperial countryman's Charles V, just previous to the anchoritish retirement of that monarch from the throne.

This splenetic disrelish of his place was evinced in almost every function pertaining to it. Proud as he was moody, he condescended to no personal mandate. Whatever special orders were necessary, their delivery was delegated to his body-servant, who in turn transferred them to their ultimate destination, through runners, alert Spanish boys or slave boys, like pages or pilot-fish within easy call continually hovering round Don Benito. So that to have beheld this undemonstrative invalid gliding about, apathetic and mute, no landsman could have dreamed that in him was lodged a dictatorship beyond which, while at sea, there was no earthly appeal.

Thus, the Spaniard, regarded in his reserve, seemed the involuntary victim of mental disorder. But, in fact, his reserve might, in some degree, have proceeded from design. If so, then here was evinced the unhealthy climax of that icy though conscientious policy, more or less adopted by all commanders of large ships, which, except in signal emergencies, obliterates alike the manifestation of sway with every trace of sociality; transforming the man into a block, or rather into a loaded canon, which, until there is call for thunder, has nothing to say.

Viewing him in this light, it seemed but a natural token of the perverse habit induced by a long course of such hard self-restraint, that, notwithstanding the present condition of his ship, the Spaniard should still persist in a demeanor, which, however harmless, or, it may be, appropriate, in a well-appointed vessel, such as the San Dominick might have been at the outset of the voyage, was anything but judicious now. But the Spaniard, perhaps, thought that it was with captains as with gods: reserve, under all events, must still be their cue. But probably this appearance of slumbering dominion might have been but an attempted disguise to conscious imbecility—not deep policy, but shallow device. But be all this as it might, whether Don Benito's manner was designed or not, the more Captain Delano noted its pervading reserve, the less he felt uneasiness at any particular manifestation of that reserve towards himself.

Neither were his thoughts taken up by the captain alone. Wonted to the quiet orderliness of the sealer's comfortable family of a crew, the noisy confusion of the San Dominick's suffering host repeatedly challenged his eye. Some prominent breaches, not only of discipline but of decency, were observed. These Captain Delano could not but ascribe, in the main, to the absence of those subordinate deck-officers to whom, along with higher duties, is intrusted what may be styled the police department of a populous ship. True, the old oakum-pickers appeared at times to act the part of monitorial constables to their countrymen, the blacks; but though occasionally succeeding in allaying trifling outbreaks now and then between man and man, they could do little or nothing toward establishing general quiet. The San Dominick was in the condition of a transatlantic emigrant ship, among whose multitude of living freight are some individuals, doubtless, as little troublesome as crates and bales; but the friendly remonstrances of such with their ruder companions are of not so much avail as the unfriendly arm of the mate. What the San Dominick wanted was, what the emigrant ship has, stern superior officers. But on these decks not so much as a fourth-mate was to be seen.

The visitor's curiosity was roused to learn the particulars of those mishaps which had brought about such absenteeism, with its consequences; because, though deriving some inkling of the voyage from the wails which at the first moment had greeted him, yet of the details no clear understanding had been had. The best account would, doubtless, be given by the captain. Yet at first the visitor was loth to ask it, unwilling to provoke some distant rebuff. But plucking up courage, he at last accosted Don Benito, renewing the expression of his benevolent interest, adding, that did he (Captain Delano) but know the particulars of the ship's misfortunes, he would, perhaps, be better able in the end to relieve them. Would Don Benito favor him with the whole story.

Don Benito faltered; then, like some somnambulist suddenly interfered with, vacantly stared at his visitor, and ended by looking down on the deck. He maintained this posture so long that Captain Delano, almost equally disconcerted, and involuntarily almost as rude, turned suddenly from him, walking forward to accost one of the Spanish seamen for the desired information. But he had hardly gone five paces, when, with a sort of eagerness, Don Benito invited him back, regretting his momentary absence of mind, and professing readiness to gratify him.

While most part of the story was being given, the two captains stood on the after part of the main-deck, a privileged spot, no one being near but the servant.

"It is now a hundred and ninety days," began the Spaniard, in his husky whisper, "that this ship, well officered and well manned, with several cabin passengers—some fifty Spaniards in all—sailed from Buenos Ayres bound to Lima, with a general cargo, hardware, Paraguay tea and the like—and," pointing forward, "that parcel of negroes, now not more than a hundred and fifty, as you see, but then numbering over three hundred souls. Off Cape Horn we had heavy gales. In one moment, by night, three of my best officers, with fifteen sailors, were lost, with the main-yard; the spar snapping under them in the slings, as they sought, with heavers, to beat down the icy sail. To lighten the hull, the heavier sacks of mata were thrown into the sea, with most of the water-pipes lashed on deck at the time. And this last necessity it was, combined with the prolonged detentions afterwards experienced, which eventually brought about our chief causes of suffering. When——"

Here there was a sudden fainting attack of his cough, brought on, no doubt, by his mental distress. His servant sustained him, and drawing a cordial from his pocket placed it to his lips. He a little revived. But unwilling to leave him unsupported while yet imperfectly restored, the black with one arm still encircled his master, at the same time keeping his eye fixed on his face, as if to watch for the first sign of complete restoration, or relapse, as the event might prove.

The Spaniard proceeded, but brokenly and obscurely, as one in a dream.

—"Oh, my God! rather than pass through what I have, with joy I would have hailed the most terrible gales; but——"

His cough returned and with increased violence; this subsiding, with reddened lips and closed eyes he fell heavily against his supporter.

"His mind wanders. He was thinking of the plague that followed the gales," plaintively sighed the servant; "my poor, poor master!" wringing one hand, and with the other wiping the mouth. "But be patient, Señor," again turning to Captain Delano, "these fits do not last long; master will soon be himself."

Don Benito reviving, went on; but as this portion of the story was very brokenly delivered, the substance only will here be set down.

It appeared that after the ship had been many days tossed in storms off the Cape, the scurvy broke out, carrying off numbers of the whites and blacks. When at last they had worked round into the Pacific, their spars and sails were so damaged, and so inadequately handled by the surviving mariners, most of whom were become invalids, that, unable to lay her northerly course by the wind, which was powerful, the unmanageable ship, for successive days and nights, was blown northwestward, where the breeze suddenly deserted her, in unknown waters, to sultry calms. The absence of the water-pipes now proved as fatal to life as before their presence had menaced it. Induced, or at least aggravated, by the more than scanty allowance of water, a malignant fever followed the scurvy; with the excessive heat of the lengthened calm, making such short work of it as to sweep away, as by billows, whole families of the Africans, and a yet larger number, proportionably, of the Spaniards, including, by a luckless fatality, every remaining officer on board. Consequently, in the smart west winds eventually following the calm, the already rent sails, having to be simply dropped, not furled, at need, had been gradually reduced to the beggars' rags they were now. To procure substitutes for his lost sailors, as well as supplies of water and sails, the captain, at the earliest opportunity, had made for Baldivia, the southernmost civilized port of Chili and South America; but upon nearing the coast the thick weather had prevented him from so much as sighting that harbor. Since which period, almost without a crew, and almost without canvas and almost without water, and, at intervals, giving its added dead to the sea, the San Dominick had been battle-dored about by contrary winds, inveigled by currents, or grown weedy in calms. Like a man lost in woods, more than once she had doubled upon her own track.

"But throughout these calamities," huskily continued Don Benito, painfully turning in the half embrace of his servant, "I have to thank those negroes you see, who, though to your inexperienced eyes appearing unruly, have, indeed, conducted themselves with less of restlessness than even their owner could have thought possible under such circumstances."

Here he again fell faintly back. Again his mind wandered; but he rallied, and less obscurely proceeded.

"Yes, their owner was quite right in assuring me that no fetters would be needed with his blacks; so that while, as is wont in this transportation, those negroes have always remained upon deck—not thrust below, as in the Guineamen—they have, also, from the beginning, been freely permitted to range within given bounds at their pleasure."

Once more the faintness returned—his mind roved—but, recovering, he resumed:

"But it is Babo here to whom, under God, I owe not only my own preservation, but likewise to him, chiefly, the merit is due, of pacifying his more ignorant brethren, when at intervals tempted to murmurings."

"Ah, master," sighed the black, bowing his face, "don't speak of me; Babo is nothing; what Babo has done was but duty."

"Faithful fellow!" cried Captain Delano. "Don Benito, I envy you such a friend; slave I cannot call him."

As master and man stood before him, the black upholding the white, Captain Delano could not but bethink him of the beauty of that relationship which could present such a spectacle of fidelity on the one hand and confidence on the other. The scene was heightened by the contrast in dress, denoting their relative positions. The Spaniard wore a loose Chili jacket of dark velvet; white small-clothes and stockings, with silver buckles at the knee and instep; a high-crowned sombrero, of fine grass; a slender sword, silver mounted, hung from a knot in his sash—the last being an almost invariable adjunct, more for utility than ornament, of a South American gentleman's dress to this hour. Excepting when his occasional nervous contortions brought about disarray, there was a certain precision in his attire curiously at variance with the unsightly disorder around; especially in the belittered Ghetto, forward of the mainmast, wholly occupied by the blacks.

The servant wore nothing but wide trowsers, apparently, from their coarseness and patches, made out of some old topsail; they were clean, and confined at the waist by a bit of unstranded rope, which, with his composed, deprecatory air at times, made him look something like a begging friar of St. Francis.

However unsuitable for the time and place, at least in the blunt-thinking American's eyes, and however strangely surviving in the midst of all his afflictions, the toilette of Don Benito might not, in fashion at least, have gone beyond the style of the day among South Americans of his class. Though on the present voyage sailing from Buenos Ayres, he had avowed himself a native and resident of Chili, whose inhabitants had not so generally adopted the plain coat and once plebeian pantaloons; but, with a becoming modification, adhered to their provincial costume, picturesque as any in the world. Still, relatively to the pale history of the voyage, and his own pale face, there seemed something so incongruous in the Spaniard's apparel, as almost to suggest the image of an invalid courtier tottering about London streets in the time of the plague.

The portion of the narrative which, perhaps, most excited interest, as well as some surprise, considering the latitudes in question, was the long calms spoken of, and more particularly the ship's so long drifting about. Without communicating the opinion, of course, the American could not but impute at least part of the detentions both to clumsy seamanship and faulty navigation. Eyeing Don Benito's small, yellow hands, he easily inferrred that the young Captain had not got into command at the hawse-hole, but the cabin-window; and if so, why wonder at incompetence, in youth, sickness, and gentility united?

But drowning criticism in compassion, after a fresh repetition of his sympathies, Captain Delano, having heard out his story, not only engaged, as in the first place, to see Don Benito and his people supplied in their immediate bodily needs, but, also, now further promised to assist him in procuring a large permanent supply of water, as well as some sails and rigging; and, though it would involve no small embarrassment to himself, yet he would spare three of his best seamen for temporary deck officers; so that without delay the ship might proceed to Conception, there fully to refit for Lima, her destined port.

Such generosity was not without its effect, even upon the invalid. His face lighted up; eager and hectic, he met the honest glance of his visitor. With gratitude he seemed overcome.

"This excitement is bad for master," whispered the servant, taking his arm, and with soothing words gently drawing him aside.

When Don Benito returned, the American was pained to observe that his hopefulness, like the sudden kindling in his cheek, was but febrile and transient.

Ere long, with a joyless mien, looking up towards the poop, the host invited his guest to accompany him there, for the benefit of what little breath of wind might be stirring.

As, during the telling of the story, Captain Delano had once or twice started at the occasional cymballing of the hatchet-polishers, wondering why such an interruption should be allowed, especially in that part of the ship, and in the ears of an invalid; and moreover, as the hatchets had anything but an attractive look, and the handlers of them still less so, it was, therefore, to tell the truth, not without some lurking reluctance, or even shrinking, it may be, that Captain Delano, with apparent complaisance, acquiesced in his host's invitation. The more so, since, with an untimely caprice of punctilio, rendered distressing by his cadaverous aspect, Don Benito, with Castilian bows, solemnly insisted upon his guest's preceding him up the ladder leading to the elevation; where, one on each side of the last step, sat for armorial supporters and sentries two of the ominous file. Gingerly enough stepped good Captain Delano between them, and in the instant of leaving them behind, like one running the gauntlet, he felt an apprehensive twitch in the calves of his legs.

But when, facing about, he saw the whole file, like so many organ-grinders, still stupidly intent on their work, unmindful of everything beside, he could not but smile at his late fidgety panic.

Presently, while standing with his host, looking forward upon the decks below, he was struck by one of those instances of insubordination previously alluded to. Three black boys, with two Spanish boys, were sitting together on the hatches, scraping a rude wooden platter, in which some scanty mess had recently been cooked. Suddenly, one of the black boys, enraged at a word dropped by one of his white companions, seized a knife, and, though called to forbear by one of the oakum-pickers, struck the lad over the head, inflicting a gash from which blood flowed.

In amazement, Captain Delano inquired what this meant. To which the pale Don Benito dully muttered, that it was merely the sport of the lad.

"Pretty serious sport, truly," rejoined Captain Delano. "Had such a thing happened on board the Bachelor's Delight, instant punishment would have followed."

At these words the Spaniard turned upon the American one of his sudden, staring, half-lunatic looks; then, relapsing into his torpor, answered, "Doubtless, doubtless, Señor."

Is it, thought Captain Delano, that this hapless man is one of those paper captains I've known, who by policy wink at what by power they cannot put down? I know no sadder sight than a commander who has little of command but the name.

"I should think, Don Benito," he now said, glancing towards the oakum-picker who had sought to interfere with the boys, "that you would find it advantageous to keep all your blacks employed, especially the younger ones, no matter at what useless task, and no matter what happens to the ship. Why, even with my little band, I find such a course indispensable. I once kept a crew on my quarterdeck thrumming mats for my cabin, when, for three days, I had given up my ship—mats, men, and all—for a speedy loss, owing to the violence of a gale, in which we could do nothing but helplessly drive before it."

"Doubtless, doubtless," muttered Don Benito.

"But," continued Captain Delano, again glancing upon the oakum-pickers and then at the hatchet-polishers, near by, "I see you keep some, at least, of your host employed."

"Yes," was again the vacant response.

"Those old men there, shaking their pows from their pulpits," continued Captain Delano, pointing to the oakum-pickers, "seem to act the part of old dominies to the rest, little heeded as their admonitions are at times. Is this voluntary on their part, Don Benito, or have you appointed them shepherds to your flock of black sheep?"

"What posts they fill, I appointed them," rejoined the Spaniard, in an acrid tone, as if resenting some supposed satiric reflection.

"And these others, these Ashantee conjurors here," continued Captain Delano, rather uneasily eyeing the brandished steel of the hatchet-polishers, where, in spots, it had been brought to a shine, "this seems a curious business they are at, Don Benito?"

"In the gales we met," answered the Spaniard, "what of our general cargo was not thrown overboard was much damaged by the brine. Since coming into calm weather, I have had several cases of knives and hatchets daily brought up for overhauling and cleaning."

"A prudent idea, Don Benito. You are part owner of ship and cargo, I presume; but none of the slaves, perhaps?"

"I am owner of all you see," impatiently returned Don Benito, "except the main company of blacks, who belonged to my late friend, Alexandro Aranda."

As he mentioned this name, his air was heart-broken; his knees shook; his servant supported him.

Thinking he divined the cause of such unusual emotion, to confirm his surmise, Captain Delano, after a pause, said: "And may I ask, Don Benito, whether—since awhile ago you spoke of some cabin passengers—the friend, whose loss so afflicts you, at the outset of the voyage accompanied his blacks."

"Yes."

"But died of the fever?"

"Died of the fever. Oh, could I but——"

Again quivering, the Spaniard paused.

"Pardon me," said Captain Delano, lowly, "but I think that, by a sympathetic experience, I conjecture, Don Benito, what it is that gives the keener edge to your grief. It was once my hard fortune to lose, at sea, a dear friend, my own brother, then super-cargo. Assured of the welfare of his spirit, its departure I could have borne like a man; but that honest eye, that honest hand—both of which had so often met mine—and that warm heart; all, all—like scraps to the dogs—to throw all to the sharks! It was then I vowed never to have for fellow-voyager a man I loved, unless, unbeknown to him, I had provided every requisite, in case of a fatality, for embalming his mortal part for interment on shore. Were your friend's remains now on board this ship, Don Benito, not thus strangely would the mention of his name affect you."

"On board this ship?" echoed the Spaniard. Then, with horrified gestures, as directed against some spectre, he unconsciously fell into the ready arms of his attendant, who, with a silent appeal toward Captain Delano, seemed beseeching him not again to broach a theme so unspeakably distressing to his master.

This poor fellow now, thought the pained American, is the victim of that sad superstition which associates goblins with the deserted body of man, as ghosts with an abandoned house. How unlike are we made! What to me, in like case, would have been a solemn satisfaction, the bare suggestion, even, terrifies the Spaniard into this trance. Poor Alexandro Aranda! what would you say could you here see your friend—who, on former voyages, when you, for months, were left behind, has, I dare say, often longed, and longed, for one peep at you—now transported with terror at the least thought of having you anyway nigh him.

At this moment, with a dreary grave-yard toll, betokening a flaw, the ship's forecastle bell, smote by one of the grizzled oakum-pickers, proclaimed ten o'clock, through the leaden calm; when Captain Delano's attention was caught by the moving figure of a gigantic black, emerging from the general crowd below, and slowly advancing toward the elevated poop. An iron collar was about his neck, from which depended a chain, thrice wound round his body; the terminating links padlocked together at a broad band of iron, his girdle.

"How like a mute Atufal moves," murmured the servant.

The black mounted the steps of the poop, and, like a brave prisoner, brought up to receive sentence, stood in unquailing muteness before Don Benito, now recovered from his attack.

At the first glimpse of his approach, Don Benito had started, a resentful shadow swept over his face; and, as with the sudden memory of bootless rage, his white lips glued together.

This is some mulish mutineer, thought Captain Delano, surveying, not without a mixture of admiration, the colossal form of the negro.

"See, he waits your question, master," said the servant.

Thus reminded, Don Benito, nervously averting his glance, as if shunning, by anticipation, some rebellious response, in a disconcerted voice, thus spoke:—

"Atufal, will you ask my pardon, now?"

The black was silent.

"Again, master," murmured the servant, with bitter upbraiding eyeing his countryman, "Again master; he will bend to master yet."

"Answer," said Don Benito, still averting his glance, "say but the one word, *pardon,* and your chains shall be off."

Upon this, the black, slowly raising both arms, let them lifelessly fall, his links clanking, his head bowed; as much as to say, "no, I am content."

"Go," said Don Benito, with inkept and unknown emotion.

Deliberately as he had come, the black obeyed.

"Excuse me, Don Benito," said Captain Delano, "but this scene surprises me; what means it, pray?"

"It means that that negro alone, of all the band, has given me peculiar cause of offense. I have put him in chains; I——"

Here he paused; his hand to his head, as if there were a swimming there, or a sudden bewilderment of memory had come over him; but meeting his servant's kindly glance seemed reassured, and proceeded:—

"I could not scourge such a form. But I told him he must ask my pardon. As yet he has not. At my command, every two hours he stands before me."

"And how long has this been?"

"Some sixty days."

"And obedient in all else? And respectful?"

"Yes."

"Upon my conscience, then," exclaimed Captain Delano, impulsively, "he has a royal spirit in him, this fellow."

"He may have some right to it," bitterly returned Don Benito, "he says he was king in his own land."

"Yes," said the servant, entering a word, "those slits in Atufal's ears once held wedges of gold; but poor Babo here, in his own land, was only a poor slave; a black man's slave was Babo, who now is the white's."

Somewhat annoyed by these conversational familarities, Captain Delano turned curiously upon the attendant, then glanced inquiringly at his master; but, as if long wonted to these little informalities, neither master nor man seemed to understand him.

"What, pray, was Atufal's offense, Don Benito?" asked Captain Delano; "if it was not something very serious, take a fool's advice, and, in view of his general docility, as well as in some natural respect for his spirit, remit him his penalty."

"No, no, master never will do that," here murmured the servant to himself, "proud Atufal must first ask master's pardon. The slave there carries the padlock, but master here carries the key."

His attention thus directed, Captain now noticed for the first, that, suspened by a slender silken cord, from Don Benito's neck, hung a key. At once, from the servant's muttered syllables, divining the key's purpose, he smiled and said:—"So, Don Benito—padlock and key—significant symbols, truly."

Biting his lip, Don Benito faltered.

Though the remark of Captain Delano, a man of such native simplicity as to be incapable of satire or irony, had been dropped in playful allusion to the Spaniard's singularly evidenced lordship over the black; yet the hypochondriac seemed some way to have taken it as a malicious reflection upon his confessed inability thus far to break down, at least, on a verbal summons, the entrenched will of the slave. Deploring this supposed misconception, yet despairing of correcting it, Captain Delano shifted the subject; but finding his companion more than ever withdrawn, as if still sourly digesting the lees of the presumed affront above-mentioned, by-and-by Captain Delano likewise became less talkative, oppressed, against his own will, by what seemed the secret vindictiveness of the morbidly sensitive Spaniard. But the good sailor, himself of a quite contrary disposition, refrained, on his part, alike from the appearance as from the feeling of resentment, and if silent, was only so from contagion.

Presently the Spaniard, assisted by his servant, somewhat discourteously crossed over from his guest; a procedure which, sensibly enough, might have been allowed to pass for idle caprice of ill-humor, had not master and man, lingering round the corner of the elevated skylight, began whispering together in low voices. This was unpleasing. And more; the moody air of the Spaniard, which at times had not been without a sort of valetudinarian stateliness, now seemed anything but dignified; while the menial familiarity of the servant lost its original charm of simple-hearted attachment.

In his embarrassment, the visitor turned his face to the other side of the ship. By so doing, his glance accidentally fell on a young Spanish sailor, a coil of rope in his hand, just stepped from the deck to the first round of the mizzen-rigging. Perhaps the man would not have been particularly noticed, were it not that, during his ascent to one of the yards, he, with a sort of covert intentness, kept his eye fixed on Captain Delano, from whom, presently, it passed, as if by a natural sequence, to the two whisperers.

His own attention thus redirected to that quarter, Captain Delano gave a slight start. From something in Don Benito's manner just then, it seemed as if the visitor had, at least partly, been the subject of the withdrawn consultation going on—a conjecture as little agreeable to the guest as it was little flattering to the host.

The singular alternations of courtesy and ill-breeding in the Spanish captain were unaccountable, except on one of two suppositions—innocent lunacy, or wicked imposture.

But the first idea, though it might naturally have occurred to an indifferent observer, and, in some respect, had not hitherto been wholly a stranger to Captain Delano's mind, yet, now that, in an incipient way, he began to regard the stranger's conduct something in the light of an intentional affront, of course the idea of lunacy was virtually vacated. But if not a lunatic, what then? Under the circumstances, would a gentleman, nay, any honest boor, act the part now acted by his host? The man was an imposter. Some low-born adventurer, masquerading as an oceanic grandee; yet so ignorant of the first requisites of mere gentlemanhood as to be betrayed into the present remarkable indecorum. That strange ceremoniousness, too, at other times evinced, seemed not uncharacteristic of one playing a part above his real level. Benito Cereno—Don Benito Cereno—a sounding name. One, too, at that period, not unknown, in the surname, to supercargoes and sea captains trading along the Spanish Main, as belonging to one of the most enterprising and extensive mercantile families in all those provinces; several members of it having titles; a sort of Castilian Rothschild, with a noble brother, or cousin, in every great trading town of South America. The alleged Don Benito was in early manhood, about twenty-nine or thirty. To assume a sort of roving cadetship in the maritime affairs of such a house, what more likely scheme for a young knave of talent and spirit? But the Spaniard was a pale invalid. Never mind. For even to the degree of simulating mortal disease, the craft of some tricksters had been known to attain. To think that, under the aspect of infantile weakness, the most savage energies might be couched—those velvets of the Spaniard but the silky paw of his fangs.

From no train of thought did these fancies come; not from within, but from without; suddenly, too, and in one throng, like hoar frost; yet as soon to vanish as the mild sun of Captain Delano's good-nature regained its meridian.

Glancing over once more towards his host—whose side-face, revealed above the skylight, was now turned towards him—he was struck by the profile, whose clearness of cut was refined by the thinness, incident to ill-health, as well as ennobled about the chin by the beard. Away with suspicion. He was a true off-shoot of a true hidalgo Cereno.

Relieved by these and other better thoughts, the visitor, lightly humming a tune, now began indifferently pacing the poop, so as not to betray to Don Benito that he had at all mistrusted incivility, much less duplicity; for such mistrust would yet be proved illusory, and by the event; though, for the present, the circumstance which had provoked that distrust remained unexplained. But when that little mystery should have been cleared up, Captain Delano thought he might extremely regret it, did he allow Don Benito to become aware that he had indulged in ungenerous surmises. In short, to the Spaniard's black-letter text, it was best, for awhile, to leave open margin.

Presently, his pale face twitching and overcast, the Spaniard, still supported by his attendant, moved over towards his guest, when, with even more than his usual embarrassment, and a strange sort of intriguing intonation in his husky whisper, the following conversation began:—

"Señor, may I ask how long you have lain at this isle?"

"Oh, but a day or two, Don Benito."

"And from what port are you last?"

"Canton."

"And there, Señor, you exchanged your sealskins for teas and silks, I think you said?"

"Yes. Silks, mostly."

"And the balance you took in specie, perhaps?

Captain Delano, fidgeting a little, answered—

"Yes; some silver; not a very great deal, though."

"Ah—well. May I ask how many men have you, Señor?"

Captain Delano slightly started, but answered—

"About five-and-twenty, all told."

"And at present, Señor, all on board, I suppose?"

"All on board, Don Benito," replied the Captain, now with satisfaction.

"And will be to-night, Señor?"

At this last question, following so many pertinacious ones, for the soul of him Captain Delano could not but look very earnestly at the questioner, who, instead of meeting the glance, with every token of craven discomposure dropped his eyes to the deck; presenting an unworthy contrast to his servant, who, just then, was kneeling at his feet, adjusting a loose shoe-buckle; his disengaged face meantime, with humble curiosity, turned openly up into his master's downcast one.

The Spaniard, still with a guilty shuffle, repeated his question:

"And—and will be to-night, Senor?"

"Yes, for aught I know," returned Captain Delano—"but nay," rallying himself into fearless truth, "some of them talked of going off on another fishing party about midnight."

"Your ships generally go—go more or less armed, I believe, Señor?"

"Oh, a six-pounder or two, in case of emergency," was the intrepidly indifferent reply, "with a small stock of muskets, sealing-spears, and cutlasses, you know."

As he thus responded, Captain Delano again glanced at Don Benito, but the latter's eyes were averted; while abruptly and awkwardly shifting the subject, he made some peevish allusion to the calm, and then, without apology, once more, with his attendant, withdrew to the opposite bulwarks, where the whispering was resumed.

At this moment, and ere Captain Delano could cast a cool thought upon what had just passed, the young Spanish sailor, before mentioned, was seen descending from the rigging. In act of stooping over to spring inboard to the deck, his voluminous, unconfined frock, or shirt, of coarse woolen, much spotted with tar, opened out far down the chest, revealing a soiled under garment of what seemed the finest linen, edged, about the neck, with a narrow blue ribbon, sadly faded and worn. At this moment the young sailor's eye was again fixed on the whispers, and Captain Delano thought he observed a lurking significance in it, as if silent signs, of some Freemason sort, had that instant been interchanged.

This once more impelled his own glance in the direction of Don Benito, and, as before, he could not but infer that himself formed the subject of the conference. He paused. The sound of the hatchet-polishing fell on his ears. He cast another swift side-look at the two. They had the air of conspirators. In connection with the late questionings, and the incident of the young sailor, these things now begat such return of involuntary suspicion, that the singular guilelessness of the American could not endure it. Plucking up a gay and humorous expression, he crossed over to the two rapidly, saying:—"Ha, Don Benito, your black here seems high in your trust; a sort of privy-counselor, in fact."

Upon this, the servant looked up with a good-natured grin, but the master started as from a venomous bite. It was a moment or two before the Spaniard sufficiently recovered himself to reply; which he did, at last, with cold constraint:—"Yes, Señor, I have trust in Babo."

Here Babo, changing his previous grin of mere animal humor into an intelligent smile, not ungratefully eyed his master.

Finding that the Spaniard now stood silent and reserved, as if involuntarily, or purposely giving hint that his guest's proximity was inconvenient just then, Captain Delano, unwilling to appear uncivil even to incivility itself, made some trivial remark and moved off; again and again turning over in his mind the mysterious demeanor of Don Benito Cereno.

He had descended from the poop, and, wrapped in thought, was passing near a dark hatchway, leading down into the steerage, when, perceiving motion there, he looked to see what moved. The same instant there was a sparkle in the shadowy hatchway, and he saw one of the Spanish sailors, prowling there, hurriedly placing his hand in the bosom of his frock, as if hiding something. Before the man could have been certain who it was that was passing, he slunk below out of sight. But enough was seen of him to make it sure that he was the same young sailor before noticed in the rigging.

What was that which so sparkled? thought Captain Delano. It was no lamp—no match—no live coal. Could it have been a jewel? But how come sailors with jewels?—or with silk-trimmed under-shirts either? Has he been robbing the trunks of the dead cabin-passengers? But if so, he would hardly wear one of the stolen articles on board ship here. Ah, ah—if, now, that was, indeed, a secret sign I saw passing between this suspicious fellow and his captain awhile since; if I could only be certain that, in my uneasiness, my senses did not deceive me, then——

Here, passing from one suspicious thing to another, his mind revolved the strange questions put to him concering his ship.

By a curious coincidence, as each point was recalled, the black wizards of Ashantee would strike up with their hatchets, as in ominous comment on the white stranger's thoughts. Pressed by such enigmas and portents, it would have been almost against nature, had not, even into the least distrustful heart, some ugly misgivings obtruded.

Observing the ship, now helplessly fallen into a current, with enchanted sails, drifting with increased rapidity seaward; and noting that, from a lately intercepted projection of the land, the sealer was hidden, the stout mariner began to quake at thoughts which he barely durst confess to himself. Above all, he began to feel a ghostly dread of Don Benito. And yet, when he roused himself, dilated his chest, felt himself strong on his legs, and cooly considered it—what did all these phantoms amount to?

Had the Spaniard any sinister scheme, it must have reference not so much to him (Captain Delano) as to his ship (the Bachelor's Delight). Hence the present drifting away of the one ship from the other, instead of favoring any such possible scheme, was, for the time, at least, opposed to it. Clearly any suspicion, combining such contradictions, must need be delusive. Beside, was it not absurd to think of a vessel in distress—a vessel by sickness almost dismanned of her crew—a vessel whose inmates were parched for water—was it not a thousand times absurd that such a craft should, at present, be of a piratical character; or her commander, either for himself or those under him, cherish any desire but for speedy relief and refreshment? But then, might not general distress, and thirst in particular, be affected? And might not that same undiminished Spanish crew, alleged to have perished off to a remnant, be at that very moment lurking in the hold? On heart-broken pretense of entreating a cup of cold water, fiends in human form had got into lonely dwellings, nor retired until a dark deed had been done. And among the Malay pirates, it was no unusual thing to lure ships after them into their treacherous harbors, or entice boarders from a declared enemy at sea, by the spectacle of thinly manned or vacant decks, beneath which prowled a hundred spears with yellow arms ready to upthrust them through the mats. Not that Captain Delano had entirely credited such things. He had heard of them—and now, as stories, they recurred. The present destination of the ship was the anchorage. There she would be near his own vessel. Upon gaining that vicinity, might not the San Dominick, like a slumbering volcano, suddenly let loose energies now hid?

He recalled the Spaniard's manner while telling his story. There was a gloomy hesitancy and subterfuge about it. It was just the manner of one making up his tale for evil purposes, as he goes. But if that story was not true, what was the truth? That the ship had unlawfully come into the Spaniard's possession? But in many of its details, especially in reference to the more calamitous parts, such as the fatalities among the seamen, the consequent prolonged beating about, the past sufferings from obstinate calms, and still continued suffering from thirst; in all these points, as well as others, Don Benito's story had corroborated not only the wailing ejaculations of the indiscriminate multitude, white and black, but likewise—what seemed impossible to be counterfeit—by the very expression and play of every human feature, which Captain Delano saw. If Don Benito's story was, throughout, an invention, then every soul on board, down to the youngest negress, was his carefully drilled recruit in the plot: an incredible inference. And yet, if there was ground for mistrusting his veracity, that inference was a legitimate one.

But those questions of the Spaniard. There, indeed, one might pause. Did they not seem put with much the same object with which the burglar or assassin, by daytime, reconnoitres the walls of a house? But, with ill purposes, to solicit such information openly of the chief person endangered, and so, in effect, setting him on his guard; how unlikely a procedure was that? Absurd, then, to suppose that those questions had been prompted by evil designs. Thus, the same conduct, which, in this instance, had raised the alarm, served to dispel it. In short, scarce any suspicion or uneasiness, however apparently reasonable at the time, which was not now, with equal apparent reason, dismissed.

At last he began to laugh at his former forebodings; and laugh at the strange ship for, in its aspect, someway siding with them, as it were; and laugh, too, at the odd-looking blacks, particularly those old scissor-grinders, the Ashantees; and those bed-ridden old knitting women, the oakum-pickers; and almost at the dark Spaniard himself, the central hobgoblin of all.

For the rest, whatever in a serious way seemed enigmatical, was now good-naturedly explained away by the thought that, for the most part, the poor invalid scarcely knew what he was about; either sulking in black vapors, or putting idle questions without sense or object. Evidently, for the present, the main was not fit to be intrusted with the ship. On some benevolent plea withdrawing the command from him, Captain Delano would yet have to send her to Conception, in charge of his second mate, a worthy person and good navigator—a plan not more convenient for the San Dominick than for Don Benito; for, relieved from all anxiety, keeping wholly to his cabin, the sick man, under the good nursing of his servant, would, probably, by the end of the passage, be in a measure restored to health, and with that he should also be restored to authority.

Such were the American's thoughts. They were tranquilizing. There was a difference between the idea of Don Benito's darkly pre-ordaining Captain Delano's fate, and Captain Delano's lightly arranging Don Benito's. Nevertheless, it was not without something of relief that the good seaman presently perceived his whaleboat in the distance. Its absence had been prolonged by unexpected detention at the sealer's side, as well as its returning trip lengthened by the continual recession of the goal.

The advancing speck was observed by the blacks. Their shouts attracted the attention of Don Benito, who, with a return of courtesy, approaching Captain Delano, expressed satisfaction at the coming of some supplies, slight and temporary as they must necessarily prove.

Captain Delano responded; but while doing so, his attention was drawn to something passing on the deck below: among the crowd climbing the landward bulwarks, anxiously watching the coming boat, two blacks, to all appearances accidentally incommoded by one of the sailors, violently pushed him aside, which the sailor someway resenting, they dashed him to the deck, despite the earnest cries of the oakum-pickers.

"Don Benito," said Captain Delano quickly, "do you see what is going on there? Look!"

But, seized by his cough, the Spaniard staggered, with both hands to his face, on the point of falling. Captain Delano would have supported him, but the servant was more alert, who, with one hand sustaining his master, with the other applied the cordial. Don Benito restored, the black withdrew his support slipping aside a little, but dutifully remaining within call of a whisper. Such discretion was here evinced as quite wiped away, in the visitor's eyes, any blemish of impropriety which might have attached to the attendant, from the indecorous conferences before mentioned; showing, too, that if the servant were to blame, it might be more the master's fault than his own, since, when left to himself, he could conduct thus well.

His glance called away from the spectacle of disorder to the more pleasing one before him, Captain Delano could not avoid again congratulating his host upon possessing such a servant, who, though perhaps a little too forward now and then, must upon the whole be invaluable to one in the invalid's situation.

"Tell me, Don Benito," he added, with a smile—"I should like to have your man here, myself—what will you take for him? Would fifty doubloons be any object?"

"Master wouldn't part with Babo for a thousand doubloons," murmured the black, overhearing the offer, and taking it in earnest, and, with the strange vanity of a faithful slave, appreciated by his master, scorning to hear so paltry a valuation put upon him by a stranger. But Don Benito, apparently hardly yet completely restored, and again interrupted by his cough, made but some broken reply.

Soon his physical distress became so great, affecting his mind, too, apparently, that, as if to screen the sad spectacle, the servant gently conducted his master below.

Left to himself, the American, to while away the time till his boat should arrive, would have pleasantly accosted some one of the few Spanish seamen he saw; but recalling something that Don Benito had said touching their ill conduct, he refrained; as a ship-master indisposed to countenance cowardice or unfaithfulness in seamen.

While, with these thoughts, standing with eye directed forward towards that handful of sailors, suddenly he thought that one or two of them returned the glance and with a sort of meaning. He rubbed his eyes, and looked again; but again seemed to see the same thing. Under a new form, but more obscure than any previous one, the old suspicions recurred, but, in the absence of Don Benito, with less of panic than before. Despite the bad account given of the sailors, Captain Delano resolved forthwith to accost one of them. Descending the poop, he made his way through the blacks, his movement drawing a queer cry from the oakum-pickers, prompted by whom, the negroes, twitching each other aside, divided before him; but, as if curious to see what was the object of this deliberate visit to their ghetto, closing in behind, in tolerable order, followed the white stranger up. His progress thus proclaimed as by mounted kings-at-arms, and escorted as by a Caffre guard of honor, Captain Delano, assuming a good-humored, off-handed air, continued to advance; now and then saying a blithe word to the negroes, and his eye curiously surveying the white faces, here and there sparsely mixed in with the blacks, like stray white pawns venturously involved in the ranks of the chess-men opposed.

While thinking which of them to select for his purpose, he chanced to observe a sailor seated on the deck engaged in tarring the strap of a large block, a circle of blacks squatted round him inquisitively eyeing the process.

The mean employment of the man was in contrast with something superior in his figure. His hand, black with continually thrusting it into the tar-pot held for him by a negro, seemed not naturally allied to his face, a face which would have been a very fine one but for its haggardness. Whether this haggardness had aught to do with criminality, could not be determined; since, as intense heat and cold, though unlike, produce like sensations, so innocence and guilt, when, through casual association with mental pain, stamping any visible impress, use one seal—a hacked one.

Not again that this reflection occurred to Captain Delano at the time, charitable man as he was. Rather another idea. Because observing so singular a haggardness combined with a dark eye, averted as in trouble and shame, and then again recalling Don Benito's confessed ill opinion of his crew, insensibly he was operated upon by certain general notions which, while disconnecting pain and abashment from virtue, invariably link them with vice.

If, indeed, there be any wickedness on board this ship, thought Captain Delano, be sure that man there has fouled his hand in it, even as now he fouls it in the pitch. I don't like to accost him. I will speak to this other, this old Jack here on the windlass.

He advanced to an old Barcelona tar, in ragged red breeches and dirty night-cap, cheeks trenched and bronzed, whiskers dense as thorn hedges. Seated between two sleepy-looking Africans, this mariner, like his younger shipmate, was employed upon some rigging—splicing a cable—the sleepy-looking blacks performing the inferior function of holding the outer parts of the ropes for him.

Upon Captain Delano's approach, the man at once hung his head below its previous level; the one necessary for business. It appeared as if he desired to be thought absorbed, with more than common fidelity, in his task. Being addressed, he glanced up, but with what seemed a furitive, diffident air, which sat strangely enough on his weather-beaten visage, much as if a grizzly bear, instead of growling and biting, should simper and cast sheep's eyes. He was asked several questions concerning the voyage—questions purposely referring to several particulars in Don Benito's narrative, not previously corroborated by those impulsive cries greeting the visitor on first coming on board. The questions were briefly answered, confirming all that remained to be confirmed of the story. The negroes about the wildlass joined in with the old sailor; but, as they became talkative, he by degrees became mute, and at length quite glum, seemed morosely unwilling to answer more questions, and yet, all the while, this ursine air was somehow mixed with his sheepish one.

Despairing of getting into unembarrassed talk with such a centaur, Captain Delano, after glancing round for a more promising countenance, but seeing none, spoke pleasantly to the blacks to make way for him; and so, amid various grins and grimaces, returned to the poop, feeling a little strange at first, he could hardly tell why, but upon the whole with regained confidence in Benito Cereno.

How plainly, thought he, did that old whiskerando yonder betray a consciousness of ill desert. No doubt, when he saw me coming, he dreaded lest I, apprised by his Captain of the crew's general misbehavior, came with sharp words for him, and so down with his head. And yet—and yet, now that I think of it, that very old fellow, if I err not, was one of those who seemed so earnestly eyeing me here awhile since. Ah, these currents spin one's head round almost as much as they do the ship. Ha, there now's a pleasant sort of sunny sight; quite sociable, too.

His attention had been drawn to a slumbering negress, partly disclosed through the lace-work of some rigging, lying, with youthful limbs carelessly disposed, under the lee of the bulwarks, like a doe in the shade of a woodland rock. Sprawling at her lapped breasts, was her wide-awake fawn, stark naked, its black little body half lifted from the deck, crosswise with its dam's; its hands, like two paws, clambering upon her; its mouth and nose ineffectually rooting to get at the mark; and meantime giving a vexatious half-grunt, blending with the composed snore of the negress.

The uncommon vigor of the child at length roused the mother. She started up, at a distance facing Capain Delano. But as if not at all concerned at the attitude in which she had been caught, delightedly she caught the child up, with maternal transports, covering it with kisses.

There's naked nature, now; pure tenderness and love, thought Captain Delano, well pleased.

This incident prompted him to remark the other negresses more particularly than before. He was gratified with their manners: like most uncivilized women, they seemed at once tender of heart and tough of constitution; equally ready to die for their infants or fight for them. Unsophisticated as leopardesses; loving as doves. Ah! thought Captain Delano, these, perhaps, are some of the very women whom Ledyard saw in Africa, and gave such a noble account of.

These natural sights somehow insensibly deepened his confidence and ease. At last he looked to see how his boat was getting on; but it was still pretty remote. He turned to see if Don Benito had returned; but he had not.

To change the scene, as well as to please himself with a leisurely observation of the coming boat, stepping over into the mizzen-chains, he clambered his way into the starboard quarter-gallery—one of those abandoned Venetian-looking water-balconies previously mentioned—retreats cut off from the deck. As his foot pressed the half-damp, half-dry sea-mosses matting the place, and a chance phantom cats-paw—an islet of breeze, unheralded, unfollowed—as this ghostly cats-paw came fanning his cheek; as his glance fell upon the row of small, round dead-lights—all closed like coppered eyes of the coffined—and the state-cabin door, once connecting with the gallery, even as the dead-lights had once looked out upon it, but now calked fast like a sarcophagus lid; and to a purple-black tarred-over, panel, threshold, and post; and he bethought him of the time when that state-cabin and this state-balcony had heard the voices of the Spanish king's officers, and the forms of the Lima viceroy's daughters had perhaps leaned where he stood—as these and other images flitted through his mind, as the cats-paw through the calm, gradually he felt rising a dreamy inquietude, like that of one who alone on the prairie feels unrest from the repose of the moon.

He leaned against the carved balustrade, again looking off toward his boat; but found his eye falling upon the ribbon grass, trailing along the ship's water-line, straight as a border of green box; and parterres of seaweed, broad ovals and crescents, floating nigh and far, with what seemed long formal alleys between, crossing the terraces of swells, and sweeping round as if leading to the grottoes below. And overhanging all was the balustrade by his arm, which, partly stained with pitch and partly embossed with moss, seemed the charred ruin of some summer-house in a grand garden long running to waste.

Trying to break one charm, he was but becharmed anew. Though upon the wide sea, he seemed in some far inland country; prisoner in some deserted chateau, left to stare at empty grounds, and peer out at vague roads, where never wagon or wayfarer passed.

But these enchantments were a little disenchanted as his eye fell on the corroded main-chains. Of an ancient style, massy and rusty in link, shackle and bolt, they seemed even more fit for the ship's present business than the one for which she had been built.

Presently he thought something moved nigh the chains. He rubbed his eyes, and looked hard. Groves of rigging were about the chains; and there, peering from behind a great stay, like an Indian from behind a hemlock, a Spanish sailor, a marlingspike in his hand, was seen, who made what seemed an imperfect gesture towards the balcony, but immediately, as if alarmed by some advancing step along the deck within, vanished into the recesses of the hempen forest, like a poacher.

What meant this? Something the man had sought to communicate, unbeknown to any one, even to his captain. Did the secret involve aught unfavorable to his captain? Were those previous misgivings of Captain Delano's about to be verified? Or, in his haunted mood at the moment, had some random, unintentional motion of the man, while busy with the stay, as if repairing it, been mistaken for a significant beckoning?

Not unbewildered, again he gazed off for his boat. But it was temporarily hidden by a rocky spur of the isle. As with some eagerness he bent forward, watching for the first shooting view of its beak, the balustrade gave way before him like charcoal. Had he not clutched an outreaching rope he would have fallen into the sea. The crash, though feeble, and the fall, though hollow, of the rotten fragments, must have been overheard. He glanced up. With sober curiosity peering down upon him was one of the old oakum-pickers, slipped from his perch to an outside boom; while below the old negro, and, invisible to him, reconnoitering from a port-hole like a fox from the mouth of its den, crouched the Spanish sailor again. From something suddenly suggested by the man's air, the mad idea now darted into Captain Delano's mind, that Don Benito's plea of indisposition, in withdrawing below, was but a pretense: that he was engaged there maturing his plot, of which the sailor, by some means gaining an inkling, had a mind to warn the stranger against; incited, it may be, by gratitude for a kind word on first boarding the ship. Was it from foreseeing some possible interference like this, that Don Benito had, beforehand, given such a bad character of his sailors, while praising the negroes; though, indeed, the former seemed as docile as the latter the contrary? The whites, too, by nature, were the shrewder race. A man with some evil design, would he not be likely to speak well of that stupidity which was blind to his depravity, and malign that intelligence from which it might be hidden? Not unlikely, perhaps. But if the whites had dark secrets concerning Don Benito, could then Don Benito be any way in complicity with the blacks? But they were too stupid. Besides, who ever heard of a white so far a renegade as to apostatize from his very species almost, by leaguing in against it with negroes? These difficulties recalled former ones. Lost in their mazes, Captain Delano, who had now regained the deck, was uneasily advancing along it, when he observed a new face; an aged sailor seated cross-legged near the main hatchway. His skin was shrunk up with wrinkles like a pelican's empty pouch; his hair frosted; his countenance grave and composed. His hands were full of ropes, which he was working into a large knot. Some blacks were about him obligingly dipping the strands for him, here and there, as the exigencies of the operation demanded.

Captain Delano crossed over to him, and stood in silence surveying the knot; his mind, by a not uncongenial transition, passing from its own entanglements to those of the hemp. For intricacy, such a knot he had never seen in an American ship, nor indeed any other. The old man looked like an Egyptian priest, making Gordian knots for the temple of Ammon. The knot seemed a combination of double-bowline-knot, treble-crown-knot, back-handed-well-knot, knot-in-and-out-knot, and jamming-knot.

At last, puzzled to comprehend the meaning of such a knot, Captain Delano addressed the knotter:—

"What are you knotting there, my man?"

"The knot," was the brief reply, without looking up.

"So it seems; but what is it for?"

"For some one else to undo," muttered back the old man, plying his fingers harder than ever, the knot being now nearly completed.

While Captain Delano stood watching him, suddenly the old man threw the knot towards him, saying in broken English—the first heard in the ship—something to this effect: "Undo it, cut it, quick." It was said lowly, but with such condensation of rapidity, that the long, slow words in Spanish, which had preceded and followed, almost operated as covers to the brief English between.

For a moment, knot in hand, and knot in head, Captain Delano stood mute; while, without further heeding him, the old man was now intent upon other ropes. Presently there was a slight stir behind Captain Delano. Turning, he saw the chained negro, Atufal, standing quietly there. The next moment the old sailor rose, muttering, and, followed by his subordinate negroes, removed to the forward part of the ship, where in the crowd he disappeared.

An elderly negro, in a clout like an infant's, and with a pepper and salt head, and a kind of attorney air, now approached Captain Delano. In tolerable Spanish, and with a good-natured, knowing wink, he informed him that the old knotter was simple-witted, but harmless; often playing his odd tricks. The negro concluded by begging the knot, for of course the stranger would not care to be troubled with it. Unconsciously, it was handed to him. With a sort of congé, the negro received it, and, turning his back, ferreted into it like a detective custom-house office after smuggled laces. Soon, with some African word, equivalent to pshaw, he tossed the knot overboard.

All this is very queer now, thought Captain Delano, with a qualmish sort of emotion; but, as one feeling incipient sea-sickness, he strove, by ignoring the symptoms, to get rid of the malady. Once more he looked off for his boat. To his delight, it was now again in view, leaving the rocky spur astern.

The sensation here experienced, after at first relieving his uneasiness, with unforeseen efficacy soon began to remove it. The less distant sight of that well-known boat—showing it, not as before, half blended with the haze, but with outline defined, so that its individuality, like a man's, was manifest; that boat, Rover by name, which, though now in strange seas, had often pressed the beach of Captain Delano's home, and, brought to its threshold for repairs, had familiarly lain there, as a Newfoundland dog; the sight of that household boat evoked a thousand trustful associations, which, contrasted with previous suspicions, filled him not only with lightsome confidence, but somehow with half humorous self-reproaches at his former lack of it.

"What, I, Amasa Delano—Jack of the Beach, as they called me when a lad—I, Amasa; the same that, duck-satchel in hand, used to paddle along the water-side to the schoolhouse made from the old hulk—I, little Jack of the Beach, that used to go berrying with cousin Nat and the rest; I to be murdered here at the ends of the earth, on board a haunted pirate-ship by a horrible Spaniard? Too nonsensical to think of! Who would murder Amasa Delano? His conscience is clean. There is some one above. Fie, fie, Jack of the Beach! you are a child indeed; a child of the second childhood, old boy; you are beginning to dote and drule, I'm afraid."

Light of heart and foot, he stepped aft, and there was met by Don Benito's servant, who, with a pleasing expression, responsive to his own present feelings, informed him that his master had recovered from the effects of his coughing fit, and had just ordered him to go present his compliments to his good guest, Don Amasa, and say that he (Don Benito) would soon have the happiness to rejoin him.

There now, do you mark that? again thought Captain Delano, walking the poop. What a donkey I was. This kind gentleman who here sends me his kind compliments, he, but ten minutes ago, dark-lantern in hand, was dodging round some old grind-stone in the hold, sharpening a hatchet for me, I thought. Well, well; these long calms have a morbid effect on the mind, I've often heard, though I never believed it before. Ha! glancing towards the boat; there's Rover; good dog; a white bone in her mouth. A pretty big bone though, seems to me.—What? Yes, she has fallen afoul of the bubbling tide-rip there. It sets her the other way, too, for the time. Patience.

It was now about noon, though, from the grayness of everything, it seemed to be getting towards dusk.

The calm was confirmed. In the far distance, away from the influence of land, the leaden ocean seemed laid out and leaded up, its course finished, soul gone, defunct. But the current from landward, where the ship was, increased; silently sweeping her further and further towards the tranced waters beyond.

Still, from his knowledge of those latitudes, cherishing hopes of a breeze, and a fair and fresh one, at any moment, Captain Delano, despite present prospects, buoyantly counted upon bringing the San Dominick safely to anchor ere night. The distance swept over was nothing; since, with a good wind, ten minutes' sailing would retrace more than sixty minutes, drifting. Meantime, one moment turning to mark "Rover" fighting the tide-rip, and the next to see Don Benito approaching, continued walking the poop.

Gradually he felt a vexation arising from the delay of his boat; this soon merged into uneasiness; and at last—his eye falling continually, as from a stage-box into the pit, upon the strange crowd before and below him, and, by-and-by, recognizing there the face—now composed to indifference—of the Spanish sailor who had seemed to beckon from the main-chains—something of his old trepidations returned.

Ah, thought he—gravely enough—this is like the ague: because it went off, it follows not that it won't come back.

Though ashamed of the relapse, he could not altogether subdue it; and so, exerting his good-nature to the utmost, insensibly he came to a compromise.

Yes, this is a strange craft; a strange history, too, and strange folks on board. But—nothing more.

By way of keeping his mind out of mischief till the boat should arrive, he tried to occupy it with turning over and over, in a purely speculative sort of way, some lesser peculiarities of the captain and crew. Among others, four curious points recurred:

First, the affair of the Spanish lad assailed with a knife by the slave boy; an act winked at by Don Benito. Second, the tyranny in Don Benito's treatment of Atufal, the black; as if a child should lead a bull of the Nile by the ring in his nose. Third, the trampling of the sailor by the two negroes; a piece of insolence passed over without so much as a reprimand. Fourth, the cringing submission to their master, of all the ship's underlings, mostly blacks; as if by the least inadvertence they feared to draw down his despotic displeasure.

Coupling these points, they seemed somewhat contradictory. But what then, thought Captain Delano, glancing towards his now nearing boat—what then? Why, Don Benito is a very capricious commander. But he is not the first of the sort I have seen; though it's true he rather exceeds any other. But as a nation—continued he in his reveries—these Spaniards are all an odd set; the very word Spaniard has a curious, conspirator, Guy-Fawkish twang to it. And yet, I dare say, Spaniards in the main are as good folks as any in Duxbury, Massachusetts. Ah good! At last "Rover" has come.

As, with its welcome freight, the boat touched the side, the oakum-pickers, with venerable gestures, sought to restrain the blacks, who, at the sight of three gurried water-casks in its bottom, and a pile of wilted pumpkins in its bow, hung over the bulwarks in disorderly raptures.

Don Benito, with his servant, now appeared; his coming, perhaps, hastened by hearing the noise. Of him Captain Delano sought permission to serve out the water, so that all might share alike, and none injure themselves by unfair excess. But sensible, and, on Don Benito's account, kind as this offer was, it was received with what seemed impatience; as if aware that he lacked energy as a commander, Don Benito, with the true jealousy of weakness, resented as an affront any interference. So, at least, Captain Delano inferred.

In another moment the casks were being hoisted in, when some of the eager negroes accidentally jostled Captain Delano, where he stood by the gangway; so that, unmindful of Don Benito, yielding to the impulse of the moment, with good-natured authority he bade the blacks stand back; to enforce his words making use of a half-mirthful, half-menacing gesture. Instantly the blacks paused, just where they were, each negro and negress suspended in his or her posture, exactly as the word had found them—for a few seconds continuing so—while, as between the responsive posts of a telegraph, an unknown syllable ran from man to man among the perched oakum-pickers. While the visitor's attention was fixed by this scene, suddenly the hatchet-polishers half rose, and a rapid cry came from Don Benito.

Thinking that at the signal of the Spaniard he was about to be massacred, Captain Delano would have sprung for his boat, but paused, as the oakum-pickers, dropping down into the crowd with earnest exclamations, forced every white and every negro back, at the same moment, with gestures friendly and familiar, almost jocose, bidding him, in substance, not be a fool. Simultaneously the hatchet-polishers resumed their seats, quietly as so many tailors, and at once, as if nothing had happend, the work of hoisting in the casks was resumed, whites and blacks singing at the tackle.

Captain Delano glanced towards Don Benito. As he saw his meagre form in the act of recovering itself from reclining in the servant's arms, into which the agitated invalid had fallen, he could not but marvel at the panic by which himself had been surprised, on the darting supposition that such a commander, who, upon a legitimate occasion, so trivial, too, as it now appeared, could lose all self-command, was, with energetic iniquity, going to bring about his murder.

The casks being on deck, Captain Delano was handed a number of jars and cups by one of the steward's aids, who, in the name of his captain, entreated him to do as he had proposed—dole out the water. He complied, with republican impartiality as to this republican element, which always seeks one level, serving the oldest white no better than the youngest black; excepting indeed, poor Don Benito, whose condition, if not rank, demanded an extra allowance. To him, in the first place, Captain Delano presented a fair pitcher of the fluid; but, thirsting as he was for it, the Spaniard quaffed not a drop until after several grave bows and salutes. A reciprocation of courtesies which the sight-loving Africans hailed with clapping of hands.

Two of the less wilted pumpkins being reserved for the cabin table, the residue were minced up on the spot for the general regalement. But the soft bread, sugar, and bottled cider, Captain Delano would have given the whites alone, and in chief Don Benito; but the latter objected; which disinterestedness not a little pleased the American; and so mouthfuls all around were given alike to whites and blacks; excepting one bottle of cider, which Babo insisted upon setting aside for his master.

Here it may be observed that as, on the first visit of the boat, the American had not permitted his men to board the ship, neither did he now; being unwilling to add to the confusion of the decks.

Not influenced by the peculiar good-humor at present prevailing, and for the time oblivious of any but benevolent thoughts, Captain Delano, who, from recent indications, counted upon a breeze within an hour or two at furthest, dispatched the boat back to the sealer, with orders for all the hands that could be spared immediately to set about rafting casks to the watering-place and filling them. Likewise he bade word be carried to his chief officer, that if, against present expectation, the ship was not brought to anchor by sunset, he need be under no concern; for as there was to be a full moon that night, he (Captain Delano) would remain on board ready to play the pilot, come the wind soon or late.

As the two captains stood together, observing the departing boat—the servant, as it happened, having just spied a spot on his master's velvet sleeve, and silently engaged rubbing it out—the American expressed his regrets that the San Dominick had no boats; none, at least, but the unseaworthy old hulk of the long-boat, which, warped as a camel's skeleton in the desert, and almost as bleached, lay pot-wise inverted amidships, one side a little tipped, furnishing a subterraneous sort of den for family groups of the blacks, mostly women and small children; who, squatting on old mats below, or perched above in the dark dome, on the elevated seats, were descried, some distance within, like a social circle of bats, sheltering in some friendly cave; at intervals, ebon flights of naked boys and girls, three or four years old, darting in and out of the den's mouth.

"Had you three or four boats now, Don Benito," said Captain Delano, "I think that, by tugging at the oars, your negroes here might help along matters some. Did you sail from port without boats, Don Benito?"

"They were stove in the gales, Señor."

"That was bad. Many men, too, you lost then. Boats and men. Those must have been hard gales, Don Benito."

"Past all speech," cringed the Spaniard.

"Tell me, Don Benito," continued his companion with increased interest, "tell me, were these gales immediately off the pitch of Cape Horn?"

"Cape Horn?—who spoke of Cape Horn?"

"Yourself did, when giving me an account of your voyage," answered Captain Delano, with almost equal astonishment at this eating of his own words, even as he ever seemed eating his own heart, on the part of the Spaniard. "You yourself, Don Benito, spoke of Cape Horn," he emphatically repeated.

The Spaniard turned, in a sort of stooping posture, pausing an instant, as one about to make a plunging exchange of elements, as from air to water.

At this moment a messenger-boy, a white, hurried by, in the regular performance of his function carrying the last expired half hour forward to the forecastle, from the cabin time-piece, to have it struck at the ship's large bell.

"Master," said the servant, discontinuing his work on the coat sleeve, and addressing the rapt Spaniard with a sort of timid apprehensiveness, as one charged with a duty, the discharge of which, it was foreseen, would prove irksome to the very person who had imposed it, and for whose benefit it was intended, "master told me never mind where he was, or how engaged, always to remind him, to a minute, when shaving-time comes. Miguel has gone to strike the half-hour afternoon. It is *now*, master. Will master go into the cuddy?"

"Ah—yes," answered the Spaniard, starting, as from dreams into realities; then turning upon Captain Delano, he said that ere long he would resume the conversation.

"Then if master means to talk more to Don Amasa," said the servant, "why not let Don Amasa sit by master in the cuddy, and master can talk, and Don Amasa can listen, while Babo here lathers and strops."

"Yes," said Captain Delano, not unpleased with this sociable plan, "yes, Don Benito, unless you had rather not, I will go with you."

"Be it so, Señor."

As the three passed aft, the American could not but think it another strange instance of his host's capriciousness, this being shaved with such uncommon punctuality in the middle of the day. But he deemed it more than likely that the servant's anxious fidelity had something to do with the matter; inasmuch as the timely interruption served to rally his master from the mood which had evidently been coming upon him.

The place called the cuddy was a light deck-cabin formed by the poop, a sort of attic to the large cabin below. Part of it had formerly been the quarters of the officers; but since their death all the partitionings had been thrown down, and the whole interior converted into one spacious and airy marine hall; for absence of fine furniture and picturesque disarray of odd appurtenances, somewhat answering to the wide, cluttered hall of some eccentric bachelor-squire in the country, who hangs his shooting-jacket and tobacco-pouch on deer antlers, and keeps his fishing-rod, tongs, and walking-stick in the same corner.

The similitude was heightened, if not originally suggested, by glimpses of the surrounding sea; since, in one aspect, the country and the ocean seem cousins-german.

The floor of the cuddy was matted. Overhead, four or five old muskets were stuck into horizontal holes along the beams. On one side was a claw-footed old table lashed to the deck; a thumbed missal on it, and over it a small, meagre crucifix attached to the bulk-head. Under the table lay a dented cutlass or two, with a hacked harpoon, among some melancholy old rigging, like a heap of poor friars' girdles. There were also two long, sharp-ribbed settees of Malacca cane, black with age, and uncomfortable to look at as inquisitors' racks, with a large, misshapen arm-chair, which, furnished with a rude barber's crotch at the back, working with a screw, seemed some grotesque engine of torment. A flag locker was in one corner, open, exposing various colored bunting, some rolled up, others half unrolled, still others tumbled. Opposite was a cumbrous washstand, of black mahogany, all of one block, with a pedestal, like a font, and over it a railed shelf, containing combs, brushes, and other implements of the toilet. A torn hammock of stained grass swung near; the sheets tossed, and the pillow wrinkled up like a brow, as if whoever slept here slept but illy, with alternate visitations of sad thoughts and bad dreams.

The further extremity of the cuddy, overhanging the ship's stern, was pierced with three openings, windows or port-holes, according as men or cannon might peer, socially or unsocially, out of them. At present neither men nor cannon were seen, though huge ring-bolts and other rusty iron fixtures of the wood-work hinted of twenty-four-pounders.

Glancing towards the hammock as he entered, Captain Delano said, "You sleep here, Don Benito?"

"Yes, Señor, since we got into mild weather."

"This seems a sort of dormitory, sitting-room, sail-loft, chapel, armory, and private closet all together, Don Benito," added Captain Delano, looking round.

"Yes, Señor; events have not been favorable to much order in my arrangements."

Here the servant, napkin on arm, made a motion as it waiting his master's good pleasure. Don Benito signified his readiness, when, seating him in the Malacca arm-chair, and for the guest's convenience drawing opposite one of the settees, the servant commenced operations by throwing back his master's collar and lossening his cravat.

There is something in the negro which, in a peculiar way, fits him for avocations about one's person. Most negroes are natural valets and hair-dressers; taking to the comb and brush congenially as to the castanets, and flourishing them apparently with almost equal satisfaction. There is, too, a smooth tact about them in this employment, with a marvelous, noiseless, gliding briskness, not ungraceful in its way, singularly pleasing to behold, and still more so to be the manipulated subject of. And above all is the great gift of good-humor. Not the mere grin or laugh is here meant. Those were unsuitable. But a certain easy cheerfulness, harmonious in every glance and gesture; as though God had set the whole negro to some pleasant tune.

When to this is added the docility arising from the unaspiring contentment of a limited mind, and that susceptibility of bland attachment sometimes inhering in indisputable inferiors, one readily perceives why those hypochondriacs, Johnson and Byron—it may be, something like the hypochrondriac Benito Cereno—took to their hearts, almost to the exclusion of the entire white race, their serving men, the negroes, Barber and Fletcher. But if there be that in the negro which exempts him from the inflicted sourness of the morbid or cynical mind, how, in his most prepossessing aspects, must he appear to a benevolent one? When at ease with respect to exterior things, Captain Delano's nature was not only benign, but familiarly and humorously so. At home, he had often taken rare satisfaction in sitting in his door, watching some free man of color at his work or play. If on a voyage he chanced to have a black sailor, invariably he was on chatty and half-gamesome terms with him. In fact, like most men of a good, blithe heart, Captain Delano took to negroes, not philanthropically, but genially, just as other men to Newfoundland dogs.

Hitherto, the circumstances in which he found the San Dominick had repressed the tendency. But in the cuddy, relieved from his former uneasiness, and, for various reasons, more sociably inclined than at any previous period of the day, and seeing the colored servant, napkin on arm, so debonair about his master, in a business so familiar as that of shaving, too, all his old weakness for negroes returned.

Among other things, he was amused with an odd instance of the African love of bright colors and fine shows, in the black's informally taking from the flag-locker a great piece of bunting of all hues, and lavishly tucking it under his master's chin for an apron.

The mode of shaving among the Spaniards is a little different from what it is with other nations. They have a basin, specifically called a barber's basin, which on one side is scooped out, so as accurately to receive the chin, against which it is closely held in lathering; which is done, not with a brush, but with soap dipped in the water of the basin and rubbed on the face.

In the present instance salt-water was used for lack of better; and the parts lathered were only the upper lip, and low down under the throat, all the rest being cultivated beard.

The preliminaries being somewhat novel to Captain Delano, he sat curiously eyeing them, so that no conversation took place, nor, for the present, did Don Benito appear disposed to renew any.

Setting down his basin, the negro searched among the razors, as for the sharpest, and having found it, gave it an additional edge by expertly strapping it on the firm, smooth, oily skin of his open palm; he then made a gesture as if to begin, but midway stood suspended for an instant, one hand elevating the razor, the other professionally dabbling among the bubbling suds on the Spaniard's lank neck. Not unaffected by the close sight of the gleaming steel, Don Benito nervously shuddered; his usual ghastliness was heightened by the lather, which lather, again, was intensified in its hue by the contrasting sootiness of the negro's body. Altogether the scene was somewhat peculiar, at least to Captain Delano, nor, as he saw the two thus postured, could he resist the vagary, that in the black he saw a headsman, and in the white a man at the block. But this was one of those antic conceits, appearing and vanishing in a breath, from which, perhaps, the best regulated mind is not always free.

Meantime the agitation of the Spaniard had a little loosened the bunting from around him, so that one broad fold swept curtain-like over the chair-arm to the floor, revealing, amid a profusion of amorial bars and ground-colors—black, blue, and yellow—a closed castle in a blood-red field diagonal with a lion rampant in a white.

"The castle and the lion," exclaimed Captain Delano—"why, Don Benito, this is the flag of Spain you use here. It's well it's only I, and not the King, that sees this," he added, with a smile, "but"—turning towards the black—"it's all one, I suppose, so the colors be gay"; which playful remark did not fail somewhat to tickle the negro.

"Now, master," he said, readjusting the flag, and pressing the head gently further back into the crotch of the chair; "now, master," and the steel glanced nigh the throat.

Again Don Benito faintly shuddered.

"You must not shake so, master. See, Don Amasa, master always shakes when I shave him. And yet master knows I never yet have drawn blood, though it's true, if master will shake so, I may some of these times. Now master," he continued. "And now, Don Amasa, please go on with your talk about the gale, and all that; master can hear, and, between times, master can answer."

"Ah yes, these gales," said Captain Delano; "but the more I think of your voyage, Don Benito, the more I wonder, not at the gales, terrible as they must have been, but at the disastrous interval following them. For here, by your account, have you been these two months and more getting from Cape Horn to St. Maria, a distance which I myself, with a good wind, have sailed in a few days. True, you had calms, and long ones, but to be becalmed for two months, that is, at least, unusual. Why, Don Benito, had almost any other gentleman told me such a story, I should have been half disposed to a little incredulity."

Here an involuntary expression came over the Spaniard, similar to that just before on the deck, and whether it was the start he gave, or a sudden gawky roll of the hull in the calm, or a momentary unsteadiness of the servant's hand, however it was, just then the razor drew blood, spots of which stained the creamy lather under the throat: immediately the black barber drew back his steel, and, remaining in his professional attitude, back to Captain Delano, and face to Don Benito, held up the trickling razor, saying, with a sort of half humorous sorrow, "See, master—you shook so—here's Babo's first blood."

No sword drawn before James the First of England, no assassination in that timid King's presence, could have produced a more terrified aspect than was now presented by Don Benito.

Poor fellow, thought Captain Delano, so nervous he can't even bear the sight of barber's blood; and this unstrung, sick man, is it credible that I should have imagined he meant to spill all my blood, who can't endure the sight of one little drop of his own? Surely, Amasa Delano, you have been beside yourself this day. Tell it not when you get home, sappy Amasa. Well, well, he looks like a murderer, doesn't he? More like as if himself were to be done for. Well, well, this day's experience shall be a good lesson.

Meantime, while these things were running through the honest seaman's mind, the servant had taken the napkin from his arm, and to Don Benito had said—"But answer Don Amasa, please, master, while I wipe this ugly stuff off the razor, and strop it again."

As he said the words, his face was turned half round, so as to be alike visible to the Spaniard and the American, and seemed, by its expression, to hint, that he was desirous, by getting his master to go on with the conversation, considerately to withdraw his attention from the recent annoying accident. As if glad to snatch the offered relief, Don Benito resumed, rehearsing to Captain Delano, that not only were the calms of unusual duration, but the ship had fallen in with obstinate currents; and other things he added, some of which were but repetitions of former statements, to explain how it came to pass that the passage from Cape Horn to St. Maria had been so exceedingly long; now and then mingling with his words, incidental praises, less qualified than before, to the blacks, for their general good conduct. These particulars were not given consecutively, the servant, at convenient times, using his razor, and so, between the intervals of shaving, the story and panegyric went on with more than usual huskiness.

To Captain Delano's imagination, now again not wholly at rest, there was something so hollow in the Spaniard's manner, with apparently some reciprocal hollowness in the servant's dusky comment of silence, that the idea flashed across him, that possibly master and man, for some unknown purpose, were acting out, both in word and deed, nay, to the very tremor of Don Benito's limbs, some juggling play before him. Neither did the suspicion of collusion lack apparent support, from the fact of those whispered conferences before mentioned. But then, what could be the object of enacting this play of the barber before him? At last, regarding the notion as a whimsy, insensibly suggested, perhaps, by the theatrical aspect of Don Benito in this harlequin ensign, Captain Delano speedily banished it.

The shaving over, the servant bestirred himself with a small bottle of scented waters, pouring a few drops on the head, and then diligently rubbing; the vehemence of the exercise causing the muscles of his face to twitch rather strangely.

His next operation was with comb, scissors, and brush; going round and round, smoothing a curl here, clipping an unruly whisker-hair there, giving a graceful sweep to the temple-lock, with other impromptu touches evincing the hands of a master; while, like any resigned gentleman in barber's hands, Don Benito bore all, much less uneasily, at least, than he had done the razoring; indeed he sat so pale and rigid now, that the negro seemed a Nubian sculptor finishing off a white statue-head.

All being over at last, the standard of Spain removed, tumbled up, and tossed back into the flag-locker, the negro's warm breath blowing away any stray hair which might have lodged down his master's neck; collar and cravat readjusted; a speck of lint whisked off the velvet lapel; all this being done; backing off a little space, and pausing with an expression of subdued self-complacency, the servant for a moment surveyed his master, as, in toilet at least, the creature of his own tasteful hands.

Captain Delano playfully complimented him upon his achievement; at the same time congratulating Don Benito.

But neither sweet waters, nor shampooing, nor fidelity, nor sociality, delighted the Spaniard. Seeing him relapsing into forbidding gloom, and still remaining seated, Captain Delano, thinking that his presence was undesired just then, withdrew, on pretense of seeing whether, as he had prophesied, any signs of a breeze were visible.

Walking forward to the main-mast, he stood awhile thinking over the scene, and not without some undefined misgivings, when he heard a noise near the cuddy, and turning, saw the negro, his hand to his cheek. Advancing, Captain Delano perceived that the cheek was bleeding. He was about to ask the cause, when the negro's wailing soliloquy enlightened him.

"Ah, when will master get better from his sickness; only the sour heart that sour sickness breeds made him serve Babo so; cutting Babo with the razor, because, only by accident, Babo had given master one little scratch; and for the first time in so many a day, too. Ah, ah, ah," holding his hand to his face.

Is it possible, thought Captain Delano; was it to wreak in private his Spanish spite against this poor friend of his, that Don Benito, by his sullen manner, impelled me to withdraw? Ah, this slavery breeds ugly passions in man.—Poor fellow!

He was about to speak in sympathy to the negro, but with a timid reluctance he now re-entered the cuddy.

Presently master and man came forth; Don Benito leaning on his servant as if nothing had happened.

But a sort of love-quarrel, after all, thought Captain Delano.

He accosted Don Benito, and they slowly walked together. They had gone but a few paces, when the steward—a tall, rajah-looking mulatto, orientally set off with a pagoda turban formed by three or four Madras handkerchiefs wound about his head, tier on tier—approaching with a salam, announced lunch in the cabin.

On their way thither, the two captains were preceded by the mulatto, who, turning round as he advanced, with continual smiles and bows, ushered them on, a display of elegance which quite completed the insignificance of the small bareheaded Babo, who, as if not unconscious of inferiority, eyed askance the graceful steward. But in part, Captain Delano imputed his jealous watchfulness to that peculiar feeling which the full-blooded African entertains for the adulterated one. As for the steward, his manner, if not bespeaking much dignity or self-respect, yet evidenced his extreme desire to please; which is doubly meritorious, as at once Christian and Chesterfieldian.

Captain Delano observed with interest that while the complexion of the mulatto was hybrid, his physiognomy was European—classically so.

"Don Benito," whispered he, "I am glad to see this usher-of-the-golden-rod of yours; the sight refutes an ugly remark once made to me by a Barbadoes planter; that when a mulatto has a regular European face, look out for him; he is a devil. But see, your steward here has features more regular than King George's of England; and yet there he nods, and bows, and smiles; a king, indeed—the king of kind hearts and polite fellows. What a pleasant voice he has, too?"

"He has, Señor."

"But tell me, has he not, so far as you have known him, always proved a good, worthy fellow?" said Captain Delano, pausing, while with a final genuflexion the steward disappeared into the cabin; "come, for the reason just mentioned, I am curious to know."

"Francesco is a good man," somewhat sluggishly responded Don Benito, like a phlegmatic appreciator, who would neither find fault nor flatter.

"Ah, I thought so. For it were strange, indeed, and not very creditable to us white-skins, if a little of our blood mixed with the African's, should, far from improving the latter's quality, have the sad effect of pouring vitriolic acid into black broth; improving the hue, perhaps, but not the wholesomeness."

"Doubtless, doubtless, Señor, but"—glancing at Babo—"not to speak of negroes, your planter's remark I have heard applied to the Spanish and Indian intermixtures in our provinces. But I know nothing about the matter," he listlessly added.

And here they entered the cabin.

The lunch was a frugal one. Some of Captain Delano's fresh fish and pumpkins, biscuit and salt beef, the reserved bottle of cider, and the San Dominick's last bottle of Canary.

As they entered, Francesco, with two or three colored aids, was hovering over the table giving the last adjustments. Upon perceiving their master they withdrew, Francesco making a smiling congé, and the Spaniard, without condescending to notice it, fastidiously remarking to his companion that he relished not superfluous attendance.

Without companions, host and guest sat down, like a childless married couple, at opposite ends of the table, Don Benito waving Captain Delano to his place, and, weak as he was, insisting upon that gentleman being seated before himself.

The negro placed a rug under Don Benito's feet, and a cushion behind his back, and then stood behind, not his master's chair, but Captain Delano's. At first, this a little surprised the latter. But it was soon evident that, in taking his position, the black was still true to his master; since by facing him he could the more readily anticipate his slightest want.

"This is an uncommonly intelligent fellow of yours, Don Benito," whispered Captain Delano across the table.

"You say true, Señor."

During the repast, the guest again reverted to parts of Don Benito's story, begging further particulars here and there. He inquired how it was that the scurvy and fever should have committed such wholesale havoc upon the whites, while destroying less than half of the blacks. As if this question reproduced the whole scene of plague before the Spaniard's eyes, miserably reminding him of his solitude in a cabin where before he had had so many friends and officers round him, his hand shook, his face became hueless, broken words escaped; but directly the sane memory of the past seemed replaced by insane terrors of the present. With starting eyes he stared before him at vacancy. For nothing was to be seen but the hand of his servant pushing the Canary over towards him. At length a few sips served partially to restore him. He made random reference to the different constitution of races, enabling one to offer more resistance to certain maladies than another. The thought was new to his companion.

Presently Captain Delano, intending to say something to his host concerning the pecuniary part of the business he had undertaken for him, especially—since he was strictly accountable to his owners—with reference to the new suit of sails, and other things of that sort; and naturally preferring to conduct such affairs in private, was desirous that the servant should withdraw; imagining that Don Benito for a few minutes could dispense with his attendance. He, however, waited awhile; thinking that, as the conversation proceeded, Don Benito, without being prompted, would perceive the propriety of the step.

But it was otherwise. At last catching his host's eye, Captain Delano, with a slight backward gesture of his thumb, whispered, "Don Benito, pardon me, but there is an interference with the full expression of what I have to say to you."

Upon this the Spaniard changed countenance; which was imputed to his resenting the hint, as in some way a reflection upon his servant. After a moment's pause, he assured his guest that the black's remaining with them could be of no disservice; because since losing his officers he had made Babo (whose original office, it now appeared, had been captain of the slaves) not only his constant attendant and companion, but in all things his confidant.

After this, nothing more could be said; though, indeed, Captain Delano could hardly avoid some little tinge of irritation upon being left ungratified in so inconsiderable a wish, by one, too, for whom he intended such solid services. But it is only his querulousness, thought he; and so filling his glass he proceeded to business.

The price of the sails and other matters was fixed upon. But while this was being done, the American observed that, though his original offer of assistance had been hailed with hectic animation, yet now when it was reduced to a business transaction, indifference and apathy were betrayed. Don Benito, in fact, appeared to submit to hearing the details more out of regard to common propriety, than from any impression that weighty benefit to himself and his voyage was involved.

Soon, his manner became still more reserved. The effort was vain to seek to draw him into social talk. Gnawed by his splenetic mood, he sat twitching his beard, while to little purpose the hand of his servant, mute as that on the wall, slowly pushed over the Canary.

Lunch being over, they sat down on the cushioned transom; the servant placing a pillow behind his master. The long continuance of the calm had now affected the atmosphere. Don Benito sighed heavily, as if for breath.

"Why not adjourn to the cuddy," said Captain Delano; "there is more air there." But the host sat silent and motionless.

Meantime his servant knelt before him, with a large fan of feathers. And Francesco coming in on tiptoes, handed the negro a little cup of aromatic waters, with which at intervals he chafed his master's brow; smoothing the hair along the temples as a nurse does a child's. He spoke no word. He only rested his eye on his master's, as if, amid all Don Benito's distress, a little to refresh his spirit by the silent sight of fidelity.

Presently the ship's bell sounded two o'clock; and through the cabin windows a slight rippling of the sea was discerned; and from the desired direction.

"There," exlaimed Captain Delano, "I told you so, Don Benito, look!"

He had risen to his feet, speaking in a very animated tone, with a view the more to rouse his companion. But though the crimson curtain of the stern-window near him that moment fluttered against his pale cheek, Don Benito seemed to have even less welcome for the breeze than the calm.

Poor fellow, thought Captain Delano, bitter experience has taught him that one ripple does not make a wind, any more than one swallow a summer. But he is mistaken for once. I will get his ship in for him, and prove it.

Briefly alluding to his weak condition, he urged his host to remain quietly where he was, since he (Captain Delano) would with pleasure take upon himself the responsibility of making the best use of the wind.

Upon gaining the deck, Captain Delano started at the unexpected figure of Atufal, monumentally fixed at the threshold, like one of those sculptured porters of black marble guarding the porches of Egyptian tombs.

But this time the start was, perhaps, purely physical. Atufal's presence, singularly attesting docility even in sullenness, was contrasted with that of the hatchet-polishers, who in patience evinced their industry; while both spectacles showed, that lax as Don Benito's general authority might be, still, whenever he chose to exert it, no man so savage or colossal but must, more or less, bow.

Snatching a trumpet which hung from the bulwarks, with a free step Captain Delano advanced to the forward edge of the poop, issuing his orders in his best Spanish. The few sailors and many negroes, all equally pleased, obediently set about heading the ship towards the harbor.

While giving some directions about setting a lower stun'n'-sail, suddenly Captain Delano heard a voice faithfully repeating his orders. Turning, he saw Babo, now for the time acting, under the pilot, his original part of captain of the slaves. This assistance proved valuable. Tattered sails and warped yards were soon brought into some trim. And no brace or halyard was pulled but to the blithe songs of the inspirited negroes.

Good fellows, thought Captain Delano, a little training would make fine sailors of them. Why see, the very women pull and sing too. These must be some of those Ashantee negresses that make such capital soldiers, I've heard. But who's at the helm. I must have a good hand there.

He went to see.

The San Dominick steered with a cumbrous tiller, with large horizontal pullies attached. At each pulley-end stood a subordinate black, and between them, at the tiller-head, the responsible post, a Spanish seaman, whose countenance evinced his due share in the general hopefulness and confidence at the coming of the breeze.

He proved the same man who had behaved with so shamefaced an air on the windlass.

"Ah,—it is you, my man," exclaimed Captain Delano—"well, no more sheep's-eyes now;—look straight forward and keep the ship so. Good hand, I trust? And want to get into the harbor, don't you?"

The man assented with an inward chuckle, grasping the tiller-head firmly. Upon this, unperceived by the American, the two blacks eyed the sailor intently.

Finding all right at the helm, the pilot went forward to the forecastle, to see how matters stood there.

The ship now had way enough to breast the current. With the approach of evening, the breeze would be sure to freshen.

Having done all that was needed for the present, Captain Delano, giving his last orders to the sailors, turned aft to report affairs to Don Benito in the cabin; perhaps additionally incited to rejoin him by the hope of snatching a moment's private chat while the servant was engaged upon deck.

From opposite sides, there were, beneath the poop, two approaches to the cabin; one further forward than the other, and consequently communicating with a longer passage. Marking the servant still above, Captain Delano, taking the nighest entrance—the one last named, and at whose porch Atufal still stood—hurried on his way, till, arrived at the cabin threshold, he paused an instant, a little to recover from his eagerness. Then, with the words of his intended business upon his lips, he entered. As he advanced toward the seated Spaniard, he heard another footstep, keeping time with his. From the opposite door, a salver in hand, the servant was likewise advancing.

"Confound the faithful fellow," thought Captain Delano; "what a vexatious coincidence."

Possibly, the vexation might have been something different, were it not for the brisk confidence inspired by the breeze. But even as it was, he felt a slight twinge, from a sudden indefinite association in his mind of Babo with Atufal.

"Don Benito," said he, "I give you joy; the breeze will hold, and will increase. By the way, you tall man and time-piece, Atufal, stands without. By your order, of course?"

Don Benito recoiled, as if at some bland satiricial touch, delivered with such adroit garnish of apparent good breeding as to present no handle for retort.

He is like one flayed alive, thought Captain Delano; where may one touch him without causing a shrink?

The servant moved before his master, adjusting a cushion; recalled to civility, the Spaniard stiffly replied: "You are right. The slave appears where you saw him, according to my command; which is, that if at the given hour I am below, he must take his stand and abide my coming."

"Ah now, pardon me, but that is treating the poor fellow like an ex-king indeed. Ah, Don Benito," smiling, "for all the license you permit in some things, I fear lest, at bottom, you are a bitter hard master."

Again Don Benito shrank; and this time, as the good sailor thought, from a genuine twinge of his conscience.

Again conversation became constrained. In vain Captain Delano called attention to the now perceptible motion of the keel gently cleaving the sea; with lack-lustre eye, Don Benito returned words few and reserved.

By-and-by, the wind having steadily risen, and still blowing right into the harbor, bore the San Dominick swiftly on. Rounding a point of land, the sealer at distance came into open view.

Meantime Captain Delano had again repaired to the deck, remaining there sometime. Having at last altered the ship's course, so as to give the reef a wide berth, he returned for a few moments below.

I will cheer up my poor friend, this time, thought he.

"Better and better, Don Benito," he cried as he blithely reentered: "there will soon be an end to your cares, at least for awhile. For when, after a long, sad voyage, you know, the anchor drops into the haven, all its vast weight seems lifted from the captain's heart. We are getting on famously, Don Benito. My ship is in sight. Look through this side-light here; there she is; all a-taunt-o! The Bachelor's Delight, my good friend. Ah, how this wind braces one up. Come, you must take a cup of coffee with me this evening. My old steward will give you as fine a cup as ever any sultan tasted. What say you, Don Benito, will you?"

At first, the Spaniard glanced feverishly up, casting a longing look towards the sealer, while with mute concern his servant gazed into his face. Suddenly the old ague of coldness returned, and dropping back to his cushions he was silent.

"You do not answer. Come, all day you have been my host; would you have hospitality all on one side?"

"I cannot go," was the response.

"What? it will not fatigue you. The ships will lie together as near as they can, without swinging foul. It will be little more than stepping from deck to deck; which is but as from room to room. Come, come, you must not refuse me."

"I cannot go," decisively and repulsively repeated Don Benito.

Renouncing all but the last appearance of courtesy, with a sort of cadaverous sullenness, and biting his thin nails to the quick, he glanced, almost glared, at his guest, as if impatient that a stranger's presence should interfere with the full indulgence of his morbid hour. Meantime the sound of the parted waters came more and more gurglingly and merrily in at the windows; as reproaching him for his dark spleen; as telling him that, sulk as he might, and go mad with it, nature cared not a jot; since, whose fault was it, pray?

But the foul mood was now at its depth, as the fair wind at its height.

There was something in the man so far beyond any mere unsociality or sourness previously evinced, that even the forbearing good-nature of his guest could no longer endure it. Wholly at a loss to account for such demeanor, and deeming sickness with eccentricity, however extreme, no adequate excuse, well satisfied, too, that nothing in his own conduct could justify it, Captain Delano's pride began to be roused. Himself became reserved. But all seemed one to the Spaniard. Quitting him, therefore, Captain Delano once more went to the deck.

The ship was now within less than two miles of the sealer. The whale-boat was seen darting over the interval.

To be brief, the two vessels, thanks to the pilot's skill, ere long in neighborly style lay anchored together.

Before returning to his own vessel, Captain Delano had intended communicating to Don Benito the smaller details of the proposed services to be rendered. But, as it was, unwilling anew to subject himself to rebuffs, he resolved, now that he had seen the San Dominick safely moored, immediately to quit her, without further allusion to hospitality or business. Indefinitely postponing his ulterior plans, he would regulate his future actions according to future circumstances. His boat was ready to receive him; but his host still tarried below. Well, thought Captain Delano, if he has little breeding, the more need to show mine. He descended to the cabin to bid a ceremonious, and, it may be, tacitly rebukeful adieu. But to his great satisfaction, Don Benito, as if he began to feel the weight of that treatment with which his slighted guest had, not indecorously, retaliated upon him, now supported by his servant, rose to his feet, and grasping Captain Delano's hand, stood tremulous; too much agitated to speak. But the good augury hence drawn was suddenly dashed, by his resuming all his previous reserve, with augumented gloom, as, with half-averted eyes, he silently reseated himself on his cushions. With a corresponding return of his own chilled feelings, Captain Delano bowed and withdrew.

He was hardly midway in the narrow corridor, dim as a tunnel, leading from the cabin to the stairs, when a sound, as of the tolling for execution in some jail-yard, fell on his ears. It was the echo of the ship's flawed bell, striking the hour, drearily reverberated in the subterranean vault. Instantly, by a fatality not to be withstood, his mind, responsive to the portent, swarmed with superstitious suspicions. He paused. In images far swifter than these sentences, the minutest details of all his former distrusts swept through him.

Hitherto, credulous good-nature had been too ready to furnish excuses for reasonable fears. Why was the Spaniard, so superfluously punctilious at times, now heedless of common propriety in not accompanying to the side his departing guest? Did indisposition forbid? Indisposition had not forbidden more irksome exertion that day. His last equivocal demeanor recurred. He had risen to his feet, grasped his guest's hand, motioned toward his hat; then, in an instant, all was eclipsed in sinister muteness and gloom. Did this imply one brief, repentant relenting at the final moment, from some iniquitous plot, followed by remorseless return to it? His last glance seemed to express a calamitous, yet acquiescent farewell to Captain Delano forever. Why decline the invitation to visit the sealer that evening? Or was the Spaniard less hardened than the Jew, who refrained not from supping at the board of him whom the same night he meant to betray? What imported all those day-long enigmas and contradictions, except they were intended to mystify, preliminary to some stealthy blow? Atufal, the pretended rebel, but punctual shadow, that moment lurked by the threshold without. He seemed a sentry, and more. Who, by his own confession, had stationed him there? Was the negro now lying in wait?

The Spaniard behind—his creature before: to rush from darkness to light was the involuntary choice.

The next moment, with clenched jaw and hand, he passed Atufal, and stood unharmed in the light. As he saw his trim ship lying peacefully at anchor, and almost within ordinary call; as he saw his household boat, with familiar faces in it, patiently rising and falling on the short waves by the San Dominick's side; and then, glancing about the decks where he stood, saw the oakum-pickers still gravely plying their fingers; and heard the low, buzzing whistle and industrious hum of the hatchet-polishers, still bestirring themselves over their endless occupation; and more than all, as he saw the benign aspect of nature, taking her innocent repose in the evening; the screened sun in the quiet camp of the west shining out like the mild light from Abraham's tent; as charmed eye and ear took in all these, with the chained figure of the black, clenched jaw and hand relaxed. Once again he smiled at the phantoms which had mocked him, and felt something like a tinge of remorse, that, by harboring them even for a moment, he should, by implication, have betrayed an atheist doubt of the ever-watchful Providence above.

There was a few minutes' delay, while, in obedience to his orders, the boat was being hooked along to the gangway. During this interval, a sort of saddened satisfaction stole over Captain Delano, at thinking of the kindly offices he had that day discharged for a stranger. Ah, thought he, after good actions one's conscience is never ungrateful, however much so the benefited party may be.

Presently, his foot, in the first act of descent into the boat, pressed the first round of the side-ladder, his face presented inward upon the deck. In the same moment, he heard his name courteously sounded; and, to his pleased surprise, saw Don Benito advancing—an unwonted energy in his air, as if, at the last moment, intent upon making amends for his recent discourtesy. With instinctive good feeling, Captain Delano, withdrawing his foot, turned and reciprocally advanced. As he did so, the Spaniard's nervous eagerness increased, but his vital energy failed; so that, the better to support him, the servant, placing his master's hand on his naked shoulder, and gently holding it there, formed himself into a sort of crutch.

When the two captains met, the Spaniard again fervently took the hand of the American, at the same time casting an earnest glance into his eyes, but, as before, too much overcome to speak.

I have done him wrong, self-reproachfully thought Captain Delano; his apparent coldness has deceived me; in no instance has he meant to offend.

Meantime, as if fearful that the continuance of the scene might too much unstring his master, the servant seemed anxious to terminate it. And so, still presenting himself as a crutch, and walking between the two captains, he advanced with them towards the gangway; while still, as if full of kindly contrition, Don Benito would not let go the hand of Captain Delano, but retained it in his, across the black's body.

Soon they were standing by the side, looking over into the boat, whose crew turned up their curious eyes. Waiting a moment for the Spaniard to relinquish his hold, the now embarrassed Captain Delano lifted his foot, to overstep the threshold of the open gangway; but still Don Benito would not let go his hand. And yet, with an agitated tone, he said, "I can go no further; here I must bid you adieu. Adieu, my dear, dear Don Amasa. Go—go!" suddenly tearing his hand loose, "go, and God guard you better than me, my best friend."

Not unaffected, Captain Delano would now have lingered; but catching the meekly admonitory eye of the servant, with a hasty farewell he descended into his boat, followed by the continual adieus of Don Benito, standing rooted in the gangway.

Seating himself in the stern, Captain Delano, making a last salute, ordered the boat shoved off. The crew had their oars on end. The bowsmen pushed the boat a sufficient distance for the oars to be lengthwise dropped. The instant that was done, Don Benito sprang over the bulwarks, falling at the feet of Captain Delano; at the same time calling towards his ship, but in tones so frenzied, that none in the boat could understand him. But, as if not equally obtuse, three sailors, from three different and distant parts of the ship, splashed into the sea, swimming after their captain, as if intent upon his rescue.

The dismayed officer of the boat eagerly asked what this meant. To which, Captain Delano, turning a disdainful smile upon the unaccountable

Spaniard, answered that, for his part, he neither knew nor cared; but it seemed as if Don Benito had taken it into his head to produce the impression among his people that the boat wanted to kidnap him. "Or else—give way for your lives," he wildly added, starting at a clattering hubbub in the ship, above which rang the tocsin of the hatchet-polishers; and seizing Don Benito by the throat he added, "this plotting pirate means murder!" Here, in apparent verification of the words, the servant, a dagger in his hand, was seen on the rail overhead, poised, in the act of leaping, as if with desperate fidelity to befriend his master to the last; while, seemingly to aid the black, the three white sailors were trying to clamber into the hampered bow. Meantime, the whole host of negroes, as if inflamed at the sight of their jeopardized captain, impended in one sooty avalanche over the bulwarks.

All this, with what preceeded, and what followed, occurred with such involutions of rapidity, that past, present, and future seemed one.

Seeing the negro coming, Captain Delano had flung the Spaniard aside, almost in the very act of clutching him, and, by the unconscious recoil, shifting his place, with arms thrown up, so promptly grappled the servant in his descent, that with dagger presented at Captain Delano's heart, the black seemed of purpose to have leaped there as to his mark. But the weapon was wrenched away, and the assailant dashed down into the bottom of the boat, which now, with disentangled oars, began to speed through the sea.

At this juncture, the left hand of Captain Delano, on one side, again clutched the half-reclined Don Benito, heedless that he was in a speechless faint, while his right foot, on the other side, ground the prostrate negro; and his right arm pressed for added speed on the after oar, his eye bent forward, encouraging his men to their utmost.

But here, the officer of the boat, who had at last succeeded in beating off the towing sailors, and was now, with face turned aft, assisting the bowsman at his oar, suddenly called to Captain Delano, to see what the black was about; while a Portuguese oarsman shouted to him to give heed to what the Spaniard was saying.

Glancing down at his feet, Captain Delano saw the freed hand of the servant aiming with a second dagger—a small one, before concealed in his wool—with this he was snakishly writhing up from the boat's bottom, at the heart of his master, his countenance lividly vindictive, expressing the centred purpose of his soul; while the Spaniard, half-choked, was vainly shrinking way, with husky words, incoherent to all but the Portuguese.

That moment, across the long-benighted mind of Captain Delano, a flash of revelation swept, illuminating, in unanticipated clearness, his host's whole mysterious demeanor, with every enigmatic event of the day, as well as the entire past voyage of the San Dominick. He smote Babo's hand down, but his own heart smote him harder. With infinite pity he withdrew his hold from Don Benito. Not Captain Delano, but Don Benito, the black, in leaping into the boat, had intended to stab.

Both the black's hands were held, as, glancing up towards the San Dominick, Captain Delano, now with scales dropped from his eyes, saw the negroes, not in misrule, not in tumult, not as if frantically concerned for Don Benito, but with mask torn away, flourishing hatchets and knives, in ferocious piratical revolt. Like delirious black dervishes, the six Ashantees danced on the poop. Prevented by their foes from springing into the water, the Spanish boys were hurrying up to the topmost spars, while such of the few Spanish sailors, not already in the sea, less alert, were described, helplessly mixed in, on deck, with the blacks.

Meantime Captain Delano hailed his own vessel, ordering the ports up, and the guns run out. But by this time the cable of the San Dominick had been cut; and the fag-end, in lashing out, whipped away the canvas shroud about the beak, suddenly revealing, as the bleached hull swung round towards the open ocean, death for the figure-head, in a human skeleton; chalky comment on the chalked words below, "*Follow your leader.*"

At the sight, Don Benito, covering his face, wailed out: "Tis he, Aranda! my murdered, unburied friend!"

Upon reaching the sealer, calling for ropes, Captain Delano bound the negro, who made no resistance, and had him hoisted to the deck. He would then have assisted the now almost helpless Don Benito up the side; but Don Benito, wan as he was, refused to move, or be moved, until the negro should have been first put below out of view. When, presently assured that it was done, he no more shrank from the ascent.

The boat was immediately dispatched back to pick up the three swimming sailors. Meantime, the guns were in readiness, though, owing to the San Dominick having glided somewhat astern of the sealer, only the aftermost one could be brought to bear. With this, they fired six times; thinking to cripple the fuitive ship by bringing down her spars. But only a few inconsiderable ropes were shot away. Soon the ship was beyond the gun's range, steering broad out of the bay; the blacks thickly clustering round the bowsprit, one moment with taunting cries towards the whites, the next with upthrown gestures hailing the now dusky moors of ocean—cawing crows escaped from the hand of the fowler.

The first impulse was to slip the cables and give chase. But, upon second thoughts, to pursue with whale-boat and yawl seemed more promising.

Upon inquiring of Don Benito what fire-arms they had on board the San Dominick, Captain Delano was answered that they had none that could be used; because, in the earlier stages of the mutiny, a cabin-passenger, since dead, had secretly put out of order the locks of what few muskets there were. But with all his remaining strength, Don Benito entreated the

American not to give chase, either with ship or boat; for the negroes had already proved themselves such desperadoes, that, in case of a present assault, nothing but a total massacre of the whites could be looked for. But, regarding this warning as coming from one whose spirit had been crushed by misery the American did not give up his design.

The boats were got ready and armed. Captain Delano ordered his men into them. He was going himself when Don Benito grasped his arm.

"What! have you saved my life, Señor, and are you now going to throw away your own?"

The officers also, for reasons connected with their interests and those of the voyage, and a duty owing to the owners, strongly objected against their commander's going. Weighing their remonstrances a moment, Captain Delano felt bound to remain; appointing his chief mate—an athletic and resolute man, who had been a privateer's-man—to head the party. The more to encourage the sailors, they were told, that the Spanish captain considered his ship good as lost; that she and her cargo, including some gold and silver, were worth more than a thousand dubloons. Take her, and no small part should be theirs. The sailors replied with a shout.

The fugitives had now almost gained an offing. It was nearly night; but the moon was rising. After hard, prolonged pulling, the boats came up on the ship's quarters, at a suitable distance laying upon their oars to discharge their muskets. Having no bullets to return, the negroes sent their yells. But, upon the second volley, Indian-like, they hurtled their hatchets. One took off a sailor's fingers. Another struck the whale-boat's bow, cutting off the rope there, and remaining stuck in the gunwale like a woodman's axe. Snatching it, quivering from its lodgment, the mate hurled it back. The returned gauntlet now stuck in the ship's broken quarter-gallery, and so remained.

The negroes giving too hot a reception, the whites kept a more respectful distance. Hovering now just out of reach of the hurtling hatchets, they, with a view to the close encounter which must soon come, sought to decoy the blacks into entirely disarming themselves of their most murderous weapons in a hand-to-hand fight, by foolishly flinging them, as missiles, short of the mark, into the sea. But, ere long, perceiving the stratagem, the negroes desisted, though not before many of them had to replace their lost hatchets with handspikes; an exchange which, as counted upon, proved, in the end, favorable to the assailants.

Meantime, with a strong wind, the ship still clove the water; the boats alternately falling behind, and pulling up, to discharge fresh volleys.

The fire was mostly directed towards the stern, since there, chiefly, the negroes, at present, were clustering. But to kill or maim the negroes was not the object. To take them, with the ship, was the object. To do it, the ship must be boarded; which could not be done by boats while she was sailing so fast.

A thought now struck the mate. Observing the Spanish boys still aloft, high as they could get, he called to them to descend to the yards, and cut adrift the sails. It was done. About this time, owing to causes hereafter to be shown, two Spaniards, in the dress of sailors, and conspicuously showing themselves, were killed; not by volleys, but by deliberate marksman's shots; while, as it afterwards appeared, by one of the general discharges, Atufal, the black, and the Spaniard at the helm likewise were killed. What now, with the loss of the sails, and loss of leaders, the ship became unmanageable to the negroes.

With creaking masts, she came heavily round to the wind; the prow slowly swinging into view of the boats, its skeleton gleaming in the horizontal moonlight, and casting a gigantic ribbed shadow upon the water. One extended arm of the ghost seemed beckoning the whites to avenge it.

"Follow your leader!" cried the mate; and, one on each bow, the boats boarded. Sealing-spears and cutlasses crossed hatchets and hand-spikes. Huddled upon the long-boat amidships, the negresses raised a wailing chant, whose chorus was the clash of the steel.

For a time, the attack wavered; the negroes wedging themselves to beat it back; the half-repelled sailors, as yet unable to gain a footing, fighting as troopers in the saddle, one leg sideways flung over the bulwarks, and one without, plying their cutlasses like carters' whips. But in vain. They were almost overborne, when, rallying themselves into a squad as one man, with a huzza, they sprang inboard, where, entangled, they involuntarily separated again. For a few breaths' space there was a vague, muffled, inner sound, as of submerged sword-fish rushing hither and thither through shoals of black-fish. Soon, in a reunited band, and joined by the Spanish seamen, the whites came to the surface, irresistibly driving the negroes toward the stern. But a barricade of casks and sacks, from side to side, had been thrown up by the mainmast. Here the negroes faced about, and though scorning peace or truce, yet fain would have had respite. But, without pause, overleaping the barrier, the unflagging sailors again closed. Exhausted, the blacks, now fought in despair. Their red tongues lolled, wolf-like, from their black mouths. But the pale sailors' teeth were set; not a word was spoken; and, in five minutes more, the ship was won.

Nearly a score of the negroes were killed. Exclusive of those by the balls, many were mangled; their wounds—mostly inflicted by the long-edged sealing-spears, resembling those shaven ones of the English at Preston Pans, made by the poled scythes of the Highlanders. On the other side, none were killed, though several were wounded; some severely, including the mate. The surviving negroes were temporarily secured, and the ship, towed back into the harbor at midnight, once more lay anchored.

Omitting the incidents and arrangements ensuing, suffice it that, after two days spent in refitting, the ships sailed in company for Conception, in Chili, and thence for Lima, in Peru; where, before the vice-regal courts, the whole affair, from the beginning, underwent investigation.

Though, midway on the passage, the ill-fated Spaniard, relaxed from constraint, showed some signs of regaining health with freewill; yet, agreeably to his own foreboding, shortly before arriving at Lima, he relapsed, finally becoming so reduced as to be carried ashore in arms. Hearing of his story and plight, one of the many religious institutions of the City of Kings opened an hospitable refuge to him, where both physician and priest were his nurses, and a member of the order volunteered to be his one special guardian and consoler, by night and by day.

The following extracts, translated from one of the official Spanish documents, will, it is hoped, shed light on the preceding narrative, as well as, in the first place, reveal the true port of departure and true history of the San Dominick's voyage, down to the time of her touching at the island of St. Maria.

But, ere the extracts come, it may be well to preface them with a remark.

The document selected, from among many others, for partial translation, contains the deposition of Benito Cereno; the first taken in the case. Some disclosures therein were, at the time, held dubious for both learned and natural reasons. The tribunal inclined to the opinion that the deponent, not undisturbed in his mind by recent events, raved of some things which could never have happened. But subsequent depositions of the surviving sailors, bearing out the revelations of their captain in several of the strangest particulars, gave credence to the rest. So that the tribunal, in its final decision, rested its capital sentences upon statements which, had they lacked confirmation, it would have deemed it but duty to reject.

I, Don Jose de Abos and Padilla, His Majesty's Notary for the Royal Revenue, and Register of this Province, and Notary Public of the Holy Crusade of this Bishopric, etc.

Do certify and declare, as much as is requisite in law, that, in the criminal cause commenced the twenty-fourth of the month of September, in the year seventeen hundred and ninety-nine, against the negroes of the ship San Dominick, the following declaration before me was made:

Declaration of the first witness Don Benito Cereno.

The same day, and month, and year, His Honor, Doctor Juan Martinez de Rozas, Councilor of the Royal Audience of this Kingdom, and learned in the law of this Intendency, ordered the captain of the ship San Dominick, Don Benito Cereno, to appear; which he did in his litter, attended by the monk Infelez; of whom he received the oath, which he took by God our

Lord, and a sign of the Cross; under which he promised to tell the truth of whatever he should know and should be asked;—and being interrogated agreeably to the tenor of the act commencing the process, he said, that on the twentieth of May last, he set sail with his ship from the port of Valparaiso, bound to that of Callao; loaded with the produce of the country beside thirty cases of hardware and one hundred and sixty blacks, of both sexes, mostly belonging to Don Alexandro Aranda, gentleman, of the city of Mendoza; that the crew of the ship consisted of thirty-six men, beside the persons who went as passengers; that the negroes were in part as follows:

[*Here, in the original, follows a list of some fifty names, descriptions, and ages, compiled from certain recovered documents of Aranda's, and also from recollections of the deponent, from which portions only are extracted.*]

—One, from about eighteen to nineteen years, named José, and this was the man that waited upon his master, Don Alexandro, and who speaks well the Spanish, having served him four or five years; . . . a mulatto, named Francesco, the cabin steward, of a good person and voice, having sung in the Valparaiso churches, native of the province of Buenos Ayres, aged about thirty-five years. . . . A smart negro, named Dago, who had been for many years a grave-digger among the Spaniards, aged forty-six years. . . . Four old negroes, born in Africa, from sixty to seventy, but sound, calkers by trade, whose names are as follows:—the first was named Muri, and he was killed (as was also his son named Diamelo); the second, Nacta; the third, Yola, likewise killed; the fourth, Ghofan; and six full-grown negroes, aged from thirty to forty-five, all raw, and born among the Ashantees—Matiliqui, Yan, Lecbe, Mapenda, Yambaio, Akim; four of whom were killed; . . . a powerful negro named Atufal, who being supposed to have been a chief in Africa, his owner set great store by him. . . . And a small negro of Senegal, but some years among the Spaniards, aged about thirty, which negro's name was Babo; . . . that he does not remember the names of the others, but that still expecting the residue of Don Alexandro's papers will be found, will then take due account of them all, and remit to the court; . . . and thirty-nine women and children of all ages.

[*The catalogue over, the deposition goes on.*]

. . . That all the negroes slept upon deck, as is customary in this navigation, and none wore fetters, because the owner, his friend Aranda, told him that they were all tractable; . . . that on the seventh day after leaving port, at three o'clock in the morning, all the Spaniards being asleep except the two officers on the watch, who were the boatswain, Juan Robles, and the carpenter, Juan Bautista Gayete, and the helmsman and his boy, the negroes revolted suddenly, wounded dangerously the boatswain and the carpenter, and successively killed eighteen men of those who were sleeping upon deck, some with handspikes and hatchets, and others by throwing them alive overboard, after tying them; that of the Spaniards upon deck, they left about seven, as he thinks, alive and tied, to manœuvre the ship, and three or four more, who hid themselves, remained also alive. Although in the act of revolt the negroes made themselves masters of the hatchway, six or seven wounded went through it to the cockpit, without any hindrance on their part; that during the act of revolt, the mate and another person, whose name he does not recollect, attempted to come up through the hatchway, but being quickly wounded, were obliged to return to the cabin; that the deponent resolved at break of day to come up the companion-way, where the negro Babo was, being the ringleader, and Atufal, who assisted him, and having spoken to them, exhorted them to cease committing such atrocities, asking them, at the same time, what they wanted and intended to do, offering himself, to obey their commands; that notwithstanding this, they threw, in his presence, three men, alive and tied, overboard; that they told the deponent to come up, and that they would not kill him; which having done, the negro Babo asked him whether there were in those seas any negro countries where they might be carried, and he answered them, No; that the negro Babo afterwards told him to carry them to Senegal, or to the neighboring islands of St. Nicholas; and he answered, that this was impossible, on account of the great distance, the necessity involved of rounding Cape Horn, the bad condition of the vessel, the want of provisions, sails, and water; but that the negro Babo replied to him he must carry them in any way; that they would do and conform themselves to everything the deponent should require as to eating and drinking; that after a long conference, being absolutely compelled to please them, for they threatened to kill all the whites if they were not, at all events, carried to Senegal, he told them that what was most wanting for the voyage was water; that they would go near the coast to take it, and thence they would proceed on their course; that the negro Babo agreed to it; and the deponent steered towards the intermediate ports, hoping to meet some Spanish or foreign vessel that would save them; that within ten or eleven days they saw the land, and continued their course by it in the vicinity of Nasca; that the deponent observed that the negroes were now restless and mutinous, because he did not effect the taking in of water, the negro Babo having required, with threats, that it should be done, without fail, the following day; he told him he saw plainly that the coast was steep, and the rivers designated in the maps were not to be found, with other reasons suitable to the circumstances; that the best way would be to go to the island of Santa Maria, where they might water easily, it being a solitary island, as the foreigners did; that the deponent did not go to Pisco, that was near, nor make any other port of the coast, because the negro Babo had intimated to him several times, that he would kill all the whites the very moment he should perceive any city, town, or settlement of any kind on the shores to which they should be carried: that having determined to go to the island of Santa Maria, as the deponent had planned, for the purpose of trying whether, on the passage or near the island itself, they could find any vessel that should favor them, or whether he could escape from it in a boat to the neighboring coast of Arruco, to adopt the necessary means he immediately changed his course, steering for the island; that the negroes Babo and Atufal held daily conferences, in which they discussed what was necessary for their design of returning to Senegal, whether they were to kill all the Spaniards, and particularly the deponent; that eight days after parting from the coast of Nasca, the deponent being on the watch a little after daybreak, and soon after the negroes had their meeting, the negro Babo came to the place where the deponent was, and told him that he had determined to kill his master, Don Alexandro Aranda, both because he and his companions could not otherwise be sure of their liberty, and that to keep the seamen in subjection, he wanted to prepare a warning of what road they should be made to take did they or any of them oppose him; and that, by means of the death of Don Alexandro, that warning would best be given; but, that what this last meant, the deponent did not at the time comprehend, nor could not, further than that the death of Don Alexandro was intended; and moreover the negro Babo proposed to the deponent to call the mate Raneds, who was sleeping in the cabin, before the thing was done, for fear, as the deponent understood it, that the mate, who was a good navigator, should be killed with Don Alexandro and the rest; that the deponent, who was the friend, from youth, of Don Alexandro, prayed and conjured, but all was useless; for the negro Babo answered him that the thing could not be prevented, and that all the Spaniards risked their death if they could attempt to frustrate his will in this matter, or any other; that, in this conflict, the deponent called the mate, Raneds, who was forced to go apart, and immediately the negro Babo commanded the Ashantee Martinqui and the Ashantee Lecbe to go and commit the murder; that those two went down with hatchets to the berth of Don Alexandro; that, yet half alive and mangled, they dragged him on deck; that they were going to throw him overboard in that state, but the negro Babo stopped them, bidding the murder be completed on the deck before him, which was done, when, by his orders, the body was carried below, forward; that nothing more was seen of it by the deponent for three days; . . . that Don Alonzo Sidonia, an old man, long resident at Valparaiso, and lately appointed to a civil office in Peru, whither he had taken passage, was at the time sleeping in the berth opposite Don Alexandro's; that awakening at his cries, suprised by them, and at the sight of the negroes with their bloody hatchets in their hands, he threw himself into the sea through a window which was near him, and was drowned, without it being in the power of the deponent to assist or take up; . . . that a short time after killing Aranda, they brought upon deck his german-cousin, of middle-age, Don Francisco Masa, of Mendoza, and the young Don Joaquin, Marques de Aramboalaza, then lately from Spain, with his Spanish servant Ponce, and the three young clerks of Aranda, José Mozairi, Lorenzo Bargas, and Hermenegildo Gandix, all of Cadiz; that Don Joaquin and Hermenegildo Gandix, the negro Babo, for purposes hereafter to appear, preserved alive, but Don Francisco Masa, José Mozairi, and Lorenzo Bargas, with Ponce the servant, beside the boatswain, Juan Robles, the boatswain's mates, Manual Viscaya and Roderigo Hurta, and four of the sailors, the negro Babo ordered to be thrown alive into the sea, although they made no resistance, nor begged for anything else but mercy; that the boatswain, Juan Robles, who knew how to swim, kept the longest above water, making acts of contrition, and, in the last words he uttered, charged this deponent to cause mass to be said for his soul to our Lady of Succor: . . . that, during the three days which followed, the deponent, uncertain what fate had befallen the remains of Don Alexandro, frequently asked the negro Babo where they were, and, if still on board, whether they were to be preserved for interment ashore, entreating him so to order it; that the negro Babo answered nothing till the fourth day, when at sunrise, the deponent coming on deck, the negro Babo showed him a skeleton, which had been substituted for the ship's proper figure-head—the image of Christopher Colon, the discoverer of the New World; that the negro Babo asked him whose skeleton that was, and whether, from its whiteness, he should not think it a white's; that, upon discovering his face, the negro Babo, coming close, said words to this effect: "Keep faith with the blacks from here to Senegal, or you shall in spirit, as now in body, follow your leader," pointing to the prow; . . . that the same morning the negro Babo took by succession each Spaniard forward, and asked him whose skeleton that was, and whether, from its whiteness, he should not think it a white's; that each Spaniard covered his face; that then to each the negro Babo repeated the words in the first place said to the deponent; . . . that they (the Spaniards), being then assembled aft, the negro Babo harangued them, saying that he had now done all; that the deponent (as navigator for the negroes) might pursue his course, warning him of all of them that they should, soul and body, go the way of Don Alexandro, if he saw them (the Spaniards), speak or plot anything against them (the negroes)—a threat which was repeated every day; that, before the events last mentioned, they had tied the cook to throw him overboard, for it is not known what thing they heard him speak, but finally the negro Babo spared his life, at the request of the deponent; that a few days after, the deponent, endeavoring not to admit any means to preserve the lives of the remaining whites, spoke to the negroes of peace and tranquillity, and agreed to draw up a paper, signed by the deponent and the sailors who could write, as also by the negro Babo, for himself and all the blacks, in which the deponent obliged himself to carry them to Senegal, and they not to kill any more, and he formally to make over to them the ship, with the cargo, with which they were for that time satisfied and quieted. . . . But the next day, the more surely to guard against the sailors' escape, the negro Babo commanded all the boats to be destroyed but the long-boat, which was unseaworthy, and another, a cutter in good condition, which knowing it would yet be wanted for towing the water casks, he had it lowered down into the hold.

. . .

[*Various particulars of the prolonged and perplexed navigation ensuing here follow, with incidents of a calamitous calm, from which portion one passage is extracted, to wit:*]

—That on the fifth day of the calm, all on board suffering much from the heat, and want of water, and five having died in fits, and mad, the negroes became irritable, and for a chance gesture, which they deemed suspicious—though it was harmless—made by the mate, Raneds, to the deponent in the act of handing a quadrant, they killed him; but that for this they afterwards were sorry, the mate being the only remaining navigator on board, except the deponent.

. . .

—That omitting other events, which daily happened, and which can only serve uselessly to recall past misfortunes and conflicts, after seventy-three days' navigation, reckoned from the time they sailed from Nasca, during which they navigated under a scanty allowance of water, and were afflicted with the calms before mentioned, they at last arrived at the island of Santa Maria, on the seventeenth of the month of August, at about six o'clock in the afternoon, at which hour they cast anchor very near the American ship, Bachelor's Delight, which lay in the same bay, commanded by the generous Captain Amasa Delano; but at six o'clock in the morning, they had already described the port, and the negroes became uneasy, as soon as at distance they saw the ship, not having expected to see one there; that the negro Babo pacified them, assuring them that no fear need be had; that straightway he ordered the figure on the bow to be covered with canvas, as for repairs, and had the decks a little set in order; that for a time the negro Babo and the negro Atufal conferred; that the negro Atufal was for sailing away, but the negro Babo would not, and, by himself, cast about what to do; that at last he came to the deponent, proposing to him to say and do all that the deponent declares to have said and done to the American captain;

. . .

that the negro Babo warned him that if he varied in the least, or uttered any word, or gave any look that should give the least intimation of the past events or present state, he would instantly kill him, with all his companions, showing a dagger, which he carried hid, saying something which, as he understood it, meant that that dagger would be alert as his eye; that the negro Babo then announced the plan to all his companions, which pleased them; that he then, the better to disguise the truth, devised many expedients, in some of them uniting deceit and defense; that of this sort was the device of the six Ashantees before named, who were his bravoes; that them he stationed on the break of the poop, as if to clean certain hatchets (in cases, which were part of the cargo), but in reality to use them, and distribute them at need, and at a given word he told them; that, among other devices, was the device of presenting Atufal, his right hand man, as chained, though in a moment the chains could be dropped; that in every particular he informed the deponent what part he was expected to enact in every device, and what story he was to tell on every occasion, always threatening him with instant death if he varied in the least: that, conscious that many of the negroes would be turbulent, the negro Babo appointed the four aged negroes, who were calkers, to keep what domestic order they could on the decks; that again and again he harangued the Spaniards and his companions, informing them of his intent, and of his devices, and of the invented story that this deponent was to tell; charging them lest any of them varied from that story; that these arrangements were made and matured during the interval of two or three hours, between their first sighting the ship and the arrival on board of Captain Amasa Delano; that this happened about half-past seven o'clock in the morning, Captain Amasa Delano coming in his boat, and all gladly receiving him; that the deponent, as well as he could force himself, acting then the part of principal owner, and a free captain of the ship, told Captain Amasa Delano, when called upon, that he came from Buenos Ayres, bound to Lima, with three hundred negroes; that off Cape Horn, and in a subsequent fever, many negroes had died; that also, by similar casualties, all the sea officers and the greatest part of the crew had died.

. . .

[*And so the deposition goes on, circumstantially recounting the fictitious story dictated to the deponent by Babo, and through the deponent imposed upon Captain Delano; and also recounting the friendly offers of Captain Delano, with other things, but all of which is here omitted. After the fictitious story, etc. the deposition proceeds:*]

. . .

—that the generous Captain Amasa Delano remained on board all the day, till he left the ship anchored at six o'clock in the evening, deponent speaking to him always of his pretended misfortunes, under the fore-mentioned principles, without having had it in his power to tell a single word, or give him the least hint, that he might know the truth and state of things; because the negro Babo, performing the office of an officious servant with all the appearance of submission of the humble slave, did not leave the deponent one moment; that this was in order to observe the deponent's actions and words, for the negro Babo understands well the Spanish; and besides, there were thereabout some others who were constantly on the watch, and likewise understood the Spanish; . . . that upon one occasion, while deponent was standing on the deck conversing with Amasa Delano, by a secret sign the negro Babo drew him (the deponent) aside, the act appearing as if originating with the deponent; that then, he being drawn aside, the negro

Babo purposed to him to gain from Amasa Delano full particulars about his ship, and crew, and arms; that the deponent asked "For what?" that the negro Babo answered he might conceive; that, grieved at the prospect of what might overtake the generous Captain Amasa Delano, the deponent at first refused to ask the desired questions, and used every argument to induce the negro Babo to give up this new design; that the negro Babo showed the point of his dagger; that, after the information had been obtained the negro Babo again drew him aside, telling him that that very night he (the deponent) would be captain of two ships, instead of one, for that, great part of the American's ship's crew being to be absent fishing, the six Ashantees, without any one else, would easily take it; that at this time he said other things to the same purpose; that no entreaties availed; that before Amasa Delano's coming on board, no hint had been given touching the capture of the American ship: that to prevent this project the deponent was powerless; . . . —that in some things his memory is confused, he cannot distinctly recall every event; . . .—that as soon as they had cast anchor at six of the clock in the evening, as has before been stated, the American Captain took leave, to return to his vessel; that upon a sudden impulse, which the deponent believes to have come from God and his angels, he, after the farewell had been said, followed the generous Captain Amasa Delano as far as the gunwale, where he stayed, under pretense of taking leave, until Amasa Delano should have been seated in his boat; that on shoving off, the deponent sprang from the gunwale into the boat, and fell into it, he knows not how, God guarding him; that—

. . .

[*Here, in the original, follows the account of what further happened at the escape, and how the San Dominick was retaken, and of the passage to the coast; including in the recital many expressions of "eternal gratitude" to the "generous Captain Amasa Delano." The deposition then proceeds with recapitulatory remarks, and a partial renumeration of the negroes, making record of their individual part in the past events, with a view to furnishing, according to command of the court, the data whereon to found the criminal sentences to be pronounced. From this portion is the following;*]

—That he believes that all the negroes, though not in the first place knowing to the design of revolt, when it was accomplished, approved it. . . . That the negro, José, eighteen years old, and in the personal service of Don Alexandro, was the one who communicated the information to the negro Babo, about the state of things in the cabin, before the revolt; that this is known, because, in the preceding midnight, he used to come from his berth, which was under his master's, in the cabin, to the deck where the ringleader and his associates were, and had secret conversations with the negro Babo, in which he was several times seen by the mate; that, one night, the mate drove him away twice; . . . that this same negro José was the one who, without being commanded to do so by the negro Babo, as Lecbe and

Martinqui were, stabbed his master, Don Alexandro, after he had been dragged half-lifeless to the deck; . . . that the mulatto steward, Francesco, was of the first band of revolters, that he was, in all things, the creature and tool of the negro Babo; that, to make his court, he, just before a repast in the cabin, proposed, to the negro Babo, poisoning a dish for the generous Captain Amasa Delano; that is known and believed, because the negroes have said it; but that the negro Babo, having another design, forbade Francesco; . . . that the Ashantee Lecbe was one of the worst of them; for that, on the day the ship was retaken, he assisted in the defense of her, with a hatchet in each hand, with one of which he wounded, in the breast, the chief mate of Amasa Delano, in the first act of boarding; this all knew; that, in sight of the deponent, Lecbe struck, with a hatchet, Don Francisco Masa, when, by the negro Babo's orders, he was carrying him to throw him overboard, alive, beside participating in the murder, before mentioned, of Don Alexandro Aranda, and others of the cabin-passengers; that, owing to the fury with which the Ashantees fought in the engagement with the boats, but this Lecbe and Yan survived; that Yan was as bad as Lecbe; that Yan was the man who, by Babo's command, willingly prepared the skeleton of Don Alexandro, in a way the negroes afterwards told the deponent, but which he, so long as reason is left him, can never divulge; that Yan and Lecbe were the two who, in a calm by night, riveted the skeleton to the bow; this also the negroes told him; that the negro Babo was he who traced the inscription below it; that the negro Babo was the plotter from first to last; he ordered every murder, and was the helm and keel of the revolt; that Atufal was his lieutenant in all; but Atufal, with his own hand, committed no murder; nor did the negro Babo; . . . that Atufal was shot, being killed in the fight with the boats, ere boarding; . . . that the negresses, of age, were knowing to the revolt, and testified themselves satisfied at the death of their master, Don Alexandro; that, had the negroes not restrained them, they would have tortured to death, instead of simply killing, the Spaniards slain by command of the negro Babo; that the negresses used their utmost influence to have the deponent made away with; that, in the various acts of murder, they sang songs and danced—not gaily, but solemnly; and before the engagement with the boats, as well as during the action, they sang melancholy songs to the negroes, and that this melancholy tone was more inflaming than a different one would have been, and was so intended; that all this is believed, because the negroes have said it.
—that of the thirty-six men of the crew, exclusive of the passengers (all of whom are now dead), which the deponent had knowledge of, six only remained alive, with four cabin-boys and ship-boys, not included with the crew; . . . —that the negroes broke an arm of one of the cabin-boys and gave him strokes with hatchets.

[*Then follow various random disclosures referring to various periods of time. The following are extracted;*]

—That during the presence of Captain Amasa Delano on board, some attempts were made by the sailors, and one by Hermenegildo Gandix, to convey hints to him of the true state of affairs; but that these attempts were ineffectual, owing to fear of incurring death, and, furthermore, owing to the devices which offered contradictions to the true state of affairs, as well as owing to the generosity and piety of Amasa Delano incapable of sounding such wickedness; . . . that Luys Galgo, a sailor about sixty years of age, and formerly of the king's navy, was one of those who sought to convey tokens to Captain Amasa Delano; but his intent, though undiscovered, being suspected, he was, on a pretense, made to retire out of sight, and at last into the hold, and there was made away with. This the negroes have since said; . . . that one of the ship-boys feeling, from Captain Amasa Delano's presence, some hopes of release, and not having enough prudence, dropped some chance-word respecting his expectations, which being overheard and understood by a slave-boy with whom he was eating at the time, the latter struck him on the head with a knife, inflicting a bad wound, but of which the boy is now healing; that likewise, not long before the ship was brought to anchor, one of the seamen, steering at the time, endangered himself by letting the blacks remark some expression in his countenance, arising from a cause similar to the above; but this sailor, by his heedful after conduct, escaped; . . . that these statements are made to show the court that from the beginning to the end of the revolt, it was impossible for the deponent and his men to act otherwise than they did; . . . —that the third clerk, Hermenegildo Gandix, who before had been forced to live among the seamen, wearing a seaman's habit, and in all respects appearing to be one for the time; he, Gandix, was killed by a musket ball fired through mistake from the boats before boarding; having in his fright run up the mizzen-rigging, calling to the boats—"don't board," lest upon their boarding the negroes should kill him; that this inducing the Americans to believe he some way favored the cause of the negroes, they fired two balls at him, so that he fell wounded from the rigging, and was drowned in the sea; . . . —that the young Don Joaquin, Marques de Aramboalaza, like Hermenegildo Gandix, the third clerk, was degraded to the office and appearance of a common seaman; that upon one occasion when Don Joaquin shrank, the negro Babo commanded the Ashantee Lecbe to take tar and heat it, and pour it upon Don Joaquin's hands; . . . —that Don Joaquin was killed owing to another mistake of the Americans, but one impossible to be avoided, as upon the approach of the boats, Don Joaquin, with a hatchet tied edge out, and upright to his hand, was made by the negroes to appear on the bulwarks; whereupon, seen with arms in his hands and in a questionable attitude, he was shot for a renegade seaman; . . . —that on the person of Don Joaquin was found secreted a jewel, which, by papers that were discovered, proved to have been meant for the shrine of our Lady of Mercy in Lima; a votive offering, beforehand prepared and guarded, to attest his gratitude, when he should have landed in Peru, his last destination, for the safe conclusion of his entire voyage from Spain; . . . —that the jewel, with the other effects of the late Don Joaquin, is in the custody of the brethren of the Hospital de Sacerdotes, awaiting the disposition of the honorable court; . . . —that, owing to the condition of the deponent, as well as the haste in which the boats departed for the attack, the Americans were not forewarned that there were, among the apparent crew, a passenger and one of the clerks disguised by the negro Babo; . . . —that, beside the negroes killed in the action, some were killed after the capture and re-anchoring at night, when shackled to the ring-bolts on deck; that these deaths were committed by the sailors, ere they could be prevented. That so soon as informed of it, Captain Amasa Delano used all his authority, and, in particular with his own hand, struck down Martinez Gola, who, having found a razor in the pocket of an old jacket of his, which one of the shackled negroes had on, was aiming it at the negro's throat; that the noble Captain Amasa Delano also wrenched from the hand of Bartholomew Barlo a dagger, secreted at the time of the massacre of the whites, with which he was in the act of stabbing a shackled negro, who, the same day, with another negro, had thrown him down and jumped upon him; . . . —that, for all the events, befalling through so long a time, during which the ship was in the hands of the negro Babo, he cannot here give account; but that, what he has said is the most substantial of what occurs to him at present, and is the truth under the oath which he has taken; which declaration he affirmed and ratified, after hearing it read to him.

He said that he is twenty-nine years of age, and broken in body and mind; that when finally dismissed by the court, he shall not return home to Chili, but betake himself to the monastery on Mount Agonia without; and signed with his honor, and crossed himself, and, for the time, departed as he came, in his litter, with the monk Infelez, to the Hospital de Sacerdotes.

Benito Cereno

Doctor Rozas

If the Deposition have served as the key to fit into the lock of the complications which precede it, then, as a vault whose door has been flung back, the San Dominick's hull lies open to-day.

Hitherto the nature of this narrative, besides rendering the intricacies in the beginning unavoidable, has more or less required that many things, instead of being set down in the order of occurrence, should be retrospectively, or irregularly given; this last is the case with the following passages, which will conclude the account:

During the long, mild voyage to Lima, there was, as before hinted, a period during which the sufferer a little recovered his health, or, at least in some degree, his tranquillity. Ere the decided relapse which came, the two captains had many cordial conversations—their fraternal unreserve in singular contrast with former withdrawments.

Again and again it was repeated, how hard it had been to enact the part forced on the Spaniard by Babo.

"Ah, my dear friend," Don Benito once said, "at those very times when you thought me so morose and ungrateful, nay, when, as you now admit, you half thought me plotting your murder, at those very times my heart was frozen; I could not look at you, thinking of what, both on board this ship and your own, hung, from other hands, over my kind benefactor. And as God lives, Don Amasa, I know not whether desire for my own safety alone could have nerved me to that leap into your boat, had it not been for the thought that, did you, unenlightened, return to your ship, you, my best friend, with all who might be with you, stolen upon, that night, in your hammocks, would never in this world have wakened again. Do but think how you walked this deck, how you sat in this cabin, every inch of ground mined into honey-combs under you. Had I dropped the least hint, made the least advance towards an understanding between us, death, explosive death—yours as mine—would have ended the scene."

"True, true," cried Captain Delano, starting, "you have saved my life, Don Benito, more than I yours; saved it, too, against my knowledge and will."

"Nay, my friend," rejoined the Spaniard, courteous even to the point of religion, "God charmed your life, but you saved mine. To think of some things you did—those smilings and chattings, rash pointings and gesturings. For less than these, they slew my mate, Raneds; but you had the Prince of Heaven's safe-conduct through all ambuscades."

"Yes, all is owing to Providence, I know: but the temper of my mind that morning was more than commonly pleasant, while the sight of so much suffering, more apparent than real, added to my good-nature, compassion, and charity, happily interweaving the three. Had it been otherwise, doubtless, as you hint, some of my interferences might have ended unhappily enough. Besides, those feelings I spoke of enabled me to get the better of momentary distrust, at times when acuteness might have cost me my life, without saving another's. Only at the end did my suspicions get the better of me, and you know how wide of the mark they then proved."

"Wide, indeed," said Don Benito, sadly; "you were with me all day; stood with me, sat with me, talked with me, looked at me, ate with me, drank with me; and yet, your last act was to clutch for a monster, not only an innocent man, but the most pitiable of all men. To such degree may malign machinations and deceptions impose. So far may even the best man err, in judging the conduct of one with the recesses of whose condition he is not acquainted. But you were forced to it; and you were in time undeceived. Would that, in both respects, it was so ever, and with all men."

"You generalize, Don Benito; and mournfully enough. But the past is passed; why moralize upon it? Forget it. See, yon bright sun has forgotten it all, and the blue sea, and the blue sky; these have turned over new leaves."

"Because they have no memory," he dejectedly replied; "because they are not human."

"But these mild trades that now fan your cheek, do they not come with a human-like healing to you? Warm friends, steadfast friends are the trades."

"With their steadfastness they but waft me to my tomb, Señor," was the foreboding response.

"You are saved," cried Captain Delano, more and more astonished and pained; "you are saved: what has cast such a shadow upon you?"

"The negro."

There was silence, while the moody man sat, slowly and unconsciously gathering his mantle about him, as if it were a pall.

There was no more conversation that day.

But if the Spaniard's melancholy sometimes ended in muteness upon topics like the above, there were others upon which he never spoke at all; on which, indeed, all his old reserves were piled. Pass over the worst, and, only to elucidate, let an item or two of these be cited. The dress, so precise and costly, worn by him on the day whose events have been narrated, had not willingly been put on. And that silver-mounted sword, apparent symbol of despotic command, was not, indeed, a sword, but the ghost of one. The scabbard, artificially stiffened, was empty.

As for the black—whose brain, not body, had schemed and led the revolt, with the plot—his slight frame, inadequate to that which it held, had at once yielded to the superior muscular strength of his captor, in the boat. Seeing all was over, he uttered no sound, and could not be forced to. His aspect seemed to say, since I cannot do deeds, I will not speak words. Put in irons in the hold, with the rest, he was carried to Lima. During the passage, Don Benito did not visit him. Nor then, nor at any time after, would he look at him. Before the tribunal he refused. When pressed by the judges he fainted. On the testimony of the sailors alone rested the legal identity of Babo.

Some months after, dragged to the gibbet at the tail of a mule, the black met his voiceless end. The body was burned to ashes; but for many days, the head, that hive of subtlety, fixed on a pole in the Plaza, met, unabashed, the gaze of the whites; and across the Plaza looked towards St. Bartholomew's church, in whose vaults slept then, as now, the recovered bones of Aranda: and across the Rimac bridge looked towards the monastery, on Mount Agonia without; where, three months after being dismissed by the court, Benito Cereno, borne on the bier, did, indeed, follow his leader.

Guy de Maupassant

(1850 - 1893)

Guy de Maupassant, the author of six novels and nearly three hundred short stories in a prolific ten years, 1880–1890, was the most important and influential French writer of short fiction in the nineteenth century. In fact, Maupassant and Anton Chekhov, whose technique the Frenchman influenced, were the two most imitated short story writers of the last century and are regarded as the fathers of the modern genre. A disciple of fellow Norman Gustave Flaubert (the author of *Madame Bovary*), Maupassant learned to apply to the short story the objective, precise manner that the master had used in the novel. He perfected the technique of distilling the essence of a scene and conveying its flavor and texture in the simplest, most natural way, a characteristic which distinguishes the modern short story from the more discursive earlier short fiction. Maupassant was a naturalist in the manner of Zola, and he presented his view of reality with the detachment of a surgeon, without sentiment. His dramatization of character is invariably from the outside, without psychological analysis. Although he frequently wrote from the point of view of society's outcasts and uncouth peasants, Maupassant was essentially a misanthrope who denied the goodness of man and saw truth and beauty as grand illusions created by an unhappy species. In the preface to his novel *Pierre et Jean* he wrote: "Each of us . . . forms for himself an illusion of the world which is poetic, sentimental, joyous, melancholy, unclear or dismal according to his nature. The writer has no other business than to reproduce faithfully this illusion. . . . The great artists are those who force humanity to accept their illusion."

Mademoiselle Fifi

The Major Graf von Farlsberg, the Prussian commandant, was reading his newspaper, lying back in a great armchair, with his booted feet on the

"Mademoiselle Fifi" from *The Complete Short Stories of Guy de Maupassant,* translated by Artine Artinian. Reprinted by permission of Doubleday & Company, Inc.

beautiful marble fireplace, where his spurs had made two holes which grew deeper every day during the three months that he had been in the château of Urville.

A cup of coffee was smoking on a small inlaid table which was stained with liquors, burnt by cigars, notched by the penknife of the victorious officer who occasionally would stop while sharpening a pencil to jot down figures or to make a drawing on it, just as it took his fancy.

When he had read his letters and the German newspapers which his baggage-master had brought him he got up, and after throwing three or four enormous pieces of green wood onto the fire—for these gentlemen were gradually cutting down the park in order to keep themselves warm—he went to the window. The rain was descending in torrents, a regular Normandy rain, which looked as if it were being poured out by some furious hand, a slanting rain, which was as thick as a curtain and which formed a kind of wall with oblique stripes and which deluged everything, a regular rain, such as one frequently experiences in the neighborhood of Rouen, which is the watering pot of France.

For a long time the officer looked at the sodden turf and at the swollen Andelle beyond it, which was overflowing its banks, and he was drumming a waltz from the Rhine on the windowpanes with his fingers, when a noise made him turn round; it was his second in command, Captain Baron von Kelweinstein.

The major was a giant with broad shoulders and a long, fair beard, which hung like a cloth onto his chest. His whole solemn person suggested the idea of a military peacock, a peacock who was carrying his tail spread out onto his breast. He had cold, gentle blue eyes and the scar from a sword cut which he had received in the war with Austria; he was said to be an honorable man as well as a brave officer.

The captain, a short, red-faced man who was tightly girthed in at the waist, had his red hair cropped quite close to his head and in certain lights almost looked as if he had been rubbed over with phosphorus. He had lost two front teeth one night, though he could not quite remember how. This defect made him speak so that he could not always be understood, and he had a bald patch on the top of his head, which made him look rather like a monk with a fringe of curly, bright golden hair round the circle of bare skin.

The commandant shook hands with him and drank his cup of coffee (the sixth that morning) at a draught, while he listened to his subordinate's report of what had occurred; and then they both went to the window and declared that it was a very unpleasant outlook. The major, who was a quiet man with a wife at home, could accommodate himself to everything, but the captain, who was rather fast, being in the habit of frequenting low resorts and much given to women, was mad at having been shut up for three months in the compulsory chastity of that wretched hole.

There was a knock at the door, and when the commandant said, "Come in," one of their automatic soldiers appeared and by his mere presence announced that breakfast was ready. In the dining room they met three other officers of lower rank: a lieutenant, Otto von Grossling, and two sublieutenants, Fritz Scheunebarg and Count von Eyrick, a very short, fair-haired man, who was proud and brutal toward men, harsh toward prisoners, and very violent.

Since he had been in France his comrades had called him nothing but "Mademoiselle Fifi." They have given him that nickname on account of his dandified style and small waist, which looked as if he wore stays, from his pale face, on which his budding mustache scarcely showed, and on account of the habit he had acquired of employing the French expression, *fi, fi donc,* which he pronounced with a slight whistle when he wished to express his sovereign contempt for persons or things.

The dining room of the château was a magnificent long room whose fine old mirrors, now cracked by pistol bullets, and Flemish tapestry, now cut to ribbons and hanging in rags in places from sword cuts, told too well what Mademoiselle Fifi's occupation was during his spare time.

There were three family portraits on the walls: a steel-clad knight, a cardinal and a judge, who were all smoking long porcelain pipes which had been inserted into holes in the canvas, while a lady in a long pointed waist proudly exhibited an enormous pair of mustaches drawn with a piece of charcoal.

The officers ate their breakfast almost in silence in that mutilated room which looked dull in the rain and melancholy under its vanquished appearance, although its old oak floor had become as solid as the stone floor of a public house.

When they had finished eating and were smoking and drinking, they began, as usual, to talk about the dull life they were leading. The bottle of brandy and of liquors passed from hand to hand, and all sat back in their chairs, taking repeated sips from their glasses and scarcely removing the long bent stems, which terminated in china bowls painted in a manner to delight a Hottentot, from their mouths.

As soon as their glasses were empty they filled them again with a gesture of resigned weariness, but Mademoiselle Fifi emptied his every minute, and a soldier immediately gave him another. They were enveloped in a cloud of strong tobacco smoke; they seemed to be sunk in a state of drowsy, stupid intoxication, in that dull state of drunkenness of men who have nothing to do, when suddenly the baron sat up and said: "By heavens! This cannot go on; we must think of something to do." And on hearing this, Lieutenant Otto and Sublieutenant Fritz, who pre-eminently possessed the grave, heavy German countenance, said: "What, Captain?"

He thought for a few moments and then replied: "What? Well, we must get up some entertainment if the commandant will allow us."

"What sort of an entertainment, Captain?" the major asked, taking his pipe out of his mouth.

"I will arrange all that, Commandant," the baron said. "I will send *Le Devoir* to Rouen, who will bring us some ladies. I know where they can be found. We will have supper here, as all the materials are at hand, and at least we shall have a jolly evening."

Graf von Farlsberg shrugged his shoulders with a smile: "You must surely be mad, my friend."

But all the other officers got up, surrounded their chief and said: "Let Captain have his own way, Commandant; it is terribly dull here."

And the major ended by yielding. "Very well," he replied, and the baron immediately sent for *Le Devoir.*

The latter was an old corporal who had never been seen to smile, but who carried out all orders of his superiors to the letter, no matter what they might be. He stood there with an impassive face while he received the baron's instructions and then went out; five minutes later a large wagon belonging to the military train, covered with a miller's tilt, galloped off as fast as four horses could take it under the pouring rain, and the officers all seemed to awaken from their lethargy; their looks brightened, and they began to talk.

Although it was raining as hard as ever, the major declared that it was not so dull, and Lieutenant von Grossling said with conviction that the sky was clearing up, while Mademoiselle Fifi did not seem to be able to keep in his place. He got up and sat down again, and his bright eyes seemed to be looking for something to destroy. Suddenly, looking at the lady with the mustaches, the young fellow pulled out his revolver and said: "You shall not see it." And without leaving his seat he aimed and with two successive bullets cut out both the eyes of the portrait.

"Let us make a mine!" he then exclaimed, and the conversation was suddenly interrupted, as if they had found some fresh and powerful subject of interest. The mine was his invention, his method of destruction and his favorite amusement.

When he left the château the lawful owner, Count Fernand d'Amoys d'Urville, had not had time to carry away or to hide anything except the plate, which had been stowed away in a hole made in one of the walls so that, as he was very rich and had good taste, the large drawing room, which opened into the dining room, had looked like the gallery in a museum before his precipitate flight.

Expensive oil paintings, water colors and drawings hung upon the walls, while on the tables, on the hanging shelves and in elegant glass cupboards there were a thousand knickknacks: small vases, statuettes, groups in Dresden china, grotesque Chinese figures, old ivory and Venetian glass, which filled the large room with their precious and fantastical array.

Scarcely anything was left now; not that the things had been stolen, for the major would not have allowed that, but Mademoiselle Fifi *would have a mine,* and on that occasion all the officers thoroughly enjoyed themselves for five minutes. The little marquis went into the drawing room to get what he wanted, and he brought back a small, delicate china teapot, which he filled with gunpowder, and carefully introduced a piece of German tinder into it, through the spout. Then he lighted it and took this infernal machine into the next room, but he came back immediately and shut the door. The Germans all stood expectantly, their faces full of childish, smiling curiosity, and as soon as the explosion had shaken the château they all rushed in at once.

Mademoiselle Fifi, who got in first, clapped his hands in delight at the sight of a terra-cotta Venus, whose head had been blown off, and each picked up pieces of porcelain and wondered at the strange shape of the fragments, while the major was looking with a paternal eye at the large drawing room which had been wrecked in such a Neronic fashion and which was strewn with the fragments of works of art. He went out first and said, with a smile: "He managed that very well!"

But there was such a cloud of smoke in the dining room mingled with the tobacco smoke that they could not breathe, so the commandant opened the window, and all the officers, who had gone into the room for a glass of cognac, went up to it.

The moist air blew into the room and brought a sort of spray with it which powdered their beards. They looked at the tall trees which were dripping with the rain, at the broad valley which was covered with mist and at the church spire in the distance which rose up like a gray point in the beating rain.

The bells had not rung since their arrival. That was the only resistance which the invaders had met with in the neighborhood. The parish priest had not refused to take in and to feed the Prussian soldiers; he had several times even drunk a bottle of beer or claret with the hostile commandant, who often employed him as a benevolent intermediary, but it was no use to ask him for a single stroke of the bells; he would sooner have allowed himself to be shot. That was his way of protesting against the invasion, a peaceful and silent protest, the only one, he said, which was suitable to a priest who was a man of mildness and not of blood; and everyone for twenty-five miles round praised Abbé Chantavoine's firmness and heroism in venturing to proclaim the public mourning by the obstinate silence of his church bells.

The whole village grew enthusiastic over his resistance and was ready to back up their pastor and to risk anything, as they looked upon that silent protest as the safeguard of the national honor. It seemed to the peasants that thus they had deserved better of their country than Belfort and Strassburg, that they had set an equally valuable example and that the name of their little village would become immortalized by that, but with that exception, they refused their Prussian conquerors nothing.

The commandant and his officers laughed among themselves at that inoffensive courage, and as the people in the whole country round showed themselves obliging and compliant toward them, they willingly tolerated their silent patriotism. Only little Count Wilhelm would have liked to force them to ring the bells. He was very angry at his superior's politic compliance with the priest's scruples, and every day he begged the commandant to allow him to sound "dingdong, dingdong" just once, only just once, just by way of a joke. And he asked it like a wheedling woman, in the tender voice of some mistress who wishes to obtain something, but the commandant would not yield, and to console *herself* Mademoiselle Fifi made a *mine* in the château.

The five men stood there together for some minutes, inhaling the moist air, and at last Sublieutenant Fritz said with a laugh: "The ladies will certainly not have fine weather for their drive." Then they separated, each to his own duties, while the captain had plenty to do in seeing about the dinner.

When they met again as it was growing dark, they began to laugh at seeing each other as dandified and smart as on the day of a grand review. The commandant's hair did not look as gray as it did in the morning, and the captain had shaved—had only kept his mustache on, which made him look as if he had a streak of fire under his nose.

In spite of the rain they left the window open, and one of them went to listen from time to time. At a quarter past six the baron said he heard a rumbling in the distance. They all rushed down, and soon the wagon drove up at a gallop with its four horses, splashed up to their backs, steaming and panting. Five women got out at the bottom of the steps, five handsome girls whom a comrade of the captain, to whom *Le Devoir* had taken his card, had selected with care.

They had not required much pressing, as they were sure of being well treated, for they had got to know the Prussians in the three months during which they had had to do with them. So they resigned themselves to the men as they did to the state of affairs. "It is part of our business, so it must be done," they said as they drove along, no doubt to allay some slight, secret scruples of conscience.

They went into the dining room immediately, which looked still more dismal in its dilapidated state when it was lighted up, while the table, covered with choice dishes, the beautiful china and glass and the plate, which had been found in the hole in the wall, where its owner had hidden it, gave to the place the look of a bandits' resort, where they were supping after committing a robbery. The captain was radiant; he took hold of the women as if he were familiar with them, appraising them, kissing them, valuing them for what they were worth as *ladies of pleasure*, and when the three young men wanted to appropriate one each he opposed them authoritatively, reserving to himself the right to apportion them justly, according to their several ranks, so as not to wound the hierarchy. Therefore, so as to avoid all discussion, jarring and suspicion of partiality, he placed them all in a line according to height and addressing the tallest, he said in a voice of command:

"What is your name?"

"Pamela," she replied, raising her voice.

Then he said: "Number one, called Pamela, is adjudged to the commandant."

Then, having kissed Blondina, the second, as a sign of proprietorship, he proffered stout Amanda to Lieutenant Otto, Eva, "the Tomato," to Sublieutenant Fritz, and Rachel, the shortest of them all, a very young, dark girl, with eyes as black as ink, a Jewess, whose snub nose confirmed by exception the rule which allots hooked noses to all her race, to the youngest officer, frail Count Wilhelm von Eyrick.

They were all pretty and plump, without any distinctive features, and all were very much alike in look and person from their daily dissipation and the life common to houses of public accommodation.

The three younger men wished to carry off their women immediately, under the pretext of finding them brushes and soap, but the captain wisely opposed this, for he said they were quite fit to sit down to dinner and that those who went up would wish for a change when they came down, and so would disturb the other couples, and his experience in such matters carried the day. There were only many kisses, expectant kisses.

Suddenly Rachel choked and began to cough until the tears came into her eyes, while smoke came through her nostrils. Under pretense of kissing her the count had blown a whiff of tobacco into her mouth. She did not fly into a rage and did not say a word, but she looked at her possessor with latent hatred in her dark eyes.

They sat down to dinner. The commandant seemed delighted; he made Pamela sit on his right and Blondina on his left and said as he unfolded his table napkin: "That was a delightful idea of yours, Captain."

Lieutenants Otto and Fritz, who were as polite as if they had been with fashionable ladies, rather intimidated their neighbors, but Baron von Kelweinstein gave the reins to all his vicious propensites, beamed, made doubtful remarks and seemed on fire with his crown of red hair. He paid them compliments in French from the other side of the Rhine and sputtered out gallant remarks, only fit for a low pothouse, from between his two broken teeth.

They did not understand him, however, and their intelligence did not seem to be awakened until he uttered nasty words and broad expressions which were mangled by his accent. Then all began to laugh at once, like mad women, and fell against each other, repeating the words which the baron then began to say all wrong, in order that he might have the pleasure of hearing them say doubtful things. They gave him as much of that stuff as he wanted, for they were drunk after the first bottle of wine and, becoming themselves once more and opening the door to their usual habits, they kissed the mustaches on the right and left of them, pinched their arms, uttered furious cries, drank out of every glass and sang French couplets and bits of German songs which they had picked up in their daily intercourse with the enemy.

Soon the men themselves, intoxicated by that which was displayed to their sight and touch, grew very amorous, shouted and broke the plates and dishes, while the soldiers behind them waited on them stolidly. The commandant was the only one who put any restraint upon himself.

Mademoiselle Fifi had taken Rachel onto his knees and, getting excited, at one moment kissed the little black curls on her neck, inhaling the pleasant warmth of her body and all the savor of her person through the slight space there was between her dress and her skin, and at another pinched her furiously through the material and made her scream, for he was seized with a species of ferocity and tormented by his desire to hurt her. He often held her close to him, as if to make her part of himself, and put his lips in a long kiss on the Jewess's rosy mouth until she lost her breath, and at last he bit her until a stream of blood ran down her chin and onto her bodice.

For the second time she looked him full in the face, and as she bathed the wound she said: "You will have to pay for that!"

But he merely laughed a hard laugh and said: "I will pay."

At dessert champagne was served, and the commandant rose, and in the same voice in which he would have drunk to the health of the Empress Augusta he drank: "To our ladies!" Then a series of toasts began, toasts worthy of the lowest soldiers and of drunkards, mingled with filthy jokes which were made still more brutal by their ignorance of the language. They got up, one after the other, trying to say something witty, forcing themselves to be funny, and the women, who were so drunk that they almost fell off their chairs, with vacant looks and clammy tongues applauded madly each time.

The captain, who no doubt wished to impart an appearance of gallantry to the orgy, raised his glass again and said: "To our victories over hearts!" Thereupon Lieutenant Otto, who was a species of bear from the Black Forest, jumped up, inflamed and saturated with drink and seized by an access of alcoholic patriotism, cried: "To our victories over France!"

Drunk as they were, the women were silent, and Rachel turned round with a shudder and said: "Look here, I know some Frenchmen in whose presence you would not dare to say that." But the little count, still holding her on his knees, began to laugh, for the wine had made him very merry, and said: "Ha! ha! ha! I have never met any of them myself. As soon as we show ourselves they run away!"

The girl, who was in a terrible rage, shouted into his face: "You are lying, you dirty scoundrel!"

For a moment he looked at her steadily, with his bright eyes upon her, as he had looked at the portrait before he destroyed it with revolver bullets, and then he began to laugh: "Ah yes, talk about them, my dear! Should we be here now if they were brave?" Then, getting excited, he exclaimed: "We are the masters! France belongs to us!" She jumped off his knees with a bound and threw herself into her chair, while he rose, held out his glass over the table and repeated: "France and the French, the woods, the fields and the houses of France belong to us!"

The others, who were quite drunk and who were suddenly seized by military enthusiasm, the enthusiasm of brutes, seized their glasses and, shouting, "Long live Prussia!" emptied them at a draught.

The girls did not protest, for they were reduced to silence and were afraid. Even Rachel did not say a word, as she had no reply to make, and then the little count put his champagne glass, which had just been refilled, onto the head of the Jewess and exclaimed: "All the women in France belong to us also!"

At that she got up so quickly that the glass upset, spilling the amber-colored wine onto her black hair, as if to baptize her, and broke into a hundred fragments as it fell onto the floor. With trembling lips she defied the looks of the officer, who was still laughing, and she stammered out in a voice choked with rage: "That—that—that—is not true—for you shall certainly not have any French women."

He sat down again, so as to laugh at his ease and, trying effectually to speak in the Parisian accent, he said: "That is good, very good! Then what did you come here for, my dear?"

She was thunderstruck and made no reply for a moment, for in her agitation she did not understand him at first, but as soon as she grasped his meaning she said to him indignantly and vehemently: "I! I am not a woman; I am only a strumpet, and that is all the Prussians want."

Almost before she had finished he slapped her full in her face, but as he was raising his hand again, as if he would strike her, she, almost mad with passion, took up a small dessert knife from the table and stabbed him right in the neck, just above the breastbone. Something that he was going to say was cut short in his throat, and he sat there with his mouth half open and a terrible look in his eyes.

All the officers shouted in horror and leaped up tumultuously, but, throwing her chair between Lieutenant Otto's legs, who fell down at full length, she ran to the window, opened it before they could seize her and jumped out into the night and pouring rain.

In two minutes Mademoiselle Fifi was dead. Fritz and Otto drew their swords and wanted to kill the women, who threw themselves at their feet and clung to their knees. With some difficulty the major stopped the slaughter and had the four terrified girls locked up in a room under the care of two soldiers. Then he organized the pursuit of the fugitive as carefully as if he were about to engage in a skirmish, feeling quite sure that she would be caught.

The table, which had been cleared immediately, now served as a bed on which to lay Fifi out, and the four officers made for the window, rigid and sobered, with the stern faces of soldiers on duty, and tried to pierce through the darkness of the night, amid the steady torrent of rain. Suddenly a shot was heard and then another a long way off, and for four hours they heard from time to time near or distant reports and rallying cries, strange words uttered as a call in guttural voices.

In the morning they all returned. Two soldiers had been killed and three others wounded by their comrades in the ardor of that chase and in the confusion of such a nocturnal pursuit, but they had not caught Rachel.

Then the inhabitants of the district were terrorized; the houses were turned topsy-turvy; the country was scoured and beaten up over and over again, but the Jewess did not seem to have left a single trace of her passage behind her.

When the general was told of it he gave orders to hush up the affair so as not to set a bad example to the army, but he severely censured the commandant, who in turn punished his inferiors. The general had said: "One does not go to war in order to amuse oneself and to caress prostitutes." And Graf von Farlsberg, in his exasperation, made up his mind to have his revenge on the district, but as he required a pretext for showing severity, he sent for the priest and ordered him to have the bell tolled at the funeral of Count von Eyrick.

Contrary to all expectation, the priest showed himself humble and most respectful, and when Mademoiselle Fifi's body left the Château d'Urville on its way to the cemetery, carried by soldiers, preceded, surrounded and followed by soldiers, who marched with loaded rifles, for the first time the bell sounded its funereal knell in a lively manner, as if a friendly hand were caressing it. At night it sounded again, and the next day and every day; it rang as much as anyone could desire. Sometimes even it would start at night and sound gently through the darkness, seized by strange joy, awakened; one could not tell why. All the peasants in the neighborhood declared that it was bewitched, and nobody except the priest and the sacristan would now go near the church tower, and they went because a poor girl was living there in grief and solitude, secretly nourished by those two men.

She remained there until the German troops departed, and then one evening the priest borrowed the baker's cart and himself drove his prisoner to Rouen. When they got there he embraced her, and she quickly went on foot to the establishment from which she had come, where the proprietress, who thought that she was dead, was very glad to see her.

A short time afterward a patriot who had no prejudices, who liked her because of her bold deed and who afterward loved her for herself, married her and made a lady of her.

Robert Louis Stevenson

(1850 - 1894)

Best known for his novels of adventure (*Treasure Island* and *Kidnapped*) and tales of fantasy and science fiction ("The Strange Case of Dr. Jekyll and Mr. Hyde"), Robert Louis Stevenson was also a superb essayist and, along with Hardy and Kipling, one of the most important nineteenth-century contributors to the modern British short story. "If our minds are fixed on contemporary themes and on the short story of the last thirty years," writes T. O. Bancroft in *The Modest Art,* a recent study of the short story, "Stevenson now has an old-fashioned air. If, however, we think of the longer history of the short story we can see that he produced a brilliant, forward-looking version of the short-story form, the outcome of an original and flamboyant personality." In his short life, which was haunted by tuberculosis, this Scotsman traveled widely and, despite his always fragile health, lived intensely. Stevenson was one of the voices of the romantic revival at the end of the nineteenth century, and in his short fiction, he combines romantic narrative with a highly polished style and compact form. Unlike twentieth-century fiction, his stories bear a pronounced moralistic note.

The Sire de Malétroit's Door

Denis de Beaulieu was not yet two-and-twenty, but he counted himself a grown man, and a very accomplished cavalier into the bargain. Lads were early formed in that rough, warfaring epoch; and when one has been in a pitched battle and a dozen raids, has killed one's man in an honourable fashion, and knows a thing or two of strategy and mankind, a certain swagger in the gait is surely to be pardoned. He had put up his horse with due care, and supped with due deliberation; and then, in a very agreeable frame of mind, went out to pay a visit in the grey of the evening. It was not a very wise proceeding on the young man's part. He would have done better to remain beside the fire or go decently to bed. For the town was full of the troops of Burgundy and England under a mixed command; and though Denis was there on safe-conduct, his safe-conduct was like to serve him little on a chance encouter.

It was September, 1429; the weather had fallen sharp; a flighty piping wind, laden with showers, beat about the township; and the dead leaves ran riot along the streets. Here and there a window was already lighted up; and the noise of men-at-arms making merry over supper within, came forth in fits and was swallowed up and carried away by the wind. The night fell swiftly; the flag of England, fluttering on the spire-top, grew ever fainter and fainter against the flying clouds—a black speck like a swallow in the tumultuous, leaden chaos of the sky. As the night fell the wind rose, and began to hoot under archways and roar amid the tree-tops in the valley below the town.

Denis de Beaulieu walked fast and was soon knocking at his friend's door; but though he promised himself to stay only a little while and make an early return, his welcome was so pleasant, and he found so much to delay him, that it was already long past midnight before he said good-bye upon the threshold. The wind had fallen again in the meanwhile; the night was as black as the grave; not a star, nor a glimmer of moonshine, slipped through the canopy of cloud. Denis was ill-acquainted with the intricate lanes of Château Landon; even by daylight he had found some trouble in picking his way; and in this absolute darkness he soon lost it altogether. He was certain of one thing only—to keep mounting the hill; for his friend's house lay at the lower end, or tail, of Château Landon, while the inn was up at the head, under the great church spire. With this clue to go upon he stumbled and groped forward, now breathing more freely in open places where there was a good slice of sky overhead, now feeling along the wall in stifling closes. It is an eerie and mysterious position to be thus submerged in opaque blackness in an almost unknown town. The silence is terrifying in its possibilities. The touch of cold window bars to the exploring hand startles the man like the touch of a toad; the inequalities of the pavement shake his heart into his mouth; a piece of denser darkness threatens an ambuscade or a chasm in the pathway; and where the air is brighter, the houses put on strange and bewildering appearances, as if to lead him farther from his way. For Denis, who had to regain his inn without attracting notice, there was real danger as well as mere discomfort in the walk; and he went warily and boldly at once, and at every corner paused to make an observation.

He had been for some time threading a lane so narrow that he could touch a wall with either hand, when it began to open out and go sharply downward. Plainly this lay no longer in the direction of his inn; but the hope of a little more light tempted him forward to reconnoitre. The lane ended in a terrace with a bartizan wall, which gave an outlook between high houses, as out of an embrasure, into the valley lying dark and formless several hundred feet below. Denis looked down, and could discern a few tree-tops waving and a single speck of brightness where the river ran across a weir. The weather was clearing up, and the sky had lightened, so as to show the outline of the heavier clouds and the dark margin of the hills. By the uncertain glimmer, the house on his left hand should be a place of some pretensions; it was surmounted by several pinnacles and turret-tops; the round stern of a chapel, with a fringe of flying buttresses, projected boldly from the main block; and the door was sheltered under a deep porch carved with figures and overhung by two long gargoyles. The windows of the chapel gleamed through their intricate tracery with a light as of many tapers, and threw out the buttresses and the peaked roof in a more intense blackness against the sky. It was plainly the hotel of some great family of the neighbourhood; and as it reminded Denis of a town house of his own at Bourges, he stood for some time gazing up at it and mentally gauging the skill of the architects and the consideration of the two families.

There seemed to be no issue to the terrace but the lane by which he had reached it; he could only retrace his steps, but he had gained some notion of his whereabouts and hoped by this means to hit the main thoroughfare and speedily regain the inn. He was reckoning without the chapter of accidents which was to make this night memorable above all others in his career; for he had not gone back above a hundred yards before he saw a light coming to meet him, and heard loud voices speaking together in the echoing narrows of the lane. It was a party of men-at-arms going the night round with torches. Denis assured himself that they had all been making free with the wine bowl, and were in no mood to be particular about safe-conducts or the niceties of chivalrous war. It was as like as not that they would kill him like a dog and leave him where he fell. The situation was inspiriting but nervous. Their own torches would conceal him from sight, he reflected; and he hoped that they would drown the noise of his footsteps with their own empty voices. If he were but fleet and silent, he might evade their notice altogether.

Unfortunately, as he turned to beat a retreat, his foot rolled upon a pebble; he fell against the wall with an ejaculation, and his sword rang loudly on the stones. Two or three voices demanded who went there—some in French, some in English; but Denis made no reply, and ran the faster down the lane. Once upon the terrace, he paused to look back. They still kept calling after him, and just then began to double the pace in pursuit, with a considerable clank of armour, and great tossing of the torchlight to and fro in the narrow jaws of the passage.

Denis cast a look around and darted into the porch. There he might escape observation, or—if that were too much to expect—was in a capital posture whether for parley or defense. So thinking, he drew his sword and tried to set his back against the door. To his surprise, it yielded behind his weight; and though he turned in a moment, continued to swing back on oiled and noiseless hinges, until it stood wide open on a black interior. When things fall out opportunely for the person concerned, he is not apt to be critical about the how or why, his own immediate personal convenience seeming a sufficient reason for the strangest oddities and revolutions in our sublunary things; and so Denis, without a moment's hesitation, stepped within and partly closed the door behind him to conceal his place of refuge. Nothing was further from his thoughts than to close it altogether; but for some inexplicable reason—perhaps by a spring or a weight—the ponderous mass of oak whipped itself out of his fingers and clanked to, with a formidable rumble and a noise like the falling of an automatic bar.

The round, at that very moment, debouched upon the terrace and proceeded to summon him with shouts and curses. He heard them ferreting in the dark corners; the stock of a lance even rattled along the outer surface of the door behind which he stood; but these gentlemen were in too high a humour to be long delayed, and soon made on down a corkscrew pathway which had escaped Denis' observation, and passed out of sight and hearing along the battlements of the town.

Denis breathed again. He gave them a few minutes' grace for fear of accidents, and then groped about for some means of opening the door and slipping forth again. The inner surface was quite smooth, not a handle, not a moulding, not a projection of any sort. He got his finger-nails round the edges and pulled, but the mass was immovable. He shook it, it was as firm as a rock. Denis de Beaulieu frowned and gave vent to a little noiseless whistle. What ailed the door? he wondered. Why was it open? How came it to shut so easily and so effectually after him? There was something obscure and underhand about all this, that was little to the young man's fancy. It looked like a snare; and yet who could suppose a snare in such a quiet by-street and in a house of so prosperous and even noble exterior? And yet—snare or no snare, intentionally or unintentionally—here he was, prettily trapped; and for the life of him he could see no way out of it again. The darkness began to weigh upon him. He gave ear; all was silent without, but within and close by he seemed to catch a faint sighing, a faint sobbing rustle, a little stealthy creak—as though many persons were at his side, holding themselves quite still, and governing even their respiration with the extreme of slyness. The idea went to his vitals with a shock, and he faced about suddenly as if to defend his life. Then, for the first time, he became aware of a light about the level of his eyes and at some distance in the interior of the house—a vertical thread of light, widening towards the bottom, such as might escape between two wings of arras over a doorway. To see anything was a relief to Denis; it was like a piece of solid ground to a man labouring in a morass; his mind seized upon it with avidity; and he stood staring at it and trying to piece together some logical conception of his surroundings. Plainly there was a flight of steps ascending from his own level to that of the illuminated doorway; and indeed he thought he could make out another thread of light, as fine as a needle and as faint as phosphorescence, which might very well be reflected along the polished wood of a handrail. Since he had begun to suspect that he was not alone, his heart had continued to beat with smothering violence, and an intolerable desire for action of any sort had possessed itself of his spirit. He was in deadly peril, he believed. What could be more natural than to mount the staircase, lift the curtain, and confront his difficulty at once? At least he would be dealing with something tangible; at least he would be no longer in the dark. He stepped slowly forward with outstretched hands, until his foot struck the bottom step; then he rapidly scaled the stairs, stood for a moment to compose his expression, lifted the arras, and went in.

He found himself in a large apartment of polished stone. There were three doors; one on each of three sides; all similarly curtained with tapestry. The fourth side was occupied by two large windows and a great stone chimneypiece, carved with the arms of the Malétroits. Denis recognized the bearing, and was gratified to find himself in such good hands. The room was strongly illuminated; but it contained little furniture except a heavy table and a chair or two, the hearth was innocent of fire, and the pavement was but sparsely strewn with rushes clearly many days old.

On a high chair beside the chimney, and directly facing Denis as he entered, sat a little old gentleman in a fur tippet. He sat with legs crossed and his hands folded, and a cup of spiced wine stood by his elbow on a bracket on the wall. His countenance had a strongly masculine cast; not properly human, but such as we see in the bull, the goat, or the domestic boar; something equivocal and wheedling, something greedy, brutal, and dangerous. The upper lip was inordinately full, as though swollen by a blow or a toothache; and the smile, the peaked eyebrows, and the small, strong eyes were quaintly and almost comically evil in expression. Beautiful white hair hung straight all round his head, like a saint's, and fell in a single curl upon the tippet. His beard and moustache were the pink of venerable sweetness. Age, probably in consequence of inordinate precautions, had left no mark upon his hands; and the Malétroit hand was famous. It would be difficult to imagine anything at once so fleshy and so delicate in design; the tapered, sensual fingers were like those of one of Leonardo's women; the fork of the thumb made a dimpled protuberance when closed; the nails were perfectly shaped, and of a dead, surprising whiteness. It rendered his aspect tenfold more redoubtable, that a man with hands like these should keep them devoutly folded like a virgin martyr—that a man with so intent and startling an expression of face should sit patiently on his seat and contemplate people with an unwinking stare, like a god, or a god's statue. His quiescence seemed ironical and treacherous, it fitted so poorly with his looks.

Such was Alain, Sire de Malétroit.

Denis and he looked silently at each other for a second or two.

"Pray step in," said the Sire de Malétroit. "I have been expecting you all the evening."

He had not risen, but he accompanied his words with a smile and a slight but courteous inclination of the head. Partly from the smile, partly from the strange musical murmur with which the Sire prefaced his observation, Denis felt a strong shudder of disgust go through his marrow. And what with disgust and honest confusion of mind, he could scarcely get words together in reply.

"I fear," he said, "that this is a double accident. I am not the person you suppose me. It seems you were looking for a visit; but for my part, nothing was further from my thoughts—nothing could be more contrary to my wishes—than this intrusion."

"Well, well," replied the old gentleman indulgently, "here you are, which is the main point. Seat yourself, my friend, and put yourself entirely at your ease. We shall arrange our little affairs presently."

Denis perceived that the matter was still complicated with some misconception, and he hastened to continue his explanation.

"Your door . . ." he began.

"About my door?" asked the other, raising his peaked eyebrows. "A little piece of ingenuity." And he shrugged his shoulders. "A hospitable fancy! By your own account, you were not desirous of making my acquaintance. We old people look for such reluctance now and then; and when it touches our honours, we cast about until we find some way of overcoming it. You arrive uninvited, but believe me, very welcome."

"You persist in error, sir," said Denis. "There can be no question between you and me. I am a stranger in this countryside. My name is Denis, damoiseau de Beaulieu. If you see me in your house, it is only—"

"My found friend," interrupted the other, "you will permit me to have my own ideas on that subject. They probably differ from yours at the present moment," he added with a leer, "but time will show which of us is in the right."

Denis was convinced he had to do with a lunatic. He seated himself with a shrug, content to wait the upshot; and a pause ensued, during which he thought he could distinguish a hurried gabbling as of prayer from behind the arras immediately opposite him. Sometimes there seemed to be but one person engaged, sometimes two; and the vehemence of the voice, low as it was, seemed to indicate either great haste or an agony of spirit. It occurred to him that this piece of tapestry covered the entrance to the chapel he had noticed from without.

The old gentleman meanwhile surveyed Denis from head to foot with a smile, and from time to time emitted little noises like a bird or a mouse, which seemed to indicate a high degree of satisfaction. This state of matters became rapidly insupportable; and Denis, to put an end to it, remarked politely that the wind had gone down.

The old gentleman fell into a fit of silent laughter, so prolonged and violent that he became quite red in the face. Denis got upon his feet at once, and put on his hat with a flourish.

"Sir," he said, "if you are in your wits, you have affronted me grossly. If you are out of them, I flatter myself I can find better employment for my brains than to talk with lunatics. My conscience is clear; you have made a fool of me from the first moment; you have refused to hear my explanations; and now there is no power under God will make me stay here any longer; and if I cannot make my way out in a more decent fashion, I will hack your door in pieces with my sword."

The Sire de Malétroit raised his right hand and wagged it at Denis with the fore and little fingers extended.

"My dear nephew," he said, "sit down."

"Nephew!" retorted Denis, "you lie in your throat"; and he snapped his fingers in his face.

"Sit down, you rogue!" cried the old gentleman, in a sudden harsh voice, like the barking of a dog. "Do you fancy," he went on, "that when I had made my little contrivance for the door I had stopped short with that? If you prefer to be bound hand and foot till your bones ache, rise and try to go away. If you choose to remain a free young buck, agreeably conversing with an old gentleman—why, sit where you are in peace, and God be with you."

"Do you mean I am a prisoner?" demanded Denis.

"I state the facts," replied the other. "I would rather leave the conclusion to yourself."

Denis sat down again. Externally he managed to keep pretty calm; but within, he was now boiling with anger, now chilled with apprehension. He no longer felt convinced that he was dealing with a madman. And if the old gentleman was sane, what, in God's name, had he to look for? What absurd or tragical adventure had befallen him? What countenance was he to assume?

While he was thus unpleasantly reflecting, the arras that overhung the chapel door was raised, and a tall priest in his robes came forth and, giving a long, keen stare at Denis, said something in an undertone to Sire de Malétroit.

"She is in a better frame of spirit?" asked the latter.

"She is more resigned, messire," replied the priest.

"Now the Lord help her, she is hard to please!" sneered the old gentleman. "A likely stripling—nor ill-born—and of her own choosing, too? Why, what more would the jade have?"

"The situation is not usual for a young damsel," said the other, "and somewhat trying to her blushes."

"She should have thought of that before she began the dance. It was none of my choosing. God knows that: but since she is in it, by our Lady, she shall carry it to the end." And then addressing Denis, "Monsieur de Beaulieu," he asked, "may I present you to my niece? She has been waiting your arrival, I may say, with even greater impatience than myself."

Denis had resigned himself with a good grace—all he desired was to know the worst of it as speedily as possible; so he rose at once, and bowed in acquiescence. The Sire de Malétroit followed his example and limped, with the assistance of the chaplain's arm, towards the chapel door. The priest pulled aside the arras, and all three entered. The building had considerable architectural pretensions. A light groining sprang from six stout columns, and hung down in two rich pendants from the centre of the vault. The place terminated behind the alter in a round end, embossed and honeycombed with a superfluity of ornament in relief, and pierced by many little windows shaped like stars, trefoils, or wheels. These windows were imperfectly glazed, so that the night air circulated freely in the chapel. The tapers, of which there must have been half a hundred burning on the alter, were unmercifully blown about; and the light went through many different phases of brilliancy and semi-eclipse. On the steps in front of the altar knelt a young girl richly attired as a bride. A chill settled over Denis as he observed her costume; he fought with desperate energy against the conclusion that was being thrust upon his mind; it could not—it should not—be as he feared.

"Blanche," said the Sire, in his most flutelike tones, "I have brought a friend to see you, my little girl; turn round and give him your pretty hand. It is good to be devout; but it is necessary to be polite, my niece."

The girl rose to her feet and turned towards the newcomer. She moved all of a piece; and shame and exhaustion were expressed in every line of her fresh young body; and she held her head down and kept her eyes upon the pavement, as she came slowly forward. In the course of her advance, her eyes fell upon Denis de Beaulieu's feet—feet of which he was justly vain, be it remarked, and wore in the most elegant accoutrement even while travelling. She paused—started, as if his yellow boots had conveyed some shocking meaning—and glanced suddenly up into the wearer's countenance. Their eyes met; shame gave place to horror and terror in her looks; the blood left her lips; with a piercing scream she covered her face with her hands and sank upon the chapel floor.

"That is not the man!" she cried. "My uncle, that is not the man!"

The Sire de Malétroit chirped agreeably. "Of course not," he said, "I expected as much. It was so unfortunate you could not remember his name."

"Indeed," she cried, "indeed, I have never seen this person till this moment—I have never so much as set eyes upon him—I never wish to see him again. Sir," she said, turning to Denis, "if you are a gentleman, you will bear me out. Have I ever seen you—have you ever seen me—before this accursed hour?"

"To speak for myself, I have never had that pleasure," answered the young man. "This is the first time, messire, that I have met with your engaging niece."

The old gentleman shrugged his shoulders.

"I am distressed to hear it," he said. "But it is never too late to begin. I had little more acquaintance with my own late lady ere I married her; which proves," he added, with a grimace, "that these impromptu marriages may often produce an excellent understanding in the long run. As the bridegroom is to have a voice in the matter, I will give him two hours to make up for lost time before we proceed with the ceremony." And he turned toward the door, followed by the clergyman.

The girl was on her feet in a moment. "My uncle, you cannot be in earnest," she said "I declare before God I will stab myself rather than be forced on that young man. The heart rises at it; God forbids such marriages; you dishonour your white hair. Oh, my uncle, pity me! There is not a woman in all the world but would prefer death to such a nuptial. Is it possible," she added, faltering—"is it possible that you do not believe me—that you still think this"—and she pointed at Denis with a tremor of anger and contempt—"that you still think *this* to be the man?"

"Frankly," said the old gentleman, pausing on the threshold, "I do. But let me explain to you once for all, Blanche de Malétroit, my way of thinking about this affair. When you took it into your head to dishonour my family and the name that I have borne, in peace and war, for more than threescore years, you forfeited, not only the right to question my designs, but that of looking me in the face. If your father had been alive, he would have spat on you and turned you out of doors. His was the hand of iron. You may bless your God you have only to deal with the hand of velvet, mademoiselle. It was my duty to get you married without delay. Out of pure goodwill, I have tried to find your own gallant for you. And I believe I have succeeded. But before God and all the holy angels, Blanche de Malétroit, if I have not, I care not one jackstraw. So let me recommend you to be polite to our young friend; for upon my word, your next groom may be less appetizing."

And with that he went out, with the chaplain at his heels; and the arras fell behind the pair.

The girl turned upon Denis with flashing eyes.

"And what, sir," she demanded, "may be the meaning of all this?"

"God knows," returned Denis gloomily. "I am a prisoner in this house, which seems full of mad people. More I know not; and nothing do I understand."

"And pray how came you here?" she asked.

He told her as briefly as he could. "For the rest," he added, "perhaps you will follow my example, and tell me the answer to all these riddles, and what, in God's name, is like to be the end of it."

She stood silent for a little, and he could see her lips tremble and her tearless eyes burn with a feverish lustre. Then she pressed her forehead in both hands.

"Alas, how my head aches!" she said wearily—"to say nothing of my poor heart! But it is due to you to know my story, unmaidenly as it must seem. I am called Blanche de Malétroit; I have been without father or mother for—oh! for as long as I can recollect, and indeed I have been most unhappy all my life. Three months ago a young captain began to stand near me every day in church. I could see that I pleased him; I am much to blame, but I was so glad that any one should love me; and when he passed me a letter, I took it home with me and read it with great pleasure. Since that time he has written many. He was so anxious to speak with me, poor fellow! and kept asking me to leave the door open some evening that we might have two words upon the stair. For he knew how much my uncle trusted me." She gave something like a sob at that, and it was a moment before she could go on. "My uncle is a hard man, but is very shrewd," she said at last. "He has performed many feats in war, and was a great person at court, and much trusted by Queen Isabeau in old days. How he came to suspect me I cannot tell; but it is hard to keep anything from his knowledge; and this morning, as we came from Mass, he took my hand in his, forced it open, and read my little billet, walking by my side all the while. When he had finished, he gave it back to me with great politeness. It contained another request to have the door left open; and this has been the ruin of us all. My uncle kept me strictly in my room until evening, and then ordered me to dress myself as you see me—a hard mockery for a young girl, do you not think so? I suppose, when he could not prevail with me to tell him the young captain's name, he must have laid a trap for him: into which, alas! you have fallen in the anger of God. I looked for much confusion; for how could I tell whether he was willing to take me for his wife on these sharp terms? He might have been trifling with me from the first; or I might have made myself too cheap in his eyes. But truly I had not looked for such a shameful punishment as this! I could not think that God would let a girl be so disgraced before a young man. And now I have told you all; and I can scarcely hope that you will not despise me."

Denis made her a respectful inclination.

"Madam," he said, "you have honoured me by your confidence. It remains for me to prove that I am not unworthy of the honour. Is Messire de Malétroit at hand?"

"I believe he is waiting in the salle without," she answered.

"May I lead you thither, madam?" asked Denis, offering his hand with his most courtly bearing.

She accepted it; and the pair passed out of the chapel, Blanche in a very drooping and shamefast condition, but Denis strutting and ruffling in the consciousness of a mission, and the boyish certainty of accomplishing it with honour.

The Sire de Malétroit rose to meet them with an ironical obeisance.

"Sir," said Denis, with the grandest possible air, "I believe I am to have some say in the matter of this marriage; and let me tell you at once, I will be no party to forcing the inclination of this young lady. Had it been freely offered to me, I should have been proud to accept her hand, for I perceive she is as good as she is beautiful; but as things are, I have now the honour, messire, of refusing."

Blanche looked at him with gratitude in her eyes; but the old gentleman only smiled and smiled, until his smile grew positively sickening to Denis.

"I am afraid," he said, "Monsieur de Beaulieu, that you do not perfectly understand the choice I have to offer you. Follow me, I beseech you, to this window." And he led the way to one of the large windows which stood open on the night. "You observe," he went on, "there is an iron ring in the upper masonry, and reeved through that, a very efficacious rope. Now, mark my words: if you should find your disinclination to my niece's person insurmountable, I shall have you hanged out of this window before sunrise. I shall only proceed to such an extremity with the greatest regret, you may believe me. For it is not at all you death that I desire, but my niece's establishment in life. At the same time, it must come to that if you prove obstinate. Your family, Monsieur de Beaulieu, is very well in its way; but if you sprang from Charlemagne, you should not refuse the hand of a Malétroit with impunity—not if she had been as common as the Paris road —not if she were as hideous as the gargoyle over my door. Neither my niece nor you, nor my own private feelings, move me at all in this matter. The honour of my house has been compromised; I believe you to be the guilty person; at least you are now in the secret; and you can hardly wonder if I request you to wipe out the stain. If you will not, your blood be on your own head! It will be no great satisfaction to me to have your interesting relics kicking their heels in the breeze below my windows; but half a loaf is better than no bread, and if I cannot cure the dishonour, I shall at least stop the scandal."

There was a pause.

"I believe there are other ways of settling such imbroglios among gentlemen," said Denis. "You wear a sword, and I hear you have used it with distinction."

The Sire de Malétroit made a signal to the chaplain, who crossed the room with long silent strides and raised the arras over the third of the three doors. It was only a moment before he let it fall again; but Denis had time to see a dusky passage full of armed men.

"When I was a little younger, I should have been delighted to honour you, Monsieur de Beaulieu." said Sire Alain; "but I am now too old. Faithful retainers are the sinews of age, and I must employ the strength I have. This is one of the hardest things to swallow as a man grows up in years; but with a little patience, even this becomes habitual. You and the lady seem to prefer the salle for what remains of your two hours; and as I have no desire to cross your preference, I shall resign it to your use with all the pleasure in the world. No haste!" he added, holding up his hand, as he saw a dangerous look come into Denis de Beaulieu's face. "If your mind revolts against hanging, it will be time enough two hours hence to throw yourself out of the window or upon the pikes of my retainers. Two hours of life are always two hours. A great many things may turn up in even as little a while as that. And besides, if I understand her appearance, my niece has still something to say to you. You will not disfigure your last hours by a want of politeness to a lady?"

Denis looked at Blanche, and she made him an imploring gesture.

It is likely that the old gentleman was hugely pleased at this symptom of an understanding; for he smiled on both, and added sweetly: "If you will give me your word of honour, Monsieur de Beaulieu, to await my return at the end of the two hours before attempting anything desperate, I shall withdraw my retainers, and let you speak in greater privacy with mademoiselle."

Denis again glanced at the girl, who seemed to beseech him to agree.

"I give you my word of honour," he said.

Messire de Malétroit bowed, and proceeded to limp about the apartment, clearing his throat the while with that odd musical chirp which had already grown so irritating in the ears of Denis de Beaulieu. He first possessed himself of some papers which lay upon the table; then he went to the mouth of the passage and appeared to give an order to the men behind the arras; and lastly he hobbled out through the door by which Denis had come in, turning upon the threshold to address a last smiling bow to the young couple, and followed by the chaplain with a hand lamp.

No sooner were they alone than Blanche advanced toward Denis with her hands extended. Her face was flushed and excited, and her eyes shone with tears.

"You shall not die!" she cried, "you shall marry me after all."

"You seem to think, madam," replied Denis, "that I stand much in fear of death."

"Oh, no, no," she said, "I see you are no poltroon. It is for my own sake —I could not bear to have you slain for such a scruple."

"I am afraid," returned Denis, "that you underrate the difficulty, madam. What you may be too generous to refuse, I may be too proud to accept. In a moment of noble feeling toward me, you forgot what you perhaps owe to others."

He had the decency to keep his eyes on the floor as he said this, and after he had finished, so as not to spy upon her confusion. She stood silent for a moment, then walked suddenly away, and falling on her uncle's chair, fairly burst out sobbing. Denis was in the acme of embarrassment. He looked round, as if to seek for inspiration, and seeing a stool, plumped down upon it for something to do. There he sat, playing with the guard of his rapier, and wishing himself dead a thousand times over, and buried in the nastiest kitchen-heap in France. His eyes wandered around the apartment, but found nothing to arrest them. There were such wide spaces between furniture, the light fell so badly and cheerlessly over all, the dark outside air looked in so coldly through the windows, that he thought he had never seen a church so vast, nor a tomb so melancholy. The regular sobs of Blanche de Malétroit measured out the time like the ticking of a clock. He read the device upon the shield over and over again, until his eyes became obscured; he stared into shadowy corners until he imagined they were swarming with horrible animals; and every now and again he awoke with a start, to remember that his last two hours were running, and death was on the march.

Oftener and oftener, as the time went on, did his glance settle on the girl herself. Her face was bowed forward and covered with her hands, and she was shaken at intervals by the convulsive hiccup of grief. Even thus she was not an unpleasant object to dwell upon, so plump and yet so fine, with a warm brown skin, and the most beautiful hair, Denis thought, in the whole world of womankind. Her hands were like her uncle's; but they were more in place at the end of her young arms, and looked infinitely soft and caressing. He remembered how her blue eyes had shone upon him, full of anger, pity, and innocence. And the more he dwelt on her perfections, the uglier death looked, and the more deeply was he smitten with penitence at her continued tears. Now he felt that no man could have the courage to leave a world which contained so beautiful a creature; and now he would have given forty minutes of this last hour to have unsaid his cruel speech.

Suddenly a hoarse and ragged peal of cockcrow rose to their ears from the dark valley below the windows. And this shattering noise in the silence all around was like a light in a dark place, and shook them both out of their reflections.

"Alas, can I do nothing to help you?" she said, looking up.

"Madam," replied Denis, with a fine irrelevancy, "if I have said anything to wound you, believe me, it was for your own sake and not for mine."

She thanked him with a tearful look.

"I feel your position cruelly," he went on. "The world has been bitter hard on you. Your uncle is a disgrace to mankind. Believe me, madam, there is no young gentleman in all France but would be glad of my opportunity, to die in doing you a momentary service."

"I know already what you can be very brave and generous," she answered. "What I *want* to know is whether I can serve you—now or afterwards," she added, with a quaver.

"Most certainly," he answered with a smile. "Let me sit beside you as if I were a friend, instead of a foolish intruder; try to forget how awkwardly we are placed to one another; make my last moments go pleasantly; and you will do me the chief service possible."

"You are very gallant," she added, with a yet deeper sadness . . . "very gallant . . . and it somehow pains me. But draw nearer, if you please, and if you find anything to say to me, you will at least make certain of a very friendly listener. Ah! Monsieur de Beaulieu, how can I look you in the face?" And she fell to weeping again with a renewed effusion.

"Madam," said Denis, taking her hand in both of his, "reflect on the little time I have before me, and the great bitterness into which I am cast by the sight of your distress. Spare me, in my last moments, the spectacle of what I cannot cure even with the sacrifice of my life."

"I am very selfish," answered Blanche. "I will be braver, Monsieur de Beaulieu, for your sake. But think if I can do you no kindness in the future—if you have no friends to whom I could carry your adieux. Charge me as heavily as you can; every burden will lighten, by so little, the invaluable gratitiude I owe you. Put it in my power to do something more for you than weep."

"My mother is married again, and has a young family to care for. My brother Guichard will inherit my fiefs; and if I am not in error, that will content him amply for my death. Life is a little vapor that passeth away, as we are told by those in holy orders. When a man is in a fair way and sees all life open in front of him, he seems to himself to make a very important figure in the world. His horse whinnies to him; the trumpets blow and the girls look out of window as he rides into town before his company; he receives many assurances of trust and regard—sometimes by express in a letter—sometimes face to face, with persons of great consequence falling on his neck. It is not wonderful if his head is turned for a time. But once he is dead, were he as brave as Hercules or as wise as Solomon, he is soon forgotten. It is not ten years since my father fell, with many other knights around him, in a very fierce encounter, and I do not think that any one of them, nor so much as the name of the fight, is now remembered. No, no, madam, the nearer you come to it, you see that death is a dark and dusty corner, where a man gets into his tomb and has the door shut after him till the judgment day. I have few friends just now, and once I am dead I shall have none."

"Ah, Monsieur de Beaulieu!" she exclaimed, "you forget Blanche de Malétroit."

"You have a sweet nature, madam, and you are pleased to estimate a little service far beyond its worth."

"It is not that," she answered. "You mistake me if you think I am easily touched by my own concerns. I say so, because you are the noblest man I have ever met; because I recognize in you a spirit that would have made even a common person famous in the land."

"And yet here I die in a mousetrap—with no more noise about it than my own squeaking," answered he.

A look of pain crossed her face, and she was silent for a little while. Then a light came into her eyes, and with a smile she spoke again.

"I cannot have my champion think meanly of himself. Anyone who gives his life for another will be met in Paradise by all the heralds and angels of the Lord God. And you have no such cause to hang your head. For—pray, do you think me beautiful?" she asked, with a deep flush.

"Indeed, madam, I do," he said.

"I am glad of that," she answered heartily. "Do you think there are many men in France who have been asked in marriage by a beautiful maiden—with her own lips—and who have refused her to her face? I know you men would half despise such a triumph! but believe me, we women know more of what is precious in love. There is nothing that should set a person higher in his own esteem; and we women would prize nothing more dearly."

"You are very good," he said; "but you cannot make me forget that I was asked in pity and not for love."

"I am not so sure of that," she replied, holding down her head. "Hear me to an end, Monsieur de Beaulieu. I know how you must despise me; I feel you are right to do so; I am too poor a creature to occupy one thought of your mind, although, alas! you must die for me this morning. But when I asked you to marry me, indeed, and indeed, it was because I respected and admired you, and loved you with my whole soul, from the very moment that you took my part against my uncle. If you had seen yourself, and how noble you looked, you would pity rather than despise me. And now," she went on, hurriedly checking him with her hand, "although I have laid aside all reserve and told you so much, remember that I know your sentiments towards me already. I would not, believe me, being nobly born, weary you with importunities into consent. I too have a pride of my own: and I declare before the holy mother of God, if you should now go back from your word already given, I would no more marry you than I would marry my uncle's groom."

Denis smiled a little bitterly.

"It is a small love," he said, "that shies at a little pride."

She made no answer, although she probably had her own thought.

"Come hither to the window," he said, with a sigh. "Here is the dawn."

And indeed the dawn was already beginning. The hollow of the sky was full of essential daylight, colourless and clean; and the valley underneath was flooded with a grey reflection. A few thin vapors clung in the coves of the forest or lay along the winding course of the river. The scene disengaged a surprising effect of stillness, which was hardly interrupted when the cocks began once more to crow among the steadings. Perhaps the same fellow who had made so horrid a clangour in the darkness not half an hour before, now sent up the merriest cheer to great the coming day. A little wind went bustling and eddying among the tree-tops underneath the windows. And still the daylight kept flooding insensibly out of the east, which was soon to grow incandescent and cast up that red-hot cannon-ball, the rising sun.

Denis looked out over all this with a bit of a shiver. He had taken her hand and retained it in his almost unconsciously.

"Has the day begun already?" she said; and then, illogically enough: "the night has been so long! Alas! what shall we say to my uncle when he returns?"

"What you will," said Denis, and he pressed her fingers in his.

She was silent.

"Blanche," he said, with a swift, uncertain, passionate utterance, "you have seen whether I fear death. You must know well enough that I would as gladly leap out of that window into the empty air as to lay a finger on you without your free and full consent. But if you care for me at all do not let me lose my life in a misapprehension; for I love you better than the whole world; and though I will die for you blithely, it would be like all the joys of Paradise to live on and spend my life in your service."

As he stopped speaking, a bell began to ring loudly in the interior of the house; and a clatter of armour in the corridor showed that the retainers were returning to their post, and the two hours were at an end.

"After all that you have heard?" she whispered, leaning toward him with her lips and eyes.

"I have heard nothing," he replied.

"The captain's name was Florimond de Champdivers," she said in his ear.

"I did not hear it," he answered, taking her supple body in his arms, and covering her wet face with kisses.

A melodious chirping was audible behind, followed by a beautiful chuckle, and the voice of Messire de Malétroit wished his new nephew a good-morning.

Leo Tolstoy

(1828 - 1910)

Leo Tolstoy was a titanic, stormy man, a remarkable social and religious reformer, and one of the world's greatest novelists. Although he grew up as a member of the landed and privileged gentry, he devoted much of his life to ameliorating the desperate living conditions of Russia's peasants. Scorning the materialism and artificial lives of both the bourgeoisie and aristocracy, Tolstoy celebrated the simple virtues of peasant life, reminding one of an almost fanatical Thoreau in his demand for simplicity. After writing his two masterpieces, *War and Peace* (1869) and *Anna Karenina* (1877), he zealously embraced an austere form of Christianity divested of church organization and ritual, and he boldy spoke out on questions of social injustice. Because of his international literary reputation, he was tolerated by the czarist government. In his old age Tolstoy, despite his fanaticism and eccentricities, was regarded as a saint and sage by the Russian masses.

The short novel *The Death of Ivan Illych* is an unforgettably powerful depiction of the death of an individual man who has squandered his *only* life. The novel is, among other things, a sustained criticism of Ivan's inauthentic life and the artificial, self-deceiving character of his society, a society most of us recognize immediately. It is not surprising that *The Death of Ivan Ilych* has become popular with those young people today who are sensitive to the alleged phoniness of their society. J. Glenn Gray, the head of the philosophy department at Colorado College, has observed that "If [the students] find Socrates wholly admirable but a size larger than life, Ivan is all too human, the anonymous Everyman of our day, painfully contemporary. I have overheard more than one of my students breathe, 'My God, he is just like my old man!'" But Ivan Ilych is like most sons, too. One of the novel's disturbing truths arises from the reader's recognition of how he, as well as Ivan and the others in the story, often refuses, by psychological trickery, to face and contemplate the awesome meaning of death and to accept death as absolute, ineluctable. Keeping the thought of one's death always in mind may be healthful and a spur to living, because, as British novelist John Fowles has written, "The more absolute death seems, the more authentic life becomes."

The Death of Ivan Ilych

I

During an interval in the Melvinski trial in the large building of the Law Courts, the members and public prosecutor met in Ivan Egorovich Shebek's private room, where the conversation turned on the celebrated Krasovski case. Fëdor Vasilievich warmly maintained that it was not subject to their jurisdiction, Ivan Egorovich maintained the contrary, while Peter Ivanovich, not having entered the discussion at the start, took no part in it but looked through the *Gazette* which had just been handed in.

"Gentlemen," he said, "Ivan Ilych has died!"

"You don't say so!"

"Here, read it yourself," replied Peter Ivanovich, handing Fëdor Vasilievich the paper still damp from the press. Surrounded by a black border were the words: "Praskovya Fëdorovna Golovina, with profound sorrow, informs relatives and friends of the demise of her beloved husband Ivan Ilych Golovin, Member of the Court of Justice, which occurred on February the 4th of this year 1882. The funeral will take place on Friday at one o'clock in the afternoon."

Ivan Ilych had been a colleague of the gentlemen present and was liked by them all. He had been ill for some weeks with an illness said to be incurable. His post had been kept open for him, but there had been conjectures that in case of his death Alexeev might receive his appointment, and that either Vinnikov or Shtabel would succeed Alexeev. So on receiving the news of Ivan Ilych's death the first thought of each of the gentlemen in that private room was of the changes and promotions it might occasion among themselves or their acquaintances.

"I shall be sure to get Shtabel's place or Vinnikov's," thought Fëdor Vasilievich. "I was promised that long ago, and the promotion means an extra eight hundred rubles a year for me besides the allowance."

"Now I must apply for my brother-in-law's transfer from Kaluga," thought Peter Ivanovich. "My wife will be very glad, and then she won't be able to say that I never do anything for her relations."

"I thought he would never leave his bed again," said Peter Ivanovich aloud. "It's very sad."

"But what really was the matter with him?"

"The doctors couldn't say—at least they could, but each of them said something different. When last I saw him I thought he was getting better."

"And I haven't been to see him since the holidays. I always meant to go."

"Had he any property?"

"I think his wife had a little—but something quite trifling."

"We shall have to go to see her, but they live so terribly far away."

"Far away from you, you mean. Everything's far away from your place."

"You see, he never can forgive my living on the other side of the river," said Peter Ivanovich, smiling at Shebek. Then, still talking of the distances between different parts of the city, they returned to the Court.

Besides considerations as to the possible transfers and promotions likely to result from Ivan Ilych's death, the mere fact of the death of a near acquaintance aroused, as usual, in all who heard of it the complacent feeling that, "it is he who is dead and not I."

Each one thought or felt, "Well, he's dead but I'm alive!" But the more intimate of Ivan Ilych's acquaintances, his so-called friends, could not help thinking also that they would now have to fulfill the very tiresome demands of propriety by attending the funeral service and paying a visit of condolence to the widow.

Fëdor Vasilievich and Peter Ivanovich had been his nearest acquaintances. Peter Ivanovich had studied law with Ivan Ilych and had considered himself to be under obligations to him.

Having told his wife at dinner-time of Ivan Ilych's death and of his conjecture that it might be possible to get her brother transferred to their circuit, Peter Ivanovich sacrificed his usual nap, put on his evening clothes, and drove to Ivan Ilych's house.

At the entrance stood a carriage and two cabs. Leaning against the wall in the hall downstairs near the cloak-stand was a coffin-lid covered with cloth of gold, ornamented with gold cord and tassels, that had been polished up with metal powder. Two ladies in black were taking off their fur cloaks. Peter Ivanovich recognized one of them as Ivan Ilych's sister, but the other was a stranger to him. His colleague Schwartz was just coming downstairs, but on seeing Peter Ivanovich enter he stopped and winked at him, as if to say: "Ivan Ilych has made a mess of things—not like you and me."

Schwartz's face with his Piccadilly whiskers and his slim figure in evening dress had as usual an air of elegant solemnity which contrasted with the playfulness of his character and had a special piquancy here, or so it seemed to Peter Ivanovich.

Peter Ivanovich allowed the ladies to precede him and slowly followed them upstairs. Schwartz did not come down but remained where he was, and Peter Ivanovich understood that he wanted to arrange where they should play bridge that evening. The ladies went upstairs to the widow's room, and Schwartz with seriously compressed lips but a playful look in his eyes, indicated by a twist of his eyebrows the room to the right where the body lay.

Peter Ivanovich, like everyone else on such occasions, entered feeling uncertain what he would have to do. All he knew was that at such times it is always safe to cross oneself. But he was not quite sure whether one should make obeisances while doing so. He therefore adopted a middle course. On entering the room he began crossing himself and made a slight movement resembling a bow. At the same time, as far as the motion of his head and arm allowed, he surveyed the room. Two young men—apparently nephews, one of whom was a high-school pupil—were leaving the room, crossing themselves as they did so. An old woman was standing motionless, and a lady with strangely arched eyebrows was saying something to her in a whisper. A vigorous, resolute Church Reader, in a frock-coat, was reading something in a loud voice with an expression that precluded any contradiction. The butler's assistant, Gerasim, stepping lightly in front of Peter Ivanovich, was strewing something on the floor. Noticing this, Peter Ivanovich was immediately aware of a faint odour of a decomposing body.

The last time he had called on Ivan Ilych, Peter Ivanovich had seen Gerasim in the study. Ivan Ilych had been particularly fond of him and he was performing the duty of a sick nurse.

Peter Ivanovich continued to make the sign of the cross, slightly inclining his head in an intermediate direction between the coffin, the Reader, and the icons on the table in a corner of the room. Afterwards, when it seemed to him that this movement of his arm in crossing himself had gone on too long, he stopped and began to look at the corpse.

The dead man lay, as dead men always lie, in a specially heavy way, his rigid limbs sunk in the soft cushions of the coffin, with the head forever bowed on the pillow. His yellow waxen brow with bald patches over his sunken temples, was thrust up in the way peculiar to the dead, the protruding nose seem to press on the upper lip. He was much changed and had grown even thinner since Peter Ivanovich had last seen him, but, as is always the case with the dead, his face was handsomer and above all more dignified than when he was alive. The expression on the face said that what was necessary had been accomplished, and accomplished rightly. Besides this there was in that expression a reproach and a warning to the living. This warning seemed to Peter Ivanovich out of place, or at least not applicable to him. He felt a certain discomfort and so he hurriedly crossed himself once more and turned and went out of the door—too hurriedly and too regardless of propriety, as he himself was aware.

Schwartz was waiting for him in the adjoining room with legs spread wide apart and both hands toying with his top-hat behind his back. The mere sight of that playful, well-groomed, and elegant figure refreshed Peter Ivanovich. He felt that Schwartz was above all these happenings and would not surrender to any depressing influences. His very look said that this incident of a church service for Ivan Ilych could not be a sufficient reason for infringing the order of the session—in other words, that it would certainly not prevent his unwrapping a new pack of cards and shuffling them that evening while a footman placed four fresh candles on the table: in fact, that there was no reason for supposing that this incident would hinder their spending the evening agreeably. Indeed he said this in a whisper as Peter Ivanovich passed him, proposing that they should meet for a game at Fëdor Vasilievich's. But apparently Peter Ivanovich was not destined to play bridge that evening. Praskovya Fëdorovna (a short, fat woman who despite all efforts to the contrary had continued to broaden steadily from her shoulders downwards and who had the same extraordinarily arched eyebrows as the lady who had been standing by the coffin), dressed all in black, her head covered with lace, came out of her own room with some other ladies, conducted them to the room where the dead body lay, and said: "The service will begin immediately. Please go in."

Schwartz, making an indefinite bow, stood still, evidently neither accepting nor declining this invitation. Praskovya Fëdorovna, recognizing Peter Ivanovich, sighed, went close up to him, took his hand, and said: "I know you were a true friend of Ivan Ilych . . ." and looked at him awaiting some suitable response. And Peter Ivanovich knew that, just as it had been the right thing to cross himself in that room, so what he had to do here was to press her hand, sigh, and say, "Believe me. . . ." So he did all this and as he did it felt that the desired results had been achieved: that both he and she were touched.

"Come with me. I want to speak to you before it begins," said the widow. "Give me your arm."

Peter Ivanovich gave her his arm and they went to the inner rooms, passing Schwartz, who winked at Peter Ivanovich compassionately.

"That does for our bridge! Don't object if we find another player. Perhaps you can cut in when you do escape," said his playful look.

Peter Ivanovich sighed still more deeply and despondently, and Praskovya Fëdorovna pressed his arm gratefully. When they reached the drawing-room, upholstered in pink cretonne and lighted by a dim lamp, they sat down at the table—she on a sofa and Peter Ivanovich on a low pouffe, the springs of which yielded spasmodically under his weight. Praskovya Fëdorovna had been on the point of warning him to take another seat, but felt that such a warning was out of keeping with her present condition and so changed her mind. As he sat down on the pouffe Peter Ivanovich recalled how Ivan Ilych had arranged this room and had consulted him regarding this pink cretonne with green leaves. The whole room was full of furniture and knick-knacks, and on her way to the sofa the lace of the widow's black shawl caught on the carved edge of the table. Peter Ivanovich rose to detach it, and the springs of the pouffe, relieved of his weight, rose also and gave him a push. The widow began detaching her shawl herself, and Peter

Ivanovich again sat down, suppressing the rebellious springs of the pouffe under him. But the widow had not quite freed herself and Peter Ivanovich got up again, and again the pouffe rebelled and even creaked. When this was all over she took out a clean cambric handkerchief and began to weep. The episode with the shawl and the struggle with the pouffe had cooled Peter Ivanovich's emotions and he sat there with a sullen look on his face. This awkward situation was interrupted by Sokolov, Ivan Ilych's butler, who came to report that the plot in the cemetery that Praskovya Fëdorovna had chosen would cost two hundred rubles. She stopped weeping and, looking at Peter Ivanovich with the air of a victim, remarked in French that it was very hard for her. Peter Ivanovich made a silent gesture signifying his full conviction that it must indeed be so.

"Please smoke," she said in a magnanimous yet crushed voice, and turned to discuss with Sokolov the price for the plot for the grave.

Peter Ivanovich while lighting his cigarette heard her inquiring very circumstantially into the prices of different plots in the cemetery and finally decide which she would take. When that was done she gave instructions about engaging the choir. Sokolov then left the room.

"I look after everything myself," she told Peter Ivanovich, shifting the albums that lay on the table; and noticing that the table was endangered by his cigarette-ash, she immediately passed him an ash-tray, saying as she did so: "I consider it an affectation to say that my grief prevents my attending to practical affairs. On the contrary, if anything can—I won't say console me, but—distract me, it is seeing to everything concerning him." She again took out her handkerchief as if preparing to cry, but suddenly, as if mastering her feeling, she shook herself and began to speak calmly. "But there is something I want to talk to you about."

Peter Invanvich bowed, keeping control of the springs of the pouffe, which immediately began quivering under him.

"He suffered terribly the last few days."

"Did he?" said Peter Ivanovich.

"Oh, terribly! He screamed unceasingly, not for minutes but for hours. For the last three days he screamed incessantly. It was unendurable. I cannot understand how I bore it; you could hear him three rooms off. Oh, what I have suffered!"

"Is it possible that he was conscious all that time?" asked Peter Ivanovich.

"Yes," she whispered. "To the last moment. He took leave of us a quarter of an hour before he died, and asked us to take Volodya away."

The thought of the sufferings of this man he had known so intimately, first as a merry little boy, then as a school-mate, and later as a grown-up colleague, suddenly struck Peter Ivanovich with horror, despite an unpleasant consciousness of his own and this woman's dissimulation. He again saw that brow, and that nose pressing down on the lip, and felt afraid for himself.

"Three days of frightful suffering and then death! Why, that might suddenly, at any time, happen to me," he thought, and for a moment felt terrified. But—he did not himself know how—the customary reflection at once occurred to him that this had happened to Ivan Ilych and not to him, and that it should not and could not happen to him, and that to think that it could would be yielding to depression which he ought not to do, as Schwartz's expression plainly showed. After which reflection Peter Ivanovich felt reassured, and began to ask with interest about the details of Ivan Ilych's death, as though death was an accident natural to Ivan Ilych but certainly not to himself.

After many details of the really dreadful physical sufferings Ivan Ilych had endured (which details he learnt only from the effect those sufferings had produced on Praskovya Fëdorovna's nerves) the widow apparently found it necessary to get to business.

"Oh, Peter Ivanovich, how hard it is! How terribly, terribly hard!" and she again began to weep.

Peter Ivanovich sighed and waited for her to finish blowing her nose. When she had done so he said, "Believe me . . ." and she again began talking and brought out what was evidently her chief concern with him—namely, to question him as to how she could obtain a grant of money from the government on the occasion of her husband's death. She made it appear that she was asking Peter Ivanovich's advice about her pension, but he soon saw that she already knew about that to the minutest detail, more even than he did himself. She knew how much could be got out of the government in consequence of her husband's death, but wanted to find out whether she could not possibly extract something more. Peter Ivanovich tried to think of some means of doing so, but after reflecting for a while and, out of propriety, condemning the government for its niggardliness, he said he thought that nothing more could be got. Then she sighed and evidently began to devise means of getting rid of her visitor. Noticing this, he put out his cigarette, rose, pressed her hand, and went out into the anteroom.

In the dining-room where the clock stood that Ivan Ilych had liked so much and had bought at an antique shop, Peter Ivanovich met a priest and a few acquaintances who had come to attend the service, and he recognized Ivan Ilych's daughter, a handsome young woman. She was in black and her slim figure appeared slimmer than every. She had a gloomy, determined, almost angry expression, and bowed to Peter Ivanovich as though he were in some way to blame. Behind her, with the same offended look, stood a wealthy young man, an examining magistrate, whom Peter Ivanovich also knew and who was her fiancé, as he had heard. He bowed mournfully to them and was about to pass into the death-chamber, when from under the stairs appeared the figure of Ivan Ilych's schoolboy son, who was extremely like his father. He seemed a little Ivan Ilych, such as Peter Ivanovich remembered when they studied law together. His tear-stained eyes had in them the look that is seen in the eyes of boys of thirteen or fourteen who are not pure-minded. When he saw Peter Ivanovich he scowled morosely and shamefacedly. Peter Ivanovich nodded to him and entered the death-chamber. The service began: candles, groans, incense, tears, and sobs. Peter Ivanovich stood looking gloomily down at his feet. He did not look once at the dead man, did not yield to any depressing influence, and was one of the first to leave the room. There was no one in the anteroom, but Gerasim darted out of the dead man's room, rummaged with his strong hands among the fur coats to find Peter Ivanovich's, and helped him on with it.

"Well, friend Gerasim," said Peter Ivanovich, so as to say something. "It's a sad affair, isn't it?"

"It's God's will. We shall all come to it some day," said Gerasim, displaying his teeth—the even, white teeth of a healthy peasant—and, like a man in the thick of urgent work, he briskly opened the front door, called the coachman, helped Peter Ivanovich into the sledge, and sprang back to the porch as if in readiness for what he had to do next.

Peter Ivanovich found the fresh air particularly pleasant after the smell of incense, the dead body, and carbolic acid.

"Where to, sir?" asked the coachman.

"It's not too late even now. . . . I'll call round on Fëdor Vasilievich."

He accordingly drove there and found them just finishing the first rubber, so that it was quite convenient for him to cut in.

II

Ivan Ilych's life had been most simple and most ordinary and therefore most terrible.

He had been a member of the Court of Justice, and died at the age of forty-five. His father had been an official who after serving in various ministries and departments in Petersburg had made the sort of career which brings men to positions from which by reason of their long service they cannot be dismissed, though they are obviously unfit to hold any responsible position, and for whom therefore posts are specially created, which though fictitious carry salaries of from six to ten thousand rubles that are not fictitious, and in receipt of which they live on to a great age.

Such was the Privy Councillor and superfluous member of various superfluous institutions, Ilya Epimovich Golovin.

He had three sons, of whom Ivan Ilych was the second. The eldest son was following in his father's footsteps only in another department, and was already approaching that stage in the service at which a similar sinecure would be reached. The third son was a failure. He had ruined his prospects in a number of positions and was now serving in the railway department. His father and brothers, and still more their wives, not merely disliked meeting him, but avoided remembering his existence unless compelled to do so. His sister had married Baron Greff, a Petersburg official of her father's type. Ivan Ilych was *le phênix de la famille* as people said. He was neither as cold and formal as his elder brother nor as wild as the younger, but was a happy mean between them—an intelligent, polished, lively, and agreeable man. He had studied with his younger brother at the School of Law, but the latter had failed to complete the course and was expelled when he was in the fifth class. Ivan Ilych finished the course well. Even when he was at the School of Law he was just what he remained for the rest of his life: a capable, cheerful, good-natured, sociable man, though strict in the fulfilment of what he considered to be his duty: and he considered his duty to be what was so considered by those in authority. Neither as a boy nor as a man was he a toady, but from early youth was by nature attracted to people of high station as a fly is drawn to the light, assimilating their ways and views of life and establishing friendly relations with them. All the enthusiasms of childhood and youth passed with leaving much trace on him; he succumbed to sensuality, to vanity, and latterly among the highest classes to liberalism, but always within limits which his instinct unfailingly indicated to him as correct.

At school he had done things which had formerly seemed to him very horrid and made him feel disgusted with himself when he did them; but when later on he saw that such actions were done by people of good position and that they did not regard them as wrong, he was able not exactly to regard them as right, but to forget about them entirely or not be at all troubled at remembering them.

Having graduated from the School of Law and qualified for the tenth rank of the civil service, and having received money from his father for his equipment, Ivan Ilych ordered himself clothes at Scharmer's, the fashionable tailor, hung a medallion inscribed *respice finem* on his watch-chain, took leave of his professor and the prince who was patron of the school, had a farewell dinner with his comrades at Donon's first-class restaurant, and with his new and fashionable portmanteau, linen, clothes, shaving and other toilet appliances, and a travelling rug, all purchased at the best shops, he set off for one of the provinces where, through his father's influence, he had been attached to the Governor as an official for special service.

In the province Ivan Ilych soon arranged as easy and agreeable a position for himself as he had had at the School of Law. He performed his official tasks, made his career, and at the same time amused himself pleasantly and decorously. Occasionally he paid official visits to country districts, where he behaved with dignity both to his superiors and inferiors, and performed the duties entrusted to him, which related chiefly to the sectarians, with an exactness and incorruptible honesty of which he could not but feel proud.

In official matters, despite his youth and taste for frivolous gaiety, he was exceedingly reserved, punctilious, and even severe; but in society he was often amusing and witty, and always good-natured, correct in his manner, and *bon enfant,* as the Governor and his wife—with whom he was like one of the family—used to say of him.

In the province he had an affair with a lady who made advances to the elegant young lawyer, and there was also a milliner; and there were carousals with aides-de-camp who visited the district, and after-supper visits to a certain outlying street of doubtful reputation; and there was too some obsequiousness to his chief and even to his chief's wife, but all this was done with such a tone of good breeding that no hard names could be applied to it. It all came under the heading of the French saying: *"Il faut que jeunesse se passe."* It was done with clean hands, in clean linen, with French phrases, and above all among people of the best society and consequently with the approval of people of rank.

So Ivan Ilych served for five years and then came a change in his official life. The new and reformed judicial institutions were introduced, and new men were needed. Ivan Ilych became such a new man. He was offered the post of examining magistrate, and he accepted it though the post was in another province and obliged him to give up the connexions he had formed and to make new ones. His friends met to give him a send-off; they had a group-photograph taken and presented him with a silver cigarette-case, and he set off to his new post.

As examining magistrate Ivan Ilych was just as *comme il faut* and decorous a man, inspiring general respect and capable of separating his official duties from his private life, as he had been when acting as an official on special service. His duties now as examining magistrate were far more interesting and attractive than before. In his former position it had been pleasant to wear an undress uniform made by Scharmer, and to pass through the crowd of petitioners and officials who were timorously awaiting an audience with the Governor, and who envied him as with free and easy gait he went straight into his chief's private room to have a cup of tea and a cigarette with him. But not many people had been directly dependent on him—only police officials and the sectarians when he went on special missions—and he liked to treat them politely, almost as comrades, as if he were letting them feel that he who had the power to crush them was treating them in this simple, friendly way. There were then but few such people. But now, as an examining magistrate, Ivan Ilych felt that everyone without exception, even the most important and self-satisfied, was in his power, and that he need only write a few words on a sheet of paper with a certain heading, and this or that important, self-satisfied person would be brought before him in the role of an accused person or a witness, and if he did not choose to allow him to sit down, would have to stand before him and answer his questions. Ivan Ilych never abused his power; he tried on the contrary to soften its expression, but the consciousness of it and of the possibility of softening its effect, supplied the chief interest and attraction of his office. In his work itself, especially in his examinations, he very soon acquired a method of eliminating all considerations irrelevant to the legal aspect of the case, and reducing even the most complicated case to a form in which it would be presented on paper only in its externals, completely excluding his personal opinion of the matter, while above all observing every prescribed formality. The work was new and Ivan Ilych was one of the first men to apply the new Code of 1864.

On taking up the post of examining magistrate in a new town, he made new acquaintances and connexions, placed himself on a new footing, and assumed a somewhat different tone. He took up an attitude of rather dignified aloofness towards the provincial authorities, but picked out the best circle of legal gentlemen and wealthy gentry living in the town and assumed a tone of slight dissatisfaction with the government, of moderate liberalism, and of enlightened citizenship. At the same time, without at all altering the elegance of his toilet, he ceased shaving his chin and allowed his beard to grow as it pleased.

Ivan Ilych settled down very pleasantly in this new town. The society there, which inclined towards opposition to the Governor, was friendly, his salary was larger, and he began to play *vint* [a form of bridge], which he found added not a little to the pleasure of life, for he had a capacity for cards, played good-humouredly, and calculated rapidly and astutely, so that he usually won.

After living there for two years he met his future wife, Praskovya Fëdorovna Mikhel, who was the most attractive, clever, and brilliant girl of the set in which he moved, and among other amusements and relaxations from his labours as examining magistrate, Ivan Ilych established light and playful relations with her.

While he had been an official on special service he had been accustomed to dance, but now as an examining magistrate it was exceptional for him to do so. If he danced now, he did it as if to show that though he served under the reformed order of things, and had reached the fifth official rank, yet when it came to dancing he could do it better than most people. So at the end of an evening he sometimes danced with Praskovya Fëdorovna, and it was chiefly during these dances that he captivated her. She fell in love with him. Ivan Ilych had at first no definite intention of marrying, but when the girl fell in love with him he said to himself: "Really, why shouldn't I marry?"

Praskovya Fëdorovna came of a good family, was not bad looking, and had some little property. Ivan Ilych might have aspired to a more brilliant match, but even this was good. He had his salary, and she, he hoped, would have an equal income. She was well connected, and was a sweet, pretty, and thoroughly correct young woman. To say that Ivan Ilych married because he fell in love with Praskovya Fëdorovna and found that she sympathized with his views of life would be as incorrect as to say that he married because his social circle approved of the match. He was swayed by both these considerations: the marriage gave him personal satisfaction, and at the same time it was considered the right thing by the most highly placed of his associates.

So Ivan Ilych got married.

The preparations for marriage and the beginning of married life, with its conjugal caresses, the new furniture, new crockery, and new linen, were very pleasant until his wife became pregnant—so that Ivan Ilych had begun to think that marriage would not impair the easy, agreeable, gay, and always decorous character of his life, approved of by society and regarded by himself as natural, but would even improve it. But from the first months of his wife's pregnancy, something new, unpleasant, depressing, and unseemly, and from which there was no way of escape, unexpectedly showed itself.

His wife, without any reason—*de gaieté de coeur* as Ivan Ilych expressed it to himself—began to disturb the pleasure and propriety of their life. She began to be jealous without any cause, expected him to devote his whole attention to her, found fault with everything, and made coarse and ill-mannered scenes.

At first Ivan Ilych hoped to escape from the unpleasantness of this state of affairs by the same easy and decorous relation to life that had served him heretofore: he tried to ignore his wife's disagreeable moods, continued to live in his usual easy and pleasant way, invited friends to his house for a game of cards, and also tried going out to his club or spending his evenings with friends. But one day his wife began upbraiding him so vigorously, using such coarse words, and continued to abuse him every time he did not fulfill her demands, so resolutely and with such evident determination not to give way till he submitted—that is, till he stayed at home and was bored just as she was—that he became alarmed. He now realized that matrimony—at any rate with Praskovya Fëdorovna—was not always conducive to the pleasures and amenities of life, but on the contrary often infringed both comfort and propriety, and that he must therefore entrench himself against such infringement. And Ivan Ilych began to seek for means of doing so. His official duties were the one thing that imposed upon Praskovya Fëdorovna, and by means of his official work and the duties attached to it he began struggling with his wife to secure his own independence.

With the birth of their child, the attempts to feed it and the various failures in doing so, and with the real and imaginary illnesses of mother and child, in which Ivan Ilych's sympathy was demanded but about which he understood nothing, the need of securing for himself an existence outside his family life became still more imperative.

As his wife grew more irritable and exacting and Ivan Ilych transferred the centre of gravity of his life more and more to his official work, so did he grow to like his work better and become more ambitious than before.

Very soon, within a year of his wedding, Ivan Ilych had realized that marriage, though it may add some comforts to life, is in fact a very intricate and difficult affair towards which in order to perform one's duty, that is, to lead a decorous life approved of by society, one must adopt a definite attitude just as towards one's official duties.

And Ivan Ilych evolved such an attitude towards married life. He only required of it those conveniences—dinner at home, housewife, and bed—which it could give him, and above all that propriety of external forms required by public opinion. For the rest he looked for light-hearted pleasure and propriety, and was very thankful when he found them, but if he met with antagonism and querulousness he at once retired into his separate fenced-off world of official duties, where he found satisfaction.

Ivan Ilych was esteemed a good official, and after three years was made Assistant Public Prosecutor. His new duties, their importance, the possibility of indicting and imprisoning anyone he chose, the publicity his speeches received, and the success he had in all these things, made his work still more attractive.

More children came. His wife became more and more querulous and ill-tempered, but the attitude Ivan Ilych had adopted towards his home life rendered him almost impervious to her grumbling.

After seven years' service in that town he was transferred to another province as Public Prosecutor. They moved, but were short of money and his wife did not like the place they moved to. Though the salary was higher the cost of living was greater, besides which two of their children died and family life became still more unpleasant for him.

Praskovya Fëdorovna blamed her husband for every inconvenience they encountered in their new home. Most of the conversations between husband and wife, especially as to the children's education, led to topics which recalled former disputes, and those disputes were apt to flare up again at any moment. There remained only those rare periods of amorousness which still came to them at times but did not last long. These were islets at which they anchored for a while and then again set out upon that ocean of veiled hostility which showed itself in their aloofness from one another. This aloofness might have grieved Ivan Ilych had he considered that it ought not to exist, but he now regarded the position as normal, and even made it the goal at which he aimed in family life. His aim was to free himself more and more from those unpleasantnesses and to give them a semblance of harmlessness and propriety. He attained this by spending less and less time with his family, and when obliged to be at home he tried to safeguard his position by the presence of outsiders. The chief thing however was that he had his official duties. The whole interest of his life now centered in the official world and that interest absorbed him. The consciousness of his power, being able to ruin anybody he wished to ruin, the importance, even the external dignity of his entry into court, or meetings with his subordinates, his success with superiors and inferiors, and above all his masterly handling of cases, of which he was conscious—all this gave him pleasure and filled his life, together with chats with his colleagues, dinners, and bridge. So that on the whole Ivan Ilych's life continued to flow as he considered it should do—pleasantly and properly.

So things continued for another seven years. His eldest daughter was already sixteen, another child had died, and only one son was left, a schoolboy and a subject of dissension. Ivan Ilych wanted to put him in the School of Law, but to spite him Praskovya Fëdorovna entered him at the High School. The daughter had been educated at home and had turned out well: the boy did not learn badly either.

III

So Ivan Ilych lived for seventeen years after his marriage. He was already a Public Prosecutor of long standing, and had declined several proposed transfers while awaiting a more desirable post, when an unanticipated and unpleasant occurrence quite upset the peaceful course of his life. He was expecting to be offered the post of presiding judge in a university town, but Happe somehow came to the front and obtained the appointment instead. Ivan Ilych became irritable, reproached Happe, and quarrelled both with him and with his immediate superiors—who became colder to him and again passed him over when other appointments were made.

This was in 1880, the hardest year of Ivan Ilych's life. It was then that it became evident on the one hand that his salary was insufficient for them to live on, and on the other that he had been forgotten, and not only this, but that what was for him the greatest and most cruel injustice appeared to others a quite ordinary occurrence. Even his father did not consider it his duty to help him. Ivan Ilych felt himself abandoned by everyone, and that they regarded his position with a salary of 3,500 rubles as quite normal and even fortunate. He alone knew that with the consciousness of the injustices done him, with his wife's incessant nagging, and with the debts he had contracted by living beyond his means, his position was far from normal.

In order to save money that summer he obtained leave of absence and went with his wife to live in the country at her brother's place.

In the country, without his work, he experienced *ennui* for the first time in his life, and not only *ennui* but intolerable depression, and he decided that it was impossible to go on living like that, and that it was necessary to take energetic measures.

Having passed a sleepless night pacing up and down the veranda, he decided to go to Petersburg and bestir himself, in order to punish those who had failed to appreciate him and to get transferred to another ministry.

Next day, despite many protests from his wife and her brother, he started for Petersburg with the sole object of obtaining a post with a salary of five thousand rubles a year. He was no longer bent on any particular department, or tendency, or kind of activity. All he now wanted was an appointment to another post with a salary of five thousand rubles, either in the administration, in the banks, with the railways, in one of the Empress Marya's Institutions, or even in the customs—but it had to carry with it a salary of five thousand rubles and be in a ministry other than that in which they had failed to appreciate him.

And this quest of Ivan Ilych's was crowned with remarkable and unexpected success. At Kursk an acquaintance of his, F. I. Ilyin, got into the first-class carriage, sat down beside Ivan Ilych, and told him of a telegram just received by the Governor of Kursk announcing that a change was about to take place in the ministry: Peter Ivanovich was to be superseded by Ivan Semënovich.

The proposed change, apart from its significance for Russia, had a special significance for Ivan Ilych, because by bringing forward a new man, Peter Petrovich, and consequently his friend Zachar Ivanovich, it was highly favourable for Ivan Ilych, since Zachar Ivanovich was a friend and colleague of his.

In Moscow this news was confirmed, and on reaching Petersburg Ivan Ilych found Zachar Ivanovich and received a definite promise of an appointment in his former department of Justice.

A week later he telegraphed to his wife: "Zachar in Miller's place. I shall receive appointment on presentation of report."

Thanks to this change of personnel, Ivan Ilych had unexpectedly obtained an appointment in his former ministry which placed him two stages above his former colleagues besides giving him five thousand rubles salary and three thousand five hundred rubles for expenses connected with his removal. All his ill humour towards his former enemies and the whole department vanished, and Ivan Ilych was completely happy.

He returned to the country more cheerful and contented than he had been for a long time. Praskovya Fëdorovna also cheered up and a truce was arranged between them. Ivan Ilych told of how he had been fêted by everybody in Petersburg, how all those who had been his enemies were put to shame and now fawned on him, how envious they were of his appointment, and how much everybody in Petersburg had liked him.

Praskovya Fëdorovna listened to all this and appeared to believe it. She did not contradict anything, but only made plans for their life in the town to which they were going. Ivan Ilych saw with delight that these plans were his plans, that he and his wife agreed, and that, after a stumble, his life was regaining its due and natural character of pleasant lightheartedness and decorum.

Ivan Ilych had come back for a short time only, for he had to take up his new duties on the 10th of September. Moreover, he needed time to settle into the new place, to move all his belongings from the province, and to buy and order many additional things; in a word, to make such arrangements as he had resolved on, which were almost exactly what Praskovya Fëdorovna too had decided on.

Now that everything had happened so fortunately, and that he and his wife were at one in their aims and moreover saw so little of one another, they got on together better than they had done since the first years of marriage. Ivan Ilych had thought of taking his family away with him at once, but the insistence of his wife's brother and her sister-in-law, who had suddenly become particularly amiable and friendly to him and his family, induced him to depart alone.

So he departed, and the cheerful state of mind induced by his success and by the harmony between his wife and himself, the one intensifying the other, did not leave him. He found a delightful house, just the thing both he and his wife had dreamt of. Spacious, lofty reception rooms in the old style, a convenient and dignified study, rooms for his wife and daughter, a study for his son—it might have been specially built for them. Ivan Ilych himself superintended the arrangements, chose the wallpapers, supplemented the furniture (preferably with antiques which he considered particularly *comme il faut*), and supervised the upholstering. Everything progressed and progressed and approached the ideal he had set himself: even when things were only half completed they exceeded his expectations. He saw what a refined and elegant character, free from vulgarity, it would all have when it was ready. On falling asleep he pictured to himself how the reception-room would look. Looking at the yet unfinished drawing-room he could see the fireplace, the screen, the what-not, the little chairs dotted here and there, the dishes and plates on the walls, and the bronzes, as they would be when everything was in place. He was pleased by the thought of how his wife and daughter, who shared his taste in this matter, would be impressed by it. They were certainly not expecting as much. He had been particularly successful in finding, and buying cheaply, antiques which gave a particularly aristocratic character to the whole place. But in his letters he intentionally understated everything in order to be able to surprise them. All this so absorbed him that his new duties—though he liked his official work—interested him less than he had expected. Sometimes he even had moments of absent-mindedness during the Court Sessions, and would consider whether he should have straight or curved cornices for his curtains. He was so interested in it all that he often did things himself, rearranging the furniture, or rehanging the curtains. Once when mounting a step-ladder to show the upholsterer, who did not understand, how he wanted the hangings draped, he made a false step and slipped, but being a strong and agile man he clung on and only knocked his side against the knob of the window frame. The bruised place was painful but the pain soon passed, and he felt particularly bright and well just then. He wrote: "I feel fifteen years younger." He thought he would have everything ready by September, but it dragged on till mid-October. But the result was charming not only in his eyes but to everyone who saw it.

In reality it was just what is usually seen in the houses of people of moderate means who want to appear rich, and therefore succeed only in resembling others like themselves: there were damasks, dark wood, plants, rugs, and dull and polished bronzes—all the things people of a certain class have in order to resemble other people of that class. His house was so like the others that it would never have been noticed, but to him it all seemed to be quite exceptional. He was very happy when he met his family at the station and brought them to the newly furnished house all lit up, where a footman in a white tie opened the door into the hall decorated with plants, and when they went on into the drawing-room, and the study uttering exclamations of delight. He conducted them everywhere, drank in their praises eagerly, and beamed with pleasure. At tea that evening, when Praskovya Fëdorovna among other things asked him about his fall, he laughed and showed them how he had gone flying and had frightened the upholsterer.

"It's a good thing I'm a bit of an athlete. Another man might have been killed, but I merely knocked myself, just here; it hurts when it's touched, but it's passing off already—it's only a bruise."

So they began living in their new home—in which, as always happens, when they got thoroughly settled in they found they were just one room short—and with the increased income, which as always was just a little (some five hundred rubles) too little, but it was all very nice.

Things went particularly well at first, before everything was finally arranged and while something had still to be done: this thing bought, that thing ordered, another thing moved, and something else adjusted. Though there were some disputes between husband and wife, they were both so well satisfied and had so much to do that it all passed off without any serious quarrels. When nothing was left to arrange it became rather dull and something seemed to be lacking, but they were then making acquaintances, forming habits, and life was growing fuller.

Ivan Ilych spent his mornings at the law courts and came home to dinner, and at first he was generally in a good humour, though he occasionally became irritable just on account of his house. (Every spot on the tablecloth or the upholstery, and every broken windowblind string, irritated him. He had devoted so much trouble to arranging it all that every disturbance of it distressed him.) But on the whole his life ran its course as he believed life should do: easily, pleasantly, and decorously.

He got up at nine, drank his coffee, read the paper, and then put on his undress uniform and went to the law courts. There the harness in which he worked had already been stretched to fit him and he donned it without a hitch: petitioners, inquiries at the chancery, the chancery itself, and the sittings public and administrative. In all this the thing was to exclude everything fresh and vital, which always disturbs the regular course of official business, and to admit only official relations with people, and then only on official grounds. A man would come, for instance, wanting some information. Ivan Ilych, as one in whose sphere the matter did not lie, would have nothing to do with him: but if the man had some business with him in his official capacity, something that could be expressed on officially stamped paper, he would do everything, positively everything he could within the limits of such relations, and in doing so would maintain the semblance of friendly human relations, that is, would observe the courtesies of life. As soon as the official relations ended, so did everything else. Ivan Ilych possessed this capacity to separate his real life from the official side of affairs and not mix the two, in the highest degree, and by long practice and natural aptitude had brought it to such a pitch that sometimes, in the manner of a virtuoso, he would even allow himself to let the human and official relations mingle. He let himself do this just because he felt that he could at any time he chose resume the strictly official attitude again and drop the human relation. And he did it all easily, pleasantly, correctly, and even artistically. In the intervals between the sessions he smoked, drank tea, chatted a little about politics, a little about general topics, a little about cards, but most of all about official appointments. Tired, but with the feelings of a virtuoso—one of the first violins who has played his part in an orchestra with precision—he would return home to find that his wife and daughter had been out paying calls, or had a visitor, and that his son had been to school, had done his homework with his tutor, and was duly learning what is taught at High Schools. Everything was as it should be. After dinner, if they had no visitors, Ivan Ilych sometimes read a book that was being much discussed at the time, and in the evening settled down to work, that is, read official papers, compared the depositions of witnesses, and noted paragraphs of the Code applying to them. This was neither dull nor amusing. It was dull when he might have been playing bridge, but if no bridge was available it was at any rate better than doing nothing or sitting with his wife. Ivan Ilych's chief pleasure was giving little dinners to which he invited men and women of good social position, and just as his drawing-room resembled all other drawing-rooms so did his enjoyable little parties resemble all other such parties.

Once they even gave a dance. Ivan Ilych enjoyed it and everything went off well, except that it led to a violent quarrel with his wife about the cakes and sweets. Praskovya Fëdorovna had made her own plans, but Ivan Ilych insisted on getting everything from an expensive confectioner and ordered too many cakes, and the quarrel occurred because some of those cakes were left over and the confectioner's bill came to forty-five rubles. It was a great and disagreeable quarrel. Praskovya Fëdorovna called him "a fool and an imbecile," and he clutched at his head and made angry allusions to divorce.

But the dance itself had been enjoyable. The best people were there, and Ivan Ilych had danced with Princess Trufonova, a sister of the distinguished founder of the Society "Bear my Burden."

The pleasures connected with his work were pleasures of ambition; his social pleasures were those of vanity; but Ivan Ilych's greatest pleasure was playing bridge. He acknowledged that whatever disagreeable incident happened in his life, the pleasure that beamed like a ray of light above everything else was to sit down to bridge with good players, not noisy partners, and of course to four-handed bridge (with five players it was annoying to have to stand out, though one pretended not to mind), to play a clever and serious game (when the cards allowed it), and then to have supper and drink a glass of wine. After a game of bridge, especially if he had won a little (to win a large sum was unpleasant), Ivan Ilych went to bed in specially good humour.

So they lived. They formed a circle of acquaintances among the best people and were visited by people of importance and by young folk. In their views as to their acquaintances, husband, wife, and daughter were entirely agreed, and tacitly and unanimously kept at arm's length and shook off the various shabby friends and relations who, with much show of affection, gushed into the drawing-room with its Japanese plates on the walls. Soon these shabby friends ceased to obtrude themselves and only the best people remained in the Golovins' set.

Young men made up to Lisa, and Petrishchev, an examining magistrate and Dmitri Ivanovich Petrishchev's son and sole heir, began to be so attentive to her that Ivan Ilych had already spoken to Praskovya Fëdorovna about it, and considered whether they should not arrange a party for them, or get up some private theatricals.

So they lived, and all went well, without change, and life flowed pleasantly.

IV

They were all in good health. It could not be called ill health if Ivan Ilych sometimes said that he had a queer taste in his mouth and felt some discomfort in his left side.

But this discomfort increased and, though not exactly painful, grew into a sense of pressure in his side accompanied by ill humour. And his irritability became worse and worse and began to mar the agreeable, easy, and correct life that had established itself in the Golovin family. Quarrels between husband and wife became more and more frequent, and soon the ease and amenity disappeared and even the decorum was barely maintained. Scenes again became frequent, and very few of those islets remained on which husband and wife could meet without an explosion. Praskovya Fëdorovna now had good reason to say that her husband's temper was trying. With characteristic exaggeration she said he had always had a dreadful temper, and that it had needed all her good nature to put up with it for twenty years. It was true that now the quarrels were started by him. His bursts of temper always came just before dinner, often just as he began to eat his soup. Sometimes he noticed that a plate or dish was chipped, or the food was not right, or his son put his elbow on the table, or his daughter's hair was not done as he liked it, and for all this he blamed Praskovya Fëdorovna. At first she retorted and said disagreeable things to him, but once or twice he fell into such a rage at the beginning of dinner that she realized it was due to some physical derangement brought on by taking food, and so she restrained herself and did not answer, but only hurried to get the dinner over. She regarded this self-restraint as highly praiseworthy. Having come to the conclusion that her husband had a dreadful temper and made her life miserable, she began to feel sorry for herself, and the more she pitied herself the more she hated her husband. She began to wish he would die; yet she did not want him to die because then his salary would cease. And this irritated her against him still more. She considered herself dreadfully unhappy just because not even his death could save her, and though she concealed her exasperation, that hidden exasperation of hers increased his irritation also.

After one scene in which Ivan Ilych had been particularly unfair and after which he had said in explanation that he certainly was irritable but that it was due to his not being well, she said that if he was ill it should be attended to, and insisted on his going to see a celebrated doctor.

He went. Everything took place as he had expected and as it always does. There was the usual waiting and the important air assumed by the doctor, with which he was so familiar (resembling that which he himself assumed in court), and the sounding and listening, and the questions which called for answers that were foregone conclusions and were evidently unnecessary, and the look of importance which implied that "if only you put yourself in our hands we will arrange everything—we know indubitably how it has to be done, always in the same way for everybody alike." It was all just as it was in the law courts. The doctor put on just the same air towards him as he himself put on towards an accused person.

The doctor said that so-and-so indicated that there was so-and-so inside the patient, but if the investigation of so-and-so did not confirm this, then he must assume that and that. If he assumed that and that, then . . . and so on. To Ivan Ilych only one question was important: was his case serious or not? But the doctor ignored that inappropriate question. From his point of view it was not the one under consideration, the real question was to decide between a floating kidney, chronic catarrh, or appendicitis. It was not a question of Ivan Ilych's life or death, but one between a floating kidney and appendicitis. And that question the doctor solved brilliantly, as it seemed to Ivan Ilych, in favour of the appendix, with the reservation that should an examination of the urine give fresh indications the matter would be reconsidered. All this was just what Ivan Ilych had himself brilliantly accomplished a thousand times in dealing with men on trial. The doctor summed up just as brilliantly, looking over his spectacles triumphantly and even gaily at the accused. From the doctor's summing up Ivan Ilych concluded that things were bad, but that for the doctor, and perhaps for everybody else, it was a matter of indifference, though for him it was bad. And this conclusion struck him painfully, arousing in him a great feeling of pity for himself and of bitterness towards the doctor's indifference to a matter of such importance.

He said nothing of this, but rose, placed the doctor's fee on the table, and remarked with a sigh: "We sick people probably often put inappropriate questions. But tell me, in general, is this complaint dangerous, or not? . . ."

The doctor looked at him sternly over his spectacles with one eye, as if to say: "Prisoner, if you will not keep to the questions put to you, I shall be obliged to have you removed from the court."

"I have already told you what I consider necessary and proper. The analysis may show something more." And the doctor bowed.

Ivan Ilych went out slowly, seated himself disconsolately in his sledge, and drove home. All the way home he was going over what the doctor had said, trying to translate those complicated, obscure, scientific phrases into plain language and find in them an answer to the question: "Is my condition bad? Is it very bad? Or is there as yet nothing much wrong?" And it seemed to him that the meaning of what the doctor had said was that it was very bad. Everything in the streets seemed depressing. The cabmen, the houses, the passers-by, and the shops, were dismal. His ache, this dull gnawing ache that never ceased for a moment, seemed to have acquired a new and more serious significance from the doctor's dubious remarks. Ivan Ilych now watched it with a new and oppressive feeling.

He reached home and began to tell his wife about it. She listened, but in the middle of his account his daughter came in with her hat on, ready to go out with her mother. She sat down reluctantly to listen to this tedious story, but could not stand it long, and her mother too did not hear him to the end.

"Well, I am very glad," she said. "Mind now to take your medicine regularly. Give me the prescription and I'll send Gerasim to the chemist's." And she went to get ready to go out.

While she was in the room Ivan Ilych had hardly taken time to breathe, but he sighed deeply when she left it.

"Well," he thought, "perhaps it isn't so bad after all."

He began taking his medicine and following the doctor's directions, which had been altered after the examination of the urine. But then it happened that there was a contradiction between the indications drawn from the examination of the urine and the symptoms that showed themselves. It turned out that what was happening differed from what the doctor had told him, and that he had either forgotten, or blundered, or hidden something from him. He could not, however, be blamed for that, and Ivan Ilych still obeyed his orders implicitly and at first derived some comfort from doing so.

From the time of his visit to the doctor, Ivan Ilych's chief occupation was the exact fulfilment of the doctor's instructions regarding hygiene and the taking of medicine, and the observation of his pain and his excretions. His chief interests came to be people's ailments and people's health. When sickness, deaths, or recoveries were mentioned in his presence, especially when the illness resembled his own, he listened with agitation which he tried to hide, asked questions, and applied what he heard to his own case.

The pain did not grow less, but Ivan Ilych made efforts to force himself to think that he was better. And he could do this so long as nothing agitated him. But as soon as he had any unpleasantness with his wife, any lack of success in his official work, or held bad cards at bridge, he was at once acutely sensible of his disease. He had formerly borne such mischances, hoping soon to adjust what was wrong, to master it and attain success, or make a grand slam. But now every mischance upset him and plunged him into despair. He would say to himself: "There now, just as I was beginning to get better and the medicine had begun to take effect, comes this accursed misfortune, or unpleasantness. . . ." And he was furious with the mishap, or with the people who were causing the unpleasantness and killing him, for he felt that this fury was killing him but could not restrain it. One would have thought that it should have been clear to him that this exasperation with circumstances and people aggravated his illness, and that he ought therefore to ignore unpleasant occurrences. But he drew the very opposite conclusion: he said that he needed peace, and he watched for everything that might disturb it and became irritable at the slightest infringement of it. His condition was rendered worse by the fact that he read medical books and consulted doctors. The progress of his disease was so gradual that he could deceive himself when comparing one day with another—the difference was so slight. But when he consulted the doctors it seemed to him that he was getting worse, and even very rapidly. Yet despite this he was continually consulting them.

That month he went to see another celebrity, who told him almost the same as the first had done but put his questions rather differently, and the interview with this celebrity only increased Ivan Ilych's doubts and fears. A friend of a friend of his, a very good doctor, diagnosed his illness again quite differently from the others, and though he predicted recovery, his questions and suppositions bewildered Ivan Ilych still more and increased his doubts. A homoeopathist diagnosed the disease in yet another way, and prescribed medicine which Ivan Ilych took secretly for a week. But after a week, not feeling any improvement and having lost confidence both in the former doctor's treatment and in this one's, he became still more despondent. One day a lady acquaintance mentioned a cure effected by a wonder-working icon. Ivan Ilych caught himself listening attentively and beginning to believe that it had occurred. This incident alarmed him. "Has my mind really weakened to such an extent?" he asked himself. "Nonsense! It's all rubbish. I mustn't give way to nervous fears but having chosen a doctor must keep strictly to his treatment. That is what I will do. Now it's all settled. I won't think about it, but will follow the treatment seriously till summer, and then we shall see. From now there must be no more of this wavering!" This was easy to say but impossible to carry out. The pain in his side oppressed him and seemed to grow worse and more incessant, while the taste in his mouth grew stranger and stranger. It seemed to him that his breath had a disgusting smell, and he was conscious of a loss of appetite and strength. There was no deceiving himself: something terrible, new, and more important than anything before in his life, was taking place within him of which he alone was aware. Those about him did not understand or would not understand it, but thought everything in the world was going on as usual. That tormented Ivan Ilych more than anything. He saw that his household, especially his wife and daughter who were in a perfect whirl of visiting, did not understand anything of it and were annoyed that he was so depressed and so exacting, as if he were to blame for it. Though they tried to disguise it he saw that he was an obstacle in their path, and that his wife had adopted a definite line in regard to his illness and kept to it regardless of anything he said or did. Her attitude was this: "You know," she would say to her friends, "Ivan Ilych can't do as other people do, and keep to the treatment prescribed for him. One day he'll take his drops and keep strictly to his diet and go to bed in good time, but the next day unless I watch him he'll suddenly forget his medicine, eat sturgeon—which is forbidden—and sit up playing cards till one o'clock in the morning."

"Oh, come, when was that?" Ivan Ilych would ask in vexation. "Only once at Peter Ivanovich's."

"And yesterday with Shebek."

"Well, even if I hadn't stayed up, this pain would have kept me awake."

"Be that as it may you'll never get well like that, but will always make us wretched."

Praskovya Fëdorovna's attitude to Ivan Ilych's illness, as she expressed it both to others and to him, was that it was his own fault and was another of the annoyances he caused her. Ivan Ilych felt that this opinion escaped her involuntarily—but that did not make it easier for him.

At the law courts too, Ivan Ilych noticed, or thought he noticed, a strange attitude towards himself. It sometimes seemed to him that people were watching him inquisitively as a man whose place might soon be vacant. Then again, his friends would suddenly begin to chaff him in a friendly way about his low spirits, as if the awful, horrible, and unheard-of thing that was going on within him, incessantly gnawing at him and irresistibly drawing him away, was a very agreeable subject for jests. Schwartz in particular irritated him by his jocularity, vivacity, and *savoir-faire,* which reminded him of what he himself had been ten years ago.

Friends came to make up a set and they sat down to cards. They dealt, bending the new cards to soften them, and he sorted the diamonds in his hand and found he had seven. His partner said "No trumps" and supported him with two diamonds. What more could be wished for? It ought to be jolly and lively. They would make a grand slam. But suddenly Ivan Ilych was conscious of that gnawing pain, that taste in his mouth, and it seemed ridiculous that in such circumstances he should be pleased to make a grand slam.

He looked at his partner Mikhail Mikhaylovich, who rapped the table with his strong hand and instead of snatching up the tricks pushed the cards courteously and indulgently towards Ivan Ilych that he might have the pleasure of gathering them up without the trouble of stretching out his hand for them. "Does he think I am too weak to stretch out my arm?" thought Ivan Ilych, and forgetting what he was doing he over-trumped his partner, missing the grand slam by three tricks. And what was most awful of all was that he saw how upset Mikhail Mikhaylovich was about it but did not himself care. And it was dreadful to realize why he did not care.

They all saw that he was suffering, and said: "We can stop if you are tired. Take a rest." Lie down? No, he was not at all tired, and he finished the rubber. All were gloomy and silent. Ivan Ilych felt that he had diffused this gloom over them and could not dispel it. They had supper and went away, and Ivan Ilych was left alone with the consciousness that his life was poisoned and was poisoning the lives of others, and that this poison did not weaken but penetrated more and more deeply into his whole being.

With this consciousness, and with physical pain besides the terror, he must go to bed, often to lie awake the greater part of the night. Next morning he had to get up again, dress, go to the law courts, speak, and write; or if he did not go out, spend at home those twenty-four hours a day each of which was a torture. And he had to live thus alone on the brink of an abyss, with no one who understood or pitied him.

V

So one month passed and then another. Just before the New Year his brother-in-law came to town and stayed at their house. Ivan Ilych was at the law courts and Praskovya Fëdorovna had gone shopping. When Ivan Ilych came home and entered his study he found his brother-in-law there—a healthy, florid man—unpacking his portmanteau himself. He raised his head on hearing Ivan Ilych's footsteps and looked up at him for a moment without a word. That stare told Ivan Ilych everything. His brother-in-law opened his mouth to utter an exclamation of surprise but checked himself, and that action confirmed it all.

"I have changed, eh?"

"Yes, there is a change."

And after that, try as he would to get his brother-in-law to return to the subjects of his looks, the latter would say nothing about it. Praskovya Fëdorovna came home and her brother went out to her. Ivan Ilych locked the door and began to examine himself in the glass, first full face, then in profile. He took up a portrait of himself taken with his wife, and compared it with what he saw in the glass. The change in him was immense. Then he bared his arms to the elbow, looked at them, drew the sleeves down again, sat down on an ottoman, and grew blacker than night.

"No, no, this won't do!" he said to himself, and jumped up, went to the table, took up some law papers, and began to read them, but could not continue. He unlocked the door and went into the reception-room. The door leading to the drawing-room was shut. He approached it on tiptoe and listened.

"No, you are exaggerating!" Praskovya Fëdorovna was saying.

"Exaggerating! Don't you see it? Why, he's a dead man! Look at his eyes—there's no light in them. But what is it that is wrong with him?"

"No one knows. Nikolaevich [that was another doctor] said something, but I don't know what. And Leshchetitsky [this was the celebrated specialist] said quite the contrary. . . ."

Ivan Ilych walked away, went to his own room, lay down, and began musing: "The kidney, a floating kidney." He recalled all the doctors had told him of how it detached itself and swayed about. And by an effort of imagination he tried to catch that kidney and arrest it and support it. So little was needed for this, it seemed to him. "No, I'll go to see Peter Ivanovich again." [That was the friend whose friend was a doctor.] He rang, ordered the carriage, and got ready to go.

"Where are you going, Jean?" asked his wife, with a specially sad and exceptionally kind look.

This exceptionally kind look irritated him. He looked morosely at her.

"I must go to see Peter Ivanovich."

He went to see Peter Ivanovich, and together they went to see his friend, the doctor. He was in, and Ivan Ilych had a long talk with him.

Reviewing the anatomical and physiological details of what in the doctor's opinion was going on inside him, he understood it all.

There was something, a small thing, in the vermiform appendix. It might all come right. Only stimulate the energy of one organ and check the activity of another, then absorption would take place and everything would come right. He got home rather late for dinner, ate his dinner, and conversed cheerfully, but could not for a long time bring himself to go back to work in his room. At last, however, he went to his study and did what was necessary, but the consciousness that he had put something aside—an important, intimate matter which he would revert to when his work was done—never left him. When he had finished his work he remembered that this intimate matter was the thought of his vermiform appendix. But he did not give himself up to it, and went to the drawing-room for tea. There were callers there, including the examining magistrate who was a desirable match for his daughter, and they were conversing, playing the piano, and singing. Ivan Ilych, as Praskovya Fëdorovna remarked, spent that evening more cheerfully than usual, but he never for a moment forgot that he had postponed the important matter of the appendix. At eleven o'clock he said good-night and went to his bedroom. Since his illness he had slept alone in a small room next to his study. He undressed and took up a novel by Zola, but instead of reading it he fell into thought, and in his imagination that desired improvement in the vermiform appendix occurred. There was the absorption and evacuation and the re-establishment of normal activity. "Yes, that's it!" he said to himself. "One need only assist nature, that's all." He remembered his medicine, rose, took it, and lay down on his back watching for the beneficent action of the medicine and for it to lessen the pain. "I need only take it regularly and avoid all injurious influences. I am already feeling better, much better." He began touching his side: it was not painful to the touch. "There, I really don't feel it. It's much better already." He put out the light and turned on his side. . . . "The appendix is getting better, absorption is occurring." Suddenly he felt the old, familiar, dull, gnawing pain, stubborn and serious. There was the same familiar loathsome taste in his mouth. His heart sank and he felt dazed. "My God! My God!" he muttered. "Again, again! and it will never cease." And suddenly the matter presented itself in a quite different aspect. "Vermiform appendix! Kidney!" he said to himself. "It's not a question of appendix or kidney, but of life and . . . death. Yes, life was there and now it is going, going and I cannot stop it. Yes. Why deceive myself? Isn't it obvious to everyone but me that I'm dying, and that it's only a question of weeks, days . . . it may happen this moment. There was light and now there is darkness. I was here and now I'm going there! Where?" A chill came over him, his breathing ceased, and he felt only the throbbing of his heart.

"When I am not, what will there be? There will be nothing. Then where shall I be when I am no more? Can this be dying? No, I don't want to!" He jumped up and tried to light the candle, felt for it with trembling hands, dropped candle and candlestick on the floor, and fell back on his pillow.

"What's the use? It makes no difference," he said to himself, staring with wide-open eyes into the darkness. "Death. Yes, death. And none of them know or wish to know it, and they have no pity for me. Now they are playing." (He heard through the door the distant sound of a song and its accompaniment.) "It's all the same to them, but they will die too! Fools! I first, and they later, but it will be the same for them. And now they are merry . . . the beasts!"

Anger choked him and he was agonizingly, unbearably miserable. "It is impossible that all men have been doomed to suffer this awful horror!" He raised himself.

"Something must be wrong. I must calm myself—must think it all over from the beginning." And he again began thinking. "Yes, the beginning of my illness: I knocked my side, but I was still quite well that day and the next. It hurt a little, then rather more. I saw the doctors, then followed despondency and anguish, more doctors, and I drew nearer to the abyss. My strength grew less and I kept coming nearer and nearer, and now I have wasted away and there is no light in my eyes. I think of the appendix—but this is death! I think of mending the appendix, and all the while here is death! Can it really be death?" Again terror seized him and he gasped for breath. He leant down and began feeling for the matches, pressing with his elbow on the stand beside the bed. It was in his way and hurt him, he grew furious with it, pressed on it still harder, and upset it. Breathless and in despair he fell on his back, expecting death to come immediately.

Meanwhile the visitors were leaving. Praskovya Fëdorovna was seeing them off. She heard something fall and came in.

"What has happened?"

"Nothing. I knocked it over accidentally."

She went out and returned with a candle. He lay there panting heavily, like a man who has run a thousand yards, and stared upwards at her with a fixed look.

"What is it, Jean?"

"No . . . o . . . thing. I upset it." ("Why speak of it? She won't understand," he thought.)

And in truth she did not understand. She picked up the stand, lit his candle, and hurried away to see another visitor off. When she came back he still lay on his back, looking upwards.

"What is it? Do you feel worse?"

"Yes."

She shook her head and sat down.

"Do you know, Jean, I think we must ask Leshchetitsky to come and see you here."

This meant calling in the famous specialist, regardless of expense. He smiled malignantly and said "No." She remained a little longer and then went up to him and kissed his forehead.

While she was kissing him he hated her from the bottom of his soul and with difficulty refrained from pushing her away.

"Good-night. Please God you'll sleep."

"Yes."

VI

Ivan Ilych saw that he was dying, and he was in continual despair.

In the depth of his heart he knew he was dying, but not only was he not accustomed to the thought, he simply did not and could not grasp it.

The syllogism he had learnt from Kiezewetter's Logic: "Caius is a man, men are mortal, therefore Caius is mortal," had always seemed to him correct as applied to Caius, but certainly not as applied to himself. That Caius—man in the abstract—was mortal, was perfectly correct, but he was not Caius, not an abstract man, but a creature quite, quite separate from all others. He had been little Vanya, with a mamma and a papa, with Mitya and Volodya, with the toys, a coachman and a nurse, afterwards with Katenka and with all the joys, griefs, and delights of childhood, boyhood, and youth. What did Caius know of the smell of that striped leather ball Vanya had been so fond of? Had Caius kissed his mother's hand like that, and did the silk of her dress rustle so for Caius? Had he rioted like that at school when the pastry was bad? Had Caius been in love like that? Could Caius preside at a session as he did? "Caius really was mortal, and it was right for him to die; but for me, little Vanya, Ivan Ilych, with all my thoughts and emotions, it's altogether a different matter. It cannot be that I ought to die. That would be too terrible."

Such was his feeling.

"If I had to die like Caius I should have known it was so. An inner voice would have told me so, but there was nothing of the sort in me and I and all my friends felt that our case was quite different from that of Caius. And now here it is!" he said to himself. "It can't be. It's impossible! But here it is. How is this? How is one to understand it?"

He could not understand it, and tried to drive this false, incorrect, morbid thought away and to replace it by other proper and healthy thoughts. But that thought, and not the thought only but the reality itself, seemed to come and confront him.

And to replace that thought he called up a succession of others, hoping to find in them some support. He tried to get back into the former current of thoughts that had once screened the thought of death from him. But strange to say, all that had formerly shut off, hidden, and destroyed his consciousness of death, no longer had that effect. Ivan Ilych now spent most of his time in attempting to re-establish that old current. He would say to himself: "I will take up my duties again—after all I used to live by them." And banishing all doubts he would go to the law courts, enter into conversation with his colleagues, and sit carelessly as was his wont, scanning the crowd with a thoughtful look and leaning both his emaciated arms on the arms of his oak chair; bending over as usual to a colleague and drawing his papers nearer he would interchange whispers with him, and then suddenly raising his eyes and sitting erect would pronounce certain words and open the proceedings. But suddenly in the midst of those proceedings the pain in his side, regardless of the stage the proceedings had reached, would begin its own gnawing work. Ivan Ilych would turn his attention to it and try to drive the thought of it away, but without success. *It* would come and stand before him and look at him, and he would be petrified and the light would die out of his eyes, and he would again begin asking himself whether *It* alone was true. And his colleagues and subordinates would see with surprise and distress that he, the brilliant and subtle judge, was becoming confused and making mistakes. He would shake himself, try to pull himself together, manage somehow to bring the sitting to a close, and return home with the sorrowful consciousness that his judicial labours could not as formerly hide from him what he wanted them to hide, and could not deliver him from *It.* And what was worst of all was that *It* drew his attention to itself not in order to make him take some action but only that he should look at *It,* look it straight in the face: look at it and, without doing anything, suffer inexpressibly.

And to save himself from this condition Ivan Ilych looked for consolations—new screens—and new screens were found and for a while seemed to save him, but then they immediately fell to pieces or rather became transparent, as if *It* penetrated them and nothing could veil *It.*

In these latter days he would go into the drawing-room he had arranged—that drawing-room where he had fallen and for the sake of which (how bitterly ridiculous it seemed) he had sacrificed his life—for he knew that his illness originated with that knock. He would enter and see that something had scratched the polished table. He would look for the cause of this and find that it was the bronze ornamentation of an album, that had got bent. He would take up the expensive album which he had lovingly arranged, and feel vexed with his daughter and her friends for their untidiness—for the album was torn here and there and some of the photographs turned upside down. He would put it carefully in order and bend the ornamentation back into position. Then it would occur to him to place all those things in another corner of the room, near the plants. He could call the footman, but his daughter or wife would come to help him. They would not agree, and his wife would contradict him, and he would dispute and grow angry. But that was all right, for then he did not think about *It.* *It* was invisible.

But then, when he was moving something himself, his wife would say: "Let the servants do it. You will hurt yourself again." And suddenly *It* would flash through the screen and he would see it. It was just a flash, and he hoped it would disappear, but he would involuntarily pay attention to his side. "It sits there as before, gnawing just the same!" And he could no longer forget *It,* but could distinctly see it looking at him from behind the flowers. "What is it all for?"

"It really is so! I lost my life over that curtain as I might have done when storming a fort. Is that possible? How terrible and how stupid. It can't be true! It can't, but it is."

He would go to his study, lie down, and again be alone with *It:* face to face with *It.* And nothing could be done with *It* except to look at it and shudder.

VII

How it happened it is impossible to say because it came about step by step, unnoticed, but in the third month of Ivan Ilych's illness, his wife, his daughter, his son, his acquaintances, the doctors, the servants, and above all he himself, were aware that the whole interest he had for other people was whether he would soon vacate his place, and at last release the living from the discomfort caused by his presence and be himself released from his sufferings.

He slept less and less. He was given opium and hypodermic injections of morphine, but this did not relieve him. The dull depression he experienced in a somnolent condition at first gave him a little relief, but only as something new, afterwards it became as distressing as the pain itself or even more so.

Special foods were prepared for him by the doctors' orders, but all those foods became increasingly distasteful and disgusting to him.

For his excretions also special arrangements had to be made, and this was a torment to him every time—a torment from the uncleanliness, the unseemliness, and the smell, and from knowing that another person had to take part in it.

But just through this most unpleasant matter, Ivan Ilych obtained comfort. Gerasim, the butler's young assistant, always came in to carry the things out. Gerasim was a clean, fresh peasant lad, grown stout on town food and always cheerful and bright. At first the sight of him, in his clean Russian peasant costume, engaged on that disgusting task embarrassed Ivan Ilych.

Once when he got up from the commode too weak to draw up his trousers, he dropped into a soft armchair and looked with horror at his bare, enfeebled thighs with the muscles so sharply marked on them.

Gerasim with a firm light tread, his heavy boots emitting a pleasant smell of tar and fresh winter air, came in wearing a clean Hessian apron, the sleeves of his print shirt tucked up over his strong, bare young arms; and refraining from looking at his sick master out of consideration for his feelings, and restraining the joy of life that beamed from his face, he went up to the commode.

"Gerasim!" said Ivan Ilych in a weak voice.

Gerasim started, evidently afraid he might have committed some blunder, and with a rapid movement turned his fresh, kind, simple young face which just showed the first downy signs of a beard.

"Yes, sir?"

"That must be very unpleasant for you. You must forgive me. I am helpless."

"Oh, why, sir," and Gerasim's eyes beamed and he showed his glistening white teeth, "what's a little trouble? It's a case of illness with you sir."

And his deft strong hands did their accustomed task, and he went out of the room stepping lightly. Five minutes later he as lightly returned.

Ivan Ilych was still sitting in the same position in the armchair.

"Gerasim," he said when the latter had replaced the freshly-washed utensil. "Please come here and help me." Gerasim went up to him. "Lift me up. It is hard for me to get up, and I have sent Dmitri away."

Gerasim went up to him, grasped his master with his strong arms deftly but gently, in the same way that he stepped—lifted him, supported him with one hand, and with the other drew up his trousers and would have set him down again, but Ivan Ilych asked to be led to the sofa. Gerasim, without an effort and without apparent pressure, led him, almost lifting him, to the sofa and placed him on it.

"Thank you. How easily and well you do it all!"

Gerasim smiled again and turned to leave the room. But Ivan Ilych felt his presence such a comfort that he did not want to let him go.

"One thing more, please move up that chair. No, the other one—under my feet. It is easier for me when my feet are raised."

Gerasim brought the chair, set it down gently in place, and raised Ivan Ilych's legs on to it. It seemed to Ivan Ilych that he felt better while Gerasim was holding up his legs.

"It's better when my legs are higher," he said. "Place that cushion under them."

Gerasim did so. He again lifted the legs and placed them, and again Ivan Ilych felt better while Gerasim held his legs. When he set them down Ivan Ilych fancied he felt worse.

"Gerasim," he said. "Are you busy now?"

"Not at all, sir," said Gerasim, who had learnt from the townsfolk how to speak to gentlefolk.

"What have you still to do?"

"What have I to do? I've done everything except chopping the logs for tomorrow."

"Then hold my legs up a bit higher, can you?"

"Of course I can. Why not?" And Gerasim raised his master's legs higher and Ivan Ilych thought that in that position he did not feel any pain at all.

"And how about the logs?"

"Don't trouble about that, sir. There's plenty of time."

Ivan Ilych told Gerasim to sit down and hold his leg, and began to talk to him. And strange to say it seemed to him that he felt better while Gerasim held his legs up.

After that Ivan Ilych would sometimes call Gerasim and get him to hold his legs on his shoulders, and he liked talking to him. Gerasim did it all easily, willingly, simply, and with a good nature that touched Ivan Ilych.

Health, strength, and vitality in other people were offensive to him, but Gerasim's strength and vitality did not mortify but soothed him.

What tormented Ivan Ilych most was the deception, the lie, which for some reason they all accepted, that he was not dying but was simply ill, and that he only need keep quiet and undergo a treatment and then something very good would result. He however knew that do what they would nothing would come of it, only still more agonizing suffering and death. This deception tortured him—their not wishing to admit what they all knew and what he knew, but wanting to lie to him concerning his terrible condition, and wishing and forcing him to participate in that lie. Those lies—lies enacted over him on the eve of his death and destined to degrade this awful, solemn act to the level of their visitings, their curtains, their sturgeon for dinner—were a terrible agony for Ivan Ilych. And strangely enough, many times when they were going through their antics over him he had been within a hairbreadth of calling out to them: "Stop lying! You know and I know that I am dying. Then at least stop lying about it!" But he had never had the spirit to do it. The awful, terrible act of his dying was, he could see, reduced by those about him to the level of a casual, unpleasant, and almost indecorous incident (as if someone entered a drawing-room diffusing an unpleasant odour) and this was done by that very decorum which he had served all his life long. He saw that no one felt for him, because no one even wished to grasp his position. Only Gerasim recognized it and pitied him. And so Ivan Ilych felt at ease only with him. He felt comforted when Gerasim supported his legs (sometimes all night long) and refused to go to bed, saying: "Don't you worry, Ivan Ilych. I'll get sleep enough later on," or when he suddenly became familiar and exclaimed: "If you weren't sick it would be another matter, but as it is, why should I grudge a little trouble?" Gerasim alone did not lie; everything showed that he alone understood the facts of the case and did not consider it necessary to disguise them, but simply felt sorry for his emaciated and enfeebled master. Once when Ivan Ilych was sending him away he even said straight out: "We shall all of us die, so why should I grudge a little trouble?"—expressing the fact that he did not think his work burdensome, because he was doing it for a dying man and hoped someone would do the same for him when his time came.

Apart from this lying, or because of it, what most tormented Ivan Ilych was that no one pitied him as he wished to be pitied. At certain moments after prolonged suffering he wished most of all (though he would have been ashamed to confess it) for someone to pity him as a sick child is pitied. He longed to be petted and comforted. He knew he was an important functionary, that he had a beard turning grey, and that therefore what he longed for was impossible, but still he longed for it. And in Gerasim's attitude towards him there was something akin to what he wished for, and so that attitude comforted him. Ivan Ilych wanted to weep, wanted to be petted and cried over, and then his colleague Shebek would come, and instead of weeping and being petted, Ivan Ilych would assume a serious, severe, and profound air, and by force of habit would express his opinion on a decision of the Court of Cassation and would stubbornly insist on that view. This falsity around him and within him did more than anything else to poison his last days.

VIII

It was morning. He knew it was morning because Gerasim had gone, and Peter the footman had come and put out the candles, drawn back one of the curtains, and begun quietly to tidy up. Whether it was morning or evening, Friday or Sunday, made no difference, it was all just the same: the gnawing, unmitigated, agonizing pain, never ceasing for an instant, the consciousness of life inexorably waning but not yet extinguished, the approach of that ever dreaded and hateful Death which was the only reality, and always the same falsity. What were days, weeks, hours, in such a case?

"Will you have some tea, sir?

"He wants things to be regular, and wishes the gentlefolk to drink tea in the morning," thought Ivan Ilych, and only said "No."

"Wouldn't you like to move onto the sofa, sir?"

"He wants to tidy up the room, and I'm in the way. I am uncleanliness and disorder," he thought, and said only:

"No, leave me alone."

The man went on bustling about. Ivan Ilych stretched out his hand. Peter came up, ready to help.

"What is it, sir?"

"My watch."

Peter took the watch which was close at hand and gave it to his master.

"Half-past eight. Are they up?"

"No, sir, except Vladimir Ivanovich" (the son) "who has gone to school. Praskovya Fëdorovna ordered me to wake her if you asked for her. Shall I do so?"

"No, there's no need to." "Perhaps I'd better have some tea," he thought, and added aloud: "Yes, bring me some tea."

Peter went to the door, but Ivan Ilych dreaded being left alone. "How can I keep him here? Oh yes, my medicine." "Peter, give me my medicine." "Why not? Perhaps it may still do me some good." He took a spoonful and swallowed it. "No, it won't help. It's all tomfoolery, all deception," he decided as soon as he became aware of the familar, sickly, hopeless taste. "No, I can't believe in it any longer. But the pain, why this pain? If it would only cease just for a moment!" And he moaned. Peter turned towards him. "It's all right. Go and fetch me some tea."

Peter went out. Left alone Ivan Ilych groaned not so much with pain, terrible though that was, as from mental anguish. Always and forever the same, always these endless days and nights. If only it would come quicker! If only *what* would come quicker? Death, darkness? . . . No, no! Anything rather than death!

When Peter returned with the tea on a tray, Ivan Ilych stared at him for a time in perplexity, not realizing who and what he was. Peter was disconcerted by the look and his embarrassment brought Ivan Ilych to himself.

"Oh, tea! All right, put it down. Only help me to wash and put on a clean shirt."

And Ivan Ilych began to wash. With pauses for rest, he washed his hands and then his face, cleaned his teeth, brushed his hair, and looked in the glass. He was terrified by what he saw, especially by the limp way in which his hair clung to his pallid forehead.

While his shirt was being changed he knew that he would be still more frightened at the sight of his body, so he avoided looking at it. Finally he was ready. He drew on a dressing-gown, wrapped himself in a plaid, and sat down in the armchair to take his tea. For a moment he felt refreshed, but soon as he begin to drink the tea he was again aware of the same taste, and the pain also returned. He finished it with an effort, and then lay down stretching out his legs, and dismissed Peter.

Always the same. Now a spark of hope flashed up, then a sea of despair rages, and always pain; always pain, always despair, and always the same. When alone he had a dreadful and distressing desire to call someone, but he knew beforehand that with others present it would be still worse. "Another dose of morphine—to lose consciousness. I will tell him, the doctor, that he must think of something else. It's impossible, impossible, to go on like this."

An hour and another pass like that. But now there is a ring at the door bell. Perhaps it's the doctor? It is. He comes in fresh, hearty, plump, and cheerful, with that look on his face that seems to say: "There now, you're in a panic about something, but we'll arrange it all for you directly!" The doctor knows this expression is out of place here, but he has put it on once for all and can't take it off—like a man who has put on a frock-coat in the morning to pay a round of calls.

The doctor rubs his hands vigorously and reassuringly.

"Brr! How cold it is! There's such a sharp frost; just let me warm myself!" he says, as if it were only a matter of waitng till he was warm, and then he would put everything right.

"Well now, how are you!"

Ivan Ilych feels that the doctor would like to say: "Well, how are our affairs?" but that even he feels that this would not do, and says instead: "What sort of a night have you had?"

Ivan Ilych looks at him as much as to say: "Are you really never ashamed of lying?" But the doctor does not wish to understand this question, and Ivan Ilych says: "Just as terrible as ever. The pain never leaves me and never subsides. If only something . . ."

"Yes, you sick people are always like that. . . . There, now I think I am warm enough. Even Praskovya Fëdorovna, who is so particular, could find no fault with my temperature. Well, now I can say good-morning," and the doctor presses his patient's hand.

Then, dropping his former playfulness, he begins with a most serious face to examine the patient, feeling his pulse and taking his temperature, and then begins the sounding and auscultation.

Ivan Ilych knows quite well and definitely that all this is nonsense and pure deception, but when the doctor, getting down on his knee, leans over him, putting his ear first higher then lower, and performs various gymnastic movements over him with a significant expression on his face, Ivan Ilych submits to it all as he used to submit to the speeches of the lawyers, though he knew very well that they were all lying and why they were lying.

The doctor, kneeling on the sofa, is still sounding him when Praskovya Fëdorovna's silk dress rustles at the door and she is heard scolding Peter for not having let her know of the doctor's arrival.

She comes in, kisses her husband, and at once proceeds to prove that she has been up a long time already, and only owing to a misunderstanding failed to be there when the doctor arrived.

Ivan Ilych looks at her, scans her all over, sets against her the whiteness and plumpness and cleanness of her hands and neck, the gloss of her hair, and the sparkle of her vivacious eyes. He hates her with his whole soul. And the thrill of hatred he feels for her makes him suffer from her touch.

Her attitude towards him and his disease is still the same. Just as the doctor had adopted a certain relation to his patient which he could not abandon, so had she formed one towards him—that he was not doing something he ought to do and was himself to blame, and that she reproached him lovingly for this—and she could not now change that attitude.

"You see he doesn't listen to me and doesn't take his medicine at the proper time. And above all he lies in a position that is no doubt bad for him—with his legs up."

She described how he made Gerasim hold his legs up.

The doctor smiled with a contemptuous affability that said: "What's to be done? These sick people do have foolish fancies of that kind, but we must forgive them."

When the examination was over the doctor looked at his watch, and then Praskovya Fëdorovna announced to Ivan Ilych that it was of course as he pleased, but she had sent today for a celebrated specialist who would examine him and have a consultation with Michael Danilovich (their regular doctor).

"Please don't raise any objections. I am doing this for my own sake," she said ironically, letting it be felt that she was doing it all for his sake and only said this to leave him no right to refuse. He remained silent, knitting his brows. He felt that he was so surrounded and involved in a mesh of falsity that it was hard to unravel anything.

Everything she did for him was entirely for her own sake, and she told him she was doing for herself what she actually was doing for herself, as if that was so incredible that he must understand the opposite.

At half-past eleven the celebrated specialist arrived. Again the sounding began and the significant conversations in his presence and in another room, about the kidneys and the appendix, and the questions and answers, with such an air of importance that again, instead of the real question of life and death which now alone confronted him, the question arose of the kidney and appendix which were not behaving as they ought to and would now be attacked by Michael Danilovich and the specialist and forced to amend their ways.

The celebrated specialist took leave of him with a serious though not hopeless look, and in reply to the timid question Ivan Ilych, with eyes glistening with fear and hope, put to him as to whether there was a chance of recovery, said that he could not vouch for it but there was a possibility. The look of hope with which Ivan Ilych watched the doctor out was so pathetic that Praskovya Fëdorovna, seeing it, even wept as she left the room to hand the doctor his fee.

The gleam of hope kindled by the doctor's encouragement did not last long. The same room, the same pictures, curtains, wallpaper, medicine bottles, were all there, and the same aching suffering body, and Ivan Ilych began to moan. They gave him a subcutaneous injection and he sank into oblivion.

It was twilight when he came to. They brought him his dinner and he swallowed some beef tea with difficulty, and then everything was the same again and night was coming on.

After dinner, at seven o'clock, Praskovya Fëdorovna came into the room in evening dress, her full bosom pushed up by her corset, and with traces of powder on her face. She had reminded him in the morning that they were going to the theatre. Sarah Bernhardt was visiting the town and they had a box, which he had insisted on their taking. Now he had forgotten about it and her toilet offended him, but he concealed his vexation when he remembered that he had himself insisted on their securing a box and going because it would be an instructive and aesthetic pleasure for the children.

Praskovya Fëdorovna came in, self-satisfied but yet with a rather guilty air. She sat down and asked how he was, but, as he saw, only for the sake of asking and not in order to learn about it, knowing that there was nothing to learn—and then went on to what she really wanted to say: that she would not on any account have gone but that the box had been taken and Helen and their daughter were going, as well as Petrishchev (the examining magistrate, their daughter's fiancé), and that it was out of the question to let them go alone; but that she would have much preferred to sit with him for a while; and he must be sure to follow the doctor's orders while she was away.

"Oh, and Fëdor Petrovich" (the fiancé) "would like to come in. May he? And Lisa?"

"All right."

Their daughter came in in full evening dress, her fresh young flesh exposed (making a show of that very flesh which in his own case caused so much suffering), strong, healthy, evidently in love, and impatient with illness, suffering, and death, because they interfered with her happiness.

Fëdor Petrovich came in too, in evening dress, his hair curled *à la Capoul,* a tight stiff collar round his long sinewy neck, an enormous white shirt-front, and narrow black trousers tightly stretched over his strong thighs. He had one white glove tightly drawn on, and was holding his opera hat in his hand.

Following him the schoolboy crept in unnoticed, in a new uniform, poor little fellow, and wearing gloves. Terribly dark shadows showed under his eyes, the meaning of which Ivan Ilych knew well.

His son had always seemed pathetic to him, and now it was dreadful to see the boy's frightened look of pity. It seemed to Ivan Ilych that Vasya was the only one besides Gerasim who understood and pitied him.

They all sat down and again asked how he was. A silence followed. Lisa asked her mother about the opera-glasses, and there was an altercation between mother and daughter as to who had taken them and where they had been put. This occasioned some unpleasantness.

Fëdor Petrovich inquired of Ivan Ilych whether he had ever seen Sarah Bernhardt. Ivan Ilych did not at first catch the question, but then replied: "No, have you seen her before?"

"Yes, in *Adrienne Lecouvreur.*"

Praskovya Fëdorovna mention some rôles in which Sarah Bernhardt was particularly good. Her daughter disagreed. Conversation sprang up as to the elegance and realism of her acting—the sort of conversation that is always repeated and is always the same.

In the midst of the conversation Fëdor Petrovich glanced at Ivan Ilych and became silent. The others also looked at him and grew silent. Ivan Ilych was staring with glittering eyes straight before him, evidently indignant with them. This had to be rectified, but it was impossible to do so. The silence had to be broken, but for a time no one dared to break it and they all became afraid that the conventional deception would suddenly become obvious and the truth become plain to all. Lisa was the first to pluck up courage and break that silence, but by trying to hide what everybody was feeling, she betrayed it.

"Well, if we are going it's time to start," she said, looking at her watch, a present from her father, and with a faint and significant smile at Fëdor Petrovich relating to something known only to them. She got up with a rustle of her dress.

They all rose, said good-night, and went away.

When they had gone it seemed to Ivan Ilych that he felt better; the falsity had gone with them. But the pain remained—that same pain and that same fear that made everything monotonously alike, nothing harder and nothing easier. Everything was worse.

Again minute followed minute and hour followed hour. Everything remained the same and there was no cessation. And the inevitable end of it all became more and more terrible.

"Yes, send Gerasim here," he replied to a question Peter asked.

IX

His wife returned late at night. She came in on tiptoe, but he heard her, opened his eyes, and made haste to close them again. She wished to send Gerasim away and to sit with him herself, but he opened his eyes and said: "No, go away."

"Are you in great pain?"

"Always the same."

"Take some opium."

He agreed and took some. She went away.

Till about three in the morning he was in a state of stupefied misery. It seemed to him that he and his pain were being thrust into a narrow, deep black sack, but though they were pushed further and further in they could not be pushed to the bottom. And this, terrible enough in itself, was accompanied by suffering. He was frightened yet wanted to fall through the sack, he struggled but yet co-operated. And suddenly he broke through, fell, and regained consciousness. Gerasim was sitting at the foot of the bed dozing quietly and patiently, while he himself lay with his emaciated stockinged legs resting on Gerasim's shoulders; the same shaded candle was there and the same unceasing pain.

"Go away, Gerasim," he whispered.

"It's all right, sir. I'll stay a while."

"No. Go away."

He removed his legs from Gerasim's shoulders, turned sideways onto his arm, and felt sorry for himself. He only waited till Gerasim had gone into the next room and then restrained himself no longer but wept like a child. He wept on account of his helplessness, his terrible loneliness, the cruelty of man, the cruelty of God, and the absence of God.

"Why hast Thou done all this? Why hast Thou brought me here? Why, why dost Thou torment me so terribly?"

He did not expect an answer and yet wept because there was no answer and could be none. The pain again grew more acute, but he did not stir and did not call. He said to himself: "Go on! Strike me! But what is it for? What have I done to Thee? What is it for?"

Then he grew quiet and not only ceased weeping but even held his breath and became all attention. It was as though he were listening not to an audible voice but to the voice of his soul, to the current of thoughts arising within him.

"What is it you want?" was the first clear conception capable of expression in words, that he heard.

"What do you want? What do you want?" he repeated to himself.

"What do I want? To live and not to suffer," he answered.

And again he listened with such concentrated attention that even his pain did not distract him.

"To live? How?" asked his inner voice.

"Why, to live as I used to—well and pleasantly."

"As you lived before, well and pleasantly?" the voice repeated.

And in imagination he began to recall the best moments of his pleasant life. But strange to say none of those best moments of his pleasant life now seemed at all what they had then seemed—none of them except the first recollections of childhood. There, in childhood, there had been something really pleasant with which it would be possible to live if it could return. But the child who had experienced that happiness existed no longer, it was like a reminiscence of somebody else.

As soon as the period began which had produced the present Ivan Ilych, all that had then seemed joys now melted before his sight and turned into something trivial and often nasty.

And the further he departed from childhood and the nearer he came to the present the more worthless and doubtful were the joys. This began with the School of Law. A little that was really good was still found there—there was lightheartedness, friendship, and hope. But in the upper classes there had already been fewer of such good moments. Then during the first years of his official career, when he was in the service of the Governor, some pleasant moments again occurred; they were the memories of love for a woman. Then all became confused and there was still less of what was good; later on again there was still less that was good, and the further he went the less there was. His marriage, a mere accident, then the disenchantment that followed it, his wife's bad breath and the sensuality and hypocrisy: then that deadly official life and those preoccupations about money, a year of it, and two, and ten, and twenty, and always the same thing. And the longer it lasted the more deadly it became. "It is as if I had been going downhill while I imagined I was going up. And that is really what it was. I was going up in public opinion, but to the same extent life was ebbing away from me. And now it is all done and there is only death."

"Then what does it mean? Why? It can't be that life is so senseless and horrible. But if it really has been so horrible and senseless, why must I die and die in agony? There is something wrong!"

"Maybe I did not live as I ought to have done," it suddenly occurred to him. "But how could that be, when I did everything properly?" he replied, and immediately dismissed from his mind this, the sole solution of all the riddles of life and death, as something quite impossible.

"Then what do you want now? To live? Live how? Live as you lived in the law courts when the usher proclaimed 'The judge is coming!' The judge is coming, the judge!" he repeated to himself. "Here he is, the judge. But I am not guilty!" he exclaimed angrily. "What is it for?" And he ceased crying, but turning his face to the wall continued to ponder on the same question: Why, and for what purpose, is there all this horror? But however much he pondered he found no answer. And whenever the thought occurred to him, as it often did, that it all resulted from his not having lived as he ought to have done, he at once recalled the correctness of his whole life and dismissed so strange an idea.

X

Another fortnight passed. Ivan Ilych now no longer left his sofa. He would not lie in bed but lay on the sofa, facing the wall nearly all the time. He suffered ever the same unceasing agonies and in his loneliness pondered always on the same insoluble question: "What is this? Can it be that it is Death?" And the inner voice answered: "Yes, it is Death."

"Why these sufferings?" And the voice answered, "For no reason—they just are so." Beyond and besides this there was nothing.

From the very beginning of his illness, ever since he had first been to see the doctor, Ivan Ilych's life had been divided between two contrary and alternating moods: now it was despair and the expectation of this uncomprehended and terrible death, and now hope and an intently interested observation of the functioning of his organs. Now before his eyes there was only a kidney or an intestine that temporarily evaded its duty, and now only that incomprehensible and dreadful death from which it was impossible to escape.

These two states of mind had alternated from the very beginning of his illness, but the further it progressed the more doubtful and fantastic became the conception of the kidney, and the more real the sense of impending death.

He had but to call to mind what he had been three months before and what he was now, to call to mind with what regularity he had been going downhill, for every possibility of hope to be shattered.

Latterly during that loneliness in which he found himself as he lay facing the back of the sofa, a loneliness in the midst of a populous town and surrounded by numerous acquaintances and relations but that yet could not have been more complete anywhere—either at the bottom of the sea or under the earth—during that terrible loneliness Ivan Ilych had lived only in memories of the past. Pictures of his past rose before him one after another. They always began with what was nearest in time and then went back to what was most remote—to his childhood—and rested there. If he thought of the stewed prunes that had been offered him that day, his mind went back to the raw shrivelled French plums of his childhood, their peculiar flavour and the flow of saliva when he sucked their stones, and along with the memory of that taste came a whole series of memories of those days: his nurse, his brother, and their toys. "No, I mustn't think of that. . . . It is too painful," Ivan Ilych said to himself, and brought himself back to the present—to the button on the back of the sofa and the creases in its morocco. "Morocco is expensive, but it does not wear well: there had been a quarrel about it. It was a different kind of quarrel and a different kind of morocco that time when we tore father's portfolio and were punished, and mamma brought us some tarts. . . ." And again his thoughts dwelt on his childhood, and again it was painful and he tried to banish them and fix his mind on something else.

Then again together with that chain of memories another series passed through his mind—of how his illness had progressed and grown worse. There also the further back he looked the more life there had been. There had been more of what was good in life and more of life itself. The two merged together. "Just as the pain went on getting worse and worse, so my life grew worse and worse," he thought. "There is one bright spot there at the back, at the beginning of life, and afterwards all becomes blacker and blacker and proceeds more and more rapidly—in inverse ratio to the square of the distance from death," thought Ivan Ilych. And the example of a stone falling downwards with increasing velocity entered his mind. Life, a series of increasing sufferings, flies further and further towards its end—the most terrible suffering. "I am flying. . . ." He shuddered, shifted himself, and tried to resist, but was already aware that resistance was impossible, and again, with eyes weary of gazing but unable to cease seeing what was before them, he stared at the back of the sofa and waited—awaiting that dreadful fall and shock and destruction.

"Resistance is impossible!" he said to himself. "If I could only understand what it is all for! But that too is impossible. An explanation would be possible if it could be said that I have not lived as I ought to. But it is impossible to say that," and he remembered all the legality, correctitude, and propriety of his life. "That at any rate can certainly not be admitted," he thought, and his lips smiled ironically as if someone could see that smile and be taken in by it. "There is no explanation! Agony, death . . . What for?"

XI

Another two weeks went by in this way and during that fortnight an event occurred that Ivan Ilych and his wife had desired. Petrishchev formally proposed. It happened in the evening. The next day Praskovya Fëdorovna came into her husband's room considering how best to inform him of it, but that very night there had been a fresh change for the worse in his condition. She found him still lying on the sofa but in a different position. He lay on his back, groaning and staring fixedly straight in front of him.

She began to remind him of his medicines, but he turned his eyes towards her with such a look that she did not finish what she was saying; so great an animosity, to her in particular, did that look express.

"For Christ's sake let me die in peace!" he said.

She would have gone away, but just then their daughter came in and went up to say good morning. He looked at her as he had done at his wife, and in reply to her inquiry about his health said dryly that he would soon free them all of himself. They were both silent and after sitting with him for a while went away.

"Is it our fault?" Lisa said to her mother. "It's as if we were to blame! I am sorry for papa, but why should we be tortured?"

The doctor came at his usual time. Ivan Ilych answered "Yes" and "No," never taking his angry eyes from him, and at last said: "You know you can do nothing for me, so leave me alone."

"We can ease your sufferings."

"You can't even do that. Let me be."

The doctor went into the drawing-room and told Praskovya Fëdorovna that the case was very serious and that the only resource left was opium to allay her husband's sufferings, which must be terrible.

It was true, as the doctor said, that Ivan Ilych's physical sufferings were terrible, but worse than the physical sufferings were his mental sufferings, which were his chief torture.

His mental sufferings were due to the fact that that night, as he looked at Gerasim's sleepy, good-natured face with its prominent cheekbones, the question suddenly occurred to him: "What if my whole life has really been wrong?"

It occurred to him that what had appeared perfectly impossible before, namely that he had not spent his life as he should have done, might after all be true. It occurred to him that his scarcely perceptible attempts to struggle against what was considered good by the most highly placed people, those scarcely noticeable impulses which he had immediately suppressed, might have been the real thing, and all the rest false. And his professional duties and the whole arrangement of his life and of his family, and all his social and official interests, might all have been false. He tried to defend all those things to himself and suddenly felt the weakness of what he was defending. There was nothing to defend.

"But if that is so," he said to himself, "and I am leaving this life with the consciousness that I have lost all that was given me and it is impossible to rectify it—what then?"

He lay on his back and began to pass his life in review in quite a new way. In the morning when he saw first his footman, then his wife, then his daughter, and then the doctor, their every word and movement confirmed to him the awful truth that had been revealed to him during the night. In them he saw himself—all that for which he had lived—and saw clearly that it was not real at all, but a terrible and huge deception which had hidden both life and death. This consciousness intensified his physical suffering tenfold. He groaned and tossed about, and pulled at his clothing which choked and stifled him. And he hated them on that account.

He was given a large dose of opium and became unconscious, but at noon his sufferings began again. He drove everybody away and tossed from side to side.

His wife came to him and said:

"Jean, my dear, do this for me. It can't do any harm and often helps. Healthy people often do it."

He opened his eyes wide.

"What? Take communion? Why? It's unnecessary! However . . ."

She began to cry.

"Yes, do, my dear. I'll send for our priest. He is such a nice man."

"All right. Very well," he muttered.

When the priest came and heard his confession, Ivan Ilych was softened and seemed to feel a relief from his doubts and consequently from his sufferings, and for a moment there came a ray of hope. He again began to think of the vermiform appendix and the possibility of correcting it. He received the sacrament with tears in his eyes.

When they laid him down again afterwards he felt a moment's ease, and the hope that he might live awoke in him again. He began to think of the operation that had been suggested to him. "To live! I want to live!" he said to himself.

His wife came in to congratulate him after his communion, and when uttering the usual conventional words she added:

"You feel better, don't you?"

Without looking at her he said "Yes."

Her dress, her figure, the expression of her face, the tone of her voice, all revealed the same thing. "This is wrong, it is not as it should be. All you have lived for and still live for is falsehood and deception, hiding life and death from you." And as soon as he admitted that thought, his hatred and his agonizing physical suffering again sprang up, and with that suffering a consciousness of the unavoidable, approaching end. And to this was added a new sensation of grinding shooting pain and a feeling of suffocation.

The expression of his face when he uttered that "yes" was dreadful. Having uttered it, he looked her straight in the eyes, turned on his face with a rapidity extraordinary in his weak state and shouted:

"Go away! Go away and leave me alone!"

XII

From that moment the screaming began that continued for three days, and was so terrible that one could not hear it through two closed doors without horror. At the moment he answered his wife he realized that he was lost, that there was no return, that the end had come, the very end, and his doubts were still unsolved and remained doubts.

"Oh! Oh! Oh!" he cried in various intonations. He had begun by screaming "I won't!" and continued screaming on the letter *O*.

For three whole days, during which time did not exist for him, he struggled in that black sack into which he was being thrust by an invisible, resistless force. He struggled as a man condemned to death struggles in the hands of the executioner, knowing that he cannot save himself. And every moment he felt that despite all his efforts he was drawing nearer and nearer to what terrified him. He felt that his agony was due to his being thrust into that black hole and still more to his not being able to get right into it. He was hindered from getting into it by his conviction that his life had been a good one. That very justification of his life held him fast and prevented his moving forward, and it caused him most torment of all.

Suddenly some force struck him in the chest and side, making it still harder to breathe, and he fell through the hole and there at the bottom was a light. What had happened to him was like the sensation one sometimes experiences in a railway carriage when one thinks one is going backwards while one is really going forwards and suddenly becomes aware of the real direction.

"Yes, it was all not the right thing," he said to himself, "but that's no matter. It can be done. But what *is* the right thing?" he asked himself, and suddenly grew quiet.

This occurred at the end of the third day, two hours before his death. Just then his schoolboy son had crept softly in and gone up to the bedside. The dying man was still screaming desperately and waving his arms. His hand fell on the boy's head, and the boy caught it, pressed it to his lips, and began to cry.

At that very moment Ivan Ilych fell through and caught sight of the light, and it was revealed to him that though his life had not been what it should have been, this could still be rectified. He asked himself, "What *is* the right thing?" and grew still, listening. Then he felt that someone was kissing his hand. He opened his eyes, looked at his son, and felt sorry for him. His wife came up to him and he glanced at her. She was gazing at him open-mouthed, with undried tears on her nose and cheek and a despairing look on her face. He felt sorry for her too.

"Yes, I am making them wretched," he thought. "They are sorry, but it will be better for them when I die." He wished to say this but had not the strength to utter it. "Besides, why speak? I must act," he thought. With a look at his wife he indicated his son and said: "Take him away . . . sorry for him . . . sorry for you too. . . ." He tried to add, "Forgive me," but said "forgo" and waved his hand, knowing that He whose understanding mattered would understand.

And suddenly it grew clear to him that what had been oppressing him and would not leave him was all dropping away at once from two sides, from ten sides, and from all sides. He was sorry for them, he must act so as not to hurt them: release them and free himself from these sufferings. "How good and how simple!" he thought. "And the pain?" he asked himself. "What has become of it? Where are you, pain?"

He turned his attention to it.

"Yes, here it is. Well, what of it? Let the pain be."

"And death . . . where is it?"

He sought his former accustomed fear of death and did not find it. "Where is it? What death?" There was no fear because there was no death.

In place of death there was light.

"So that's what it is!" he suddenly exclaimed aloud. "What joy!"

To him all this happened in a single instant, and the meaning of that instant did not change. For those present his agony continued for another two hours. Something rattled in his throat, his emaciated body twitched, then the gasping and rattle became less and less frequent.

"It is finished!" said someone near him.

He heard these words and repeated them in his soul.

"Death is finished," he said to himself. "It is no more!"

He drew in a breath, stopped in the midst of a sigh, stretched out, and died.

Thomas Hardy

(1840 - 1928)

Thomas Hardy was a gentle humanist and lover of all living creatures who viewed human life as a tragedy governed by chance and irrational fate. Although he regarded himself as a meliorist—one who believes man may improve the world by his own efforts—and rejected the label of pessimist, Hardy in his novels and short stories presented a decidedly somber vision of the world. His characters are the playthings of forces beyond their control, being buffeted by nature and society. For Hardy God apparently was not in his heaven and all was not right with the world; in fact, if God did exist, this "President of the Immortals" was possibly indifferent to man's suffering. In the face of this discouraging human condition, Hardy's heroes and heroines, like those of Hemingway, struggle and dance and achieve character and dignity by stoical endurance and acceptance of fate. Known best for his novels, which wonderfully mix tragedy and romance (for example, *The Return of the Native* and *Tess of the D'Urbervilles*), Hardy was also a lyric poet and an important contributor to the emerging modern British short story. Like other Victorian writers, Hardy was not seriously concerned with the short story as a form, and many of his tales are diffuse, rambling, overplotted, and freighted with an excessive burden of picturesque local color. Nevertheless, he could, in his best stories, hold to a unity of theme and time, conveying the drama by means of sharply focused scenes much as a modern short story writer would. He is especially good at evoking the life and atmosphere of rural England and its simple folk.

The Three Strangers

Among the few features of agricultural England which retain an appearance but little modified by the lapse of centuries, may be reckoned the long, grassy and furzy downs, coombs, or ewe-leases, as they are called according to their kind, that fill a large area of certain counties in the south and south-west. If any mark of human occupation is met with hereon, it usually takes the form of the solitary cottage of some shepherd.

Fifty years ago such a lonely cottage stood on such a down, and may possibly be standing there now. In spite of its loneliness, however, the spot, by actual measurement, was not three miles from a county-town. Yet that affected it little. Three miles of irregular upland, during the long inimical seasons, with their sleets, snows, rains, and mists, afford withdrawing space enough to isolate a Timon or a Nebuchadnezzar; much less, in fair weather, to please that less repellent tribe, the poets, philosophers, artists, and others who "conceive and meditate of pleasant things."

Some old earthen camp or barrow, some clump of trees, at least some starved fragment of ancient hedge is usually taken advantage of in the erection of these forlorn dwellings. But, in the present case, such a kind of shelter had been disregarded. Higher Crowstairs, as the house was called, stood quite detached and undefended. The only reason for its precise situation seemed to be the crossing of two footpaths at right angles hard by, which may have crossed there and thus for a good five hundred years. Hence the house was exposed to the elements on all sides. But, though the wind up here blew unmistakably when it did blow, and the rain hit hard whenever it fell, the various weathers of the winter season were not quite so formidable on the down as they were imagined to be by dwellers on low ground. The raw rimes were not so pernicious as in the hollows, and the frosts were scarcely so severe. When the shepherd and his family who tenanted the house were pitied for their sufferings from the exposure, they said that upon the whole they were less inconvenienced by "wuzzes and flames" (hoarses and phlegms) than when they had lived by the stream of a snug neighbouring valley.

The night of March 28, 182—, was precisely one of the nights that were wont to call forth these expressions of commiseration. The level rainstorm smote walls, slopes, and hedges like the clothyard shafts of Senlac and Crecy. Such sheep and outdoor animals as had no shelter stood with their buttocks to the winds; while the tails of little birds trying to roost on some scraggy thorn were blown inside-out like umbrellas. The gable-end of the cottage was stained with wet, and the eavesdroppings flapped against the wall. Yet never was commiseration for the shepherd more misplaced. For that cheerful rustic was entertaining a large party in glorification of the christening of his second girl.

The guests had arrived before the rain began to fall, and they were all now assembled in the chief or living-room of the dwelling. A glance into the apartment at eight o'clock on this eventful evening would have resulted in the opinion that it was as cosy and comfortable a nook as could be wished for in boisterous weather. The calling of its inhabitant was proclaimed by a number of highly-polished sheep-crooks without stems that were hung ornamentally over the fireplace, the curl of each shining crook varying from the antiquated type engraved in the patriarchal pictures of old family Bibles to the most approved fashion of the last local sheep-fair. The room was lighted by half-a-dozen candles, having wicks only a trifle smaller than the grease which enveloped them, in candlesticks that were never used but at high-days, holy-days, and family feasts. The lights were scattered about the room, two of them standing on the chimney-piece. This position of candles was in itself significant. Candles on the chimney-piece always meant a party.

On the hearth, in front of a back-brand to give substance, blazed a fire of thorns, that crackled "like the laughter of the fool."

Nineteen persons were gathered here. Of these, five women, wearing gowns of various bright hues, sat in chairs along the wall; girls shy and not shy filled the window-bench; four men, including Charley Jake the hedge-carpenter, Elijah New the parish-clerk, and John Pitcher, a neighbouring dairyman, the shepherd's father-in-law, lolled in the settle; a young man and maid, who were blushing over tentative *pourparlers* on a life-companionship, sat beneath the corner-cupboard; and an elderly engaged man of fifty or upward moved restlessly about from spots where his betrothed was not to the spot where she was. Enjoyment was pretty general, and so much the more prevailed in being unhampered by conventional restrictions. Absolute confidence in each other's good opinion begat perfect ease, while the finishing stroke of manner, amounting to a truly princely serenity, was lent to the majority by the absence of any expression or trait denoting that they wished to get on in the world, enlarge their minds, or do any eclipsing thing whatever—which nowadays so generally nips the bloom and *bonhomie* of all except the two extremes of the social scale.

Shepherd Fennel had married well, his wife being a dairyman's daughter from a vale at a distance, who brought fifty guineas in her pocket —and kept them there, till they should be required for ministering to the needs of a coming family. This frugal woman had been somewhat exercised as to the character that should be given to the gathering. A sit-still party had its advantages; but an undisturbed position of ease in chairs and settles was apt to lead on the men to such an unconscionable deal of toping that they would sometimes fairly drink the house dry. A dancing-party was the alternative; but this, while avoiding the foregoing objection on the score of good drink, had a counterbalancing disadvantage in the matter of good victuals, the ravenous appetites engendered by the exercise causing immense havoc in the buttery. Shepherdess Fennel fell back upon the intermediate plan of mingling short dances with short periods of talk and singing, so as to hinder any ungovernable rage in either. But this scheme was entirely confined to her own gentle mind: the shepherd himself was in the mood to exhibit the most reckless phases of hospitality.

The fiddler was a boy of those parts, about twelve years of age, who had a wonderful dexterity in jigs and reels, though his fingers were so small and short as to necessitate a constant shifting for the high notes, from which he scrambled back to the first position with sounds not of unmixed purity of tone. At seven the shrill tweedle-dee of this youngster had begun, accompanied by a booming ground-bass from Elijah New, the parish-clerk, who had thoughtfully brought with him his favourite musical instrument, the serpent. Dancing was instantaneous, Mrs. Fennel privately enjoining the players on no account to let the dance exceed the length of a quarter of an hour.

But Elijah and the boy in the excitement of their position quite forgot the injunction. Moreover, Oliver Giles, a man of seventeen, one of the dancers, who was enamoured of his partner, a fair girl of thirty-three rolling years, had recklessly handed a new crown-piece to the musicians, as a bribe to keep going as long as they had muscle and wind. Mrs. Fennel, seeing the steam begin to generate on the countenances of her guests, crossed over and touched the fiddler's elbow and put her hand on the serpent's mouth. But they took no notice, and fearing she might lose her character of genial hostess if she were to interfere too markedly, she retired and sat down helpless. And so the dance whizzed on with cumulative fury, the performers moving in their planet-like courses, direct and retrograde, from apogee to perigee, till the hand of the well-kicked clock at the bottom of the room had travelled over the circumference of an hour.

While these cheerful events were in course of enactment within Fennel's pastoral dwelling an incident having considerable bearing on the party had occurred in the gloomy night without. Mrs. Fennel's concern about the growing fierceness of the dance corresponded in point of time with the ascent of a human figure to the solitary hill of Higher Crowstairs from the direction of the distant town. This personage strode on through the rain without a pause, following the little-worn path which, further on in its course, skirted the shepherd's cottage.

It was nearly the time of full moon, and on this account, though the sky was lined with a uniform sheet of dripping cloud, ordinary objects out of doors were readily visible. The sad wan light revealed the lonely pedestrian to be a man of supple frame; his gait suggested that he had somewhat passed the period of perfect and instinctive agility, though not so far as to be otherwise than rapid of motion when occasion required. At a rough guess, he might have been about forty years of age. He appeared tall, but a recruiting sergeant, or other person accustomed to the judging of men's heights by the eye, would have discerned that this was chiefly owing to his gauntness, and that he was not more than five-feet-eight or nine.

Notwithstanding the regularity of his tread there was caution in it, as in that of one who mentally feels his way; and despite the fact that it was not a black coat nor a dark garment of any sort that he wore, there was something about him which suggested that he naturally belonged to the black-coated tribes of men. His clothes were of fustian, and his boots hobnailed, yet in his progress he showed not the mud-accustomed bearing of hobnailed and fustianed peasantry.

By the time that he had arrived abreast of the shepherd's premises the rain came down, or rather came along, with yet more determined violence. The outskirts of the little settlement partially broke the force of wind and rain, and this induced him to stand still. The most salient of the shepherd's domestic erections was an empty sty at the forward corner of his hedgeless garden, for in these latitudes the principle of masking the homelier features of your establishment by a conventional frontage was unknown. The traveller's eye was attracted to this small building by the pallid shine of the wet slates that covered it. He turned aside, and, finding it empty, stood under the pent-roof for shelter.

While he stood the boom of the serpent within the adjacent house, and the lesser strains of the fiddler, reached the spot as an accompaniment to the surging hiss of the flying rain on the sod, its louder beating on the cabbage-leaves of the garden, on the straw hackles of eight or ten beehives just discernible by the path, and its dripping from the eaves into a row of buckets and pans that had been placed under the walls of the cottage. For at Higher Crowstairs, as at all such elevated domiciles, the grand difficulty of housekeeping was an insufficiency of water; and a casual rainfall was utilized by turning out, as catchers, every utensil that the house contained. Some queer stories might be told of the contrivances for economy in suds and dish-waters that are absolutely necessitated in upland habitations during the droughts of summer. But at this season there were no such exigencies; a mere acceptance of what the skies bestowed was sufficient for an abundant store.

At last the notes of the serpent ceased and the house was silent. This cessation of activity aroused the solitary pedestrian from the reverie into which he had lapsed, and, emerging from the shed, with an apparently new intention, he walked up the path to the house-door. Arrived here, his first act was to kneel down on a large stone beside the row of vessels, and to drink a copious draught from one of them. Having quenched his thirst he rose and lifted his hand to knock, but paused with his eye upon the panel. Since the dark surface of the wood revealed absolutely nothing, it was evident that he must be mentally looking through the door, as if he wished to measure thereby all the possibilities that a house of this sort might include, and how they might bear upon the question of his entry.

In his indecision he turned and surveyed the scene around. Not a soul was anywhere visible. The garden-path stretched downward from his feet, gleaming like the track of a snail; the roof of the little well (mostly dry), the well-cover, the top rail of the garden-gate, were varnished with the same dull liquid glaze; while, far away in the vale, a faint whiteness of more than usual extent showed that the rivers were high in the meads. Beyond all this winked a few bleared lamplights through the beating drops

—lights that denoted the situation of the county-town from which he had appeared to come. The absence of all notes of life in that direction seemed to clinch his intentions, and he knocked at the door.

Within, a desultory chat had taken the place of movement and musical sound. The hedge-carpenter was suggesting a song to the company, which nobody just then was inclined to undertake, so that the knock afforded a not unwelcome diversion.

"Walk in!" said the shepherd promptly.

The latch clicked upward, and out of the night our pedestrian appeared upon the door-mat. The shepherd arose, snuffed two of the nearest candles, and turned to look at him.

Their light disclosed that the stranger was dark in complexion and not unprepossessing as to feature. His hat, which for a moment he did not remove, hung low over his eyes, without concealing that they were large, open, and determined, moving with a flash rather than a glance round the room. He seemed pleased with his survey, and, baring his shaggy head, said, in a rich deep voice, "The rain is so heavy, friends, that I ask leave to come in and rest awhile."

"To be sure, stranger," said the shepherd. "And faith, you've been lucky in choosing your time, for we are having a bit of a fling for a glad cause—though, to be sure, a man could hardly wish that glad cause to happen more than once a year."

"Nor less," spoke up a woman. "For 'tis best to get your family over and done with, as soon as you can, so as to be all the earlier out of the fag o't."

"And what may be this glad cause?" asked the stranger.

"A birth and christening," said the shepherd.

The stranger hoped his host might not be made unhappy either by too many or too few of such episodes, and being invited by a gesture to a pull at the mug, he readily acquiesced. His manner, which, before entering, had been so dubious, was now altogether that of a careless and candid man.

"Late to be traipsing athwart this coomb—hey?" said the engaged man of fifty.

"Late it is, master, as you say.—I'll take a seat in the chimney-corner, if you have nothing to urge against it, ma'am; for I am a little moist on the side that was next the rain."

Mrs. Shepherd Fennel assented, and made room for the self-invited comer, who, having got completely inside the chimney-corner, stretched out his legs and his arms with the expansiveness of a person quite at home.

"Yes, I am rather cracked in the vamp," he said freely, seeing that the eyes of the shepherd's wife fell upon his boots, "and I am not well fitted either. I have had some rough times lately, and have been forced to pick up what I can get in the way of wearing, but I must find a suit better fit for working-days when I reach home."

"One of hereabouts?" she inquired.

"Not quite that—further up the country."

"I thought so. And so be I; and by your tongue you come from my neighbourhood."

"But you would hardly have heard of me," he said quickly. "My time would be long before yours, ma'am, you see."

This testimony to the youthfulness of his hostess had the effect of stopping her cross-examination.

"There is only one thing more wanted to make me happy," continued the new-comer. "And that is a little baccy, which I am sorry to say I am out of."

"I'll fill your pipe," said the shepherd.

"I must ask you to lend me a pipe likewise."

"A smoker, and no pipe about 'ee?"

"I have dropped it somewhere on the road."

The shepherd filled and handed him a new clay pipe, saying, as he did so, "Hand me your baccy-box—I'll fill that too, now I am about it."

The man went through the movement of searching his pockets.

"Lost that too?" said his entertainer, with some surprise.

"I am afraid so," said the man with some confusion. "Give it to me in a screw of paper." Lighting his pipe at the candle with a suction that drew the whole flame into the bowl, he resettled himself in the corner and bent his looks upon the faint steam from his damp legs, as if he wished to say no more.

Meanwhile the general body of guests had been taking little notice of this visitor by reason of an absorbing discussion in which they were engaged with the band about a tune for the next dance. The matter being settled, they were about to stand up when an interruption came in the shape of another knock at the door.

At sound of the same the man in the chimney-corner took up the poker and began stirring the brands as if doing it thoroughly were the one aim of his existence; and a second time the shepherd said, "Walk in!" In a moment another man stood upon the straw-woven doormat. He too was a stranger.

This individual was one of a type radically different from the first. There was more of the commonplace in his manner, and a certain jovial cosmopolitanism sat upon his features. He was several years older than the first arrival, his hair being slightly frosted, his eyebrows bristly, and his whiskers cut back from his cheeks. His face was rather full and flabby, and yet it was not altogether a face without power. A few grog-blossoms marked the neighbourhood of his nose. He flung back his long drab greatcoat, revealing that beneath it he wore a suit of cinder-gray shade throughout, large heavy seals, of some metal or other that would take a polish, dangling from his fob as his only personal ornament. Shaking the water-drops from his low-crowned glazed hat, he said, "I must ask for a few minutes' shelter, comrades, or I shall be wetted to my skin before I get to Casterbridge."

"Make yourself at home, master," said the shepherd, perhaps a trifle less heartily than on the first occasion. Not that Fennel had the least tinge of niggardliness in his composition; but the room was far from large, spare chairs were not numerous, and damp companions were not altogether desirable at close quarters for the women and girls in their bright-coloured gowns.

However, the second comer, after taking off his greatcoat, and hanging his hat on a nail in one of the ceiling-beams as if he had been specially invited to put it there, advanced and sat down at the table. This had been pushed so closely into the chimney-corner, to give all available room to the dancers, that its inner edge grazed the elbow of the man who had ensconced himself by the fire; and thus the two strangers were brought into close companionship. They nodded to each other by way of breaking the ice of unacquaintance, and the first stranger handed his neighbour the family mug—a huge vessel of brown ware, having its upper edge worn away like a threshold by the rub of whole generations of thirsty lips that had gone the way of all flesh, and bearing the following inscription burnt upon its rotund side in yellow letters:—

THERE IS NO FUN
UNTILL I CUM

The other man, nothing loth, raised the mug to his lips, and drank on, and on, and on—till a curious blueness overspread the countenance of the shepherd's wife, who had regarded with no little surprise the first stranger's free offer to the second of what did not belong to him to dispense.

"I knew it!" said the toper to the shepherd with much satisfaction. "When I walked up your garden before coming in, and saw the hives all of a row, I said to myself, 'Where there's bees there's honey, and where there's honey there's mead.' But mead of such a truly comfortable sort as this I really didn't expect to meet in my older days." He took yet another pull at the mug, till it assumed an ominous elevation.

"Glad you enjoy it!" said the shepherd warmly.

"It is goodish mead," assented Mrs. Fennel, with an absence of enthusiasm which seemed to say that it was possible to buy praise for one's cellar at too heavy a price. "It is trouble enough to make—and really I hardly think we shall make any more. For honey sells well, and we ourselves can make shift with a drop o' small mead and metheglin for common use from the comb-washings."

"O, but you'll never have the heart!" reproachfully cried the stranger in cinder-gray, after taking up the mug a third time and setting it down empty. "I love mead, when 'tis old like this, as I love to go to church o' Sundays or to relieve the needy any day of the week."

"Ha, ha, ha!" said the man in the chimney-corner, who, in spite of the taciturnity induced by the pipe of tobacco, could not or would not refrain from this slight testimony to his comrade's humour.

Now the old mead of those days, brewed of the purest first-year or maiden honey, four pounds to the gallon—with its due complement of white of eggs, cinnamon, ginger, cloves, mace, rosemary, yeast, and processes of working, bottling, and cellaring—tasted remarkably strong; but it did not taste so strong as it actually was. Hence, presently, the stranger in cinder-gray at the table, moved by its creeping influence, unbuttoned his waistcoat, threw himself back in his chair, spread his legs, and made his presence felt in various ways.

"Well, well, as I say," he resumed, "I am going to Casterbridge, and to Casterbridge I must go. I should have been almost there by this time; but the rain drove me into your dwelling, and I'm not sorry for it."

"You don't live in Casterbridge?" said the shepherd.

"Not as yet; though I shortly mean to move there."

"Going to set up in trade, perhaps?"

"No, no," said the shepherd's wife. "It is easy to see that the gentleman is rich, and don't want to work at anything."

The cinder-gray stranger paused, as if to consider whether he would accept that definition of himself. He presently rejected it by answering, "Rich is not quite the word for me, dame. I do work, and I must work. And even if I only get to Casterbridge by midnight I must begin work there at eight to-morrow morning. Yes, het or wet, blow or snow, famine or sword, my day's work to-morrow must be done."

"Poor man! Then, in spite o' seeming, you be worse off than we?" replied the shepherd's wife.

"'Tis the nature of my trade, men and maidens. 'Tis the nature of my trade more than my poverty. . . . But really and truly I must up and off, or I shan't get a lodging in the town." However, the speaker did not move, and directly added, "There's time for one more draught of friendship before I go; and I'd perform it at once if the mug were not dry."

"Here's a mug o' small," said Mrs. Fennel. "Small, we call it, though to be sure 'tis only the first wash o' the combs."

"No," said the stranger disdainfully. "I won't spoil your first kindness by partaking o' your second."

"Certainly not," broke in Fennel. "We don't increase and multiply every day, and I'll fill the mug again." He went away to the dark place under the stairs where the barrel stood. The shepherdess followed him.

"Why should you do this?" she said reproachfully, as soon as they were alone. "He's emptied it once, though it held enough for ten people; and now he's not contented wi' the small, but must needs call for more o' the strong! And a stranger unbeknown to any of us. For my part, I don't like the look o' the man at all."

"But he's in the house, my honey; and 'tis a wet night, and a christening. Daze it, what's a cup of mead more or less? There'll be plenty more next bee-burning."

"Very well—this time, then," she answered, looking wistfully at the barrel. "But what is the man's calling, and where is he one of, that he should come in and join us like this?"

"I don't know. I'll ask him again."

The catastrophe of having the mug drained dry at one pull by the stranger in cinder-gray was effectually guarded against this time by Mrs. Fennel. She poured out his allowance in a small cup, keeping the large one at a discreet distance from him. When he had tossed off his portion the shepherd renewed his inquiry about the stranger's occupation.

The latter did not immediately reply, and the man in the chimney-corner, with sudden demonstrativeness, said, "Anybody may know my trade—I'm a wheelwright."

"A very good trade for these parts," said the shepherd.

"And anybody may know mine—if they've the sense to find it out," said the stranger in cinder-gray.

"You may generally tell what a man is by his claws," observed the hedge-carpenter, looking at his own hands. "My fingers be as full of thorns as an old pin-cushion is of pins."

The hands of the man in the chimney-corner instinctively sought the shade, and he gazed into the fire as he resumed his pipe. The man at the table took up the hedge-carpenter's remark, and added smartly, "True; but the oddity of my trade is that, instead of setting a mark upon me, it sets a mark upon my customers."

No observation being offered by anybody in elucidation of this enigma the shepherd's wife once more called for a song. The same obstacles presented themselves as at the former time—one had no voice, another had forgotten the first verse. The stranger at the table, whose soul had now risen to a good working temperature, relieved the difficulty by exclaiming that, to start the company, he would sing himself. Thrusting one thumb into the arm-hole of his waistcoat, he waved the other hand in the air, and, with an extemporizing gaze at the shining sheep-crooks above the mantelpiece, began:—

O my trade it is the rarest one,
Simple shepherds all—
My trade is a sight to see;
For my customers I tie, and take them up on high,
And waft 'em to a far countree!

The room was silent when he had finished the verse—with one exception, that of the man in the chimney-corner, who, at the singer's word, "Chorus!" joined him in a deep bass voice of musical relish—

And waft 'em to a far countree!

Oliver Giles, John Pitcher the dairyman, the parish-clerk, the engaged man of fifty, the row of young women against the wall, seemed lost in thought not of the gayest kind. The shepherd looked meditatively on the ground, the shepherdess gazed keenly at the singer, and with some suspicion; she was doubting whether this stranger were merely singing an old song from recollection, or was composing one there and then for the occasion. All were as perplexed at the obscure revelation as the guests at Belshazzar's Feast, except the man in the chimney-corner, who quietly said, "Second verse, stranger," and smoked on.

The singer thoroughly moistened himself from his lips inwards, and went on with the next stanza as requested:—

My tools are but common ones,
Simple shepherds all—
My tools are no sight to see:
A little hempen string, and a post whereon to swing,
Are implements enough for me!

Shepherd Fennel glanced round. There was no longer any doubt that the stranger was answering his question rhythmically. The guests one and all started back with suppressed exclamations. The young woman engaged to the man of fifty fainted half-way, and would have proceeded, but finding him wanting in alacrity for catching her she sat down trembling.

"O, he's the—!" whispered the people in the background, mentioning the name of an ominous public officer. "He's come to do it! 'Tis to be at Casterbridge jail to-morrow—the man for sheep-stealing—the poor clock-maker we heard of, who used to live away at Shottsford and had no work to do—Timothy Summers, whose family were a-starving, and so he went out of Shottsford by the high-road, and took a sheep in open daylight, defying the farmer and the farmer's wife and the farmer's lad, and every man jack among 'em. He" (and they nodded towards the stranger of the deadly trade) "is come from up the country to do it because there's not enough to do in his own county-town, and he's got the place here now our own county man's dead; he's going to live in the same cottage under the prison wall."

The stranger in cinder-gray took no notice of this whispered string of observations, but again wetted his lips. Seeing that his friend in the chimney-corner was the only one who reciprocated his joviality in any way, he held out his cup towards that appreciative comrade, who also held out his own. They clinked together, the eyes of the rest of the room hanging upon the singer's actions. He parted his lips for the third verse; but at that moment another knock was audible upon the door. This time the knock was faint and hesitating.

The company seemed scared; the shepherd looked with consternation towards the entrance, and it was with some effort that he resisted his alarmed wife's deprecatory glance, and uttered for the third time the welcoming words, "Walk in!"

The door was gently opened, and another man stood upon the mat. He, like those who had preceded him, was a stranger. This time it was a short, small personage, of fair complexion, and dressed in a decent suit of dark clothes.

"Can you tell me the way to ——?" he began: when gazing round the room to observe the nature of the company amongst whom he had fallen, his lighted on the stranger in cinder-gray. It was just at the instant when the latter, who had thrown his mind into his song with such a will that he scarcely heeded the interruption, silenced all whispers and inquiries by bursting into his third verse:—

To-morrow is my working day,
Simple shepherds all—
To-morrow is a working day for me:
For the farmer's sheep is slain, and the lad who did it ta'en,
And on his soul may God ha' merc-y!

The stranger in the chimney-corner, waving cups with the singer so heartily that his mead splashed over on the hearth, repeated in his bass voice as before:—

And on his soul may God ha' merc-y!

All this time the third stranger had been standing in the doorway. Finding now that he did not come forward or go on speaking, the guests particularly regarded him. They noticed to their surprise that he stood before them the picture of abject terror—his knees trembling, his hand shaking so violently that the door-latch by which he supported himself rattled audibly: his white lips were parted, and his eyes fixed on the merry officer of justice in the middle of the room. A moment more and he had turned, closed the door, and fled.

"What a man can it be?" said the shepherd.

The rest, between the awfulness of their late discovery and the odd conduct of this third visitor, looked as if they knew not what to think, and said nothing. Instinctively they withdrew further and further from the grim gentleman in their midst, whom some of them seemed to take for the Prince of Darkness himself, till they formed a remote circle, an empty space of floor being left between them and him—

. . . circulus, cujus centrum diabolus.

The room was so silent—though there were more than twenty people in it—that nothing could be heard but the patter of the rain against the window-shutters, accompanied by the occasional hiss of a stray drop that fell down the chimney into the fire, and the steady puffing of the man in the corner, who had now resumed his pipe of long clay.

The stillness was unexpectedly broken. The distant sound of a gun reverberated through the air—apparently from the direction of the county-town.

"Be jiggered!" cried the stranger who had sung the song, jumping up.

"What does that mean?" asked several.

"A prisoner escaped from the jail—that's what it means."

All listened. The sound was repeated, and none of them spoke but the man in the chimney-corner, who said quietly, "I've often been told that in this county they fire a gun at such times; but I never heard it till now."

"I wonder if it is *my* man?" murmured the personage in cinder-gray.

"Surely it is!" said the shepherd unvoluntarily. "And surely we've zeed him! That little man who looked in at the door by now, and quivered like a leaf when he zeed ye and heard your song!"

"His teeth chattered, and the breath went out of his body," said the dairyman.

"And his heart seemed to sink within him like a stone," said Oliver Giles.

"And he bolted as if he'd been shot at," said the hedge-carpenter.

"True—his teeth chattered, and his heart seemed to sink; and he bolted as if he'd been shot at," slowly summed up the man in the chimney-corner.

"I didn't notice it," remarked the hangman.

"We were all a-wondering what made him run off in such fright," faltered one of the women against the wall, "and now 'tis explained!"

The firing of the alarm-gun went on at intervals, low and sullenly, and their suspicions became a certainty. The sinister gentleman in cinder-gray roused himself. "Is there a constable here?" he asked, in thick tones. "If so, let him step forward."

The engaged man of fifty stepped quavering out from the wall, his betrothed beginning to sob on the back of the chair.

"You are a sworn constable?"

"I be, sir."

"Then pursue the criminal at once, with assistance, and bring him back here. He can't have gone far."

"I will, sir, I will—when I've got my staff. I'll go home and get it, and come sharp here, and start in a body."

"Staff!—never mind your staff; the man'll be gone!"

"But I can't do nothing without my staff—can I, William, and John, and Charles Jake? No; for there's the king's royal crown a painted on en in yaller and gold, and the lion and the unicorn, so as when I raise en up and hit my prisoner, 'tis made a lawful blow thereby. I wouldn't 'tempt to take up a man without my staff—no, not I. If I hadn't the law to gie me courage, why, instead o' my taking up him he might take up me!"

"Now, I'm a king's man myself, and can give you authority enough for this," said the formidable officer in gray. "Now then, all of ye, be ready. Have ye any lanterns?"

"Yes—have ye any lanterns?—I demand it!" said the constable.

"And the rest of you able-bodied——"

"Able-bodied man—yes—the rest of ye!" said the constable.

"Have you some good stout staves and pitchforks——"

"Staves and pitchforks—in the name o' the law! And take 'em in yer hands and go in quest, and do as we in authority tell ye!"

Thus aroused, the men prepared to give chase. The evidence was, indeed, though circumstantial, so convincing, that but little argument was needed to show the shepherd's guests that after what they had seen it would look very much like connivance if they did not instantly pursue the unhappy third stranger, who could not as yet have gone more than a few hundred yards over such uneven country.

A shepherd is always well provided with lanterns; and, lighting these hastily, and with hurdle-staves in their hands, they poured out of the door, taking a direction along the crest of the hill, away from the town, the rain having fortunately a little abated.

Disturbed by the noise, or possibly by unpleasant dreams of her baptism, the child who had been christened began to cry heart-brokenly in the room overhead. These notes of grief came down through the chinks of the floor to the ears of the women below, who jumped up one by one, and seemed glad of the excuse to ascend and comfort the baby, for the incidents of the last half-hour greatly oppressed them. Thus in the space of two or three minutes the room on the ground-floor was deserted quite.

But it was not for long. Hardly had the sound of footsteps died away when a man returned round the corner of the house from the direction the pursuers had taken. Peeping in at the door, and seeing nobody there, he entered leisurely. It was the stranger of the chimney-corner, who had gone out with the rest. The motive of his return was shown by his helping himself to a cut piece of skimmer-cake that lay on a ledge beside where he had sat, and which he had apparently forgotten to take with him. He also poured out half a cup more mead from the quantity that remained, ravenously eating and drinking these as he stood. He had not finished when another figure came in just as quietly—his friend in cinder-gray.

"O—you here?" said the latter, smiling. "I thought you had gone to help in the capture." And this speaker also revealed the object of his return by looking solicitously round for the fascinating mug of old mead.

"And I thought you had gone," said the other, continuing his skimmer-cake with some effort.

"Well, on second thoughts, I felt there were enough without me," said the first confidentially, "and such a night as it is, too. Besides, 'tis the business o' the Government to take care of its criminals—not mine."

"True; so it is. And I felt as you did, that there were enough without me."

"I don't want to break my limbs running over the humps and hollows of this wild country."

"Nor I neither, between you and me."

"These shepherd-people are used to it—simple-minded souls, you know, stirred up to anything in a moment. They'll have him ready for me before the morning, and no trouble to me at all."

"They'll have him, and we shall have saved ourselves all labour in the matter."

"True, true. Well, my way is to Casterbridge; and 'tis as much as my legs will do to take me that far. Going the same way?"

"No, I am sorry to say! I have to get home over there" (he nodded indefinitely to the right), "and I feel as you do, that it is quite enough for my legs to do before bedtime."

The other had by this time finished the mead in the mug, after which, shaking hands heartily at the door, and wishing each other well, they went their several ways.

In the meantime the company of pursuers had reached the end of the hog's-back elevation which dominated this part of the down. They had decided on no particular plan of action; and, finding that the man of the baleful trade was no longer in their company, they seemed quite unable to form any such plan now. They descended in all directions down the hill, and straightway several of the party fell into the snare set by Nature for all misguided midnight ramblers over this part of the cretaceous formation. The "lanchets," or flint slopes, which belted the escarpment at intervals of a dozen yards, took the less cautious ones unawares, and losing their footing on the rubbly steep they slid sharply downwards, the lanterns rolling from their hands to the bottom, and there lying on their sides till the horn was scorched through.

When they had again gathered themselves together the shepherd, as the man who knew the country best, took the lead, and guided them round these treacherous inclines. The lanterns, which seemed rather to dazzle their eyes and warn the fugitive than to assist them in the exploration, were extinguished, due silence was observed; and in this more rational order they plunged into the vale. It was a grassy, briery, moist defile, affording some shelter to any person who had sought it; but the party perambulated it in vain, and ascended on the other side. Here they wandered apart, and after an interval closed together again to report progress. At the second time of closing in they found themselves near a lonely ash, the single tree on this part of the coomb, probably sown there by a passing bird some fifty years before. And here, standing a little to one side of the trunk, as motionless as the trunk itself, appeared the man they were in quest of, his outline being well defined against the sky beyond. The band noiselessly drew up and faced him.

"Your money or your life!" said the constable sternly to the still figure.

"No, no," whispered John Pitcher. "'Tisn't our side ought to say that. That's the doctrine of vagabonds like him, and we be on the side of the law."

"Well, well," replied the constable impatiently; "I must say something, mustn't I? and if you had all the weight o' this undertaking upon your mind, perhaps you'd say the wrong thing too!—Prisoner at the bar, surrender, in the name of the Father—the Crown, I mane!"

The man under the tree seemed now to notice them for the first time, and, giving them no opportunity whatever for exhibiting their courage, he strolled slowly towards them. He was, indeed, the little man, the third stranger; but his trepidation had in a great measure gone.

"Well, travellers," he said, "did I hear ye speak to me?"

"You did: you've got to come and be our prisoner at once!" said the constable. "We arrest 'ee on the charge of not biding in Casterbridge jail in a decent proper manner to be hung to-morrow morning. Neighbours, do your duty, and seize the culpet!"

On hearing the charge the man seemed enlightened, and, saying not another word, resigned himself with preternatural civility to the search-party, who, with their staves in their hands, surrounded him on all sides, and marched him back towards the shepherd's cottage.

It was eleven o'clock by the time they arrived. The light shining from the open door, a sound of men's voices within, proclaimed to them as they approached the house that some new events had arisen in their absence. On entering they discovered the shepherd's living-room to be invaded by two officers from Casterbridge jail, and a well-known magistrate who lived at the nearest country-seat, intelligence of the escape having become generally circulated.

"Gentlemen," said the constable, "I have brought back your man—not without risk and danger; but every one must do his duty! He is inside this circle of able-bodied persons, who have lent me useful aid, considering their ignorance of Crown work. Men, bring forward your prisoner!" And the third stranger was led to the light.

"Who is this?" said one of the officials.

"The man," said the constable.

"Certainly not," said the turnkey; and the first corroborated his statement.

"But how can it be otherwise?" asked the constable.

"Or why was he so terrified at sight o' the singing instrument of the law who sat there?" Here he related the strange behaviour of the third stranger on entering the house during the hangman's song.

"Can't understand it," said the officer coolly. "All I know is that it is not the condemned man. He's quite a different character from this one; a gauntish fellow, with dark hair and eyes, rather good-looking, and with a musical bass voice that if you heard it once you'd never mistake as long as you lived."

"Why souls—'twas the man in the chimney-corner!"

"Hey—what?" said the magistrate, coming forward after inquiring particulars from the shepherd in the background. "Haven't you got the man after all?"

"Well, sir," said the constable, "he's the man we were in search of, that's true; and yet he's not the man we were in search of. For the man we were in search of was not the man we wanted, sir, if you understand my every-day way; for 'twas the man in the chimney-corner!"

"A pretty kettle of fish altogether!" said the magistrate. "You had better start for the other man at once."

The prisoner now spoke for the first time. The mention of the man in the chimney-corner seemed to have moved him as nothing else could do. "Sir," he said, stepping forward to the magistrate, "take no more trouble about me. The time is come when I may as well speak. I have done nothing; my crime is that the condemned man is my brother. Early this afternoon I left home at Shottsford to tramp it all the way to Casterbridge jail to bid him farewell. I was benighted, and called here to rest and ask the way. When I opened the door I saw before me the very man, my brother, that I thought to see in the condemned cell at Casterbridge. He was in this chimney-corner; and jammed close to him, so that he could not have got out if he had tried, was the executioner who'd come to take his life, singing a song about it and not knowing that it was his victim who was close by, joining in to save appearances. My brother threw a glance of agony at me, and I knew he meant, 'Don't reveal what you see; my life depends on it.' I was so terror-struck that I could hardly stand, and not knowing what I did, I turned and hurried away."

The narrator's manner and tone had the stamp of truth, and his story made a great impression on all around.

"And do you know where your brother is at the present time?" asked the magistrate.

"I do not. I have never seen him since I closed this door."

"I can testify to that, for we've been between ye ever since," said the constable.

"Where does he think to fly to?—what is his occupation?"

"He's a watch-and-clock-maker, sir."

"A said 'a was a wheelwright—a wicked rogue," said the constable.

"The wheels of clocks and watches he meant, no doubt," said Shepherd Fennel. "I thought his hand were palish for's trade."

"Well, it appears to me that nothing can be gained by retaining this poor man in custody," said the magistrate; "your business lies with the other, unquestionably."

And so the little man was released off-hand; but he looked nothing the less sad on that account, it being beyond the power of magistrate or constable to raze out the written troubles in his brain, for they concerned another whom he regarded with more solicitude than himself. When this was done, and the man had gone his way, the night was found to be so far advanced that it was deemed useless to renew the search before the next morning.

Next day, accordingly, the quest for the clever sheep-stealer became general and keen, to all appearance at least. But the intended punishment was cruelly disproportioned to the transgression, and the sympathy of a great many country-folk in that district was strongly on the side of the fugitive. Moreover, his marvellous coolness and daring in hob-and-nobbling with the hangman, under the unprecedented circumstances of the shepherd's party won their admiration. So that it may be questioned if all those who ostensibly made themselves so busy in exploring woods and fields and lanes were quite so thorough when it came to the private examination of their own lofts and out-houses. Stories were afloat of a mysterious figure being occasionally seen in some old overgrown trackway or other, remote from turnpike roads; but when a search was instituted in any of these suspected quarters nobody was found. Thus the days and weeks passed without tidings.

In brief, the bass-voiced man of the chimney-corner was never recaptured. Some said that he went across the sea, others that he did not, but buried himself in the depths of a populous city. At any rate, the gentleman in cinder-gray never did his morning's work at Casterbridge, nor met anywhere at all, for business purposes, the genial comrade with whom he had passed an hour of relaxation in the lonely house on the slope of the coomb.

The grass has long been green on the graves of Shepherd Fennel and his frugal wife; the guests who made up the christening party have mainly followed their entertainers to the tomb; the baby in whose honour they all had met is a matron in the sere and yellow leaf. But the arrival of the three strangers at the shepherd's that night, and the details connected therewith, is a story as well known as ever in the country about Higher Crowstairs.

Anton Chekhov

(1860 - 1904)

The importance of Anton Chekhov as a short story writer and as an influence on the development of the genre could hardly be exaggerated. In fact, with him the modern short story came fully of age. Born in the provinces, the grandson of a serf, Chekhov came to Moscow to study medicine and in 1884 received his medical degree from the University of Moscow. While a student he contributed anecdotes and humorous stories to popular magazines in order to support himself and his parents. Though written hastily, these pieces served to force Chekhov to write concisely. Encouraged by professional writers, Chekhov began to write more carefully in 1888 and he abandoned the popular press for *New Times* (comparable to *Harper's* or *The Atlantic*). While still a practicing doctor, he experimented with actionless plots and impressionism and contrasted the beauty and ephemeral quality of life with the ugliness and despair he saw about him. Chekhov read Tolstoy and was sympathetic toward the idea of social reform, but he himself was not an activist. He once said, "I haven't acquired a political, philosophical outlook on life. I keep changing it every month, and I therefore have to confine myself to descriptions of how my characters love, get married, beget children, talk, and die." With isolation, loneliness, and frustration as common themes, Chekhov, like Maupassant, wrote of the submerged classes, the oppression of the peasants and the wasted lives of the aristocrats. Toward the end of his short life Chekhov enjoyed remarkable success as a realistic playwright, blending comedy and pathos in an irresistible mixture.

The Lady with a Dog

I

They said that a new face had appeared on the sea front: a lady with a dog. Dmitry Dmitrich Gurov, who had already been at Yalta for two weeks

A new translation by Richard G. Kappler, Associate Professor of Foreign Languages, Washington State University. Printed here with his permission.

and had got the hang of the place, also was growing interested in new faces. Sitting in the pavilion at Vernet's he saw a young woman passing along the sea front, a slight little blonde in a beret. After her trotted a white Pomeranian.

And afterwards he met her in the city garden and in the park several times each day. She walked alone with the white Pomeranian and always wore the same beret. Nobody knew who she was and they called her simply "the lady with a dog."

"If she's without her husband and without friends," reflected Gurov, "then there wouldn't be any harm in getting acquainted with her."

He hadn't quite reached forty, but he already had a twelve-year-old daughter and two sons in school. He married early when he was still an advanced student and now his wife seemed twice as old as he. She was a tall woman with dark brows, stiff, dignified, and sedate and, as she herself termed it, "an intellectual." She read a great deal, omitted the Russian hard sign in her letters, called her husband not Dmitry but "Dee-mee-tree," and he secretly considered her none too clever, narrow-minded and unattractive, was afraid of her and didn't like to stay home. He had begun to be unfaithful to her long ago, betrayed her often and probably on this account, spoke of women almost always harshly, and when they were discussed in his presence always summarily described them as:

"The inferior race!"

It seemed to him that he had been so tempered by bitter experience that he could call them whatever he pleased, but just the same he couldn't get along even two days without the "inferior race." In the company of men he was bored, not at home. With them he was taciturn, cold, but when he found himself among women he felt unconstrained and knew what to talk about with them and how to conduct himself; it was even easy for him not to talk at all in their presence. In his looks and character, in his entire nature, there was something attractive and elusive that drew women to him, that lured them. He was aware of this and he himself was attracted to them by some force or other.

Repeated experience—and bitter experience at that—had long ago taught him that every rapprochement which relieves the monotony of life so pleasantly at first and seems such a sweet and sprightly affair—in the case of "proper" persons, especially Moscow men, sluggish and indecisive as they are—inevitably develops into an extremely complicated undertaking, and the situation in the very end becomes burdensome. But at the time of each new encounter with an interesting woman this experience somehow just slipped out of his mind. He wanted to live fully and everything seemed so simple and amusing.

And now one evening as he was dining in the public garden, the lady in the beret leisurely came up to occupy the next table. Her expression, walk, dress told him that she came from upper-class society, was married, was in

Yalta for the first time, was alone, and was bored here. . . . In stories about the laxness of holiday resort morals there are many myths. He scoffed at these and knew that such tales are mainly made up by people who would commit sin readily if they but knew how to go about it. But when the lady sat down at a neighboring table just three paces away, he recalled these stories about easy conquests, about escapades into the hills, and the alluring thought of a quick and fleeting affair with a strange woman whose first and last name he didn't even know suddenly overpowered him.

Affably he caught the attention of the Pomeranian and when the dog came up he wagged his finger at him. The Pom began to growl. Gurov again wagged his finger.

The lady glanced at him and immediately lowered her eyes.

"He doesn't bite," she said and blushed.

"May I give him a bone?" And when she nodded her head, he asked amiably, "Have you been in Yalta long?"

"About five days."

"And I'm already putting in the second week here."

They fell silent briefly.

"The time goes by fast, but meanwhile it's so dull here!" she said, not looking at him.

"That's just a habit people get of saying it's boring here. Your vacationer lives off somewhere in Belev or Zhizdro[1]—and he's not bored there, but as soon as he comes here it's: 'Ugh, how boring! Ugh, the dust!' You'd think he came from Grenada!"

She began to laugh. Then they both went on eating in silence like two strangers. But after supper they went out together and there began the playful, light conversation of two free and contented people without a care where they go or what they talk about. They strolled and chatted about how oddly the sea was lit up. The water was of a lilac hue, so soft and warm, and over it shone a golden strip of light from the moon. They talked about how stifling it was after such a hot day. Gurov related that he was from Moscow, by training a philologist, but that he worked in a bank; that he at one time had been preparing to sing in a private opera company, but that he had thrown it up; that he had two houses in Moscow. . . . And from her he found out that she had grown up in Petersburg, but was married in S—, where she had already lived two years, that she'd be about a month more in Yalta and that perhaps her husband, who felt like taking a rest, might come down after her. She couldn't at all explain where her husband was working —whether he was on a Provincial Government Board or on a Provincial Zemstvo[2] Council and this was funny even to her. And in addition, Gurov found out that her name was Anna Sergeevna.

[1] Hinterland.

[2] A local administrative body in czarist Russia.

Later on up in his room by himself, he thought about her and that tomorrow she would surely meet him again. It was bound to happen. While going to bed, he recalled that not very long ago she was still a girl at school, studying just exactly as his daughter was now. He recalled how much shyness and awkwardness there was in her laughter still and in her conversation with a stranger. This must have been the first time in her life that she was alone in such circumstances, where men walked behind her, looked at her and spoke to her with only a single, secret purpose in mind—one she could hardly help guessing. He recalled her slender, delicate neck, the beautiful grey eyes.

"There's something pathetic about her just the same," he thought to himself and fell asleep.

II

A week had passed since they had became acquainted. It was a holiday. In the hotel rooms it was stifling and in the streets gusts of wind spiraled up the dust and blew off hats. They felt like drinking all day long and Gurov often stopped in at the pavilion and offered Anna Sergeevna syrup and water or ice cream. There was no place to escape the heat.

In the evening, when the wind had somewhat subsided, they went to the pier to see the steamer come in. On the wharf there were many people strolling. They had come to meet those they knew and were holding bouquets. And here two peculiarities of the dressy Yalta crowd struck the eye: the elderly ladies were attired like the young ones and there were many generals.

On account of the choppiness of the sea, the steamer arrived late, as the sun was setting, and before pulling in at the wharf it took a long time docking. Anna Sergeevna looked through her lorgnette at the steamer and at the passengers as though seeking someone she knew, and when she turned to Gurov her eyes were shining. She talked a good deal, her questions were abrupt and disconnected and she herself immediately forgot what she had asked about; then she lost her lorgnette in the crowd.

The smartly dressed crowd dispersed and faces were no longer visible. The wind had died completely, but Gurov and Anna were still standing as though waiting for someone to get off the steamer. By this time Anna Sergeevna had lapsed into silence and sniffed her flowers—not looking at Gurov.

"The weather's a bit better this evening," he said. "Where shall we go now? We might go for a drive?"

She said nothing in reply.

Just then he looked at her intently and all at once embraced her and kissed her on the lips. The moist smell of the flowers overpowered him and immediately he glanced behind him: had anyone seen them?

"Let's go to your place. . . ." he murmured.

And they both went away quickly.

It was stifling in her room; it reeked of the perfume she had bought in a Japanese shop. Gurov, as he gazed at her, was thinking: "Such meetings just don't happen in my life."

He recalled from his past all those carefree, good-natured women, who were gay in their love-making and grateful to him for the pleasure he gave, be it ever so brief, and also such types—as, for example, his wife—who loved without sincerity, with their superfluous chatter, their affectation, their hysteria, with an expression as though to suggest that all this was not love or passion but something far more significant; and then he thought of the two or three so very beautiful cold women on whose faces there suddenly flashed a rapacious expression, an obstinate desire to take and grasp from life more than it could give, and these were women not in their first youth—capricious, unreasonable, imperious, unintelligent. And when Gurov lost interest in them, their beauty stirred up in him a feeling of hatred and the lace on their linen then reminded him of the scales on a snake.

But here there was always that same shyness and awkwardness of inexperienced youth, an uneasy feeling; and there was an impression of embarrassment, just as though someone suddenly had knocked at the door. Anna Sergeevna, this "lady with a dog," regarded what had happened in a special, very serious way—actually as her downfall. Or so it seemed, and to Gurov this was odd and inappropriate. Her features were drooping and lifeless and on either side of her face her long hair hung sadly and, sunk in a melancholy pose, she looked just like the woman taken in adultery in an old-fashioned painting.

"It's dreadful," she said. "Now you'll be the first one not to respect me."

There was a watermelon on the hotel room table. Gurov cut himself a slice and began to eat leisurely. At least a half-hour passed in silence.

Anna Sergeevna was touching. From her person emanated the purity of a decent, naïve woman with little experience in life. A solitary candle burning on the table hardly lit up her face, but it was evident that she was troubled in spirit.

"Why should I stop respecting you?" asked Gurov. "You don't know yourself what you are saying."

"May God forgive me!" she said and her eyes filled with tears. "This is terrible."

"You don't have to justify yourself."

"How can I justify myself? I am a no-good, fallen woman. I despise myself and couldn't think of justification. I haven't deceived my husband but rather myself. And not only now. I've been deceiving myself for a long time. My husband is perhaps an honest, good man, but he's just a lackey! I don't know what he does where he works, but I only know that he's a lackey. I was twenty when I married him and tormented by curiosity. I felt there was something better. You know there must be—I said to myself—a better life. I wanted to see life! To see more and more of life. . . . I was burning with curiosity. You cannot understand it, but I swear to God, I could no longer control myself. Something was happening to me. I couldn't hold myself back—I told my husband I was ill and came here! And here I kept wandering about in a stupor, like a madwoman. . . . And now I have become a common, good-for-nothing woman whom everyone can despise!"

Gurov was already bored listening to her. Her naïve tone and this confession, so unexpected and out of place, irritated him. But for the tears in her eyes one might think she were joking or playing a part.

"I don't understand," he said gently. "Just what is it you want?"

She hid her face in his chest and snuggled up to him.

"Believe me, believe me, I beg you," she said. "I love an honest, clean life and sin to me is vile. I don't know myself what I am doing. Simple believers would say: 'The Devil led her astray,' and now I can say of myself that the Devil has led me astray."

"Don't, don't. . . ." he murmured.

He looked into her fixed, frightened eyes, kissed her, spoke softly and lovingly, and she gradually became calm and cheerful again; then they both broke into laughter.

Later when they went out, there wasn't a soul on the sea front. The town with its cypresses had a rather funereal look, but the sea was still roaring and beating against the shore. A solitary sailboat was rolling on the waves and on it sleepily twinkled a tiny lantern.

They hailed a cabby and drove to Oreanda.

"Just now down in the lobby I found out your last name. On the board was written von Dideritz," said Gurov. "Is your husband a German?"

"No, his grandfather, it seems, was German, but he is Russian Orthodox himself."

At Oreanda they sat on a bench, not far from the church, looking down at the sea in silence. Yalta was barely visible through the morning mist. On the mountain peaks white clouds hung motionless. The foliage on the trees was still, but the cicadas were chirping and the monotonous, rumbling roar of the sea, carried up from below, bespoke of the peace, of the eternal sleep that waits in store for us. Thus it roared below when neither Yalta nor Oreanda were yet here, roars now and will roar just as indifferently and deafly when we are gone. And in this changelessness, in this complete indifference to the life and death of each one of us, is inscribed the token of our eternal salvation, of the uninterrupted movement of life on earth, of the uninterrupted process of perfection. Sitting beside the young woman, who appeared so pretty in the light of dawn, Gurov, calmed and enchanted by the sight of this fabulous setting—the sea, the mountains, the clouds, the open sky—thought: in considering the matter, if we forget about the higher aims of existence and our own human worth, how beautiful everything is in this world, everything moreover that we think and do ourselves.

Some man or other, probably a watchman, came up, glanced at them and went his way. Even this incident seemed so mysterious and also beautiful. They could see the steamer arriving from Theodosia all lit up with the morning rays, the lights on board already extinguished.

"There's dew on the grass," said Anna Sergeevna after a period of silence.

"Yes, it's time to go back."

They returned to town.

Then each noon they met on the sea front, breakfasted together, dined, strolled, exulted in the sea. She complained that she slept badly and that her heart beat anxiously. She kept asking the very same questions, prompted at times by jealousy and at times by her fear he didn't respect her enough. And often in the public garden or in the park, when no one was around, he would suddenly draw her to him and kiss her passionately. The absolute leisure, these kisses in broad daylight, with the backward glance in fear someone would see them, the heat, smell of the sea and the flashing kaleidoscope before their eyes of idle, well-dressed, well-fed people fairly made a new man of him. He told Anna Sergeevna how pretty she was, how attractive. He was impatiently passionate, never taking a step away from her, whereas she was often pensive and kept asking him to confess that he didn't respect her, didn't love her in the least, and only regarded her as a lewd woman. Almost every evening, rather late, they would drive somewhere out of town, to Oreanda or to the waterfall. And each jaunt was a success; the impressions they received were each time unfailingly beautiful and sublime.

They were expecting her husband to arrive. But a letter came from him in which he announced that he was having trouble with his eyes and he implored his wife to return home with all possible speed. Anna Sergeevna made haste to depart.

"It's just as well I'm leaving," she said to Gurov. "It's simply fate."

She took a horse carriage to the nearest station and he accompanied her. It was an all-day drive. When she settled in the car of the express train, and when the second warning bell rang, she said:

"Let me take one more look at you. . . . Let me look once more! There we are!"

She didn't cry, but felt low, positively ill and her face was quivering.

"I will think about you and remember," she said. "God be with you! Think kindly of me! We are saying good-bye forever and it has to be so, since we ought never to have met. Well, God be with you!"

The train took off quickly, its lights soon disappeared and within a minute not even a sound could be heard from it, so that it seemed that everything were conspiring purposely to put an end as quickly as possible to this sweet oblivion, this madness. Remaining alone on the platform and gazing into the dark distance, Gurov heard the grating sound of the katydids and the humming of the telegraph wires with such awareness as though he had just then awakened from sleep. And he thought that here was still one more affair or adventure in his life and that it too had ended and remained but a memory. He was feeling let down, melancholy and even somewhat repentant, for actually this young woman whom he would never see again was not happy with him. He had been kind to her and sincere, but just the same in his whole treatment of her, in his voice and caresses, there underlay a hint of the light irony, the rather fulsome arrogance of a man who had attained his end and who was moreover almost twice her age. And all the while she kept calling him kind, exceptional, noble: evidently he appeared to her other than what he was in reality, so that he involuntarily had deceived her.

Here at the station there was already the scent of autumn; the evening was cool.

"It's about time for me to head north, too," thought Gurov, leaving the station. "High time!"

III

At home in Moscow everything was already quite winterlike: the stoves were burning and in the mornings when the children were getting ready for school and were drinking their tea it was dark and nanny would light up the lamp for a short time. The frosts had already begun. When the first snow comes on the first day for sleigh riding, it is pleasant to see the white earth, the white roofs, to breathe softly and wonderfully and at this time to recall one's youthful years. The old lindens and birches, white with hoarfrost, have a good-natured look to them. They seem closer to the heart than cypresses and palms and in their presence one no longer cares to think about mountains and the sea.

Gurov was a Moscovite. He returned to Moscow on a fine, frosty day, and when he put on his fur coat and warm gloves and strolled along the Petrovka, and when on Saturday evening he heard the ringing of the church bells, then the recent trip and the places where he stayed lost all their charm for him. Little by little he drifted back into Moscow life, avidly read through three newspapers daily, and then declared that on principle he didn't read Moscow papers. He was already drawn into restaurants, clubs, dinners, anniversary parties and he was flattered that well-known lawyers and artists often visited his home and that at the physician's club he played cards with a medical specialist. By this time he managed to consume an entire portion of *selyanka,* a fish or meat potage, right on the skillet.

About a month would pass, it seemed to him, and Anna Sergeevna would become, as it were, befogged in his memory and he would only occasionally dream of her with her touching smile as he had dreamt of all the the others. But a month more went by, the deep winter set in and in his mind's eyes everything was clear just as though it were only yesterday that he had taken leave of Anna Sergeevna. And the recollections flamed up more and more strongly. The voices of the children preparing their lessons would waft into the quiet of evening in his study. He would hear a love song or the organ in a restaurant, or the blizzard would howl in the chimney —then everything would come alive in his memory: what happened on the wharf, the early morning with the mist on the mountains, the steamer from Theodosia and the kiss. He paced for a long time about his room recollecting and smiling and then the recollections turned into dreams. It wasn't that he exactly dreamt of Anna Sergeevna, but she seemed to pace after him everywhere like a shadow and follow him. When he closed his eyes it was as though he could see her alive and she seemed to him more beautiful, younger and tenderer then she really had been, and he seemed to himself better than he actually had been then in Yalta. In the evening she peered at him from the bookshelf, from the fireplace, from the corner. He could hear her breathing and the gentle rustling of her dress. On the street he followed women with his looks as though seeking someone who resembled her. . . .

And now he began to be tormented by a strong desire to share his memories with someone. But at home, of course, he dared not speak of his love, and when away from home there was nobody either among his tenants or at the bank. Besides what was there to talk about? Had he really been in love at the time? Had there actually been anything beautiful, edifying or even interesting in his relations with Anna Sergeevna? And so he found himself talking in generalities about love and women and nobody could guess what it was all about. Only his wife wrinkled her dark brows and remarked:

"Really, Dimitry, the role of lady's man doesn't suit you at all!"

One evening upon leaving the physicians' club with his card partner, a civil servant, he couldn't restrain himself and exlaimed:

"If you only knew what a fascinating woman I met in Yalta!"

The civil servant got into his sleigh and drove off, but suddenly turned around and shouted:

"Dmitry Dmitrich!"

"What?"

"You were right just now, the sturgeon was a little tainted!"

These words, though trite in themselves, suddenly revolted Gurov and seemed to him degrading and dirty. What barbaric habits, what awful people! What stupifying nights, what dull, meaningless days: frenzied card games, gluttony, drunkenness, constant jabbering always about the same thing. Useless activity and conversation always on the same topics cut out the best part of his time, the best portion of his energy, so that in the end was left only a truncated, uninspiring, nonsensical kind of life. It was just as though he were sitting in a madhouse or convict labor camp and it was impossible to escape anywhere. Seething with revulsion Gurov couldn't sleep all night and afterward passed the whole day with a headache. And on the ensuing nights he slept badly, sitting up in bed and thinking or else pacing from corner to corner. The children irritated him, the bank annoyed him, and he had no inclination to go anywhere or talk about anything.

In December during the holidays, he packed his things, and told his wife he was going away to Petersburg to do some favor for a young man, and took off for S ——. Why? He wasn't exactly certain himself. He wanted just to see Anna Sergeevna and have a chat with her and, if possible, to arrange a rendezvous.

He arrived at S —— in the morning and took the best room in a hotel where the whole floor was carpeted with a grey military stuff and on the table there was an inkstand, grey with dust, representing a rider on horseback, arm upraised with hat in hand, but whose head had been broken off. The porter gave him the necessary information. Von Dideritz lived on Old Pottery Street in his own home. This was not far from the hotel. He lived well, as a matter of fact, on a grand scale and kept his own horses. Everyone in town knew him. The porter pronounced the name "Drideritz."

Taking his time, Gurov went to Old Pottery Street and found the house. Just in front of the house stretched a high, grey fence topped with spikes.

"You'd want to escape from that sort of fence," Gurov thought, looking first at the windows and then at the fence.

He weighed the situation: today is a holiday and probably her husband is at home. So it would be tactless to barge into the house and embarrass her. On the other hand, if he sent a note then it might fall into her husband's hands and ruin everything. The best thing would be to pin his hopes on a chance encounter. So he continued to walk up and down the street by the fence waiting for this opportunity. He saw a beggar enter the gate only to be attacked by the dogs and then an hour later he heard someone playing the piano and the sounds that reached him were weak and indistinct. It must have been Anna Sergeevna playing. The front door opened suddenly and out came some old woman and behind her trotted the familiar white Pomeranian. Gurov wanted to call the dog, but suddenly his heart began to beat and he became so nervous he couldn't remember the dog's name.

He kept walking and began hating the grey fence more and more. He already thought irritably that Anna Sergeevna had forgotten about him and perhaps was by this time amusing herself with someone else, which was natural enough for a young woman who had to look at that damned fence from morning till night. He went back to his room and sat for a long time on the sofa not knowing what to do. Then he had dinner and took a long nap.

"How idiotic and upsetting all this is," he thought when he woke up, and glancing through the dark windows saw it was already evening. "Here I've overslept for some reason. Now what am I going to do this evening?"

He sat on the bed, which was covered with a cheap, grey, hospital-type blanket and scolded himself in vexation:

"This is what you get for that lady with the dog! This is an amorous adventure for you! And you just sit here!"

Just that morning at the station a poster with great big letters had struck his eyes—they were presenting the premiere of *The Geisha Girl.* He remember this and took off for the theatre.

"Most likely she goes to first night performances," he thought.

The theatre was jammed. And here, just as in all provincial theatres, the air was hazy above the chandeliers, the people in the gallery were stirring about noisily, and in the front rows before the beginning of the performance the local fops were standing with their hands behind their backs. And there in the governor's box, right in front, sat the governor's daughter in a feather boa, but the governor himself sat modestly concealed behind the drapes and only his hands could be seen. The curtain kept swaying and the orchestra took forever to tune up. During the whole time people that were coming in and taking their seats, Gurov searched avidly with his eyes.

At last Anna Sergeevna entered. She sat in the third row and when Gurov glanced at her his heart was wrung and he understood clearly that now for him there was no other closer, dearer, more important person in the whole world. This little woman, part of the provincial crowd, in no way distinguished, with a lorgnette in her hand like everyone carried, now filled his whole life, was its grief, joy, the only happiness he now wished for himself. And to the strains of the terrible orchestra, the awful local violins, he thought how fine she was. He thought and dreamed.

A young man with thin sideburns, very tall and stooping, entered with Anna Sergeevna and sat by her. At every step he nodded his head and it seemed was forever bowing. No doubt, this was her husband, whom she in an access of bitter feeling when in Yalta, had called a "lackey." And indeed with his long body, his whiskers and little bald spot, there was a certain lackey-like servility about him. He smiled sweetly and in his buttonhole shone some kind of academic decoration exactly like a porter's badge with a number on it.

During the first intermission her husband went out to smoke and she remained at her seat. Gurov, who was also sitting in the orchestra, went up to her and, forcing a smile, said in a shaking voice:

"Hello!"

She glanced at him and turned pale, then looked again in alarm not quite believing her eyes and tightly squeezed her fan and lorgnette together in her hands, evidently struggling with herself so as not to fall in a faint.

Neither said a word. She was sitting, he standing up and, frightened by her embarrassment, couldn't make up his mind to sit down beside her. The sounds of violins tuning up and flutes were heard and suddenly the situation became awful. It seemed as though people were looking at them from all the loges. But all at once she got up and dashed to the exit. He followed behind her and they both went at random through the corridors and up and down staircases. Before their eyes people in judicial, school, and provincial uniforms passed rapidly all wearing decorations. Ladies flitted past and they passed by fur coats hanging on the walls. A draught was blowing heavy with the odor of tobacco smoke. And Gurov, whose heart was pounding thought:

"O Lord, why do these people have to be here, that orchestra . . . ?"

And at that moment he suddenly remembered how on that evening when he took Anna Sergeevna to the station he told himself that it was all over and that they would never see each other again. But how far off the end still was!

On a narrow, gloomy stairway on which was written "Entrance to the gallery," she stopped.

"How you frightened me!" she said, breathing hard, still quite pale and stunned. "Oh, how you frightened me! I'm half dead! Why did you come? Why?"

"But understand, Anna, understand," he mumbled hastily in a low voice. "I beg you try to understand."

She looked at him with alarm, with entreaty, with love. She looked at him intently as though to engrave his features more deeply in her memory.

"I have suffered so much," she continued, not listening to him. "All the while I have thought only about you. And I wanted to forget, forget! But why have you come?"

A little above on the landing two schoolboys were smoking and looking down, but Gurov didn't care. He drew Anna Sergeevna to him and began kissing her face, cheeks, hands.

"What are you doing, what are you doing?" she said in fear, pushing him away from her. "We must be mad. Go away today, go right now. I pray you by all that's holy! I beg you . . . someone's coming up!"

Someone was coming up the stairs from below.

"You must go away," Anna Sergeevna went on in a whisper. "Do you hear, Dmitry Dmitrich? I'll come to you in Moscow. I have never been happy. I'm unhappy now and never, never will be happy, never! Don't make me suffer still more! I swear I'll come to Moscow. But now we must part! My sweet, good, dearest, we must part!"

She pressed his hand and began to go down quickly, looking back at him all the while, and from her eyes it was really quite evident she was not happy. Gurov stood a little while listening and then when everything had quieted down, took his coat off the hook and went out of the theatre.

IV

And Anna Sergeevna began to come to Moscow to visit him. Once every two or three months she left S—— and told her husband that she was going to consult a specialist about a female complaint—and her husband believed and didn't believe her. When she came to Moscow, she stayed at the Slavonic Bazaar Hotel and immediately sent a messenger in a red cap to Gurov. Gurov would go to see her and nobody in Moscow knew about it.

He was going to her thus one winter morning (the messenger had been to his home the evening before and didn't find him in). Beside him walked his daughter, who wanted him to accompany her to school since it was on his way. A heavy, damp snow was piling up.

"Three degrees above freezing now and just the same it is snowing," said Gurov to his daughter, "but actually the warmth is only on the surface of the earth. In the upper layers of the atmosphere the temperature is quite different."

"Papa, and why doesn't it thunder in winter?"

He explained this, too. He spoke and thought that here he was going to a rendezvous and not a living soul knew of it and probably would never know. He was leading two lives: the evident one which everyone whom it concerned could see and know about—full of conventional truth and conventional deceit, just exactly like the lives of his acquaintances and friends—and the other life he was carrying on in secret. And by some strange coincidence, perhaps accidental, everything that was for him important, interesting, indispensable, in which he was sincere and did not deceive himself, which formed the kernel of his life, was secretly hidden from others, whereas what was for him a lie, a shell under which he hid to conceal the truth as, for example, his job at the bank, discussions at the club, his "inferior race," going with his wife to anniversary parties—all this was on the surface. And he judged others by himself. He couldn't believe what he saw and always supposed that every other man led his real, most interesting life under a veil of mystery, under cover of night. Each man's personal existence was carried on in secret and perhaps, on this account, every civilized man was so nervously concerned that his personal secret remain inviolate.

After he took his daughter to school, Gurov set off for the Slavonic Bazaar Hotel. He hung up his fur coat downstairs, went up and quietly knocked at the door. Anna Sergeevna, wearing his favorite grey dress, worn out from travelling and expectation, had been waiting for him since the evening before. She was pale and glanced at him without a smile. Hardly had he entered when she pressed up against his chest. It was as though they hadn't seen each other for two years. Their kiss was long and lingering.

"Well, how are you getting on there?" he asked. "What's new?"

"Wait just a moment, I'll tell you. . . . Right now, I can't."

She couldn't speak, she was weeping so much. She turned away from him and pressed a handkerchief to her eyes.

Well, let her cry herself out and I'll just sit down meanwhile, he concluded and sat in an armchair.

Then he rang to ask them to bring up some tea and all the while he was drinking his tea she stood with her face to the window. She wept from emotion, from the mournful awareness that their life had taken such a sad turn—they had to see one another only secretly, they were obliged to hide from people like thieves! Weren't their lives in fact wrecked?

"Oh, do stop!" he said.

For him it was evident that their love was far from finished and they had no idea just when it would be. Anna Sergeevna was becoming all the more strongly attached to him; she adored him and it would be unthinkable to tell her that all of this would sometime have to have an end. Besides, she wouldn't even believe it.

He went up to her and took her by the shoulders, to caress her, to cheer her with a little joke and just then he caught sight of himself in the looking glass.

His head was already getting grey and it seemed to him strange that he had got so old during these last years and had lost his good looks. The shoulders upon which his hands lay were warm and pulsating. He felt compassion for this live body, still so warm and beautiful, but probably already near the point where it would begin to fade and wither as had his own person. Why did she love him so? He always seemed to women other than he really was and they loved in him, not his real self, but the man they had created in their imaginations and whom they were avidly seeking throughout their lives; and then when they became aware of their error, they loved him just the same. And not one of them had ever been happy with him. The time passed, he made liaisons, broke them off and went his way, but he was never in love. He had experienced every conceivable type of relationship, but there was never love.

And it was only now when he was getting grey, that he had fallen in love—*comme il faut*—genuinely, for the first time in his life.

Anna Sergeevna and he loved one another like close kinsfolk, like husband and wife, like tender friends. It seemed to them that they were destined for one another by fate itself and it was incomprehensible that he should have a wife and she a husband. They were just like two birds of passage, a male and female, who had been caught and made to dwell in separated cages. They had forgiven one another for everything they had been ashamed of in the past, and they forgave everything in the present and felt that this love had changed them both.

Formerly in moments of anguish, he consoled himself with whatever rationalization first came into his head, but now he was no longer capable of reasoning. He felt a deep compassion for her and wanted to be sincere, tender. . . .

"'Stop, my darling," he said. "You've cried enough. Now let's have a talk and we'll think of something."

Then they talked things over for a long while, discussing how they could deliver themselves from the necessity of hiding, deceiving, living in different towns and not seeing each other for long periods. How could they free themselves from their unbearable chains?

"How? How?" he asked, gripping his head in his hands. "How?"

And it seemed that in just a little while a solution would be found and then a fine new life would begin; and it was clear to them both that the end was still far far away and that the most complex and difficult part was only just beginning.

Henry James

(1843 - 1916)

In a well-known essay, "Paleface and Redskin," Philip Rahv observed that the "creative mind in America is fragmented and one-sided," that American writers have tended to gravitate toward one of two distinct poles. They have either glorified experience, energy, *élan* (the redskins) or they have emphasized consciousness, sensibility, delicate emotional states (the palefaces). ". . . While the redskin glories in his Americanism," Professor Rahv wrote, "to the paleface it is a source of endless ambiguities. Sociologically they can be distinguished as patrician vs. plebeian, and in their aesthetic ideals one is drawn to allegory and the distillations of symbolism, whereas the other inclines to a gross, riotous naturalism." Henry James, who was born in New York City but settled in London as a young man and ultimately became a British citizen, was a consummate paleface, a cosmopolitan patrician who once said, "I have not the least hesitation in saying that I aspire to write in such a way that it would be impossible to an outsider to say whether at a given moment I am an American writing about England or an Englishman writing about America." Although it may be unimportant whether James is classified as a British or an American writer, it is worth noting that he repeatedly examined the ambiguous relationship between American and European cultures. In his fiction James played many variations on the theme of an innocent and awkward American confronted by refined but slightly decadent and unscrupulous Europeans. Like Hawthorne, another paleface who influenced him, James was drawn to "the distillations of symbolism" rather than traditional realism, and he enjoyed exploring the psychological motivations of his characters, what he called "the atmosphere of the mind." The author of several important, fascinating, sometimes difficult novels (*The Portrait of a Lady,* 1881, *The Wings of the Dove,* 1902, and *The Ambassadors,* 1903, being three of the best), James also wrote 112 tales, many of which are more like short novels than stories. In discussing his shorter narratives he made the distinction between an "anecdote," which dramatizes an interesting incident that happens to a single person, and a "picture," which cannot develop into a dramatic action, such as "The Beast in the Jungle." Often long-winded, James was considerably less successful in the short story than in the novel because, as his biographer Leon Edel has said, his tales belong to an era of greater leisure and patience than the twentieth century. Nevertheless, in such short narratives as "The Beast in the Jungle," James writes at the height of his powers and creates nothing short of a masterpiece.

The Beast in the Jungle

I

What determined the speech that startled him in the course of their encounter scarcely matters, being probably but some words spoken by himself quite without intention—spoken as they lingered and slowly moved together after their renewal of acquaintance. He had been conveyed by friends an hour or two before to the house at which she was staying; the party of visitors at the other house, of whom he was one, and thanks to whom it was his theory, as always, that he was lost in the crowd, had been invited over to luncheon. There had been after luncheon much dispersal, all in the interest of the original motive, a view of Weatherend itself and the fine things, intrinsic features, pictures, heirlooms, treasures of all the arts, that made the place almost famous; and the great rooms were so numerous that guests could wander at their will, hang back from the principal group and in cases where they took such matters with the last seriousness give themselves up to mysterious appreciations and measurements. There were persons to be observed, singly or in couples, bending toward objects in out-of-the-way corners with their hands on their knees and their heads nodding quite as with the emphasis of an excited sense of smell. When they were two they either mingled their sounds of ecstasy or melted into silences of even deeper import, so that there were aspects of the occasion that gave it for Marcher much the air of the "look round," previous to a sale highly advertised, that excites or quenches, as may be, the dream of acquisition. The dream of acquisition at Weatherend would have had to be wild indeed, and John Marcher found himself, among such suggestions, disconcerted almost equally by the presence of those who knew too much and by that of those who knew nothing. The great rooms caused so much poetry and history to press upon him that he needed some straying apart to feel in a proper relation with them, though this impulse was not, as happened, like the gloating of some of his companions, to be compared to the movement of a dog sniffing a cupboard. It had an issue promptly enough in a direction that was not to have been calculated.

"The Beast in the Jungle" by Henry James. New York: Charles Scribner's Sons, Publishers.

It led, briefly, in the course of the October afternoon, to his closer meeting with May Bartram, whose face, a reminder, yet not quite a remembrance, as they sat much separated at a very long table, had begun merely by troubling him rather pleasantly. It affected him as the sequel of something of which he had lost the beginning. He knew it, and for the time quite welcomed it, as a continuation, but didn't know what it continued, which was an interest or an amusement the greater as he was also somehow aware—yet without a direct sign from her—that the young woman herself hadn't lost the thread. She hadn't lost it, but she wouldn't give it back to him, he saw, without some putting forth of his hand for it; and he not only saw that, but saw several things more, things odd enough in the light of the fact that at the moment some accident of grouping brought them face to face he was still merely fumbling with the idea that any contact between them in the past would have had no importance. If it had had no importance he scarcely knew why his actual impression of her should so seem to have so much; the answer to which, however, was that in such a life as they all appeared to be leading for the moment one could but take things as they came. He was satisfied, without in the least being able to say why, that this young lady might roughly have ranked in the house as a poor relation; satisfied also that she was not there on a brief visit, but was more or less a part of the establishment—almost a working, a remunerated part. Didn't she enjoy at periods a protection that she paid for by helping, among other services, to show the place and explain it, deal with the tiresome people, answer questions about the dates of the building, the style of the furniture, the authorship of the pictures, the favourite haunts of the ghost? It wasn't that she looked as if you could have given her shillings—it was impossible to look less so. Yet when she finally drifted toward him, distinctly handsome, though ever so much older—older than when he had seen her before—it might have been as an effect of her guessing that he had, within the couple of hours, devoted more imagination to her than to all the others put together, and had thereby penetrated to a kind of truth that the others were too stupid for. She *was* there on harder terms than any one; she was there as a consequence of things suffered, one way and another, in the interval of years; and she remembered him very much as she was remembered—only a good deal better.

By the time they at last thus came to speech they were alone in one of the rooms—remarkable for a fine portrait over the chimney-place—out of which their friends had passed, and the charm of it was that even before they had spoken they had practically arranged with each other to stay behind for talk. The charm, happily, was in other things too—partly in there being scarce a spot at Weatherend without something to stay behind for. It was in the way the autumn day looked into the high windows as it waned; the way the red light, breaking at the close from under a low sombre sky, reached out in a long shaft and played over old wainscots, old tapestry, old gold, old colour. It was most of all perhaps in the way she came to him as if, since she had been turned on to deal with the simpler sort, he might, should he choose to keep the whole thing down, just take her mild attention for a part of her general business. As soon as he heard her voice, however, the gap was filled up and the missing link supplied; the slight irony he divined in her attitude lost its advantage. He almost jumped at it to get there before her. "I met you years and years ago in Rome. I remember all about it." She confessed to disappointment—she had been so sure he didn't; and to prove how well he did he began to pour forth the particular recollections that popped up as he called for them. Her face and her voice, all at his service now, worked the miracle—the impression operating like the torch of a lamplighter who touches into flame, one by one, a long row of gas-jets. Marcher flattered himself the illumination was brilliant, yet he was really still more pleased on her showing him, with amusement, that in his haste to make everything right he had got most things rather wrong. It hadn't been at Rome—it had been at Naples; and it hadn't been eight years before—it had been more nearly ten. She hadn't been, either, with her uncle and aunt, but with her mother and her brother; in addition to which it was not with the Pembles *he* had been, but with the Boyers, coming down in their company from Rome—a point on which she inisted, a little to his confusion, and as to which she had her evidence in hand. The Boyers she had known, but didn't know the Pembles, though she had heard of them, and it was the people he was with who had made them acquainted. The incident of the thunderstorm that had raged round them with such violence as to drive them for refuge into an excavation—this incident had not occurred at the Palace of the Caesars, but at Pompeii, on an occasion when they had been present there at an important find.

He accepted her amendments, he enjoyed her corrections, though the moral of them was, she pointed out, that he *really* didn't remember the least thing about her; and he only felt it as a drawback that when all was made strictly historic there didn't appear much of anything left. They lingered together still, she neglecting her office—for from the moment he was so clever she had no proper right to him—and both neglecting the house, just waiting as to see if a memory or two more wouldn't again breathe on them. It hadn't taken them many minutes, after all, to put down on the table, like the cards of a pack, those that constituted their respective hands; only what came out was that the pack was unfortunately not perfect—that the past, invoked, invited, encouraged, could give them, naturally, no more than it had. It had made them anciently meet—her at twenty, him at twenty-five; but nothing was so strange, they seemed to say to each other, as that, while so occupied, it hadn't done a little more for them. They looked at each other as with the feeling of an occasion missed; the present would have been so much better if the other, in the far distance, in the foreign land, hadn't been so stupidly meagre. There weren't apparently, all counted, more than a dozen little old things that had succeeded in coming to pass between them; trivialities of youth, simplicities of freshness, stupidities of ignorance, small possible germs, but too deeply buried—too deeply (didn't it seem?) to sprout after so many years. Marcher could only feel he ought to have rendered her some service—saved her from a capsized boat in the Bay or at least recovered her dressing-bag, filched from her cab in the streets of Naples by a lazzarone with a stiletto. Or it would have been nice if he could have been taken with fever all alone at his hotel, and she could have come to look after him, to write to his people, to drive him out in convalescence. *Then* they would be in possession of the something or other that their actual show seemed to lack. It yet somehow presented itself, this show, as too good to be spoiled; so that they were reduced for a few minutes more to wondering a little helplessly why—since they seemed to know a certain number of the same people—their reunion had been so long averted. They didn't use that name for it, but their delay from minute to minute to join the others was a kind of confession that they didn't quite want it to be a failure. Their attempted supposition of reasons for their not having met but showed how little they knew of each other. There came in fact a moment when Marcher felt a positive pang. It was vain to pretend she was an old friend, for all the communities were wanting, in spite of which it was an old friend that he saw she would have suited him. He had new ones enough—was surrounded with them for instance on the stage of the other house; as a new one he probably wouldn't have so much as noticed her. He would have liked to invent something, get her to make-believe with him that some passage of a romantic or critical kind *had* originally occurred. He was really almost reaching out in imagination—as against time—for something that would do, and saying to himself that if it didn't come this sketch of a fresh start would show for quite awkwardly bungled. They would separate, and now for no second or no third chance. They would have tried and not succeeded. Then it was, just at the turn, as he afterwards made it out to himself, that, everything else failing, she herself decided to take up the case and, as it were, save the situation. He felt as soon as she spoke that she had been consciously keeping back what she said and hoping to get on without it; a scruple in her that immensely touched him when, by the end of three or four minutes more, he was able to measure it. What she brought out, at any rate, quite cleared the air and supplied the link—the link it was so odd he should frivolously have managed to lose.

"You know you told me something I've never forgotten and that again and again has made me think of you since; it was that tremendously hot day when we went to Sorrento, across the bay, for the breeze. What I allude to was what you said to me, on the way back, as we sat under the awning of the boat enjoying the cool. Have you forgotten?"

He had forgotten and was even more surprised than ashamed. But the great thing was that he saw in this no vulgar reminder of any "sweet" speech. The vanity of women had long memories, but she was making no claim on him of a compliment or a mistake. With another woman, a totally different one, he might have feared the recall of possibly even some imbecile "offer." So, in having to say that he had indeed forgotten, he was conscious rather of a loss than of a gain; he already saw an interest in the matter of her mention. "I try to think—but I give it up. Yet I remember the Sorrento day."

"I'm not very sure you do," May Bartram after a moment said; "and I'm not very sure I ought to want you to. It's dreadful to bring a person back at any time to what he was ten years before. If you've lived away from it," she smiled, "so much the better."

"Ah if *you* haven't why should I?" he asked

"Lived away, you mean, from what I myself was?"

"From what *I* was. I was of course an ass," Marcher went on; "but I would rather know from you just the sort of ass I was than—from the moment you have something in your mind—not know anything."

Still, however, she hesitated. "But if you've completely ceased to be that sort—?"

"Why I can then all the more bear to know. Besides, perhaps I haven't."

"Perhaps. Yet if you haven't," she added, "I should suppose you'd remember. Not indeed that *I* in the least connect with my impression the invidious name you use. If I had only thought you foolish," she explained, "the thing I speak of wouldn't so have remained with me. It was about yourself." She waited as if it might come to him, but in only meeting her eyes in wonder, he gave no sign, she burnt her lips.

"Has it ever happened?"

Then it was that, while he continued to stare, a light broke for him and the blood slowly came to his face, which began to burn with recognition. "Do you mean I told you—?" But he faltered, lest what came to him shouldn't be right, lest he should only give himself away.

"It was something about yourself that it was natural one shouldn't forget—that is if one remembered you at all. That's why I ask you," she smiled, "if the thing you then spoke of has ever come to pass?"

Oh then he saw, but he was lost in wonder and found himself embarassed. This, he also saw, made her sorry for him, as if her allusion had been a mistake. It took him but a moment, however, to feel it hadn't been, much as it had been a surprise. After the first little shock of it her knowledge on the contrary began, even if rather strangely, to taste sweet to him. She was the only other person in the world then who would have it, and she had had it all these years, while the fact of his having so breathed his secret had unaccountably faded from him. No wonder they couldn't have met as if nothing had happened. "I judge," he finally said, "that I know what you mean. Only I had strangely enough lost any sense of having taken you so far into my confidence."

"Is it because you've taken so many others as well?"

"I've taken nobody. Not a creature since then."

"So that I'm the only person who knows?"

"The only person in the world."

"Well," she quickly replied, "I myself have never spoken. I've never, never repeated of you what you told me." She looked at him so that he perfectly believed her. Their eyes met over it in such a way that he was without a doubt. "And I never will."

She spoke with an earnestness that, as if almost excessive, put him at ease about her possible derision. Somehow the whole question was a new luxury to him—that is from the moment she was in possession. If she didn't take the sarcastic view she clearly took the sympathetic, and that was what he had had, in all the long time, from no one whomsoever. What he felt was that he couldn't at present have begun to tell her, and yet could profit perhaps exquisitely by the accident of having done so of old. "Please don't then. We're just right as it is."

"Oh I am," she laughed, "if you are!" To which she added: "Then you do still feel in the same way?"

It was impossible to him not to take to himself that she was really interested, and it all kept coming as a sort of revelation. He had thought of himself so long as abominably alone, and lo he wasn't alone a bit. He hadn't been, it appeared, for an hour—since those moments on the Sorrento boat. It was *she* who had been, he seemed to see as he looked at her—she who had been made so by the graceless fact of his lapse of fidelity. To tell her what he had told her—what had it been but to ask something of her? something that she had given, in her charity, without his having, by a remembrance, by a return of the spirit, failing another encounter, so much as thanked her. What he had asked of her had been simply at first not to laugh at him. She had beautifully not done so for ten years, and she was not doing so now. So he had endless gratitude to make up. Only for that he must see just how he had figured to her. "What, exactly, was the account I gave—?"

"Of the way you did feel? Well, it was very simple. You said you had had from your earliest time, as the deepest thing within you, the sense of being kept for something rare and strange, possibly prodigious and terrible, that was sooner or later to happen to you, that you had in your bones the foreboding and the conviction of, and that would perhaps overwhelm you."

"Do you call that very simple?" John Marcher asked.

She thought a moment. "It was perhaps because I seemed, as you spoke, to understand it."

"You do understand it?" he eagerly asked.

Again she kept her kind eyes on him. "You still have the belief?"

"Oh!" he exclaimed helplessly. There was too much to say.

"Whatever it's to be," she clearly made out, "it hasn't yet come."

He shook his head in complete surrender now. "It hasn't yet come. Only, you know, it isn't anything I'm to *do,* to achieve in the world, to be distinguished or admired for. I'm not such an ass as *that.* It would be much better, no doubt, if I were."

"It's to be something you're merely to suffer?"

"Well, say to wait for—to have to meet, to face, to see suddenly break out in my life; possibly destroying all further consciousness, possibly annihilating me; possibly, on the other hand, only altering everything, striking at the root of all my world and leaving me to the consequences, however they shape themselves."

She took this in, but the light in her eyes continued for him not to be that of mockery. "Isn't what you describe perhaps but the expectation—or at any rate the sense of danger, familiar to so many people—of falling in love?"

John Marcher wondered. "Did you ask me that before?"

"No—I wasn't so free-and-easy then. But it's what strikes me now."

"Of course," he said after a moment, "it strikes you. Of course it strikes *me.* Of course what's in store for me may be no more than that. The only thing is," he went on, "that I think if it had been that I should by this time know."

"Do you mean because you've *been* in love?" And then as he but looked at her in silence: "You've been in love, and it hasn't meant such a cataclysm, hasn't proved the great affair?"

"Here I am, you see. It hasn't been overwhelming."

"Then it hasn't been love," said May Bartram.

"Well, I at least thought it was. I took it for that—I've taken it till now. It was agreeable, it was delightful, it was miserable," he explained. "But it wasn't strange. It wasn't what *my* affair's to be."

"You want something all to yourself—something that nobody else knows or *has* known?"

"It isn't a question of what I 'want'—God knows I don't want anything. It's only a question of the apprehension that haunts me—that I live with day by day."

He said this so lucidly and consistently that he could see it further impose itself. If she hadn't been interested before she'd have been interested now. "Is it a sense of coming violence?"

Evidently now too again he liked to talk of it. "I don't think of it as—when it does come—necessarily violent. I only think of it as natural and as of course above all unmistakable. I think of it simply as the thing. *The* thing will of itself appear natural."

"Then how will it appear strange?"

Marcher bethought himself. "It won't—to *me.*"

"To whom then?"

"Well," he replied, smiling at last, "say to you."

"Oh then I'm to be present?"

"Why you *are* present—since you know."

"I see," She turned it over. "But I mean at the catastrophe."

At this, for a minute, their lightness gave way to their gravity; it was as if the long look they exchanged held them together. "It will only depend on yourself—if you'll watch with me."

"Are you afraid?" she asked.

"Don't leave me *now,*" he went on.

"Are you afraid?" she repeated.

"Do you think me simply out of my mind?" he pursued instead of answering. "Do I merely strike you as a harmless lunatic?"

"No," said May Bartram. "I understand you. I believe you."

"You mean you feel how my obsession—poor old thing!—may correspond to some possible reality?"

"To some possible reality."

"Then you *will* watch with me?"

She hesitated, then for the third time put her question. "Are you afraid?"

"Did I tell you I was—at Naples?"

"No, you said nothing about it."

"Then I don't know. And I should *like* to know," said John Marcher. "You'll tell me yourself whether you think so. If you'll watch with me you'll see."

"Very good then." They had been moving by this time across the room, and at the door, before passing out, they paused as for the full wind-up of their understanding. "I'll watch with you," said May Bartram.

II

The fact that she "knew"—knew and yet neither chaffed him nor betrayed him—had in a short time begun to constitute between them a goodly bond, which became more marked when, within the year that followed their afternoon at Weatherend, the opportunities for meeting multiplied. The event that thus promoted these occasions was the death of the ancient lady her great-aunt, under whose wing, since losing her mother, she had to such an extent found shelter, and who, though but the widowed mother of the new successor to the property, had succeeded—thanks to a high tone and a high temper—in not forfeiting the supreme position at the great house. The deposition of this personage arrived but with her death, which, followed by many changes, made in particular a difference for the young woman in whom Marcher's expert attention had recognised from the first a dependent with a pride that might ache though it didn't bristle. Nothing for a long time had made him easier than the thought that the aching must have been much soothed by Miss Bartram's now finding herself able to set up a small home in London. She had acquired property, to an amount that made that luxury just possible, under her aunt's extremely complicated will, and when the whole matter began to be straightened out, which indeed took time, she let him know that the happy issue was at last in view. He had seen her again before that day, both because he had more than once accompanied the ancient lady to town and because he had paid another visit to the friends who so conveniently made of Weatherend one of the charms of their own hospitality. These friends had taken him back there; he had achieved there again with Miss Bartram some quiet detachment; and he had in London succeeded in persuading her to more than one brief absence from her aunt. They went together, on these latter occasions, to the National Gallery and the South Kensington Museum, where, among vivid reminders, they talked of Italy at large—not now attempting to recover, as at first, the taste of their youth and their ignorance. That recovery, the first day at Weatherend, had served its purpose well, had given them quite enough; so that they were, to Marcher's sense, no longer hovering about the headwaters of their stream, but had felt their boat pushed sharply off and down the current.

They were literally afloat together; for our gentleman this was marked, quite as marked as that the fortunate cause of it was just the buried treasure of her knowledge. He had with his own hands dug up this little hoard, brought to light—that is to within reach of the dim day constituted by their discretions and privacies—the object of value the hiding-place of which he had, after putting it into the ground himself, so strangely, so long forgotten. The rare luck of his having again just stumbled on the spot made him indifferent to any other question; he would doubtless have devoted more time to the odd accident of his lapse of memory if he hadn't been moved to devote so much to the sweetness, the comfort, as he felt, for the future, that this accident itself had helped to keep fresh. It had never entered into his plan that any one should "know," and mainly for the reason that it wasn't in him to tell any one. That would have been impossible, for nothing but the amusement of a cold world would have waited on it. Since, however, a mysterious fate had opened his mouth betimes, in spite of him, he would count that a compensation and profit by it to the utmost. That the right person *should* know tempered the asperity of his secret more even than his shyness had permitted him to imagine; and May Bartram was clearly right, because—well, because there she was. Her knowledge simply settled it; he would have been sure enough by this time had she been wrong. There was that in his situation, no doubt, that disposed him too much to see her as a mere confidant, taking all her light for him from the fact—the fact only—of her interest in his predicament; from her mercy, sympathy, seriousness, her consent not to regard him as the funniest of the funny. Aware, in fine, that her price for him was just in her giving him this constant sense of his being admirably spared, he was careful to remember that she had also a life of her own, with things that might happen to *her*, things that in friendship one should likewise take account of. Something fairly remarkable came to pass with him, for that matter, in this connexion —something represented by a certain passage of his consciousness, in the suddenest way, from one extreme to the other.

He had though himself, so long as nobody knew, the most disinterested person in the world, carrying his concentrated burden, his perpetual suspense, ever so quietly, holding his tongue about it, giving others no glimpse of it nor of its effect upon his life, asking of them no allowance and only making on his side all those that were asked. He hadn't disturbed people with the queerness of their having to know a haunted man, though he had had moments of rather special temptation on hearing them say they were foresooth "unsettled." If they were as unsettled as he was—he who had never been settled for an hour in his life—they would know what it meant. Yet it wasn't, all the same, for him to make them, and he listened to them civilly enough. This was why he had such good—though possibly such rather colourless—manners; this was why, above all, he could regard himself, in a greedy world, as decently—as in fact perhaps even a little sublimely—unselfish. Our point is accordingly that he valued this character quite sufficiently to measure his present danger of letting it lapse, against which he promised himself to be much on his guard. He was quite ready, none the less, to be selfish just a little, since surely no more charming occasion for it had come to him. "Just a little," in a word, was just as much as Miss Bartram, taking one day with another, would let him. He never would be in the least coercive, and would keep well before him the lines on which consideration for her—the very highest—ought to proceed. He would thoroughly establish the heads under which her affairs, her requirements, her peculiarities—he went so far as to give them the latitude of that name—would come into their intercourse. All this naturally was a sign of how much he took the intercourse itself for granted. There was nothing more to be done about *that.* It simply existed; had sprung into being with her first penetrating question to him in the autumn light there at Weatherend. The real form it should have taken on the basis that stood out large was the form of their marrying. But the devil in this was that the very basis itself put marrying out of the question. His conviction, his apprehension, his obsession, in short, wasn't a privilege he could invite a woman to share; and that consequence of it was precisely what was the matter with him. Something or other lay in wait for him amid the twists and the turns of the months and the years, like a crouching beast in the jungle. It signified little whether the crouching beast were destined to slay him or to be slain. The definite point was the inevitable spring of the creature; and the definite lesson from that was that a man of feeling didn't cause himself to be accompanied by a lady on a tiger-hunt. Such was the image under which he had ended by figuring his life.

They had at first, none the less, in the scattered hours spent together, made no allusion to that view of it; which was a sign he was handsomely alert to give that he didn't expect, that he in fact didn't care, always to be talking about it. Such a feature in one's outlook was really like a hump on one's back. The difference it made every minute of the day existed quite independently of discussion. One discussed of course *like* a hunchback, for there was always, if nothing else, the hunchback face. That remained, and she was watching him; but people watched best, as a general thing in silence, so that such would be predominantly the manner of their vigil. Yet he didn't want, at the same time, to be tense and solemn; tense and solemn was what he imagined he too much showed for with other people. The thing to be, with the one person who knew, was easy and natural—to make the reference rather than be seeming to avoid it, to avoid it rather than be seeming to make it, and to keep it in any case, familiar, facetious even, rather than pedantic and portentous. Some such consideration as the latter was doubtless in his mind for instance when he wrote pleasantly to Miss Bartram that perhaps the great thing he had so long felt as in the lap of the gods was no more than this circumstance, which touched him so nearly, of her acquiring a house in London. It was the first allusion they had yet again made, needing any other hitherto so little; but when she replied, after having given him the news, that she was by no means satisfied with such a trifle as the climax to so special a suspense, she almost set him wondering if she hadn't even a larger conception of singularity for him than he had for himself. He was at all events destined to become aware little by little, as time went by, that she was all the while looking at his life, judging it, measuring it, in the light of the thing she knew, which grew to be at last, with the consecration of the years, never mentioned between them save as "the real truth" about him. That had always been his own form of reference to it, but she adopted the form so quietly that, looking back at the end of a period, he knew there was no moment at which it was traceable that she had, as he might say, got inside his idea, or exchanged the attitude of beautifully indulging for that of still more beautifully believing him.

It was always open to him to accuse her of seeing him but as the most harmless of maniacs, and this, in the long run—since it covered so much ground—was his easiest description of their friendship. He had a screw loose for her, but she liked him in spite of it and was practically, against the rest of the world, his kind wise keeper, unremunerated but fairly amused and, in the absence of other near ties, not disreputably occupied. The rest of the world of course thought him queer, but she, she only, knew how, and above all why, queer; which was precisely what enabled her to dispose the concealing veil in the right folds. She took his gaiety from him—since it had to pass with them for gaiety—as she took everything else; but she certainly so far justified by her unerring touch his finer sense of the degree to which he had ended by convincing her. *She* at least never spoke of the secret of his life except as "the real truth about you," and she had in fact a wonderful way of making it seem, as such, the secret of her own life too. That was in fine how he so constantly felt her as allowing for him; he couldn't on the whole call it anything else. He allowed for himself, but she, exactly, allowed still more; partly because, better placed for a sight of the matter, she traced his unhappy perversion through reaches of its course into which he could scarce follow it. He knew how he felt, but, besides knowing that, she knew how he *looked* as well; he knew each of the things of importance he was insidiously kept from doing, but she could add up the amount they made, understand how much, with a lighter weight on his spirit, he might have done, and thereby establish how, clever as he was, he fell short. Above all she was in the secret of the difference between the forms he went through—those of his little office under Government, those of caring for his modest patrimony, for his library, for his garden in the country, for the people in London whose invitations he accepted and repaid—and the detachment that reigned beneath them and that made of all behaviour, all that could in the least be called behaviour, a long act of dissimulation. What it had come to was that he wore a mask painted with the social simper, out of the eye-holes of which there looked eyes of an expression not in the least matching the other features. This the stupid world, even after years, had never more than half-discovered. It was only May Bartram who had, and she achieved, by an art indescribable, the feat of at once—or perhaps it was only alternately—meeting the eyes from in front and mingling her own vision, as from over his shoulder, with their peep through the apertures.

So while they grew older together she did watch with him, and so she let this association give shape and colour to her own existence. Beneath *her* forms as well detachment had learned to sit, and behaviour had become for her, in the social sense, a false account of herself. There was but one account of her that would have been true all the while and that she could give straight to nobody, least of all to John Marcher. Her whole attitude was a virtual statement, but the perception of that only seemed called to take its place for him as one of the many things necessarily crowded out of his consciousness. If she had moreover, like himself, to make sacrifices to their real truth, it was to be granted that her compensation might have affected her as more prompt and more natural. They had long periods, in this London time, during which, when they were together, a stranger might have listened to them without in the least pricking up his ears; on the other hand the real truth was equally liable at any moment to rise to the surface, and the auditor would then have wondered indeed what they were talking about. They had from an early hour made up their mind that society was, luckily, unintelligent, and the margin allowed them by this had fairly become one of their commonplaces. Yet there were still moments when the situation turned almost fresh—usually under the effect of some expression drawn from herself. Her expressions doubtless repeated themselves, but her intervals were generous. "What saves us, you know, is that we answer so completely to so usual an appearance: that of the man and woman whose friendship has become such a daily habit—or almost—as to be at last indispensable." That for instance was a remark she had frequently enough had occasion to make, though she had given it at different times different developments. What we are especially concerned with is the turn it happened to take from her one afternoon when he had come to see her in honour of her birthday. This anniversary had fallen on a Sunday, at a season of thick fog and general outward gloom; but he had brought her his customary offering, having known her now long enough to have established a hundred small traditions. It was one of his proofs to himself, the present he made her on her birthday, that he hadn't sunk into real selfishness. It was mostly nothing more than a small trinket, but it was always fine of its kind, and he was regularly careful to pay for it more than he thought he could afford. "Our habit saves you at least, don't you see? because it makes you, after all, for the vulgar, indistinguishable from other men. What's the most inveterate mark of men in general? Why the capacity to spend endless time with dull women—to spend it I won't say without being bored, but without minding that they are, without being driven off at a tangent by it; which comes to the same thing. I'm your dull woman, a part of the daily bread for which you pray at church. That covers your tracks more than anything."

"And what covers yours?" asked Marcher, whom his dull woman could mostly to this extent amuse. "I see of course what you mean by your saving me, in this way and that, so far as other people are concerned—I've seen it all along. Only what is it that saves *you?* I often think, you know, of that."

She looked as if she sometimes thought of that too, but rather in a different way. "Where other people, you mean, are concerned?"

"Well, you're really so in with me, you know—as a sort of result of my being so in with yourself. I mean of my having such an immense regard for you, being so tremendously mindful of all you've done for me. I sometimes ask myself if it's quite fair. Fair I mean to have so involved and—since one may say it—interested you. I almost feel as if you hadn't really had time to do anything else."

"Anything else but be interested?" she asked. "Ah what else does one ever want to be? If I've being 'watching' with you, as we long ago agreed I was to do, watching's always in itself an absorption."

"Oh certainly," John Marcher said, "if you hadn't had your curiosity—! Only doesn't it sometimes come to you as time goes on that your curiosity isn't being particularly repaid?"

May Bartram had a pause. "Do you ask that, by any chance, because you feel at all that yours isn't? I mean because you have to wait so long."

Oh he understood what she meant! "For the thing to happen that never does happen? For the beast to jump out? No, I'm just where I was about it. It isn't a matter as to which I can *choose,* I can decide for a change. It isn't one as to which there *can* be a change. It's in the lap of the gods. One's in the hands of one's law—there one is. As to the form the law will take, the way it will operate, that's its own affair."

"Yes," Miss Bartram replied; "of course one's fate's coming, of course it *has* come in its own form and its own way, all the while. Only, you know, the form and the way in your case were to have been—well, something so exceptional and, as one may say, so particulary *your* own."

Something in this made him look at her with suspicion. "You say 'were to *have* been,' as if in your heart you had begun to doubt."

"Oh!" she vaguely protested.

"As if you believed," he went on, "that nothing will now take place."

She shook her head slowly but rather inscrutably. "You're far from my thought."

He continued to look at her. "What then is the matter with you?"

"Well," she said after another wait, "the matter with me is simply that I'm more sure than ever my curiosity, as you call it, will be but too well repaid."

They were frankly grave now; he had got up from his seat, had turned once more about the little drawing-room to which, year after year, he brought his inevitable topic; in which he had, as he might have said, tasted their intimate community with every sauce, where every object was as familiar to him as the things of his own house and the very carpets were worn with his fitful walk very much as the desks in old counting-houses are worn by the elbows of generations of clerks. The generations of his nervous moods had been at work there, and the place was the written history of his whole middle life. Under the impression of what his friend had just said he knew himself, for some reason, more aware of these things: which made him, after a moment, stop again before her. "Is it possibly that you've grown afraid?"

"Afraid?" He thought, as she repeated the word, that his question had made her, a little, change colour; so that, lest he should have touched on a truth, he explained very kindly: "You remember that that was what you asked *me* long ago—that first day at Weatherend."

"Oh yes, and you told me you didn't know—that I was to see for myself. We've said little about it since, even in so long a time."

"Precisely," Marcher interposed—"quite as if it were too delicate a matter for us to make free with. Quite as if we might find, on pressure, that I *am* afraid. For then," he said, "we shouldn't, should we? quite know what to do."

She had for the time no answer to this question. "There have been days when I thought you were. Only, of course," she added, "there have been days when we have thought almost anything."

"Everything. Oh!" Marcher softly groaned as with a gasp, half-spent, at the face, more uncovered just then than it had been for a long while, of the imagination always with them. It had always had its incalcuable moments of glaring out, quite as with the very eyes of the very Beast, and, used as he was to them, they could still draw from him the tribute of a sigh that rose from the depths of his being. All they had thought, first and last, rolled over him; the past seemed to have been reduced to mere barren speculation. This in fact was what the place had just struck him as so full of—the simplification of everything but the state of suspense. That remained only by seeming to hang in the void surrounding it. Even his original fear, if fear it had been, had lost itself in the desert. "I judge, however," he continued, "that you see I'm not afraid now."

"What I see, as I make it out, is that you've achieved something almost unprecedented in the way of getting used to danger. Living with it so long and so closely you've lost your sense of it; you know it's there, but you're indifferent, and you cease even, as of old, to have to whistle in the dark. Considering what the danger is," May Bartram wound up, "I'm bound to say I don't think your attitude could well be surpassed."

John Marcher faintly smiled. "It's heroic?"

"Certainly—call it that."

It was what he would have liked indeed to call it. "I *am* then a man of courage?"

"That's what you were to show me."

He still, however, wondered. "But doesn't the man of courage know what he's afraid of—or *not* afraid of? I don't know *that,* you see. I don't focus it. I can't name it. I only know I'm exposed."

"Yes, but exposed—how shall I say?—so directly. So intimately. That's surely enough."

"Enough to make you feel then—as what we may call the end and the upshot of our watch—that I'm not afraid?"

"You're not afraid. But it isn't," she said, "the end of our watch. That is it isn't the end of yours. You've everything still to see."

"Then why haven't *you?*" he asked. He had had, all along, to-day, the sense of her keeping something back, and he still had it. As this was his first impression of that it quite made a date. The case was the more marked as she didn't at first answer; which in turn made him go on. "You know something I don't." Then his voice, for that of a man of courage, trembled a little. "You know what's to happen." Her silence, with the face she showed, was almost a confession—it made him sure. "You know, and you're afraid to tell me. It's so bad that you're afraid I'll find out.

All this might be true, for she did look as if, unexpectedly to her he had crossed some mystic line that she had secretly drawn round her. Yet she might, after all, not have worried; and the real climax was that he himself, at all events, needn't. "You'll never find out."

III

It was all to have made, none the less, as I have said, a date; which came out in the fact that again and again, even after long intervals, other things that passed between them were in relation to this hour but the character of recalls and results. Its immediate effect had been indeed rather to lighten insistence—almost to provoke a reaction; as if their topic had dropped by its own weight and as if moreover, for that matter, Marcher had been visited by one of his occasional warnings against egotism. He had kept up, he felt, and very decently on the whole, his consciousness of the importance of not being selfish, and it was true that he had never sinned in that direction without promptly enough trying to press the scales the other way. He often repaired his fault, the season permitting, by inviting his friend to accompany him to the opera; and it not infrequently thus happened that, to show he didn't wish her to have but one sort of food for her mind, he was the cause of her appearing there with him a dozen nights in the month. It even happened that, seeing her home at such times, he occasionally went in with her to finish, as he called it, the evening, and, the better to make his point, sat down to the frugal but always careful little supper that awaited his pleasure. His point was made, he thought, by his not eternally insisting with her on himself; made for instance, at such hours, when it befell that, her piano at hand and each of them familiar with it, they went over passages of the opera together. It chanced to be on one of these occasions, however, that he reminded her of her not having answered a certain question he had put to her during the talk that had taken place between them on her last birthday. "What is it that saves *you?*"—saved her, he meant, from that appearance of variation from the usual human type. If he had practically escaped remark, as she pretended, by doing, in the most important particular, what most men do—find the answer to life in patching up an alliance of a sort with a woman no better than himself—how had she escaped it, and how could the alliance, such as it was, since they must suppose it had been more or less noticed, have failed to make her rather positively talked about?

"I never said," May Bartram replied, "that it hadn't made me a good deal talked about."

"Ah well then you're not 'saved.'"

"It hasn't been a question for me. If you've had your woman I've had," she said, "my man."

"And you mean that makes you all right?"

Oh it was always as if there were so much to say! "I don't know why it shouldn't make me—humanly, which is what we're speaking of—as right as it makes you."

"I see," Marcher returned. "'Humanly,' no doubt, as showing that you're living for something. Not, that is, just for me and my secret."

May Bartram smiled. "I don't pretend it exactly shows that I'm not living for you. It's my intimacy with you that's in question"

He laughed as he saw what she meant. "Yes, but since, as you say, I'm only, so far as people make out, ordinary, you're—aren't you?—no more than ordinary either. You help me to pass for a man like another. So if I *am,* as I understand you, you're not compromised. Is that it?"

She had another of her waits, but she spoke clearly enough. "That's it. It's all that concerns me—to help you to pass for a man like another."

He was careful to acknowledge the remark handsomely. "How kind, how beautiful, you are to me! How shall I every repay you?"

She had her last grave pause, as if there might be a choice of ways. But she chose. "By going on as you are."

It was into this going on as he was that they relapsed, and really for so long a time that the day inevitably came for a further sounding of their depths. These depths, constantly bridged over by a structure firm enough in spite of its lightness and of its occasional oscillation in the somewhat vertiginous air, invited on occasion, in the interest of their nerves, a dropping of the plummet and a measurement of the abyss. A difference had been made moreover, once for all, by the fact that she had all the while not appeared to feel the need of rebutting his charge of an idea within her that he didn't dare to express—a charge uttered just before one of the fullest of their later discussions ended. It had come up for him then that she "knew" something and that what she knew was bad—too bad to tell him. When he had spoken of it as visibly so bad that she was afraid he might find it out, her reply had left the matter too equivocal to be let alone and yet, for Marcher's special sensibility, almost too formidable again to touch. He circled about it at a distance that alternately narrowed and widened and that still wasn't much affected by the consciousness in him that there was nothing she could "know," after all, any better than he did. She had no source of knowledge he hadn't equally—except of course that she might have finer nerves. That was what women had where they were interested; they made out things, where people were concerned, that the people often couldn't have made out for themselves. Their nerves, their sensibility, their imagination, were conductors and revealers, and the beauty of May Bartram was in particular that she had given herself so to his case. He felt in these days what, oddly enough, he had never felt before, the growth of a dread of losing her by some catastrophe—some catastrophe that yet wouldn't at all be *the* catastrophe: partly because she had almost of a sudden begun to strike him as more useful to him than ever yet, and partly by reason of an appearance of uncertainty in her health, coincident and equally new. It was characteristic of the inner detachment he had hitherto so successfully cultivated and to which our whole account of him is a reference, it was characteristic that his complications, such as they were, had never yet seemed so as at this crisis to thicken about him, even to the point of making him ask himself if he were, by any chance, of a truth, within sight or sound, within touch or reach, within the immediate jurisdiction, of the thing that waited.

When the day came, as come it had to, that his friend confessed to him her fear of a deep disorder in her blood, he felt somehow the shadow of a change and the chill of a shock. He immediately began to imagine aggravations and disasters, and above all to think of her peril as the direct menace for himself of personal privation. This indeed gave him one of those partial recoveries of equanimity that were agreeable to him—it showed him that what was still first in his mind was the loss she herself might suffer. "What if she should have to die before knowing, before seeing—?" It would have been brutal, in the early stages of her trouble, to put that question to her; but it had immediately sounded for him to his own concern, and the possibility was what most made him sorry for her. If she did "know," moreover, in the sense of her having had some—what should he think?—mystical irresistible light, this would make the matter not better, but worse, inasmuch as her original adoption of his own curiosity had quite become the basis of her life. She had been living to see what would *be* to be seen, and it would quite lacerate her to have to give up before the accomplishment of the vision. These reflections, as I say, quickened his generosity; yet, make them as he might, he saw himself, with the lapse of the period, more and more disconcerted. It lapsed for him with a strange steady sweep, and the oddest oddity was that it gave him, independently of the threat of much inconvenience, almost the only positive surprise his career, if career it could be called, had yet offered him. She kept the house as she had never done; he had to go to her to see her—she could meet him nowhere now, though there was scarce a corner of their loved old London in which she hadn't in the past, at one time or another, done so; and he found her always seated by her fire in the deep old-fashioned chair she was less and less able to leave. He had been struck one day, after an absence exceeding his usual measure, with her suddenly looking much older to him than he had ever thought of her being, then he recognised that the suddenness was all on his side—he had just simply and suddenly noticed. She looked older because inevitably, after so many years, she *was* old, or almost; which was of course true in still greater measure of her companion. If she was old, or almost, John Marcher assuredly was, and yet it was her showing of the lesson, not his own, that brought the truth home to him. His surprises began here; when once they had begun they multiplied; they came rather with a rush: it was as if, in the oddest way in the world, they had all been kept back, sown in a thick cluster, for the late afternoon of life, the time at which for people in general the unexpected has died out.

One of them was that he should have caught himself—for he *had* so done—*really* wondering if the great accident would take form now as nothing more than his being condemned to see this charming woman, this admirable friend, pass away from him. He had never so unreservedly qualified her as while confronted in thought with such a possibility; in spite of which there was small doubt for him that as an answer to his long riddle the mere effacement of even so fine a feature of his situation would be an abject anti-climax. It would represent, as connected with his past attitude, a drop of dignity under the shadow of which his existence could only become the most grotesque of failures. He had been far from holding it a failure—long as he had waited for the appearance that was to make it a success. He had waited for quite another thing, not for such a thing as that. The breath of his good faith came short, however, as he recognised how long he had waited, or how long at least his companion had. That she, at all events, might be recorded as having waited in vain—this affected him sharply, and all the more because of his at first having done little more than amuse himself with the idea. It grew more grave as the gravity of her condition grew, and the state of mind it produced in him, which he himself ended by watching as if it had been some definite disfigurement of his outer person, may pass for another of his surprises. This conjoined itself still with another, the really stupefying consciousness of a question that he would have allowed to shape itself had he dared. What did everything mean—what, that is, did *she* mean, she and her vain waiting and her probable death and the soundless admonition of it all—unless that, at this time of day, it was simply, it was overwhelmingly too late? He had never at any stage of his queer consciousness admitted the whisper of such a correction; he had never till within these last few months been so false to his conviction as not to hold that what was to come to him had time, whether *he* struck himself as having it or not. That at last, at last, he certainly hadn't it, to speak of, or had it but in the scantiest measure—such, soon enough, as things went with him, became the inference with which his old obsession had to reckon: and this it was not helped to do by the more and more confirmed appearance that the great vagueness casting the long shadow in which he had lived had, to attest itself, almost no margin left. Since it was in Time that he was to have met his fate, so it was in Time that his fate was to have acted; and as he waked up to the sense of no longer being young, which was exactly the sense of being stale, just as that, in turn, was the sense of being weak, he waked up to another matter beside. It all hung together; they were subject, he and the great vagueness, to an equal and indivisible law. When the possibilities themselves had accordingly turned stale, when the secret of the gods had grown faint, had perhaps even quite evaporated, that, and that only, was failure. It wouldn't have been failure to be bankrupt, dishonoured, pilloried, hanged; it was failure not to be anything. And so, in the dark valley into which his path had taken its unlooked-for twist, he wondered not a little as he groped. He didn't care what awful crash might overtake him, with what ignominy or what monstrosity he might yet be associated—since he wasn't after all too utterly old to suffer—if it would only be decently proportionate to the posture he had kept, all his life, in the threatened presence of it. He had but one desire left—that he shouldn't have been "sold."

IV

Then it was that, one afternoon, while the spring of the year was young and new she met all in her own way his frankest betrayal of these alarms. He had gone in late to see her, but evening hadn't settled and she was presented to him in that long fresh light of waning April days which affects us often with sadness sharper than the greyest hours of autumn. The week had been warm, the spring was supposed to have begun early, and May Bartram sat, for the first time in the year, without a fire; a fact that, to Marcher's sense, gave the scene of which she formed part a smooth and ultimate look, an air of knowing, in its immaculate order and cold meaningless cheer, that it would never see a fire again. Her own aspect—he could scarce have said why—intensified this note. Almost as white as wax, with the marks and signs in her face as numerous and as fine as if they had been etched by a needle, with soft white draperies relieved by a faded green scarf on the delicate tone of which the years had further refined, she was the picture of a serene and exquisite but impenetrable sphinx, whose head, or indeed all whose person, might have been powdered with silver. She was a sphinx, yet with her white petals and green fronds she might have been a lily too—only an artificial lily, wonderfully imitated and constantly kept, without dust or stain, though not exempt from a slight droop and a complexity of faint creases, under some clear glass bell. The perfection of household care, of high polish and finish, always reigned in her rooms, but they now looked most as if everything had been wound up, tucked in, put away, so that she might sit with folded hands and with nothing more to do. She was "out of it," to Marcher's vision; her work was over; she communicated with him as across some gulf or from some island of rest that she had already reached, and it made him feel strangely abandoned. Was it—or rather wasn't it—that if for so long she had been watching with him the answer to their question must have swum into her ken and taken on its name, so that her occupation was verily gone? He had as much as charged her with this in saying to her, many months before, that she even then knew something she was keeping from him. It was a point he had never since ventured to press, vaguely fearing as he did that it might become a difference, perhaps a disagreement between them. He had in his later time turned nervous, which was what he in all the other years had never been; and the oddity was that his nervousness should have waited till he had begun to doubt, should have held off so long as he was sure. There was something, it seemed to him, that the wrong word would bring down on his head, something that would so at least ease off his tension. But he wanted not to speak the wrong word; that would make everything ugly. He wanted the knowledge he lacked to drop on him, if drop it could, by its own august weight. If she was to forsake him it was surely for her to take leave. This was why he didn't directly ask her again what she knew; but it was also why, approaching the matter from another side, he said to her in the course of his visit: "What do you regard as the very worst that at this time of day *can* happen to me?"

He had asked her that in the past often enough; they had, with the odd irregular rhythm of their intensities and avoidances, exchanged ideas about it and then had seen the ideas washed away by cool intervals, washed like figures traced in sea-sand. It had ever been the mark of their talk that the oldest allusions in it required but a little dismissal and reaction to come out again, sounding for the hour as new. She could thus at present meet his enquiry quite freshly and patiently. "Oh yes, I've repeatedly thought, only it always seemed to me of old that I couldn't quite make up my mind. I thought of dreadful things, between which it was difficult to choose; and so must you have done."

"Rather! I feel now as if I had scarce done anything else. I appear to myself to have spent my life in thinking of nothing *but* dreadful things. A great many of them I've at different times named to you, but there were others I couldn't name."

"They were too, too dreadful?"

"Too, too dreadful—some of them."

She looked at him a minute, and there came to him as he met it an inconsequent sense that her eyes, when one got their full clearness, were still as beautiful as they had been in youth, only beautiful with a strange cold light—a light that somehow was a part of the effect, it it wasn't rather a part of the cause, of the pale hard sweetness of the season and the hour. "And yet," she said at last, "there are horrors we've mentioned."

It deepened the strangeness to see her, as such a figure in such a picture, talk of "horrors," but she was to do in a few minutes something stranger yet—though even of this he was to take the full measure but afterwards—and the note of it already trembled. It was, for the matter of that, one of the signs that her eyes were having again the high flicker of their prime. He had to admit, however, what she said. "Oh yes, there were times when we did go far." He caught himself in the act of speaking as if it all were over. Well, he wished it were; and the consummation depended for him clearly more and more on his friend.

But she had now a soft smile. "Oh far—!"

It was oddly ironic. "Do you mean you're prepared to go further?"

She was frail and ancient and charming as she continued to look at him, yet it was rather as if she had lost the thread. "Do you consider that we went far?"

"Why I thought it the point you were just making—that we *had* looked most things in the face."

"Including each other?" She still smiled. "But you're quite right. We've had together great imaginations, often great fears; but some of them have been unspoken."

"Then the worst—we haven't faced that. I *could* face it, I believe, if I knew what you think it. I feel," he explained, "as if I had lost my power to conceive such things." And he wondered if he looked as blank as he sounded. "It's spent."

"Then why do you assume," she asked, "that mine isn't?

"Because you've given me signs to the contrary. It isn't a question for you of conceiving, imagining, comparing. It isn't a question now of choosing." At last he came out with it. "You know something I don't. You've shown me that before."

These last words had affected her, he made out in a moment, exceedingly, and she spoke with firmness. "I've shown you, my dear, nothing."

He shook his head. "You can't hide it."

"Oh, oh!" May Bartram sounded over what she couldn't hide. It was almost a smothered groan.

"You admitted it months ago, when I spoke of it to you as of something you were afraid I should find out. Your answer was that I couldn't, that I wouldn't, and I don't pretend I have. But you had something therefore in mind, and I now see how it must have been, how it still is, the possibility that, of all possibilities, has settled itself for you as the worst. This," he went on, "is why I appeal to you. I'm only afraid of ignorance to-day—I'm not afraid of knowledge." And then as for a while she said nothing: "What makes me sure is that I see in your face and feel here, in this air and amid these appearances, that you're out of it. You've done. You've had your experience. You leave me to my fate."

Well, she listened, motionless and white in her chair, as on a decision to be made, so that her manner was fairly an avowal, though still, with a small fine inner stiffness, an imperfect surrender. "It *would* be the worst," she finally let herself say. "I mean the thing I've never said."

It hushed him a moment. "More monstrous than all the monstrosities we've named?"

"More monstrous. Isn't that what you sufficiently express," she asked, "in calling it the worst?"

Marcher thought. "Assuredly—if you mean, as I do, something that includes all the loss and all the shame that are thinkable."

"It would if it *should* happen," said May Bartram. "What we're speaking of, remember, is only my idea."

"It's your belief," Marcher returned. "That's enough for me. I feel your beliefs are right. Therefore if, having this one, you give me no more light on it, you abandon me."

"No, no!" she repeated. "I'm with you—don't you see?—still." And as to make it more vivid to him she rose from her chair—a movement she seldom risked in these days—and showed herself, all draped and all soft, in her fairness and slimness. "I haven't forsaken you."

It was really, in its effort against weakness, a generous assurance, and had the success of the impulse not, happily, been great, it would have touched him to pain more than to pleasure. But the cold charm in her eyes had spread, as she hovered before him, to all the rest of her person, so that it was for the minute almost a recovery of youth. He couldn't pity her for that; he could only take her as she showed—as capable even yet of helping him. It was as if, at the same time, her light might at any instant go out; wherefore he must make the most of it. There passed before him with intensity th(three or four things he wanted most to know; but the question that came of itself to his lips really covered the others. "Then tell me if I shall consciously suffer."

She promptly shook her head. "Never!"

It confirmed the authority he imputed to her, and it produced on him an extraordinary effect. "Well, what's better than that? Do you call that the worst?"

"You think nothing is better?" she asked.

She seemed to mean something so special that he again sharply wondered, though still with the dawn of a prospect of relief. "Why not, if one doesn't *know?*" After which, as their eyes, over his question, met in a silence, the dawn deepened and something to his purpose came prodigiously out of her very face. His own, as he took it in, suddenly flushed to the forehead, and he gasped with the force of a perception to which, on the instant, everything fitted. The sound of his gasp filled the air; then he became articulate. "I see—if I don't suffer!"

In her own look, however, was doubt. "You see what?"

"Why what you mean—what you've always meant."

She again shook her head. "What I mean isn't what I've always meant. It's different."

"It's something new?"

She hung back from it a little. "Something new. It's not what you think. I see what you think."

His divination drew breath then; only her correction might be wrong. "It isn't that I *am* a blockhead?" he asked between faintness and grimness. "It isn't that it's all a mistake?"

"A mistake?" she pityingly echoed. *That* possibility, for her, he saw, would be monstrous; and if she guaranteed him the immunity from pain it would accordingly not be what she had in mind. "Oh no," she declared; "it's nothing of that sort. You've been right."

Yet he couldn't help asking himself if she weren't, thus pressed, speaking but to save him. It seemed to him he should be most in a hole if his history should prove all a platitude. "Are you telling me the truth, so that I shan't have been a bigger idiot that I can bear to know? I *haven't* lived with a vain imagination, in the most besotted illusion? I haven't waited but to see the door shut in my face?"

She shook her head again. "However the case stands *that* isn't the truth. Whatever the reality, it *is* a reality. The door isn't shut. The door's open," said May Bartram.

"Then something's to come?"

She waited once again, always with her cold sweet eyes on him. "It's never too late." She had with her gliding step, diminished the distance between them, and she stood nearer to him, close to him, a minute, as if still charged with the unspoken. Her movement might have been for some finer emphasis of what she was at once hesitating and deciding to say. He had been standing by the chimney-piece, fireless and sparely adorned, a small perfect old French clock and two morsels of rosy Dresden constituting all its furniture; and her hand grasped the shelf while she kept him waiting, grasped it a little as for support and encouragement. She only kept him waiting, however; that is he only waited. It had become suddenly, from her movement and attitude, beautiful and vivid to him that she had something more to give him; her wasted face delicately shone with it—it glittered almost as with the white lustre of silver in her expression. She was right, incontestably, for what he saw in her face was the truth, and strangely, without consequence, while their talk of it as dreadful was still in the air, she appeared to present it as inordinately soft. This, prompting bewilderment, made him but gape the more gratefully for her revelation, so that they continued for some minutes silent, her face shining at him, her contact imponderably pressing, and his stare all kind but all expectant. The end, none the less, was that what he had expected failed to come to him. Something else took place instead, which seemed to consist at first in the mere closing of her eyes. She gave way at the same instant to a slow fine shudder, and though he remained staring—though he stared in fact but the harder—turned off and regained her chair. It was the end of what she had been intending, but it left him thinking only of that.

"Well, you don't say—?"

She had touched in her passage a bell near the chimney and had sunk back strangely pale. "I'm afraid I'm too ill."

"Too ill to tell me?" It sprang up sharp to him, and almost to his lips, the fear she might die without giving him light. He checked himself in time from so expressing his question, but she answered as if she had heard the words.

"Don't you know—now?"

"'Now'—?" She had spoken as if some difference had been made within the moment. But her maid, quickly obedient to her bell, was already with them. "I know nothing." And he was afterwards to say to himself that he must have spoken with odious impatience, such an impatience as to show that, supremely disconcerted, he washed his hands of the whole question.

"Oh!" said May Bartram.

"Are you in pain?" he asked as the woman went to her.

"No," said May Bartram.

Her maid, who had put an arm round her as if to take her to her room, fixed on him eyes that appealingly contradicted her; in spite of which, however, he showed once more his mystification. "What then has happened?"

She was once more, with her companion's help, on her feet, and, feeling withdrawal imposed on him, he had blankly found his hat and gloves and had reached the door. Yet he waited for her answer. "What *was* to," she said.

V

He came back the next day, but she was then unable to see him, and as it was literally the first time this had occurred in the long stretch of their acquaintance he turned away, defeated and sore, almost angry—or feeling at least that such a break in their custom was really the beginning of the end—and wandered alone with his thoughts, especially with the one he was least able to keep down. She was dying and he would lose her; she was dying and his life would end. He stopped in the Park, into which he had passed, and stared before him at his recurrent doubt. Away from her the doubt pressed again; in her presence he had believed her, but as he felt his forlorness he threw himself into the explanation that, nearest at hand, had most of a miserable warmth for him and least of a cold torment. She had deceived him to save him—to put him off with something in which he should be able to rest. What could the thing that was to happen to him be, after all, but just this thing that had begun to happen? Her dying, her death, his consequent solitude—*that* was what he had figured as the Beast in the Jungle, that was what had been in the lap of the gods. He had had her word for it as he left her—what else on earth could she have meant? It wasn't a thing of a monstrous order; not a fate rare and distinguished; not a stroke of fortune that overwhelmed and immortalised; it had only the stamp of the common doom. But poor Marcher at this hour judged the common doom sufficient. It would serve his turn, and even as the consummation of infinite waiting he would bend his pride to accept it. He sat down on a bench in the twilight.

He hadn't been a fool. Something had *been,* as she had said, to come. Before he rose indeed it had quite struck him that the final fact really matched with the long avenue through which he had had to reach it. As sharing his suspense and as giving herself all, giving her life, to bring it to an end, she had come with him every step of the way. He had lived by her aid, and to leave her behind would be cruelly, damnably to miss her. What could be more overwhelming than that?

Well, he was to know within the week, for though she kept him a while at bay, left him restless and wretched during a series of days on each of which he asked about her only again to have to turn away, she ended his trial by receiving him where she had always received him. Yet she had been brought out at some hazard into the presence of so many of the things that were consciously, vainly, half their past, and there was scant service left in the gentleness of her mere desire, all too visible, to check his obsession and wind up his long trouble. That was clearly what she wanted, the one thing more for her own peace while she could still put out her hand. He was so affected by her state that, once seated by her chair he was moved to let everything go; it was she herself therefore who brought him back, took up again, before she dismissed him, her last word of the other time. She showed how she wished to leave their business in order. "I'm not sure you understood. You've nothing to wait for more. It *has* come."

Oh how he looked at her! "Really?"

"Really."

"The thing that, as you said, *was* to?"

"The thing that we began in our youth to watch for."

Face to face with her once more he believed her; it was a claim to which he had so abjectly little to oppose. "You mean that it has come as a positive definite occurrence, with a name and a date?"

"Positive. Definite. I don't know about the 'name,' but oh with a date!"

He found himself again too helplessly at sea. "But come in the night—come and passed me by?"

May Bartram had her strange faint smile. "Oh no, it hasn't passed you by!"

"But if I haven't been aware of it and it hasn't touched me—?"

"Ah your not being aware of it"—and she seemed to hesitate an instant to deal with this—"your not being aware of it is the strangeness *in* the strangeness. It's the wonder *of* the wonder." She spoke as with the softness almost of a sick child, yet now at last, at the end of all, with the perfect straightness of a sibyl. She visibly knew that she knew, and the effect on him was of something co-ordinate, in its high character, with the law that had ruled him. It was the true voice of the law; so on her lips would the law itself have sounded. "It *has* touched you," she went on. "It has done its office. It has made you all its own."

"So utterly without my knowing it?"

"So utterly without your knowing it." His hand, as he leaned to her, was on the arm of her chair, and, dimly smiling always now, she placed her own on it. "It's enough if *I* know it."

"Oh!" he confusedly breathed, as she herself of late so often had done.

"What I long ago said is true. You'll never know now, and I think you ought to be content. You've *had* it," said May Bartram.

"But had what?"

"Why what was to have marked you out. The proof of your law. It has acted. I'm too glad," she then bravely added, "to have been able to see what it's *not.*"

He continued to attach his eyes to her, and with the sense that it was all beyond him, and that *she* was too, he would still have sharply challenged her hadn't he so felt it an abuse of her weakness to do more than take devoutly what she gave him, take it hushed as to a revelation. If he did speak, it was out of the fore-knowledge of his loneliness to come. "If you're glad of what it's 'not' it might then have been worse?"

She turned her eyes away, she looked straight before her; with which after a moment: "Well, you know our fears."

He wondered. "It's something then we never feared?"

On this slowly she turned to him. "Did we ever dream, with all our dreams, that we should sit and talk of it thus?"

He tried for a little to make out that they had; but it was as if their dreams, numberless enough, were in solution in some thick cold mist through which thought lost itself. "It might have been that we couldn't talk?"

"Well"—she did her best for him—"not from this side. This, you see," she said, "is the *other* side."

"I think," poor Marcher returned, "that all sides are the same to me." Then, however, as she gently shook her head in correction: "We mightn't, as it were, have got across—?"

"To where we are—no. We're *here*"—she made her weak emphasis.

"And much good does it do us!" was her friend's frank comment.

"It does us the good it can. It does us the good that *it* isn't here. It's past. It's behind," said May Bartram. "Before—" but her voice dropped.

He had got up, not to tire her, but it was hard to combat his yearning. She after all told him nothing but that his light had failed—which he knew well enough without her. "Before—?" he blankly echoed.

"Before, you see, it was always to *come.* That kept it present."

"Oh I don't care what comes now! Besides," Marcher added, "it seems to me I liked it better present, as you say, than I can like it absent with *your* absence."

"Oh mine!"—and her pale hands made light of it.

"With the absence of everything." He had a dreadful sense of standing there before her for—so far as anything but this proved, this bottomless drop was concerned—the last time of their life. It rested on him with a weight he felt he could scarce bear, and this weight it apparently was that still pressed out what remained in him of speakable protest. "I believe you; but I can't begin to pretend I understand. *Nothing,* for me, is past; nothing *will* pass till I pass myself, which I pray my stars may be as soon as possible. Say, however," he added, "that I've eaten my cake, as you contend, to the last crumb—how can the thing I've never felt at all be the thing I was marked out to feel?"

She met him perhaps less directly, but she met him unperturbed. "You take your 'feelings' for granted. You were to suffer your fate. That was not necessarily to know it."

"How in the world—when what is such knowledge but suffering?"

She looked up at him a while in silence. "No—you don't understand."

"I suffer," said John Marcher.

"Don't, don't!"

"How can I help at least *that?*"

"Don't!" May Bartram repeated.

She spoke it in a tone so special, in spite of her weakness, that he stared an instant—stared as if some light, hitherto hidden, had shimmered across his vision. Darkness again closed over it, but the gleam had already become for him an idea. "Because I haven't the right—?"

"Don't *know*—when you needn't," she mercifully urged. "You needn't—for we shouldn't."

"Shouldn't?" If he could but know what she meant!

"No—it's too much."

"Too much?" he still asked but, with a mystification that was the next moment of a sudden to give way. Her words, if they meant something, affect him in this light—the light also of her wasted face—as meaning *all,* and the sense of what knowledge had been for herself came over him with a rush which broke through into a question. "Is it of that then you're dying?"

She but watched him, gravely at first, as to see, with this, where he was, and she might have seen something or feared something that moved her sympathy. "I would live for you still—if I could." Her eyes closed for a little, as if, withdrawn into herself, she were for a last time trying. "But I can't!" she said as she raised them again to take leave of him.

She couldn't indeed, as but too promptly and sharply appeared, and he had no vision of her after this that was anything but darkness and doom. They had parted for ever in that strange talk; access to her chamber of pain, rigidly guarded, was almost wholly forbidden him; he was feeling now moreover, in the face of doctors, nurses, the two or three relatives attracted doubtless by the presumption of what she had to "leave," how few were the rights, as they were called in such cases, that he had to put forward, and how odd it might even seem that their intimacy shouldn't have given him more of them. The stupidest fourth cousin had more, even though she had been nothing in such a person's life. She had been a feature of features in *his,* for what else was it to have been so indispensable? Strange beyond saying were the ways of existence, baffling for him the anomaly of his lack, as he felt it to be, of producible claim. A woman might have been, as it were, everything to him, and it might yet present him in no connexion that any one seemed held to recognise. If this was the case in these closing weeks it was the case more sharply on the occasion of the last offices rendered, in the great grey London cemetery, to what had been mortal, to what had been precious, in his friend. The concourse at her grave was not numerous, but he saw himself treated as scarce more nearly concerned with it than if there had been a thousand others. He was in short from this moment face to face with the fact that he was to profit extraordinarily little by the interest May Bartram had taken in him. He couldn't quite have said what he expected, but he hadn't surely expected this approach to a double privation. Not only had her interest failed him, but he seemed to feel himself unattended—and for a reason he couldn't seize—by the distinction, the dignity, the propriety, if nothing else, of the man markedly bereaved. It was as if in the view of society he had not *been* markedly bereaved, as if there still failed some sign or proof of it, and as if none the less his character could never be affirmed nor the deficiency ever made up. There were moments as the weeks went by when he would have liked, by some almost aggressive act to take his stand on the intimacy of his loss, in order that it *might* be questioned and his retort, to the relief of his spirit, so recorded; but the moments of an irritation more helpless followed fast on these, the moments during which, turning things over with a good conscience but with a bare horizon, he found himself wondering if he oughtn't to have begun, so to speak, further back.

He found himself wondering indeed at many things, and this last speculation had others to keep it company. What could he have done, after all, in her lifetime, without giving them both, as it were, away? He couldn't have made known she was watching him, for that would have published the superstition of the Beast. This was what closed his mouth now—now that the Jungle had been threshed to vacancy and that the Beast had stolen away. It sounded too foolish and too flat; the difference for him in this particular, the extinction in his life of the element of suspense, was such as in fact to surprise him. He could scarce have said what the effect resembled; the abrupt cessation, the positive prohibition, of music perhaps, more than anything else, in some place all adjusted and all accustomed to sonority and to attention. If he could at any rate have conceived lifting the veil from his image at some moment of the past (what had he done, after all, if not lift it to *her?*) so to do this to-day, to talk to people at large of the Jungle cleared and confide to them that he now felt it as safe, would have been not only to see them listen as to a goodwife's tale, but really to hear himself tell one. What it presently came to in truth was that poor Marcher waded through his beaten grass, where no life stirred, where no breath sounded, where no evil eye seemed to gleam from a possible lair, very much as if vaguely looking for the Beast, and still more as if acutely missing it. He walked about in an existence that had grown strangely more spacious, and, stopping fitfully in places where the undergrowth of life struck him as closer, asked himself yearningly, wondered secretly and sorely, if it would have lurked here or there. It would have at all events *sprung;* what was at least complete was his belief in the truth itself of the assurance given him. The change from his old sense to his new was absolute and final: what was to happen *had* so absolutely and finally happened that he was as little able to know a fear for his future as to know a hope; so absent in short was any question of anything still to come. He was to live entirely with the other question, that of his unidentified past, that of his having to see his fortune impenetrably muffled and masked.

The torment of this vision became then his occupation; he couldn't perhaps have consented to live but for the possibility of guessing. She had told him, his friend, not to guess, she had forbidden him, so far as he might, to know, and she had even in a sort denied the power in him to learn: which were so many things, precisely, to deprive him of rest. It wasn't that he wanted, he argued for fairness, that anything past and done should repeat itself; it was only that he shouldn't, as an anticlimax, have been taken sleeping so sound as not to be able to win back by an effort of thought the lost stuff of consciousness. He declared to himself at moments that he would either win it back or have done with consciousness for ever; he made this idea his one motive in fine, and made it so much his passion that none other, to compare with it, seemed ever to have touched him. The lost stuff of consciousness became thus for him as a strayed or stolen child to an unappeasable father; he hunted it up and down very much as if he were knocking at the doors and enquiring of the police. This was the spirit in which, inevitably, he set himself to travel; he started on a journey that was to be as long as he could make it; it danced before him that, as the other side of the globe couldn't possibly have less to say to him, it might, by a possibility of suggestion, have more. Before he quitted London, however, he made a pilgrimage to May Bartram's grave, took his way to it through the endless avenues of the grim suburban metropolis, sought it out in the wilderness of tombs, and, though he had come but for the renewal of the act of farewell, found himself, when he had at last stood by it, beguiled into long intensities. He stood for an hour, powerless to turn away and yet powerless to penetrate the darkness of death; fixing with his eyes her inscribed name and date, beating his forehead against the fact of the secret they kept, drawing his breath, while he waited, as if some sense would in pity of him rise from the stones. He kneeled on the stones, however, in vain; they kept what they concealed;

and if the face of the tomb did become a face for him it was because her two names became a pair of eyes that didn't know him. He gave them a last long look, but no palest light broke.

VI

He stayed away, after this, for a year; he visited the depths of Asia, spending himself on scenes of romantic interest, of superlative sanctity; but what was present to him everywhere was that for a man who had known what *he* had known the world was vulgar and vain. The state of mind in which he had lived for so many years shone out to him, in reflection, as a light that colored and refined, a light beside which the glow of the East was garish cheap and thin. The terrible truth was that he had lost—with everything else—a distinction as well; the things he saw couldn't help being common when he had become common to look at them. He was simply now one of them himself—he was in the dust, without a peg for the sense of difference; and there were hours when, before the temples of gods and the sepulchres of kings, his spirit turned for nobleness of association to the barely discriminated slab in the London suburb. That had become for him, and more intensely with time and distance, his one witness of a past glory. It was all that was left to him for proof or pride, yet the past glories of Pharaohs were nothing to him as he thought of it. Small wonder then that he came back to it on the morrow of his return. He was drawn there this time as irresistibly as the other, yet with a confidence, almost, that was doubtless the effect of the many months that had elapsed. He had lived, in spite of himself, into his change of feeling, and in wandering over the earth had wandered, as might be said, from the circumference to the centre of his desert. He had settled to his safety and accepted perforce his extinction; figuring to himself, with some colour, in the likeness of certain little old men he remembered to have seen, of whom, all meagre and wizened as they might look, it was related that they had in their time fought twenty duels or been loved by ten princesses. They indeed had been wondrous for others while he was but wondrous for himself; which, however, was exactly the cause of his haste to renew the wonder by getting back, as he might put it, into his own presence. That had quickened his steps and checked his delay. If his visit was prompt it was because he had been separated so long from the part of himself that alone he now valued.

It's accordingly not false to say that he reached his goal with a certain elation and stood there again with a certain assurance. The creature beneath the sod *knew* of his rare experience, so that, strangely now, the place had lost for him its mere blankness of expression. It met him in mildness—not, as before, in mockery; it wore for him the air of conscious greeting that we find, after absence, in things that have closely belonged to us and which seem to confess of themselves to the connexion. The plot of ground, the graven tablet, the tended flowers affected him so as belonging to him that he resembled for the hour a contented landlord reviewing a piece of property. Whatever had happened—well, had happened. He had not come back this time with the vanity of that question, his former worrying "What, *what?*" now practically so spent. Yet he would none the less never again so cut himself off from the spot; he would come back to it every month, for if he did nothing else by its aid he at least held up his head. It thus grew for him, in the oddest way, a positive resource; he carried out his idea of periodical returns, which took their place at last among the most inveterate of his habits. What it all amounted to, oddly enough, was that in his finally so simplified world this garden of death gave him the few square feet of earth on which he could still most live. It was as if, being nothing anywhere else for any one, nothing even for himself, he were just everything here, and if not for a crowd of witnesses or indeed for any witness but John Marcher, then by clear right of the register that he could scan like an open page. The open page was the tomb of his friend, and *there* were the facts of the past, there the truth of his life, there the backward reaches in which he could lose himself. He did this from time to time with such effect that he seemed to wander through the old years with his hand in the arm of a companion who was, in the most extraordinary manner, his other, his younger self; and to wander, which was more extraordinary yet, round and round a third presence—not wandering she, but stationary, still, whose eyes, turning with his revolution, never ceased to follow him, and whose seat was his point, so to speak, of orientation. Thus in short he settled to live—feeding all on the sense that he once *had* lived, and dependent on it not alone for a support but for an identity.

It sufficed him in its way for months and the year elapsed; it would doubtless even have carried him further but for an accident, superficially slight, which moved him, quite in another direction, with a force beyond any of his impressions of Egypt or of India. It was a thing of the merest chance—the turn, as he afterwards felt, of a hair, though he was indeed to live to believe that if light hadn't come to him in this particular fashion it would still have come in another. He was to live to believe this, I say, though he was not to live, I may not less definitely mention, to do much else. We allow him at any rate the benefit of the conviction, struggling up for him at the end, that, whatever might have happened or not happened, he would have come round of himself to the light. The incident of an autumn day had put the match to the train laid from of old by his misery. With the light before him he knew that even of late his ache had only been smothered. It was strangely drugged but it throbbed; at the touch it began to bleed. And the touch, in the event, was the face of a fellow mortal. This face, one grey afternoon when the leaves were thick in the alleys, looked into Marcher's own, at the cemetery, with an expression like the cut of a blade.

He felt it, that is, so deep down that he winced at the steady thrust. The person who so mutely assaulted him was a figure he had noticed, on reaching his own goal, absorbed by a grave a short distance away, a grave apparently fresh, so that the emotion of the visitor would probably match it for frankness. This fact alone forbade further attention, though during the time he stayed he remained vaguely conscious of his neighbour, a middle-aged man apparently, in mourning, whose bowed back, among the clustered monuments and mortuary yews, was constantly presented. Marcher's theory that these were elements in contact with which he himself revived, had suffered, on this occasion, it may be granted, a marked, an excessive check. The autumn day was dire for him as none had recently been, and he rested with a heaviness he had not yet known on the low stone table that bore May Bartram's name. He rested without power to move, as if some spring in him, some spell vouchsafed, had suddenly been broken for ever. If he could have done that moment as he wanted he would simply have stretched himself on the slab that was ready to take him, treating it as a place prepared to receive his last sleep. What in all the wide world had he now to keep awake for? He stared before him with the question, and it was then that, as one of the cemetery walks passed near him, he caught the shock of the face.

His neighbour at the other grave had withdrawn, as he himself, with force enough in him, would have done by now, and was advancing along the path on his way to one of the gates. This brought him close, and his pace was slow, so that—and all the more as there was a kind of hunger in his look—the two men were for a minute directly confronted. Marcher knew him at once for one of the deeply stricken—a perception so sharp that nothing else in the picture comparatively lived, neither his dress, his age, nor his presumable character and class; nothing lived but the deep ravage of the features he showed. He *showed* them—that was the point; he was moved, as he passed, by some impulse that was either a signal for sympathy or, more possibly, a challenge to an opposed sorrow. He might have already been aware of our friend, might have at some previous hour have noticed in him the smooth habit of the scene, with which the state of his own senses so scantly consorted, and might thereby have been stirred as by an overt discord. What Marcher was at all events conscious of was in the first place that the image of scarred passion presented to him was conscious too—of something that profaned the air; and in the second that, roused, startled, shocked, he was yet the next moment looking after it, as it went, with envy. The most extraordinary thing that had happened to him—though he had given that name to other matters as well—took place, after his immediate vague stare, as a consequence of this impression. The stranger passed, but the raw glare of his grief remained, making our friend wonder in pity what wrong, what wound it expressed, what injury not to be healed. What had the man *had,* to make him by the loss of it so bleed and yet live?

Something—and this reached him with a pang—that *he,* John Marcher, hadn't; the proof of which was precisely John Marcher's arid end. No passion had ever touched him, for this was what passion meant; he had survived and maundered and pined, but where had been *his* deep ravage? The extraordinary thing we speak of was the sudden rush of the result of this question. The sight that had just met his eyes named to him, as in letters of quick flame, something he had utterly, insanely missed, and what he had missed made these things a train of fire, made them mark themselves in an anguish of inward throbs. He had seen *outside* of his life, not learned it within, the way a woman was mourned when she had been loved for herself: such was the force of his conviction of the meaning of the stranger's face, which still flared for him as a smoky torch. It hadn't come to him, the knowledge, on the wings of experience; it had brushed him, jostled him, upset him, with the disrespect of chance, the insolence of accident. Now that the illumination had begun, however, it blazed to the zenith, and what he presently stood there gazing at was the sounded void of his life. He gazed, he drew breath, in pain; he turned in his dismay, and, turning, he had before him in sharper incision than ever the open page of his story. The name on the table smote him as the passage of his neighbour had done, and what it said to him, full in the face, was that *she* was what he had missed. This was the awful thought, the answer to all the past, the vision at the dread clearness of which he grew as cold as the stone beneath him. Everything fell together, confessed, explained, overwhelmed; leaving him most of all stupefied at the blindness he had cherished. The fate he had been marked for he had met with a vengeance—he had emptied the cup to the lees; he had been the man of his time, *the* man, to whom nothing on earth was to have happened. That was the rare stroke—that was his visitation. So he saw it, as we say, in pale horror, while the pieces fitted and fitted. So *she* had seen it while he didn't, and so she served at this hour to drive the truth home. It was the truth, vivid and monstrous, that all the while he had waited the wait was itself his portion. This the companion of his vigil had at a given moment made out, and she had then offered him the chance to baffle his doom. One's doom, however, was never baffled, and on the day she told him his own had come down she had seen him but stupidly stare at the escape she offered him.

The escape would have been to love her; then, *then* he would have lived. *She* had lived—who could say now with what passion?—since she had loved him for himself; whereas he had never thought of her (ah how it hugely glared at him!) but in the chill of his egotism and the light of her use. Her spoken words came back to him—the chain stretched and stretched. The Beast had lurked indeed, and the Beast, at its hour, had sprung; it had sprung in that twilight of the cold April when, pale, ill, wasted, but all beautiful, and perhaps even then recoverable, she had risen from her chair to stand before him and let him imaginably guess. It had sprung as he didn't guess; it had sprung as she hopelessly turned from him, and the mark, by the time he left her, had fallen where it *was* to fall. He had justified his fear and achieved his fate; he had failed, with the last exactitude, of all he was to fail of; and a moan now rose to his lips as he remembered she had prayed he mightn't know. This horror of waking—*this* was knowledge, knowledge under the breath of which the very tears in his eyes seemed to freeze. Through them, none the less, he tried to fix it and hold it; he kept it there before him so that he might feel the pain. That at least, belated and bitter, had something of the taste of life. But the bitterness suddenly sickened him, and it was as if, horribly, he saw, in the truth, in the cruelty of his image, what had been appointed and done. He saw the Jungle of his life and saw the lurking Beast; then, while he looked, perceived it, as by a stir of the air, rise, huge and hideous, for the leap that was to settle him. His eyes darkened—it was close; and, instinctively turning, in his hallucination, to avoid it, he flung himself, face down, on the tomb.

Stephen Crane

(1871 - 1900)

Stephen Crane, who died of tuberculosis before reaching his twenty-ninth birthday, was a great writer of short fiction and a precursor of the revolutionary character of much twentieth-century American literature. Carl and Mark Van Doren didn't exaggerate when they said, "Modern American fiction may be said to begin with Stephen Crane." (Hemingway ascribed this honor to Mark Twain.) What distinguished Crane from other American writers at the end of the nineteenth century were his choice of subjects, his detached and ironic perspective, and his scrupulously clean style. He wrote the first naturalist novel in America, *Maggie: A Girl of the Streets* (1892), and the first impressionistic novel, *The Red Badge of Courage* (1895). A journalist who reported on wars and the uglier side of life, Crane rebelled against the literary gentility which was fashionable at the end of the century. "I renounced the clever school of literature," he wrote. "It seemed to me that there must be something more in life than to sit and cudgel one's brains for the clever and witty expedients." He was an unusually honest writer who recorded the truth of external reality, using a vivid, almost photographic technique with as little distortion as possible.

The Bride Comes to Yellow Sky

I

The great Pullman was whirling onward with such dignity of motion that a glance from the window seemed simply to prove that the plains of Texas were pouring eastward. Vast flats of green grass, dull-hued spaces of mesquit and cactus, little groups of frame houses, woods of light and tender trees, all were sweeping into the east, sweeping over the horizon, a precipice.

A newly married pair had boarded this coach at San Antonio. The man's face was reddened from many days in the wind and sun, and a direct result of his new black clothes was that his brick-colored hands were constantly performing in a most conscious fashion. From time to time he looked down respectfully at his attire. He sat with a hand on each knee, like a man waiting in a barber's shop. The glances he devoted to other passengers were furtive and shy.

The bride was not pretty, nor was she very young. She wore a dress of blue cashmere, with small reservations of velvet here and there, and with steel buttons abounding. She continually twisted her head to regard her puff sleeves, very stiff, straight, and high. They embarrassed her. It was quite apparent that she had cooked, and that she expected to cook, dutifully. The blushes caused by the careless scrutiny of some passengers as she had entered the car were strange to see upon this plain, under-class countenance, which was drawn in placid, almost emotionless lines.

They were evidently very happy. "Ever been in a parlor car before?" he asked, smiling with delight.

"No," she answered; "I never was. It's fine, ain't it?"

"Great! And then after a while we'll go forward to the diner, and get a big lay-out. Finest meal in the world. Charge a dollar."

"Oh, do they?" cried the bride. "Charge a dollar? Why, that's too much—for us—ain't it, Jack?"

"Not this trip, anyhow," he answered bravely. "We're going to go the whole thing."

Later he explained to her about the trains. "You see, it's a thousand miles from one end of Texas to the other; and this train runs right across it, and never stops but four times." He had the pride of an owner. He pointed out to her the dazzling fittings of the coach; and in truth her eyes opened wider as she contemplated the sea-green figured velvet, the shining brass, silver, and glass, the wood that gleamed as darkly brilliant as the surface of a pool of oil. At one end a bronze figure sturdily held a support for a separated chamber, and at convenient places on the ceiling were frescos in olive and silver.

To the minds of the pair, their surroundings reflected the glory of their marriage that morning in San Antonio; this was the environment of their new estate; and the man's face in particular beamed with an elation that made him appear ridiculous to the Negro porter. This individual at times surveyed them from afar with an amused and superior grin. On other occasions he bullied them with skill in ways that did not make it exactly plain to them that they were being bullied. He subtly used all the manners of the most unconquerable kind of snobbery. He oppressed them; but of this oppression they had small knowledge, and they speedily forgot that infrequently a number of travelers covered them with stares of derisive enjoyment. Historically there was supposed to be something infinitely humorous in their situation.

"We are due in Yellow Sky at 3:42," he said, looking tenderly into her eyes.

"Oh, are we?" she said, as if she had not been aware of it. To evince surprise at her husband's statement was part of her wifely amiability. She took from a pocket a little silver watch; and as she held it before her, and stared at it with a frown of attention, the new husband's face shone.

"I bought it in San Anton' from a friend of mine," he told her gleefully.

"It's seventeen minutes past twelve," she said, looking up at him with a kind of shy and clumsy coquetry. A passenger, noting this play, grew excessively sardonic, and winked at himself in one of the numerous mirrors.

At last they went to the dining car. Two rows of Negro waiters, in glowing white suits, surveyed their entrance with the interest, and also the equanimity, of men who had been forewarned. The pair fell to the lot of a waiter who happened to feel pleasure in steering them through their meal. He viewed them with the manner of a fatherly pilot, his countenance radiant with benevolence. The patronage, entwined with the ordinary deference, was not plain to them. And yet, as they returned to their coach, they showed in their faces a sense of escape.

To the left, miles down a long purple slope, was a little ribbon of mint where moved the keening Rio Grande. The train was approaching it at an angle, and the apex was Yellow Sky. Presently it was apparent that, as the distance from Yellow Sky grew shorter, the husband became commensurately restless. His brick-red hands were more insistent in their prominence. Occasionally he was even rather absent-minded and faraway when the bride leaned forward and addressed him.

As a matter of truth, Jack Potter was beginning to find the shadow of a deed weigh upon him like a leaden slab. He, the town marshal of Yellow Sky, a man known, liked, and feared in his corner, a prominent person, had gone to San Antonio to meet a girl he believed he loved, and there, after the usual prayers, had actually induced her to marry him, without consulting Yellow Sky for any part of the transaction. He was now bringing his bride before an innocent and unsuspecting community.

Of course people in Yellow Sky married as it pleased them, in accordance with a general custom; but such was Potter's thought of his duty to his friends, or of their idea of his duty, or of an unspoken form which does not control men in these matters, that he felt he was heinous. He had committed an extraordinary crime. Face to face with this girl in San Antonio, and spurred by his sharp impulse, he had gone headlong over all the social hedges. At San Antonio he was like a man hidden in the dark. A knife to sever any friendly duty, any form, was easy to his hand in that remote city. But the hour of Yellow Sky—the hour of daylight—was approaching.

He knew full well that his marriage was an important thing to his town. It could only be exceeded by the burning of the new hotel. His friends could not forgive him. Frequently he had reflected on the advisability of telling them by telegraph, but a new cowardice had been upon him. He feared to do it. And now the train was hurrying him toward a scene of amazement, glee, and reproach. He glanced out of the window at the line of haze swinging slowly in toward the train.

Yellow Sky had a kind of brass band, which played painfully, to the delight of the populace. He laughed without heart as he thought of it. If the citizens could dream of his prospective arrival with his bride, they would parade the band at the station and escort them, amid cheers and laughing congratulations, to his adobe home.

He resolved that he would use all the devices of speed and plainscraft in making the journey from the station to his house. Once within that safe citadel, he could issue some sort of vocal bulletin, and then not go among the citizens until they had time to wear off a little of their enthusiasm.

The bride looked anxiously at him. "What's worrying you, Jack?"

He laughed again. "I'm not worrying, girl; I'm only thinking of Yellow Sky."

She flushed in comprehension.

A sense of mutual guilt invaded their minds and developed a finer tenderness. They looked at each other with eyes softly aglow. But Potter often laughed the same nervous laugh; the flush upon the bride's face seemed quite permanent.

The traitor to the feelings of Yellow Sky narrowly watched the speeding landscape. "We're nearly there," he said.

Presently the porter came and announced the proximity of Potter's home. He held a brush in his hand, and, with all his airy superiority gone, he brushed Potter's new clothes as the latter slowly turned this way and that way. Potter fumbled out a coin and gave it to the porter, as he had seen others do. It was a heavy and muscle-bound business, as that of a man shoeing his first horse.

The porter took their bag, and as the train began to slow they moved forward to the hooded platform of the car. Presently the two engines and their long string of coaches rushed into the station of Yellow Sky.

"They have to take water here," said Potter, from a constricted throat and in mournful cadence, as one announcing death. Before the train stopped his eye had swept the length of the platform, and he was glad and astonished to see there was none upon it but the station agent, who, with a slightly hurried and anxious air, was walking toward the water tanks. When the train had halted, the porter alighted first, and placed in position a little temporary step.

"Come on, girl," said Potter, hoarsely. As he helped her down they each laughed on a false note. He took the bag from the Negro, and bade his wife cling to his arm. As they slunk rapidly away, his handdog glance perceived that they were unloading the two trunks, and also that the station agent, far ahead near the baggage car, had turned and was running toward him, making gestures. He laughed, and groaned as he laughed, when he noted the first effect of his marital bliss upon Yellow Sky. He gripped his wife's arm firmly to his side, and they fled. Behind them the porter stood, chuckling fatuously.

II

The California express on the Southern Railway was due at Yellow Sky in twenty-one minutes. There were six men at the bar of the Weary Gentleman saloon. One was a drummer who talked a great deal and rapidly; three were Texans who did not care to talk at that time; and two were Mexican sheep-herders, who did not talk as a general practice in the Weary Gentleman saloon. The barkeeper's dog lay on the boardwalk that crossed in front of the door. His head was on his paws, and he glanced drowsily here and there with the constant vigilance of a dog that is kicked on occasion. Across the sandy street were some vivid green grass-plots, so wonderful in appearance, amid the sands that burned near them in a blazing sun, that they caused a doubt in the mind. They exactly resembled the grass mats used to represent lawns on the stage. At the cooler end of the railway station, a man without a coat sat in a tilted chair and smoked his pipe. The fresh-cut bank of the Rio Grande circled near the town, and there could be seen beyond it a great plum-colored plain of mesquit.

Save for the busy drummer and his companions in the saloon, Yellow Sky was dozing. The newcomer leaned gracefully upon the bar, and recited many tales with the confidence of a bard who has come upon a new field.

"—and at the moment that the old man fell downstairs with the bureau in his arms, the old woman was coming up with two scuttles of coal, and of course—"

The drummer's tale was interrupted by a young man who suddenly appeared in the open door. He cried: "Scratchy Wilson's drunk, and has turned loose with both hands." The two Mexicans at once set down their glasses and faded out of the rear entrance of the saloon.

The drummer, innocent and jocular, answered: "All right, old man. S'pose he has? Come in and have a drink, anyhow."

But the information had made such an obvious cleft in every skull in the room that the drummer was obliged to see its importance. All had become instantly solemn. "Say," said he, mystified, "what is this?" His three companions made the introductory gesture of eloquent speech; but the young man at the door forestalled them.

"It means, my friend," he answered, as he came into the saloon, "that for the next two hours this town won't be a health resort."

The barkeeper went to the door, and locked and barred it, reaching out of the window, he pulled in heavy wooden shutters, and barred them. Immediately a solemn, chapel-like gloom was upon the place. The drummer was looking from one to another.

"But say," he cried, "what is this, anyhow? You don't mean there is going to be a gun fight?"

"Don't know whether there'll be a fight or not," answered one man, grimly, "but there'll be some shootin'—some good shootin'."

The young man who had warned them waved his hand. "Oh, there'll be a fight fast enough, if any one wants it. Anybody can get a fight out there in the street. There's a fight just waiting."

The drummer seemed to be swayed between the interest of a foreigner and a perception of personal danger.

"What did you say his name was?" he asked.

"Scratchy Wilson," they answered in chorus.

"And will he kill anybody? What are you going to do? Does this happen often? Does he rampage around like this once a week or so? Can he break in that door?"

"No, he can't break down that door," replied the barkeeper. "He's tried it three times. But when he comes you'd better lay down on the floor, stranger. He's dead sure to shoot at it, and a bullet may come through."

Thereafter the drummer kept a strict eye upon the door. The time had not yet been called for him to hug the floor, but, as a minor precaution, he sidled near to the wall. "Will he kill anybody?" he said again.

The men laughed low and scornfully at the question.

"He's out to shoot, and he's out for trouble. Don't see any good in experimentin' with him."

"But what do you do in a case like this? What do you do?"

A man responded: "Why, he and Jack Potter—"

"But," in chorus the other men interrupted, "Jack Potter's in San Anton'."

"Well, who is he? What's he got to do with it?"

"Oh, he's the town marshal. He goes out and fights Scratchy when he gets on one of these tears."

"Wow!" said the drummer, mopping his brow. "Nice job he's got."

The voices had toned away to mere whisperings. The drummer wished to ask further questions, which were born of an increasing anxiety and bewilderment; but when he attempted them, the men merely looked at him in irritation and motioned him to remain silent. A tense waiting hush was upon them. In the deep shadows of the room their eyes shone as they listened for sounds from the street. One man made three gestures at the barkeeper; and the latter, moving like a ghost, handed him a glass and a bottle. The man poured a full glass of whisky, and set down the bottle noiselessly. He gulped the whisky in a swallow, and turned again toward the door in immovable silence. The drummer saw that the barkeeper, without a sound, had taken a Winchester from beneath the bar. Later he saw this individual beckoning to him, so he tiptoed across the room.

"You better come with me back of the bar."

"No, thanks," said the drummer, perspiring; "I'd rather be where I can make a break for the back door."

Whereupon the man of bottles made a kindly but peremptory gesture. The drummer obeyed it, and, finding himself seated on a box with his head below the level of the bar, balm was laid upon his soul at sight of various zinc and copper fittings that bore a resemblance to armor plate. The barkeeper took a seat comfortably upon an adjacent box.

"You see," he whispered, "this here Scratchy Wilson is a wonder with a gun—a perfect wonder; and when he goes on the war-trail, we hunt our holes—naturally. He's about the last one of the old gang that used to hang out along the river here. He's a terror when he's drunk. When he's sober he's all right—kind of simple—wouldn't hurt a fly—nicest fellow in town. But when he's drunk—whoo!"

There were periods of stillness. "I wish Jack Potter was back from San Anton'," said the barkeeper. "He shot Wilson up once—in the leg—and he would sail in and pull out the kinks in this thing."

Presently they heard from a distance the sound of a shot, followed by three wild yowls. It instantly removed a bond from the men in the darkened saloon. There was a shuffling of feet. They looked at each other. "Here he comes," they said.

III

A man in a maroon-colored flannel shirt, which had been purchased for purposes of decoration, and made principally by some Jewish women on the East Side of New York, rounded a corner and walked into the middle of the main street of Yellow Sky. In either hand the man held a long, heavy, blue-black revolver. Often he yelled, and these cries rang through a semblance of a deserted village, shrilly flying over the roofs in a volume that seemed to have no relation to the ordinary vocal strength of a man. It was as if the surrounding stillness formed the arch of a tomb over him. These cries of ferocious challenge rang against walls of silence. And his boots had red tops with gilded imprints, of the kind beloved in winter by little sledding boys on the hillsides of New England.

The man's face flamed in a rage begot of whisky. His eyes, rolling, and yet keen for ambush, hunted the still doorways and windows. He walked with the creeping movement of the midnight cat. As it occurred to him, he roared menacing information. The long revolvers in his hands were as easy as straws; they were moved with an electric swiftness. The little fingers of each hand played sometimes in a musician's way. Plain from the low collar of the shirt, the cords of his neck straightened and sank, straightened and sank, as passion moved him. The only sounds were his terrible invitations. The calm adobes preserved their demeanor at the passing of this small thing in the middle of the street.

There was no offer of fight—no offer of fight. The man called to the sky. There were no attractions. He bellowed and fumed and swayed his revolvers here and everywhere.

The dog of the barkeeper of the Weary Gentleman saloon had not appreciated the advance of events. He yet lay dozing in front of his master's door. At sight of the dog, the man paused and raised his revolver humorously. At sight of the man, the dog sprang up and walked diagonally away, with a sullen head, and growling. The man yelled, and the dog broke into a gallop. As it was about to enter an alley, there was a loud noise, a whistling, and something spat the ground directly before it. The dog screamed, and, wheeling in terror, galloped headlong in a new direction. Again there was a noise, a whistling, and sand was kicked viciously before it. Fear-stricken, the dog turned and flurried like an animal in a pen. The man stood laughing, his weapons at his hips.

Ultimately the man was attracted by the closed door of the Weary Gentleman saloon. He went to it and, hammering with a revolver, demanded drink.

The door remaining imperturbable, he picked a bit of paper from the walk, and nailed it to the framework with a knife. He then turned his back contemptuously upon this popular resort and, walking to the opposite side of the street and spinning there on his heel quickly and lithely, fired at the bit of paper. He missed it by a half-inch. He swore at himself, and went away. Later he comfortably fusilladed the windows of his most intimate friend. The man was playing with this town; it was a toy for him.

But still there was no offer of fight. The name of Jack Potter, his ancient antagonist, entered his mind, and he concluded that it would be a glad thing if he should go to Potter's house, and by bombardment induce him to come out and fight. He moved in the direction of his desire, chanting Apache scalp-music.

When he arrived at it, Potter's house presented the same still front as had the other adobes. Taking up a strategic position, the man howled a challenge. But this house regarded him as might a great stone god. It gave no sign. After a decent wait, the man howled further challenges, mingling with them wonderful epithets.

Presently there came the spectacle of a man churning himself into deepest rage over the immobility of a house. He fumed at it as the winter wind attacks a prairie cabin in the North. To the distance there should have gone the sound of a tumult like the fighting of two hundred Mexicans. As necessity bade him, he paused for breath or to reload his revolvers.

IV

Potter and his bride walked sheepishly and with speed. Sometimes they laughed together shamefacedly and low.

"Next corner, dear," he said finally.

They put forth the efforts of a pair walking bowed against a strong wind. Potter was about to raise a finger to point the first appearance of the new home when, as they circled the corner, they came face to face with a man in a maroon-colored shirt, who was feverishly pushing cartridges into a large revolver. Upon the instant the man dropped his revolver to the ground and, like lightning, whipped another from its holster. The second weapon was aimed at the bridegroom's chest.

There was a silence. Potter's mouth seemed to be merely a grave for his tongue. He exhibited an instinct to at once loosen his arm from the woman's grip, and he dropped the bag to the sand. As for the bride, her face had gone as yellow as old cloth. She was a slave to hideous rites, gazing at the apparitional snake.

The two men faced each other at a distance of three paces. He of the revolver smiled with a new and quiet ferocity.

"Tried to sneak up on me," he said. "Tried to sneak up on me!" His eyes grew more baleful. As Potter made a slight movement, the man thrust his revolver venomously forward. "No; don't you do it, Jack Potter. Don't you move a finger toward a gun just yet. Don't you move an eyelash. The time has come for me to settle with you, and I'm goin' to do it my own way, and loaf along with no interferin'. So if you don't want a gun bent on you, just mind what I tell you."

Potter looked at his enemy. "I ain't got a gun on me, Scratchy," he said. "Honest, I ain't." He was stiffening and steadying, but yet somewhere at the back of his mind a vision of the Pullman floated: the sea-green figured velvet, the shining brass, silver, and glass, the wood that gleamed as darkly brilliant as the surface of a pool of oil—all the glory of the marriage, the environment of the new estate. "You know I fight when it comes to fighting, Scratchy Wilson; but I ain't got a gun on me. You'll have to do all the shootin' yourself."

His enemy's face went livid. He stepped forward, and lashed his weapon to and fro before Potter's chest. "Don't you tell me you ain't got no gun on you, you whelp. Don't tell me no lie like that. There ain't a man in Texas ever seen you without no gun. Don't take me for no kid." His eyes blazed with light, and his throat worked like a pump.

"I ain't takin' you for no kid," answered Potter. His heels had not moved an inch backward. "I'm takin' you for a damn fool. I tell you I ain't got a gun, and I ain't. If you're goin' to shoot me up, you better begin now; you'll never get a chance like this again."

So much enforced reasoning had told on Wilson's rage; he was calmer. "If you ain't got a gun, why ain't you got a gun?" he sneered. "Been to Sunday school?"

"I ain't got a gun because I've just come from San Anton' with my wife. I'm married," said Potter. "And if I'd thought there was going to be any galoots like you prowling around when I brought my wife home, I'd had a gun, and don't you forget it."

"Married!" said Scratchy, not at all comprehending.

"Yes, married. I'm married," said Potter, distinctly.

"Married?" said Scratchy. Seemingly for the first time, he saw the drooping, drowning woman at the other man's side. "No!" he said. He was like a creature allowed a glimpse of another world. He moved a pace backward, and his arm, with the revolver, dropped to his side. "Is this the lady?" he asked.

"Yes; this is the lady," answered Potter.

There was another period of silence.

"Well," said Wilson at last, slowly, "I s'pose it's all off now."

"It's all off if you say so, Scratchy. You know I didn't make the trouble." Potter lifted his valise.

"Well, I 'low it's off, Jack," said Wilson. He was looking at the ground. "Married!" He was not a student of chivalry; it was merely that in the presence of this foreign condition he was a simple child of the earlier plains. He picked up his starboard revolver, and, placing both weapons in their holsters, he went away. His feet made funnel-shaped tracks in the heavy sand.

Rudyard Kipling

(1865 - 1936)

Rudyard Kipling, a chauvinistic Englishman who unashamedly applauded his country's imperialism under Queen Victoria, was born in India and worked in that British colony as a journalist, story writer, and poet until the early 1890's when he married an American and settled in England. Partly because he flattered the spirit of his age and class in England, he was an enormously popular poet and story writer in his own time, but his literary reputation has dimmed drastically since his death. Nevertheless, Kipling contributed significantly to the making of the British short story as we know it. From his newspaper work and his reading of nineteenth-century continental writers, Kipling learned the need for exact, carefully chosen details and economy in the short story. Although a prolific writer, he usually had difficulty with plot and was not successful as a novelist except for the episodic *Kim.* Like Richard Wagner in music, Kipling tended to exaggerate feelings and actions, and consequently there is sometimes a hint of artificiality in his fiction despite his realism.

The Gardener

Every one in the village knew that Helen Turrell did her duty by all her world, and by none more honourably than by her only brother's unfortunate child. The village knew, too, that George Turrell had tried his family severely since early youth, and were not surprised to be told that, after many fresh starts given and thrown away, he, an Inspector of Indian Police, had entangled himself with the daughter of a retired non-commissioned officer, and had died of a fall from a horse a few weeks before his child was born. Mercifully, George's father and mother were both dead, and though Helen, thirty-five and independent, might well have washed her hands of the whole disgraceful affair, she most nobly took charge, though she was, at the time, under threat of lung trouble which had driven her to the South of France. She arranged for the passage of the child and a nurse from Bombay, met them at Marseilles, nursed the baby through an attack of infantile dysentery due to the carelessness of the nurse, whom she had had to dismiss, and at last, thin and worn but triumphant, brought the boy late in the autumn, wholly restored, to her Hampshire home.

All these details were public property, for Helen was as open as the day, and held that scandals are only increased by hushing them up. She admitted that George had always been rather a black sheep, but things might have been much worse if the mother had insisted on her right to keep the boy. Luckily, it seemed that people of that class would do almost anything for money, and, as George had always turned to her in his scrapes, she felt herself justified—her friends agreed with her—in cutting the whole non-commissioned officer connection, and giving the child every advantage. A christening, by the Rector, under the name of Michael, was the first step. So far as she knew herself, she was not, she said, a child-lover, but, for all his faults, she had been very fond of George, and she pointed out that little Michael had his father's mouth to a line; which made something to build upon.

As a matter of fact, it was the Turrell forehead, broad, low, and well-shaped, with the widely-spaced eyes beneath it, that Michael had most faithfully reproduced. His mouth was somewhat better cut than the family type. But Helen, who would concede nothing good to his mother's side, vowed he was a Turrell all over, and, there being no one to contradict, the likeness was established.

In a few years Michael took his place, as accepted as Helen had always been—fearless, philosophical, and fairly good-looking. At six, he wished to know why he could not call her "Mummy," as other boys called their mothers. She explained that she was only his auntie, and that aunties were not quite the same as mummies, but that, if it gave him pleasure, he might call her "Mummy" at bedtime, for a pet-name between themselves.

Michael kept his secret most loyally, but Helen, as usual, explained the fact to her friends; which when Michael heard, he raged.

"Why did you tell? *Why* did you tell?" came at the end of the storm.

"Because it's always best to tell the truth," Helen answered, her arm round him as he shook in his cot.

"All right, but when the troof's ugly I don't think it's nice."

"Don't you, dear?"

"No, I don't, and"—she felt the small body stiffen—"now you've told, I won't call you 'Mummy' any more—not even at bedtimes."

"But isn't that rather unkind?" said Helen, softly.

"I don't care! I don't care! You've hurted me in my insides and I'll hurt you back. I'll hurt you as long as I live!"

"Don't, oh, don't talk like that, dear! You don't know what____"

"I will! And when I'm dead I'll hurt you worse!"

"Thank goodness, I shall be dead long before you, darling."

"Huh! Emma says, 'Never know your luck.'" (Michael had been talking to Helen's elderly, flat-faced maid.) "Lots of little boys die quite soon. So'll I. *Then* you'll see!"

Helen caught her breath and moved towards the door, but the wail of "Mummy! Mummy!" drew her back again, and the two wept together.

At ten years old, after two terms at a prep school, something or somebody gave him the idea that his civil status was not quite regular. He attacked Helen on the subject, breaking down her stammered defences with the family directness.

"'Don't believe a word of it," he said, cheerily, at the end. "People wouldn't have talked like they did if my people had been married. But don't you bother, Auntie. I've found out all about my sort in English Hist'ry and the Shakespeare bits. There was William the Conqueror to begin with, and —oh, heaps more, and they all got on first-rate. 'Twon't make any difference to you, my being *that*—will it?"

"As if anything could____" she began.

"All right. We won't talk about it any more if it makes you cry." He never mentioned the thing again of his own will, but when, two years later, he skilfully managed to have measles in the holidays, as his temperature went up to the appointed one hundred and four he muttered of nothing else, till Helen's voice, piercing at last his delirium, reached him with assurance that nothing on earth or beyond could make any difference between them.

The terms at his public school and the wonderful Christmas, Easter, and Summer holidays followed each other, variegated and glorious as jewels on a string; and as jewels Helen treasured them. In due time Michael developed his own interests, which ran their courses and gave way to others; but his interest in Helen was constant and increasing throughout. She repaid it with all that she had of affection or could command of counsel and money; and since Michael was no fool, the War took him just before what was like to have been a most promising career.

He was to have gone up to Oxford, with a scholarship, in October. At the end of August he was on the edge of joining the first holocaust of public-school boys who threw themselves into the Line; but the captain of his

O.T.C., where he had been sergeant for nearly a year, headed him off and steered him directly to a commission in a battalion so new that half of it still wore the old Army red, and the other half was breeding meningitis through living overcrowdedly in damp tents. Helen had been shocked at the idea of direct enlistment.

"But it's in the family," Michael laughed.

"You don't mean to tell me that you believed that old story all this time?" said Helen. (Emma, her maid, had been dead now several years.) "I gave you my word of honour—and I give it again—that—that it's all right. It is indeed."

"Oh, *that* doesn't worry me. It never did," he replied valiantly. "What I meant was, I should have got into the show earlier if I'd enlisted—like my grandfather."

"Don't talk like that! Are you afraid of it's ending so soon, then?"

"No such luck. You know what K. says."

"Yes. But my banker told me last Monday it couldn't *possibly* last beyond Christmas—for financial reasons."

"'Hope he's right, but our Colonel—and he's a Regular—says it's going to be a long job."

Michael's battalion was fortunate in that, by some chance which meant several "leaves," it was used for coast-defense among shallow trenches on the Norfolk coast; thence sent north to watch the mouth of a Scotch estuary, and, lastly, held for weeks on a baseless rumour of distant service. But, the very day that Michael was to have met Helen for four whole hours at a railway-junction up the line, it was hurled out, to help make good the wastage of Loos, and he had only just time to send her a wire of farewell.

In France luck again helped the battalion. It was put down near the Salient, where it led a meritorious and unexacting life, while the Somme was being manufactured; and enjoyed the peace of the Armentières and Laventie sectors when that battle began. Finding that it had sound views on protecting its own flanks and could dig, a prudent Commander stole it out of its own Division, under pretence of helping to lay telegraphs, and used it round Ypres at large.

A month later, and just after Michael had written Helen that there was nothing special doing and therefore no need to worry, a shell-splinter dropping out of a wet dawn killed him at once. The next shell uprooted and laid down over the body what had been the foundation of a barn wall, so neatly that none but an expert would have guessed that anything unpleasant had happened.

By this time the village was old in experience of war, and, English fashion, had evolved a ritual to meet it. When the postmistress handed her seven-year-old daughter the official telegram to take to Miss Turrell, she observed to the Rector's gardener: "It's Miss Helen's turn now." He replied, thinking of his own son: "Well, he's lasted longer than some." The child herself came to the front-door weeping aloud, because Master Michael had often given her sweets. Helen, presently, found herself pulling down the house-blinds one after one with great care, and saying earnestly to each: "Missing *always* means dead." Then she took her place in the dreary procession that was impelled to go through an inevitable series of unprofitable emotions. The Rector, of course, preached hope and prophesied word, very soon, from a prison camp. Several friends, too, told her perfectly truthful tales, but always about other women, to whom, after months and months of silence, their missing had been miraculously restored. Other people urged her to communicate with infallible Secretaries of organisations who could communicate with benevolent neutrals, who could extract accurate information from the most secretive of Hun prison commandants. Helen did and wrote and signed everything that was suggested or put before her.

Once, on one of Michael's leaves, he had taken her over a munition factory, where she saw the progress of a shell from blank-iron to the all but finished article. It struck her at the time that the wretched thing was never left alone for a single second; and "I'm being manufactured into a bereaved next-of-kin," she told herself, as she prepared her documents.

In due course, when all the organisations had deeply or sincerely regretted their inability to trace, etc., something gave way within her and all sensation—save of thankfulness for the release—came to an end in blessed passivity. Michael had died and her world had stood still and she had been one with the full shock of that arrest. Now she was standing still and the world was going forward, but it did not concern her—in no way or relation did it touch her. She knew this by the ease with which she could slip Michael's name into talk and incline her head to the proper angle, at the proper murmur of sympathy.

In the blessed realisation of that relief, the Armistice with all its bells broke over her and passed unheeded. At the end of another year she had overcome her physical loathing of the living and returned young, so that she could take them by the hand and almost sincerely wish them well. She had no interest in any aftermath, national or personal, of the War, but, moving at an immense distance, she sat on various relief committees and held strong views—she heard herself delivering them—about the site of the proposed village War Memorial.

Then there came to her, as next of kin, an official intimation, backed by a page of a letter to her in indelible pencil, a silver identity-disc, and a watch, to the effect that the body of Lieutenant Michael Turrell had been found, identified, and re-interred in Hagenzeele Third Military Cemetery—the letter of the row and the grave's number in that row duly given.

So Helen found herself moved on to another process of the manufacture—to a world full of exultant or broken relatives, now strong in the certainty that there was an altar upon earth where they might lay their love. These soon told her, and by means of time-tables made clear, how easy it was and how little it interfered with life's affairs to go and see one's grave.

"*So* different," as the Rector's wife said, "if he'd been killed in Mesopotamia, or even Gallipoli."

The agony of being waked up to some sort of second life drove Helen across the Channel, where, in a new world of abbreviated titles, she learnt that Hagenzeele Third could be comfortably reached by an afternoon train which fitted in with the morning boat, and that there was a comfortable little hotel not three kilometres from Hagenzeele itself, where one could spend quite a comfortable night and see one's grave next morning. All this she had from a Central Authority who lived in a board and tarpaper shed on the skirts of a razed city full of whirling lime-dust and blown papers.

"By the way," said he, "you know your grave, of course?"

"Yes, thank you," said Helen, and showed its row and number typed on Michael's own little typewriter. The officer would have checked it, out of one of his many books; but a large Lancashire woman thrust between them and bade him tell her where she might find her son, who had been corporal in the A.S.C. His proper name, she sobbed, was Anderson, but, coming of respectable folk, he had of course enlisted under the name of Smith; and had been killed at Dickiebush, in early 'Fifteen. She had not his number nor did she know which of his two Christian names he might have used with his alias; but her Cook's tourist ticket expired at the end of Easter week, and if by then she could not find her child she should go mad. Whereupon she fell forward on Helen's breast; but the officer's wife came out quickly from a little bedroom behind the office, and the three of them lifted the woman on to the cot.

"They are often like this," said the officer's wife, loosening the tight bonnet-strings. "Yesterday she said he'd been killed at Hooge. Are you sure you know your grave? It makes such a difference."

"Yes, thank you," said Helen, and hurried out before the woman on the bed should begin to lament again.

Tea in a crowded mauve and blue-striped wooden structure, with a false front, carried her still further into the nightmare. She paid her bill beside a stolid, plain-featured Englishwoman, who, hearing her inquire about the train to Hagenzeele, volunteered to come with her.

"I'm going to Hagenzeele myself," she explained. "Not to Hagenzeele Third; mine is Sugar Factory, but they call it La Rosière now. It's just south of Hagenzeele Three. Have you got your room at the hotel there?"

"Oh yes, thank you. I've wired."

"That's better. Sometimes the place is quite full, and at others there's hardly a soul. But they've put bathrooms into the old Lion d'Or—that's the hotel on the west side of Sugar Factory—and it draws off a lot of people, luckily."

"It's all new to me. This is the first time I've been over."

"Indeed! This is my ninth time since the Armistice. Not on my own account. *I* haven't lost any one, thank God—but, like every one else, I've a lot of friends at home who have. Coming over as often as I do, I find it helps them to have some one just look at the—the place and tell them about it afterwards. And one can take photos for them, too. I get quite a list of commissions to execute." She laughed nervously and tapped her slung Kodak. "There are two or three to see at Sugar Factory this time, and plenty of others in the cemeteries all about. My system is to save them up, and arrange them, you know. And when I've got enough commissions for one area to make it worth while, I pop over and execute them. It *does* comfort people."

"I suppose so," Helen answered, shivering as they entered the little train.

"Of course it does. (Isn't it lucky we've got window-seats?) It must do or they wouldn't ask one to do it, would they? I've a list of quite twelve or fifteen commissions here"—she tapped the Kodak again—"I must sort them out to-night. Oh, I forgot to ask you. What's yours?"

"My nephew," said Helen. "But I was very fond of him."

"Ah yes! I sometimes wonder whether *they* know after death? What do you think?"

"Oh, I don't—I haven't dared to think much about that sort of thing," said Helen, almost lifting her hands to keep her off.

"Perhaps that's better," the woman answered. "The sense of loss must be enough, I expect. Well, I won't worry you any more."

Helen was grateful, but when they reached the hotel Mrs. Scarsworth (they had exchanged names) insisted on dining at the same table with her, and after the meal, in the little, hideous salon full of low-voiced relatives, took Helen through her "commissions" with biographies of the dead, where she happened to know them, and sketches of their next of kin. Helen endured till nearly half-past nine, ere she fled to her room.

Almost at once there was a knock at her door and Mrs. Scarsworth entered; her hands, holding the dreadful list, clasped before her.

"Yes—yes—*I* know," she began. "Your're sick of me, but I want to tell you something. You—you aren't married are you? Then perhaps you won't. . . . But it doesn't matter. I've *got* to tell some one. I can't go on any longer like this."

"But please ——" Mrs. Scarsworth had backed against the shut door, and her mouth worked dryly.

"In a minute," she said. "You—you know about these graves of mine

I was telling you about downstairs, just now? They really *are* commissions. At least several of them are." Her eye wandered round the room. "What extraordinary wall-papers they have in Belgium, don't you think? . . . Yes. I swear they are commissions. But there's *one,* d'you see, and—and he was more to me than anything else in the world. Do you understand?"

Helen nodded.

"More than any one else. And, of course, he oughtn't to have been. He ought to have been nothing to me. But he *was.* He *is.* That's why I do the commissions, you see. That's all."

"But why do you tell me?" Helen asked desperately.

"Because I'm *so* tired of lying. Tired of lying—always lying—year in and year out. When I don't tell lies I've got to act 'em and I've got to think 'em, always. *You* don't know what that means. He was everything to me that he oughtn't to have been—the one real thing—the only thing that ever happened to me in all my life; and I've had to pretend he wasn't. I've had to watch every word I said, and think out what lie I'd tell next, for years and years!"

"How many years?" Helen asked.

"Six years and four months before, and two and three-quarters after. I've gone to him eight times, since. To-morrow'll make the ninth, and—and I can't—I *can't* go to him again with nobody in the world knowing. I want to be honest with some one before I go. Do you understand? It doesn't matter about *me.* I was never truthful, even as a girl. But it isn't worthy of *him.* So—so I—I had to tell you. I can't keep it up any longer. Oh, I can't!"

She lifted her joined hands almost to the level of her mouth, and brought them down sharply, still joined, to full arms' length below her waist. Helen reached forward, caught them, bowed her head over them, and murmured: "Oh, my dear! My dear!" Mrs. Scarsworth stepped back, her face all mottled.

"My God!" said she. "Is *that* how you take it?"

Helen could not speak, the woman went out; but it was a long while before Helen was able to sleep.

Next morning Mrs. Scarsworth left early on her round of commissions, and Helen walked alone to Hagenzeele Third. The place was still in the making, and stood some five or six feet above the metalled road, which it flanked for hundreds of yards. Culverts across a deep ditch served for entrances through the unfinished boundary wall. She climbed a few wooden-faced earthen steps and then met the entire crowded level of the thing in one held breath. She did not know that Hagenzeele Third counted twenty-one thousand dead already. All she saw was a merciless sea of black crosses, bearing little strips of stamped tin at all angles across their faces. She could distinguish no order or arrangement in their mass; nothing but a waist-high wilderness as of weeds stricken dead, rushing at her. She went forward, moved to the left and the right hopelessly, wondering by what guidance she should ever come to her own. A great distance away there was a line of whiteness. It proved to be a block of some two or three hundred graves whose headstones had already been set, whose flowers were planted out, and whose new-sown grass showed green. Here she could see clear-cut letters at the ends of the rows, and, referring to her slip, realised that it was not here she must look.

A man knelt behind a line of headstones—evidently a gardener, for he was firming a young plant in the soft earth. She went towards him, her paper in her hand. He rose at her approach and without prelude or salutation asked: "Who are you looking for?"

"Lieutenant Michael Turrell—my nephew," said Helen slowly and word for word, as she had many thousands of times in her life.

The man lifted his eyes and looked at her with infinite compassion before he turned from the fresh-sown grass towards the naked black crosses.

"Come with me," he said, "and I will show you where your son lies."

When Helen left the Cemetery she turned for a last look. In the distance she saw the man bending over his young plants; and she went away, supposing him to be the gardener.

George Moore

(1852 - 1933)

Born in Ireland in 1852, George Moore lived a bohemian life in Paris in the 1870's, associating with the leading French novelists, poets, and impressionist painters. Stimulated and influenced by the writings and remarks of Emile Zola, Stéphane Mallarmé, and Paul Verlaine—the forces behind the naturalist and symbolist movements—Moore later called himself Zola's ricochet and introduced naturalism into the British novel with his *A Mummer's Wife* (1884). A mercurial man and writer, he continually experimented with literary techniques and styles, and he quite rightly said of himself, "I came into the world apparently with a nature like a smooth sheet of wax, bearing no impress but capable of receiving any." Moore's realistic novel, *Esther Waters* (1894), is his best known fictional work, but his masterpiece may be the three-volume *Hail and Farewell* (1914), a controversial, highly personal record of the Irish Literary Renaissance in the first decade of this century. He contributed significantly to the developing British short story with *Celibates* (1895), a collection of psychological studies, and *The Untilled Field* (1903), a group of austere, concentrated stories which captures the paralysis and stagnation of Irish rural life. It appears that Moore influenced the James Joyce of *Dubliners* who depicted the spiritual paralysis in Dublin. "Home Sickness," which is taken from *The Untilled Field,* deals with the peculiarly Irish problem of exile, and Frank O'Connor, the late Irish short-story writer and critic, doubted "if Irish literature has produced a better short story than 'Home Sickness.'"

Home Sickness

He told the doctor he was due in the bar-room at eight o'clock in the morning; the bar-room was in a slum in the Bowery; and he had only been able to keep himself in health by getting up at five o'clock and going for long walks in Central Park.

"A sea voyage is what you want," said the doctor. "Why not go to Ireland for two or three months? You will come back a new man."

"I'd like to see Ireland again."

And then he began to wonder how the people at home were getting on. The doctor was right. He thanked him, and three weeks afterwards he landed in Cork.

As he sat in the railway carriage he recalled his native village—he could see it and its lake, and then the fields one by one, and the roads. He could see a large piece of rocky land—some three or four hundred acres of headland stretching out into the winding lake. Upon this headland the peasantry had been given permission to build their cabins by former owners of the Georgian house standing on the pleasant green hill. The present owners considered the village a disgrace, but the villagers paid high rents for their plots of ground, and all the manual labour that the Big House required came from the village: the gardeners, the stable helpers, the house and the kitchen maids.

He had been thirteen years in America, and when the train stopped at his station, he looked round to see if there were any changes in it. It was just the same blue limestone station-house as it was thirteen years ago. The platform and the sheds were the same, and there were five miles of road from the station to Duncannon. The sea voyage had done him good, but five miles were too far for him to-day; the last time he had walked the road, he had walked it in an hour and a half, carrying a heavy bundle on a stick.

He was sorry he did not feel strong enough for the walk; the evening was fine, and he would meet many people coming home from the fair, some of whom he had known in his youth, and they would tell him where he could get a clean lodging. But the carman would be able to tell him that; he called the car that was waiting at the station, and soon he was answering questions about America. But Bryden wanted to hear of those who were still living in the old country, and after hearing the stories of many people he had forgotten, he heard that Mike Scully, who had been away in a situation for many years as a coachman in the King's County, had come back and built a fine house with a concrete floor. Now there was a good loft in Mike Scully's house, and Mike would be pleased to take in a lodger.

Bryden remembered that Mike had been in a situation at the Big House; he had intended to be a jockey, but had suddenly shot up into a fine tall man, and had had to become a coachman instead. Bryden tried to recall the face, but he could only remember a straight nose, and a somewhat dusky complexion. Mike was one of the heroes of his childhood, and his youth floated before him, and he caught glimpses of himself, something that was more than a phantom and less than a reality. Suddenly his reverie was broken: the carman pointed with his whip, and Bryden saw a tall, finely-built, middle-aged man coming through the gates, and the driver said:—

"There's Mike Scully."

Mike had forgotten Bryden even more completely than Bryden had forgotten him, and many aunts and uncles were mentioned before he began to understand.

"You've grown into a fine man, James," he said, looking at Bryden's great width of chest. "But you are thin in the cheeks, and you're sallow in the cheeks too."

"I haven't been very well lately—that is one of the reasons I have come back; but I want to see you all again."

Bryden paid the carman, wished him "God-speed," and he and Mike divided the luggage between them, Mike carrying the bag and Bryden the bundle, and they walked round the lake, for the townland was at the back of the demesne; and while they walked, James proposed to pay Mike ten shillings a week for his board and lodging.

He remembered the woods thick and well-forested; now they were windworn, the drains were choked, and the bridge leading across the lake inlet was falling away. Their way led between long fields where herds of cattle were grazing; the road was broken—Bryden wondered how the villagers drove their carts over it, and Mike told him that the landlord could not keep it in repair, and he would not allow it to be kept in repair out of the rates, for then it would be a public road, and he did not think there should be a public road through his property.

At the end of many fields they came to the village, and it looked a desolate place, even on this fine evening, and Bryden remarked that the county did not seem to be as much lived in as it used to be. It was at once strange and familiar to see the chickens in the kitchen; and, wishing to re-knit himself to the old habits, he begged of Mrs. Scully not to drive them out, saying he did not mind them. Mike told his wife that Bryden was born in Duncannon, and when he mentioned Bryden's name she gave him her hand, after wiping it in her apron, saying he was heartily welcome, only she was afraid he would not care to sleep in a loft.

"Why wouldn't I sleep in a loft, a dry loft! You're thinking a good deal of America over here," said he, "but I reckon it isn't all you think it. Here you work when you like and you sit down when you like; but when you have had a touch of blood-poisoning as I had, and when you have seen young people walking with a stick, you think that there is something to be said for old Ireland."

"Now won't you be taking a sup of milk? You'll be wanting a drink after travelling," said Mrs. Scully.

And when he had drunk the milk Mike asked him if he would like to go inside or if he would like to go for a walk.

"Maybe it is sitting down you would like to be."

And they went into the cabin, and started to talk about the wages a man could get in America, and the long hours of work.

And after Bryden had told Mike everything about America that he thought would interest him, he asked Mike about Ireland. But Mike did not seem to be able to tell him much that was of interest. They were all very poor—poorer, perhaps, than when he left them.

"I don't think anyone except myself has a five pound note to his name."

Bryden hoped he felt sufficiently sorry for Mike. But after all Mike's life and prospects mattered little to him. He had come back in search of health; and he felt better already; the milk had done him good, and the bacon and cabbage in the pot sent forth a savoury odour. The Scullys were very kind, they pressed him to make a good meal; a few weeks of country air and food, they said, would give him back the health he had lost in the Bowery; and when Bryden said he was longing for a smoke, Mike said there was no better sign than that. During his long illness he had never wanted to smoke, and he was a confirmed smoker.

It was comfortable to sit by the mild peat fire watching the smoke of their pipes drifting up the chimney, and all Bryden wanted was to be let alone; he did not want to hear of anyone's misfortunes, but about nine o'clock a number of villagers came in, and their appearance was depressing. Bryden remembered one or two of them—he used to know them very well when he was a boy; their talk was as depressing as their appearance, and he could feel no interest whatever in them. He was not moved when he heard that Higgins the stone-mason was dead; he was not affected when he heard that Mary Kelly, who used to go to do the laundry at the Big House, had married; he was only interested when he heard she had gone to America. No, he had not met her there, America is a big place. Then one of the peasants asked him if he remembered Patsy Carabine, who used to do the gardening at the Big House. Yes, he remembered Patsy well. Patsy was in the poor-house. He had not been able to do any work on account of his arm; his house had fallen in; he had given up his holding and gone into the poorhouse. All this was very sad, and to avoid hearing any further unpleasantness, Bryden began to tell them about America. And they sat round listening to him; but all the talking was on his side; he wearied of it; and looking round the group he recognised a ragged hunchback with grey hair; twenty years ago he was a young hunchback, and, turning to him, Bryden asked him if he were doing well with his five acres.

"Ah, not much. This has been a bad season. The potatoes failed; they were watery—there is no diet in them."

These peasants were all agreed that they could make nothing out of their farms. Their regret was that they had not gone to America when they were young; and after striving to take an interest in the fact that O'Connor had lost a mare and foal worth forty pounds Bryden began to wish himself back in the slum. And when they left the house he wondered if every evening would be like the present one. Mike piled fresh sods on the fire, and he hoped it would show enough light in the loft for Bryden to undress himself by.

The cackling of some geese in the road kept him awake, and the loneliness of the country seemed to penetrate to his bones, and to freeze the marrow in them. There was a bat in the loft—a dog howled in the distance—and then he drew the clothes over his head. Never had he been so unhappy, and the sound of Mike breathing by his wife's side in the kitchen added to his nervous terror. Then he dozed a little; and lying on his back he dreamed he was awake, and the men he had seen sitting round the fireside that evening seemed to him like spectres come out of some unknown region of morass and reedy tarn. He stretched out his hands for his clothes, determined to fly from this house, but remembering the lonely road that led to the station he fell back on his pillow. The geese still cackled, but he was too tired to be kept awake any longer. He seemed to have been asleep only a few minutes when he heard Mike calling him. Mike had come half way up the ladder and was telling him that breakfast was ready. "What kind of breakfast will he give me?" Bryden asked himself as he pulled on his clothes. There were tea and hot griddle cakes for breakfast, and there were fresh eggs; there was sunlight in the kitchen and he liked to hear Mike tell of the work he was going to do in the fields. Mike rented a farm of about fifteen acres, at least ten of it was grass; he grew an acre of potatoes and some corn, and some turnips for his sheep. He had a nice bit of meadow, and he took down his scythe, and as he put the whetstone in his belt Bryden noticed a second scythe, and he asked Mike if he should go down with him and help him to finish the field.

"You haven't done any mowing this many a year; I don't think you'd be of much help. You'd better go for a walk by the lake, but you may come in the afternoon if you like and help to turn the grass over."

Bryden was afraid he would find the lake shore very lonely, but the magic of returning health is the sufficient distraction for the convalescent, and the morning passed agreeably. The weather was still and sunny. He could hear the ducks in the reeds. The hours dreamed themselves away, and it became his habit to go to the lake every morning. One morning he met the landlord, and they walked together, talking of the country, of what it had been, and the ruin it was slipping into. James Bryden told him that ill health had brought him back to Ireland; and the landlord lent him his boat, and Bryden rowed about the islands, and resting upon his oars he looked at the old castles, and remembered the pre-historic raiders that the landlord had told him about. He came across the stones to which the lake dwellers had tied their boats, and these signs of ancient Ireland were pleasing to Bryden in his present mood.

As well as the great lake there was a smaller lake in the bog where the villagers cut their turf. This lake was famous for its pike, and the landlord allowed Bryden to fish there, and one evening when he was looking for a frog with which to bait his line he met Margaret Dirken driving home the cows for the milking. Margaret was the herdsman's daughter, and she lived in a cottage near the Big House; but she came up to the village whenever there was a dance, and Bryden had found himself opposite to her in the reels. But until this evening he had had little opportunity of speaking to her, and he was glad to speak to someone, for the evening was lonely, and they stood talking together.

"You're getting your health again," she said. "You'll soon be leaving us."

"I'm in no hurry."

"You're grand people over there; I hear a man is paid four dollars a day for his work."

"And how much," said James, "has he to pay for his food and for his clothes?"

Her cheeks were bright and her teeth small, white and beautifully even; and a woman's soul looked at Bryden out of her soft Irish eyes. He was troubled and turned aside, and catching sight of a frog looking at him out of a tuft of grass he said:—

"I have been looking for a frog to put upon my pike line."

The frog jumped right and left, and nearly escaped in some bushes, but he caught it and returned with it in his hand.

"It is just the kind of frog a pike will like," he said. "Look at its great white belly and its bright yellow back."

And without more ado he pushed the wire to which the hook was fastened through the frog's fresh body, and dragging it through the mouth he passed the hooks through the hind legs and tied the line to the end of the wire.

"I think," said Margaret, "I must be looking after my cows; it's time I got them home."

"Won't you come down to the lake while I set my line?"

She thought for a moment and said:—

"No, I'll see you from here."

He went down the the reedy tarn, and at his approach several snipe got up, and they flew above his head uttering sharp cries. His fishing-rod was a long hazel stick, and he threw the frog as far as he could into the lake. In doing this he roused some wild ducks; a mallard and two ducks got up, and they flew towards the larger lake. Margaret watched them; they flew in a line with an old castle; and they had not disappeared from view when Bryden came towards her, and he and she drove the cows home together that evening.

They had not met very often when she said, "James, you had better not come here so often calling to me."

"Don't you wish me to come?"

"Yes, I wish you to come well enough, but keeping company is not the custom of the country, and I don't want to be talked about."

"Are you afraid the priest would speak against us from the altar?"

"He has spoken against keeping company, but it is not so much what the priest says, for there is no harm in talking."

"But if you are going to be married there is no harm in walking out together."

"Well, not so much, but marriages are made differently in these parts; there is not much courting here."

And next day it was known in the village that James was going to marry Margaret Dirken.

His desire to excel the boys in dancing had aroused much gaiety in the parish, and for some time past there had been dancing in every house where there was a floor fit to dance upon; and if the cottager had no money to pay for a barrel of beer, James Bryden, who had money, sent him a barrel, so that Margaret might get her dance. She told him that they sometimes crossed over into another parish where the priest was not so averse to dancing, and James wondered. And next morning at Mass he wondered at their simple fervour. Some of them held their hands above their heads as they prayed, and all this was very new and very old to James Bryden. But the obedience of these people to their priest surprised him. When he was a lad they had not been so obedient, or he had forgotten their obedience; and he listened in mixed anger and wonderment to the priest who was scolding his parishioners, speaking to them by name, saying that he had heard there was dancing going on in their homes. Worse than that, he said he had seen boys and girls loitering about the roads, and the talk that went on was of one kind—love. He said that newspapers containing love-stories were finding their way into the people's houses, stories about love, in which there was nothing elevating or ennobling. The people listened, accepting the priest's opinion without question. And their submission was pathetic. It was the submission of a primitive people clinging to religious authority, and Bryden contrasted the weakness and incompetence of the people about him with the modern restlessness and cold energy of the people he had left behind him.

One evening, as they were dancing, a knock came to the door, and the piper stopped playing, and the dancers whispered:—

"Some one has told on us; it is the priest."

And the awe-stricken villagers crowded round the cottage fire, afraid to open the door. But the priest said that if they did not open the door he would put his shoulder to it and force it open. Bryden went towards the door, saying he would allow no one to threaten him, priest or no priest, but Margaret caught his arm and told him that if he said anything to the priest, the priest would speak against them from the altar, and they would be shunned by the neighbours. It was Mike Scully who went to the door and let the priest in, and he came in saying they were dancing their souls into hell.

"I've heard of your goings on," he said—"of your beer-drinking and dancing. I will not have it in my parish. If you want that sort of thing you had better go to America."

"If that is intended for me, sir, I will go back tomorrow. Margaret can follow."

"It isn't the dancing, it's the drinking I'm opposed to," said the priest, turning to Bryden.

"Well, no one has drunk too much, sir," said Bryden.

"But you'll sit here drinking all night," and the priest's eyes went towards the corner where the women had gathered, and Bryden felt that the priest looked on the women as more dangerous than the porter. "It's after midnight," he said, taking out his watch.

By Bryden's watch it was only half-past eleven, and while they were arguing about the time Mrs. Scully offered Bryden's umbrella to the priest, for in his hurry to stop the dancing the priest had gone out without his; and, as if to show Bryden that he bore him no ill-will, the priest accepted the loan of the umbrella, for he was thinking of the big marriage fee that Bryden would pay him.

"I shall be badly off for the umbrella to-morrow," Bryden said, as soon as the priest was out of the house. He was going with his father-in-law to a fair. His father-in-law was learning him how to buy and sell cattle. And his father-in-law was saying that the country was mending, and that a man might become rich in Ireland if he only had a little capital. Bryden had the capital, and Margaret had an uncle on the other side of the lake who would leave her all he had, that would be fifty pounds, and never in the village of Duncannon had a young couple begun life with so much prospect of success as would James Bryden and Margaret Dirken.

Some time after Christmas was spoken of as the best time for the marriage; James Bryden said that he would not be able to get his money out of America before the spring. The delay seemed to vex him, and he seemed anxious to be married, until one day he recieved a letter from America, from a man who had served in the bar with him. This friend wrote to ask Bryden if he were coming back. The letter was no more than a passing wish to see Bryden again. Yet Bryden stood looking at it, and everyone wondered what could be in the letter. It seemed momentous, and they hardly believed him when he said it was from a friend who wanted to know if his health were better. He tried to forget the letter, and he looked at the worn fields, divided by walls of loose stones, and a great longing came upon him.

The smell of the Bowery slum had come across the Atlantic, and had found him out in this western headland; and one night he awoke from a dream in which he was hurling some drunken customer through the open doors into the darkness. He had seen his friend in his white duck jacket throwing drink from glass into glass amid the din of voices and strange accents; he had heard the clang of money as it was swept into the till, and his sense sickened for the bar-room. But how should he tell Margaret Dirken that he could not marry her? She had built her life upon this marriage. He could not tell her that he would not marry her . . . yet he must go. He felt as if he were being hunted; the thought that he must tell Margaret that he could not marry her hunted him day after day as a weasel hunts a rabbit. Again and again he went to meet her with the intention of telling her that he did not love her, that their lives were not for one another, that it had all been a mistake, and that happily he had found out it was a mistake soon enough. But Margaret, as if she guessed what he was about to speak of, threw her arms about him and begged him to say he loved her, and that they would be married at once. He agreed that he loved her, and that they would be married at once. But he had not left her many minutes before the feeling came upon him that he could not marry her—that he must go away. The smell of the bar-room hunted him down. Was it for the sake of the money that he might make there that he wished to go back? No, it was not the money. What then? His eyes fell on the bleak country, on the little fields divided by bleak walls; he remembered the pathetic ignorance of the people, and it was these things that he could not endure. It was the priest who came to forbid the dancing. Yes, it was the priest. As he stood looking at the line of the hills the bar-room seemed by him. He heard the politicians, and the excitement of politics was in his blood again. He must go away from this place—he must get back to the bar-room. Looking up he saw the scanty orchard, and he hated the spare road that led to the village, and he hated the little hill at the top of which the village began, and he hated more than all other places the house where he was to live with Margaret Dirken—if he married her. He could see it from where he stood—by the edge of the lake, with twenty acres of pasture land about it, for the landlord had given up part of his demesne land to them.

He caught sight of Margaret, and he called to her to come through the stile.

"I have just had a letter from America."

"About the money?" she said.

"Yes, about the money. But I shall have to go over there."

He stood looking at her, seeking for words; and she guessed from his embarrassment that he would say to her that he must go to America before they were married.

"Do you mean, James, you will have to go at once?"

"Yes," he said, "at once. But I shall come back in time to be married in August. It will only mean delaying our marriage a month."

They walked on a little way talking; every step he took James felt that he was a step nearer the Bowery slum. And when they came to the gate Bryden said:—

"I must hasten or I shall miss the train."

"But," she said, "you are not going now—you are not going to-day?"

"Yes, this morning. It is seven miles. I shall have to hurry not to miss the train."

And then she asked him if he would ever come back.

"Yes," he said, "I am coming back."

"If you are coming back, James, why not let me go with you?"

"You could not walk fast enough. We should miss the train."

"One moment, James. Don't make me suffer; tell me the truth. You are not coming back. Your clothes—where shall I send them?"

He hurried away, hoping he would come back. He tried to think that he liked the country he was leaving, that it would be better to have a farmhouse and live there with Margaret Dirken than to serve drinks behind a counter in the Bowery. He did not think he was telling her a lie when he said he was coming back. Her offer to forward his clothes touched his heart, and at the end of the road he stood and asked himself if he should go back to her. He would miss the train if he waited another minute, and he ran on. And he would have missed the train if he had not met a car. Once he was on the car he felt himself safe—the country was already behind him. The train and the boat at Cork were mere formulae; he was already in America.

The moment he landed he felt the thrill of home that he had not found in his native village, and he wondered how it was that the smell of the bar seemed more natural than the smell of the fields, and the roar of crowds more welcome than the silence of the lake's edge. However, he offered up a thanksgiving for his escape, and entered into negotiations for the purchase of the bar-room.

. . .

He took a wife, she bore him sons and daughters, the bar-room prospered, property came and went; he grew old, his wife died, he retired from business, and reached the age when a man begins to feel there are not many years in front of him, and that all he has had to do in life has been done. His children married, lonesomeness began to creep about him; in the evening, when he looked into the fire-light, a vague, tender reverie floated up, and Margaret's soft eyes and name vivified the dusk. His wife and children passed out of mind, and it seemed to him that a memory was the only real thing he possessed, and the desire to see Margaret again grew intense. But she was an old woman, she had married, maybe she was dead. Well, he would like to be buried in the village where he was born.

There is an unchanging, silent life within every man that none knows but himself, and his unchanging, silent life was his memory of Margaret Dirken. The bar-room was forgotten and all that concerned it, and the things he saw most clearly were the green hillside, and the bog lake and the rushes about it, and the greater lake in the distance, and behind it the blue lines of wandering hills.

The Modern Period

Joseph Conrad

(1857 - 1924)

Joseph Conrad, who became a great British novelist, was born Josef Teodor Konrad Nalcez Korzeniowski of Polish parents in the Ukraine and spoke virtually no English before becoming a British seaman in 1878. As seaman and later officer, he sailed to Asia, South America, and Africa, locations which would play an essential part in his novels. In 1895 Conrad published his first novel, *Almayer's Folly,* and although the book was only a partial success, he decided to abandon the sea for a writing career. Because he often used his sea experiences in exotic lands for settings, he was known for many years as merely a writer of sea adventures. Although the public did not accept Conrad's fiction for many years with more than tepid interest, he was sustained to some extent by the praise of critics and fellow novelists, including Henry James, John Galsworthy, Stephen Crane, and Ford Madox Ford. Ironically, it was not until 1913 and the publication of one of his lesser novels, *Chance,* that he became the darling of the mass readers. Between *Almayer's Folly* and *Chance,* Conrad wrote several excellent novels, including *The Nigger of the Narcissus* (1897), *Heart of Darkness* (1899), *Lord Jim* (1900), and *Nostromo* (1904). Conrad said of himself, "I have been called a writer of the sea, a descriptive writer, a romantic writer—and also a realist. But as a matter of fact all my concern has been with the 'ideal' value of things, events, and people. That and nothing else." A perceptive psychologist, Conrad examined the moral ambiguities of human actions and how ideals often clash with reality and man's imperfections. Believing that men cannot cut themselves off from humanity and remain whole, he frequently dramatized situations in which men must risk involvement with others or perish in solitary confinement. *The Secret Sharer* is a suspenseful, artful psychological novel of a young and insecure sea captain and his sympathetic relationship with a fugitive (a kind of alter ego) whom he protects from the authorities. This psychological voyage presents many problems and the reader must follow it carefully from the dreamy description of the first paragraph.

The Secret Sharer

I

On my right hand there were lines of fishing stakes resembling a mysterious system of half-submerged bamboo fences, incomprehensible in its division of the domain of tropical fishes, and crazy of aspect as if abandoned forever by some nomad tribe of fishermen now gone to the other end of the ocean; for there was no sign of human habitation as far as the eye could reach. To the left a group of barren islets, suggesting ruins of stone walls, towers, and block-houses, had its foundations set in a blue sea that itself looked solid, so still and stable did it lie below my feet; even the track of light from the westering sun shone smoothly, without that animated glitter which tells of an imperceptible ripple. And when I turned my head to take a parting glance at the tug which had just left us anchored outside the bar, I saw the straight line of the flat shore joined to the stable sea, edge to edge, with a perfect and unmarked closeness, in one leveled floor half brown, half blue under the enormous dome of the sky. Corresponding in their insignificance to the islets of the sea, two small clumps of trees, one on each side of the only fault in the impeccable joint, marked the mouth of the river Meinam we had just left on the first preparatory stage of our homeward journey; and, far back on the inland level, a larger and loftier mass, the grove surrounding the great Paknam pagoda, was the only thing on which the eye could rest from the vain task of exploring the monotonous sweep of the horizon. Here and there gleams as of a few scattered pieces of silver marked the windings of the great river; and on the nearest of them, just within the bar, the tug steaming right into the land became lost to my sight, hull and funnel and masts, as though the impassive earth had swallowed her up without an effort, without a tremor. My eye followed the light cloud of her smoke, now here, now there, above the plain, according to the devious curves of the stream, but always fainter and farther away, till I lost it at last behind the miter-shaped hill of the great pagoda. And then I was left alone with my ship, anchored at the head of the Gulf of Siam.

She floated at the starting point of a long journey, very still in an immense stillness, the shadows of her spars flung far to the eastward by the setting sun. At that moment I was alone on her decks. There was not a sound in her—and around us nothing moved, nothing lived, not a canoe on the water, not a bird in the air, not a cloud in the sky. In this breathless pause at the threshold of a long passage we seemed to be measuring our fitness for a long and arduous enterprise, the appointed task of both our existences to be carried out, far from all human eyes, with only sky and sea for spectators and for judges.

There must have been some glare in the air to interfere with one's sight, because it was only just before the sun left us that my roaming eyes made out beyond the highest ridge of the principal islet of the group something which did away with the solemnity of perfect solitude. The tide of darkness flowed on swiftly; and with tropical suddenness a swarm of stars came out above the shadowy earth, while I lingered yet, my hand resting lightly on my ship's rail as if on the shoulder of a trusted friend. But, with all that multitude of celestial bodies staring down at one, the comfort of quiet communion with her was gone for good. And there were also disturbing sounds by this time—voices, footsteps forward; the steward flitted along the main deck, a busily ministering spirit; a hand bell tinkled urgently under the poop deck. . . .

I found my two officers waiting for me near the supper table, in the lighted cuddy. We sat down at once, and as I helped the chief mate, I said:

"Are you aware that there is a ship anchored inside the islands? I saw her mastheads above the ridge as the sun went down."

He raised sharply his simple face, overcharged by a terrible growth of whisker, and emitted his usual ejaculations: "Bless my soul, sir! You don't say so!"

My second mate was a sound-cheeked, silent young man, grave beyond his years, I thought; but as our eyes happened to meet I detected a slight quiver on his lips. I looked down at once. It was not my part to encourage sneering on board my ship. It must be said, too, that I knew very little of my officers. In consequence of certain events of no particular significance, except to myself, I had been appointed to the command only a fortnight before. Neither did I know much of the hands forward. All these people had been together for eighteen months or so, and my position was that of the only stranger on board. I mention this because it has some bearing on what is to follow. But what I felt most was my being a stranger to the ship; and if all the truth must be told, I was somewhat of a stranger to myself. The youngest man on board (barring the second mate), and untried as yet by a position of the fullest responsibility, I was willing to take the adequacy of the others for granted. They had simply to be equal to their tasks: but I wondered how far I should turn out faithful to that ideal conception of one's own personality every man sets up for himself secretly.

Meantime the chief mate, with an almost visible effect of collaboration on the part of his round eyes and frightful whiskers, was trying to evolve a theory of the anchored ship. His dominant trait was to take all things into earnest consideration. He was of a painstaking turn of mind. As he used to say, he "liked to account to himself" for practically everything that came in his way, down to a miserable scorpion he had found in his cabin a week before. The why and the wherefore of that scorpion—how it got on board and came to select his room rather than the pantry (which was a dark place and more what a scorpion would be partial to), and how on earth it managed to drown itself in the inkwell of his writing desk—had exercised him infinitely. The ship within the islands was much more easily accounted for; and just as we were about to rise from the table he made his pronouncement. She was, he doubted not, a ship from home lately arrived. Probably she drew too much water to cross the bar except at the top of spring tides. Therefore she went into that natural harbor to wait for a few days in preference to remaining in an open roadstead.

"That's so," confirmed the second mate, suddenly, in his slightly hoarse voice. "She draws over twenty feet. She's the Liverpool ship *Sephora* with a cargo of coal. Hundred and twenty-three days from Cardiff."

We looked at him in surprise.

"The tugboat skipper told me when he came on board for your letters, sir," explained the young man. "He expects to take her up the river the day after tomorrow."

After thus overwhelming us with the extent of his information he slipped out of the cabin. The mate observed regretfully that he "could not account for that young fellow's whims." What prevented him telling us all about it at once, he wanted to know.

I detained him as he was making a move. For the last two days the crew had had plenty of hard work, and the night before they had very little sleep. I felt painfully that I—a stranger—was doing something unusual when I directed him to let all hands turn in without setting an anchor watch. I proposed to keep on deck myself till one o'clock or thereabouts. I would get the second mate to relieve me at that hour.

"He will turn out the cook and the steward at four," I concluded, "and then give you a call. Of course at the slightest sign of any sort of wind we'll have the hands up and make a start at once."

He concealed his astonishment. "Very well, sir." Outside the cuddy he put his head in the second mate's door to inform him of my unheard-of caprice to take a five hour's anchor watch on myself. I heard the other raise his voice incredulously—"What? The Captain himself?" Then a few more murmurs, a door closed, then another. A few moments later I went on deck.

My strangeness, which had made me sleepless, had prompted that unconventional arrangement, as if I had expected in those solitary hours of the night to get on terms with the ship of which I knew nothing, manned by men of whom I knew very little more. Fast alongside a wharf, littered like any ship in port with a tangle of unrelated things, invaded by unrelated shore people. I had hardly seen her yet properly. Now, as she lay cleared for sea, the stretch of her main deck seemed to me very fine under the stars. Very fine, very roomy for her size, and very inviting. I descended the poop and paced the waist, my mind picturing to myself the coming passage through the Malay Archipelago, down the Indian Ocean, and up the Atlantic. All its phases were familiar enough to me, every characteristic, all the alternatives which were likely to face me on the high seas—everything! . . . except the novel responsibility of command. But I took heart from the reasonable thought that the ship was like other ships, the men like other men, and that the sea was not likely to keep any special surprises expressly for my discomfiture.

Arrived at that comforting conclusion, I bethought myself of a cigar and went below to get it. All was still down there. Everybody at the after end of the ship was sleeping profoundly. I came out again on the quarter-deck, agreeably at ease in my sleeping suit on the warm breathless night, barefooted, a flowing cigar in my teeth, and, going forward, I was met by the profound silence of the fore end of the ship. Only as I passed the door of the forecastle I heard a deep, quiet, trustful sigh of some sleeper inside. And suddenly I rejoiced in the great security of the sea as compared with the unrest of the land, in my choice of that untempted life presenting no disquieting problems. invested with an elementary moral beauty by the absolute straightforwardness of its appeal and by the singleness of its purpose.

The riding light in the forerigging burned with a clear, untroubled, (as if symbolic,) flame, confident and bright in the mysterious shades of the night. Passing on my way aft along the other side of the ship, I observed that the rope side ladder, put over, no doubt, for the master of the tug when he came to fetch away our letters, had not been hauled in as it should have been. I became annoyed at this, for exactitude in some small matters is the very soul of discipline. Then I reflected that I had myself peremptorily dismissed my officers from duty, and by my own act had prevented the anchor watch being formally set and things properly attended to. I asked myself whether it was wise ever to interfere with the established routine of duties even from the kindest of motives. My action might have made me appear eccentric. Goodness only knew how that absurdly whiskered mate would "account" for my conduct, and what the whole ship thought of that informality of their new captain. I was vexed with myself.

Not from compunction certainly, but, as it were mechanically, I proceeded to get the ladder in myself. Now a side ladder of that sort is a light affair and comes in easily, yet my vigorous tug, which should have brought it flying on board, merely recoiled upon my body in a totally unexpected jerk. What the devil! . . . I was so astounded by the immovableness of that ladder that I remained stock-still, trying to account for it to myself like that imbecile mate of mine. In the end, of course, I put my head over the rail.

The side of the ship made an opaque belt of shadow on the darkling glassy shimmer of the sea. But I saw at once something elongated and pale floating very close to the ladder. Before I could form a guess a faint flash of phosphorescent light, which seemed to issue suddenly from the naked body of a man, flickered in the sleeping water with the elusive, silent play of summer lightning in a night sky. With a gasp I saw revealed to my stare a pair of feet, the long legs, a broad livid back immersed right up to the neck in the greenish cadaverous glow. One hand, awash, clutched the bottom rung of the ladder. He was complete but for the head. A headless corpse! The cigar dropped out of my gaping mouth with a tiny plop and a short hiss quite audible in the absolute stillness of all things under heaven. At that I suppose he raised up his face, a dimly pale oval in the shadow of the ship's side. But even then I could only barely make out down there the shape of his black-haired head. However, it was enough for the horrid, frost-bound sensation which had gripped me about the chest to pass off. The moment of vain exclamations was past, too. I only climbed on the spare spar and leaned over the rail as far as I could, to bring my eyes nearer to that mystery floating alongside.

As he hung by the ladder, like a resting swimmer, the sea lightning played about his limbs at every stir; and he appeared in it ghastly, silvery, fishlike. He remained as mute as a fish, too. He made no motion to get out of the water, either. It was inconceivable that he should not attempt to come on board, and strangely troubling to suspect that perhaps he did not want to. And my first words were prompted by just that troubled incertitude.

"What's the matter?" I asked in my ordinary tone, speaking down to the face upturned exactly under mine.

"Cramp," it answered, no louder. Then slightly anxious, "I say, no need to call anyone."

"I was not going to," I said.

"Are you alone on deck?"

"Yes."

I had somehow the impression that he was on the point of letting go the ladder to swim away beyond my ken—mysterious as he came. But, for the moment, this being appearing as if he had risen from the bottom of the sea (it was certainly the nearest land to the ship) wanted only to know the time. I told him. And he, down there, tentatively:

"I suppose your captain's turned in?"

"I am sure he isn't," I said.

He seemed to struggle with himself, for I heard something like the low, bitter murmur of doubt. "What's the good?" His next words came out with a hesitating effort.

"Look here, my man. Could you call him out quietly?"

I thought the time had come to declare myself.

"*I* am the captain,"

I heard a "By Jove!" whispered at the level of the water. The phosphorescence flashed in the swirl of the water all about his limbs, his other hand seized the ladder.

"My name's Leggatt."

The voice was calm and resolute. A good voice. The self-possession of that man had somehow induced a corresponding state in my self. It was very quietly that I remarked:

"You must be a good swimmer."

"Yes, I've been in the water practically since nine o'clock. The question for me now is whether I am to let go this ladder and go on swimming till I sink from exhaustion, or—to come on board here."

I felt this was no mere formula of desperate speech, but a real alternative in the view of a strong soul. I should have gathered from this that he was young; indeed, it is only the young who are ever confronted by such clear issues. But at the time it was pure intuition on my part. A mysterious communication was established already between us two—in the face of that silent, darkened tropical sea. I was young, too; young enough to make no comment. The man in the water began suddenly to climb up the ladder, and I hastened away from the rail to fetch some clothes.

Before entering the cabin I stood still, listening in the lobby at the foot of the stairs. A faint snore came through the closed door of the chief mate's room. The second mate's door was on the hook, but the darkness in there was absolutely soundless. He, too, was young and could sleep like a stone. Remained the steward, but he was not likely to wake up before he was called. I got a sleeping suit out of my room and, coming back on deck, saw the naked man from the sea sitting on the main hatch, glimmering white in the darkness, his elbows on his knees and his head in his hands. In a moment he had concealed his damp body in a sleeping suit of the same gray-stripe pattern as the one I was wearing and followed me like my double on the poop. Together we moved right aft, barefooted, silent.

"What is it?" I asked in a deadened voice, taking the lighted lamp out of the binnacle, and raising it to his face.

"An ugly business."

He had rather regular features; a good mouth; light eyes under somewhat heavy, dark eyebrows; a smooth, square forehead; no growth on his cheeks; a small, brown mustache, and a well-shaped, round chin. His expression was concentrated, meditative, under the inspecting light of the lamp I held up to his face; such as a man thinking hard in solitude might wear. My sleeping suit was just right for his size. A well-knit young fellow of twenty-five at most. He caught his lower lip with the edge of white, even teeth.

"Yes," I said, replacing the lamp in the binnacle. The warm, heavy tropical night closed upon his head again.

"There's a ship over there," he murmured.

"Yes, I know. The *Sephora.* Did you know of us?"

"Hadn't the slightest idea. I am the mate of her—" He paused and corrected himself. "I should say I *was.*"

"Aha! Something wrong?"

"Yes. Very wrong indeed. I've killed a man."

"What do you mean? Just now?"

"No, on the passage. Weeks ago. Thirty-nine south. When I say a man—"

"Fit of temper," I suggested, confidently.

The shadowy, dark head, like mine, seemed to nod imperceptibly above the ghostly gray of my sleeping suit. It was, in the night, as though I had been faced by my own reflection in the depths of a somber and immense mirror.

"A pretty thing to have to own up to for a Conway boy," murmured my double, distinctly.

"You're a Conway boy?"

"I am," he said, as if startled. Then, slowly . . . "Perhaps you too—"

It was so; but being a couple of years older I had left before he joined. After a quick interchange of dates a silence fell; and I thought suddenly of my absurd mate with his terrific whiskers and the "Bless my soul—you don't say so" type of intellect. My double gave me an inkling of his thoughts by saying: "My father's a parson in Norfolk. Do you see me before a judge and jury on that charge? For myself I can't see the necessity. There are follows that an angel from heaven— And I am not that. He was one of those creatures that are just simmering all the time with a silly sort of wickedness. Miserable devils that have no business to live at all. He wouldn't do his duty and wouldn't let anybody else do theirs. But what's the good of talking! You know well enough the sort of ill-conditioned snarling cur—"

He appealed to me as if our experiences had been as identical as our clothes. And I knew well enough the pestiferous danger of such a character where there are no means of legal repression. And I knew well enough also that my double there was no homicidal ruffian. I did not think of asking him for details, and he told me the story roughly in brusque, disconnected sentences. I needed no more. I saw it all going on as though I were myself inside that other sleeping suit.

"It happened while we were setting a reefed foresail, at dusk. Reefed foresail! You understand the sort of weather. The only sail we had left to keep the ship running; so you may guess what it had been like for days. Anxious sort of job, that. He gave me some of his cursed insolence at the sheet. I tell you I was overdone with this terrific weather that seemed to have no end to it. Terrific, I tell you—and a deep ship. I believe the fellow himself was half crazed with funk. It was no time for gentlemanly reproof, so I turned round and felled him like an ox. He up and at me. We closed just as an awful sea made for the ship. All hands saw it coming and took to the rigging, but I had him by the throat, and went on shaking him like a rat, the men above us yelling, 'Look out! look out!' Then a crash as if the sky had fallen on my head. They say that for over ten minutes hardly anything was to be seen of the ship—just the three masts and a bit of the forecastle head and of the poop all awash driving along in a smother of foam. It was a miracle that they found us, jammed together behind the forebits. It's clear that I meant business, because I was holding him by the throat still when they picked us up. He was black in the face. It was too much for them. It seems they rushed us aft together, gripped as we were, screaming 'Murder!' like a lot of lunatics, and broke into the cuddy. And the ship running for her life, touch and go all the time, any minute her last in a sea fit to turn your hair gray only a-looking at it. I understand that the skipper, too, started raving like the rest of them. The man had been deprived of sleep for more than a week, and to have this sprung on him at the height of a furious gale nearly drove him out of his mind. I wonder they didn't fling me overboard after getting the carcass of their precious shipmate out of my fingers. They had rather a job to separate us, I've been told. A sufficiently fierce story to make an old judge and a respectable jury sit up a bit. The first thing I heard when I came to myself was the maddening howling of that endless gale, and on that the voice of the old man. He was hanging on to my bunk, staring into my face out of his sou'wester.

"'Mr. Leggatt, you have killed a man. You can act no longer as chief mate of this ship.'"

His care to subdue his voice made it sound monotonous. He rested a hand on the end of the skylight to steady himself with, and all that time did not stir a limb, so far as I could see. "Nice little tale for a quiet tea party," he concluded in the same tone.

One of my hands, too, rested on the end of the skylight; neither did I stir a limb, so far as I knew. We stood less than a foot from each other. It occurred to me that if old "Bless my soul—you don't say so" were to put his head up the companion and catch sight of us, he would think he was seeing double, or imagine himself come upon a scene of weird witchcraft; the strange captain having a quiet confabulation by the wheel with his own gray ghost. I became very much concerned to prevent anything of the sort. I heard the other's soothing undertone.

"My father's a parson in Norfolk," it said. Evidently he had forgotten he had told me this important fact before. Truly a nice little tale.

"You had better slip down into my stateroom now," I said, moving off stealthily. My double followed my movements; our bare feet made no sound; I let him in, closed the door with care, and, after giving a call to the second mate, returned on deck for my relief.

"Not much sign of any wind yet," I remarked when he approached.

"No sir. Not much," he assented, sleepily, in his hoarse voice, with just enough deference, no more, and barely suppressing a yawn.

"Well, that's all you have to look out for. You have got your orders."

"Yes, sir."

I paced a turn or two on the poop and saw him take up his position face forward with his elbow in the ratlines of the mizzen rigging before I went below. The mate's faint snoring was still going on peacefully. The cuddy lamp was burning over the table on which stood a vase with flowers, a polite attention from the ship's provision merchant—the last flowers we should see for the next three months at the very least. Two bunches of bananas hung from the beam symmetrically, one on each side of the rudder casing. Everything was as before in the ship—except that two of her captain's sleeping suits were simultaneously in us, one motionless in the cuddy, the other keeping very still in the captain's stateroom.

It must be explained here that my cabin had the form of the capital letter L, the door being with the angle and opening into the short part of the letter. A couch was to the left, the bed place to the right; my writing desk and the chronometers' table faced the door. But anyone opening it, unless he stepped right inside, had no view of what I call the long (or vertical) part of the letter. It contained some lockers surmounted by a bookcase; and a few clothes, a thick jacket or two, caps, oilskin coat, and such like, hung on hooks. There was at the bottom of that part a door opening into my bathroom, which could be entered also directly from the saloon. But that way was never used.

The mysterious arrival had discovered the advantage of this particular shape. Entering my room, lighted strongly by a big bulkhead lamp swung on gimbals above my writing desk, I did not see him anywhere till he stepped out quietly from behind the coats hung in the recessed part.

"I heard somebody moving about, and went in there at once," he whispered.

I, too, spoke under my breath.

"Nobody is likely to come in here without knocking and getting permission."

He nodded. His face was thin and the sunburn faded, as though he had been ill. And no wonder. He had been, I heard presently, kept under arrest in his cabin for nearly seven weeks. But there was nothing sickly in his eyes or in his expression. He was not a bit like me, really; yet, as we stood leaning over my bed place, whispering side by side, with our dark heads together and our backs to the door, anybody bold enough to open it stealthily would have been treated to the uncanny sight of a double captain busy talking in whispers with his other self.

"But all this doesn't tell me how you came to hang on to our side ladder," I inquired, in the hardly audible murmurs we used, after he had told me something more of the proceedings on board the *Sephora* once the bad weather was over.

"When we sighted Java Head I had had time to think all those matters out several times over. I had six weeks of doing nothing else, and with only an hour or so every evening for a tramp on the quarterdeck."

He whispered, his arms folded on the side of my bed place, staring through the open port. And I could imagine perfectly the manner of this thinking out—a stubborn if not a steadfast operation; something of which I should have been perfectly incapable.

"I reckoned it would be dark before we closed with the land," he continued, so low that I had to strain my hearing near as we were to each other, shoulder touching shoulder almost. "So I asked to speak to the old man. He always seemed very sick when he came to see me—as if he could not look me in the face. You know, that foresail saved the ship. She was too deep to have run long under bare poles. And it was I that managed to set it for him. Anyway, he came. When I had him in my cabin—he stood by the door looking at me as if I had the halter round my neck already—I asked him right away to leave my cabin door unlocked at night while the ship was going through Sundra Straits. There would be the Java coast within two or three miles, off Angier Point. I wanted nothing more. I've had a prize for swimming my second year in the Conway."

"I can believe it," I breathed out.

"God only knows why they locked me in every night. To see some of their faces you'd have thought they were afraid I'd go about at night strangling people. Am I a murdering brute? Do I look it? By Jove! if I had been he wouldn't have trusted himself like that into my room. You'll say I might have chucked him aside and bolted out, there and then—it was dark already. Well, no. And for the same reason I wouldn't think of trying to smash the door. There would have been a rush to stop me at the noise, and I did not mean to get into a confounded scrimmage. Somebody else might have got killed—for I would not have broken out only to get chucked back, and I did not want any more of that work. He refused, looking more sick than ever. He was afraid of the men, and also of that old second mate of his who had been sailing with him for years—a gray-headed old humbug; and his steward, too, had been with him devil knows how long—seventeen years or more—a dogmatic sort of loafer who hated me like poison, just because I was the chief mate. No chief mate ever made more than one voyage in the *Sephora,* you know. Those two old chaps ran the ship. Devil only knows what the skipper wasn't afraid of (all his nerve went to pieces altogether in that hellish spell of bad weather we had)—of what the law would do to him—of his wife, perhaps. Oh, yes! she's on board. Though I don't think she would have meddled. She would have been only too glad to have me out of the ship in any way. The 'brand of Cain' business, don't you see. That's all right. I was ready enough to go off wandering on the face of the earth—and that was price enough to pay for an Abel of that sort. Anyhow, he wouldn't listen to me. 'This thing must take its course. I represent the law here.' He was shaking like a leaf. 'So you won't?' 'No!' 'Then I hope you will be able to sleep on that,' I said, and turned my back on him. 'I wonder that *you* can,' cries he, and locks the door.

"Well after that, I couldn't. Not very well. That was three weeks ago. We have had a slow passage through the Java Sea; drifted about Carimata for ten days. When we anchored here they thought, I suppose, it was all right. The nearest land (and that's five miles) is the ship's destination; the consul would soon set about catching me; and there would have been no object in bolting to these islets there. I don't suppose there's a drop of water on them. I don't know how it was, but tonight that steward, after bringing me my supper, went out to let me eat it, and left the door unlocked. And I ate it—all there was, too. After I had finished I strolled out on the quarter-deck. I don't know that I meant to do anything. A breath of fresh air was all I wanted, I believe. Then a sudden temptation came over me. I kicked off my slippers and was in the water before I had made up my mind fairly. Somebody heard the splash and they raised an awful hullabaloo. 'He's gone! Lower the boats! He's committed suicide! No, he's swimming.' Certainly I was swimming. It's not so easy for a swimmer like me to commit suicide by drowning. I landed on the nearest islet before the boat left the ship's side. I heard them pulling about in the dark, hailing, and so on, but after a bit they gave up. Everything quieted down and the anchorage became as still as death. I sat down on a stone and began to think. I felt certain they would start searching for me at daylight. There was no place to hide on those stony things—and if there had been, what would have been the good? But now I was clear of that ship, I was not going back. So after a while I took off all my clothes, tied them up in a bundle with a stone inside, and dropped them in the deep water on the outer side of that islet. That was suicide enough for me. Let them think what they liked, but I didn't mean to drown myself. I meant to swim till I sank—but that's not the same thing. I struck out for another of these little islands, and it was from that one that I first saw your riding light. Something to swim for. I went on easily, and on the way I came upon a flat rock a foot or two above water. In the daytime, I dare say, you might make it out with a glass from your poop. I scrambled up on it and rested myself for a bit. Then I made another start. That last spell must have been over a mile."

His whisper was getting fainter and fainter, and all the time he stared straight out through the porthole, in which there was not even a star to be seen. I had not interrupted him. There was something that made comment impossible in his narrative, or perhaps in himself; a sort of feeling, a quality which I can't find a name for. And when he ceased, all I found was a futile whisper: "So you swam for our light?"

"Yes—straight for it. It was something to swim for. I couldn't see any stars low down because the coast was in the way, and I couldn't see the land, either. The water was like glass. One might have been swimming in a confounded thousand-feet deep cistern with no place for scrambling out anywhere; but what I didn't lie was the notion of swimming round and round like a crazed bullock before I gave out; and as I didn't mean to go back . . . No. Do you see me being hauled back, stark naked, off one of these little islands by the scruff of the neck and fighting like a wild beast? Somebody would have got killed for certain, and I did not want any of that. So I went on. Then your ladder—"

"Why didn't you hail the ship?" I asked, a little louder.

He touched my shoulder lightly. Lazy footsteps came right over our heads and stopped. The second mate had crossed from the other side of the poop and might have been hanging over the rail for all we knew.

"He couldn't hear us talking—could he?" My double breathed into my very ear, anxiously.

His anxiety was an answer, a sufficient answer, to the question I had put to him. An answer containing all the difficulty of that situation. I closed the porthole quietly, to make sure. A louder word might have been overheard.

"Who's that?" he whispered then.

"My second mate. But I don't know much more of the fellow than you do."

And I told him a little about myself. I had been appointed to take charge while I least expected anything of the sort, not quite a fortnight ago. I didn't know either the ship or the people. Hadn't had the time in port to look about me or size anybody up. And as to the crew, all they knew was that I was appointed to take the ship home. For the rest, I was almost as much of a stranger on board as himself, I said. And at the moment I felt it most acutely. I felt that it would take very little to make me a suspect person in the eyes of the ship's company.

He had turned about meantime; and we, the two strangers in the ship, faced each other in identical attitudes.

"You ladder—" he murmured, after a silence. "Who'd have thought of finding a ladder hanging over at night in a ship anchored out here! I felt just then a very unpleasant faintness. After the life I've been leading for nine weeks, anybody would have got out of condition. I wasn't capable of swimming round as far as your rudder chains. And, lo and behold! there was a ladder to get hold of. After I gripped it I said to myself, 'What's the good?' When I saw a man's head looking over I thought I would swim away presently and leave him shouting—in whatever langugage it was. I didn't mind being looked at. I—I liked it. And then you speaking to me so quietly—as if you had expected me—made me hold on a little longer. It had been a confounded lonely time—I don't mean while swimming. I was glad to talk a little to somebody that didn't belong to the *Sephora*. As to asking for the captain, that was a mere impulse. It could have been no use, with all the ship knowing about me and the other people pretty certain to be round here in the morning. I don't know—I wanted to be seen, to talk with somebody, before I went on. I don't know what I would have said. . . . 'Fine night, isn't it?' or something of the sort."

"Do you think they will be round here presently?" I asked with some incredulity.

"Quite likely," he said, faintly.

He looked extremely haggard all of a sudden. His head rolled on his shoulders.

"H'm. We shall see then. Meantime get into that bed," I whispered. "Want help? There."

It was a rather high bed place with a set of drawers underneath. This amazing swimmer really needed the lift I gave him by seizing his leg. He tumbled in, rolled over on his back, and flung one arm across his eyes. And then, with his face nearly hidden, he must have looked exactly as I used to look in that bed. I gazed upon my other self for a while before drawing across carefully the two green serge curtains which ran on a brass rod. I thought for a moment of pinning them together for greater safety, but I sat down on the couch, and once there I felt unwilling to rise and hunt for a pin. I would do it in a moment. I was extremely tired, in a peculiarly intimate way, by the strain of stealthiness, by the effort of whispering and the general secrecy of this excitement. It was three o'clock by now and I had been on my feet since nine, but I was not sleepy; I could not have gone to sleep. I sat there, fagged out, looking at the curtains, trying to clear my mind of the confused sensation of being in two places at once, and greatly bothered by an exasperating knocking in my head. It was a relief to discover suddenly that it was not in my head at all, but on the outside of the door. Before I could collect myself the words "Come in" were out of my mouth, and the steward entered with a tray, bringing in my morning coffee. I had slept, after all, and I was so frightened that I shouted, "This way! I am here, steward," as though he had been miles away. He put down the tray on the table next the couch and only then said, very quietly, "I can see you are here, sir." I felt him give me a keen look, but I dared not meet his eyes just then. He must have wondered why I had drawn the curtains of my bed before going to sleep on the couch. He went out, hooking the door open as usual.

I heard the crew washing decks above me. I knew I would have been told at once if there had been any wind. Calm, I thought, and I was doubly vexed. Indeed, I felt dual more than ever. The steward reappeared suddenly in the doorway. I jumped up from the couch so quickly that he gave a start.

"What do you want here?"

"Close your port, sir—they are washing decks."

"It is closed," I said, reddening.

"Very well, sir." But he did not move from the doorway and returned my stare in an extraordinary, equivocal manner for a time. Then his eyes wavered, all his expression changed, and in a voice unusually gentle, almost coaxingly:

"May I come in to take the empty cup away, sir?"

"Of course!" I turned my back on him while he popped in and out. Then I unhooked and closed the door and even pushed the bolt. This sort of thing could not go on very long. The cabin was as hot as an oven, too. I took a peep at my double, and discovered that he had not moved, his arm was still over his eyes; but his chest heaved; his hair was wet; his chin glistened with perspiration. I reached over him and opened the port.

"I must show myself on deck," I reflected.

Of course, theoretically, I could do what I liked, with no one to say nay to me within the whole circle of the horizon; but to lock my cabin door and take the key away I did not dare. Directly I put my head out of the companion I saw the group of my two officers, the second mate barefooted, the chief mate in long India-rubber boots, near the break of the poop, and the steward halfway down the poop ladder talking to them eagerly. He happened to catch sight of me and dived, the second ran down on the main deck shouting some order or other, and the chief mate came to meet me, touching his cap.

There was a sort of curiosity in his eye that I did not like. I don't know whether the steward had told them that I was "queer" only, or downright drunk, but I know the man meant to have a good look at me. I watched him coming with a smile which, as he got into point-blank range, took effect and froze his very whiskers. I did not give him time to open his lips.

"Square the yards by lifts and braces before the hands go to breakfast."

It was the first particular order I had given on board that ship; and I stayed on deck to see it executed, too. I had felt the need of asserting myself without loss of time. That sneering young cub got taken down a peg or two on that occasion, and I also seized the opportunity of having a good look at the face of every foremast man as they filed past me to go to the after braces. At breakfast time, eating nothing myself, I presided with such frigid dignity that the two mates were only too glad to escape from the cabin as soon as decency permitted; and all the time the dual working of my mind distracted me almost to the point of insanity. I was constantly watching myself, my secret self, as dependent on my actions as my own personality, sleeping in that bed, behind that door which faced me as I sat at the head of the table. It was very much like being mad, only it was worse because one was aware of it.

I had to shake him for a solid minute, but when at last he opened his eyes it was in the full possession of his senses, with an inquiring look.

"All's well so far," I whispered. "Now you must vanish into the bathroom."

He did so, as noiseless as a ghost, and then I rang for the steward, and facing him bodly, directed him to tidy up my stateroom while I was having my bath—"and be quick about it." As my tone admitted of no excuses, he said, "Yes, sir," and ran off to fetch his dustpan and brushes. I took a bath and did most of my dressing, splashing, and whistling softly for the steward's edification, while the secret sharer of my life stood drawn up bolt upright in that little space, his face looking very sunken in daylight, his eyelids lowered under the stern, dark line of his eyebrows drawn together by a slight frown.

When I left him there to go back to my room the steward was finishing dusting. I sent for the mate and engaged him in some insignificant conversation. It was, as it were, trifling with the terrific character of his whiskers; but my object was to give him an opportunity for a good look at my cabin. And then I could at last shut, with a clear conscience, the door of my stateroom and get my double back into the recessed part. There was nothing else for it. He had to sit still on a small folding stool, half smothered by the heavy coats hanging there. We listened to the steward going into the bathroom out of the saloon, filling the water bottles there, scrubbing the bath, setting things to rights, whisk, bang, clatter—out again into the saloon—turn the key—click. Such was my scheme for keeping my second self invisible. Nothing better could be contrived under the circumstances. And there we sat; I at my writing desk ready to appear busy with some papers, he behind me out of sight of the door. It would not have been prudent to talk in daytime; and I could not have stood the excitement of that queer sense of whispering to myself. Now and then, glancing over my shoulder, I saw him far back there, sitting rigidly on the low stool, his bare feet close together, his arms folded, his head hanging on his breast—and perfectly still. Anybody would have taken him for me.

I was fascinated by it myself. Every moment I had to glance over my shoulder. I was looking at him when a voice outside the door said:

"Beg pardon, sir."

"Well!" . . . I kept my eyes on him, and so when the voice outside the door announced, "There's a ship's boat coming our way, sir," I saw him give a start—the first movement he had made for hours. But he did not raise his bowed head.

"All right. Get the ladder over."

I hesitated. Should I whisper something to him? But what? His immobility seemed to have been never disturbed. What could I tell him he did not know already? . . . Finally I went on deck.

II

The skipper of the *Sephora* had a thin red whisker all round his face, and the sort of complexion that goes with hair of that color; also the particular, rather smeary shade of blue in the eyes. He was not exactly a showy figure; his shoulders were high, his stature but middling—one leg slightly more bandy than the other. He shook hands, looking vaguely around. A spiritless tenacity was his main characteristic, I judged. I behaved with a politeness which seemed to disconcert him. Perhaps he was shy. He mumbled to me as if he were ashamed of what he was saying; gave his name (it was something like Archbold—but at this distance of years I hardly am sure), his ship's name, and a few other particulars of that sort, in the manner of a criminal making a reluctant and doleful confession. He had had terrible weather on the passage out—terrible—terrible—wife aboard, too.

By this time we were seated in the cabin and the steward brought in a tray with a bottle and glasses. "Thanks! No." Never took liquor. Would have some water, though. He drank two tumblerfuls. Terrible thirsty work. Ever since daylight had been exploring the islands round his ship.

"What was that for—fun?" I asked, with an appearance of polite interest.

"No!" He sighed. "Painful duty."

As he persisted in his mumbling and I wanted my double to hear every word, I hit upon the notion of informing him that I regretted to say I was hard of hearing.

"Such a young man, too!" he nodded, keeping his smeary blue, unintelligent eyes fastened upon me. "What was the cause of it—some disease?" he inquired, without the least sympathy and as if he thought that, if so, I'd got no more than I deserved.

"Yes; disease," I admitted in a cheerful tone which seemed to shock him. But my point was gained, because he had to raise his voice to give me his tale. It is not worth while to record that version. It was just over two months since all this had happened, and he had thought so much about it that he seemed completely muddled as to its bearings, but still immensely impressed.

"What would you think of such a thing happening on board your own ship? I've had the *Sephora* for these fifteen years. I am a well-know shipmaster."

He was densely distressed—and perhaps I should have sympathized with him if I had been able to detach my mental vision from the unsuspected sharer of my cabin as though he were my second self. There he was on the other side of the bulkhead, four or five feet from us, no more, as we sat in the saloon. I looked politely at Captain Archbold (if that was his name), but it was the other I saw, in a gray sleeping suit, seated on a low stool, his bare feet close together, his arms folded, and every word said between us falling into the ears of his dark head bowed on his chest.

"I have been at sea now, man and boy, for seven-and-thirty years, and I've never heard of such a thing happening in an English ship. And that it should be my ship. Wife on board, too."

I was hardly listening to him.

"Don't you think," I said, "that the heavy sea which, you told me, came aboard just then might have killed the man? I have seen the sheer weight of a sea kill a man very neatly, by simply breaking his neck."

"Good God!" he uttered, impressively, fixing his smeary blue eyes on me. "The sea! No man killed by the sea ever looked like that." He seemed positively scandalized at my suggestion. And as I gazed at him certainly not prepared for anything original on his part, he advanced his head close to mine and thrust his tongue out at me so suddenly that I couldn't help starting back.

After scoring over my calmness in this graphic way he nodded wisely. If I had seen the sight, he assured me, I would never forget it as long as I lived. The weather was too bad to give the corpse a proper sea burial. So next day at dawn they took it up on the poop, covering its face with a bit of bunting; he read a short prayer, and then, just as it was, in its oilskins and long boots, they launched it amongst those mountainous seas that seemed ready every moment to swallow up the ship herself and the terrified lives on board of her.

"That reefed foresail saved you," I threw in.

"Under God—it did," he exclaimed fervently. "It was by a special mercy, I firmly believe, that it stood some of those hurricane squalls."

"It was the setting of that sail which—" I began.

"God's own hand in it," he interrupted me. "Nothing less could have done it. I don't mind telling you that I hardly dared give the order. It seemed impossible that we could touch anything without losing it, and then our last hope would have been gone."

The terror of that gale was on him yet. I let him go on for a bit, then said, casually—as if returning to a minor subject:

"You were very anxious to give up your mate to the shore people, I believe?"

He was. To the law. His obscure tenacity on that point had in it something incomprehensible and a little awful; something, as it were, mystical, quite apart from his anxiety that he should not be suspected of "countenancing any doings of that sort." Seven-and-thirty virtuous years at sea, of which over twenty of immaculate command, and the last fifteen in the *Sephora,* seemed to have laid him under some pitiless obligation.

"And you know," he went on, groping shame-facedly amongst his feelings, "I did not engage that young fellow. His people had some interest with my owners. I was in a way forced to take him on. He looked very smart, very gentlemanly, and all that. But do you know—I never liked him, somehow. I am a plain man. You see, he wasn't exactly the sort for the chief mate of a ship like the *Sephora.*"

I had become so connected in thoughts and impressions with the secret sharer of my cabin that I felt as if I, personally, were being given to understand that I, too, was not the sort that would have done for the chief mate of a ship like the *Sephora.* I had no doubt of it in my mind.

"Not at all the style of man. You understand," he insisted, superfluously, looking hard at me.

I smiled urbanely. He seemed at a loss for a while.

"I suppose I must report a suicide."

"Beg pardon?"

"Sui-cide! That's what I'll have to write to my owners directly I get in."

"Unless you manage to recover him before tomorrow," I assented, dispassionately. . . . "I mean, alive."

He mumbled something which I really did not catch, and I turned my ear to him in a puzzled manner. He fairly bawled:

"The land—I say, the mainland is at least seven miles off my anchorage."

"About that."

My lack of excitement, of curiosity, of surprise, of any sort of pronounced interest, began to arouse his distrust. But except for the felicitous pretense of deafness I had not tried to pretend anything. I had felt utterly incapable of playing the part of ignorance properly, and therefore was afraid to try. It is also certain that he had brought some ready-made suspicions with him, and that he viewed my politeness as a strange and unnatural phenomenon. And yet how else could I have received him? Not heartily! That was impossible for psychological reasons, which I need not state here. My only object was to keep off his inquiries. Surlily? Yes, but surliness might have provoked a point-blank question. From its novelty to him and from it nature, punctilious courtesy was the manner best calculated to restrain the man. But there was the danger of his breaking through my defense bluntly. I could not, I think, have met him by a direct lie, also for psychological (not moral) reasons. If he had only known how afraid I was of his putting my feeling of identity with the other to the test! But, strangely enough—(I thought of it only afterwards)—I believe that he was not a little disconcerted by the reverse side of the weird situation, by something in me that reminded him of the man he was seeking—suggested a mysterious similitude to the young fellow he had distrusted and disliked from the first.

However that might have been, the silence was not very prolonged. He took another oblique step.

"I reckon I had no more than a two-mile pull to your ship. Not a bit more."

"And quite enough, too, in this awful heat," I said.

Another pause full of mistrust followed. Necessity, they say, is mother of invention, but fear, too, is not barren of ingenious suggestions. And I was afraid he would ask me point-blank for news of my other self.

"Nice little saloon, isn't it?" I remarked, as if noticing for the first time the way his eyes roamed from one closed door to the other. "And very well fitted out, too. Here, for instance," I continued, reaching over the back of my seat negligently and flinging the door open, "is my bathroom."

He made an eager movement, but hardly gave it a glance. I got up, shut the door of the bathroom, and invited him to have a look round, as if I were very proud of my accommodation. He had to rise and be shown round, but he went through the business without any raptures whatever.

"And now we'll have a look at my stateroom," I declared, in a voice as loud as I dared to make it, crossing the cabin to the starboard side with purposely heavy steps.

He followed me in and gazed around. My intelligent double had vanished. I played my part.

"Very convenient—isn't it?"

"Very nice. Very comf. . ." He didn't finish and went out brusquely as if to escape from some unrighteous wiles of mine. But it was not to be. I had been too frightened not to feel vengeful; I felt I had him on the run, and I meant to keep him on the run. My polite insistence must have had something menacing in it, because he gave in suddenly. And I did not let him off a single item; mate's room, pantry, storerooms, the very sail locker which was also under the poop—he had to look into them all. When at last I showed him out on the quarter-deck he drew a long, spiritless sigh, and mumbled dismally that he must really be going back to his ship now. I desired my mate, who had joined us, to see to the captain's boat.

The man of whiskers gave a blast on the whistle which he used to wear hanging round his neck, and yelled, "*Sephora's* away!" My double down there in my cabin must have heard, and certainly could not feel more relieved than I. Four fellows came running out from somewhere forward and went over the side, while my own men, appearing on deck too, lined the rail. I escorted my visitor to the gangway ceremoniously, and nearly overdid it. He was a tenacious beast. On the very ladder he lingered, and in that unique, guiltily conscientious manner of sticking to the point:

"I say . . . you . . . you don't think that—"

I covered his voice loudly:

"Certainly not. . . . I am delighted. Good-by."

I had an idea of what he meant to say, and just saved myself by the privilege of defective hearing. He was too shaken generally to insist, but my mate, close witness of that parting, looked mystified and his face took on a thoughtful cast. As I did not want to appear as if I wished to avoid all communication with my officers, he had the opportunity to address me.

"Seems a very nice man. His boat's crew told our chaps a very extraordinary story, if what I am told by the steward is true. I suppose you had it from the captain, sir?"

"Yes. I had a story from the captain."

"A very horrible affair—isn't it, sir?"

"It is."

"Beats all these tales we hear about murders in Yankee ships."

"I don't think it beats them. I don't think it resembles them in the least."

"Bless my soul—you don't say so! But of course I've no acquaintance whatever with American ships, not I, so I couldn't go against your knowledge. It's horrible enough for me. . . . But the queerest part is that those fellows seemed to have some idea the man was hidden aboard here. They had really. Did you ever hear of such a thing?"

"Preposterous—isn't it?"

We were walking to and fro athwart the quarter-deck. No one of the crew forward could be seen (the day was Sunday), and the mate pursued:

"There was some little dispute about it. Our chaps took offense. 'As if we would harbor a thing like that,' they said. 'Wouldn't you like to look for him in our coalhole?' Quite a tiff. But they made it up in the end. I suppose he did drown himself. Don't you, sir?"

"I don't suppose anything."

"You have no doubt in the matter, sir?"

"None whatever."

I left him suddenly. I felt I was producing a bad impression, but with my double down there it was most trying to be on deck. And it was almost as trying to be below. Altogether a nerve-trying situation. But on the whole I felt less torn in two when I was with him. There was no one in the whole ship whom I dared take into my confidence. Since the hands had got to know his story, it would have been impossible to pass him off for anyone else, and an accidental discovery was to be dreaded now more than ever. . . .

The steward being engaged in laying the table for dinner, we could talk only with out eyes when I first went down. Later in the afternoon we had a cautious try at whispering. The Sunday quietness of the ship was against us; the stillness of air and water around her was against us; the elements, the men were against us—everything was against us in our secret partnership; time itself—for this could not go on forever. The very trust in Providence was, I suppose, denied to his guilt. Shall I confess that this thought cast me down very much? And as to the chapter of accidents which counts for so much in the book of success, I could only hope that it was closed. For what favorable accident could be expected?

"Did you hear everything?" were my first words as soon as we took up our position side by side, leaning over my bed place.

He had. And the proof of it was his earnest whisper, "The man told you he hardly dared to give the order."

I understood the reference to be to that saving foresail.

"Yes. He was afraid of it being lost in the setting."

"I assure you he never gave the order. He may think he did, but he never gave it. He stood there with me on the break of the poop after the main topsail blew away, and whimpered about our last hope—positively whimpered about it and nothing else—and the night coming on! To hear one's skipper go on like that in such weather was enough to drive any fellow out of his mind. It worked me up into a sort of desperation. I just took it into my own hands and went away from him, boiling, and—But what's the use telling you? *You* know! . . . Do you think that if I had not been pretty fierce with them I should have got the men to do anything? Not it! The bo's'n perhaps? Perhaps! It wasn't a heavy sea—it was a sea gone mad! I suppose the end of the world will be something like that; and a man may have the heart to see it coming once and be done with it—but to have to face it day after day—I don't blame anybody. I was precious little better than the rest. Only—I was an officer of that old coal wagon, anyhow—"

"I quite understand," I conveyed that sincere assurance into his ear. He was out of breath with whispering; I could hear him pant slightly. It was all very simple. The same strung-up force which had given twenty-four men a chance, at least, for their lives, had, in a sort of recoil, crushed an unworthy mutinous existence.

But I had no leisure to weigh the merits of the matter—footsteps in the saloon, a heavy knock. "There's enough wind to get under way with, sir." Here was the call of a new claim upon my thoughts and even upon my feelings.

"Turn the hands up," I cried through the door. "I'll be on deck directly."

I was going out to make the acquaintance of my ship. Before I left the cabin our eyes met—the eyes of the only two strangers on board. I pointed to the recessed part where the little campstool awaited him and laid my finger on my lips. He made a gesture—somewhat vague—a little mysterious, accompanied by a faint smile, as if of regret.

This is not the place to enlarge upon the sensations of a man who feels for the first time a ship move under his feet to his own independent word. In my case they were not unalloyed. I was not wholly alone with my command; for there was that stranger in my cabin. Or rather, I was not completely and wholly with her. Part of me was absent. That mental feeling of being in two places at once affected me physically as if the mood of secrecy had penetrated my very soul. Before an hour had elapsed since the ship had begun to move, having occasion to ask the mate (he stood by my side) to take a compass bearing of the Pagoda, I caught myself reaching up to his ear in whispers. I say I caught myself, but enough had escaped to startle the man. I can't describe it otherwise than by saying that he shied. A grave, preoccupied manner, as though he were in possession of some perplexing intelligence, did not leave him henceforth. A little later I moved away from the rail to look at the compass with such a stealthy gait that the helmsman noticed it—and I could not help noticing the unusual roundness of his eyes. These are trifling instances, though it's to no commander's advantage to be suspected of ludicrous eccentricities. But I was also more seriously affected. There are to a seaman certain words, gestures, that should in given conditions come as naturally, as instinctively as the winking of a menaced eye. A certain order should spring on to his lips without thinking; a certain sign should get itself made, so to speak, without reflection. But all unconscious alertness had abandoned me. I had to make an effort of will to recall myself back (from the cabin) to the conditions of the moment. I felt that I was appearing an irresolute commander to those people who were watching me more or less critically.

And, besides, there were the scares. On the second day out, for instance, coming off the deck in the afternoon (I had straw slippers on my bare feet) I stopped at the open pantry door and spoke to the steward. He was doing something there with his back to me. At the sound of my voice he nearly jumped out of his skin, as the saying is, and incidentally broke a cup.

"What on earth's the matter with you?" I asked, astonished.

He was extremely confused. "Beg your pardon, sir. I made sure you were in your cabin."

"You see I wasn't."

"No, sir. I could have sworn I had heard you moving in there not a moment ago. It's most extraordinary . . . very sorry, sir."

I passed on with an inward shudder. I was so identified with my secret double that I did not even mention the fact in those scanty, fearful whispers we exchanged. I suppose he had made some slight noise of some kind or other. It would have been miraculous if he hadn't at one time or another. And yet, haggard as he appeared, he looked always perfectly self-controlled, more than calm—almost invulnerable. On my suggestion he remained almost entirely in the bathroom, which, upon the whole, was the safest place. There could be really no shadow of an excuse for anyone ever wanting to go in there, once the steward had done with it. It was a very tiny place. Sometimes he reclined on the floor, his legs bent, his head sustained on one elbow. At others I would find him on the campstool, sitting in his gray sleeping suit and with his cropped dark hair like a patient, unmoved convict. At night I would smuggle him into my bed place, and we would whisper together, with the regular footfalls of the officers of the watch passing and repassing over our heads. It was an infinitely miserable time. It was lucky that some tins of fine preserves were stowed in a locker in my stateroom; hard bread I could always get hold of; and so he lived on stewed chicken, *pate de foie gras,* asparagus, cooked oysters, sardines—

on all sorts of abominable sham delicacies out of tins. My earlymorning coffee he always drank; and it was all I dared do for him in that respect.

Every day there was the horrible maneuvering to go through so that my room and then the bathroom should be done in the usual way. I came to hate the sight of the steward, to abhor the voice of that harmless man. I felt that it was he who would bring on the disaster of discovery. It hung like a sword over our heads.

The fourth day out, I think (we were then working down the east side of the Gulf of Siam, tack for tack, in light winds and smooth water)—the fourth day, I say, of this miserable juggling with the unavoidable, as we sat at our evening meal, that man, whose slightest movement I dreaded, after putting down the dishes ran up on deck busily. This could not be dangerous. Presently he came down again; and then it appeared that he had remembered a coat of mine which I had thrown over a rail to dry after having been wetted in a shower which had passed over the ship in the afternoon. Sitting stolidly at the head of the table I became terrified at the sight of the garment on his arm. Of course he made for my door. There was no time to lose.

"Steward," I thundered. My nerves were so shaken that I could not govern my voice and conceal my agitation. This was the sort of thing that made my terrifically whiskered mate tap his forehead with his forefinger. I had detected him using that gesture while talking on deck with a confidential air to the carpenter. It was too far to hear a word, but I had no doubt that this pantomime could only refer to the strange new captain.

"Yes, sir," the pale-faced steward turned resignedly to me. It was this maddening course of being shouted at, checked without rhyme or reason, arbitrarily chased out of my cabin, suddenly called into it, sent flying out of his pantry on incomprehensible errands, that accounted for the growing wretchedness of his expression.

"Where are you going with that coat?"

"To your room, sir."

"Is there another shower coming?"

"I'm sure I don't know, sir. Shall I go up again and see, sir?"

"No! never mind."

My object was attained, as of course my other self in there would have heard everything that passed. During this interlude my two officers never raised their eyes off their respective plates; but the lip of that confounded cub, the second mate, quivered visibly.

I expected the steward to hook my coat on and come out at once. He was very slow about it; but I dominated my nervousness sufficiently not to shout after him. Suddenly I became aware (it could be heard plainly enough) that the fellow for some reason or other was opening the door of the bathroom. It was the end. The place was literally not big enough to swing a cat in. My voice died in my throat and I went stony all over. I expected to hear a yell of suprise and terror, and made a movement, but had not the strength to get on my legs. Everything remained still. Had my second self taken the poor wretch by the throat? I don't know what I could have done next moment if I had not seen the steward come out of my room, close the door, and then stand quietly by the sideboard.

"Saved," I thought. "But, no! Lost! Gone! He was gone!"

I laid my knife and fork down and leaned back in my chair. My head swam. After a while, when sufficiently recovered to speak in a steady voice, I instructed my mate to put the ship round at eight o'clock himself.

"I won't come on deck," I went on. "I think I'll turn in, and unless the wind shifts I don't want to be disturbed before midnight. I feel a bit seedy."

"You did look middling bad a little while ago," the chief mate remarked without showing any great concern.

They both went out, and I stared at the steward clearing the table. There was nothing to be read on that wretched man's face. But why did he avoid my eyes, I asked myself. Then I thought I should like to hear the sound of his voice.

"Steward!"

"Sir!" Startled as usual.

"Where did you hang up that coat?"

"In the bathroom, sir." The usual anxious tone. "It's not quite dry yet, sir."

For some time longer I sat in the cuddy. Had my double vanished as he had come? But of his coming there was an explanation, whereas his disappearance would be inexplicable. . . . I went slowly into my dark room, shut the door, lighted the lamp, and for a time dared not turn round. When at last I did I saw him standing bolt-upright in the narrow recessed part. It would not be true to say I had a shock, but an irresistible doubt of his bodily existence flitted through my mind. Can it be, I asked myself, that he is not visible to other eyes than mine? It was like being haunted. Motionless, with a grave face, he raised his hands slightly at me in a gesture which meant clearly, "Heavens! what a narrow escape!" Narrow indeed. I think I had come creeping quietly as near insanity as any man who has not actually gone over the border. That gesture restrained me, so to speak.

The mate with the terrific whiskers was now putting the ship on the other tack. In the moment of profound silence which follows upon the hands going to their stations I heard on the poop his raised voice: "Hard alee!" and the distant shout of the order repeated on the maindeck. The sails, in that light breeze, made but a faint fluttering noise. It ceased. The ship was coming round slowly; I held my breath in the renewed stillness of expectation; one wouldn't have thought that there was a single living soul on her decks. A sudden brisk shout, "Mainsail haul!" broke the spell, and in the noisy cries and rush overhead of the men running away with the main brace we two, down in my cabin, came together in our usual position by the bed place.

He did not wait for my question. "I heard him fumbling here and just managed to squat myself down in the bath," he whispered to me. "The fellow only opened the door and put his arm in to hang the coat up. All the same—"

"I never thought of that," I whispered back, even more appalled than before at the closeness of the shave, and marveling at that something unyielding in his character which was carrying him through so finely. There was no agitation in his whisper. Whoever was being driven distracted, it was not he. He was sane. And the proof of his sanity was continued when he took up the whispering again.

"It would never do for me to come to life again."

It was something that a ghost might have said. But what he was alluding to was his old captain's reluctant admission of the theory of suicide. It would obviously serve his turn—if I had understood at all the view which seemed to govern the unalterable purpose of his action.

"You must maroon me as soon as ever you can get amongst these islands off the Cambodge shore," he went on.

"Maroon you! We are not living in a boy's adventure tale," I protested. His scornful whispering took me up.

"We aren't indeed! There's nothing of a boy's tale in this. But there's nothing else for it. I want no more. You don't suppose I am afraid of what can be done to me? Prison or gallows or whatever they may please. But you don't see me coming back to explain such things to an old fellow in a wig and twelve respectable tradesmen, do you? What can they know whether I am guilty or not—or of *what* I am guilty, either? That's my affair. What does the Bible say? 'Driven off the face of the earth.' Very well, I am off the face of the earth now. As I came at night so I shall go."

"Impossible!" I murmured. "You can't."

"Can't? . . . Not naked like a soul on the Day of Judgment. I shall freeze on to this sleeping-suit. The Last Day is not yet—and . . . you have understood thoroughly. Didn't you?"

I felt suddenly ashamed of myself. I may say truly that I understood—and my hesitation in letting that man swim away from my ship's side had been a mere sham sentiment, a sort of cowardice.

"It can't be done now till next night," I breathed out. "The ship is on the off-shore tack and the wind may fail us."

"As long as I know that you understand," he whispered. "But of course you do. It's a great satisfaction to have got somebody to understand. You seem to have been there on purpose." And in the same whisper, as if we two whenever we talked had to say things to each other which were not fit for the world to hear, he added, "It's very wonderful."

We remained side by side talking in our secret way—but sometimes silent or just exchanging a whispered word or two at long intervals. And as usual he stared through the port. A breath of wind came now and again into our faces. The ship might have been moored in dock, so gently and on an even keel she slipped through the water, that did not murmur even at our passage, shadowy and silent like a phantom sea.

At midnight I went on deck, and to my mate's great surprise put the ship round on the other tack. His terrible whiskers flitted round me in silent criticism. I certainly should not have done it if it had been only a question of getting out of that sleepy gulf as quickly as possible. I believe he told the second mate, who relieved him, that it was a great want of judgment. The other only yawned. That intolerable cub shuffled about so sleepily and lolled against the rails in such a slack, improper fashion that I came down on him sharply.

"Aren't you properly awake yet?"

"Yes, sir! I am awake."

"Well, then, be good enough to hold yourself as if you were. And keep a lookout. If there's any current we'll be closing with some islands before daylight."

The east side of the gulf is fringed with islands, some solitary, others in groups. On the blue background of the high coast they seem to float on silvery patches of calm water, arid and gray, or dark green and rounded like clumps of evergreen bushes, with the larger ones, a mile or two long, showing the outlines of ridges, ribs of gray rock under the dank mantle of matted leafage. Unkown to trade, to travel, almost to geography, the manner of life they harbor is an unsolved secret. There must be villages—settlements of fishermen at least—on the largest of them, and some communication with the world is probably kept up by native craft. But all that forenoon, as we headed for them, fanned along by the faintest of breezes, I saw no sign of man or canoe in the field of the telescope I kept on pointing at the scattered group.

At noon I gave no orders for a change of course, and the mate's whiskers became much concerned and seemed to be offering themselves unduly to my notice. At last I said:

"I am going to stand right in. Quite in—as far as I can take her."

The stare of extreme surprise imparted an air of ferocity also to his eyes, and he looked truly terrific for a moment.

"We're not doing well in the middle of the gulf," I continued, casually. "I am going to look for the land breezes tonight."

"Bless my soul! Do you mean, sir, in the dark amongst the lot of all them islands and reefs and shoals?"

"Well—if there are any regular land breezes at all on this coast one must get close inshore to find them, mustn't one?"

"Bless my soul!" he exclaimed again under his breath. All that afternoon he wore a dreamy, contemplative appearance which in him was a mark of perplexity. After dinner I went into my stateroom as if I meant to take some rest. There we two bent our dark heads over a half-unrolled chart lying on my bed.

"There," I said. "It's got to be Koh-ring. I've been looking at it ever since sunrise. It has got two hills and a low point. It must be inhabited. And on the coast opposite there is what looks like the mouth of a biggish river—with some town, no doubt, not far up. It's the best chance for you that I can see."

"Anything. Koh-ring let it be."

He looked thoughtfully at the chart as if surveying chances and distances from a lofty height—and following with his eyes his own figure wandering on the blank land of Cochin-China, and then passing off that piece of paper clean out of sight into uncharted regions. And it was as if the ship had two captains to plan her course for her. I had been so worried and restless running up and down that I had not had the patience to dress that day. I had remained in my sleeping suit, with straw slippers and a soft floppy hat. The closeness of the heat in the gulf had been most oppressive, and the crew were used to see me wandering in that airy attire.

"She will clear the south point as she heads now," I whispered into his ear. "Goodness only knows when, though, but certainly after dark. I'll edge her in to half a mile, as far as I may be able to judge in the dark—"

"Be careful," he murmured, warningly—and I realized suddenly that all my future, the only future for which I was fit, would perhaps go irretrievably to pieces in any mishap to my first command.

I could not stop a moment longer in the room. I motioned him to get out of sight and made my way on the poop. That unplayful cub had the watch. I walked up and down for a while thinking things out, then beckoned him over.

"Send a couple of hands to open the two quarter-deck ports," I said, mildly.

He actually had the impudence, or else so forgot himself in his wonder at such an incomprehensible order, as to repeat:

"Open the quarter-deck ports! What for, sir?"

"The only reason you need concern yourself about is because I tell you to do so. Have them open wide and fastened properly."

He reddened and went off, but I believe made some jeering remark to the carpenter as to the sensible practice of ventilating a ship's quarterdeck. I know he popped into the mate's cabin to impart the fact to him because the whiskers came on deck, as it were by chance, and stole glances at me from below—for signs of lunacy or drunkenness, I suppose.

A little before supper, feeling more restless than ever, I rejoined, for a moment, my second self. And to find him sitting so quietly was surprising, like something against nature, inhuman.

I developed my plan in a hurried whisper.

"I shall stand in as close as I dare and then put her round. I will presently find means to smuggle you out of here into the sail-locker, which communicates with the lobby. But there is an opening, a sort of square for hauling the sails out, which gives straight on the quarter-deck and which is never closed in fine weather, so as to give air to the sails. When the ship's way is deadened in stays and all the hands are aft at the main-braces you will have a clear road to slip out and get overboard through the open quarter-deck port. I've had them both fastened up. Use a rope's end to lower yourself into the water so as to avoid a splash—you know. It could be heard and cause some beastly complication."

He kept silent for a while, then whispered, "I understand."

"I won't be there to see you go," I began with an effort. "The rest . . . I only hope I have understood, too."

"You have. From first to last"—and for the first time there seemed to be a faltering, something strained in his whisper. He caught hold of my arm, but the ringing of the supper bell made me start. He didn't, though; he only released his grip.

After supper I didn't come below again till well past eight o'clock. The faint, steady breeze was loaded with dew; and the wet, darkened sails held all there was of propelling power in it. The night, clear and starry, sparkled darkly, and the opaque, lightless patches shifting slowly against the low stars were the drifting islets. On the port bow there was a big one more distant and shadowily imposing by the great space of sky it eclipsed.

On opening the door I had a back view of my very own self looking at a chart. He had come out of the recess and was standing near the table.

"Quite dark enough," I whispered.

He stepped back and leaned against my bed with a level, quiet glance. I sat on the couch. We had nothing to say to each other. Over our heads the officer of the watch moved here and there. Then I heard him move quickly. I knew what that meant. He was making for the companion; and presently his voice was outside my door.

"We are drawing in pretty fast, sir. Land looks rather close."

"Very well," I answered. "I am coming on deck directly."

I waited till he was gone out of the cuddy, then rose. My double moved too. The time had come to exchange our last whispers, for neither of us was ever to hear each other's natural voice.

"Look here!" I opened a drawer and took out three sovereigns. "Take this anyhow. I've got six and I'd give you the lot, only I must keep a little money to buy some fruit and vegetables for the crew from native boats as we go through Sunda Straits."

He shook his head.

"Take it," I urged him, whispering desperately. "No one can tell what—"

He smiled and slapped meaningly the only pocket of the sleeping jacket. It was not safe, certainly. But I produced a large old silk handkerchief of mine, and tying the three pieces of gold in a corner, pressed it on him. He was touched, I suppose, because he took it at last and tied it quickly round his waist under the jacket, on his bare skin.

Our eyes met; several seconds elapsed, till, our glances still mingled, I extended my hand and turned the lamp out. Then I passed through the cuddy, leaving the door of my room wide open. . . . "Steward!"

He was still lingering in the pantry in the greatness of his zeal, giving a rub-up to a plated cruet stand the last thing before going to bed. Being careful not to wake up the mate, whose room was opposite, I spoke in an undertone.

He looked round anxiously. "Sir!"

"Can you get me a little hot water from the galley?"

"I am afraid, sir, the galley fire's been out for some time now."

"Go and see."

He flew up the stairs.

"Now," I whispered, loudly, into the saloon—too loudly, perhaps, but I was afraid I couldn't make a sound. He was by my side in an instant—the double captain slipped past the stairs—through a tiny dark passage . . . a sliding door. We were in the sail locker, scrambling on our knees over the sails. A sudden thought struck me. I saw myself wandering barefooted, bareheaded, the sun beating on my dark poll. I snatched off my floppy hat and tried hurriedly in the dark to ram it on my other self. He dodged and fended off silently. I wonder what he thought had come to me before he understood and suddenly desisted. Our hands met gropingly, lingered united in a steady, motionless clasp for a second. . . . No word was breathed by either of us when they separated.

I was standing quietly by the pantry door when the steward returned.

"Sorry, sir. Kettle barely warm. Shall I light the spirit lamp?"

"Never mind."

I came out on deck slowly. It was now a matter of conscience to shave the land as close as possible—for now he must go overboard whenever the ship was put in stays. Must! There could be no going back for him. After a moment I walked over to leeward and my heart flew into my mouth at the nearness of the land on the bow. Under any other circumstances I would not have held on a minute longer. The second mate had followed me anxiously.

I looked on till I felt I could command my voice.

"She will weather," I said in a quiet tone.

"Are you going to try that, sir?" he stammered out incredulously.

I took no notice of him and raised my tone just enough to be heard by the helmsman.

"Keep her good full."

"Good full, sir."

The wind fanned my cheek, the sails slept, the world was silent. The strain of watching the dark loom of the land grow bigger and denser was too much for me. I had shut my eyes—because the ship must go closer. She must! The stillness was intolerable. Were we standing still?

When I opened my eyes the second view started my heart with a thump. The black southern hill of Koh-ring seemed to hang right over the ship like a towering fragment of the everlasting night. On that enormous mass of blackness there was not a gleam to be seen, not a sound to be heard. It was gliding irresistibly towards us and yet seemed already within reach of the hand. I saw the vague figures of the watch grouped in the waist, gazing in awed silence.

"Are you going on, sir?" inquired an unsteady voice at my elbow.

I ignored it. I had to go on.

"Keep her full. Don't check her way. That won't do now," I said, warningly.

"I can't see the sails very well," the helmsman answered me, in strange, quavering tones.

Was she close enough? Already she was, I won't say in the shadow of the land, but in the very blackness of it, already swallowed up as it were, gone too close to be recalled, gone from me altogether.

"Give the mate a call," I said to the young man who stood at my elbow as still as death. "And turn all hands up."

My tone had a borrowed loudness reverberated from the height of the land. Several voices cried out together: "We are all on deck, sir."

Then stillness again, with the great shadow gliding closer, towering higher, without a light, without a sound. Such a hush had fallen on the ship that she might have been a bark of the dead floating in slowly under the very gate of Erebus.

"My God! Where are we?"

It was the mate moaning at my elbow. He was thunderstruck, and as it were deprived of the moral support of his whiskers. He clapped his hands and absolutely cried out, "Lost!"

"Be quiet," I said, sternly.

He lowered his tone, but I saw the shadowy gesture of his despair. "What are we doing here?"

"Looking for the land wind."

He made as if to tear his hair, and addressed me recklessly.

"She will never get out. You have done it, sir. I knew it'd end in something like this. She will never weather, and you are too close now to stay. She'll drift ashore before she's round. O my God!"

I caught his arm as he was raising it to batter his poor devoted head, and shook it violently.

"She's ashore already," he wailed, trying to tear himself away.

"Is she? . . . Keep good full there!"

"Good full, sir," cried the helmsman in a frightened, thin, childlike voice.

I hadn't let go the mate's arm and went on shaking it. "Ready about, do you hear? You go forward"—shake—"and stop there"—shake—"and hold your noise"—shake—"and see these head-sheets properly overhauled"—shake, shake—shake.

And all the time I dared not look towards the land lest my heart should fail me. I released my grip at last and he ran forward as if fleeing for dear life.

I wondered what my double there in the sail locker thought of this commotion. He was able to hear everything—and perhaps he was able to understand why, on my conscience, it had to be thus close—no less. My first order "Hard alee!" re-echoed ominously under the towering shadow of Koh-ring as if I had shouted in a mountain gorge. And then I watched the land intently. In that smooth water and light wind it was impossible to feel the ship coming-to. No! I could not feel her. And my second self was making now ready to slip out and lower himself overboard. Perhaps he was gone already . . . ?

The great black mass brooding over our very mastheads began to pivot away from the ship's side silently. And now I forgot the secret stranger ready to depart, and remembered only that I was a total stranger to the ship. I did not know her. Would she do it? How was she to be handled?

I swung the mainyard and waited helplessly. She was perhaps stopped, and her very fate hung in the balance, with the black mass of Koh-ring like the gate of the everlasting night towering over her taffrail. What would she do now? Had she way on her yet? I stepped to the side swiftly, and on the shadowy water I could see nothing except a faint phosphorescent flash revealing the glassy smoothness of the sleeping surface. It was impossible to tell—and I had not learned yet the feel of my ship. Was she moving? What I needed was something easily seen, a piece of paper, which I could throw overboard and watch. I had nothing on me. To run down for it I didn't dare. There was no time. All at once my strained, yearning stare distinguished a white object floating within a yard of the ship's side. White on the black water. A phosphorescent flash passed under it. What was that thing? I recognized my own floppy hat. It must have fallen off his head . . . and he didn't bother. Now I had what I wanted—the saving mark for my eyes. But I hardly thought of my other self, now gone from the ship, to be hidden forever from all friendly faces, to be a fugitive and a vagabond on the earth, with no brand of the curse on his sane forehead to stay a slaying hand . . . too proud to explain.

And I watched the hat—the expression of my sudden pity for his mere flesh. It had been meant to save his homeless head from the dangers of the sun. And now—behold—it was saving the ship, by serving me for a mark to help out the ignorance of my strangeness. Ha! It was drifting forward, warning me just in time that the ship had gathered sternway.

"Shift the helm," I said in a low voice to the seaman standing still like a statue.

The man's eyes glistened wildly in the binnacle light as he jumped round to the other side and spun round the wheel.

I walked to the break of the poop. On the overshadowed deck all hands stood by the forebraces waiting for my order. The stars ahead seemed to be gliding from right to left. And all was so still in the world that I heard the quiet remark, "She's round," passed in a tone of intense relief between two seamen.

"Let go and haul."

The foreyards ran round with a great noise, amidst cheery cries. And now the frightful whiskers made themselves heard giving various orders. Already the ship was drawing ahead. And I was alone with her. Nothing! no one in the world should stand now between us, throwing a shadow on the way of silent knowledge and mute affection, the perfect communion of a seaman with his first command.

Walking to the taffrail, I was in time to make out, on the very edge of a darkness thrown by a towering black mass like the very gateway of Erebus—yes, I was in time to catch an evanescent glimpse of my white hat left behind to mark the spot where the secret sharer of my cabin and of my thoughts, as though he were my second self, had lowered himself into the water to take his punishment: a free man, a proud swimmer striking out for a new destiny.

Thomas Mann

(1875 - 1955)

Thomas Mann, one of the giants of the twentieth-century novel, was born into one of the wealthiest and most respected families in Lübeck, Germany, in 1875. Although he briefly experimented with a career in business, Mann was determined to be a writer and he succeeded in publishing several stories before *Buddenbrooks* (1900), his first novel. Twenty-four years later he completed *The Magic Mountain,* a long philosophical novel that probes the values and assumptions of Western culture. In 1929 Mann was awarded a Nobel Prize for his fiction. He fled from Germany when the Nazis came to power and denounced Hitler as a barbarian. The Nazis stripped him of his citizenship and burned his books. After a short exile in Switzerland, Mann came to the United States and in 1944 became an American citizen. In much of his fiction Mann was concerned with the spiritual center of man, weighing the influence of time and culture on the individual. Like Henry James, he was especially interested in—and frequently dramatized—the relationship of the artist to his society.

Little Lizzy

There are marriages which the imagination, even the most practised literary one, cannot conceive. You must just accept them, as you do in the theatre when you see the ancient and doddering married to the beautiful and gay, as the given premises on which the farce is mechanically built up.

Yes, the wife of Jacoby the lawyer was lovely and young, a woman of unusual charm. Some years—shall we say thirty years?—ago, she had been christened with the names of Anna, Margarete, Rosa, Amalie; but the name she went by was always Amra, composed of the initials of her four real ones;

it suited to perfection her somewhat exotic personality. Her soft, heavy hair, which she wore parted on one side and brushed straight back above her ears from the narrow temples, had only the darkness of the glossy chestnut; but her skin displayed the dull, dark sallowness of the south and clothed a form which southern suns must have ripened. Her slow, voluptuous, indolent presence suggested the harem; each sensuous, lazy movement of her body strengthened the impression that with her the head was entirely subordinate to the heart. She needed only to have looked at you once, with her artless brown eyes, lifting her brows in the pathetically narrow forehead, horizontally, in a quaint way she had, for you to be certain of that. But she herself was not so simple as not to know it too. Quite simply, she avoided exposing herself, she spoke seldom and little—and what is there to say against a woman who is both beautiful and silent? Yes, the word "simple" is probably the last which should be applied to her. Her glance was artless; but also it had a kind of luxurious cunning—you could see that she was not dull, also that she might be a mischief-maker. In profile her nose was rather too thick; but her full, large mouth was utterly lovely, if also lacking in any expression save sensuality.

This disturbing phenomenon was the wife of Jacoby the lawyer, a man of forty. Whoever looked at him was bound to be amazed at the fact. He was stout, Jacoby the lawyer; but stout is not the word, he was a perfect colossus of a man! His legs, in their columnar clumsiness and the slate-grey trousers he always wore, reminded one of an elephant's. His round, fat-upholstered back was that of a bear; and over the vast round of his belly his funny little grey jacket was held by a single button strained so tight that when it was unbuttoned the jacket came wide open with a pop. Scarcely anything which could be called a neck united this huge torso with the little head atop. The head had narrow watery eyes, a squabby nose, and a wee mouth between cheeks drooping with fullness. The upper lip and the round head were covered with harsh, scanty, light-coloured bristles that showed the naked skin, as on an overfed dog. There was no doubt that Jacoby's fatness was not of a healthy kind. His gigantic body, tall as well as stout, was not muscular, but flabby. The blood would sometimes rush to his puffy face, then ebb away leaving it of a yellowish pallor; the mouth would be drawn and sour.

Jacoby's practice was a limited one; but he was well-to-do, partly from his wife's side; and the childless pair lived in a comfortable apartment in the Kaiserstrasse and entertained a good deal. This must have been Frau Amra's taste, for it is unthinkable that the lawyer could have cared for it; he participated with an enthusiasm of a peculiarly painful kind. This fat man's character was the oddest in the world. No human being could have been politer, more accommodating, more complaisant than he. But you unconsciously knew that this over-obligingness was somehow forced, that its true source was an inward insecurity and cowardice—the impression it gave was not very pleasant. A man who despises himself is a very ugly sight;

worse still when vanity combines with his cowardice to make him wish to please. This was the case, I should say, with Jacoby: his obsequiousness was almost crawling, it went beyond the bounds of personal decency. He was quite capable of saying to a lady as he escorted her to table: "My dear lady, I am a disgusting creature, but will you do me the honour?" No humour would be mingled with the remark; it was simply cloying, bitter, self-tortured—in a word, disgusting, as he said.

The following once actually happened: the lawyer was taking a walk, and a clumsy porter with a hand-cart ran over his foot. Too late the man stopped his cart and turned round—whereupon Jacoby, quite pale and dazed, his cheeks shaking up and down, took off his hat and stuttered: "I b-beg your pardon." A thing like that is infuriating. But this extraordinary colossus seemed perpetually to suffer from a plague of conscience. When he took a walk with his wife on the Lerchenberg, the Corso of the little city, he would roll his eyes round at Amra, walking with her wonderful elastic gait at his side, and bow so anxiously, diligently, and zealously in all directions that he seemed to be begging pardon of all the lieutenants they met for being in unworthy possession of such a beautiful wife. His mouth had a pathetically ingratiating expression, as though he wanted to disarm their scorn.

I have already hinted that the reason why Amra married Jacoby is unfathomable. As for him, he was in love with her; ardently, as people of his physical make-up seldom are, and with such anxious humility as fitted the rest of his character. Sometimes, late in the evening, he would enter their large sleeping-chamber with its high windows and flowered hangings—softly, so softly that there was no sound, only the slow shaking of floor and furniture. He would come up to Amra's massive bed, where she already lay, kneel down, and with infinite caution take her hand. She would lift her brows in a level line, in the quaint way she had, and look at her husband, abject before her in the dim light, with a look of malice and sensuality combined. With his puffy, trembling hands he would softly stroke back the sleeve and press his tragic fat face into the soft brown flesh of her wrist, where little blue veins stood out. And he would speak to her, in a shaking, half-smothered voice, as a sensible man in everyday life never speaks:

"Amra, my dear Amra! I am not disturbing you? You were not asleep yet? Dear God! I have been thinking all day how beautiful you are and how much I love you. I beg you to listen, for it is so very hard to express what I feel: I love you so much that sometimes my heart contracts and I do not know where to turn. I love you beyond my strength. You do not understand that, I know; but you believe it, and you must say, just one single time, that you are a little grateful to me. For, you see, such a love as mine to you is precious, it has its value in this life of ours. And that you will never betray or deceive me, even if you cannot love me, just out of gratitude for this love. I have come to you to beg you, as seriously, as fervently as I can . . ." here the lawyer's speech would be dissolved in sobs, in low, bitter weeping, as he knelt. Amra would feel moved; she would stroke her husband's bristles and say over and over, in the soothing, contemptuous sing-song one uses to a dog who comes to lick one's feet: "Yes, yes, good doggy, good doggy!"

And this behaviour of Amra's was certainly not that of a moral woman. For to relieve my mind of the truth which I have so far withheld, she did already deceive her husband; she betrayed him for the embraces of a gentleman named Alfred Läutner, a gifted young musician, who at twenty-seven had made himself a small reputation with amusing little compositions. He was a slim young chap with a provocative face, a flowing blond mane, and a sunny smile in his eyes, of which he was quite aware. He belonged to the present-day race of small artists, who do not demand the utmost of themselves, whose first requirement is to be jolly and happy, who employ their pleasing little talents to heighten their personal charms. It pleases them to play in society the rôle of the naïve genius. Consciously childlike, entirely unmoral and unscrupulous, merry and self-satisfied as they are, and healthy enough to enjoy even their disorders, they are agreeable even in their vanity, so long as that has not been wounded. But woe to these wretched little poseurs when serious misfortune befalls them, with which there is no coquetting, and when they can no longer be pleasant in their own eyes. They will not know how to be wretched decently and in order, they do not know how to attack the problem of suffering. They will be destroyed. All that is a story in itself. But Herr Alfred Läutner wrote pretty things, mostly waltzes and mazurkas. They would have been rather too gay and popular to be considered music as I understand it, if each of them had not contained a passage of some originality, a modulation, a harmonic phrasing, some sort of bold effect that betrayed wit and invention, which was evidently the point of the whole and which made it interesting to genuine musicians. Often these two single measures would have a strange plaintive, melancholy tone which would come out abruptly in the midst of a piece of dance-music and as suddenly be gone.

Amra Jacoby was on fire with guilty passion for this young man, and as for him he had not enough moral fibre to resist her seductions. They met here, they met there, and for some years an immoral relation had subsisted between them, known to the whole town, who laughed at it behind the lawyer's back. But what did he think? Amra was not sensitive enough to betray herself on account of a guilty conscience, so we must take it as certain that, however heavy the lawyer's heart, he could cherish no definite suspicions.

Spring had come, rejoicing all hearts; and Amra conceived the most charming idea.

"Christian," said she—Jacoby's name was Christian—"let us give a party, a beer party to celebrate the new beer—of course quite simply, but let's have a lot of people."

"Certainly," said the lawyer, "but could we not have it a little later?"

To which Amra made no reply, having passed on to the consideration of details.

"It will be so large that we cannot have it here, we must hire a place, some sort of outdoor restaurant where there is plenty of room and fresh air. You see that, of course. The place I am thinking of is Wendelin's big hall at the foot of the Lerchenberg. The hall is independent of the restaurant and brewery, connected by a passage only. We can decorate it for the occasion and set up long tables, drink our bock, and dance—we must have music and even perhaps some sort of entertainment. There is a little stage, as I happen to know, that makes it very suitable. It will be a very original party and no end of fun."

The lawyer's face had gone a pale yellow as she spoke, and the corners of his mouth went down. He said:

"My dear Amra! How delightful it will be! I can leave it all to you, you are so clever. Make any arrangements you like."

. . .

And Amra made her arrangements. She took counsel of various ladies and gentlemen, she went in person to hire the hall, she even formed a committee of people who were invited or who volunteered to co-operate in the entertainment. These were exclusively men, except for the wife of Herr Hildebrandt, an actor at the Hoftheater, who was herself a singer. Then there was Herr Hildebrandt, and Assessor Witznagel, a young painter, Alfred Läutner the musician, and some students brought in by Herr Witznagel, who were to do Negro dances.

A week after Amra had made her plan, this committee met in Amra's drawing-room in the Kaiserstrasse—a small, crowded, overheated room, with a heavy carpet, a sofa with quantities of cushions, a fan palm, English leather chairs, and a splay-legged mahogany table with a velvet cover, upon which rested several large illustrated morocco-bound volumes. There was a fireplace too, with a small fire still burning, and on the marble chimney-top were plates of dainty sandwiches, glasses, and two decanters of sherry. Amra reclined in one corner of the sofa under the fan palm, with her legs crossed. She had the beauty of a warm summer night. A thin blouse of light-coloured silk covered her bosom, but her skirt was of heavy dark stuff embroidered with large flowers. Sometimes she put up one hand to brush back the chestnut hair from her narrow forehead. Frau Hildebrandt sat beside her on the sofa; she had red hair and wore riding clothes. Opposite the two all the gentlemen formed a semicircle—among them Jacoby himself, in the lowest chair he could find. He looked unutterably wretched, kept drawing a long breath and swallowing as though struggling against increasing nausea. Herr Alfred Läutner was in tennis clothes—he would not take a chair, but leaned decoratively against the chimney-piece, saying merrily that he could not sit still so long.

Herr Hildebrandt talked sonorously about English songs. He was a most respectable gentleman, in a black suit, with a Roman head and an assured manner—in short a proper actor for a court theatre, cultured, knowledgeable, and with enlightened tastes. He liked to hold forth in condemnation of Ibsen, Zola, and Tolstoi, all of whom had the same objectionable aims. But today he was benignly interested in the small affair under discussion.

"Do you know that priceless song 'That's Maria!'?" he asked. "Perhaps it is a little racy—but very effective. And then" so-and-so—he suggested other songs, upon which they came to an agreement and Frau Hildebrandt said that she would sing them. The young painter, who had sloping shoulders and a very blond beard, was to give a burlesque conjuring turn. Herr Hildebrandt offered to impersonate various famous characters. In short, everything was developing nicely, the programme was apparently arranged, when Assessor Witznagel, who had command of fluent gesture and a good many duelling scars, suddenly took the word.

"All very well, ladies and gentlemen, it looks like being most amusing. But if I may say so, it still lacks something; it wants some kind of high spot, a climax as it were, something a bit startling, perhaps, to round the thing off. I leave it to you, I have nothing particular in mind, I only think . . ."

"That is true enough!" Alfred Läutner's tenor voice came from the chimney-piece where he leaned. "Witznagel is right. We need a climax. Let us put our heads together!" He settled his red belt and looked engagingly about him.

"Well, if we do not consider the famous characters as the high spot," said Herr Hildebrandt. Everybody agreed with the Assessor. Something piquant was wanted for the principal number. Even Jacoby nodded, and murmured: "Yes, yes, something jolly and striking. . . ." They all reflected.

At the end of a minute's pause, which was broken only by stifled exclamations, an extraordinary thing happened. Amra was sitting reclined among the cushions, gnawing as busily as a mouse at the pointed nail of her little finger. She had a very odd look on her face: a vacant, almost an irresponsible smile, which betrayed a sensuality both tormented and cruel. Her eyes, very bright and wide, turned slowly to the chimney-piece, where for a second they met the musician's. Then suddedly she jerked her whole body to one side as she sat, in the direction of her husband. With both hands in her lap she stared into his face with an avid and clinging gaze, her own growing visibly paler, and said in her rich, slow voice:

"Christian, suppose you come on at the end as a *chanteuse,* in a red satin baby frock, and do a dance."

The effect of these few words was tremendous. The young painter essayed to laugh good-humouredly; Herr Hildebrandt, stony-faced, brushed a crumb from his sleeve; his wife coloured up, a rare thing for her; the students coughed and used their handkerchiefs loudly; and Herr Assessor Witznagel simply left the field and got himself a sandwich. The lawyer sat huddled on his little chair, yellow in the face, with a terrified smile. He looked all round the circle, and stammered:

"But, my God . . . I—I—I am not up to—not that I—I beg pardon, but . . ."

Alfred Läutner had lost his insouciant expression; he even seemed to have reddened a little, and he thrust out his neck to peer searchingly into Amra's face. He looked puzzled and upset.

But she, Amra, holding the same persuasive pose, went on with the same impressiveness:

"And you must sing, too, Christian, a song which Herr Läutner shall compose, and he can accompany you on the piano. We could not have a better or more effective climax."

There was a pause, an oppressive pause. Then this extraordinary thing happened, that Herr Läutner, as it were seized upon and carried away by his excitement, took a step forward and his voice fairly trembled with enthusiasm as he said:

"Herr Jacoby, that is a priceless idea, and I am more than ready to compose something. You must have a dance and song, anything else is unthinkable as a wind-up to our affair. You will see, it will be the best thing I have ever written or ever shall write. In a red satin baby frock. Oh, your wife is an artist, only an artist could have hit upon the idea! Do say yes, I beg of you. I will do my part, you will see, it will be an achievement."

Here the circle broke up and the meeting became lively. Out of politeness, or out of malice, the company began to storm the lawyer with entreaties—Frau Hildebrandt went so far as to say, quite loudly, in her Brünnhilde voice:

"Herr Jacoby, after all, you are such a jolly and entertaining man!"

But the lawyer had pulled himself together and spoke, a little yellow, but with a strong effort at resolution:

"But listen to me, ladies and gentlemen—what can I say to you? It isn't my line, believe me. I have no comic gift, and besides . . . in short, no, it is quite impossible, alas!"

He stuck obstinately to his refusal, and Amra no longer insisted, but sat still with her absent look. Herr Läutner was silent too, staring in deep abstraction at a pattern in the rug. Herr Hildebrandt changed the subject, and presently the committee meeting broke up without coming to a final decision about the "climax."

On the evening of the same day Amra had gone to bed and was lying there with her eyes wide open; her husband came lumbering into the bedroom, drew a chair up beside the bed, dropped into it, and said, in a low, hesitating voice:

"Listen, Amra; to be quite frank, I am feeling very disturbed. I refused them today—I did not mean to be offensive—goodness knows I did not mean that. Or do you seriously feel that—I beg you to tell me."

Amra was silent for a moment, while her brows rose slowly. Then she shrugged her shoulders and said:

"I do not know, my dear friend, how to answer you. You behaved in a way I should not have expected from you. You were unfriendly, you refused to support our enterprise in a way which they flatteringly considered to be indispensable to it. To put it mildly, you disappointed everybody and upset the whole company with your rude lack of compliance. Whereas it was your duty as host—"

The lawyer hung his head and sighed heavily. He said:

"Believe me, Amra, I had no intention to be disobliging. I do not like to offend anybody; if I have behaved badly I am ready to make amends. It is only a joke, after all, an innocent little dressing-up—why not? I will not upset the whole affair, I am ready to . . ."

The following afternoon Amra went out again to "make preparations." She drove to Number 78 Holzstrasse and went up to the second storey, where she had an appointment. And when she lay relaxed by the expression of her love she pressed her lover's head passionately to her breast and whispered:

"Write it for four hands. We will accompany him together while he sings and dances. I will see to the costume myself."

And an extraordinary shiver, a suppressed and spasmodic burst of laughter went through the limbs of both.

For anyone who wants to give a large party out of doors Herr Wendelin's place on the slope of the Lerchenberg is to be recommended. You enter it from the pretty suburban street through a tall trellised gateway and pass into the parklike garden, in the centre of which stands a large hall, connected only by a narrow passage with restaurant, kitchen, and brewery. It is a large, brightly painted wooden hall, in an amusing mixture of Chinese and Renaissance styles. It has folding doors which stand open in good weather to admit the woodland air, and it will hold a great many people.

On this evening as the carriages rolled up they were greeted from afar by the gleam of coloured lights. The whole gateway, the trees, and the hall itself were set thick with lanterns, while the interior made an entrancing sight. Heavy garlands were draped across the ceiling and studded with paper lanterns. Hosts of electric lights hung among the decorations of the walls, which consisted of pine boughs, flags, and artificial flowers; the whole hall was brilliantly lighted. The stage had foliage plants grouped on either side, and a red curtain with a painted design of a presiding genius hovering in the air. A long row of decorated tables ran almost the whole length of the hall. And at these tables the guests of Attorney Jacoby were doing themselves well on cold roast veal and bock beer. There were certainly more than a hundred and fifty people: officers, lawyers, business men, artists, upper officials, with their wives and daughters. They were quite simply dressed, in black coats and light spring toilettes, for this was a jolly, informal occasion. The gentlemen carried their mugs in person to the big casks against one of the walls; the spacious, festive, brightly lighted room was filled with a heavy sweetish atmosphere of evergreen boughs, flowers, beer, food, and human beings; and there was a clatter and buzz of laughter and talk—the loud, simple talk and the high, good-natured, unrestrained, carefree laughter of the sort of people there assembled.

The attorney sat shapeless and helpless at one end of the table, near the stage. He drank little and now and then addressed a laboured remark to his neighbour, Frau Regierungsrat Havermann. He breathed offensively, the corners of his mouth hung down, he stared fixedly with his bulging watery eyes into the lively scene, with a sort of melancholy remoteness, as though there resided in all this noisy merriment something inexpressibly painful and perplexing.

Large fruit tarts were now being handed round for the company to cut from; they drank sweet wine with these, and the time for the speeches arrived. Herr Hildebrandt celebrated the new brew in a speech almost entirely composed of classical quotations, even Greek. Herr Witznagel, with florid gestures and ingenious turns of phrase, toasted the ladies, taking a handful of flowers from the nearest vase and comparing each flower to some feminine charm. Amra Jacoby, who sat opposite him in a pale-yellow silk frock, he called "a lovelier sister of the Maréchal Niel."

Then she nodded meaningfully to her husband, brushing back her hair from her forehead; whereupon the fat man arose and almost ruined the whole atmosphere by stammering a few words with painful effort, smiling a repulsive smile. Some half-hearted bravos rewarded him, then there was an oppressive pause, after which jollity resumed its sway. All smoking, all a little elevated by drink, they rose from table and with their own hands and a great deal of noise removed the tables from the hall to make way for the dancing.

It was after eleven and high spirits reigned supreme. Some of the guests streamed out into the brightly lighted garden to get the fresh air; others stood about the hall in groups, smoking, chatting, drawing beer from the kegs, and drinking it standing. Then a loud trumpet call sounded from the stage, summoning everybody to the entertainment. The band arrived and took its place before the curtains; rows of chairs were put in place and red programmes distributed on them; the gentlemen ranged themselves along the walls. There was an expectant hush.

The band played a noisy overture, and the curtains parted to reveal a row of Negroes horrifying to behold in their barbaric costumes and their blood-red lips, gnashing their teeth and emitting savage yells.

Certainly the entertainment was the crowning success of Amra's party. As it went on, the applause grew more and more enthusiastic. Frau Hildebrandt came on in a powdered wig, pounded with a shepherdess' crook on the floor and sang—in too large a voice—"That's Maria!" A conjuror in a dress coat covered with orders performed the most amazing feats; Herr Hildebrandt impersonated Goethe, Bismarck, and Napoleon in an amazingly lifelike manner; and a newspaper editor, Dr. Wiesensprung, improvised a humorous lecture which had as its theme bock beer and its social significance. And now the suspense reached its height, for it was time for the last, the mysterious number which appeared on the programme framed in a laurel wreath and was entitled: "*Little Lizzy.* Song and Dance. Music by Alfred Läutner."

A movement swept through the hall, and people's eyes met as the band sat down at their instruments and Alfred Läutner came from the doorway where he had been lounging with a cigarette between his pouting lips to take his place beside Amra Jacoby at the piano, which stood in the centre of the stage in front of the curtains. Herr Läutner's face was flushed and he turned over his manuscript score nervously; Amra for her part was rather pale. She leaned one arm on the back of her chair and looked loweringly at the audience. The bell rang, the pianists played a few bars of an insignificant accompaniment, the curtains parted, little Lizzy appeared.

The whole audience stiffened with amazement as that tragic and bedizened bulk shambled with a sort of bear-dance into view. It was Jacoby. A wide, shapeless garment of crimson satin, without folds, fell to his feet; it was cut out above to make a repulsive display of the fat neck, stippled with white powder. The sleeves consisted merely of a shoulder puff, but the flabby arms were covered by long lemon-coloured gloves; on the head perched a high blond wig with a swaying green feather. And under the wig was a face, a puffy, pasty, unhappy, and desperately mirthful face, with cheeks that shook pathetically up and down and little red-rimmed eyes that strained in anguish towards the floor and saw nothing else at all. The fat man hoisted himself with effort from one leg to the other, while with his hands he either held up his skirts or else weakly raised his index fingers—these two gestures he had and knew no others. In a choked and gasping voice he sang, to the accompaniment of the piano.

The lamentable figure exhaled more than ever a cold breath of anguish. It killed every light-hearted enjoyment and lay like an oppressive weight upon the assembled audience. Horror was in the depths of all these spellbound eyes, gazing at this pair at the piano and at that husband there. The monstrous, unspeakable scandal lasted five long minutes.

Then came a moment which none of those present will forget as long as they live. Let us picture to ourselves what happened in that frightful and frightfully involved little instant of time.

You know of course the absurd little jingle called "Lizzy." And you remember the lines:

I can polka until I am dizzy,
I can waltz with the best and beyond,
I'm the popular pet, little Lizzy,
Who makes all the menfolks so fond—

which form the trivial and unlovely refrain to three longish stanzas. Alfred Läutner had composed a new setting to the verses I have quoted, and it was, as he had said it would be, his masterpiece. He had, that is, brought to its highest pitch his little artifice of introducing into a fairly vulgar and humorous piece of hackwork a sudden phrase of genuine creative art. The melody, in C-sharp major, had been in the first bars rather pretty and perfectly banal. At the beginning of the refrain the rhythm became livelier and dissonances occurred, which by means of the constant accentuation of a B-natural made one expect a transition into F-sharp major. These dissonances went on developing until the word "beyond"; and after the "I'm the" a culmination into F-sharp major should have followed. Instead of which the most surprising thing happened. That is, through a harsh turn, by means of an inspiration which was almost a stroke of genius, the key changed to F-major, and this little interlude which followed, with the use of both pedals on the long-drawn-out first syllable of the word "Lizzy," was indescribably, almost gruesomely effective. It was a complete surprise, an abrupt assault on the nerves, it shivered down the back, it was a miracle, a revelation, it was like a curtain suddenly torn away to reveal something nude.

And on the F-major chord Attorney Jacoby stopped dancing. He stood still, he stood as though rooted to the stage with his two forefingers lifted, one a little lower than the other. The word "Lizzy" stuck in his throat, he was dumb; almost at the same time the accompaniment broke sharp off, and the incredible, absurd, and ghastly figure stood there frozen, with his head thrust forward like a steer's, staring with inflamed eyes straight before him. He stared into the brightly lighted, decorated, crowded hall, in which, like an exhalation from all these people, the scandal hung and thickened into visibility. He stared at all these upturned faces, foreshortened and distorted by the lighting, into these hundreds of pairs of eyes all directed with the same knowing expression upon himself and the two at the piano. In a frightful stillness, unbroken by the smallest sound, his gaze travelled slowly and uneasily from the pair to the audience, from the audience to the pair, while his eyes widened more and more. Then knowledge seemed to flash across his face, like a sudden rush of blood, making it red as the frock he wore, only to give way to a waxen yellow pallor—and the fat man collapsed, making the platform creak beneath his weight.

For another moment the stillness reigned. Then there came shrieks, hubbub ensued, a few gentlemen took heart to spring upon the platform, among them a young doctor—and the curtains were drawn together.

Amra Jacoby and Alfred Läutner still sat at the piano. They had turned a little away from each other, and he, with his head bent, seemed to be listening to the echo of his F-major chord, while she, with her birdlike brain, had not yet grasped the situation, but gazed round her with vacant face.

The young doctor came back presently. He was a little Jewish gentleman with a serious face and a small pointed beard. Some people surrounded him at the door with questions—to which he replied with a shrug of the shoulders and the words:

"All over."

James Joyce

(1882 - 1941)

James Joyce was a colossal literary genius—probably the greatest of this century—who dedicated himself to his art as religiously as any priest dedicates himself to God and man. A Jesuit-educated Irishman, Joyce repudiated both his religion and country when he was in his early twenties, and after graduating from University College (Dublin) in 1902, he left Ireland for Paris. He rightly believed that his native country, dominated as it was by the Roman Catholic Church, would stifle his freedom to create. Although he sometimes expressed disdain for Ireland, Joyce repeatedly recreated Dublin in his fiction, making the city the setting of all his narrative works. He struggled for ten years in Trieste teaching English at a Berlitz school in order to support his wife and two children. By 1917 Joyce was able to attract as a sponsor a wealthy woman who appreciated his genius and from this time until his death he was able to devote himself full-time to writing. *Dubliners,* a collection of fifteen stories from which "A Little Cloud" is taken, was written almost ten years before it was published in 1914. It was, according to the author, "a chapter of the moral history of my country and I chose Dublin because that city seemed to me the centre of paralysis." These stories first appeared to most readers as mean, naturalistic sketches of frustration, deception, and corruption, but they actually are carefully constructed and surprisingly complex, and are imbedded with many enriching symbols. Joyce had great difficulty persuading anyone to publish his stories, and not only because, as it was alleged, the book maligned Ireland. The subjects and the manner of telling had never appeared before in the British short story. (It was eight years before a second edition was published, in 1922, the year *Ulysses* appeared.) Commenting on Joyce as a short-story writer, H. E. Bates remarked that his originality arose "solely from Joyce's power to transmute life (a Christmas party, a suicide, a drunken clerk . . .), to render it naturalistically and yet compassionately, objectively and yet with rare beauty of emotional tone." Strangely enough, Joyce wrote no stories after *Dubliners.* In 1916 he published *A Portrait of the Artist as a Young Man,* an autobiographical novel of a young man's growing consciousness of art and his proud, defiant decision to become a writer and flee Ireland. *Ulysses* (1922) is probably his best known work, though many of those talking about it have never read it through. A long, sometimes difficult novel, *Ulysses* slowly recounts the thoughts and actions of a few Dubliners on one day, June 16, 1904. Joyce ingeniously structured the characters and events on *The Odyssey,* and the novel parallels Homer's epic from beginning to end. It is a great comic masterpiece and one of the most impressive novels of the twentieth century.

A Little Cloud

Eight years before he had seen his friend off at the North Wall and wished him godspeed. Gallaher had got on. You could tell that at once by his travelled air, his well-cut tweed suit, and fearless accent. Few fellows had talents like his and fewer still could remain unspoiled by such success. Gallaher's heart was in the right place and he had deserved to win. It was something to have a friend like that.

Little Chandler's thoughts ever since lunch-time had been of his meeting with Gallaher, of Gallaher's invitation and of the great city London where Gallaher lived. He was called Little Chandler because, though he was but slightly under the average stature, he gave one the idea of being a little man. His hands were white and small, his frame was fragile, his voice was quiet and his manners were refined. He took the greatest care of his fair silken hair and moustache and used perfume discreetly on his handkerchief. The half-moons of his nails were perfect and when he smiled you caught a glimpse of a row of childish white teeth.

As he sat at his desk in the King's Inns he thought what changes those eight years had brought. The friend whom he had known under a shabby and necessitous guise had become a brilliant figure on the London Press. He turned often from his tiresome writing to gaze out of the office window. The glow of a late autumn sunset covered the grass plots and walks. It cast a shower of kindly golden dust on the untidy nurses and decrepit old men who drowsed on the benches; it flickered upon all the moving figures—on the children who ran screaming along the gravel paths and on everyone who passed through the gardens. He watched the scene and thought of life; and (as always happened when he thought of life) he became sad. A gentle melancholy took possession of him. He felt how useless it was to struggle against fortune, this being the burden of wisdom which the ages had bequeathed to him.

He remembered the books of poetry upon his shelves at home. He had bought them in his bachelor days and many an evening, as he sat in the little room off the hall, he had been tempted to take one down from the bookshelf and read out something to his wife. But shyness had always held him back; and so the books had remained on their shelves. At times he repeated lines to himself and this consoled him.

When his hour had struck he stood up and took leave of his desk and of his fellow-clerks punctiliously. He emerged from under the feudal arch of the King's Inns, a neat modest figure, and walked swiftly down Henrietta Street. The golden sunset was wanning and the air had grown sharp. A horde of grimy children populated the street. They stood or ran in the roadway or crawled up the steps before the gaping doors or squatted like mice upon the thresholds. Little Chandler gave them no thought. He picked his way deftly through all that minute vermin-like life and under the shadow of the gaunt spectral mansions in which the old nobility of Dublin had roystered. No memory of the past touched him, for his mind was full of a present joy.

He had never been in Corless's but he knew the value of the name. He knew that people went there after the theatre to eat oysters and drink liqueurs; and he had heard that the waiters there spoke French and German. Walking swiftly by at night he had seen cabs drawn up before the door and richly dressed ladies, escorted by cavaliers, alight and enter quickly. They wore noisy dresses and many wraps. Their faces were powdered and they caught up their dresses, when they touched earth, like alarmed Atalantas. He had always passed without turning his head to look. It was his habit to walk swiftly in the street even by day and whenever he found himself in the city late at night he hurried on his way apprehensively and excitedly. Sometimes, however, he courted the causes of his fear. He chose the darkest and narrowest streets and, as he walked boldy forward, the silence that was spread about his footsteps troubled him, the wandering, silent figures troubled him; and at times a sound of low fugitive laughter made him tremble like a leaf.

He turned to the right towards Capel Street. Ignatius Gallaher on the London Press! Who would have thought it possible eight years before? Still, now that he reviewed the past, Little Chandler could remember many signs of future greatness in his friend. People used to say that Ignatius was wild. Of course, he did mix with a rakish set of fellows at that time, drank freely and borrowed money on all sides. In the end he had got mixed up in some shady affair, some money transaction: at least, that was one version of his flight. But nobody denied him talent. There was always a certain . . . something in Ignatius Gallaher that impressed you in spite of yourself. Even when he was out at elbows and at his wits' end for money he kept up a bold face. Little Chandler remembered (and the remembrance brought a slight flush of pride to his cheek) one of Ignatius Gallaher's sayings when he was in a tight corner:

"Half time now, boys," he used to say light-heartedly. "Where's my considering cap?"

That was Ignatius Gallaher all out; and, damn it, you couldn't but admire him for it.

Little Chandler quickened his pace. For the first time in his life he felt superior to the people he passed. For the first time his soul revolted against the dull inelegance of Capel Street. There was no doubt about it: if you wanted to succeed you had to go away. You could do nothing in Dublin. As he crossed Grattan Bridge he looked down the river towards the lower quays and pitied the poor stunted houses. They seemed to him a band of tramps, huddled together along the riverbanks, their old coats covered with dust and soot, stupefied by the panorama of sunset and waiting for the first chill of night to bid them arise, shake themselves and begone. He wondered whether he could write a poem to express his idea. Perhaps Gallaher might be able to get it into some London paper for him. Could he write something original? He was not sure what idea he wished to express but the thought that a poetic moment had touched him took life within him like an infant hope. He stepped onward bravely.

Every step brought him nearer to London, farther from his own sober inartistic life. A light began to tremble on the horizon of his mind. He was not so old—thirty-two. His temperament might be said to be just at the point of maturity. There were so many different moods and impressions that he wished to express in verse. He felt them within him. He tried to weigh his soul to see if it was a poet's soul. Melancholy was the dominant note of his temperament, he thought, but it was a melancholy tempered by recurrences of faith and resignation and simple joy. If he could give expression to it in a book of poems perhaps men would listen. He would never be popular: he saw that. He could not sway the crowd but he might appeal to a little circle of kindred minds. The English critics, perhaps, would recognise him as one of the Celtic school by reason of the melancholy tone of his poems; besides that, he would put in allusions. He began to invent sentences and phrases from the notice which his book would get. "*Mr. Chandler has the gift of easy and graceful verse.*" . . . "*A wistful sadness pervades these poems.*" . . . "*The Celtic note.*" It was a pity his name was not more Irish-looking. Perhaps it would be better to insert his mother's name before the surname: Thomas Malone Chandler, or better still: T. Malone Chandler. He would speak to Gallaher about it.

He pursued his revery so ardently that he passed his street and had to turn back. As he came near Corless's his former agitation began to overmaster him and he halted before the door in indecision. Finally he opened the door and entered.

The light and noise of the bar held him at the doorways for a few moments. He looked about him, but his sight was confused by the shining of many red and green wine-glasses. The bar seemed to him to be full of people and he felt that the people were observing him curiously. He glanced quickly to right and left (frowning slightly to make his errand appear serious), but when his sight cleared a little he saw that nobody had turned to look at him: and there, sure enough, was Ignatius Gallaher leaning with his back against the counter and his feet planted far apart.

"Hallo, Tommy, old hero, here you are! What is it to be? What will you have? I'm taking whisky: better stuff than we get across the water. Soda? Lithia? No mineral? I'm the same. Spoils the flavour. . . . Here, *garcon,* bring us two halves of malt whisky, like a good fellow. . . . Well, and how have you been pulling along since I saw you last? Dear God, how old we're getting! Do you see any signs of aging in me—eh, what? A little grey and thin on the top—what?"

Ignatius Gallaher took off his hat and displayed a large closely cropped head. His face was heavy, pale and clean-shaven. His eyes, which were of bluish slate-colour, relieved his unhealthy pallor and shone out plainly above the vivid orange tie he wore. Between these rival features the lips appeared very long and shapeless and colourless. He bent his head and felt with two sympathetic fingers the thin hair at the crown. Little Chandler shook his head as a denial. Ignatius Gallaher put on his hat again.

"It pulls you down," he said, "Press life. Always hurry and scurry, looking for copy and sometimes not finding it: and then, always to have something new in your stuff. Damn proofs and printers, I say, for a few days. I'm deuced glad, I can tell you, to get back to the old country. Does a fellow good, a bit of a holiday. I feel a ton better since I landed again in dear dirty Dublin. . . . Here you are, Tommy. Water? Say when."

Little Chandler allowed his whisky to be very much diluted.

"You don't know what's good for you, my boy," said Ignatius Gallaher. "I drink mine neat."

"I drink very little as a rule," said Little Chandler modestly. "An odd half-one or so when I meet any of the old crowd: that's all."

"Ah, well," said Ignatius Gallaher, cheerfully, "here's to us and to old times and old acquaintance."

They clinked glasses and drank the toast.

"I met some of the old gang today," said Ignatius Gallaher. "O'Hara seems to be in a bad way. What's he doing?"

"Nothing," said Little Chandler. "He's gone to the dogs."

"But Hogan has a good sit, hasn't he?"

"Yes; he's in the Land Commission."

"I met him one night in London and he seemed to be very flush. . . . Poor O'Hara! Boose, I suppose?"

"Other things, too," said Little Chandler shortly.

Ignatius Gallaher laughed.

"Tommy," he said, "I see you haven't changed an atom. You're the very same serious person that used to lecture me on Sunday mornings when I had a sore head and a fur on my tongue. You'd want to knock about a bit in the world. Have you never been anywhere even for a trip?"

"I've been to the Isle of Man," said Little Chandler.

Ignatius Gallaher laughed.

"The Isle of Man!" he said. "Go to London or Paris: Paris, for choice. That'd do you good."

"Have you seen Paris?"

"I should think I have! I've knocked about there a little."

"And is it really so beautiful as they say?" asked Little Chandler.

He sipped a little of his drink while Ignatius Gallaher finished his boldly.

"Beautiful?" said Ignatius Gallaher, pausing on the word and on the flavour of his drink. "It's not so beautiful, you know. Of course, it is beautiful. . . . But it's the life of Paris; that's the thing. Ah, there's no city like Paris for gaiety, movement, excitement. . . ."

Little Chandler finished his whisky and, after some trouble, succeeded in catching the barman's eye. He ordered the same again.

"I've been to the Moulin Rouge," Ignatius Gallaher continued when the barman had removed their glasses, "and I've been to all the Bohemian cafés. Hot stuff! Not for a pious chap like you, Tommy."

Little Chandler said nothing until the barman returned with two glasses: then he touched his friend's glass lightly and reciprocated the former toast. He was beginning to feel somewhat disillusioned. Gallaher's accent and way of expressing himself did not please him. There was something vulgar in his friend which he had not observed before. But perhaps it was only the result of living in London amid the bustle and competition of the Press. The old personal charm was still there under this new gaudy manner. And, after all, Gallaher had lived, he had seen the world. Little Chandler looked at his friend enviously.

"Everything in Paris is gay," said Ignatius Gallaher. "They believe in enjoying life—and don't you think they're right? If you want to enjoy yourself properly you must go to Paris. And, mind you, they've a great feeling for the Irish there. When they heard I was from Ireland they were ready to eat me, man."

Little Chandler took four or five sips from his glass.

"Tell me," he said, "is it true that Paris is so . . . immoral as they say?"

Ignatius Gallaher made a catholic gesture with his right arm.

"Every place is immoral," he said. "Of course you do find spicy bits in Paris. Go to one of the students' balls, for instance. That's lively, if you like, when the *cocottes* begin to let themselves loose. You know what they are, I suppose?"

"I've heard of them," said Little Chandler.

Ignatius Gallaher drank off his whisky and shook his head.

"Ah," he said, "you may say what you like. There's no woman like the Parisienne—for style, for go."

"Then it is an immoral city," said Little Chandler, with timid insistence—"I mean, compared with London or Dublin?"

"London!" said Ignatius Gallaher. "It's six of one and half-a-dozen of the other. You ask Hogan, my boy. I showed him a bit about London when he was over there. He'd open your eye. . . . I say, Tommy, don't make punch of that whisky: liquor up."

"No, really. . . ."

"O, come on, another one won't do you any harm. What is it? The same again, I suppose?"

"Well . . . all right."

"*François,* the same again. . . . Will you smoke Tommy?"

Ignatius Gallaher produced his cigar-case. The two friends lit their cigars and puffed at them in silence until their drinks were served.

"I'll tell you my opinion," said Ignatius Gallaher, emerging after some time from the clouds of smoke in which he had taken refuge, "it's a rum world. Talk of immorality! I've heard of cases—what am I saying?—I've known them: cases of . . . immorality. . . ."

Ignatius Gallaher puffed thoughtfully at his cigar and then, in a calm historian's tone, he proceeded to sketch for his friend some pictures of the corruption which was rife abroad. He summarised the vices of many capitals and seemed inclined to award the palm to Berlin. Some things he could not vouch for (his friends had told him), but of others he had had personal experience. He spared neither rank nor caste. He revealed many of the secrets of religious houses on the Continent and described some of the practices which were fashionable in high society and ending by telling, with details, a story about an English duchess—a story which he knew to be true. Little Chandler was astonished.

"Ah, well," said Ignatius Gallaher, "here we are in old jog-along Dublin where nothing is known of such things."

"How dull you must find it," said Little Chandler, "after all the other places you've seen!"

"Well," said Ignatius Gallaher, "it's a relaxation to come over here, you know. And, after all, it's the old country, as they say, isn't it? You can't help having a certain feeling for it. That's human nature. . . . But tell me something about yourself. Hogan told me you had . . . tasted the joys of connubial bliss. Two years ago, wasn't it?"

Little Chandler blushed and smiled.

"Yes," he said. "I was married last May twelve months."

"I hope it's not too late in the day to offer my best wishes," said Ignatius Gallaher. "I didn't know your address or I'd have done so at the time."

He extended his hand, which Little Chandler took.

"Well, Tommy," he said, "I wish you and yours every joy in life, old chap, and tons of money, and may you never die till I shoot you. And that's the wish of a sincere friend, an old friend. You know that?"

"I know that," said Little Chandler.

"Any youngsters?" said Ignatius Gallaher.

Little Chandler blushed again.

"We have one child," he said.

"Son or daughter?"

"A little boy."

Ignatius Gallaher slapped his friend sonorously on the back.

"Bravo," he said, "I wouldn't doubt you, Tommy."

Little Chandler smiled, looked confusedly at his glass and bit his lower lip with three childishly white front teeth.

"I hope you'll spend an evening with us," he said, "before you go back. My wife will be delighted to meet you. We can have a little music and ——"

"Thanks awfully, old chap," said Ignatius Gallaher, "I'm sorry we didn't meet earlier. But I must leave tomorrow night."

"Tonight, perhaps . . . ?"

"I'm awfully sorry, old man. You see I'm over here with another fellow, clever young chap he is too, and we arranged to go to a little card-party. Only for that . . ."

"O, in that case . . ."

"But who knows?" said Ignatius Gallaher considerately. "Next year I may take a little skip over here now that I've broken the ice. It's only a pleasure deferred."

"Very well," said Little Chandler, "the next time you come we must have an evening together. That's agreed now, isn't it?"

"Yes, that's agreed," said Ignatius Gallaher. "Next year if I come, *parole d' honneur.*"

"And to clinch the bargain," said Little Chandler, "we'll just have one more now."

Ignatius Gallaher took out a large gold watch and looked at it.

"Is it to be the last?" he said. "Because you know, I have an a.p."

"O, yes, positively," said Little Chandler.

"Very well, then," said Ignatius Gallaher, "let us have another one as a *deoc an doruis*—that's good vernacular for a small whisky, I believe."

Little Chandler ordered the drinks. The blush which had risen to his face a few moments before was establishing itself. A trifle made him blush at any time: and now he felt warm and excited. Three small whiskies had gone to his head and Gallaher's strong cigar had confused his mind, for he was a delicate and abstinent person. The adventure of meeting Gallaher after eight years, of finding himself with Gallaher in Corless's surrounded by lights and noise, of listening to Gallaher's stories and of sharing for a brief space Gallaher's vagrant and triumphant life, upset the equipoise of his sensitive nature. He felt acutely the contrast between his own life and his friend's, and it seemed to him unjust. Gallaher was his inferior in birth and education. He was sure that he could do something better than his friend had ever done, or could ever do, something higher than mere tawdry journalism if he only got the chance. What was it that stood in his way? His unfortunate timidity! He wished to vindicate himself in some way, to assert his manhood. He saw behind Gallaher's refusal of his invitation. Gallaher was only patronising him by his friendliness just as he was patronising Ireland by his visit.

The barman brought their drinks. Little Chandler pushed one glass towards his friend and took up the other boldly.

"Who knows?" he said, as they lifted their glasses. "When you come next year I may have the pleasure of wishing long life and happiness to Mr. and Mrs. Ignatius Gallaher."

Ignatius Gallaher in the act of drinking closed one eye expressively over the rim of his glass. When he had drunk he smacked his lips decisively, set down his glass and said:

"No blooming fear of that, my boy. I'm going to have my fling first and see a bit of life and the world before I put my head in the sack—if I ever do."

"Some day you will," said Little Chandler calmly.

Ignatius Gallaher turned his orange tie and slate-blue eyes full upon his friend.

"You think so?" he said.

"You'll put your head in the sack," repeated Little Chandler stoutly, "like everyone else if you can find the girl."

He had slightly emphasised his tone and he was aware that he had betrayed himself; but, though the colour had heightened in his cheek, he did not flinch from his friend's gaze. Ignatius Gallaher watched him for a few moments and then said:

"If every it occurs, you may bet your bottom dollar there'll be no mooning and spooning about it. I mean to marry money. She'll have a good fat account at the bank or she won't do for me."

Little Chandler shook his head.

"Why, man alive," said Ignatius Gallaher, vehemently, "do you know what it is? I've only to say the word and tomorrow I can have the woman and the cash. You don't believe it? Well, I know it. There are hundreds—what am I saying?—thousands of rich Germans and Jews, rotten with money, that'd only be too glad. . . . You wait a while, my boy. See if I don't play my cards properly. When I go about a thing I mean business, I tell you. You just wait."

He tossed his glass to his mouth, finished his drink and laughed loudly. Then he looked thoughtfully before him and said in a calmer tone:

"But I'm in no hurry. They can wait. I don't fancy tying myself up to one woman, you know."

He imitated with his mouth the act of tasting and made a wry face.

"Must get a bit stale, I should think," he said.

Little Chandler sat in the room of the hall, holding a child in his arms. To save money they kept no servant but Annie's young sister Monica came for an hour or so in the morning and an hour or so in the evening to help. But Monica had gone home long ago. It was a quarter to nine. Little Chandler had come home late for tea and, moreover, he had forgotten to bring Annie home the parcel of coffee from Bewley's. Of course she was in a bad humour and gave him short answers. She said she would do without any tea but when it came near the time at which the shop at the corner closed she decided to go out herself for a quarter of a pound of tea and two pounds of sugar. She put the sleeping child deftly in his arms and said:

"Here. Don't waken him."

A little lamp with a white china shade stood upon the table and its light fell over a photograph which was enclosed in a frame of crumpled horn. It was Annie's photograph. Little Chandler looked at it, pausing at the thin tight lips. She wore the pale blue summer blouse which he had brought her home as a present one Saturday. It had cost him ten and elevenpence; but what an agony of nervousness it had cost him! How he had suffered that day, waiting at the shop door until the shop was empty, standing at the counter and trying to appear at his ease while the girl piled ladies' blouses before him, paying at the desk and forgetting to take up the odd penny of his change, being called back by the cashier, and finally, striving to hide his blushes as he left the shop by examining the parcel to see if it was securely tied. When he brought the blouse home Annie kissed him and said it was very pretty and stylish; but when she heard the price she threw the blouse on the table and said it was a regular swindle to charge ten and elevenpence for it. At first she wanted to take it back but when she tried it on she was delighted with it, especially with the make of the sleeves, and kissed him and said he was very good to think of her.

Hm! . . .

He looked coldly into the eyes of the photograph and they answered coldly. Certainly they were pretty and the face itself was pretty. But he found something mean in it. Why was it so unconscious and ladylike? The composure of the eyes irritated him. They repelled him and defied him: there was no passion in them, no rapture. He thought of what Gallaher had said about rich Jewesses. Those dark Oriental eyes, he thought, how full they are of passion, of voluptuous longing! . . . Why had he married the eyes in the photograph?

He caught himself up at the question and glanced nervously round the room. He found something mean in the pretty furniture which he had bought for his house on the hire system. Annie had chosen it herself and it reminded him of her. It too was prim and pretty. A dull resentment against his life awoke within him. Could he not escape from his little house? Was it too late for him to try to live bravely like Gallaher? Could he go to

London? There was the furniture still to be paid for. If he could only write a book and get it published, that might open the way for him.

A volume of Byron's poems lay before him on the table. He opened it cautiously with his left hand lest he should waken the child and began to read the first poem in the book:

> Hushed are the winds and still the evening gloom,
>   Not e'en a Zephyr wanders through the grove,
> Whilst I return to view my Margaret's tomb
>   And scatter flowers on the dust I love.

He paused. He felt the rhythm of the verse about him in the room. How melancholy it was! Could he, too, write like that, express the melancholy of his soul in verse? There were so many things he wanted to describe: his sensation of a few hours before on Grattan Bridge, for example. If he could get back again into that mood. . . .

The child awoke and began to cry. He turned from the page and tried to hush it: but it would not be hushed. He began to rock it to and fro in his arms but its wailing cry grew keener. He rocked it faster while his eyes began to read the second stanza:

> Within this narrow cell reclines her clay,
>   That clay where once . . .

It was useless. He couldn't read. He couldn't do anything. The wailing of the child pierced the drum of his ear. It was useless, useless! He was a prisoner for life. His arms trembled with anger and suddenly bending to the child's face he shouted:

"Stop!"

The child stopped for an instant, had a spasm of fright and began to scream. He jumped up from his chair and walked hastily up and down the room with the child in his arms. It began to sob piteously, losing its breath for four or five seconds, and then bursting out anew. The thin walls of the room echoed the sound. He tried to soothe it but it sobbed more convulsively. He looked at the contracted and quivering face of the child and began to be alarmed. He counted seven sobs without a break between them and caught the child to his breast in fright. If it died! . . .

The door was burst open and a young woman ran in, panting.

"What is it? What is it?" she cried.

The child, hearing its mother's voice, broke out into a paroxysm of sobbing.

"It's nothing, Annie . . . it's nothing. . . . He began to cry. . . . "

She flung her parcels on the floor and snatched the child from him.

"What have you done to him?" she cried, glaring into his face.

Litte Chandler sustained for one moment the gaze of her eyes and his heart closed together as he met the hatred in them. He began to stammer:

"It's nothing. . . . He . . . he began to cry. . . . I couldn't . . . I didn't do anything. . . . What?"

Giving no heed to him she began to walk up and down the room, clasping the child tightly in her arms and murmuring:

"My little man! My little mannie! Was 'ou frightened, love? . . . There now, love! There now! . . . Lambabaun! Mamma's little lamb of the world! . . . There now!"

Little Chandler felt his cheeks suffused with shame and he stood back out of the lamplight. He listened while the paroxysm of the child's sobbing grew less and less; and tears of remorse started to his eyes.

D. H. Lawrence

(1885 - 1930)

"My great religion," D. H. Lawrence said, "is a belief in the blood, the flesh, as being wiser than the intellect," later adding that "the final aim is not to *know,* but to *be.*" (One hears the soft applause of some contemporary youth.) Lawrence celebrated the solitary, uncompromising individual in his fiction, and William Troy's remark was apt: "All of his novels . . . are object-lessons in the consequences of losing self-identity." Concerned with the problem of remaining a *human* being in spite of the dehumanizing forces in our industrialized civilization, he deplored the mindless damage to man and nature by industry and technology. In his novels and stories he emphasized erotic love as an antidote to the demoralizing, increasingly insane tendencies of the modern world, and he believed that the all-important self could grow only by engaging the core of another self, by penetrating the *persona* (mask) of another. Lawrence thought of the sex act as a kind of mystical experience in which the two poles of human life are joined. (Lawrence wrote in his novel *Women in Love,* "She was for him what he was for her, the immemorial magnificence of the *other reality,* mystic and palpable.") Not surprisingly, many of his best stories, including "Odour of Chrysanthemums," center on man-woman relationships. Because of his candor on sexual matters, Lawrence has often been wrongly considered a pornographer and, startling as it may seem in our climate of openness, his *Lady Chatterley's Lover* (1928) was not published in the United States in an unexpurgated edition until 1960, and only then after a legal struggle. His posthumous reputation as a "dirty" writer stands in ironic contrast to his aims. "I always labor at the same thing," Lawrence wrote, "to make the sex relation valid and precious, instead of shameful." Although probably best known for his novels (*Sons and Lovers* is a modern classic), Lawrence was an excellent short-story writer and literary critic. Although he had a penchant for discursive moralizing in his novels, Lawrence is often self-effacing, precise, and magnificent in his stories, though he was not overly concerned with the genre's forms. "Odour of Chrysanthemums" was his first published story and remains one of his best.

Odour of Chrysanthemums

I

The small locomotive engine, Number 4, came clanking, stumbling down from Selston with seven full wagons. It appeared round the corner with loud threats of speed, but the colt that it startled from among the gorse, which still flickered indistinctly in the raw afternoon, out-distanced it at a canter. A woman, walking up the railway line to Underwood, drew back into the hedge, held her basket aside, and watched the footplate of the engine advancing. The trucks[1] thumped heavily past, one by one, with slow inevitable movement, as she stood insignificantly trapped between the jolting black wagons and the hedge; then they curved away towards the coppice where the withered oak leaves dropped noiselessly, while the birds, pulling at the scarlet hips beside the track, made off into the dusk that had already crept into the spinney[2]. In the open, the smoke from the engine sank and cleaved to the rough grass. The fields were dreary and forsaken, and in the marshy strip that led to the whimsey[3], a reedy pit-pond, the fowls had already abandoned their run among the alders, to roost in the tarred fowl-house. The pit-bank loomed up beyond the pond, flames like red sores licking its ashy sides, in the afternoon's stagnant light. Just beyond rose the tapering chimneys and the clumsy black headstocks of Brinsley Colliery. The two wheels were spinning fast up against the sky, and the winding engine rapped out its little spasms. The miners were being turned up.

The engine whistled as it came into the wide bay of railway lines beside the colliery, where rows of trucks stood in harbour.

Miners, single, trailing and in groups, passed like shadows diverging home. At the edge of the ribbed level of sidings squat a low cottage, three steps down from the cinder track. A large bony vine clutched at the house, as if to claw down the tiled roof. Round the bricked yard grew a few wintry primroses. Beyond, the long garden sloped down to a bush-covered brook course. There were some twiggy apple trees, winter-crack trees, and ragged cabbages. Beside the path hung dishevelled pink chrysanthemums, like pink cloths hung on bushes. A woman came stooping out of the felt-covered fowl-house, half-way down the garden. She closed and padlocked the door, then drew herself erect, having brushed some bits from her white apron.

She was a tall woman of imperious mien, handsome, with definite black eyebrows. Her smooth black hair was parted exactly. For a few moments she stood steadily watching the miners as they passed along the railway: then she turned towards the brook course. Her face was calm and set, her mouth was closed with disillusionment. After a moment she called:

[1] Open freight cars.

[2] Thicket.

[3] Machine to lift ore from a mine.

"John!" There was no answer. She waited, and then said distinctly:

"Where are you?"

"Here!" replied a child's sulky voice from among the bushes. The woman looked piercingly through the dusk.

"Are you at that brook?" she asked sternly.

For answer the child showed himself before the raspberry-canes that rose like whips. He was a small, sturdy boy of five. He stood quite still, defiantly.

"Oh!" said the mother conciliated. "I thought you were down at that wet brook—and you remember what I told you____"

The boy did not move or answer.

"Come, come on in," she said more gently, "it's getting dark. There's your grandfather's engine coming down the line!"

The lad advanced slowly, with resentful, taciturn movement. He was dressed in trousers and waistcoat of cloth that was too thick and hard for the size of the garments. They were evidently cut down from a man's clothes.

As they went slowly towards the house he tore at the ragged wisps of chrysanthemums and dropped the petals in handfuls among the path.

"Don't do that—it does look nasty," said his mother. He refrained, and she, suddenly pitiful, broke off a twig with three or four wan flowers and held them against her face. When mother and son reached the yard her hand hesitated, and instead of laying the flower aside, she pushed it in her apron-band. The mother and son stood at the foot of the three steps looking across the bay of lines at the passing home of the miners. The trundle of the small train was imminent. Suddenly the engine loomed past the house and came to a stop opposite the gate.

The engine-driver, a short man with round grey beard, leaned out of the cab high above the woman.

"Have you got a cup of tea?" he said in a cheery, hearty fashion.

It was her father. She went in, saying she would mash. Directly, she returned.

"I didn't come to see you on Sunday," began the little grey-bearded man.

"I didn't expect you," said his daughter.

The engine-driver winced; then, reassuming his cheery, airy manner, he said:

"Oh, have you heard then? Well, and what do you think____?"

"I think it is soon enough," she replied.

At her brief censure the little man made an impatient gesture, and said coaxingly, yet with dangerous coldness:

"Well, what's a man to do? It's no sort of life for a man of my years, to sit at my own hearth like a stranger. And if I'm going to marry again it may as well be soon as late—what does it matter to anybody?"

The woman did not reply, but turned and went into the house. The man in the engine-cab stood assertive, till she returned with a cup of tea and a piece of bread and butter on a plate. She went up the steps and stood near the footplate of the hissing engine.

"You needn't 'a' brought me bread an' butter," said her father. "But a cup of tea"—he sipped appreciatively—"it's very nice." He sipped for a moment or two, then: "I hear as Walter's got another bout on," he said.

"When hasn't he?" said the woman bitterly.

"I heerd tell of him in the 'Lord Nelson' braggin' as he was going to spend that b——afore he went: half a sovereign that was."

"When?" asked the woman.

A' Sat'day night—I know that's true."

"Very likely," she laughed bitterly. "He gives me twenty-three shillings."

"Aye, it's a nice thing, when a man can do nothing with his money but make a beast of himself!" said the grey whiskered man. The woman turned her head away. Her father swallowed the last of his tea and handed her the cup.

"Aye," he sighed, wiping his mouth. "It's a settler[4], it is ——" He put his hand on the lever. The little engine strained and groaned, and the train rumbled towards the crossing. The woman again looked across the metals. Darkness was settling over the spaces of the railway and trucks: the miners, in grey sombre groups, were still passing home. The winding engine pulsed hurriedly, with brief pauses. Elizabeth Bates looked at the dreary flow of men, then she went indoors. Her husband did not come.

The kitchen was small and full of firelight; red coals piled glowing up the chimney mouth. All the life of the room seemed in the white, warm hearth and the steel fender reflecting the red fire. The cloth was laid for tea; cups glinted in the shadows. At the back, where the lowest stairs protruded into the room, the boy sat struggling with a knife and piece of whitewood. He was almost hidden in the shadow. It was half-past four. They had but to await the father's coming to begin tea. As the mother watched her son's sullen little struggle with the wood, she saw herself in his silence and pertinacity; she saw the father in her child's indifference to all but himself. She seemed to be occupied by her husband. He had probably gone past his home, slunk past his own door, to drink before he came in, while his dinner spoiled and wasted in waiting. She glanced at the clock, then took the potatoes to strain them in the yard. The garden and fields beyond the brook were closed in uncertain darkness. When she rose with the saucepan, leaving the drain steaming into the night behind her, she saw the yellow lamps were lit along the high road that went up the hill away beyond the space of the railway lines and the field.

Then again she watched the men trooping home, fewer now and fewer. Indoors the fire was sinking and the room was dark red. The woman

[4] Crushing blow.

put her saucepan on the hob, and set a batter-pudding near the mouth of the oven. Then she stood unmoving. Directly, gratefully, came quick young steps to the door. Someone hung on the latch a moment, then a little girl entered and began pulling off her outdoor things, dragging a mass of curls, just ripening from gold to brown, over her eyes with her hat.

Her mother chid her for coming late from school, and said she would have to keep her at home the dark winter days.

"Why, mother, it's hardly a bit dark yet. The lamp's not lighted, and my father's not home."

"No, he isn't. But it's a quarter to five! Did you see anything of him?"

The child became serious. She looked at her mother with large, wistful blue eyes.

"No, mother, I've never seen him. Why? Has he come up an' gone past, to Old Brinsley? He hasn't, mother, 'cos I never saw him."

"He'd watch that," said the mother bitterly, "he'd take care as you didn't see him. But you may depend upon it, he's seated in the 'Prince o' Wales.' He wouldn't be this late."

The girl looked at her mother piteously.

"Let's have our teas, mother, should we?" said she.

The mother called John to table. She opened the door once more and looked out across the darkness of the lines. All was deserted: she could not hear the winding-engines.

"Perhaps," she said to herself, "he's stopped to get some ripping done."

They sat down to tea. John, at the end of the table near the door, was almost lost in the darkness. Their faces were hidden from each other. The girl crouched against the fender slowly moving a thick piece of bread before the fire. The lad, his face a dusky mark on the shadow, sat watching her who was transfigured in the red glow.

"I do think it's beautiful to look in the fire," said the child.

"Do you?" said her mother. "Why?"

"It's so red, and full of little caves—and it feels so nice, and you can fair smell it."

"It'll want mending directly," replied her mother, "and then if your father comes he'll carry on and say there never is a fire when a man comes home sweating from the pit. A public-house is always warm enough."

There was silence till the boy said complainingly: "Make haste, our Annie."

"Well, I am doing! I can't make the fire do it no faster, can I?"

"She keeps wafflin' it about so's to make 'er slow," grumbled the boy.

"Don't have such an evil imagination, child," replied the mother.

Soon the room was busy in the darkness with the crisp sound of crunching. The mother ate very little. She drank her tea determinedly, and sat thinking. When she rose her anger was evident in the stern unbending of her head. She looked at the pudding in the fender, and broke out:

"It is a scandalous thing as a man can't even come home to his dinner! If it's crozzled up to a cinder I don't see why I should care. Past his very door he goes to get to a public-house, and here I sit with his dinner waiting for him____"

She went out. As she dropped piece after piece of coal on the red fire, the shadows fells on the walls, till the room was almost in total darkness.

"I canna see," grumbled the invisible John. In spite of herself, the mother laughed.

"You know the way to your mouth," she said. She set the dust-pan outside the door. When she came again like a shadow on the hearth, the lad repeated, complaining sulkily:

"I canna see."

"Good gracious!" cried the mother irritably, "you're as bad as your father if it's a bit dusk!"

Nevertheless, she took a paper spill from a sheaf on the mantelpiece and proceeded to light the lamp that hung from the ceiling in the middle of the room. As she reached up, her figure displayed itself just rounding with maternity.

"Oh, mother ____!" exclaimed the girl.

"What?" said the woman, suspended in the act of putting the lamp-glass over the flame. The copper reflector shone handsomely on her, as she stood with uplifted arm, turning to face her daughter.

"You've got a flower in your apron!" said the child, in a little rapture at this unusual event.

"Goodness me!" exclaimed the woman, relieved. "One would think the house was afire." She replaced the glass and waited a moment before turning up the wick. A pale shadow was seen floating vaguely on the floor.

"Let me smell!" said the child, still rapturously, coming forward and putting her face to her mother's waist.

"Go along, silly!" said the mother, turning up the lamp. The light revealed their suspense so that the woman felt it almost unbearable. Annie was still bending at her waist. Irritably, the mother took the flowers out from her apron-band.

"Oh, mother—don't take them out!" Annie cried, catching her hand and trying to replace the sprig.

"Such nonsense!" said the mother, turning away. The child put the pale chrysanthemums to her lips, murmuring:

"Don't they smell beautiful!"

Her mother gave a short laugh.

"No," she said, "not to me. It was chrysanthemums when I married him, and chrysanthemums when you were born, and the first time they ever brought him home drunk, he'd got brown chrysanthemums in his button-hole."

She looked at the children. Their eyes and their parted lips were wondering. The mother sat rocking in silence for some time. Then she looked at the clock.

"Twenty minutes to six!" In a tone of fine bitter carelessness she continued: "Eh, he'll not come now till they bring him. There he'll stick! But he needn't come rolling in here in his pit-dirt, for *I* won't wash him. He can lie on the floor ____Eh, what a fool I've been, what a fool! And this is what I came here for, to this dirty hole, rats and all, for him to slink past his very door. Twice last week—he's begun now____"

She silenced herself, and rose to clear the table.

While for an hour or more the children played, subduedly intent, fertile of imagination, united in fear of the mother's wrath, and in dread of their father's home-coming. Mrs. Bates sat in her rocking-chair making a "singlet" of thick cream-coloured flannel, which gave a dull wounded sound as she tore off the grey edge. She worked at her sewing with energy, listening to the children, and her anger wearied itself, lay down to rest, opening its eyes from time to time and steadily watching, its ears raised to listen. Sometimes even her anger quailed and shrank, and the mother suspended her sewing, tracing the footsteps that thudded along the sleepers outside; she would lift her head sharply to bid the children "hush," but she recovered herself in time, and the footsteps went past the gate, and the children were not flung out of their play-world.

But at last Annie sighed, and gave in. She glanced at her wagon of slippers, and loathed the game. She turned plaintively to her mother.

"Mother!"—but she was inarticulate.

John crept out like a frog from under the sofa. His mother glanced up.

"Yes," she said, "just look at those shirt-sleeves!"

The boy held them out to survey them, saying nothing. Then somebody called in a hoarse voice away down the line, and suspense bristled in the room, till two people had gone by outside, talking.

"It is time for bed," said the mother.

"My father hasn't come," wailed Annie plaintively. But her mother was primed with courage.

"Never mind. They'll bring him when he does come—like a log." She meant there would be no scene. "And he may sleep on the floor till he wakes himself. I know he'll not go to work to-morrow after this!"

The children had their hands and faces wiped with a flannel. They were very quiet. When they had put on their night-dresses, they said their prayers, the boy mumbling. The mother looked down at them, at the brown silken bush of intertwining curls in the nape of the girl's neck, at the little black head of the lad, and her heart burst with anger at their father, who caused all three such distress. The children hid their faces in her skirts for comfort.

When Mrs. Bates came down, the room was strangely empty, with a tension of expectancy. She took up her sewing and stitched for some time without raising her head. Meantime her anger was tinged with fear.

II

The clock struck eight and she rose suddenly, dropping her sewing on her chair. She went to the stair-foot door, opened it, listening. Then she went out, locking the door behind her.

Something scuffled in the yard, and she started, though she knew it was only the rats with which the place was over-run. The night was very dark. In the great bay of railway lines, bulked with trucks, there was no trace of light, only away back she could see a few yellow lamps at the pit-top, and the red smear of the burning pit-bank on the night. She hurried along the edge of the track, then, crossing the converging lines, came to the stile by the white gates, whence she emerged on the road. Then the fear which had led her shrank. People were walking up to New Brinsley; she saw the lights in the houses; twenty yards farther on were the broad windows of the "Prince of Wales," very warm and bright, and the loud voices of men could be heard distinctly. What a fool she had been to imagine that anything had happened to him! He was merely drinking over there at the "Prince of Wales." She faltered. She had never yet been to fetch him, and she never would go. So she continued her walk towards the long straggling line of houses, standing back on the highway. She entered a passage between the dwellings.

"Mr. Rigley?—Yes! Did you want him? No, he's not in at this minute."

The raw-boned woman leaned forward from her dark scullery and peered at the other, upon whom fell a dim light through the blind of the kitchen window.

"Is it Mrs. Bates?" she asked in a tone tinged with respect.

"Yes. I wondered if your Master was at home. Mine hasn't come yet."

"Asn't 'e! Oh, Jack's been 'ome an' 'ad 'is dinner an' gone out. 'E's just gone for 'alf an hour afore bed-time. Did you call at the 'Prince of Wales'?"

"No ——"

"No, you didn't like ——! It's not very nice." The other woman was indulgent. There was an awkward pause. "Jack never said nothink about—about your Master," she said.

"No!—I expect he's stuck in there!"

Elizabeth Bates said this bitterly, and with recklessness. She knew that the woman across the yard was standing at her door listening, but she did not care. As she turned:

"Stop a minute! I'll just go an' ask Jack if 'e knows anythink," said Mrs. Rigley.

"Oh no—I wouldn't like to put ——!"

"Yes, I will, if you'll just step inside an' see as th' childer doesn't come downstairs and set theirselves afire."

Elizabeth Bates, murmuring a remonstrance, stepped inside. The other woman apologised for the state of the room.

The kitchen needed apology. There were little frocks and trousers and childish undergarments on the squab and on the floor, and a litter of playthings everywhere. On the black American cloth of the table were pieces of bread and cake, crusts, slops, and a teapot with cold tea.

"Eh, ours is just as bad," said Elizabeth Bates, looking at the woman, not at the house. Mrs. Rigley put a shawl over her head and hurried out, saying:

"I shanna be a minute."

The other sat, noting with faint disapproval the general untidiness of the room. Then she fell to counting the shoes of various sizes scattered over the floor. There were twelve. She sighed and said to herself: "No wonder!"—glancing at the litter. There came the scratching of two pairs of feet on the yard, and the Rigleys entered. Elizabeth Bates rose. Rigley was a big man, with very large bones. His head looked particularly bony. Across his temple was a blue scar, caused by a wound got in the pit, a wound in which the coal-dust remained blue like tattooing.

"'Asna 'e come whoam yit?" asked the man, without any form of greeting, but with deference and sympathy. "I couldna say wheer he is—'e's non ower theer!"—he jerked his head to signify the "Prince of Wales."

"'E's 'appen gone up to th' 'Yew'," said Mrs. Rigley.

There was another pause. Rigley had evidently something to get off his mind:

"Ah left 'im finishin' a stint," he began. "Loose-all 'ad bin gone about ten minutes when we com'n away, an' I shouted: 'Are ter comin', Walt?' an' 'e said: 'Go on, Ah shanna be but a'ef a minnit,' so we com'n ter th' bottom, me an' Bowers, thinkin' as 'e wor just behint, an' 'ud come up i' th' next bantle ____"

He stood perplexed, as if answering a charge of deserting his mate. Elizabeth Bates, now again certain of disaster, hastened to reassure him:

"I expect 'e's gone up to th' 'Yew Tree', as you say. It's not the first time. I've fretted myself into a fever before now. He'll come home when they carry him."

"Ay, isn't it too bad!" deplored the other woman.

"I'll just step up to Dick's an' see if 'e *is* theer," offered the man, afraid of appearing alarmed, afraid of taking liberties.

"Oh, I wouldn't think of bothering you that far," said Elizabeth Bates, with emphasis, but he knew she was glad of his offer.

As they stumbled up the entry, Elizabeth Bates heard Rigley's wife run across the yard and open her neighbour's door. At this, suddenly all the blood in her body seemed to switch away from her heart.

"Mind!" warned Rigley. "Ah've said many a time as Ah'd fill up them ruts in this entry, sumb'dy 'll be breakin' their legs yit."

She recovered herself and walked quickly along with the miner.

"I don't like leaving the children in bed, and nobody in the house," she said.

"No, you dunna!" he replied courteously. They were soon at the gate of the cottage.

"Well, I shanna be many minnits. Dunna you be frettin' now, 'e'll be all right," said the butty.

"Thank you very much, Mr. Rigley," she replied.

"You're welcome!" he stammered, moving away. "I shanna be many minnits."

The house was quiet. Elizabeth Bates took off her hat and shawl, and rolled back the rug. When she had finished, she sat down. It was a few minutes past nine. She was startled by the rapid chuff of the winding-engine at the pit, and the sharp whirr of the brakes on the rope as it descended. Again she felt the painful sweep of her blood, and she put her hand to her side, saying aloud: "Good gracious!—it's only the nine o'clock deputy going down," rebuking herself.

She sat still, listening. Half an hour of this, and she was wearied out.

"What am I working myself up like this for?" she said pitiably to herself, "I s'll only be doing myself some damage."

She took out her sewing again.

At a quarter to ten there were footsteps. One person! She watched for the door to open. It was an elderly woman, in a black bonnet and a black woollen shawl—his mother. She was about sixty years old, pale, with blue eyes, and her face all wrinkled and lamentable. She shut the door and turned to her daughter-in-law peevishly.

"Eh, Lizzie, whatever shall we do, whatever shall we do!" she cried.

Elizabeth drew back a little, sharply.

"What is it, mother?" she said.

The elder woman seated herself on the sofa.

"I don't know, child, I can't tell you!"—she shook her head slowly. Elizabeth sat watching her, anxious and vexed.

"I don't know," replied the grandmother, sighing very deeply. "There's no end to my troubles, there isn't. The things I've gone through, I'm sure it's enough ——!" She wept without wiping her eyes, the tears running.

"But mother," interrupted Elizabeth, "what do you mean? What is it?"

The grandmother slowly wiped her eyes. The fountains of her tears were stopped by Elizabeth's directness. She wiped her eyes slowly.

"Poor child! Eh, you poor thing!" she moaned. "I don't know what we're going to do, I don't—and you as you are—it's a thing, it is indeed!"

Elizabeth waited.

"Is he dead?" she asked, and at the words her heart swung violently, though she felt a slight flush of shame at the ultimate extravagance of the question. Her words sufficiently frightened the old lady, almost brought her to herself.

"Don't say so, Elizabeth! We'll hope it's not as bad as that; no, may the

Lord spare us that, Elizabeth. Jack Rigley came just as I was sittin' down to a glass afore going to bed, an' 'e said: ''Appen you'll go down th' line, Mrs. Bates. Walt's had an accident. 'Appen you'll go an' sit wi' 'er till we can get him home.' I hadn't time to ask him a word afore he was gone. An' I put my bonnet on an' come straight down, Lizzie. I thought to myself: 'Eh, that poor blessed child, if anybody should come an' tell her of a sudden, there's no knowin' what'll 'appen to 'er.' You mustn't let it upset you, Lizzie—or you know what to expect. How long is it, six months—or is it five, Lizzie? Ay!"—the old woman shook her head—"time slips on, it slips on! Ay!"

Elizabeth's thoughts were busy elsewhere. If he was killed—would she be able to manage on the little pension and what she could earn?—she counted up rapidly. If he was hurt—they wouldn't take him to the hospital—how tiresome he would be to nurse!—but perhaps she'd be able to get him away from the drink and his hateful ways. She would—while he was ill. The tears offered to come to her eyes at the picture. But what sentimental luxury was this she was beginning? She turned to consider the children. At any rate she was absolutely necessary for them. They were her business.

"Ay!" repeated the old woman, "it seems but a week or two since he brought me his first wages. Ay—he was a good lad, Elizabeth, he was, in his way. I don't know why he got to be such a trouble, I don't. He was a happy lad at home, only full of spirits. But there's no mistake he's been a handful of trouble, he has! I hope the Lord'll spare him to mend his ways. I hope so, I hope so. You've had a sight o' trouble with him, Elizabeth, you have indeed. But he was a jolly enough lad wi' me, he was, I can assure you. I don't know how it is. . . ."

The old woman continued to muse aloud, a monotonous irritating sound, while Elizabeth thought concentratedly, startled once, when she heard the winding-engine chuff quickly, and the brakes skirr with a shriek. Then she heard the engine more slowly, and the brakes made no sound. The old woman did not notice. Elizabeth waited in suspense. The mother-in-law talked, with lapses into silence.

"But he wasn't your son, Lizzie, an' it makes a difference. Whatever he was, I remember him when he was little, an' I learned to understand him and to make allowances. You've got to make allowances for them ——"

It was half-past ten, and the old woman was saying: "But it's trouble from beginning to end; you're never too old for trouble, never too old for that ——" when the gate banged back, and there were heavy feet on the steps.

"I'll go, Lizzie, let me go," cried the old woman, rising. But Elizabeth was at the door. It was a man in pit-clothes.

"They're bringin' 'im, Missis," he said. Elizabeth's heart halted a moment. Then it surged on again, almost suffocating her.

"Is he—is it bad?" she asked.

The man turned away, looking at the darkness:

"The doctor says 'e'd been dead hours. 'E saw 'im i' th' lamp-cabin."

The old woman, who stood just behind Elizabeth, dropped into a chair, and folded her hands, crying: "Oh, my boy, my boy!"

"Hush!" said Elizabeth, with a sharp twitch of a frown. "Be still, mother, don't waken th' children: I wouldn't have them down for anything!"

The old woman moaned softly, rocking herself. The man was drawing away. Elizabeth took a step forward.

"How was it?" she asked.

"Well, I couldn't say for sure," the man replied, very ill at ease. "'E wor finishin' a stint an' th' butties 'ad gone, an' a lot o' stuff come down atop 'n 'im."

"And crushed him?" cried the widow, with a shudder.

"No," said the man, "it fell at th' back of 'im. 'E wor under th' face, an' it niver touched 'im. It shut 'im in. It seems 'e wor smothered."

Elizabeth shrank back. She heard the old woman behind her cry:

"What—what did 'e say it was?"

The man replied, more loudly: "'E wor smothered!"

Then the old woman wailed aloud, and this relieved Elizabeth.

"Oh, mother," she said, putting her hand on the old woman, "don't waken th' children, don't waken th' children."

She wept a little, unknowing, while the old mother rocked herself and moaned. Elizabeth remembered that they were bringing him home, and she must be ready. "They'll lay him in the parlour," she said to herself, standing a moment pale and perplexed.

Then she lighted a candle and went into the tiny room. The air was cold and damp, but she could not make a fire, there was no fireplace. She set down the candle and looked round. The candlelight glittered on the lustre-glasses, on the two vases that held some of the pink chrysanthemums, and on the dark mahogany. There was a cold, deathly smell of chrysanthemums in the room. Elizabeth stood looking at the flowers. She turned away, and calculated whether there would be room to lay him on the floor, between the couch and the chiffonier. She pushed the chairs aside. There would be room to lay him down and to step round him. Then she fetched the old red tablecloth, and another old cloth, spreading them down to save her bit of carpet. She shivered on leaving the parlour; so, from the dresser drawer she took a clean shirt and put it at the fire to air. All the time her mother-in-law was rocking herself in the chair and moaning.

"You'll have to move from there, mother," said Elizabeth. "They'll be bringing him in. Come in the rocker."

The old mother rose mechanically, and seated herself by the fire, continuing to lament. Elizabeth went into the pantry for another candle, and there, in the little pent-house under the naked tiles, she heard them coming. She stood still in the pantry doorway, listening. She heard them pass the end of the house, and come awkwardly down the three steps, a jumble of shuffling footsteps and muttering voices. The old woman was silent. The men were in the yard.

Then Elizabeth heard Matthews, the manager of the pit, say: "You go in first, Jim. Mind!"

The door came open, and the two women saw a collier backing into the room, holding one end of a stretcher, on which they could see the nailed pit-boots of the dead man. The two carriers halted, the man at the head stooping to the lintel of the door.

"Wheer will you have him?" asked the manager, a short, white-bearded man.

Elizabeth roused herself and came from the pantry carrying the unlighted candle.

"In the parlour," she said.

"In there, Jim!" pointed the manager, and the carriers backed round into the tiny room. The coat with which they had covered the body fell off as they awkwardly turned through the two doorways, and the women saw their man, naked to the waist, lying stripped for work. The old woman began to moan in a low voice of horror.

"Lay th' stretcher at th' side," snapped the manager, "an' put 'im on th' cloths. Mind now, mind! Look you now ____!"

One of the men had knocked off a vase of chrysanthemums. He stared awkwardly, then they set down the stretcher. Elizabeth did not look at her husband. As soon as she could get in the room, she went and picked up the broken vase and the flowers.

"Wait a minute!" she said.

The three men waited in silence while she mopped up the water with a a duster.

"Eh, what a job, what a job, to be sure!" the manager was saying, rubbing his brow with trouble and perplexity. "Never knew such a thing in my life, never! He'd no busines to ha' been left. I never knew such a thing in my life! Fell over him clean as a whistle, an' shut him in. Not four foot of space, there wasn't—yet it scarce bruised him."

He looked down at the dead man, lying prone, half naked, all grimed with coal-dust.

"'Sphyxiated', the doctor said. It *is* the most terrible job I've ever known. Seems as if it was done o' purpose. Clean over him, an' shut 'im in, like a mouse-trap"—he made a sharp, descending gesture with his hand.

The colliers standing by jerked aside their heads in hopeless comment.

The horror of the thing bristled upon them all.

Then they heard the girl's voice upstairs calling shrilly: "Mother, mother—who is it? Mother, who is it?"

Elizabeth hurried to the foot of the stairs and opened the door:

"Go to sleep!" she commanded sharply. "What are you shouting about? Go to sleep at once—there's nothing ____"

Then she began to mount the stairs. They could hear her on the boards, and on the plaster floor of the little bedroom. They could hear her distinctly:

"What's the matter now?—what's the matter with you, silly thing?" —her voice was much agitated, with an unreal gentleness.

"I thought it was some men come," said the plaintive voice of the child. "Has he come?"

"Yes, they've brought him. There's nothing to make a fuss about. Go to sleep now, like a good child."

They could hear her voice in the bedroom, they waited whilst she covered the children under the bedclothes.

"Is he drunk?" asked the girl, timidly, faintly.

"No! No—he's not! He's—he's asleep."

"Is he asleep downstairs?"

"Yes—and don't make a noise."

There was silence for a moment, then the men heard the frightened child again:

"What's that noise?"

"It's nothing, I tell you, what are you bothering for?"

The noise was the grandmother moaning. She was oblivious of everything, sitting on her chair rocking and moaning. The manager put his hand on her arm and bade her "Sh—sh!!"

The old woman opened her eyes and looked at him. She was shocked by this interruption, and seemed to wonder.

"What time is it?" the plaintive thin voice of the child, sinking back unhappily into sleep, asked this last question.

"Ten o'clock," answered the mother more softly. Then she must have bent down and kissed the children.

Matthews beckoned to the men to come away. They put on their caps and took up the stretcher. Stepping over the body, they tiptoed out of the house. None of them spoke till they were far from the wakeful children.

When Elizabeth came down she found her mother alone on the parlour floor, leaning over the dead man, the tears dropping on him.

"We must lay him out," the wife said. She put on the kettle, then returning knelt at the feet, and began to unfasten the knotted leather laces. The room was clammy and dim with only one candle, so that she had to bend her face almost to the floor. At last she got off the heavy boots and put them away.

"You must help me now," she whispered to the old woman. Together they stripped the man.

When they arose, saw him lying in the naïve dignity of death, the woman stood arrested in fear and respect. For a few moments they remained still, looking down, the old mother whimpering. Elizabeth felt countermanded. She saw him, how utterly inviolable he lay in himself. She had nothing to do with him. She could not accept it. Stooping, she laid her hand on him, in claim. He was still warm, for the mine was hot where he had died. His mother had his face between her hands, and was murmuring incoherently. The old tears fell in succession as drops from wet leaves; the mother was not weeping, merely her tears flowed. Elizabeth embraced the body of her husband, with cheek and lips. She seemed to be listening, inquiring, trying to get some connection. But she could not. She was driven away. He was impregnable.

She rose, went into the kitchen, where she poured warm water into a bowl, brought soap and flannel and a soft towel.

"I must wash him," she said.

Then the old mother rose stiffly, and watched Elizabeth as she carefully washed his face, carefully brushing the big blond moustache from his mouth with the flannel. She was afraid with a bottomless fear, so she ministered to him. The old woman, jealous, said:

"Let me wipe him!"—and she kneeled on the other side drying slowly as Elizabeth washed, her big black bonnet sometimes brushing the dark head of her daughter-in-law. They worked thus in silence for a long time. They never forgot it was death, and the touch of the man's dead body gave them strange emotions, different in each of the women; a great dread possessed them both, the mother felt the lie was given to her womb, she was denied; the wife felt the utter isolation of the human soul, the child within her was a weight apart from her.

At last it was finished. He was a man of handsome body, and his face showed no traces of drink. He was blond, full-fleshed, with fine limbs. But he was dead.

"Bless him," whispered his mother, looking always at his face, and speaking out of sheer terror. "Dear lad—bless him!" She spoke in a faint, sibilant ecstasy of fear and mother love.

Elizabeth sank down again to the floor, and put her face against his neck, and trembled and shuddered. But she had to draw away again. He was dead, and her living flesh had no place against his. A great dread and weariness held her: she was so unavailing. Her life was gone like this.

"White as milk he is, clear as a twelve-month baby, bless him, the darling!" the old mother murmured to herself. "Not a mark on him, clear and clean and white, beautiful as ever a child was made," she murmured with pride. Elizabeth kept her face hidden.

"He went peaceful, Lizzie—peaceful as sleep. Isn't he beautiful, the lamb? Ay—he must ha' made his peace, Lizzie. 'Appen he made it all right, Lizzie, shut in there. He'd have time. He wouldn't look like this if he hadn't made his peace. The lamb, the dear lamb. Eh, but he had a hearty laugh. I loved to hear it. He had the heartiest laugh, Lizzie, as a lad ——"

Elizabeth looked up. The man's mouth was fallen back, slightly open under the cover of the moustache. The eyes, half shut, did not show glazed in the obscurity. Life with its smoky burning gone from him, had left him apart and utterly alien to her. And she knew what a stranger he was to her. In her womb was ice of fear, because of this separate stranger with whom she had been living as one flesh. Was this what it all meant—utter, intact separateness, obscured by heat of living? In dread she turned her face away. The fact was too deadly. There had been nothing between them, and yet they had come together, exchanging their nakedness repeatedly. Each time he had taken her, they had been two isolated beings, far apart as now. He was no more responsible than she. That child was like ice in her womb. For as she looked at the dead man, her mind, cold and detached, said clearly: "Who am I? What have I been doing? I have been fighting a husband who did not exist. *He* existed all the time. What wrong have I done? What was that I have been living with? There lies the reality, this man." And her soul died in her for fear: she knew she had never seen him, he had never seen her, they had met in the dark and had fought in the dark, not knowing whom they met nor whom they fought. And now she saw, and turned silent in seeing. For she had been wrong. She had said he was something he was not; she had felt familiar with him. Whereas he was apart all the while, living as she never lived, feeling as she never felt.

In fear and shame she looked at his naked body, that she had known falsely. And he was the father of her children. Her soul was torn from her body and stood apart. She looked at his naked body and was ashamed, as if she had denied it. After all, it was itself. It seemed awful to her. She looked at his face, and she turned her own face to the wall. For his look was other than hers, his way was not her way. She had denied him what he was—she saw it now. She had refused him as himself. And this had been her life, and his life. She was grateful to death, which restored the truth. And she knew she was not dead.

And all the while her heart was bursting with grief and pity for him. What had he suffered? What stretch of horror for this helpless man! She was rigid with agony. She had not been able to help him. He had been cruelly injured, this naked man, this other being, and she could make no reparation. There were the children—but the children belonged to life. This dead man had nothing to do with them. He and she were the only channels through which life had flowed to issue in the children. She was a mother—but how awful she knew it now to have been a wife. And he, dead now, how awful he must have felt it to be a husband. She felt that in the next world he would be a stranger to her. If they met there, in the beyond, they would only be ashamed of what had been before. The children had come, for some mysterious reason, out of both of them. But the children did not unite them. Now he was dead, she knew how eternally he was apart from her, how eternally he had nothing more to do with her. She saw this episode of her life closed. They had denied each other in life. Now he had withdrawn. An anguish came over her. It was finished then: it had become hopeless between them long before he died. Yet he had been her husband. But how little!

"Have you got his shirt, 'Lizabeth?"

Elizabeth turned without answering, though she strove to weep and behave as her mother-in-law expected. But she could not, she was silenced. She went into the kitchen and returned with the garment.

"It is aired," she said, grasping the cotton shirt here and there to try. She was almost ashamed to handle him; what right had she or anyone to lay hands on him; but her touch was humble on his body. It was hard work to clothe him. He was so heavy and inert. A terrible dread gripped her all the while: that he could be so heavy and utterly inert, unresponsive, apart. The horror of the distance between them was almost too much for her—it was so infinite a gap she must look across.

At last it was finished. They covered him with a sheet and left him lying, with his face bound. And she fastened the door of the little parlour, lest the children should see what was lying there. Then, with peace sunk heavy on her heart, she went about making tidy the kitchen. She knew she submitted to life, which was her immediate master. But from death, her ultimate master, she winced with fear and shame.

Franz Kafka

(1883 - 1924)

When he died of consumption in 1924 Franz Kafka was merely an undiscovered experimenter with fiction who had worked as a civil servant in a prosaic insurance office for the Austrian government. Today he is acknowledged as a European artist of unusual originality who belongs in the first rank of modern writers. Born into a comfortable Jewish middle-class family in what is now Czechoslovakia, Kafka studied law at a German university in Prague. (He wrote his stories in German, often about the impersonal, inexorable nature of the law.) During the day he worked as a bureaucrat, or something very much like one, and in the evening this unhappy bachelor created fictions about the boredom, frustration, and isolation in his own life and in the modern world. Kafka's originality, which obviously was bound up with his own psychological problems, lay in his ability to express cogently, by means of allegory and symbolism, modern man's sense of alienation and bewilderment before it became fashionable to do so. He anticipated the European writers of the 1940's and 1950's; and, not surprisingly, he has been associated with existential philosophy. The central figure in Kafka's fiction is a victim, that omnipresent character in modern literature. Kafka's protagonist is estranged or cut off from his peculiar world, or in contemporary parlance, he is alienated. Manipulated by pitiless and incomprehensible forces, this "little" man feels impotent and inadequate; here Kafka anticipated the feelings of millions of dazed souls in today's world. Because he is cut off from his society without really knowing why, the protagonist feels a vague but persistent guilt, and often he attempts to find salvation by social acceptance. Kafka's fiction has often been compared to a nightmare, and there is a decided dream-like quality about his narratives. With impressive artistic skill, he renders fantasy real, presenting the bizarre (for example, man turned into an insect) as wholly understandable, even natural. And although his novels and stories are difficult and rich in subtle meanings, his style is lucid, without many metaphors.

The Metamorphosis

I

As Gregor Samsa awoke one morning from uneasy dreams he found himself transformed in his bed into a gigantic insect. He was lying on his hard, as it were armor-plated, back and when he lifted his head a little he could see his dome-like brown belly divided into stiff arched segments on top of which the bed quilt could hardly keep in position and was about to slide off completely. His numerous legs, which were pitifully thin compared to the rest of his bulk, waved helplessly before his eyes.

What has happened to me? he thought. It was no dream. His room, a regular human bedroom, only rather too small, lay quiet between the four familiar walls. Above the table on which a collection of cloth samples was unpacked and spread out—Samsa was a commercial traveler—hung the picture which he had recently cut out of an illustrated magazine and put into a pretty gilt frame. It showed a lady, with a fur cap on and a fur stole, sitting upright and holding out to the spectator a huge fur muff into which the whole of her forearm had vanished!

Gregor's eyes turned next to the window, and the overcast sky—one could hear rain drops beating on the window gutter—made him quite melancholy. What about sleeping a little longer and forgetting all this nonsense, he thought, but it could not be done, for he was accustomed to sleep on his right side and in his present condition he could not turn himself over. However violently he forced himself towards his right side he always rolled on to his back again. He tried it at least a hundred times, shutting his eyes to keep from seeing his struggling legs, and only desisted when he began to feel in his side a faint dull ache he had never experienced before.

Oh God, he thought, what an exhausting job I've picked on! Traveling about day in, day out. It's much more irritating work than doing the actual business in the office, and on top of that there's the trouble of constant traveling, of worrying about train connections, the bed and irregular meals, casual acquaintances that are always new and never become intimate friends. The devil take it all! He felt a slight itching up on his belly; slowly pushed himself on his back nearer to the top of the bed so that he could lift his head more easily; identified the itching place which was surrounded by many small white spots the nature of which he could not understand and made to touch it with a leg, but drew the leg back immediately, for the contact made a cold shiver run through him.

He slid down again into his former position. This getting up early, he thought, makes one quite stupid. A man needs his sleep. Other commercials live like harem women. For instance, when I come back to the hotel of a morning to write up the orders I've got, these others are only sitting down to breakfast. Let me just try that with my chief; I'd be sacked on the spot. Anyhow, that might be quite a good thing for me, who can tell? If I didn't have to hold my hand because of my parents I'd have given notice long ago, I'd have gone to the chief and told him exactly what I think of him. That would knock him endways from his desk! It's a queer way of doing, too, this sitting on high at a desk and talking down to employees, especially when they have to come quite near because the chief is hard of hearing. Well, there's still hope; once I've saved enough money to pay back my parents' debts to him—that should take another five or six years—I'll do it without fail. I'll cut myself completely loose then. For the moment, though, I'd better get up, since my train goes at five.

He looked at the alarm clock ticking on the chest. Heavenly Father! he thought. It was half-past six o'clock and the hands were quietly moving on, it was even past the half-hour, it was getting on toward a quarter to seven. Had the alarm clock not gone off? From the bed one could see that it had been properly set for four o'clock; of course it must have gone off. Yes, but was it possible to sleep quietly through that ear-splitting noise? Well, he had not slept quietly, yet apparently all the more soundly for that. But what was he to do now? The next train went at seven o'clock; to catch that he would need to hurry like mad and his samples weren't even packed up, and he himself wasn't feeling particularly fresh and active. And even if he did catch the train he wouldn't avoid a row with the chief, since the firm's porter would have been waiting for the five o'clock train and would have long since reported his failure to turn up. The porter was a creature of the chief's, spineless and stupid. Well, supposing he were to say he was sick? But that would be most unpleasant and would look suspicious, since during his five years' employment he had not been ill once. The chief himself would be sure to come with the sick-insurance doctor, would reproach his parents with their son's laziness and would cut all excuses short by referring to the insurance doctor, who of course regarded all mankind as perfectly healthy malingerers. And would he be so far wrong on this occasion? Gregor really felt quite well, apart from a drowsiness that was utterly superfluous after such a long sleep, and he was even unusually hungry.

As all this was running through his mind at top speed without his being able to decide to leave his bed—the alarm clock had just struck a quarter to seven—there came a cautious tap at the door behind the head of his bed. "Gregor," said a voice—it was his mother's—"it's a quarter to seven. Hadn't you a train to catch?" That gentle voice! Gregor had a shock as he heard his own voice answering hers, unmistakably his own voice, it was true, but with a persistent horrible twittering squeak behind it like an undertone, and left the words in their clear shape only for the first moment and then rose up reverberating round them to destroy their sense, so that one could not be sure one had heard them rightly. Gregor wanted to answer at length and explain everything, but in the circumstances he confined himself to saying: "Yes, yes, thank you, Mother, I'm getting up now." The wooden door between them must have kept the change in his voice from being noticeable outside, for his mother contented herself with this statement and shuffled away. Yet this brief exchange of words had made the other members of the family aware that Gregor was still in the house, as they had not expected, and at one of the side doors his father was already knocking, gently, yet with his fist, "Gregor, Gregor," he called, "what's the matter with you?" And after a little while he called again in a deeper voice: "Gregor! Gregor!" At the other side door his sister was saying in a low, plaintive tone: "Gregor? Aren't you well? Are you needing anything?" He answered them both at once: "I'm just ready," and did his best to make his voice sound as normal as possible by enunciating the words very clearly and leaving long pauses between them. So his father went back to his breakfast, but his sister whispered: "Gregor, open the door, do." However, he was not thinking of opening the door, and felt thankful for the prudent habit he had acquired in traveling of locking all doors during the night, even at home.

His immediate intention was to get up quietly without being disturbed, to put on his clothes and above all eat his breakfast, and only then to consider what else was to be done, since in bed, he was well aware, his meditations would come to no sensible conclusion. He remembered that often enough in bed he had felt small aches and pains, probably caused by awkward postures, which had proved purely imaginary once he got up, and he looked forward eagerly to seeing this morning's delusions gradually fall away. That the change in his voice was nothing but the precursor of a severe chill, a standing ailment of commercial travelers, he had not the least possible doubt.

To get rid of the quilt was quite easy; he had only to inflate himself a little and it fell off by itself. But the next move was difficult, especially because he was so uncommonly broad. He would have needed arms and hands to hoist himself up; instead he had only the numerous little legs which never stopped waving in all directions and which he could not control in the least. When he tried to bend one of them it was the first to stretch itself straight; and did he succeed at last in making it do what he wanted, all the other legs meanwhile waved the more wildly in a high degree of unpleasant agitation. "But what's the use of lying idle in bed," said Gregor to himself.

He thought that he might get out of bed with the lower part of his body first, but this lower part, which he had not yet seen and of which he could form no clear conception, proved too difficult to move; it shifted so slowly; and when finally, almost wild with annoyance, he gathered his forces together and thrust out recklessly, he had miscalculated the direction and bumped heavily against the lower end of the bed, and the stinging pain he felt informed him that precisely this lower part of his body was at the moment probably the most sensitive.

So he tried to get the top part of himself out first, and cautiously moved his head towards the edge of the bed. That proved easy enough, and despite its breadth and mass the bulk of his body at last slowly followed the movement of his head. Still, when he finally got his head free over the edge of the bed he felt too scared to go on advancing, for after all if he let himself fall in this way it would take a miracle to keep his head from being injured. And at all costs he must not lose consciousness now, precisely now; he would rather stay in bed.

But when after a repetition of the same efforts he lay in his former position again, sighing, and watched his little legs struggling against each other more wildly than ever, if that were possible, and saw no way of bringing any order into this arbitrary confusion, he told himself again that it was impossible to stay in bed and that the most sensible course was to risk everything for the smallest hope of getting away from it. At the same time he did not forget meanwhile to remind himself that cool reflection, the coolest possible, was much better than desperate resolves. In such moments he focused his eyes as sharply as possible on the window, but unfortunately, the prospect of the morning fog, which muffled even the other side of the narrow street, brought him little encouragement and comfort. "Seven o'clock already," he said to himself when the alarm clock chimed again, "seven o'clock already and still such a thick fog." And for a little while he lay quiet, breathing lightly, as if perhaps expecting such complete repose to restore all things to their real and normal condition.

But then he said to himself: "Before it strikes a quarter past seven I must be quite out of this bed, without fail. Anyhow, by that time someone will have come from the office to ask for me, since it opens before seven." And he set himself to rocking his whole body at once in a regular rhythm, with the idea of swinging it out of the bed. If he tipped himself out in that way he could keep his head from injury by lifting it at an acute angle when he fell. His back seemed to be hard and was not likely to suffer from a fall on the carpet. His biggest worry was the loud crash he would not be able to help making, which would probably cause anxiety, if not terror, behind all the doors. Still, he must take the risk.

When he was already half out of the bed—the new method was more a game than an effort, for he needed only to hitch himself across by rocking to and fro—it struck him how simple it would be if he could get help. Two strong people—he thought of his father and the servant girl—would be amply sufficient; they would only have to thrust their arms under his convex back, lever him out of the bed, bend down with their burden and then be patient enough to let him turn himself right over on to the floor, where it was to be hoped his legs would then find their proper function. Well, ignoring the fact that the doors were all locked, ought he really to call for help? In spite of his misery he could not suppress a smile at the very idea of it.

He had got so far that he could barely keep his equilibrium when he rocked himself strongly, and he would have to nerve himself very soon for the final decision since in five minutes' time it would be a quarter past seven—when the front doorbell rang. "That's someone from the office," he said to himself, and grew almost rigid, while his little legs only jigged about all the faster. For a moment everything stayed quiet. "They're not going to open the door," said Gregor to himself, catching at some kind of irrational hope. But then of course the servant girl went as usual to the door with her heavy tread and opened it. Gregor needed only to hear the first good morning of the visitor to know immediately who it was—the chief clerk himself. What a fate, to be condemned to work for a firm where the smallest omission at once gave rise to the gravest suspicion! Were all employees in a body nothing but scoundrels, was there not among them one single loyal devoted man who, had he wasted only an hour or so of the firm's time in a morning, was so tormented by conscience as to be driven out of his mind and actually incapable of leaving his bed? Wouldn't it really have been sufficient to send an apprentice to inquire—if any inquiry were necessary at all—did the chief clerk himself have to come and thus indicate to the entire family, an innocent family, that this suspicious circumstance could be investigated by no one less versed in affairs than himself? And more through the agitation caused by these reflections than through any act of will Gregor swung himself out of bed with all his strength. There was a loud thump, but it was not really a crash. His fall was broken to some extent by the carpet, his back, too, was less stiff than he thought, and so there was merely a dull thud, not so very startling. Only he had not lifted his head carefully enough and had hit it; he turned it and rubbed it on the carpet in pain and irritation.

"That was something falling down in there," said the chief clerk in the next room to the left. Gregor tried to suppose to himself that something like what had happened to him today might some day happen to the chief clerk; one really could not deny that it was possible. But as if in brusque reply to this supposition the chief clerk took a couple of firm steps in the next-door room and his patent leather boots creaked. From the right-hand room his sister was whispering to inform him of the situation: "Gregor, the chief clerk's here." "I know," muttered Gregor to himself; but he didn't dare to make his voice loud enough for his sister to hear it.

"Gregor," said his father now from the left-hand room, "the chief clerk has come and wants to know why you didn't catch the early train. We don't know what to say to him. Besides, he wants to talk to you in person. So open the door, please. He will be good enough to excuse the untidiness of your room." "Good morning, Mr. Samsa," the chief clerk was calling amiably meanwhile. "He's not well," said his mother to the visitor, while his father was still speaking through the door, "he's not well, sir, believe me. What else would make him miss a train! The boy thinks about nothing but his work. It makes me almost cross the way he never goes out in the evenings; he's been here the last eight days and has stayed at home every single evening. He just sits there quietly at the table reading a newspaper or looking through railway timetables. The only amusement he gets is doing fretwork. For instance, he spent two or three evenings cutting out a little picture frame; you would be surprised to see how pretty it is; it's hanging in his room; you'll see it in a minute when Gregor opens the door. I must say I'm glad you've come, sir; we should never have got him to unlock the door by ourselves; he's so obstinate; and I'm sure he's unwell, though he wouldn't have it to be so this morning." "I'm just coming," said Gregor slowly and carefully, not moving an inch for fear of losing one word of the conversation. "I can't think of any other explanation, madam," said the chief clerk, "I hope it's nothing serious. Although on the other hand I must say that we men of business—fortunately or unfortunately—very often simply have to ignore any slight indisposition, since business must be attended to." "Well, can the chief clerk come in now?" asked Gregor's father impatiently, again knocking on the door. "No," said Gregor. In the left-hand room a painful silence followed this refusal, in the right-hand room his sister began to sob.

Why didn't his sister join the others? She was probably newly out of bed and hadn't even begun to put on her clothes yet. Well, why was she crying? Because he wouldn't get up and let the chief clerk in, because he was in danger of losing his job, and because the chief would begin dunning his parents again for the old debts? Surely these were things one didn't need to worry about for the present. Gregor was still at home and not in the least thinking of deserting the family. At the moment, true, he was lying on the carpet and no one who knew the condition he was in could seriously expect him to admit the chief clerk. But for such a small discourtesy, which could plausibly be explained away somehow later on, Gregor could hardly be dismissed on the spot. And it seemed to Gregor that it would be much more sensible to leave him in peace for the present than to trouble him with tears and entreaties. Still, of course, their uncertainty bewildered them all and excused their behavior.

"Mr. Samsa," the chief clerk called now in a louder voice, "what's the matter with you? Here you are barricading yourself in your room, giving only 'yes' and 'no' for answers, causing your parents a lot of unnecessary trouble and neglecting—I mention this only in passing—neglecting your business duties in an incredible fashion. I am speaking here in the name of your parents and of your chief, and I beg you quite seriously to give me an immediate and precise explanation. You amaze me, you amaze me. I thought you were a quiet, dependable person, and now all at once you seem bent on making a disgraceful exhibition of yourself. The chief did hint to me early this morning a possible explanation for your disappearance—with reference to the cash payments that were entrusted to you recently—but I almost pledged my solemn word of honor that this could not be so. But now that I see how incredibly obstinate you are, I no longer have the slightest desire to take your part at all And your position in the firm is not so unassailable. I came with the intention of telling you all this in private, but since you are wasting my time so needlessly I don't see why your parents shouldn't hear it too. For some time past your work has been most unsatisfactory this is not the season of the year for a business boom, of course, we admit that, but a season of the year for doing no business at all, that does not exist, Mr. Samsa, must not exist."

"But, sir," cried Gregor, beside himself and in his agitation forgetting everything else, "I'm just going to open the door this very minute. A slight illness, an attack of giddiness, has kept me from getting up. I'm still lying in bed. But I feel all right again. I'm getting out of bed now. Just give me a moment or two longer! I'm not quite so well as I thought. But I'm all right, really. How a thing like that can suddenly strike one down! Only last night I was quite well, my parents can tell you, or rather I did have a slight presentiment. I must have showed some sign of it. Why didn't I report it at the office! But one always thinks that an indisposition can be got over without staying in the house. Oh sir, do spare my parents! All that you're reproaching me with now has no foundation; no one has ever said a word to me about it. Perhaps you haven't looked at the last orders I sent in. Anyhow, I can still catch the eight o'clock train, I'm much the better for my few hours' rest. Don't let me detail you here, sir; I'll be attending to business very soon, and do be good enough to tell the chief so and to make my excuses to him!"

And while all this tumbling out pell-mell and Gregor hardly knew what he was saying, he had reached the chest quite easily, perhaps because of the practice he had had in bed, and was now trying to lever himself upright by means of it. He meant actually to open the door, actually to show himself and speak to the chief clerk; he was eager to find out what the others, after all their insistence, would say at the sight of him. If they were horrified then the responsibility was no longer his and he could stay quiet. But if they took it calmly, then he had no reason either to be upset, and could really get to the station for the eight o'clock train if he hurried. At first he slipped down a few times from the polished surface of the chest, but at length with a last heave he stood upright; he paid no more attention to the pains in the lower part of his body, however they smarted. Then he let himself fall against the back of a near-by chair, and clung with his little legs to the edges of it. That brought him into control of himself again and he stopped speaking, for now he could listen to what the chief clerk was saying.

"Did you understand a word of it?" the chief clerk was asking; "surely he can't be trying to make fools of us?" "Oh dear," cried his mother, in tears, "perhaps he's terribly ill and we're tormenting him. Grete! Grete!" she called out then. "Yes Mother?" called his sister from the other side. They were calling to each other across Gregor's room. "You must go this minute for the doctor. Gregor is ill. Go for the doctor, quick. Did you hear how he was speaking?" "That was no human voice," said the chief clerk in a voice noticeably low beside the shrillness of the mother's. "Anna! Anna!" his father was calling through the hall to the kitchen, clapping his hands, "get a locksmith at once!" And the two girls were already running through the hall with a swish of skirts—how could his sister have got dressed so quickly?—and were tearing the front door open. There was no sound of its closing again, they had evidently left it open, as one does in houses where some great misfortune has happened.

But Gregor was now much calmer. The words he uttered were no longer understandable, apparently, although they seemed clear enough to him, even clearer than before, perhaps because his ear had grown accustomed to the sound of them. Yet at any rate people now believed that something was wrong with him, and were ready to help him. The positive certainty with which these first measures had been taken comforted him. He felt himself drawn once more into the human circle and hoped for great and remarkable results from both the doctor and the locksmith, without really distinguishing precisely between them. To make his voice as clear as possible for the decisive conversation that was now imminent he coughed a little, as quietly as he could, of course, since this noise too might not sound like a human cough for all he was able to judge. In the next room meanwhile there was complete silence. Perhaps his parents were sitting at the table with the chief clerk, whispering, perhaps they were all leaning against the door and listening.

Slowly Gregor pushed the chair towards the door, then let go of it, caught hold of the door for support—the soles at the end of his little legs were somewhat sticky—and rested against it for a moment after his efforts. Then he set himself to turning the key in the lock with his mouth. It seemed, unhappily, that he hadn't really any teeth—what could he grip the key with?—but on the other hand his jaws were certainly very strong; with their help he did manage to set the key in motion, heedless of the fact that he was undoubtedly damaging them somewhere, since a brown fluid issued from his mouth, flowed over the key and dripped on the floor. "Just listen to that," said the chief clerk next door; "he's turning the key." That was a great encouragement to Gregor; but they should all have shouted encouragement to him, his father and mother too: "Go on, Gregor," they should have called out, "keep going, hold on to that key!" And in the belief that they were all following his efforts intently, he clenched his jaws recklessly on the key with all the force at his command. As the turning of the key progressed he circled round the lock, holding on now only with his mouth, pushing on the key, as required, or pulling it down again with all the weight of his body. The louder click of the finally yielding lock literally quickened Gregor. With a deep breath of relief he said to himself: "So I didn't need the locksmith," and laid his head on the handle to open the door wide.

Since he had to pull the door towards him, he was still invisible when it was really wide open. He had to edge himself slowly round the near half of the double door, and to do it very carefully if he was not to fall plump upon his back just on the threshold. He was still carrying out this difficult manoeuvre, with no time to observe anything else, when he heard the chief clerk utter a loud "Oh!"—it sounded like a gust of wind—and now he could see the man, standing as he was nearest to the door, clapping one hand before his open mouth and slowly backing away as if driven by some invisible steady pressure. His mother—in spite of the chief clerk's being there her hair was still undone and sticking up in all directions—first clasped her hands and looked at his father, then took two steps toward Gregor and fell on the floor among her outspread skirts, her face quite hidden on her breast. His father knotted his fist with a fierce expression on his face as if he meant to knock Gregor back into his room, then looked uncertainly round the living room, covered his eyes with his hands and wept till his great chest heaved.

Gregor did not go now into the living room, but leaned against the inside of the firmly shut wing of the door, so that only half his body was visible and his head above it bending sideways to look at the others. The light had meanwhile strengthened; on the other side of the street one could see clearly a section of the endlessly long, dark gray building opposite—it was a hospital—abruptly punctuated by its row of regular windows; the rain was still falling, but only in large single discernible and literally singly splashing drops. The breakfast dishes were set out on the table lavishly, for breakfast was the most important meal of the day to Gregor's father, who lingered it out for hours over various newspapers. Right opposite Gregor on the wall hung a photograph of himself in military service, as a lieutenant, hand on sword, a carefree smile on his face, inviting one to respect his uniform and military bearing. The door leading to the hall was open, and one could see that the front door stood open too, showing the landing beyond and the beginning of the stairs going down.

"Well," said Gregor, knowing perfectly that he was the only one who had retained any composure, "I'll put my clothes on at once, pack up my samples and start off. Will you only let me go? You see, sir, I'm not obstinate, and I'm willing to work; traveling is a hard life, but I couldn't live without it. Where are you going, sir? To the office? Yes? Will you give a true account of all this? One can be temporarily incapacitated, but that's just the moment for remembering former services and bearing in mind that later on, when the incapacity has been got over, one will certainly work with all the more industry and concentration. I'm loyally bound to serve the chief, you know that very well. Besides, I have to provide for my parents and my sister. I'm in great difficulties, but I'll get out of them again. Don't make things any worse for me than they are. Stand up for me in the firm. Travelers are not popular there, I know. People think they earn sacks of money and just have a good time. A prejudice there's no particular reason for revising. But you, sir, have a more comprehensive view of affairs than the rest of the staff, yes, let me tell you in confidence, a more comprehensive view than the chief himself, who, being the owner, lets his judgment easily be swayed against one of his employees. And you know very well that the traveler, who is never seen in the office almost the whole year round, can so easily fall a victim to gossip and ill luck and unfounded complaints, which he mostly knows nothing about, except when he comes back exhausted from his rounds, and only then suffers in person from their evil consequences, which he can no longer trace back to the original causes. Sir, sir, don't go away without a word to me to show that you think me in the right at least to some extent!"

But at Gregor's very first words the chief clerk had already backed away and only stared at him with parted lips over one twitching shoulder. And while Gregor was speaking he did not stand still one moment but stole away towards the door, without taking his eyes off Gregor, yet only an inch at a time, as if obeying some secret injunction to leave the room. He was already at the hall, and the suddenness with which he took his last step out of the living room would have made one believe he had burned the sole of his foot. Once in the hall he stretched his right arm before him towards the staircase, as if some supernatural power were waiting there to deliver him.

Gregor perceived that the chief clerk must on no account be allowed to go away in this frame of mind if his position in the firm were not to be endangered to the utmost. His parents did not understand this so well; they had convinced themselves in the course of years that Gregor was settled for life in this firm, and besides they were so preoccupied with their immediate troubles that all foresight had forsaken them. Yet Gregor had this foresight. The chief clerk must be detained, soothed, persuaded and finally won over; the whole future of Gregor and his family depended on it! If only his sister had been there! She was intelligent; she had begun to cry while Gregor was still lying quietly on his back. And no doubt the chief clerk, so partial to ladies, would have been guided by her; she would have shut the door of the flat and in the hall talked him out of his horror. But she was not there, and Gregor would have to handle the situation himself. And without remembering that he was still unaware what powers of movement he possessed, without even remembering that his words in all possibility, indeed in all likelihood, would again be unintelligible, he let go the wing of the door, pushed himself through the opening, started to walk towards the chief clerk, who was already ridiculously clinging with both hands to the railing on the landing; but immediately, as he was feeling for support, he fell down with a little cry upon all his numerous legs. Hardly was he down when he experienced for the first time this morning a sense of physical comfort; his legs had firm ground under them; they were completely obedient, as he noted with joy; they even strove to carry him forward in whatever direction he chose; and he was inclined to believe that a final relief from all his sufferings was at hand. But in the same moment as he found himself on the floor, rocking with suppressed eagerness to move, not far from his mother, indeed just in front of her, she, who had seemed so completely crushed, sprang all at once to her feet, her arms and fingers outspread, cried: "Help, for God's sake, help!" bent her head down as if to see Gregor better, yet on the contrary kept backing senselessly away; had quite forgotten that the laden table stood behind her; sat upon it hastily, as if in absence of mind, when she bumped into it, and seemed altogether unaware that the big coffee pot beside her was upset and pouring coffee in a flood over the carpet.

"Mother, Mother," said Gregor in a low voice, and looked up at her. The chief clerk, for the moment, had quite slipped from his mind; instead, he could not resist snapping his jaws together at the sight of the steaming coffee. That made his mother scream again, she fled from the table and fell into the arms of his father, who hastened to catch her. But Gregor had now no time to spare for his parents; the chief clerk was already on the stairs; with his chin on the banisters he was taking one last backward look. Gregor made a spring, to be as sure as possible of overtaking him; the chief clerk must have divined his intention, for he leaped down several steps and vanished; he was still yelling "Ugh!" and it echoed through the whole staircase.

Unfortunately, the flight of the chief clerk seemed completely to upset Gregor's father, who had remained relatively calm until now, for instead of running after the man himself, or at least not hindering Gregor in his pursuit, he seized in his right hand the walking stick which the chief clerk had left behind on a chair, together with a hat and greatcoat, snatched in his left hand a large newspaper from the table and began stamping his feet and flourishing the stick and the newspaper to drive Gregor back into his room. No entreaty of Gregor's availed, indeed no entreaty was even understood, however humbly he bent his head his father only stamped on the floor the more loudly. Behind his father his mother had torn open a window, despite the cold weather, and was leaning far out of it with her face in her hands. A strong draught set in from the street to the staircase, the window curtains blew in, the newspaper on the table fluttered, stray pages whisked over the floor. Pitilessly Gregor's father drove him back, hissing and crying "Shoo!" like a savage. But Gregor was quite unpracticed in walking backwards, it really was a slow business. If he only had a chance to turn round he could get back to his room at once, but he was afraid of exasperating his father by the slowness of such a rotation and at any moment the stick in his father's hand might hit him a fatal blow on the back or on the head.

In the end, however, nothing else was left for him to do since to his horror he observed that in moving backwards he could not even control the direction he took; so, keeping an anxious eye on his father all the time over his shoulder, he began to turn round as quickly as he could, which was in reality very slowly. Perhaps his father noted his good intentions, for he did not interfere except every now and then to help him in the manoeuvre from a distance with the point of the stick. If only he would have stopped making that unbearable hissing noise! It made Gregor quite lose his head. He had turned almost completely round when the hissing noise so distracted him that he even turned a little the wrong way again. But when at last his head was fortunately right in front of the doorway, it appeared that his body was too broad simply to get through the opening. His father, of course, in his present mood was far from thinking of such a thing as opening the other half of the door, to let Gregor have enough space. He had merely the fixed idea of driving Gregor back into his room as quickly as possible. He would never have suffered Gregor to make the circumstantial preparations for standing up on end and perhaps slipping his way through the door. Maybe he was now making more noise than ever to urge Gregor forward, as if no obstacle impeded him; to Gregor, anyhow, the noise in his rear sounded no longer like the voice of one single father; this was really no joke, and Gregor thrust himself—come what might—into the doorway. One side of his body rose up, he was tilted at an angle in the doorway, his flank was quite bruised, horrid blotches stained the white door, soon he was stuck fast and, left to himself, could not have moved at all, his legs on one side fluttered trembling in the air, those on the other were crushed painfully to the floor—when from behind his father gave a strong push which was literally a deliverance and he flew far into the room, bleeding freely. The door was slammed behind him with the stick, and then at last there was silence.

II

Not until it was twilight did Gregor awake out of a deep sleep, more like a swoon than a sleep. He would certainly have waked up of his own accord not much later, for he felt himself sufficiently rested and well-slept, but it seemed to him as if a fleeting step and a cautious shutting of the door leading into the hall had aroused him. The electric lights in the street cast a pale sheen here and there on the ceiling and the upper surfaces of the furniture, but down below, where he lay, it was dark. Slowly, awkwardly trying out his feelers, which he now first learned to appreciate, he pushed his way to the door to see what had been happening there. His left side felt like one single long, unpleasantly tense scar, and he had actually to limp on his two rows of legs. One little leg, moreover, had been severely damaged in the course of that morning's events—it was almost a miracle that only one had been damaged—and trailed uselessly behind him.

He had reached the door before he discovered what had really drawn him to it: the smell of food. For there stood a basin filled with fresh milk in which floated little sops of white bread. He could almost have laughed with joy, since he was now still hungrier than in the morning, and he dipped his head almost over the eyes straight into the milk. But soon in disappointment he withdrew it again; not only did he find it difficult to feed because of his tender left side—and he could only feed with the palpitating collaboration of his whole body—he did not like the milk either, although milk had been his favorite drink and that was certainly why his sister had set it there for him, indeed it was almost with repulsion that he turned away from the basin and crawled back to the middle of the room.

He could see through the crack of the door that the gas was turned on in the living room, but while usually at this time his father made a habit of reading the afternoon newspaper in a loud voice to his mother and occasionally to his sister as well, not a sound was now to be heard. Well, perhaps his father had recently given up this habit of reading aloud, which his sister had mentioned so often in conversation and in her letters. But there was the same silence all around, although the flat was certainly not empty of occupants. "What a quiet life our family has been leading," said Gregor to himself, and as he sat there motionless staring into the darkness he felt great pride in the fact that he had been able to provide such a life for his parents and sister in such a fine flat. But what if all the quiet, the comfort, the contentment were now to end in horror? To keep himself from being lost in such thoughts Gregor took refuge in movement and crawled up and down the room.

Once during the long evening one of the side doors was opened a little and quickly shut again, later the other side door too; someone had apparently wanted to come in and then thought better of it. Gregor now stationed himself immediately before the living room door, determined to persuade any hesitating visitor to come in or at least to discover who it might be; but the door was not opened again and he waited in vain. In the early morning, when the doors were locked, they had all wanted to come in, now that he had opened one door and the other had apparently been opened during the day, no one came in and even the keys were on the other side of the doors.

It was late at night before the gas went out in the living room, and Gregor could easily tell that his parents and his sister had all stayed awake until then, for he could clearly hear the three of them stealing away on tiptoe. No one was likely to visit him, not until the morning, that was certain; so he had plenty of time to meditate at his leisure on how he was to arrange his life afresh. But the lofty, empty room in which he had to lie flat on the floor filled him with an apprehension he could not account for, since it had been his very own room for the past five years—and with a half-unconscious action, not without a slight feeling of shame, he scuttled under the sofa, where he felt comfortable at once, although his back was a little cramped and he could not lift his head up, and his only regret was that his body was too broad to get the whole of it under the sofa.

He stayed there all night, spending the time partly in a light slumber, from which his hunger kept waking him up with a start, and partly in worrying and sketching vague hopes, which all led to the same conclusion, that he must lie low for the present and, by exercising patience and the utmost consideration, help the family to bear the inconvenience he was bound to cause them in his present condition.

Very early in the morning, it was still almost night, Gregor had the chance to test the strength of his new resolutions, for his sister, nearly fully dressed, opened the door from the hall and peered in. She did not see him at once, yet when she caught sight of him under the sofa—well, he had to be somewhere, he couldn't have flown away, could he?—she was so startled that without being able to help it she slammed the door shut again. But as if regretting her behavior she opened the door again immediately and came in on tiptoe, as if she were visiting an invalid or even a stranger. Gregor had pushed his head forward to the very edge of the sofa and watched her. Would she notice that he had left the milk standing, and not for lack of hunger, and would she bring in some other kind of food more to his taste? If she did not do it of her own accord, he would rather starve than draw her attention to the fact, although he felt a wild impulse to dart out from under the sofa, throw himself at her feet and beg her for something to eat. But his sister at once noticed, with surprise, that the basin was still full, except for a little milk that had been spilt all around it, she lifted it immediately, not with her bare hands, true, but with a cloth and carried it away. Gregor was wildly curious to know what she would bring instead, and made various speculations about it. Yet what she actually did next, in the goodness of her heart, he could never have guessed at. To find out what he liked she brought him a whole selection of food, all set out on an old newspaper. There were old, half-decayed vegetables, bones from last night's supper covered with a white sauce that had thickened; some raisins and almonds; a piece of cheese that Gregor would have called uneatable two days ago; a dry roll of bread, a buttered roll, and a roll both buttered and salted. Besides all that, she set down again the same basin, into which she had poured some water, and which was apparently to be reserved for his exclusive use. And with fine tact, knowing that Gregor would not eat in her presence, she withdrew quickly and even turned the key, to let him understand that he could take his ease as much as he liked. Gregor's legs all whizzed towards the food. His wounds must have healed completely, moreover, for he felt no disability, which amazed him and made him reflect how more than a month ago he had cut one finger a little with a knife and had still suffered pain from the wound only the day before yesterday. Am I less sensitive now? he thought, and sucked greedily at the cheese, which above all the other edibles attracted him at once and strongly. One after another and with tears of satisfaction in his eyes he quickly devoured the cheese, the vegetables and the sauce; the fresh food, on the other hand, had no charms for him, he could not even stand the smell of it and actually dragged away to some little distance the things he could eat. He had long finished his meal and was only lying lazily on the same spot when his sister turned the key slowly as a sign for him to retreat. That roused him at once, although he was nearly asleep, and he hurried under the sofa again. But it took considerable self-control for him to stay under the sofa, even for the short time his sister was in the room, since the large meal had swollen his body somewhat and he was so cramped he could hardly breathe. Slight attacks of breathlessness afflicted him and his eyes were starting a little out of his head as he watched his unsuspecting sister sweeping together with a broom not only the remains of what he had eaten but even the things he had not touched, as if these were now of no use to anyone, and hastily shoveling it all into a bucket, which she covered with a wooden lid and carried away. Hardly had she turned her back when Gregor came from under the sofa and stretched and puffed himself out.

In this manner Gregor was fed, once in the early morning while his parents and the servant girl were still asleep, and a second time after they had all had their midday dinner, for then his parents took a short nap and the servant girl could be sent out on some errand or other by his sister. Not that they would have wanted him to starve, of course, but perhaps they could not have borne to know more about his feeding than from hearsay, perhaps too his sister wanted to spare them such little anxieties wherever possible, since they had quite enough to bear as it was.

Under what pretext the doctor and the locksmith had been got rid of on the first morning Gregor could not discover, for since what he said was not understood by the others it never struck any of them, not even his sister, that he could understand what they said, and so whenever his sister came into his room he had to content himself with hearing her utter only a sigh now and then and an occasional appeal to the saints. Later on, when she had got a little used to the situation—of course she could never get completely used to it—she sometimes threw out a remark which was kindly meant or could be so interpreted. "Well, he liked his dinner today," she would say when Gregor had made a good clearance of his food; and when he had not eaten, which gradually happened more and more often, she would say almost sadly: "Everything's been left standing again."

But although Gregor could get no news directly, he overheard a lot from the neighboring rooms, and as soon as voices were audible, he would run to the door of the room concerned and press his whole body against it. In the first few days especially there was no conversation that did not refer to him somehow, even if only indirectly. For two whole days there were family consultations at every mealtime about what should be done; but also between meals the same subject was discussed, for there were always at least two members of the family at home, since no one wanted to be alone in the flat to leave it quite empty was unthinkable. And on the very first of these days the household cook—it was not quite clear what and how much she knew of the situation—went down on her knees to his mother and begged leave to go, and when she departed, a quarter of an hour later, gave thanks for her dismissal with tears in her eyes as if for the greatest benefit that could have been conferred on her, and without any prompting swore a solemn oath that she would never say a single word to anyone about what had happened.

Now Gregor's sister had to cook too, helping her mother; true, the cooking did not amount to much, for they ate scarcely anything. Gregor was always hearing one of the family vainly urging another to eat and getting no answer but: "Thanks, I've had all I want," or something similar. Perhaps they drank nothing either. Time and again his sister kept asking his father if he wouldn't like some beer and offered kindly to go and fetch it herself, and when he made no answer suggested that she could ask the concierge to fetch it, so that he need feel no sense of obligation, but then a round "No" came from his father and no more was said about it.

In the course of that very first day Gregor's father explained the family's financial position and prospects to both his mother and his sister. Now and then he rose from the table to get some voucher or memorandum out of the small safe he had rescued from the collapse of his business five years earlier. One could hear him opening the complicated lock and rustling papers out and shutting it again. This statement made by his father was the first cheerful information Gregor had heard since his imprisonment. He had been of the opinion that nothing at all was left over from his father's business, at least his father had never said anything to the contrary, and of course he had not asked him directly. At that time Gregor's sole desire was to do his utmost to help the family to forget as soon as possible the catastrophe which had overwhelmed the business and thrown them all into a state of complete despair. And so he had set to work with unusual ardor and almost overnight had become a commercial traveler instead of a little clerk, with of course much greater chances of earning money, and his success was immediately translated into good round coin which he could lay on the table for his amazed and happy family. These had been fine times, and they had never recurred, at least not with the same sense of glory, although later on Gregor had earned so much money that he was able to meet the expenses of the whole household and did so. They had simply got used to it, both the family and Gregor; the money was gratefully accepted and gladly given, but there was no special uprush of warm feeling. With his sister alone had he remained intimate, and it was a secret plan of his that she, who loved music, unlike himself, and could play movingly on the violin, should be sent next year to study at the Conservatorium, despite the great expense that would entail, which must be made up in some other way. During his brief visits home the Conservatorium was often mentioned in the talks he had with his sister, but always merely as a beautiful dream which could never come true, and his parents discouraged even these innocent references to it; yet Gregor had made up his mind firmly about it and meant to announce the fact with due solemnity on Christmas Day.

Such were the thoughts, completely futile in his present condition, that went through his head as he stood clinging upright to the door and listening. Sometimes out of sheer weariness he had to give up listening and let his head fall negligently against the door, but he always had to pull himself together again at once, for even the slight sound his head made was audible next door and brought all conversation to a stop. "What can he be doing now?" his father would say after a while, obviously turning towards the door, and only then would the interrupted conversation gradually be set going again.

Gregor was now informed as amply as he could wish—for his father tended to repeat himself in his explanations, partly because it was a long time since he had handled such matters and partly because his mother could not always grasp things at once—that a certain amount of investments, a very small amount it was true, had survived the wreck of their fortunes and had even increased a little because the dividends had not been touched meanwhile. And besides that, the money Gregor brought home every month—he had kept only a few dollars for himself—had never been quite used up and now amounted to a small capital sum. Behind the door Gregor nodded his head eagerly, rejoiced at this evidence of unexpected thrift and foresight. True, he could really have paid off some more of his father's debts to the chief with this extra money, and so brought much nearer the day on which he could quit his job, but doubtless it was better the way his father had arranged it.

Yet this capital was by no means sufficient to let the family live on the interest of it; for one year, perhaps, or at the most two, they could live on the principal, that was all. It was simply a sum that ought not to be touched and should be kept for a rainy day; money for living expenses would have to be earned. Now his father was still hale enough but an old man, and he had done no work for the past five years and could not be expected to do much; during these five years, the first years of leisure in his laborious though unsuccessful life, he had grown rather fat and become sluggish. And Gregor's old mother, how was she to earn a living with her asthma, which troubled her even when she walked through the flat and kept her lying on a sofa every other day panting for breath beside an open window? And was his sister to earn her bread, she who was still a child of seventeen and whose life hitherto had been so pleasant, consisting as it did in dressing herself nicely, sleeping long, helping in the housekeeping, going out to a few modest entertainments and above all playing the violin? At first whenever the need for earning money was mentioned Gregor let go his hold on the door and threw himself down on the cool leather sofa beside it, he felt so hot with shame and grief.

Often he just lay there the long nights through without sleeping at all, scrabbling for hours on the leather. Or he nerved himself to the great effort of pushing an armchair to the window, then crawled up over the window sill and, braced against the chair, leaned against the window panes, obviously in some recollection of the sense of freedom that looking out of a window always used to give him. For in reality day by day things that were even a little way off were growing dimmer to his sight; the hospital across the street, which he used to execrate for being all too often before his eyes, was now quite beyond his range of vision, and if he had not known that he lived in Charlotte Street, a quiet street but still a city street, he might have believed that his window gave on a desert waste where gray sky and gray land blended indistinguishably into each other. His quick-witted sister only needed to observe twice that the armchair stood at the window; after that whenever she had tidied the room she always pushed the chair back to the same place at the window and even left the inner casements open.

If he could have spoken to her and thanked her for all she had to do for him, he could have borne her ministrations better; as it was, they oppressed him. She certainly tried to make as light as possible of whatever was disagreeable in her task, and as time went on she succeeded, of course, more and more, but time brought more enlightenment to Gregor too. The very way she came in distressed him. Hardly was she in the room when she rushed to the window, without even taking time to shut the door, careful as she was usually to shield the sight of Gregor's room from the others, and as if she were almost suffocating tore the casements open with hasty fingers, standing then in the open draught for a while even in the bitterest cold and drawing deep breaths. The noisy scurry of hers upset Gregor twice a day; he would crouch trembling under the sofa all the time, knowing quite well that she would certainly have spared him such a disturbance had she found it at all possible to stay in his presence without opening the window.

On one occasion, about a month after Gregor's metamorphosis, when there was surely no reason for her to be still startled at his appearance, she came a little earlier than usual and found him gazing out of the window, quite motionless, and thus well placed to look like a bogey. Gregor would not have been surprised had she not come in at all, for she could not immediately open the window while he was there, but not only did she retreat, she jumped back as if in alarm and banged the door shut; a stranger might well have thought that he had been lying in wait for her there meaning to bite her. Of course he hid himself under the sofa at once, but he had to wait until midday before she came again, and she seemed more ill at ease than usual. This made him realize how repulsive the sight of him still was to her, and that it was bound to go on being repulsive, and what an effort it must cost her not to run away even from the sight of the small portion of his body that stuck out from under the sofa. In order to spare her that, therefore, one day he carried a sheet on his back to the sofa—it cost him four hours' labor —and arranged it there in such a way as to hide him completely, so that even if she were to bend down she could not see him. Had she considered the sheet unnecessary, she would certainly have stripped it off the sofa again, for it was clear enough that this curtaining and confining of himself was not likely to conduce to Gregor's comfort, but she left it where it was, and Gregor even fancied that he caught a thankful glance from her eye when he lifted the sheet carefully a very little with his head to see how she was taking the new arrangement.

For the first fortnight his parents could not bring themselves to the point of entering his room, and he often heard them expressing their appreciation of his sister's activities, whereas formerly they had frequently scolded her for being as they thought a somewhat useless daughter. But now, both of them often waited outside the door, his father and his mother, while his sister tidied his room, and as soon as she came out she had to tell them exactly how things were in the room, what Gregor had eaten, how he had conducted himself this time and whether there was not perhaps some slight improvement in his condition. His mother, moreover, began relatively soon to want to visit him, but his father and sister dissuaded her at first with arguments which Gregor listened to very attentively and altogether approved. Later, however, she had to be held back by main force, and when she cried out: "Do let me in to Gregor, he is my unfortunate son! Can't you understand that I must go to him?" Gregor thought that it might be well to have her come in, not every day, of course, but perhaps once a week; she understood things, after all, much better than his sister, who was only a child despite the efforts she was making and had perhaps taken on so difficult a task merely out of childish thoughtlessness.

Gregor's desire to see his mother was soon fulfilled. During the daytime he did not want to show himself at the window, out of consideration for his parents, but he could not crawl very far around the few square yards of floor space he had, nor could he bear lying quietly at rest all during the night, while he was fast losing any interest he had ever taken in food, so that for mere recreation he had formed the habit of crawling crisscross over the walls and ceiling. He especially enjoyed hanging suspended from the ceiling; it was much better than lying on the floor; one could breathe more freely; one's body swung and rocked lightly; and in the almost blissful absorption induced by this suspension it could happen to his own surprise that he let go and fell plump on the floor. Yet he now had his body much better under control than formerly, and even such a big fall did him no harm. His sister at once remarked the new distraction Gregor had found for himself—he left traces behind him of the sticky stuff on his soles wherever he crawled—and she got the idea in her head of giving him as wide a field as possible to crawl in and of removing the pieces of furniture that hindered him, above all the chest of drawers and the writing desk. But that was more than she could manage all by herself; she did not dare ask her father to help her; and as for the servant girl, a young creature of sixteen who had had the courage to stay on after the cook's departure, she could not be asked to help, for she had begged as an especial favor that she might keep the kitchen door locked and open it only on a definite summons; so there was nothing left but to apply to her mother at an hour when her father was out. And the old lady did come, with exclamations of joyful eagerness, which, however, died away at the door of Gregor's room. Gregor's sister, of course, went in first, to see that everything was in order before letting his mother enter. In great haste Gregor pulled the sheet lower and tucked it more in folds so that it really looked as if it had been thrown accidentally over the sofa. And this time he did not peer out from under it; he renounced the pleasure of seeing his mother on this occasion and was only glad that she had come at all. "Come in, he's out of sight," said his sister, obviously leading her mother in by the hand. Gregor could now hear the two women struggling to shift the heavy old chest from its place, and his sister claiming the greater part of the labor for herself, without listening to the admonitions of her mother who feared she might overstrain herself. It took a long time. After at least a quarter of an hour's tugging his mother objected that the chest had better be left where it was, for in the first place it was too heavy and could never be got out before his father came home, and standing in the middle of the room like that would only hamper Gregor's movements, while in the second place it was not at all certain that removing the furniture would be doing a service to Gregor. She was inclined to think to the contrary; the sight of the naked walls made her own heart heavy, and why shouldn't Gregor have the same feeling, considering that he had been used to his furniture for so long and might feel forlorn without it. "And doesn't it look," she concluded in a low voice —in fact she had been almost whispering all the time as if to avoid letting Gregor, whose exact whereabouts she did not know, hear even the tones of her voice, for she was convinced that he could not understand her words— "doesn't it look as if we were showing him, by taking away his furniture, that we have given up hope of his ever getting better and are just leaving him coldly to himself? I think it would be best to keep his room exactly as it has always been, so that when he comes back to us he will find everything unchanged and be able all the more easily to forget what has happened in between."

On hearing these words from his mother Gregor realized that the lack of all direct human speech for the past two months together with the monotony of family life must have confused his mind, otherwise he could not account for the fact that he had quite earnestly looked forward to having his room emptied of furnishing. Did he really want his warm room, so comfortably fitted with old family furniture, to be turned into a naked den in which he would certainly be able to crawl unhampered in all directions but at the price of shedding simultaneously all recollection of his human background? He had indeed been so near the brink of forgetfulness that only the voice of his mother, which he had not heard for so long, had drawn him back from it. Nothing should be taken out of his room; everything must stay as it was; he could not dispense with the good influence of the furniture on his state of mind; and even if the furniture did hamper him in his senseless crawling round and round, that was no drawback but a great advantage.

Unfortunately his sister was of the contrary opinion; she had grown accustomed, and not without reason, to consider herself an expert in Gregor's affairs as against her parents, and so her mother's advice was now enough to make her determined on the removal not only of the chest and the writing desk, which had been her first intention, but of all the furniture except the indispensable sofa. This determination was not, of course, merely the outcome of childish recalcitrance and of the self-confidence she had recently developed so unexpectedly and at such cost; she had in fact perceived that Gregor needed a lot of space to crawl about in, while on the other hand he never used the furniture at all, so far as could be seen. Another factor might have been also the enthusiastic temperament of an adolescent girl, which seeks to indulge itself on every opportunity and which now tempted Grete to exaggerate the horror of her brother's circumstances in order that she might do all the more for him. In a room where Gregor lorded it all alone over empty walls no one save herself was likely ever to set foot.

And so she was not to be moved from her resolve by her mother, who seemed moreover to be ill at ease in Gregor's room and therefore unsure of herself, was soon reduced to silence and helped her daughter as best she could to push the chest outside. Now, Gregor could do without the chest, if need be, but the writing desk he must retain. As soon as the two women had got the chest out of his room, groaning as they pushed it, Gregor stuck his head out from under the sofa to see how he might intervene as kindly and cautiously as possible. But as bad luck would have it, his mother was the first to return, leaving Grete clasping the chest in the room next door where she was trying to shift it all by herself, without of course moving it from the spot. His mother however was not accustomed to the sight of him, it might sicken her and so in alarm Gregor backed quickly to the other end of the sofa, yet could not prevent the sheet from swaying a little in front. That was enough to put her on the alert. She paused, stood still for a moment and then went back to Grete.

Although Gregor kept reassuring himself that nothing out of the way was happening, but only a few bits of furniture were being changed round, he soon had to admit that all this trotting to and fro of the two women, their little ejaculations and the scraping of furniture along the floor affected him like a vast disturbance coming from all sides at once, and however much he tucked in his head and legs and cowered to the very floor he was bound to confess that he would not be able to stand it for long. They were clearing his room out; taking away everything he loved; the chest in which he kept his fret saw and other tools was already dragged off; they were now loosening the writing desk which had almost sunk into the floor, the desk at which he had done all his homework when he was at the commercial academy, at the grammar school before that, and, yes, even at the primary school—he had no more time to waste in weighing the good intentions of the two women, whose existence he had by now almost forgotten, for they were so exhausted that they were laboring in silence and nothing could be heard but the heavy scuffling of their feet.

And so he rushed out—the women were just leaning against the writing desk in the next room to give themselves a breather—and four times changed his direction, since he really did not know what to rescue first, then on the wall opposite, which was already otherwise cleared, he was struck by the picture of the lady muffled in so much fur and quickly crawled up to it and pressed himself to the glass, which was a good surface to hold on to and comforted his hot belly. This picture at least, which was entirely hidden beneath him, was going to be removed by nobody. He turned his head towards the door of the living room so as to observe the women when they came back.

They had not allowed themselves much of a rest and were already coming; Grete had twined her arm round her mother and was almost supporting her. "Well, what shall we take now?" said Grete, looking round. Her eyes met Gregor's from the wall. She kept her composure, presumably because of her mother, bent her head down to her mother, to keep her from looking up, and said, although in a fluttering, unpremeditated voice: "Come, hadn't we better go back to the living room for a moment?" Her intentions were clear enough to Gregor, she wanted to bestow her mother in safety and then chase him down from the wall. Well, just let her try it! He clung to his picture and would not give it up. He would rather fly in Grete's face.

But Grete's words had succeeded in disquieting her mother, who took a step to one side, caught sight of the huge brown mass on the flowered wallpaper, and before she was really conscious that what she saw was Gregor screamed in a loud, hoarse voice: "Oh God, oh God!" fell with outspread arms over the sofa as if giving up and did not move. "Gregor!" cried his sister, shaking her fist and glaring at him. This was the first time she had directly addressed him since his metamorphosis. She ran into the next room for some aromatic essence with which to rouse her mother from her fainting fit. Gregor wanted to help too—there was still time to rescue the picture—but he was stuck fast to the glass and had to tear himself loose; he then ran after his sister into the next room as if he could advise her, as he used to do; but then had to stand helplessly behind her; she meanwhile searched among various small bottles and when she turned round started in alarm at the sight of him; one bottle fell on the floor and broke; a splinter of glass cut Gregor's face and some kind of corrosive medicine splashed him; without pausing a moment longer Grete gathered up all the bottles she could carry and ran to her mother with them; she banged the door shut with her foot. Gregor was now cut off from his mother, who was perhaps nearly dying because of him; he dared not open the door for fear of frightening away his sister, who had to stay with her mother; there was nothing he could do but wait; and harassed by self-reproach and worry he began now to crawl to an fro, over everything, walls, furniture and ceiling, and finally in his despair, when the whole room seemed to be reeling round him, fell down on to the middle of the big table.

A little while elapsed, Gregor was still lying there feebly and all around was quiet, perhaps that was a good omen. Then the doorbell rang. The servant girl was of course locked in her kitchen, and Grete would have to open the door. It was his father. "What's been happening?" were his first words; Grete's face must have told him everything. Grete answered in a muffled voice, apparently hiding her head on his breast: "Mother has been fainting, but she's better now. Gregor's broken loose." "Just what I expected," said his father, "just what I've been telling you, but you women would never listen." It was clear to Gregor that his father had taken the worst interpretation of Grete's all too brief statement and was assuming that Gregor had been guilty of some violent act. Therefore Gregor must now try to propitiate his father, since he had neither time nor means for an explanation. And so he fled to the door of his own room and crouched against it, to let his father see as soon as he came in from the hall that his son had the good intention of getting back into his room immediately and that it was not necessary to drive him there, but that if only the door were opened he would disappear at once.

Yet his father was not in the mood to perceive such fine distinctions. "Ah!" he cried as soon as he appeared in a tone which sounded at once angry and exultant. Gregor drew his head back from the door and lifted it to look at his father. Truly, this was not the father he had imagined to himself; admittedly he had been too absorbed of late in his new recreation of crawling over the ceiling to take the same interest as before in what was happening elsewhere in the flat, and he ought really to be prepared for some changes. And yet, and yet, could that be his father? The man who used to lie wearily sunk in bed whenever Gregor set out on a business journey; who welcomed him back of an evening lying in a long chair in a dressing gown; who could not really rise to his feet but only lifted his arms in greeting, and on the rare occasions when he did go out with his family, on one or two Sundays a year and on high holidays, walked between Gregor and his mother, who were slow walkers anyhow, even more slowly than they did, muffled in his old greatcoat, shuffling laboriously forward with every step and, whenever he wanted to say anything, nearly always came to a full stop and gathered his escort around him? Now he was standing there in fine shape; dressed in a smart blue uniform with gold buttons, such as bank messengers wear; his strong double chin bulged over the stiff high collar of his jacket; from under his bushy eyebrows his black eyes darted fresh and penetrating glances; his onetime tangled white hair had been combed flat on either side of a shining and carefully exact parting. He pitched his cap, which bore a gold monogram, probably the badge of some bank, in a wide sweep across the whole room on to a sofa and with the tail-ends of his jacket thrown back, his hands in his trouser pockets, advanced with a grim visage towards Gregor. Likely enough he did not himself know what he meant to do; at any rate he lifted his feet uncommonly high, and Gregor was dumfounded at the enormous size of his shoe soles. But Gregor could not risk standing up to him, aware as he had been from the very first day of his new life that his father believed only the severest measures suitable for dealing with him. And so he ran before his father, stopping when he stopped and scuttling forward again when his father made any kind of move. In this way they circled the room several times without anything decisive happening, indeed the whole operation did not even look like a pursuit because it was carried out so slowly. And so Gregor did not leave the floor, for he feared that his father might take as a piece of peculiar wickedness any excursion of his over the walls or the ceiling. All the same, he could not stay this course much longer, for while his father took one step he had to carry out a whole series of movements. He was already beginning to feel breathless, just as in his former life his lungs had not been very dependable. As he was staggering along, trying to concentrate his energy on running, hardly keeping his eyes open; in his dazed state never even thinking of any other escape than simply going forward; and having almost forgotten that the walls were free to him, which in this room were well provided with finely carved pieces of furniture full of knobs and crevices—suddenly something lightly flung landed close behind him and rolled before him. It was an apple; a second apple followed immediately; Gregor came to a stop in alarm; there was no point in running on, for his father was determined to bombard him. He had filled his pockets with fruit from the dish on the sideboard and was now shying apple after apple, without taking particularly good aim for the moment. The small red apples rolled about the floor as if magnetized and cannoned into each other. An apple thrown without much force grazed Gregor's back and glanced off harmlessly. But another following immediately landed right on his back and sank in; Gregor wanted to drag himself forward, as if this startling, incredible pain could be left behind him; but he felt as if nailed to the spot and flattened himself out in a complete derangement of all his senses. With his last conscious look he saw the door of his room being torn open and his mother rushing out ahead of his screaming sister, in her underbodice, for her daughter had loosened her clothing to let her breathe more freely and recover from her swoon, he saw his mother rushing towards his father, leaving one after another behind her on the floor her loosened petticoats, stumbling over her petticoats straight to his father and embracing him, in complete union with him—but here Gregor's sight began to fail—with her hands clasped round his father's neck as she begged for her son's life.

III

The serious injury done to Gregor, which disabled him for more than a month—the apple went on sticking in his body as a visible reminder, since no one ventured to remove it—seemed to have made even his father recollect that Gregor was a member of the family, despite his present unfortunate and repulsive shape, and ought not to be treated as an enemy, that, on the contrary, family duty required the suppression of disgust and the exercise of patience, nothing but patience.

And although his injury had impaired, probably for ever, his powers of movement, and for the time being it took him long, long minutes to creep across his room like an old invalid—there was no question now of crawling up the wall—yet in his own opinion he was sufficiently compensated for this worsening of his condition by the fact that towards evening the living-room door, which he used to watch intently for an hour or two beforehand, was always thrown open, so that lying in the darkness of his room, invisible to the family, he could see them all at the lamp-lit table and listen to their talk, by general consent as it were, very different from his earlier eavesdropping.

True, their intercourse lacked the lively character of former times, which he had always called to mind with a certain wistfulness in the small hotel bedrooms where he had been wont to throw himself down, tired out, on damp bedding. They were now mostly very silent. Soon after supper his father would fall asleep in his armchair; his mother and sister would admonish each other to be silent; his mother, bending low over the lamp, stitched at fine sewing for an underwear firm; his sister, who had taken a job as a salesgirl, was learning shorthand and French in the evenings on the chance of bettering herself. Sometimes his father woke up, and as if quite unaware that he had been sleeping said to his mother: "What a lot of sewing you're doing today!" and at once fell asleep again, while the two women exchanged a tired smile.

With a kind of mulishness his father persisted in keeping his uniform on even in the house; his dressing gown hung uselessly on its peg and he slept fully dressed where he sat, as if he were ready for service at any moment and even here only at the beck and call of his superior. As a result, his uniform, which was not brand-new to start with, began to look dirty, despite all the loving care of the mother and sister to keep it clean, and Gregor often spent whole evenings gazing at the many greasy spots on the garment, gleaming with gold buttons always in a high state of polish, in which the old man sat sleeping in extreme discomfort and yet quite peacefully.

As soon as the clock struck ten his mother tried to rouse his father with gentle words and to persuade him after that to get into bed, for sitting there he could not have a proper sleep and that was what he needed most, since he had to go on duty at six. But with the mulishness that had obsessed him since he became a bank messenger, he always insisted on staying longer at the table, although he regularly fell asleep again and in the end only with the greatest trouble could be got out of his armchair and into his bed. However insistently Gregor's mother and sister kept urging him with gentle reminders, he would go on slowly shaking his head for a quarter of an hour, keeping his eyes shut, and refuse to get to his feet. The mother plucked at his sleeve, whispering endearments in his ear, the sister left her lessons to come to her mother's help, but Gregor's father was not to be caught. He would only sink down deeper in his chair. Not until the two women hoisted him up by the armpits did he open his eyes and look at them both, one after the other, usually with the remark: "This is a life. This is the peace and quiet of my old age." And leaning on the two of them he would heave himself up, with difficulty, as if he were a great burden to himself, suffer them to lead him as far as the door and then wave them off and go on alone, while the mother abandoned her needlework and the sister her pen in order to run after him and help him farther.

Who could find time, in this overworked and tired-out family, to bother about Gregor more than was absolutely needful? The household was reduced more and more; the servant girl was turned off; a gigantic bony charwoman with white hair flying round her head came in morning and evening to do the rough work; everything else was done by Gregor's mother, as well as great piles of sewing. Even various family ornaments, which his mother and sister used to wear with pride at parties and celebrations, had to be sold, as Gregor discovered of an evening from hearing them all discuss the prices obtained. But what they lamented most was the fact that they could not leave the flat which was much too big for their present circumstances, because they could not think of any way to shift Gregor. Yet Gregor saw well enough that consideration for him was not the main difficulty preventing the removal, for they could have easily shifted him in some suitable box with a few air holes in it; what really kept them from moving into another flat was rather their own complete hopelessness and the belief that they had been singled out for a misfortune such as had never happened to any of their relations or acquaintances. They fulfilled to the uttermost all that the world demands of poor people, the father fetched breakfast for the small clerks in the bank, the mother devoted her energy to making underwear for strangers, the sister trotted to and from behind the counter at the behest of customers, but more than this they had not the strength to do. And the wound in Gregor's back began to nag at him afresh when his mother and sister, after getting his father into bed, came back again, left their work lying, drew close to each other and sat cheek by cheek; when his mother, pointing towards his room, said: "Shut that door now, Grete," and he was left again in darkness, while next door the women mingled their tears or perhaps sat dry-eyed staring at the table.

Gregor hardly slept at all by night or by day. He was often haunted by the idea that next time the door opened he would take the family's affairs in hand again just as he used to do; once more, after this long interval, there appeared in his thoughts the figures of the chief and the chief clerk, the commercial travelers and the apprentices, the porter who was so dull-witted, two or three friends in other firms, a chambermaid in one of the rural hotels, a sweet and fleeting memory, a cashier in a milliner's shop, whom he had wooed earnestly but too slowly—they all appeared, together with strangers or people he had quite forgotten, but instead of helping him and his family they were one and all unapproachable and he was glad when they vanished. At other times he would not be in the mood to bother about his family, he was only filled with rage at the way they were neglecting him, and although he had no clear idea of what he might care to eat he would make plans for getting into the larder to take the food that was after all his due, even if he were not hungry. His sister no longer took thought to bring him what might especially please him, but in the morning and at noon before she went to business hurriedly pushed into his room with her foot any food that was available, and in the evening cleared it out again with one sweep of the broom, heedless of whether it had been merely tasted, or —as most frequently happened—left untouched. The cleaning of his room, which she now did always in the evenings, could not have been more hastily done. Streaks of dirt stretched along the walls, here and there lay balls of dust and filth, At first Gregor used to station himself in some particularly filthy corner when his sister arrived, in order to reproach her with it, so to speak. But he could have sat there for weeks without getting her to make any improvement; she could see the dirt as well as he did, but she had simply made up her mind to leave it alone. And yet, with a touchiness that was new to her, which seemed anyhow to have infected the whole family, she jealously guarded her claim to be the sole caretaker of Gregor's room. His mother once subjected his room to a thorough cleaning, which was achieved only by means of several buckets of water—all this dampness of course upset Gregor too and he lay widespread, sulky and motionless on the sofa—but she was well punished for it. Hardly had his sister noticed the changed aspect of his room that evening than she rushed in high dudgeon into the living room and, despite the imploringly raised hands of her mother, burst into a storm of weeping, while her parents—her father had of course been startled out of his chair—looked on at first in helpless amazement; then they too began to go into action; the father reproached the mother on his right for not having left the cleaning of Gregor's room to his sister; shrieked at the sister on his left that never again was she to be allowed to clean Gregor's room; while the mother tried to pull the father into his bedroom, since he was beyond himself with agitation; the sister, shaken with sobs, then beat upon the table with her small fists; and Gregor hissed loudly with rage because not one of them thought of shutting the door to spare him such a spectacle and so much noise.

Still, even if the sister, exhausted by her daily work, had grown tired of looking after Gregor as she did formerly, there was no need for his mother's intervention or for Gregor's being neglected at all. The charwoman was there. This old widow, whose strong bony frame had enabled her to survive the worst a long life could offer, by no means recoiled from Gregor. Without being in the least curious she had once by chance opened the door of his room and at the sight of Gregor, who, taken by surprise, began to rush to and fro although no one was chasing him, merely stood there with her arms folded. From that time she never failed to open his door a little for a moment, morning and evening, to have a look at him. At first she even used to call him to her, with words which apparently she took to be friendly, such as "Come along, then, you old dung beetle!" or "Look at the old dung beetle, then!" To such allocutions Gregor made no answer, but stayed motionless where he was, as if the door had never been opened. Instead of being allowed to disturb him so senselessly whenever the whim took her, she should rather have been ordered to clean out his room daily, that charwoman! Once, early in the morning—heavy rain was lashing on the windowpanes, perhaps a sign that spring was on the way—Gregor was so exasperated when she began addressing him again that he ran at her, as if to attack her, although slowly and feebly enough. But the charwoman instead of showing fright merely lifted high a chair that happened to be beside the door, and as she stood there with her mouth wide open it was clear that she meant to shut it only when she brought the chair down on Gregor's back. "So you're not coming any nearer?" she asked, as Gregor turned away again, and quietly put the chair back into the corner.

Gregor was now eating hardly anything. Only when he happened to pass the food laid out for him did he take a bit of something in his mouth as a pastime, kept it there for an hour at a time and usually spat it out again. At first he thought it was chagrin over the state of his room that prevented him from eating, yet he soon got used to the various changes in his room. It had become a habit in the family to push into his room things there was no room for elsewhere, and there were plenty of these now, since one of the rooms had been let to three lodgers. These serious gentlemen—all three of them with full beards, as Gregor once observed through a crack in the door—had a passion for order, not only in their own room but, since they were now members of the household, in all its arrangements, especially in the kitchen. Superfluous, not to say dirty, objects they could not bear. Besides, they had brought with them most of the furnishings they needed. For this reason many things could be dispensed with that it was no use trying to sell but that should not be thrown away either. All of them found their way into Gregor's room. The ash can likewise and the kitchen garbage can. Anything that was not needed for the moment was simply flung into Gregor's room by the charwoman, who did everything in a hurry; fortunately Gregor usually saw only the object, whatever it was, and the hand that held it. Perhaps she intended to take the things away again as time and opportunity offered, or to collect them until she could throw them all out in a heap, but in fact they just lay wherever she happened to throw them, except when Gregor pushed his way through the junk and shifted it somewhat, at first out of necessity, because he had not room enough to crawl, but later with increasing enjoyment, although after such excursions, being sad and weary to death, he would lie motionless for hours. And since the lodgers often ate their supper at home in the common living room, the living room door stayed shut many an evening, yet Gregor reconciled himself quite easily to the shutting of the door, for often enough on evenings when it was opened he had disregarded it entirely and lain in the darkest corner of his room, quite unnoticed by the family. But on one occasion the charwoman left the door open a little and it stayed ajar even when the lodgers came in for supper and the lamp was lit. They set themselves at the top end of the table where formerly Gregor and his father and mother had eaten their meals, unfolded their napkins and took knife and fork in hand. At once his mother appeared in the other doorway with a dish of meat and close behind her his sister with a dish of potatoes piled high. The food steamed with a thick vapor. The lodgers bent over the food set before them as if to scrutinize it before eating, in fact the man in the middle, who seemed to pass for an authority with the other two, cut a piece of meat as it lay on the dish, obviously to discover if it were tender or should be sent back to the kitchen. He showed satisfaction, and Gregor's mother and sister, who had been watching anxiously, breathed freely and began to smile.

The family itself took its meals in the kitchen. None the less, Gregor's father came into the living room before going into the kitchen and with one prolonged bow, cap in hand, made a round of the table. The lodgers all stood up and murmured something in their beards. When they were alone again they ate their food in almost complete silence. It seemed remarkable to Gregor that among the various noises coming from the table he could always distinguish the sound of their masticating teeth, as if this were a sign to Gregor that one needed teeth in order to eat, and that with toothless jaws even of the finest make one could do nothing. "I'm hungry enough," said Gregor sadly to himself, "but not for that kind of food. How these lodgers are stuffing themselves, and here am I dying of starvation!"

On that very evening—during the whole of his time there Gregor could not remember ever having heard the violin—the sound of violin-playing came from the kitchen. The lodgers had already finished their supper, the one in the middle had brought out a newspaper and given the other two a page apiece, and now they were leaning back at ease reading and smoking. When the violin began to play they pricked up their ears, got to their feet, and went on tiptoe to the hall door where they stood huddled together. Their movements must have been heard in the kitchen, for Gregor's father called out: "Is the violin-playing disturbing you, gentlemen? It can be stopped at once." "On the contrary," said the middle lodger, "could not Fräulein Samsa come and play in this room, beside us, where it is much more convenient and comfortable?" "Oh certainly," cried Gregor's father, as if he were the violin-player. The lodgers came back into the living room and waited. Presently Gregor's father arrived with the music stand, his mother carrying the music and his sister with the violin. His sister quietly made everything ready to start playing; his parents, who had never let rooms before and so had an exaggerated idea of the courtesy due to lodgers, did not venture to sit down on their own chairs; his father leaned against the door, the right hand thrust between two buttons of his livery coat, which was formally buttoned up; but his mother was offered a chair by one of the lodgers and, since she left the chair just where he had happened to put it, sat down in a corner to one side.

Gregor's sister began to play; the father and mother, from either side, intently watched the movements of her hands. Gregor, attracted by the playing, ventured to move forward a little until his head was actually inside the living room. He felt hardly any surprise at his growing lack of consideration for the others; there had been a time when he prided himself on being considerate. And yet just on this occasion he had more reason than ever to hide himself, since owing to the amount of dust which lay thick in his room and rose into the air at the slightest movement, he too was covered with dust; fluff and hair remnants of food trailed with him, caught on his back and along his sides; his indifference to everything was much too great for him to turn on his back and scrape himself clean on the carpet, as once he had done several times a day. And in spite of his condition, no shame deterred him from advancing a little over the spotless floor of the living room.

To be sure no one was aware of him. The family was entirely absorbed in the violin-playing; the lodgers, however, who first of all had stationed themselves, hands in pockets, much too close behind the music stand so that they could all have read the music, which must have bothered his sister, had soon retreated to the window, half-whispering with downbent heads, and stayed there while his father turned an anxious eye on them. Indeed, they were making it more than obvious that they had been disappointed in their expectation of hearing good or enjoyable violin-playing, that they had had more than enough of the performance and only out of courtesy suffered a continued disturbance of their peace. From the way they all kept blowing the smoke of their cigars high in the air through nose and mouth one could divine their irritation. And yet Gregor's sister was playing so beautifully. Her face leaned sideways, intently and sadly her eyes followed the notes of music. Gregor crawled a little farther forward and lowered his head to the ground so that it might be possible for his eyes to meet hers. Was he an animal, that music had such an effect upon him? He felt as if the way were opening before him to the unknown nourishment he craved. He was determined to push forward till he reached his sister, to pull at her skirt and so let her know that she was to come into his room with her violin, for no one here appreciated her playing as he would appreciate it. He would never let her out of his room, at least, not so long as he lived; his frightful appearance would become, for the first time, useful to him; he would watch all the doors of his room at once and spit at intruders; but his sister should need no constraint, she should stay with him of her own free will; she should sit beside him on the sofa, bend down her ear to him and hear him confide that he had had the firm intention of sending her to the Conservatorium, and that, but for his mishap, last Christmas—surely Christmas was long past?—he would have announced it to everybody without allowing a single objection. After this confession his sister would be so touched that she would burst into tears, and Gregor would then raise himself to her shoulder and kiss her on the neck, which, now that she went to business, she kept free of any ribbon or collar.

"Mr. Samsa!" cried the middle lodger, to Gregor's father, and pointed, without wasting any more words, at Gregor, now working himself slowly forwards. The violin fell silent, the middle lodger first smiled to his friends with a shake of the head and then looked at Gregor again. Instead of driving Gregor out, his father seemed to think it more needful to begin by soothing down the lodgers, although they were not at all agitated and apparently found Gregor more entertaining than the violin-playing. He hurried towards them and, spreading out his arms, tried to urge them back into their own room and at the same time to block their view of Gregor. They now began to be really a little angry, one could not tell whether because of the old man's behavior or because it had just dawned on them that all unwittingly they had such a neighbor as Gregor next door. They demanded explanations of his father, they waved their arms like him, tugged uneasily at their beards, and only with reluctance backed towards their room. Meanwhile Gregor's sister, who stood there as if lost when her playing was so abruptly broken off, came to life again, pulled herself together all at once after standing for a while holding violin and bow in nervelessly hanging hands and staring at her music, pushed her violin into the lap of her mother, who was still sitting in her chair fighting asthmatically for breath, and ran into the lodgers' room to which they were now being shepherded by her father rather more quickly than before. One could see the pillows and blankets on the beds flying under her accustomed fingers and being laid in order. Before the lodgers had actually reached their room she had finished making the beds and slipped out.

The old man seemed once more to be so possessed by his mulish self-assertiveness that he was forgetting all the respect he should show to his lodgers. He kept driving them on and driving them on until in the very door of the bedroom the middle lodger stamped his foot loudly on the floor and so brought him to a halt. "I beg to announce," said the lodger, lifting one hand and looking also at Gregor's mother and sister, "that because of the disgusting conditions prevailing in this household and family"—here he spat on the floor with emphatic brevity—"I give you notice on the spot. Naturally I won't pay you a penny for the days I have lived here, on the contrary I shall consider bringing an action for damages against you, based on claims—believe me—that will be easily susceptible of proof." He ceased and stared straight in front of him, as if he expected something. In fact his two friends at once rushed into the breach with these words: "And we too give notice on the spot." On that he seized the door-handle and shut the door with a slam.

Gregor's father, groping with his hands, staggered forward and fell into his chair; it looked as if he were stretching himself there for his ordinary evening nap, but the marked jerkings of his head, which was as if uncontrollable, showed that he was far from asleep. Gregor had simply stayed quietly all the time on the spot where the lodgers had espied him. Disappointment at the failure of his plan, perhaps also the weakness arising from extreme hunger, made it impossible for him to move. He feared, with a fair degree of certainty, that at any moment the general tension would discharge itself in a combined attack upon him, and he lay waiting. He did not react even to the noise made by the violin as it fell off his mother's lap from under her trembling fingers and gave out a resonant note.

"My dear parents," said his sister, slapping her hand on the table by way of introduction, "things can't go on like this. Perhaps you don't realize that, but I do. I won't utter my brother's name in the presence of this creature, and so all I say is: we must try to get rid of it. We've tried to look after it and to put up with it as far as is humanly possible, and I don't think anyone could reproach us in the slightest."

"She is more than right," said Gregor's father to himself. His mother, who was still choking for lack of breath, began to cough hollowly into her hand with a wild look in her eyes.

His sister rushed over to her and held her forehead. His father's thoughts seemed to have lost their vagueness at Grete's words, he sat more upright, fingering his service cap that lay among the plates still lying on the table from the lodgers' supper, and from time to time looked at the still form of Gregor.

"We must try to get rid of it," his sister now said explicitly to her father, since her mother was coughing too much to hear a word, "it will be the death of both of you, I can see that coming. When one has to work as hard as we do, all of us, one can't stand this continual torment at home on top of it. At least I can't stand it any longer." And she burst into such a passion of sobbing that her tears dropped on her mother's face, where she wiped them off mechanically.

"My dear," said the old man sympathetically, and with evident understanding, "but what can we do?"

Gregor's sister merely shrugged her shoulders to indicate the feeling of helplessness that had now overmastered her during her weeping fit, in contrast to her former confidence.

"If he could understand us," said her father, half questioningly; Grete, still sobbing, vehemently waved a hand to show how unthinkable that was.

"If he could understand us," repeated the old man, shutting his eyes to consider his daughter's conviction that understanding was impossible, "then perhaps we might come to some agreement with him. But as it is—"

"He must go," cried Gregor's sister, "that's the only solution, Father. You must just try to get rid of the idea that this is Gregor. The fact that we've believed it for so long is the root of all our trouble. But how can it be Gregor? If this were Gregor, he would have realized long ago that human beings can't live with such a creature, and he'd have gone away on his own accord. Then we wouldn't have any brother, but we'd be able to go on living and keep his memory in honor. As it is, this creature persecutes us, drives away our lodgers, obviously wants the whole apartment to himself and would have us all sleep in the gutter. Just look, Father," she shrieked all at once, "he's at it again!" And in an access of panic that was quite incomprehensible to Gregor she even quitted her mother, literally thrusting the chair from her as if she would rather sacrifice her mother than stay so near to Gregor, and rushed behind her father, who also rose up, being simply upset by her agitation, and half-spread his arms out as if to protect her.

Yet Gregor had not the slightest intention of frightening anyone, far less his sister. He had only begun to turn around in order to crawl back to his room, but it was certainly a startling operation to watch, since because of his disabled condition he could not execute the difficult turning movements except by lifting his head and then bracing it against the floor over and over again. He paused and looked round. His good intentions seemed to have been recognized; the alarm had only been momentary. Now they were all watching him in melancholy silence. His mother lay in her chair, her legs stiffly outstretched and pressed together, her eyes almost closing for sheer weariness; his father and his sister were sitting beside each other, his sister's arm around the old man's neck.

Perhaps I can go on turning round now, thought Gregor, and began his labors again. He could not stop himself from panting with the effort, and had to pause now and then to take breath. Nor did anyone harass him, he was left entirely to himself. When he had completed the turn-round he began at once to crawl straight back. He was amazed at the distance separating him from his room and could not understand how in his weak state he had managed to accomplish the same journey so recently, almost without remarking it. Intent on crawling as fast as possible, he barely noticed that not a single word, not an ejaculation from his family, interfered with his progress. Only when he was already in the doorway did he turn his head round, not completely, for his neck muscles were getting stiff, but enough to see that nothing had changed behind him except that his sister had risen to her feet. His last glance fell on his mother, who was not quite overcome by sleep.

Hardly was he well inside his room when the door was hastily pushed shut, bolted and locked. The sudden noise in his rear startled him so much that his little legs gave beneath him. It was his sister who had shown such haste. She had been standing ready waiting and had made a light spring forward, Gregor had not even heard her coming, and she cried "At last!" to her parents as she turned the key in the lock.

"And what now?" said Gregor to himself, looking round in the darkness. Soon he made the discovery that he was now unable to stir a limb. This did not surprise him, rather it seemed unnatural that he should ever actually have been able to move on these feeble little legs. Otherwise he felt relatively comfortable. True, his whole body was aching, but it seemed that the pain was gradually growing less and would finally pass away. The rotting apple in his back and the inflamed area around it, all covered with soft dust, already hardly troubled him. He thought of his family with tenderness and love. The decision that he must disappear was one that he held to even more strongly than his sister, if that were possible. In this state of vacant and peaceful meditation he remained until the tower clock struck three in the morning. The first broadening of light in the world outside the window entered his consciousness once more. Then his head sank to the floor of its own accord and from his nostrils came the last faint flicker of his breath.

When the charwoman arrived early in the morning—what between her strength and her impatience she slammed all the doors so loudly, never mind how often she had been begged not to do so, that no one in the whole apartment could enjoy any quiet sleep after her arrival—she noticed nothing unusual as she took her customary peep into Gregor's room. She thought he was lying motionless on purpose, pretending to be in the sulks; she credited him with every kind of intelligence. Since she happened to have the long-handled broom in her hand she tried to tickle him up with it from the doorway. When that too produced no reaction she felt provoked and poked at him a little harder, and only when she had pushed him along the floor without meeting any resistance was her attention aroused. It did not take her long to establish the truth of the matter, and her eyes widened, she let out a whistle, yet did not waste much time over it but tore open the door of the Samsas' bedroom and yelled into the darkness at the top of her voice: "Just look at this, it's dead; it's lying here dead and done for!"

Mr. and Mrs. Samsa started up in their double bed and before they realized the nature of the charwoman's announcement had some difficulty in overcoming the shock of it. But then they got out of bed quickly, one on either side, Mr. Samsa throwing a blanket over his shoulders, Mrs. Samsa in nothing but her nightgown; in this array they entered Gregor's room. Meanwhile the door of the living room opened, too, where Grete had been sleeping since the advent of the lodgers; she was completely dressed as if she had not been to bed, which seemed to be confirmed also by the paleness of her face. "Dead?" said Mrs. Samsa, looking questioningly at the charwoman, although she could have investigated for herself, and the fact was obvious enough without investigation. "I should say so," said the charwoman, proving her words by pushing Gregor's corpse a long way to one side with her broomstick. Mrs. Samsa made a movement as if to stop her, but checked it. "Well," said Mr. Samsa, "now thanks be to God." He crossed himself, and the three women followed his example. Grete, whose eyes never left the corpse, said: "Just see how thin he was. It's such a long time since he's eaten anything. The food came out again just as it went in." Indeed, Gregor's body was completely flat and dry, as could only now be seen when it was no longer supported by the legs and nothing prevented one from looking closely at it.

"Come in beside us, Grete, for a little while," said Mrs. Samsa with a tremulous smile, and Grete, not without looking back at the corpse, followed her parents into their bedroom. The charwoman shut the door and opened the window wide. Although it was so early in the morning a certain softness was perceptible in the fresh air. After all, it was already the end of March.

The three lodgers emerged from their room and were surprised to see no breakfast; they had been forgotten. "Where's our breakfast?" said the middle lodger peevishly to the charwoman. But she put her finger to her lips and hastily, without a word, indicated by gestures that they should go into Gregor's room. They did so and stood, their hands in the pockets of their somewhat shabby coats, around Gregor's corpse in the room where it was now fully light.

At that the door of the Samsas' bedroom opened and Mr. Samsa appeared in his uniform, his wife on one arm, his daughter on the other. They all looked a little as if they had been crying; from time to time Grete hid her face on her father's arm.

"Leave my house at once!" said Mr. Samsa, and pointed to the door without disengaging himself from the women. "What do you mean by that?" said the middle lodger, taken somewhat aback, with a feeble smile. The two others put their hands behind them and kept rubbing them together, as if in gleeful expectation of a fine set-to in which they were bound to come off the winners. "I mean just what I say," answered Mr. Samsa, and advanced in a straight line with his two companions towards the lodger. He stood his ground at first quietly, looking at the floor as if his thoughts were taking a new pattern in his head. "Then let us go, by all means," he said, and looked up at Mr. Samsa as if in a sudden access of humility he were expecting some renewed sanction for this decision. Mr. Samsa merely nodded briefly once or twice with meaning eyes. Upon that the lodger really did go with long strides into the hall, his two friends had been listening and had quite stopped rubbing their hands for some moments and now went scuttling after him as if afraid that Mr. Samsa might get into the hall before them and cut them off from their leader. In the hall they all three took their hats from the rack, their sticks from the umbrella stand, bowed in silence and quitted the apartment. With a suspiciousness which proved quite unfounded Mr. Samsa and the two women followed them out to the landing; leaning over the banister they watched the three figures slowly but surely going down the long stairs, vanishing from sight at a certain turn of the staircase on every floor and coming into view again after a moment or so; the more they dwindled, the more the Samsa family's interest in them dwindled, and when a butcher's boy met them and passed them on the stairs coming up proudly with a tray on his head, Mr. Samsa and the two women soon left the landing and as if a burden had been lifted from them went back into their apartment.

They decided to spend this day in resting and going for a stroll; they had not only deserved such a respite from work, but absolutely needed it. And so they sat down at the table and wrote three notes of excuse, Mr. Samsa to his board of management, Mrs. Samsa to her employer and Grete to the head of her firm. While they were writing, the charwoman came in to say that she was going now, since her morning's work was finished. At first they only nodded without looking up, but as she kept hovering there they eyed her irritably. "Well?" said Mr. Samsa. The charwoman stood grinning in the doorway as if she had good news to impart to the family but meant not to say a word unless properly questioned. The small ostrich feather standing upright on her hat, which had annoyed Mr. Samsa ever since she was engaged, was waving gaily in all directions. "Well, what is it then?" asked Mrs. Samsa, who obtained more respect from the charwoman than the others. "Oh," said the charwoman, giggling so amiably that she could not at once continue, "just this, you don't need to bother about how to get rid of the thing next door. It's been seen to already." Mrs. Samsa and Grete bent over their letters again, as if preoccupied; Mr. Samsa, who perceived that she was eager to begin describing it all in detail, stopped her with a decisive hand. But since she was not allowed to tell her story, she remembered the great hurry she was in, being obviously deeply huffed:

"Bye, everybody," she said, whirling off violently, and departed with a frightful slamming of doors.

"She'll be given notice tonight," said Mr. Samsa, but neither from his wife nor his daughter did he get any answer, for the charwoman seemed to have shattered again the composure they had barely achieved. They rose, went to the window and stayed there, clasping each other tight. Mr. Samsa turned in his chair to look at them and quietly observed them for a little. Then he called out: "Come along, now, do. Let bygones be bygones. And you might have some consideration for me." The two of them complied at once, hastened to him, caressed him and quickly finished their letters.

Then they all three left the apartment together, which was more than they had done for months, and went by tram into the open country outside the town. The tram, in which they were the only passengers, was filled with warm sunshine. Leaning comfortably back in their seats they canvassed their prospects for the future, and it appeared on closer inspection that these were not at all bad, for the jobs they had got, which so far they had never really discussed with each other, were all three admirable and likely to lead to better things later on. The greatest immediate improvement in their condition would of course arise from moving to another house; they wanted to take a smaller and cheaper but also better situated and more easily run apartment than the one they had, which Gregor had selected. While they were thus conversing, it struck both Mr. and Mrs. Samsa, almost at the same moment, as they became aware of their daughter's increasing vivacity, that in spite of all the sorrow of recent times, which had made her cheeks pale, she had bloomed into a pretty girl with a good figure. They grew quieter and half unconsciously exchanged glances of complete agreement, having come to the conclusion that it would soon be time to find a good husband for her. And it was like a confirmation of their new dreams and excellent intentions that at the end of their journey their daughter sprang to her feet first and stretched her young body.

Sherwood Anderson

(1876 - 1941)

Sherwood Anderson was one of the first truly original American writers of this century and one who strongly influenced a whole generation of younger men in the 1920s. Hemingway, who followed Anderson's revolutionary thrust, was indebted to him for his sentence rhythms and syntax, and Faulkner said of Anderson, "He was the father of my generation of American writers and the tradition of American writing which our successors will carry on." Anderson himself was influenced by Theodore Dreiser and the prevailing winds of naturalism in the second decade of the century, but his own works are much more than mere slices of life in the naturalistic tradition. One of the first American writers to make use of Freudian psychology in his fiction, Anderson was less interested in surface reality than in the pathetic internal realities of his characters, and he has been called the most subjective American writer despite his detached literary manner. Most of his best stories are sympathetic probings into the minds of ordinary people who are thwarted by social conventions and pressures from realizing their true potential, men and women often overwhelmed by the complexity of the industrial age. He succeeds in presenting the everyday life of ordinary but usually sensitive Midwesterners. A literary rebel in many ways, Anderson abandoned the formal conventions of the short story begun by Poe, saying, "The plot notion did seem to me to poison all story-telling. What was wanted, I thought, was form, not plot. . . ." His style, which is occasionally slack and awkward, is usually effective in its naturalness and informality.

Death

The stairway leading up to Doctor Reefy's office, in the Heffner Block above the Paris Dry Goods store, was but dimly lighted. At the head of the stairway hung a lamp with a dirty chimney that was fastened by a bracket to the wall. The lamp had a tin reflector, brown with rust and covered with dust. The people who went up the stairway followed with their feet the feet of many who had gone before. The soft boards of the stairs had yielded under the pressure of feet and deep hollows marked the way.

At the top of the stairway a turn to the right brought you to the doctor's door. To the left was a dark hallway filled with rubbish. Old chairs, carpenter's horses, step ladders and empty boxes lay in the darkness waiting for shins to be barked. The pile of rubbish belonged to the Paris Dry Goods Company. When a counter or a row of shelves in the store became useless, clerks carried it up the stairway and threw it on the pile.

Doctor Reefy's office was as large as a barn. A stove with a round paunch sat in the middle of the room. Around its base was piled sawdust, held in place by heavy planks nailed to the floor. By the door stood a huge table that had once been a part of the furniture of Herrick's Clothing Store and that had been used for displaying custom-made clothes. It was covered with books, bottles, and surgical instruments. Near the edge of the table lay three or four apples left by John Spaniard, a tree nurseryman who was Doctor Reefy's friend, and who had slipped the apples out of his pocket as he came in at the door.

At middle age Doctor Reefy was tall and awkward. The grey beard he later wore had not yet appeared, but on the upper lip grew a brown mustache. He was not a graceful man, as when he grew older, and was much occupied with the problem of disposing of his hands and feet.

On summer afternoons, when she had been married many years and when her son George was a boy of twelve or fourteen, Elizabeth Willard sometimes went up the worn steps to Doctor Reefy's office. Already the woman's naturally tall figure had begun to droop and to drag itself listlessly about. Ostensibly she went to see the doctor because of her health, but on the half dozen occasions when she had been to see him the outcome of the visits did not primarily concern her health. She and the doctor talked of that but they talked most of her life, of their two lives and of the ideas that had come to them as they lived their lives in Winesburg.

In the big empty office the man and the woman sat looking at each other and they were a good deal alike. Their bodies were different, as were also the color of their eyes, the length of their noses, and the circumstances of their existence, but something inside them meant the same thing, wanted the same release, would have left the same impression on the memory of an onlooker. Later, and when he grew older and married a young wife, the doctor often talked to her of the hours spent with the sick woman and expressed a good many things he had been unable to express to Elizabeth. He was almost a poet in his old age and his notion of what happened took a poetic turn. "I had come to the time in my life when prayer became necessary and so I invented gods and prayed to them," he said. "I did not say my prayers in words nor did I kneel down but sat perfectly still in my chair. In the late afternoon when it was hot and quiet on Main Street or in the winter when the days were gloomy, the gods came into the office and I thought no one knew about them. Then I found that this woman Elizabeth knew, that she worshipped also the same gods. I have a notion that she came to the office because she thought the gods would be there but she was happy to find herself not alone just the same. It was an experience that cannot be explained, although I suppose it is always happening to men and women in all sorts of places."

. . .

On the summer afternoons when Elizabeth and the doctor sat in the office and talked of their two lives they talked of other lives also. Sometimes the doctor made philosophic epigrams. Then he chuckled with amusement. Now and then after a period of silence, a word was said or a hint given that strangely illuminated the life of the speaker, a wish became a desire, or a dream, half dead, flared suddenly into life. For the most part the words came from the woman and she said them without looking at the man.

Each time she came to see the doctor the hotel keeper's wife talked a little more freely and after an hour or two in his presence went down the stairway into Main Street feeling renewed and strengthened against the dullness of her days. With something approaching a girlhood swing to her body she walked along, but when she had got back to her chair by the window of her room and when darkness had come on and a girl from the hotel dining room brought her dinner on a tray, she let it grow cold. Her thoughts ran away to her girlhood with its passionate longing for adventure and she remembered the arms of men that had held her when adventure was a possible thing for her. Particularly she remembered one who had for a time been her lover and who in the moment of his passion had cried out to her more than a hundred times, saying the same words madly over and over: "You dear! You dear! You lovely dear!" The words, she thought, expressed something she would have liked to have achieved in life.

In her room in the shabby old hotel the sick wife of the hotel keeper began to weep and, putting her hands to her face, rocked back and forth. The words of her one friend, Doctor Reefy, rang in her ears. "Love is like a wind stirring the grass beneath trees on a black night," he had said. "You must not try to make love definite. It is the divine accident of life. If you try to be definite and sure about it and to live beneath the trees, where soft night winds blow, the long hot day of disappointment comes swiftly and the gritty dust from passing wagons gathers upon lips inflamed and made tender by kisses."

Elizabeth Willard could not remember her mother who had died when she was but five years old. Her girlhood had been lived in the most haphazard manner imaginable. Her father was a man who had wanted to be let alone and the affairs of the hotel would not let him alone. He also had lived and died a sick man. Every day he arose with a cheerful face, but by ten o'clock in the morning all the joy had gone out of his heart. When a guest complained of the fare in the hotel dining room or one of the girls who made up the beds got married and went away, he stamped on the floor and swore. At night when he went to bed he thought of his daughter growing up among the stream of people that drifted in and out of the hotel and was overcome with sadness. As the girl grew older and began to walk out in the evening with men he wanted to talk to her, but when he tried was not successful. He always forgot what he wanted to say and spent the time complaining of his own affairs.

In her girlhood and young womanhood Elizabeth had tried to be a real adventurer in life. At eighteen life had so gripped her that she was no longer a virgin but, although she had a half dozen lovers before she married Tom Willard, she had never entered upon an adventure prompted by desire alone. Like all the women in the world, she wanted a real lover. Always there was something she sought blindly, passionately, some hidden wonder in life. The tall beautiful girl with the swinging stride who had walked under the trees with men was forever putting out her hand into the darkness and trying to get hold of some other hand. In all the babble of words that fell from the lips of the men with whom she adventured she was trying to find what would be for her the true word.

Elizabeth had married Tom Willard, a clerk in her father's hotel, because he was at hand and wanted to marry at the time when the determination to marry came to her. For a while, like most young girls, she thought marriage would change the face of life. If there was in her mind a doubt of the outcome of the marriage with Tom she brushed it aside. Her father was ill and near death at the time and she was perplexed because of the meaningless outcome of an affair in which she had just been involved. Other girls of her age in Winesburg were marrying men she had always known, grocery clerks or young farmers. In the evening they walked in Main Street with their husbands and when she passed they smiled happily. She began to think that the fact of marriage might be full of some hidden significance. Young wives with whom she talked spoke softly and shyly. "It changes things to have a man of your own," they said.

On the evening before her marriage the perplexed girl had a talk with her father. Later she wondered if the hours alone with the sick man had not led to her decision to marry. The father talked of his life and advised the daughter to avoid being led into another such muddle. He abused Tom Willard, and that led Elizabeth to come to the clerk's defense. The sick man became excited and tried to get out of bed. When she would not let him walk about he began to complain. "I've never been let alone," he said. "Although I've worked hard I've not made the hotel pay. Even now I owe money at the bank. You'll find that out when I'm gone."

The voice of the sick man became tense with earnestness. Being unable to arise, he put out his hand and pulled the girl's head down beside his own. "There's a way out," he whispered. "Don't marry Tom Willard or anyone else here in Winesburg. There is eight hundred dollars in a tin box in my trunk. Take it and go away."

Again the sick man's voice became querulous. "You've got to promise," he declared. "If you won't promise not to marry, give me your word that you'll never tell Tom about the money. It is mine and if I give it to you I've the right to make that demand. Hide it away. It is to make up to you for my failure as a father. Some time it may prove to be a door, a great open door to you. Come now, I tell you I'm about to die, give me your promise."

. . .

In Doctor Reefy's office, Elizabeth, a tired gaunt old woman at forty-one, sat in a chair near the stove and looked at the floor. By a small desk near the window sat the doctor. His hands played with a lead pencil that lay on the desk. Elizabeth talked of her life as a married woman. She became impersonal and forgot her husband, only using him as a lay figure to give point to her tale. "And then I was married and it did not turn out at all," she said bitterly. "As soon as I had gone into it I began to be afraid. Perhaps I knew too much before and then perhaps I found out too much during my first night with him. I don't remember.

"What a fool I was. When father gave me the money and tried to talk me out of the thought of marriage, I would not listen. I thought of what the girls who were married had said of it and I wanted marriage also. It wasn't Tom I wanted, it was marriage. When father went to sleep I leaned out of the window and thought of the life I had led. I didn't want to be a bad woman. The town was full of stories about me. I even began to be afraid Tom would change his mind."

The woman's voice began to quiver with excitement. To Doctor Reefy, who without realizing what was happening had begun to love her, there came an odd illusion. He thought that as she talked the woman's body was changing, that she was becoming younger, straighter, stronger. When he could not shake off the illusion his mind gave it a professional twist. "It is good for both her body and her mind, this talking," he muttered.

The woman began telling of an incident that had happened one afternoon a few months after her marriage. Her voice became steadier. "In the late afternoon I went for a drive alone," she said. "I had a buggy and a little grey pony I kept in Moyer's Livery. Tom was painting and repapering rooms in the hotel. He wanted money and I was trying to make up my mind to tell him about the eight hundred dollars father had given to me. I couldn't decide to do it. I didn't like him well enough. There was always paint on his hands and face during those days and he smelled of paint. He was trying to fix up the old hotel, make it new and smart."

The excited woman sat up very straight in her chair and made a quick girlish movement with her hand as she told of the drive alone on the spring afternoon. "It was cloudy and a storm threatened," she said. "Black clouds made the green of the trees and the grass stand out so that the colors hurt my eyes. I went out Trunion Pike a mile or more and then turned into a side road. The little horse went quickly along up hill and down. I was impatient. Thoughts came and I wanted to get away from my thoughts. I began to beat the horse. The black clouds settled down and it began to rain. I wanted to go at a terrible speed, to drive on and on forever. I wanted to get out of town, out of my clothes, out of my marriage, out of my body, out of everything. I almost killed the horse, making him run, and when he could not run any more I got out of the buggy and ran afoot into the darkness until I fell and hurt my side. I wanted to run away from everything but I wanted to run towards something too. Don't you see, dear, how it was?"

Elizabeth sprang out of the chair and began to walk about in the office. She walked as Doctor Reefy thought he had never seen anyone walk before. To her whole body there was a swing, a rhythm that intoxicated him. When she came and knelt on the floor beside his chair he took her into his arms and began to kiss her passionately. "I cried all the way home," she said, as she tried to continue the story of her wild ride, but he did not listen. "You dear! You lovely dear! Oh you lovely dear!" he muttered and thought he held in his arms not the tired-out woman of forty-one but a lovely and innocent girl who had been able by some miracle to project herself out of the husk of the body of the tired-out woman.

Doctor Reefy did not see the woman he had held in his arms again until after her death. On the summer afternoon in the office when he was on the point of becoming her lover a half grotesque little incident brought his love-making quickly to an end. As the man and woman held each other tightly heavy feet came tramping up the office stairs. The two sprang to their feet and stood listening and trembling. The noise on the stairs was made by a clerk from the Paris Dry Goods Company. With a loud bang he threw an empty box on the pile of rubbish in the hallway and then went heavily down the stairs. Elizabeth followed him almost immediately. The thing that had come to life in her as she talked to her one friend died suddenly. She was hysterical, as was also Doctor Reefy, and did not want to continue the talk. Along the street she went with the blood still singing in her body, but when she turned out of Main Street and saw ahead the lights of the New Willard House, she began to tremble and her knees shook so that for a moment she thought she would fall in the street.

The sick woman spent the last few months of her life hungering for death. Along the road of death she went, seeking, hungering. She personified the figure of death and made him now a strong black-haired youth running over hills, now a stern quiet man marked and scarred by the business of living. In the darkness of her room she put out her hand, thrusting it from under the covers of her bed, and she thought that death like a living thing put out his hand to her. "Be patient, lover," she whispered. "Keep yourself young and beautiful and be patient."

On the evening when disease laid its heavy hand upon her and defeated her plans for telling her son George of the eight hundred dollars hidden away, she got out of bed and crept half across the room pleading with death for another hour of life. "Wait, dear! The boy! The boy! The boy!" she pleaded as she tried with all of her strength to fight off the arms of the lover she had wanted so earnestly.

. . .

Elizabeth died one day in March in the year when her son George became eighteen, and the young man had but little sense of the meaning of her death. Only time could give him that. For a month he had seen her lying white and still and speechless in her bed, and then one afternoon the doctor stopped him in the hallway and said a few words.

The young man went into his own room and closed the door. He had a queer empty feeling in the region of his stomach. For a moment he sat staring at the floor and then jumping up went for a walk. Along the station platform he went, and around through residence streets past the high-school building, thinking almost entirely of his own affairs. The notion of death could not get hold of him and he was in fact a little annoyed that his mother had died on that day. He had just received a note from Helen White, the daughter of the town banker, in answer to one from him. "Tonight I could have gone to see her and now it will have to be put off," he thought half angrily.

Elizabeth died on a Friday afternoon at three o'clock. It had been cold and rainy in the morning but in the afternoon the sun came out. Before she died she lay paralyzed for six days unable to speak or move and with only her mind and her eyes alive. For three of the six days she struggled, thinking of her boy, trying to say some few words in regard to his future, and in her eyes there was an appeal so touching that all who saw it kept the memory of the dying woman in their minds for years. Even Tom Willard, who had always half resented his wife, forgot his resentment and the tears ran out of his eyes and lodged in his mustache. The mustache had begun to turn grey and Tom colored it with dye. There was oil in the preparation he used for the purpose and the tears, catching in the mustache and being brushed away by his hand, formed a fine mist-like vapor. In his grief Tom Willard's face looked like the face of a little dog that has been out a long time in bitter weather.

George came home along Main Street at dark on the day of his mother's death and, after going to his own room to brush his hair and clothes, went along the hallway and into the room where the body lay. There was a candle on the dressing table by the door and Doctor Reefy sat in a chair by the bed. The doctor arose and started to go out. He put out his hand as though to greet the younger man and then awkwardly drew it back again. The air of the room was heavy with the presence of the two self-conscious human beings, and the man hurried away.

The dead woman's son sat down in a chair and looked at the floor. He again thought of his own affairs and definitely decided he would make a change in his life, that he would leave Winesburg. "I will go to some city. Perhaps I can get a job on some newspaper," he thought, and then his mind turned to the girl with whom he was to have spent this evening and again he was half angry at the turn of events that had prevented his going to her.

In the dimly lighted room with the dead woman the young man began to have thoughts. His mind played with thoughts of life as his mother's mind had played with the thought of death. He closed his eyes and imagined that the red young lips of Helen White touched his own lips. His body trembled and his hands shook. And then something happened. The boy sprang to his feet and stood stiffly. He looked at the figure of the dead woman under the sheets and shame for his thoughts swept over him so that he began to weep. A new notion came into his mind and he turned and looked guiltily about as though afraid he would be observed.

George Willard became possessed of a madness to lift the sheet from the body of his mother and look at her face. The thought that had come into his mind gripped him terribly. He became convinced that not his mother but someone else lay in the bed before him. The conviction was so real that it was almost unbearable. The body under the sheets was long and in death looked young and graceful. To the boy, held by some strange fancy, it was unspeakably lovely. The feeling that the body before him was alive, that in another moment a lovely woman would spring out of the bed and confront him, became so overpowering that he could not bear the suspense. Again and again he put out his hand. Once he touched and half lifted the white sheet that covered her, but his courage failed and he, like Doctor Reefy, turned and went out of the room. In the hallway outside the door he stopped and trembled so that he had to put a hand against the wall to support himself. "That's not my mother. That's not my mother in there," he whispered to himself and again his body shook with fright and uncertainty. When Aunt Elizabeth Swift, who had come to watch over the body, came out of an adjoining room he put his hand into hers and began to sob, shaking his head from side to side, half blind with grief. "My mother is dead," he said, and then forgetting the woman he turned and stared at the door through which he had just come. "The dear, the dear, oh the lovely dear," the boy, urged by some impulse outside himself, muttered aloud.

. . .

As for the eight hundred dollars the dead woman had kept hidden so long and that was to give George Willard his start in the city, it lay in the tin box behind the plaster by the foot of his mother's bed. Elizabeth had put it there a week after her marriage, breaking the plaster away with a stick. Then she got one of the workmen her husband was at that time employing about the hotel to mend the wall. "I jammed the corner of the bed against it," she had explained to her husband, unable at the moment to give up her dream of release, the release that after all came to her but twice in her life, in the moments when her lovers Death and Doctor Reefy held her in their arms.

Katherine Mansfield

(1888 - 1923)

Like Chekhov, Stevenson, D. H. Lawrence, and Camus, Katherine Mansfield (a pseudonym for Kathleen Beauchamp) lived the mature years of her life with the unresting threat and uncertainty of tuberculosis, the disease which finally killed her in her thirty-fifth year. Her brief writing career covered a mere ten years and most of her mature, polished stories were written after 1916 and the deep shock of losing her brother in World War I. Born in 1888 in Wellington, New Zealand, the daughter of a successful businessman, Katherine Mansfield decided in 1908 to settle in England with the hope of becoming a writer. Her first years in London were disastrous and heavy with suffering. She stumbled into an unhappy marriage, became pregnant by a paramour, and lost her child by a miscarriage. She later married John Middleton Murry, a successful magazine editor, and settled down to a reasonably stable life. One of the very few writers in English who established her reputation by short stories alone, Katherine Mansfield wrote delicate, very feminine stories of great intensity concerning ordinary people. A careful reader of Chekhov, she often moved indirectly toward her subject and concerned herself more with the character, his way of life, and atmosphere than with plot. Her prose possesses a tender, suggestive quality much like poetry.

The Doll's House

When dear old Mrs. Hay went back to town after staying with the Burnells she sent the children a doll's house. It was so big that the carter and Pat carried it into the courtyard, and there it stayed, propped up on two wooden boxes beside the feed-room door. No harm could come of it; it was summer. And perhaps the smell of paint would have gone off by the time it had to be taken in. For, really, the smell of paint coming from that doll's house ("Sweet of old Mrs. Hay, of course; most sweet and generous!")—but the smell of paint was quite enough to make any one seriously ill, in Aunt Beryl's opinion. Even before the sacking was taken off. And when it was. . . .

There stood the doll's house, a dark, oily, spinach green, picked out with bright yellow. Its two solid little chimneys, glued on to the roof, were painted red and white, and the door, gleaming with yellow varnish, was like a little slab of toffee. Four windows, real windows, were divided into panels by a broad streak of green. There was actually a tiny porch, too, painted yellow, with big lumps of congealed paint hanging along the edge.

But perfect, perfect little house! Who could possibly mind the smell? It was part of the joy, part of the newness.

"Open it quickly, some one!"

The hook at the side was stuck fast. Pat pried it open with his pen-knife, and the whole house-front swung back, and—there you were, gazing at one and the same moment into the drawing-room and dining-room, the kitchen and two bedrooms. That is the way for a house to open! Why don't all houses open like that? How much more exciting than peering through the slit of a door into a mean little hall with a hatstand and two umbrellas! That is—isn't it?—what you long to know about a house when you put your hand on the knocker. Perhaps it is the way God opens houses at dead of night when He is taking a quiet turn with an angel. . . .

"O-oh!" The Burnell children sounded as though they were in despair. It was too marvellous; it was too much for them. They had never seen anything like it in their lives. All the rooms were papered. There were pictures on the walls, painted on the paper, with gold frames complete. Red carpet covered all the floors except the kitchen; red plush chairs in the drawing-room, green in the dining-room; tables, beds with real bedclothes, a cradle, a stove, a dresser with tiny plates and one big jug. But what Kezia liked more than anything, what she liked frightfully, was the lamp. It stood in the middle of the dining-room table, an exquisite little amber lamp with a white globe. It was even filled all ready for lighting, though, of course, you couldn't light it. But there was something inside that looked like oil, and that moved when you shook it.

The father and mother dolls, who sprawled very stiff as though they had fainted in the drawing-room, and their two little children asleep upstairs, were really too big for the doll's house. They didn't look as though they belonged. But the lamp was perfect. It seemed to smile at Kezia, to say, "I live here." The lamp was real.

The Burnell children could hardly walk to school fast enough the next morning. They burned to tell everybody, to describe, to—well—to boast about their doll's house before the school-bell rang.

"I'm to tell," said Isabel, "because I'm the eldest. And you two can join in after. But I'm to tell first."

There was nothing to answer. Isabel was bossy, but she was always right, and Lottie and Kezia knew too well the powers that went with being eldest. They brushed through the thick buttercups at the road edge and said nothing.

"And I'm to choose who's to come and see it first. Mother said I might."

For it had been arranged that while the doll's house stood in the courtyard they might ask the girls at school, two at a time, to come and look. Not to stay to tea, of course, or to come traipsing through the house. But just to stand quietly in the courtyard while Isabel pointed out the beauties, and Lottie and Kezia looked pleased. . . .

But hurry as they might, by the time they had reached the tarred palings of the boys' playground the bell had begun to jangle. They only just had time to whip off their hats and fall into line before the roll was called. Never mind. Isabel tried to make up for it by looking very important and mysterious and by whispering behind her hands to the girls near her, "Got something to tell you at playtime."

Playtime came and Isabel was surrounded. The girls of her class nearly fought to put their arms round her, to walk away with her, to beam flatteringly, to be her special friend. She held quite a court under the huge pine trees at the side of the playground. Nudging, giggling together, the little girls pressed up close. And the only two who stayed outside the ring were the two who were always outside, the little Kelveys. They knew better than to come anywhere near the Burnells.

For the fact was, the school the Burnell children went to was not at all the kind of place their parents would have chosen if there had been any choice. But there was none. It was the only school for miles. And the consequence was all the children in the neighbourhood, the Judge's little girls, the doctor's daughters, the storekeeper's children, the milkman's, were forced to mix together. Not to speak of there being an equal number of rude, rough little boys as well. But the line had to be drawn somewhere. It was drawn at the Kelveys. Many of the children, including the Burnells, were not allowed even to speak to them. They walked past the Kelveys with their heads in the air, and as they set the fashion in all matters of behaviour, the Kelveys were shunned by everybody. Even the teacher had a special voice for them, and a special smile for the other children when Lil Kelvey came up to her desk with a bunch of dreadfully common-looking flowers.

They were the daughters of a spry, hardworking little washerwoman, who went about from house to house by the day. This was awful enough. But where was Mr. Kelvey? Nobody knew for certain. But everybody said he was in prison. So they were the daughters of a washerwoman and a gaolbird. Very nice company for other people's children! And they looked it. Why Mrs. Kelvey made them so conspicuous was hard to understand. The truth was they were dressed in "bits" given to her by the people for whom she worked. Lil, for instance, who was a stout, plain child, with big freckles, came to school in a dress made from a green art-serge table-cloth of the Burnells', with red plush sleeves from the Logans' curtains. Her hat, perched on top of her high forehead, was a grown-up woman's hat, once the property of Miss Lecky, the postmistress. It was turned up at the back and trimmed with a large scarlet quill. What a little guy she looked! It was impossible not to laugh. And her little sister, our Else, wore a long white dress, rather like a nightgown, and a pair of little boy's boots. But whatever our Else wore she would have looked strange. She was a tiny wishbone of a child, with cropped hair and enormous solemn eyes—a little white owl. Nobody had ever seen her smile; she scarcely ever spoke. She went through life holding on to Lil, with a piece of Lil's skirt screwed up in her hand. Where Lil went our Else followed. In the playground, on the road going to and from school, there was Lil marching in front and our Else holding on behind. Only when she wanted anything, or when she was out of breath, our Else gave Lil a tug, a twitch, and Lil stopped and turned round. The Kelveys never failed to understand each other.

Now they hovered at the edge; you couldn't stop them listening. When the little girls turned round and sneered, Lil, as usual, gave her silly, shamefaced smile, but our Else only looked.

And Isabel's voice, so very proud, went on telling. The carpet made a great sensation, but so did the beds with real bedclothes, and the stove with an oven door.

When she finished Kezia broke in. "You've forgotten the lamp, Isabel."

"Oh, yes," said Isabel, "and there's a teeny little lamp, all made of yellow glass, with a white globe that stands on the dining-room table. You couldn't tell it from a real one."

"The lamp's best of all," cried Kezia. She thought Isabel wasn't making half enough of the little lamp. But nobody paid any attention. Isabel was choosing the two who were to come back with them that afternoon and see it. She chose Emmie Cole and Lena Logan. But when the others knew they were all to have a chance, they couldn't be nice enough to Isabel. One by one they put their arms round Isabel's waist and walked her off. They had something to whisper to her, a secret. "Isabel's *my* friend."

Only the little Kelveys moved away forgotten; there was nothing more for them to hear.

Days passed, and as more children saw the doll's house, the fame of it spread. It became the one subject, the rage. The one question was, "Have you seen Burnells' doll's house? Oh, ain't it lovely!" "Haven't you seen it? Oh, I say!"

Even the dinner hour was given up to talking about it. The little girls sat under the pines eating their thick mutton sandwiches and big slabs of johnny cake spread with butter. While always, as near as they could get, sat the Kelveys, our Else holding on to Lil, listening too, while they chewed their jam sandwiches out of a newspaper soaked with large red blobs. . . .

"Mother," said Kezia, "can't I ask the Kelveys just once?"

"Certainly not, Kezia."

"But why not?"

"Run away, Kezia; you know quite well why not."

At last everybody had seen it except them. On that day the subject rather flagged. It was the dinner hour. The children stood together under the pine trees, and suddenly, as they looked at the Kelveys eating out of their paper, always by themselves, always listening, they wanted to be horrid to them. Emmie Cole started the whisper.

"Lil Kelvey's going to be a servant when she grows up."

"O-oh, how awful!" said Isabel Burnell, and she made eyes at Emmie.

Emmie swallowed in a very meaning way and nodded to Isabel as she'd seen her mother do on those occasions.

"It's true—it's true—it's true," she said.

Then Lena Logan's little eyes snapped. "Shall I ask her?" she whispered.

"Bet you don't," said Jessie May.

"Pooh, I'm not frightened," said Lena. Suddenly she gave a little squeal and danced in front of the other girls. "Watch! Watch me! Watch me now!" said Lena. And sliding, gliding, dragging one foot, giggling behind her hand, Lena went over to the Kelveys.

Lil looked up from her dinner. She wrapped the rest quickly away. Our Else stopped chewing. What was coming now?

"Is it true you're going to be a servant when you grow up, Lil Kelvey?" shrilled Lena.

Dead silence. But instead of answering, Lil only gave her silly, shamefaced smile. She didn't seem to mind the question at all. What a sell for Lena! The girls began to titter.

Lena couldn't stand that. She put her hands on her hips; she shot forward. "Yah, yer father's in prison!" she hissed, spitefully.

This was such a marvellous thing to have said that the little girls rushed away in a body, deeply, deeply excited, wild with joy. Some one found a long rope, and they began skipping. And never did they skip so high, run in and out so fast, or do such daring things as on that morning.

In the afternoon Pat called for the Burnell children with the buggy and they drove home. There were visitors. Isabel and Lottie, who liked visitors, went upstairs to change their pinafores. But Kezia thieved out at the back. Nobody was about; she began to swing on the big white gates of the courtyard. Presently, looking along the road, she saw two little dots. They grew bigger, they were coming towards her. Now she could see that one was in front and one close behind. Now she could see that they were the Kelveys. Kezia stopped swinging. She slipped off the gate as if she was going to run away. Then she hesitated. The Kelveys came nearer, and beside them walked their shadows, very long, stretching right across the road with their heads in the buttercups. Kezia clambered back on the gate; she had made up her mind; she swung out.

"Hullo," she said to the passing Kelveys.

They were so astounded that they stopped. Lil gave her silly smile. Our Else stared.

"You can come and see our doll's house if you want to," said Kezia, and she dragged one toe on the ground. But at that Lil turned red and shook her head quickly.

"Why not?" asked Kezia.

Lil gasped, then she said, "Your ma told our ma you wasn't to speak to us."

"Oh, well," said Kezia. She didn't know what to reply. "It doesn't matter. You can come and see our doll's house all the same. Come on. Nobody's looking."

But Lil shook her head still harder.

"Don't you want to?" asked Kezia.

Suddenly there was a twitch, a tug at Lil's skirt. She turned round. Our Else was looking at her with big, imploring eyes; she was frowning; she wanted to go. For a moment Lil looked at our Else very doubtfully. But then our Else twitched her skirt again. She started forward. Kezia led the way. Like two little stray cats they followed across the courtyard to where to doll's house stood.

"There it is," said Kezia.

There was a pause. Lil breathed loudly, almost snorted; our Else was still as a stone.

"I'll open it for you," said Kezia kindly. She undid the hook and they looked inside.

"There's the drawing-room and the dining-room, and that's the—"

"Kezia!"

Oh, what a start they gave!

"Kezia!"

It was Aunt Beryl's voice. They turned round. At the back door stood Aunt Beryl, staring as if she couldn't believe what she saw.

"How dare you ask the little Kelveys into the courtyard?" said her cold, furious voice. "You know as well as I do, you're not allowed to talk to them. Run away, children, run away at once. And don't come back again," said Aunt Beryl. And she stepped into the yard and shooed them out as if they were chickens.

"Off you go immediately!" she called, cold and proud.

They did not need telling twice. Burning with shame, shrinking together, Lil huddling along like her mother, our Else dazed, somehow they crossed the big courtyard and squeezed through the white gate.

"Wicked, disobedient little girl!" said Aunt Beryl bitterly to Kezia, and she slammed the doll's house to.

The afternoon had been awful. A letter had come from Willie Brent, a terrifying, threatening letter, saying if she did not meet him that evening in Pulman's Bush, he'd come to the front door and ask the reason why! But now that she had frightened those little rats of Kelveys and given Kezia a good scolding, her heart felt lighter. That ghastly pressure was gone. She went back to the house humming.

When the Kelveys were well out of sight of Burnells', they sat down to rest on a big red drain-pipe by the side of the road. Lil's cheeks were still burning; she took off the hat with the quill and held it on her knee. Dreamily they looked over the hay paddocks, past the creek, to the group of wattles where Logan's cows stood waiting to be milked. What were their thoughts?

Presently our Else nudged up close to her sister. But now she had forgotten the cross lady. She put out a finger and stroked her sister's quill; she smiled her rare smile.

"I seen the little lamp," she said, softly.

Then both were silent once more.

Ernest Hemingway

(1899 - 1961)

Ernest Hemingway, unquestionably the most famous American writer of the twentieth century, made his literary reputation in the 1920's with two novels, *The Sun Also Rises* (1926) and *A Farewell to Arms* (1929), and two collections of short stories, *In Our Time* (1925) and *Men Without Women* (1927). Although he continued to write until 1961, Hemingway seldom achieved in his later fiction, especially in his novels, the quality that distinguished his first efforts, and I don't believe it would be unfair to say that his popular reputation was inflated because Hemingway the adventurer, hunter, fighter, drinker, and lover was confused with Hemingway the writer. Since his suicide in Idaho in 1961, his stock as a novelist has fallen several points and the critical consensus today is that posterity will remember him less as a novelist than as an original stylist and an innovator in and master of the short story. In fact, Hemingway revolutionized the American short story and was, I believe, the most important single influence on the form in this century. In *The Modern Short Story,* H. E. Bates writes that "Hemingway broke up every known type-face with which the American short story had ever been set, and cut for it a more austere, revolutionary, and yet more classic design than it had ever known." Aiming at a lucid rendering of the immediacy of ordinary experience, Hemingway abandoned literary language for colloquial speech even in narrative and greatly simplified sentence structures and diction. By uncommon economy and simplification he succeeded in presenting directly to the reader sharp, immediately recognizable pictures and scenes. Note how Hemingway creates a well-focused picture with the simplest words in the first two sentences of *A Farewell to Arms:* "In the late summer of that year we lived in a house in a village that looked across the river and the plain to the mountains. In the bed of the river there were pebbles and boulders, dry and white in the sun, and the water was clear and swiftly moving and blue in the channels." Because he generally withholds analysis or comment on the action, Hemingway gives a distinct impression of objectivity. Thematically, Hemingway's fiction remained more or less the same from *In Our Time* to *The Old Man and the Sea* (1952). In the latter novel he wrote, ". . . Man is not made for defeat. A man can be destroyed but not defeated." The Hemingway character, knowing that the harvest of his life will be thin and that inevitably he will be destroyed, lives according to a few simple virtues (courage, honesty, fair play) to preserve a transitory human victory over the chaos and nothingness that surround him. Hemingway's world is a violent one in which traditional values have collapsed and all that matters is how one performs one's duties to oneself. Finally, there is in this great writer's world a preoccupation with death, the great destroyer.

The Capital of the World

Madrid is full of boys named Paco, which is the diminutive of the name Francisco, and there is a Madrid joke about a father who came to Madrid and inserted an advertisement in the personal columns of *El Liberal* which said: PACO MEET ME AT HOTEL MONTANA NOON TUESDAY ALL IS FORGIVEN PAPA and how a squadron of Guardia Civil had to be called out to disperse the eight hundred young men who answered the advertisement. But this Paco, who waited on table at the Pension Luarca, had no father to forgive him, nor anything for the father to forgive. He had two older sisters who were chambermaids at the Luarca, who had gotten their place through coming from the same small village as a former Luarca chambermaid who had proven hardworking and honest and hence given her village and its products a good name; and these sisters had paid his way on the auto-bus to Madrid and gotten him his job as an apprentice waiter. He came from a village in a part of Extramadura where conditions were incredibly primitive, food scarce, and comforts unknown and he had worked hard ever since he could remember.

He was a well built boy with very black, rather curly hair, good teeth and a skin that his sisters envied, and he had a ready and unpuzzled smile. He was fast on his feet and did his work well and he loved his sisters, who seemed beautiful and sophisticated; he loved Madrid, which was still an unbelievable place, and he loved his work which, done under bright lights, with clean linen, the wearing of evening clothes, and abundant food in the kitchen, seemed romantically beautiful.

There were from eight to a dozen other people who lived at the Luarca and ate in the dining room but for Paco, the youngest of the three waiters who served at table, the only ones who really existed were the bull fighters.

Second-rate matadors lived at that pension because the address in the Calle San Jeronimo was good, the food was excellent and the room and board was cheap. It is necessary for a bull fighter to give the appearance, if not of prosperity, at least of respectability, since decorum and dignity rank above courage as the virtues most highly prized in Spain, and bull fighters stayed at the Luarca until their last pesetas were gone. There is no record of any bull fighter having left the Luarca for a better or more expensive hotel; second-rate bull fighters never became first rate; but the descent from the Luarca was swift since any one could stay there who was making anything at all and a bill was never presented to a guest unasked until the woman who ran the place knew that the case was hopeless.

At this time there were three full matadors living at the Luarca as well as two very good picadors, and one excellent banderillero. The Luarca was luxury for the picadors and the banderilleros who, with their families in Seville, required lodging in Madrid during the Spring season; but they were well paid and in the fixed employ of fighters who were heavily contracted during the coming season and the three of these subalterns would probably make much more apiece than any of the three matadors. Of the three matadors one was ill and trying to conceal it; one had passed his short vogue as a novelty; and the third was a coward.

The coward had at one time, until he had received a peculiarly atrocious horn wound in the lower abdomen at the start of his first season as a full matador, been exceptionally brave and remarkably skillful and he still had many of the hearty mannerisms of his days of success. He was jovial to excess and laughed constantly with and without provocation. He had, when successful, been very addicted to practical jokes but he had given them up now. They took an assurance that he did not feel. This matador had an intelligent, very open face and he carried himself with much style.

The matador who was ill was careful never to show it and was meticulous about eating a little of all the dishes that were presented at the table. He had a great many handkerchiefs which he laundered himself in his room and, lately, he had been selling his fighting suits. He had sold one, cheaply, before Christmas and another in the first week of April. They had been very expensive suits, had always been well kept and he had one more. Before he had become ill he had been a very promising, even a sensational, fighter and, while he himself could not read, he had clippings which said that in his debut in Madrid he had been better than Belmonte. He ate alone at a small table and looked up very little.

The matador who had once been a novelty was very short and brown and very dignified. He also ate alone at a separate table and he smiled very rarely and never laughed. He came from Valladolid, where the people are extremely serious, and he was a capable matador; but his style had become old-fashioned before he had ever succeeded in endearing himself to the public through his virtues, which were courage and a calm capability, and his name on a poster would draw no one to a bull ring. His novelty had been that he was so short that he could barely see over the bull's withers, but there were other short fighters, and he had never succeeded in imposing himself on the public's fancy.

Of the picadors one was a thin, hawk-faced, gray-haired man, lightly built but with legs and arms like iron, who always wore cattle-men's boots under his trousers, drank too much every evening and gazed amorously at any woman in the pension. The other was huge, dark, brown-faced, good-looking, with black hair like an Indian and enormous hands. Both were great picadors although the first was reputed to have lost much of his ability through drink and dissipation, and the second was said to be too headstrong and quarrelsome to stay with any matador more than a single season.

The banderillero was middle-aged, gray, cat-quick in spite of his years and, sitting at the table he looked a moderately prosperous business man. His legs were still good for this season, and when they should go he was intelligent and experienced enough to keep regularly employed for a long time. The difference would be that when his speed of foot would be gone he would always be frightened where now he was assured and calm in the ring and out of it.

On this evening every one had left the dining room except the hawk-faced picador who drank too much, the birthmarked-faced auctioneer of watches at the fairs and festivals of Spain, who also drank too much, and two priests from Galicia who were sitting at a corner table and drinking if not too much certainly enough. At that time wine was included in the price of the room and board at the Luarca and the waiters had just brought fresh bottles of Valdepeñas to the tables of the auctioneer, then to the picador and, finally, to the two priests.

The three waiters stood at the end of the room. It was the rule of the house that they should all remain on duty until the diners whose tables they were responsible for should all have left, but the one who served the table of the two priests had an appointment to go to an Anarcho-Syndicalist meeting and Paco had agreed to take over his table for him.

Upstairs the matador who was ill was lying face down on his bed alone. The matador who was no longer a novelty was sitting looking out of his window preparatory to walking out to the café. The matador who was a coward had the older sister of Paco in his room with him and was trying to get her to do something which she was laughingly refusing to do. This matador was saying "Come on, little savage."

"No," said the sister. "Why should I?"

"For a favor."

"You've eaten and now you want me for dessert."

"Just once. What harm can it do?"

"Leave me alone. Leave me alone, I tell you."

"It is a very little thing to do."

"Leave me alone, I tell you."

Down in the dining room the tallest of the waiters, who was overdue at the meeting, said "Look at those black pigs drink."

"That's no way to speak," said the second waiter. "They are decent clients. They do not drink too much."

"For me it is a good way to speak," said the tall one. "There are the two curses of Spain, the bulls and the priests."

"Certainly not the individual bull and the individual priest," said the second waiter.

"Yes," said the tall waiter. "Only through the individual can you attack the class. It is necessary to kill the individual bull and the individual priest. All of them. Then there are no more."

"Save it for the meeting," said the other waiter.

"Look at the barbarity of Madrid," said the tall waiter. "It is now half-past eleven o'clock and these are still guzzling."

"They only started to eat at ten," said the other waiter. "As you know there are many dishes. That wine is cheap and these have paid for it. It is not a strong wine."

"How can there be solidarity of workers with fools like you?" asked the tall waiter.

"Look," said the second waiter who was a man of fifty. "I have worked all my life. In all that remains of my life I must work. I have no complaints against work. To work is normal."

"Yes, but the lack of work kills."

"I have always worked," said the older waiter. "Go on to the meeting. There is no necessity to stay."

"You are a good comrade," said the tall waiter. "But you lack all ideology."

"*Mejor si me falta eso que el otro,*" said the older waiter (meaning it is better to lack that than work). "Go on to the *mitin.*"

Paco had said nothing. He did not yet understand politics but it always gave him a thrill to hear the tall waiter speak of the necessity for killing the priests and the Guardia Civil. The tall waiter represented to him revolution and revolution also was romantic. He himself would like to be a good Catholic, a revolutionary, and have a steady job like this, while, at the same time, being a bullfighter.

"Go on to the meeting, Ignacio," he said. "I will respond for your work."

"The two of us," said the older waiter.

"There isn't enough for one," said Paco. "Go on to the meeting."

"*Pues, me voy,*" said the tall waiter. "And thanks."

In the meantime, upstairs, the sister of Paco had gotten out of the embrace of the matador as skilfully as a wrestler breaking a hold and said, now angry, "These are the hungry people. A failed bullfighter. With your ton-load of fear. If you have so much of that, use it in the ring."

"That is the way a whore talks."

"A whore is also a woman, but I am not a whore."

"You'll be one."

"Not through you."

"Leave me," said the matador who, now, repulsed and refused, felt the nakedness of his cowardice returning.

"Leave you? What hasn't left you?" said the sister. "Don't you want me to make up the bed? I'm paid to do that."

"Leave me," said the matador, his broad good-looking face wrinkled into a contortion that was like crying. "You whore. You dirty little whore."

"Matador," she said, shutting the door. "My matador."

Inside the room the matador sat on the bed. His face still had the contortion which, in the ring, he made into a constant smile which frightened those people in the first rows of seats who knew what they were watching. "And this," he was saying aloud. "And this. And this."

He could remember when he had been good and it had only been three years before. He could remember the weight of the heavy gold-brocaded fighting jacket on his shoulders on that hot afternoon in May when his voice had still been the same in the ring as in the café, and how he sighted along the point-dipping blade at the place in the top of the shoulders where it was dusty in the short-haired black hump of muscle above the wide, wood-knocking, splintered-tipped horns that lowered as he went in to kill, and how the sword pushed in as easy as into a mound of stiff butter with the palm of his hand pushing the pommel, his left arm crossed low, his left shoulder forward, his weight on his left leg, and then his weight wasn't on his leg. His weight was on his lower belly and as the bull raised his head the horn was out of sight in him and he swung over on it twice before they pulled him off it. So now when he went in to kill, and it was seldom, he could not look at the horns and what did any whore know about what he went through before he fought? And what had they been through that laughed at him? They were all whores and they knew what they could do with it.

Down in the dining room the picador sat looking at the priests. If there were women in the room he stared at them. If there were no women he would stare with enjoyment at a foreigner, *un inglés,* but lacking women or strangers, he now stared with enjoyment and insolence at the two priests. While he stared the birth-marked auctioneer rose and folding his napkin went out, leaving over half the wine in the last bottle he had ordered. If his accounts had been paid up at the Luarca he would have finished the bottle.

The two priests did not stare back at the picador. One of them was saying, "It is ten days since I have been here waiting to see him and all day I sit in the ante-chamber and he will not receive me."

"What is there to do?"

"Nothing. What can one do? One cannot go against authority."

"I have been here for two weeks and nothing. I wait and they will not see me."

"We are from the abandoned country. When the money runs out we can return."

"To the abandoned country. What does Madrid care about Galicia? We are a poor province."

"One understands the action of our brother Basilio."

"Still I have no real confidence in the integrity of Basilio Alvarez."

"Madrid is where one learns to understand. Madrid kills Spain."

"If they would simply see one and refuse."

"No. You must be broken and worn out by waiting."

"Well, we shall see. I can wait as well as another."

At this moment the picador got to his feet, walked over to the priests' table and stood, gray-headed and hawk-faced, staring at them and smiling.

"A torero," said one priest to the other.

"And a good one," said the picador and walked out of the dining room, gray-jacketed, trim-waisted, bow-legged, in tight breeches over his high-heeled cattleman's boots that clicked on the floor as he swaggered quite steadily, smiling to himself. He lived in a small, tight, professional world of personal efficiency, nightly alcoholic triumph, and insolence. Now he lit a cigar and tilting his hat at an angle in the hallway went out to the café.

The priests left immediately after the picador, hurriedly conscious of being the last people in the dining room, and there was no one in the room now but Paco and the middle-aged waiter. They cleared the tables and carried the bottles into the kitchen.

In the kitchen was the boy who washed the dishes. He was three years older than Paco and was very cynical and bitter.

"Take this," the middle-aged waiter said, and poured out a glass of the Valdepeñas and handed it to him.

"Why not?" the boy took the glass.

"Tu, Paco?" the older waiter asked.

"Thank you," said Paco. The three of them drank.

"I will be going," said the middle-aged waiter.

"Good night," they told him.

He went out and they were alone. Paco took a napkin one of the priests had used and standing straight, his heels planted, lowered the napkin and with head following the movement, swung his arms in the motion of a slow sweeping veronica. He turned and advancing his right foot slightly, made the second pass, gained a little terrain on the imaginary bull and made a third pass, slow, perfectly timed and suave, then gathered the napkin to his waist and swung his hips away from the bull in a media-veronica.

The dishwasher, whose name was Enrique, watched him critically and sneeringly.

"How is the bull?" he said.

"Very brave," said Paco. "Look."

Standing slim and straight he made four more perfect passes, smooth, elegant and graceful.

"And the bull?" asked Enrique standing against the sink, holding his wine glass and wearing his apron.

"Still has lots of gas," said Paco.

"You make me sick," said Enrique.

"Why?"

"Look."

Enrique removed his apron and citing the imaginary bull he sculptured four perfect, languid gypsy veronicas and ended up with a rebolera that made the apron swing in a stiff arc past the bull's nose as he walked away from him.

"Look at that," he said. "And I wash dishes."

"Why?"

"Fear," said Enrique. "*Miedo.* The same fear you would have in a ring with a bull."

"No," said Paco. "I wouldn't be afraid."

"*Leche!*" said Enrique. "Every one is afraid. But a torero can control his fear so that he can work the bull. I went in an amateur fight and I was so afraid I couldn't keep from running. Every one thought it was very funny. So would you be afraid. If it wasn't for fear every bootblack in Spain would be a bullfighter. You, a country boy, would be frightened worse than I was."

"No," said Paco.

He had done it too many times in his imagination. Too many times he had seen the horns, seen the bull's wet muzzle, the ear twitching, then the head go down and the charge, the hoofs thudding and the hot bull pass him as he swung the cape, to re-charge as he swung the cape again, then again, and again, and again, to end winding the bull around him in his great media-veronica, and walk swingingly away, with bull hairs caught in the gold ornaments of his jacket from the close passes; the bull standing hypnotized and the crowd applauding. No, he would not be afraid. Others, yes. Not he. He knew that he could do it anyway. He had confidence. "I wouldn't be afraid," he said.

Enrique said, "*Leche,*" again.

Then he said, "If we should try it?"

"How?"

"Look," said Enrique. "You think of the bull but you do not think of the horns. The bull has such force that the horns rip like a knife, they stab like a bayonet, and they kill like a club. Look," he opened a table drawer and took out two meat knives. "I will bind these to the legs of a chair. Then I will play bull for you with the chair held before my head. The knives are the horns. If you make those passes then they mean something."

"Lend me your apron," said Paco. "We'll do it in the dining room."

"No," said Enrique, suddenly not bitter. "Don't do it, Paco."

"Yes," said Paco. "I'm not afraid."

"You will be when you see the knives come."

"We'll see," said Paco. "Give me the apron."

At this time, while Enrique was binding the two heavy-bladed razor-sharp meat knives fast to the legs of the chair with two soiled napkins holding the half of each knife, wrapping them tight and then knotting them, the two chambermaids, Paco's sisters, were on their way to the cinema to see Greta Garbo in "Anna Christie." Of the two priests, one was sitting in his underwear reading his breviary and the other was wearing a night-shirt and saying the rosary. All the bullfighters except the one who was ill had made their evening appearance at the Café Fornos, where the big, dark-haired picador was playing billiards, the short, serious matador was sitting at a crowded table before a coffee and milk, along with the middle-aged banderillero and other serious workmen.

The drinking, gray-headed picador was sitting with a glass of cazalas brandy before him staring with pleasure at a table where the matador whose courage was gone sat with another matador who had renounced the sword to become a banderillero again, and two very houseworn-looking prostitutes.

The auctioneer stood on the street corner talking with friends. The tall waiter was at the Anarcho-Syndicalist meeting waiting for an opportunity to speak. The middle-aged waiter was seated on the terrace of the Café Alvarez drinking a small beer. The woman who owned the Luarca was already asleep in her bed, where she lay on her back with the bolster between her legs; big, fat, honest, clean, easy-going, very religious and never having ceased to miss or pray daily for her husband, dead, now, twenty years. In his room, alone, the matador who was ill lay face down on his bed with his mouth against a handerchief.

Now, in the deserted dining room, Enrique tied the last knot in the napkins that bound the knives to the chair legs and lifted the chair. He pointed the legs with the knives on them forward and held the chair over his head with the two knives pointing straight ahead, one on each side of his head.

"It's heavy," he said. "Look, Paco. It is very dangerous. Don't do it." He was sweating.

Paco stood facing him, holding the apron spread, holding a fold of it bunched in each hand, thumbs up, first finger down, spread to catch the eye of the bull.

"Charge straight," he said. "Turn like a bull. Charge as many times as you want."

"How will you know when to cut the pass?" asked Enrique. "It's better to do three and then a media."

"All right," said Paco. "But come straight. Huh, torito! Come on, little bull!"

Running with head down Enrique came toward him and Paco swung the apron just ahead of the knife blade as it passed close in front of his belly and as it went by it was, to him, the real horn, white-tipped, black, smooth, and as Enrique passed him and turned to rush again it was the hot, blood-flanked mass of the bull that thudded by, then turned like a cat and came again as he swung the cape slowly. Then the bull turned and came again and, as he watched the onrushing point, he stepped his left foot two inches too far forward and the knife did not pass, but had slipped in as easily as into a wineskin and there was a hot scalding rush above and around the sudden inner rigidity of steel and Enrique shouting. "Ay! Ay! Let me get it out! Let me get it out!" and Paco slipped forward on the chair, the apron cape still held, Enrique pulling on the chair as the knife turned in him, in him, Paco.

The knife was out now and he sat on the floor in the widening warm pool.

"Put the napkin over it. Hold it!" said Enrique. "Hold it tight. I will run for the doctor. You must hold in the hemorrhage."

"There should be a rubber cup," said Paco. He had seen that used in the ring.

"I came straight," said Enrique, crying. "All I wanted was to show the danger."

"Don't worry," said Paco, his voice sounding far away. "But bring the doctor."

In the ring they lifted you and carried you, running with you, to the operating room. If the femoral artery emptied itself before you reached there they called the priest.

"Advise one of the priests," said Paco, holding the napkin tight against his lower abdomen. He could not believe that this had happened to him.

But Enrique was running down the Carrera San Jeromino to the all-night first-aid station and Paco was alone, first sitting up, then huddled over, then slumped on the floor, until it was over, feeling his life go out of him as dirty water empties from a bathtub when the plug is drawn. He was frightened and he felt faint and he tried to say an act of contrition and he remembered how it started but before he had said, as fast as he could, "Oh, my God, I am heartily sorry for having offended Thee who art worthy of all my love and I firmly resolve . . . ," he felt too faint and he was lying face down on the floor and it was over very quickly. A severed femoral artery empties itself faster than you can believe.

As the doctor from the first-aid station came up the stairs accompanied by a policeman who held on to Enrique by the arm, the two sisters of Paco were still in the moving-picture palace of the Gran Via, where they were intensely disappointed in the Garbo film, which showed the great star in miserable low surroundings when they had been accustomed to see her surrounded by great luxury and brilliance. The audience disliked the film thoroughly and were protesting by whistling and stamping their feet. All the other people from the hotel were doing almost what they had been doing when the accident happened, except that the two priests had finished their devotions and were preparing for sleep, and the gray-haired picador had moved his drink over to the table with the two houseworn prostitutes. A little later he went out of the café with one of them. It was the one for whom the matador who had lost his nerve had been buying drinks.

The boy Paco had never known about any of this nor about what all these people would be doing on the next day and on other days to come. He had no idea how they really lived nor how they ended. He did not even realize they ended. He died, as the Spanish phrase has it, full of illusions. He had not had time in his life to lose any of them, nor even, at the end, to complete an act of contrition.

He had not even had time to be disappointed in the Garbo picture which disappointed all Madrid for a week.

Isaac Babel

(1894 - 1941)

A careful craftsman and wonderfully imaginative artist, Isaac Babel shows in his fiction how the short story succinctly records an insight, an epiphany. Speaking for many other story writers, Babel once wrote, "Tolstoy was able to describe what happened to him minute by minute, he remembered it all, whereas I, evidently, only have it in me to describe the most interesting five minutes I've experienced in twenty-four hours." Regarded as the best short story writer of the Soviet period of Russian literature, Babel began writing when he was fifteen and a few years later came under the guidance of Maxim Gorky. Many of his stories capture the violence, pathos, and irony of the Russian revolution and the resistance of the peasants to government forces. Sometimes compared to Hemingway because of his subjects and his realistic, detached presentation, Babel wrote stories which are extremely concise, direct, even abrupt. In the late 1920s and early 1930s this gentle Jew enjoyed critical and popular favor, but in the monstrous Stalinist purges of 1937–1939 he was arrested, imprisoned, and secretly executed. His works were banned and he became in effect a non-person. In 1964 his works were resuscitated in the Soviet Union, and in 1969 two of his works, edited by his daughter Nathalie, were published in translation in the United States.

The Sin of Jesus

Arina was a servant at the hotel. She lived next to the main staircase, while Serega, the janitor's helper, he lived over the backstairs. Between them there was shame. On Palm Sunday Arina gave Serega a present—twins. Water flows, stars shine, a man lusts, and soon Arina was big again, her sixth month was rolling by—they're slippery, a woman's months. And now Serega must go into the army. There's a mess for you!

So Arina goes and says: "No sense, Sergunia, there's no sense in my waiting for you. For four years we'll be parted, and in four years, whatever way you look at it, I'll be sure to bring two or three more into this world. It's like walking around with your skirt turned up, working at the hotel. Whoever stops here, he's your master, let him be a Jew, let him be anybody at all. By the time you come home, my insides will be no good any more, I'll be a used-up woman, no match for you."

"That's so," Serega nodded.

"There's many that want me. Trofimych the contractor—but he's no gentleman. And Isai Abramych, the warden of Nikolo-Sviatski church, a feeble old man, but anyway I'm sick to the stomach of your murderous strength. I tell you this now, and I say it like I would at confession, I've got the wind plain knocked out of me. . . . I'll spill my load in three months, then I'll take the baby to the orphanage and marry the old man."

When Serega heard this, he took off his belt and beat her like a hero, right on the belly.

"Look out there," Arina says to him, "go soft on the belly, it's your stuffing, no one else's. . . ."

There was no end to the beating, no end to the man's tears and the woman's blood, but that is neither here nor there.

Then the woman came to Jesus Christ.

"So and so," she says, "Lord Jesus. I am the woman Arina from the Hotel Madrid and Louvre, the one on Tverskaya Street. Working at the hotel, it's like going around with your skirt up. Just let a man stop there, and he's your lord and master, let him be a Jew, let him be anybody at all. There is another slave of yours walking the earth, the janitor's helper, Serega. Last year on Palm Sunday I bore him twins. . . ."

And so she described it all to the Lord.

"And what if Serega were not to go into the army at all?" the Saviour suggested.

Isaac Babel's "The Sin of Jesus" translated by Mirra Ginsburg, is reprinted from *The Partisan Review* Anthology, pp. 313–316 with the permission of *Partisan Review;* Joan Daves, Society of Author's Representatives; and Gunther Stuhlmann, Literary Agent.

"Try and get away with it—not with the policeman around. He'll drag him off as sure as daylight. . . ."

"Oh yes, the policeman," the Lord bowed his head, "I never thought of him. . . . Then perhaps you ought to live in purity for a while? . . ."

"For four years?" the woman cried. "To hear you talk, all people should deny their animal nature. That's just your old ways all over again. And where will the increase come from? No, you'd better give me some sensible advice. . . ."

The Lord's cheeks turned scarlet, the woman's words had touched a tender spot. But he said nothing. You cannot kiss your own ear—even God knows that.

"I'll tell you what, God's servant, glorious sinner, maiden Arina," the Lord proclaimed in all his glory, "I have a little angel here in heaven, hanging around uselessly. His name is Alfred. Lately he's gotten out of hand altogether, keeps crying and nagging all the time: 'What have you done to me, Lord, why did you turn me into an angel in my twentieth year, and me a hale young fellow?' So I'll give you Alfred the angel as a husband for four years. He'll be your prayer, he'll be your protection, and he'll be your solace. And as for offspring, you've nothing to worry about—you can't bear a duckling from him, let alone a baby, for there's a lot of fun in him, but no seriousness. . . ."

"That's just what I need," the maid Arina wept gratefully. "Their seriousness takes me to the doorstep of the grave three times every two years. . . ."

"You'll have a sweet respite, God's child Arina, may your prayer be light as a song. Amen."

And so it was decided. Alfred was brought in—a frail young fellow, delicate, two wings fluttering behind his pale-blue shoulders, rippling with rosy lights like two doves playing in heaven. Arina threw her hefty arms about him, weeping out of tenderness, out of her woman's soft heart.

"Alfred, my soul, my consolation, my bridegroom. . . ."

In parting, the Lord gave her strict instructions to take off the angel's wings every night before he went to bed. His wings were attached to hinges, like a door, and every night she was to take them off and wrap them in a clean sheet, because they were brittle, his wings, and could snap as he tossed in bed—for what were they made of but the sighs of babes, no more than that.

For the last time the Lord blessed the union, while the choir of bishops, called in for the occasion, rendered thunderous praises. No food was served, not a crumb—that wasn't the style in heaven—and then Arina and Alfred, their arms about each other, ran down a silken ladder, straight back to earth. They came to Petrovka, where nothing but the best is sold—the woman would do right by her Alfred!—(and he, if one might say so, not only lacking socks, but altogether natural just as his mother bore him)—

and she bought him patent leather half-boots, checked jersey trousers, a fine hunting jacket, and an electric blue vest.

"The rest," she says, "we'll find at home. . . ."

That day Arina begged off from work. Serega came, raised a fuss, but she did not even come out to him, only said from behind her locked door:

"Sergei Nifantich, I am at present laving my feet and beg you to retire without more noise. . . ."

He went away without a word—the angel's power was already beginning to manifest itself!

In the evening Arina set out a supper fit for a merchant—the woman had devilish vanity! A half-pint of vodka, wine on the side, a Danube herring with potatoes, a samovar of tea. When Alfred had partaken of all these earthly blessings, he keeled over in a dead sleep. Quick as a wink, Arina lifted off his wings from the hinges, packed them away, and carried him to bed in her arms.

There it lies, the snowy wonder on the eiderdown pillows of her tattered, sinful bed, sending forth a heavenly radiance; moon-silver shafts of light pass and repass, alternate with red ones, float across the room, sway over his shiny feet. Arina weeps and rejoices, sings and prays. Arina, thou hast been granted a happiness unheard of on this battered earth, blessed art thou among women!

They had drunk the vodka to the last drop, and now it took effect. As soon as they fell asleep, she went and rolled over on top of Alfred with her hot, six-months'-big belly. Not enough for her to sleep with an angel, not enough that nobody beside her spat at the wall, snored and snorted—that wasn't enough for the clumsy, ravening slut. No, she had to warm her belly too, her burning belly big with Serega's lust. And so she smothered him in her fuddled sleep, smothered him in the midst of her rejoicing like a week-old babe, crushed him under her bloated weight, and he gave up the ghost, and his wings, wrapped in her sheet, wept pale tears.

Dawn came—and all the trees bowed low to the ground. In distant northern forests each fir tree turned into a priest, each fir tree bent its knees in silent worship.

Once more the woman stands before the Lord's throne—broad in the shoulders, mighty, the young corpse drooping in her huge red arms.

"Behold, Lord. . . ."

But here the gentle heart of Jesus could endure no longer, and he cursed the woman in his anger:

"As it is on earth, so shall it be with you, Arina, from this day on. . . ."

"How is it then, Lord," the woman replied in a scarce audible voice, "was it I who made my body heavy, was it I that brewed vodka on earth, was it I that created a woman's soul, stupid and lonely? . . ."

"I don't wish to be bothered with you," exclaimed the Lord Jesus, "you've smothered my angel, you filthy scum. . . ."

And Arina was thrown back to earth on a putrid wind, straight down to Tverskaya Street, to the Hotel Madrid and Louvre, where she was doomed to spend her days. And once there—the sky's the limit. Serega was carousing, drinking away his last days, seeing as he was a recruit. The contractor Trofimych, just come from Koloma, took one look at Arina, hefty and red-cheeked: "Oh, you cute little belly," he says, and so forth.

Isai Abramych, the old codger, heard about this cute little belly and he is right there, too, wheezing toothlessly:

"I cannot wed you lawfully," he says, "after all that happened. However, I can lie with you the same as anyone. . . ."

The old man ought to be lying in cold mother earth instead of thinking such things, but no, he too must take his turn at spitting into her soul. It was like everybody breaking off a chain—kitchen boys, merchants, foreigners. A trading man—he likes to have his fun.

And that is the end of my tale.

Before she was laid up, because three months had rolled by in the meantime, Arina went out into the backyard, behind the janitor's rooms, raised her monstrous huge belly to the silken sky and said stupidly:

"See, Lord, what a belly. They hammer at it like peas out of a bursting pod. And what's the sense in it—I cannot see. And furthermore, I have no wish to see. . . ."

With his tears Jesus washed Arina when he heard these words, on his knees the Saviour dropped before her.

"Forgive me, Arinushka, forgive your sinful God. What have I done to you? . . ."

But Arina shook her head and would not listen.

"There's no forgiveness for you, Jesus Christ," she said, "no forgiveness at all, none."

William Faulkner

(1897 - 1962)

William Faulkner was *the* great American literary genius of this century and the only major American novelist to create, in a series of novels and short stories, an imaginary, thoroughly believable world inhabited by scores of unforgettable characters. Faulkner's literary world is called Yoknapatawpha County, Mississippi, covers 2400 square miles, and, according to its creator, contains 6298 whites and 9313 blacks. It is a dramatic, violent, colorful county. A Southerner by birth and rearing, Faulkner recounts the moral and cultural crises of the South and its proud people. As Irving Howe has said, "The world of Yoknapatawpha, though of great fascination simply as a spectacle of drama and event, is also the setting for a complex moral chronicle in which a popular myth and an almost legendary past yield something quite rare in American literature: a deep sense of the burdens and grandeur of history." But Faulkner is really much more than a regional artist splashing in local color and culture; his imaginary world is a microcosm of the suffering real world, the world in which men lust and sacrifice and show themselves to be heroes and cowards. He dramatizes three types of men: aristocrats, men deeply touched and sometimes paralyzed by the past; poor whites, who work hard, trade shrewdly and sometimes grasp at life greedily without scruple or inhibition; and blacks and Indians, simple, natural people in touch with the wellsprings of life. Reminding one of Thoreau, Faulkner viewed society and its conventions as perverting and alienating man from the reality of sensation and immediate experience, and he saw modern man as a spiritual cripple, ruefully divorced from nature by abstractions and materialism. Society and nature are antipodes, but Faulkner does not romanticize nature, for he understood its cruelty and arbitrariness. And yet it is by maintaining contact with nature that civilized man makes himself whole. Edmond Volpe, writing about Faulkner, has observed, "In the woods, man, within the pattern of natural existence, strips away the layers of artificiality imposed upon him by society and bares the vital forces of his inner being. By confronting his essential self, he acknowledges his relation to the world of nature, its cyclical pattern of death and regeneration, and hence his own role in that pattern."

The Old People

I

At first there was nothing. There was the faint, cold, steady rain, the gray and constant light of the late November dawn, with the voices of the hounds converging somewhere in it and toward them. Then Sam Fathers, standing just behind the boy as he had been standing when the boy shot his first running rabbit with his first gun and almost with the first load it ever carried, touched his shoulder and he began to shake, not with any cold. Then the buck was there. He did not come into sight; he was just there, looking not like a ghost but as if all of light were condensed in him and he were the source of it, not only moving in it but disseminating it, already running, seen first as you always see the deer, in that split second after he has already seen you, already slanting away in that first soaring bound, the antlers even in that dim light looking like a small rocking-chair balanced on his head.

"Now," Sam Fathers said, "shoot quick, and slow."

The boy did not remember that shot at all. He would live to be eighty, as his father and his father's twin brother and their father in his turn had lived to be, but he would never hear that shot nor remember even the shock of the gun-butt. He didn't even remember what he did with the gun afterward. He was running. Then he was standing over the buck where it lay on the wet earth still in the attitude of speed and not looking at all dead, standing over it shaking and jerking, with Sam Fathers beside him again, extending the knife. "Don't walk up to him in front," Sam said. "If he ain't dead, he will cut you all to pieces with his feet. Walk up to him from behind and take him by the horn first, so you can hold his head down until you can jump away. Then slip your other hand down and hook your fingers in his nostrils."

The boy did that—drew the head back and the throat taut and drew Sam Father's knife across the throat and Sam stooped and dipped his hands in the hot smoking blood and wiped them back and forth across the boy's face. Then Sam's horn rang in the wet gray woods and again and again;

there was a boiling wave of dogs about them, with Tennie's Jim and Boon Hogganbeck whipping them back after each had had a taste of the blood, then the men, the true hunters—Walter Ewell whose rifle never missed, and Major de Spain and old General Compson and the boy's cousin, McCaslin Edmonds, grandson of his father's sister, sixteen years his senior and, since both he and McCaslin were only children and the boy's father had been nearing seventy when he was born, more his brother than his cousin and more his father than either—sitting their horses and looking down at them: at the old man of seventy who had been a Negro for two generations now but whose face and bearing were still those of the Chickasaw chief who had been his father; and the white boy of twelve with the prints of the bloody hands on his face, who had nothing to do now but stand straight and not let the trembling show.

"Did he do all right, Sam?" his cousin McCaslin said.

"He done all right," Sam Fathers said.

They were the white boy, marked forever, and the old dark man sired on both sides by savage kings, who had marked him, whose bloody hands had merely formally consecrated him to that which, under the man's tutelage, he had already accepted, humbly and joyfully, with abnegation and with pride too; the hands, the touch, the first worthy blood which he had been found at last worthy to draw, joining him and the man forever, so that the man would continue to live past the boy's seventy years and then eighty years, long after the man himself had entered the earth as chiefs and kings entered it;—the child, not yet a man, whose grandfather had lived in the same country and in almost the same manner as the boy himself would grow up to live, leaving his descendants in the land in his turn as his grandfather had done, and the old man past seventy whose grandfathers had owned the land long before the white men ever saw it and who had vanished from it now with all their kind, what of blood they left behind them running now in another race and for a while even in bondage and now drawing toward the end of its alien and irrevocable course, barren, since Sam Fathers had no children.

His father was Ikkemotubbe himself, who had named himself Doom. Sam told the boy about that—how Ikkemotubbe, old Issetibbeha's sister's son, had run away to New Orleans in his youth and returned seven years later with a French companion calling himself the Chevalier Soeur-Blonde de Vitry, who must have been the Ikkemotubbe of his family too and who was already addressing Ikkemotubbe as *Du Homme;*—returned, came home again, with his foreign Aramis and the quadroon slave woman who was to be Sam's mother, and a gold-laced hat and coat and a wicker wine-hamper containing a litter of month-old puppies and a gold snuff-box filled with a white powder resembling fine sugar. And how he was met at the River landing by three or four companions of his bachelor youth, and while the light of a smoking torch gleamed on the glittering braid of the hat and coat Doom squatted in the mud of the land and took one of the puppies from the hamper and put a pinch of the white powder on its tongue and the puppy died before the one who was holding it could cast it away. And how they returned to the Plantation where Issetibbeha, dead now, had been succeeded by his son, Doom's fat cousin Moketubbe, and the next day Moketubbe's eight-year-old son died suddenly and that afternoon, in the presence of Moketubbe and most of the others (the People, Sam Fathers called them) Doom produced another puppy from the wine-hamper and put a pinch of the white powder on its tongue and Moketubbe abdicated and Doom became in fact The Man which his French friend already called him. And how on the day after that, during the ceremony of accession, Doom pronounced a marriage between the pregnant quadroon and one of the slave men which he had just inherited (that was how Sam Fathers got his name, which in Chickasaw had been Had-Two-Fathers) and two years later sold the man and woman and the child who was his own son to his white neighbor, Carothers McCaslin.

That was seventy years ago. The Sam Fathers whom the boy knew was already sixty—a man not tall, squat rather, almost sedentary, flabby-looking though he actually was not, with hair like a horse's mane which even at seventy showed no trace of white and a face which showed no age until he smiled, whose only visible trace of Negro blood was a slight dullness of the hair and the fingernails, and something else which you did notice about the eyes, which you noticed because it was not always there, only in repose and not always then—something not in their shape nor pigment but in their expression, and the boy's cousin McCaslin told him what that was: not the heritage of Ham, not the mark of servitude but of bondage; the knowledge that for a while that part of his blood had been the blood of slaves. "Like an old lion or a bear in a cage," McCaslin said. "He was born in the cage and has been in it all his life, he knows nothing else. Then he smells something. It might be anything, any breeze blowing past anything and then into his nostrils. But there for a second was the hot sand or the cane-brake that he never saw himself, might not even know if he did see it and probably does know he couldn't hold his own with it if he got back to it. But that's not what he smells then. It was the cage he smelled. He hadn't smelled the cage until that minute. Then the hot sand or the brake blew into his nostrils and blew away, and all he could smell was the cage. That's what makes his eyes look like that."

"Then let him go!" the boy cried. "Let him go!"

His cousin laughed shortly. Then he stopped laughing, making the sound, that is. It had never been laughing. "His cage aint McCaslins," he said. "He was a wild man. When he was born, all his blood on both sides, except the little white part, knew things that had been tamed out of our blood so long ago that we have not only forgotten them, we have to live together in herds to protect ourselves from our own sources. He was the direct son not only of a warrior but of a chief. Then he grew up and began to learn things, and all of a sudden one day he found out that he had been betrayed, the blood of the warriors and chiefs had been betrayed. Not by his father," he added quickly. "He probably never held it against old Doom for selling him and his mother into slavery, because he probably believed the damage was already done before then and it was the same warriors' and chiefs' blood in him and Doom both that was betrayed through the black blood which his mother gave him. Not betrayed by the black blood and not wilfully betrayed by his mother, but betrayed by her all the same, who had bequeathed him not only the blood of slaves but even a little of the very blood which had enslaved it; himself his own battleground, the scene of his own vanquishment and the mausoleum of his defeat. His cage aint us," McCaslin said. "Did you ever know anybody yet, even your father and Uncle Buddy, that ever told him to do or not do anything that he ever paid any attention to?"

That was true. The boy first remembered him as sitting in the door of the plantation blacksmith-shop, where he sharpened plow-points and mended tools and even did rough carpenter-work when he was not in the woods. And sometimes, even when the woods had not drawn him, even with the shop cluttered with work which the farm waited on, Sam would sit there, doing nothing at all for half a day or a whole one, and no man, neither the boy's father and twin uncle in their day nor his cousin McCaslin after he became practical though not yet titular master, ever to say to him, "I want this finished by sundown" or "why wasn't this done yesterday?" And once each year, in the late fall, in November, the boy would watch the wagon, the hooped canvas top erected now, being loaded—the food, hams and sausage from the smokehouse, coffee and flour and molasses from the commissary, a whole beef killed just last night for the dogs until there would be meat in camp, the crate containing the dogs themselves, then the bedding, the guns, the horns and lanterns and axes, and his cousin McCaslin and Sam Fathers in their hunting clothes would mount to the seat and with Tennie's Jim sitting on the dog-crate they would drive away to Jefferson, to join Major de Spain and General Compson and Boon Hogganbeck and Walter Ewell and go on into the big bottom of the Tallahatchie where the deer and bear were, to be gone two weeks. But before the wagon was even loaded the boy would find that he could watch no longer. He would go away, running almost, to stand behind the corner where he could not see the wagon and nobody could see him, not crying, holding himself rigid except for trembling, whispering to himself: "Soon now. Soon now. Just three more years" (or two more or one more) "and I will be ten. Then Cass said I can go."

White man's work, when Sam did work. Because he did nothing else: farmed no alloted acres of his own, as the other ex-slaves of old Carothers McCaslin did, performed no field-work for daily wages as the younger and newer Negroes did—and the boy never knew just how that had been settled between Sam and old Carothers, or perhaps with old Carothers' twin sons after him. For, although Sam lived among the Negroes, in a cabin among the other cabins in the quarters, and consorted with Negroes (what of consorting with anyone Sam did after the boy got big enough to walk alone from the house to the blacksmith-shop and then to carry a gun) and dressed like them and talked like them and even went with them to the Negro church now and then, he was still the son of that Chickasaw chief and the Negroes knew it. And, it seemed to the boy, not only Negroes. Boon Hogganbeck's grandmother had been a Chickasaw woman too, and although the blood had run white since and Boon was a white man, it was not chief's blood. To the boy at least, the difference was apparent immediately you saw Boon and Sam together, and even Boon seemed to know it was there—even Boon, to whom in his tradition it had never occurred that anyone might be better born than himself. A man might be smarter, he admitted that, or richer (luckier, he called it) but not better born. Boon was a mastiff, absolutely faithful, dividing his fidelity equally between Major de Spain and the boy's cousin McCaslin, absolutely dependent for his very bread and dividing that impartially too between Major de Spain and McCaslin, hardy, generous, courageous enough, a slave to all the appetites and almost unratiocinative. In the boy's eyes at least it was Sam Fathers, the Negro, who bore himself not only toward his cousin McCaslin and Major de Spain but toward all white men, with gravity and dignity and without servility or recourse to that impenetrable wall of ready and easy mirth which Negroes sustain between themselves and white men, bearing himself toward his cousin McCaslin not only as one man to another but as an older man to a younger.

He taught the boy the woods, to hunt, when to shoot and when not to shoot, when to kill and when not to kill, and better, what to do with it afterward. Then he would talk to the boy, the two of them sitting beneath the close fierce stars on a summer hilltop while they waited for the hounds to bring the fox back within hearing, or beside a fire in the November or December woods while the dogs worked out a coon's trail along the creek, or fireless in the pitch dark and heavy dew of April mornings while they squatted beneath a turkey-roost. The boy would never question him; Sam did not react to questions. The boy would just wait and then listen and Sam would begin, talking about the old days and the People whom he had not had time ever to know and so could not remember (he did not remember ever having seen his father's face), and in place of whom the other race into which his blood had run supplied him with no substitute.

And as he talked about those old times and those dead and vanished men of another race from either that the boy knew, gradually to the boy those old times would cease to be old times and would become a part of the boy's present, not only as if they had happened yesterday but as if they were still happening, the men who walked through them actually walking in breath and air and casting an actual shadow on the earth they had not quitted. And more: as if some of them had not happened yet but would occur tomorrow, until at last it would seem to the boy that he himself had not come into existence yet, that none of his race nor the other subject race which his people had brought with them into the land had come here yet; that although it had been his grandfather's and then his father's and uncle's and was now his cousin's and someday would be his own land which he and Sam hunted over, their hold upon it actually was a trivial and without reality as the now faded and archaic script in the chancery book in Jefferson which allocated it to them and that it was he, the boy, who was the guest here and Sam Father's voice the mouthpiece of the host.

Until three years ago there had been two of them, the other a full-blood Chickasaw, in a sense even more incredibly lost than Sam Fathers. He called himself Jobaker, as if it were one word. Nobody knew his history at all. He was a hermit, living in a foul little shack at the forks of the creek five miles from the plantation and about that far from any other habitation. He was a market hunter and fisherman and he consorted with nobody, black or white; no Negro would even cross his path and no man dared approach his hut except Sam. And perhaps once a month the boy would find them in Sam's shop—two old men squatting on their heels on the dirt floor, talking in a mixture of Negroid English and flat hill dialect and now and then a phrase of that old tongue which as time went on and the boy squatted there too listening, he began to learn. Then Jobaker died. That is, nobody had seen him in some time. Then one morning Sam was missing, nobody, not even the boy, knew when nor where, until that night when some Negroes hunting in the creek bottom saw the sudden burst of flame and approached. It was Jobaker's hut, but before they got anywhere near it, someone shot at them from the shadows beyond it. It was Sam who fired, but nobody ever found Jobaker's grave.

The next morning, sitting at breakfast with his cousin, the boy saw Sam pass the dining-room window and he remembered then that never in his life before had he seen Sam nearer the house than the blacksmith-shop. He stopped eating even; he sat there and he and his cousin both heard the voices from beyond the pantry door, then the door opened and Sam entered, carrying his hat in his hand but without knocking as anyone else on the place except a house servant would have done, entered just far enough for the door to close behind him and stood looking at neither of them—the Indian face above the nigger clothes, looking at something over their heads or at something not even in the room.

"I want to go," he said. "I want to go to the Big Bottom to live."

"To live?" the boy's cousin said.

"At Major de Spain's and your camp, where you go to hunt," Sam said.

"I could take care of it for you all while you aint there. I will build me a little house in the woods, if you rather I didn't stay in the big one."

"What about Isaac here?" his cousin said. "How will you get away from him? Are you going to take him with you?" But still Sam looked at neither them, standing just inside the room with that face which showed nothing, which showed that he was an old man only when it smiled.

"I want to go," he said. "Let me go."

"Yes," the cousin said quietly. "Of course. I'll fix it with Major de Spain. You want to go soon?"

"I'm going now," Sam said. He went out. And that was all. The boy was nine then; it seemed perfectly natural that nobody, not even his cousin McCaslin, should argue with Sam. Also, since he was nine now, he could understand that Sam could leave him and their days and nights in the woods together without any wrench. He believed that he and Sam both knew that this was not only temporary but that exigencies of his maturing, of that for which Sam had been training him all his life some day to dedicate himself, required it. They had settled that one night last summer while they listened to the hounds bringing a fox back up the creek valley; now the boy discerned in that very talk under the high, fierce August stars a presage, a warning, of this moment today. "I done taught you all there is of this settled country," Sam said. "You can hunt it good as I can now. You are ready for the Big Bottom now, for bear and deer. Hunter's meat," he said. "Next year you will be ten. You will write your age in two numbers and you will be ready to become a man. Your pa" (Sam always referred to the boy's cousin as his father, establishing even before the boy's orphanhood did that relation between them not of the ward to his guardian and kinsman and chief and head of his blood, but of the child to the man who sired his flesh and his thinking too) "promised you can go with us then." So the boy could understand Sam's going. But he couldn't understand why now, in March, six months before the moon for hunting.

"If Jobaker's dead like they say," he said, "and Sam hasn't got anybody but us at all kin to him, why does he want to go to the Big Bottom now, when it will be six months before we get there?"

"Maybe that's what he wants," McCaslin said. "Maybe he wants to get away from you a little while."

But that was all right. McCaslin and other grown people often said things like that and he paid no attention to them, just as he paid no attention to Sam saying he wanted to go to the Big Bottom to live. After all, he would have to live there for six months, because there would be no use in going at all if he was going to turn right around and come back. And, as Sam himself had told him, he already knew all about hunting in this settled country that Sam or anybody else could teach him. So it would be all right. Summer, then the bright days after the first frost, then the cold and himself on the wagon with McCaslin this time and the moment would come and he would draw the blood, the big blood which would make him a man, a hunter, and Sam would come back home with them and he too would have outgrown the child's pursuit of rabbits and 'possums. Then he too would make one before the winter fire, talking of the old hunts and the hunts to come as hunters talked.

So Sam departed. He owned so little that he could carry it. He walked. He would neither let McCaslin send him in the wagon, nor take a mule to ride. No one saw him go even. He was just gone one morning, the cabin which had never had very much in it, vacant and empty, the shop in which there never had been very much done, standing idle. Then November came at last, and now the boy made one—himself and his cousin McCaslin and Tennie's Jim, and Major de Spain and General Compson and Walter Ewell and Boon and old Uncle Ash to do the cooking, waiting for them in Jefferson with the other wagon, and the surrey in which he and McCaslin and General Compson and Major de Spain would ride.

Sam was waiting at the camp to meet them. If he was glad to see them, he did not show it. And if, when they broke camp two weeks later to return home, he was sorry to see them go, he did not show that either. Because he did not come back with them. It was only the boy who returned, returning solitary and alone to the settled familiar land, to follow for eleven months the childish business of rabbits and such while he waited to go back, having brought with him, even from his brief first sojourn, an unforgettable sense of the big woods—not a quality dangerous or particularly inimical, but profound, sentient, gigantic and brooding, amid which he had been permitted to go to and fro at will unscathed, why he knew not, but dwarfed and, until he had drawn honorably blood worthy of being drawn, alien.

Then November, and they would come back. Each morning Sam would take the boy out to the stand allotted him. It would be one of the poorer stands of course, since he was only ten and eleven and twelve and he had never even seen a deer running yet. But they would stand there, Sam a little behind him and without a gun himself, as he had been standing when the boy shot the running rabbit when he was eight years old. They would stand there in the November dawns, and after a while they would hear the dogs. Sometimes the chase would sweep up and pass quite close, belling and invisible; once they heard the two heavy reports of Boon Hogganbeck's old gun with which he had never killed anything larger than a squirrel and that sitting, and twice they heard the flat unreverberant clap of Walter Ewell's rifle, following which you did not even wait to hear his horn.

"I'll never get a shot," the boy said. "I'll never kill one."

"Yes you will," Sam said. "You wait. You'll be a hunter. You'll be a man."

But Sam wouldn't come out. They would leave him there. He would come as far as the road where the surrey waited, to taking the riding horses back, and that was all. The men would ride the horses and Uncle Ash and Tennie's Jim and the boy would follow in the wagon with Sam, with the camp equipment and the trophies, the meat, the heads, the antlers, the good ones, the wagon winding on among the tremendous gums and cypresses and oaks where no axe save that of the hunter had ever sounded, between the impenetrable walls of cane and brier—the two changing yet constant walls just beyond which the wilderness whose mark he had brought away forever on his spirit even from that first two weeks seemed to lean, stooping a little, watching them and listening, not quite inimical because they were too small, even those such as Walter and Major de Spain and old General Compson who had killed many deer and bear, their sojourn too brief and too harmless to excite to that, but just brooding, secret, tremendous, almost inattentive.

Then they would emerge, they would be out of it, the line as sharp as the demarcation of a doored wall. Suddenly skeleton cotton- and cornfields would flow away on either hand, gaunt and motionless beneath the gray rain; there would be a house, barns, fences, where the hand of man had clawed for an instant, holding, the wall of the wilderness behind them now, tremendous and still and seemingly impenetrable in the gray and fading light, the very tiny orifice through which they had emerged apparently swallowed up. The surrey would be waiting, his cousin McCaslin and Major de Spain and General Compson and Walter and Boon dismounted beside it. Then Sam would get down from the wagon and mount one of the horses and, with the others on a rope behind him, he would turn back. The boy would watch him for a while against that tall and secret wall, growing smaller and smaller against it, never looking back. Then he would enter it, returning to what the boy believed, and thought that his cousin McCaslin believed, was his loneliness and solitude.

II

So the instant came. He pulled trigger and Sam Fathers marked his face with the hot blood which he had spilled and he ceased to be a child and became a hunter and a man. It was the last day. They broke camp that afternoon and went out, his cousin and Major de Spain and General Compson and Boon on the horses, Walter Ewell and the Negroes in the wagon with him and Sam and his hide and antlers. There could have been (and were) other trophies in the wagon. But for him they did not exist, just as for all practical purposes he and Sam Fathers were still alone together as they had been that morning. The wagon wound and jolted between the slow and shifting yet constant walls from beyond and above which the wilderness watched them pass, less than inimical now and never to be inimical again since the buck still and forever leaped, the shaking gun-barrels coming constantly and forever steady at last, crashing, and still out of his instant of immortality the buck sprang, forever immortal;—the wagon jolting and bouncing on, the moment of the buck, the shot, Sam Fathers and himself and the blood with which Sam had marked him forever one with the wilderness which had accepted him since Sam said that he had done all right, when suddenly Sam reined back and stopped the wagon and they all heard the unmistakable and unforgettable sound of a deer breaking cover.

Then Boon shouted from beyond the bend of the trail and while they sat motionless in the halted wagon, Walter and the boy already reaching for their guns, Boon came galloping back, flogging his mule with his hat, his face wild and amazed as he shouted down at them. Then the other riders came around the bend, also spurring.

"Get the dogs!" Boon cried "Get the dogs! If he had a nub on his head, he had fourteen points! Laying right there by the road in that pawpaw thicket! If I'd a knowed he was there, I could have cut his throat with my pocket knife!"

"Maybe that's why he run," Walter said. "He saw you never had your gun." He was already out of the wagon with his rifle. Then the boy was out too with his gun, and the other riders came up and Boon got off his mule somehow and was scrabbling and clawing among the duffel in the wagon, still shouting, "Get the dogs! Get the dogs!" And it seemed to the boy too that it would take them forever to decide what to do—the old men in whom the blood ran cold and slow, in whom during the intervening years between them and himself the blood had become a different and colder substance from that which ran in him and even in Boon and Walter.

"What about it, Sam?" Major de Spain said. "Could the dogs bring him back?"

"We wont need the dogs," Sam said. "If he dont hear the dogs behind him, he will circle back in here about sundown to bed."

"All right," Major de Spain said. "You boys take the horses. We'll go on out to the road in the wagon and wait there." He and General Compson and McCaslin got into the wagon and Boon and Walter and Sam and the boy mounted the horses and turned back and out of the trail. Sam led them for an hour through the gray and unmarked afternoon whose light was little different from what it had been at dawn and which would become darkness without any gradation between. Then Sam stopped them.

"This is far enough," he said. "He'll be coming upwind, and he dont want to smell the mules." They tied the mounts in a thicket. Sam led them on foot now, unpathed through the markless afternoon, the boy pressing close behind him, the two others, or so it seemed to the boy, on his heels. But they were not. Twice Sam turned his head slightly and spoke back to him across his shoulder, still walking: "You got time. We'll get there fore he does."

So he tried to go slower. He tried deliberately to decelerate the dizzy rushing of time in which the buck which he had not even seen was moving, which it seemed to him must be carrying the buck farther and farther and more and more irretrievably away from them even though there were no dogs behind him now to make him run, even though, according to Sam, he must have completed his circle now and was heading back toward them. They went on; it could have been another hour or twice that or less than half, the boy could not have said. Then they were on a ridge. He had never been in here before and he could not see that it was a ridge. He just knew that the earth had risen slightly because the underbrush had thinned a little, the ground sloping invisibly away toward a dense wall of cane. Sam stopped. "This is it," he said. He spoke to Walter and Boon: "Follow this ridge and you will come to two crossings. You will see the tracks. If he crosses, it will be at one of these three."

Walter looked about for a moment. "I know it," he said "I've even seen your deer. I was in here last Monday. He aint nothing but a yearling."

"A yearling?" Boon said. He was panting from the walking. His face still looked a little wild. "If the one I saw was any yearling, I'm still in kindergarden."

"Then I must have seen a rabbit," Walter said. "I always heard you quit school altogether two years before the first grade."

Boon glared at Walter. "If you dont want to shoot him, get out of the way," he said. "Set down somewhere. By God, I—"

"Aint nobody going to shoot him standing here," Sam said quietly.

"Sam's right," Walter said. He moved, slanting the worn, silver-colored barrel of his rifle downward to walk with it again. "A little more moving and a little more quiet too. Five miles is still Hogganbeck range, even if he wasn't downwind." They went on. The boy could still hear Boon talking, though presently that ceased too. Then once more he and Sam stood motionless together against a tremendous pin oak in a little thicket, and again there was nothing. There was only the soaring and sombre solitude in the dim light, there was the thin murmur of the faint cold rain which had not ceased all day. Then, as if it had waited for them to find their positions and become still, the wilderness breathed again. It seemed to lean inward above them, above himself and Sam and Walter and Boon in their separate lurking-places, tremendous, attentive, impartial and omniscient, the buck moving in it somewhere, not running yet since he had not been pursued, not frightened yet and never fearsome but just alert also as they were alert, perhaps already circling back, perhaps quite near, perhaps conscious also of the eye of the ancient immortal Umpire. Because he was just twelve then, and that morning something had happened to him: in less than a second he had ceased forever to be the child he was yesterday. Or perhaps that made no difference, perhaps even a city-bred man, let alone a child, could not have understood it; perhaps only a country-bred one could comprehend loving the life he spills. He began to shake again.

"I'm glad it's started now," he whispered. He did not move to speak; only his lips shaped the expiring words: "Then it will be gone when I raise the gun—"

Nor did Sam. "Hush," he said.

"Is he that near?" the boy whispered. "Do you think—"

"Hush," Sam said. So he hushed. But he could not stop the shaking. He did not try, because he knew it would go away when he needed the steadiness—had not Sam Fathers already consecrated and absolved him from weakness and regret too?—not from love and pity for all which lived and ran and then ceased to live in a second in the very midst of splendor and speed, but from weakness and regret. So they stood motionless, breathing deep and quiet and steady. If there had been any sun, it would be near to setting now; there was a condensing, a densifying, of what he had thought was the gray and unchanging light until he realised suddenly that it was his own breathing, his heart, his blood—something, all things, and that Sam Fathers had marked him indeed, not as a mere hunter, but with something Sam had had in his turn of his vanished and forgotten people. He stopped breathing then; there was only his heart, his blood, and in the following silence the wilderness ceased to breathe also, leaning, stooping overhead with its breath held, tremendous and impartial and waiting. Then the shaking stopped too, as he had known it would, and he drew back the two heavy hammers of the gun.

Then it had passed. It was over. The solitude did not breathe again yet; it had merely stopped watching him and was looking somewhere else, even turning its back on him, looking on away up the ridge at another point, and the boy knew as well as if he had seen him that the buck had come to the edge of the cane and had either seen or scented them and faded back into it. But the solitude did not breathe again. It should have suspired again then but it did not. It was still facing, watching, what it had been watching and it was not here, not where he and Sam stood; rigid, not breathing himself, he thought, cried *No! No!,* knowing already that it was too late, thinking with the old despair of two and three years ago: *I'll never get a shot.* Then he heard it—the flat single clap of Walter Ewell's rifle which never missed. Then the mellow sound of the horn came down the ridge and something went out of him and he knew then he had never expected to get the shot at all.

"I reckon that's it," he said. "Walter got him." He had raised the gun slightly without knowing it. He lowered it again and had lowered one of the hammers and was already moving out of the thickets when Sam spoke.

"Wait."

"Wait?" the boy cried. And he would remember that—how he turned upon Sam in the truculence of a boy's grief over the missed opportunity, the missed luck. "What for? Dont you hear that horn?"

And he would remember how Sam was standing. Sam had not moved. He was not tall, squat rather and broad, and the boy had been growing fast for the past year or so and there was not much difference between them in height, yet Sam was looking over the boy's head and up the ridge toward the sound of the horn and the boy knew that Sam did not even see him; that Sam knew he was still there beside him but he did not see the boy. Then the boy saw the buck. It was coming down the ridge, as if it were walking out of the very sound of the horn which related its death. It was not running, it was walking, tremendous, unhurried, slanting and tilting its head to pass the antlers through the undergrowth, and the boy standing with Sam beside him now instead of behind him as Sam always stood, and the gun still partly aimed and one of the hammers still cocked.

Then it saw them. And still it did not begin to run. It just stopped for an instant, taller than any man, looking at them; then its muscles suppled, gathered. It did not even alter its course, not fleeing, not even running, just moving with that winged and effortless ease with which deer move, passing within twenty feet of them, its head high and the eye not proud and not haughty but just full and wild and unafraid, and Sam standing beside the boy now, his right arm raised at full length, palm-outward, speaking in that tongue which the boy had learned from listening to him and Jobaker in the blacksmith-shop, while up the ridge Walter Ewell's horn was still blowing them in to a dead buck.

"Oleh, Chief," Sam said. "Grandfather."

When they reached Walter, he was standing with his back toward them, quite still, bemused almost, looking down at his feet. He didn't look up at all.

"Come here, Sam," he said quietly. When they reached him he still did not look up, standing above a little spike buck which had still been a fawn last spring. "He was so little I pretty near let him go," Walter said. "But just look at the track he was making. It's pretty near big as a cow's. If there were any more tracks here besides the ones he is laying in, I would swear there was another buck here that I never even saw."

III

It was dark when they reached the road where the surrey waited. It was turning cold, the rain had stopped, and the sky was beginning to blow clear. His cousin and Major de Spain and General Compson had a fire going. "Did you get him?" Major de Spain said.

"Got a goodsized swamp-rabbit with spike horns," Walter said. He slid the little buck down from his mule. The boy's cousin McCaslin looked at it.

"Nobody saw the big one?" he said.

"I dont even believe Boon saw it," Walter said. "He probably jumped somebody's stray cow in that thicket." Boon started cursing, swearing at Walter and Sam for not getting the dogs in the first place and at the buck and all.

"Never mind," Major de Spain said. "He'll be here for us next fall. Let's get started home."

It was after midnight when they let Walter out at his gate two miles from Jefferson and later still when they took General Compson to his house and then returned to Major de Spain's, where he and McCaslin would spend the rest of the night, since it was still seventeen miles home. It was cold, the sky was clear now; there would be a heavy frost by sunup and the ground was already frozen beneath the horses' feet and the wheels and beneath their own feet as they crossed Major de Spain's yard and entered the house, the warm dark house, feeling their way up the dark stairs until Major de Spain found a candle and lit it, and into the strange room and the big deep bed, the still cold sheets until they began to warm to their bodies and at last the shaking stopped and suddenly he was telling McCaslin about it while McCaslin listened quietly until he had finished. "You dont believe it," the boy said. "I know you dont—"

"Why not?" McCaslin said. "Think of all that has happened here, on this earth. All the blood hot and strong for living, pleasuring, that has soaked back into it. For grieving and suffering too, of course, but still getting something out of it for all that, getting a lot out of it, because after all you dont have to continue to bear what you believe is suffering; you can always choose to stop that, put an end to that. And even suffering and grieving is better than nothing; there is only one thing worse than not being alive, and that's shame. But you cant be alive forever, and you always wear out life long before you have exhausted the possibilities of living. And all that must be somewhere; all that could not have been invented and created just to be thrown away. And the earth is shallow; there is not a great deal of it before you come to rock. And the earth dont want to just keep things, hoard them; it wants to use them again. Look at the seed, the acorns, at what happens even to carrion when you try to bury it: it refuses too, seethes and struggles too until it reaches light and air again, hunting the sun still. And they—" the boy saw his hand in silhouette for a moment against the window beyond which, accustomed to the darkness now, he could see sky where the scoured and icy stars glittered "—they dont want it, need it. Besides, what would it want, itself, knocking around out there, when it never had enough time about the earth as it was, when there is plenty of room about the earth, plenty of places still unchanged from what they were when the blood used and pleasured in them while it was still blood?"

"But we want them," the boy said. "We want them too. There is plenty of room for us and them too."

"That's right," McCaslin said. "Suppose they dont have substance, cant cast a shadow—"

"But I saw it!" the boy cried. "I saw him!"

"Steady," McCaslin said. For an instant his hand touched the boy's flank beneath the covers. "Steady. I know you did. So did I. Sam took me in there once after I killed my first deer."

Elizabeth Bowen

(1899)

Elizabeth Bowen, known equally well for her short stories and novels, was born in Dublin, Ireland, in 1899. This Anglo-Irish writer is the author of eight novels, including *The House in Paris* (1935) and *The Death of the Heart* (1938), and six volumes of stories, the first published in 1923. A keen observer of sophisticated persons and the sights and sounds of place, she is often concerned with depicting the subtle relationship between character and environment. With the most delicate strokes she creates moods out of landscapes and rooms, moods that are sometimes more memorable than the characters. In "The Demon Lover" Miss Bowen evokes a sinister atmosphere from a careful description of the setting enveloping Mrs. Drover.

The Demon Lover

Towards the end of her day in London Mrs. Drover went round to her shut-up house to look for several things she wanted to take away. Some belonged to herself, some to her family, who were by now used to their country life. It was late August; it had been a steamy, showery day; at the moment the trees down the pavement glittered in an escape of humid yellow afternoon sun. Against the next batch of clouds, already piling up ink-dark, broken chimneys and parapets stood out. In her once familiar street, as in any unused channel, an unfamiliar queerness had silted up; a cat wove itself in and out of railings, but no human eye watched Mrs. Drover's return. Shifting some parcels under her arm, she slowly forced round her latchkey in an unwilling lock, then gave the door, which had warped, a push with her knee. Dead air came out to meet her as she went in.

The staircase window had been boarded up, no light came down into the hall. But one door, she could just see, stood ajar, so she went quickly through into the room and unshuttered the big window in there. Now the prosaic woman, looking about her, was more perplexed than she knew by everything that she saw, by traces of her long former habit of life—the yellow smoke-stain up the white marble mantelpiece, the ring left by a vase on the top of the escritoire; the bruise in the wallpaper where, on the door being thrown open widely, the china handle had always hit the wall. The piano, having gone away to be stored, had left what looked like claw-marks on its part of the parquet. Though not much dust had seeped in, each object wore a film of another kind; and, the only ventilation being the chimney, the whole drawing-room smelled of the cold hearth. Mrs. Drover put down her parcels on the escritoire and left the room to proceed upstairs; the things she wanted were in a bedroom chest.

She had been anxious to see how the house was—the part-time caretaker she shared with some neighbours was away this week on his holiday, known to be not yet back. At the best of times he did not look in often, and she was never sure that she trusted him. There were some cracks in the structure, left by the last bombing, on which she was anxious to keep an eye. Not that one could do anything—

A shaft of refracted daylight now lay across the hall. She stopped dead and stared at the hall table—on this lay a letter addressed to her.

She thought first—then the caretaker *must* be back. All the same, who, seeing the house shuttered, would have dropped a letter in at the box? It was not a circular, it was not a bill. And the post office redirected, to the address in the country, everything for her that came through the post. The caretaker (even if he *were* back) did not know she was due in London to-day—her call here had been planned to be a surprise—so his negligence in the matter of this letter, leaving it to wait in the dusk and the dust, annoyed her. Annoyed, she picked up the letter, which bore no stamp. But it cannot be important, or they would know. . . . She took the letter rapidly upstairs with her, without a stop to look at the writing till she reached what had been her bedroom, where she let in light. The room looked over the garden and other gardens; the sun had gone in; as the clouds sharpened and lowered, the trees and rank lawns seemed already to smoke with dark. Her reluctance to look again at the letter came from the fact that she felt intruded upon—and by someone contemptuous of her ways. However, in the tenseness preceding the fall of rain she read it: it was a few lines.

Dear Kathleen,

You will not have forgotten that to-day is our anniversary, and the day we said. The years have gone by at once slowly and fast. In view of the fact that nothing has changed, I shall rely upon you to keep your promise. I was sorry to see you leave London, but was satisfied that you would be back in time. You may expect me, therefore, at the hour arranged.

Until then . . .

K.

Mrs. Drover looked for the date: it was to-day's. She dropped the letter on to the bed-springs, then picked it up to see the writing again—her lips, beneath the remains of lipstick, beginning to go white. She felt so much the change in her own face that she went to the mirror, polished a clear patch in it and looked at once urgently and stealthily in. She was confronted by a woman of forty-four, with eyes starting out under a hat-brim that had been rather carelessly pulled down. She had not put on any more powder since she left the shop where she ate her solitary tea. The pearls her husband had given her on their marriage hung loose round her now rather thinner throat, slipping into the V of the pink wool jumper her sister knitted last autumn as they sat round the fire. Mrs. Drover's most normal expression was one of controlled worry, but of assent. Since the birth of the third of her little boys, attended by a quite serious illness, she had had an intermittent muscular flicker to the left of her mouth, but in spite of this she could always sustain a manner that was at once energetic and calm.

Turning from her own face as precipitately as she had gone to meet it, she went to the chest where the things were, unlocked it, threw up the lid and knelt to search. But as rain began to come crashing down she could not keep from looking over her shoulder at the stripped bed on which the letter lay. Behind the blanket of rain the clock of the church that still stood struck six—with rapidly heightening apprehension she counted each of the slow strokes. "The hour arranged. . . . My God," she said, "*what* hour? How should I . . . ? After twenty-five years. . . ."

The young girl talking to the soldier in the garden had not ever completely seen his face. It was dark; they were saying good-bye under a tree. Now and then—for it felt, from not seeing him at this intense moment, as though she had never seen him at all—she verified his presence for these few moments longer by putting out a hand, which he each time pressed, without very much kindness, and painfully, on to one of the breast buttons of his uniform. That cut of the button on the palm of her hand was, principally, what she was to carry away. This was so near the end of a leave from France that she could only wish him already gone. It was August 1916. Being not kissed, being drawn away from and looked at intimidated

Kathleen till she imagined spectral glitters in the place of his eyes. Turning away and looking back up the lawn she saw, through branches of trees, the drawing-room window alight: she caught a breath for the moment when she could go running back there into the safe arms of her mother and sister, and cry: "What shall I do, what shall I do? He has gone."

Hearing her catch her breath, her fiancé said, without feeling: "Cold?"

"You're going away such a long way."

"Not so far as you think."

"I don't understand?"

"You don't have to," he said. "You will. You know what we said."

"But that was—suppose you—I mean, suppose."

"I shall be with you," he said, "sooner or later. You won't forget that. You need do nothing but wait."

Only a little more than a minute later she was free to run up the silent lawn. Looking in through the window at her mother and sister, who did not for the moment perceive her, she already felt that unnatural promise drive down between her and the rest of all human kind. No other way of having given herself could have made her feel so apart, lost and foresworn. She could not have plighted a more sinister troth.

Kathleen behaved well when, some months later, her fiancé was reported missing, presumed killed. Her family not only supported her but were able to praise her courage without stint because they could not regret, as a husband for her, the man they knew almost nothing about. They hoped she would, in a year or two, console herself—and had it been only a question of consolation things might have gone much straighter ahead. But her trouble, behind just a little grief, was a complete dislocation from everything. She did not reject other lovers, for these failed to appear: for years she failed to attract men—and with the approach of her thirties she became natural enough to share her family's anxiousness on this score. She began to put herself out, to wonder; and at thirty-two she was very greatly relieved to find herself being courted by William Drover. She married him, and the two of them settled down in this quiet, arboreal part of Kensington: in this house the years piled up, her children were born and they all lived till they were driven out by the bombs of the next war. Her movements as Mrs. Drover were circumscribed, and she dismissed any idea that they were still watched.

As things were—dead or living the letter-writer sent her only a threat. Unable, for some minutes, to go on kneeling with her back exposed to the empty room, Mrs. Drover rose from the chest to sit on an upright chair whose back was firmly against the wall. The desuetude of her former bedroom, her married London home's whole air of being a cracked cup from which memory, with its reassuring power, had either evaporated or leaked away, made a crisis—and at just this crisis the letter-writer had, knowledgeably, struck. The hollowness of the house this evening cancelled years on years of voices, habits and steps. Through the shut windows she only heard rain on the roofs around. To rally herself, she said she was in a mood—and, for two or three seconds shutting her eyes, told herself that she had imagined the letter. But she opened them—there it lay on the bed.

On the supernatural side of the letter's entrance she was not permitting her mind to dwell. Who, in London, knew she meant to call at the house to-day? Evidently, however, this had been known. The caretaker, *had* he come back, had had no cause to expect her: he would have taken the letter in his pocket, to forward it, at his own time, through the post. There was no other sign that the caretaker had been in—but, if not? Letters dropped in at doors of deserted houses do not fly or walk to tables in halls. They do not sit on the dust of empty tables with the air of certainty that they will be found. There is needed some human hand—but nobody but the caretaker had a key. Under circumstances she did not care to consider, a house can be entered without a key. It was possible that she was not alone now. She might be being waited for, downstairs. Waited for—until when? Until "the hour arranged." At least that was not six o'clock: six had struck.

She rose from the chair and went over and locked the door.

The thing was, to get out. To fly? No, not that: she had to catch her train. As a woman whose utter dependability was the keystone of her family life she was not willing to return to the country, to her husband, her little boys and her sister, without the objects she had come up to fetch. Resuming work at the chest she set about making up a number of parcels in a rapid, fumbling-decisive way. These, with her shopping parcels, would be too much to carry; these meant a taxi—at the thought of the taxi her heart went up and her normal breathing resumed. I will ring up the taxi now; the taxi cannot come too soon: I shall hear the taxi out there running its engine, till I walk camly down to it through the hall. I'll ring up—But no: the telephone is cut off. . . . She tugged at a knot she had tied wrong.

The idea of flight. . . . He was never kind to me, not really. I don't remember him kind at all. Mother said he never considered me. He was set on me, that was what it was—not love. Not love, not meaning a person well. What did he do, to make me promise like that? I can't remember—But she found that she could.

She remembered with such dreadful acuteness that the twenty-five years since then dissolved like smoke and she instinctively looked for the weal left by the button on the palm of her hand. She remembered not only all that he said and did but the complete suspension of *her* existence during that August week. I was not myself—they all told me so at the time. She remembered—but with one white burning blank as where acid has dropped on a photograph: *under no conditions* could she remember his face.

So, wherever he may be waiting, I shall not know him. You have no time to run from a face you do not expect.

The thing was to get to the taxi before any clock struck what could be the hour. She would slip down the street and round the side of the square to where the square gave on the main road. She would return in the taxi, safe, to her own door, and bring the solid driver into the house with her to pick up the parcels from room to room. The idea of the taxi driver made her decisive, bold: she unlocked her door, went to the top of the staircase and listened down.

She heard nothing—but while she was hearing nothing the *passe* air of the staircase was disturbed by a draught that travelled up to her face. It emanated from the basement: down there a door or window was being opened by someone who chose this moment to leave the house.

The rain had stopped; the pavements steamily shone as Mrs. Drover let herself out by inches from her own front door into the empty street. The unoccupied houses opposite continued to meet her look with their damaged stare. Making towards the thoroughfare and the taxi, she tried not to keep looking behind. Indeed, the silence was so intense—one of those creeks of London silence exaggerated this summer by the damage of war—that no tread could have gained on hers unheard. Where her street debouched on the square where people went on living she grew conscious of and checked her unnatural pace. Across the open end of the square two buses impassively passed each other; women, a perambulator, cyclists, a man wheeling a barrow signalized, once again, the ordinary flow of life. At the square's most populous corner should be—and was—the short taxi rank. This evening, only one taxi—but this, although it presented its blank rump, appeared already to be alertly waiting for her. Indeed, without looking round the driver started his engine as she panted up from behind and put her hand on the door. As she did so, the clock struck seven. The taxi faced the main road: to make the trip back to her house it would have to turn—she had settled back on the seat and the taxi *had* turned before she, surprised by its knowing movement, recollected that she had not "said where." She leaned forward to scratch at the glass panel that divided the driver's head from her own.

The driver braked to what was almost a stop, turned round and slid the glass panel back: the jolt of this flung Mrs. Drover forward till her face was almost into the glass. Through the aperture driver and passenger, not six inches between, remained for an eternity eye to eye. Mrs. Drover's mouth hung open for some seconds before she could issue her first scream. After that she continued to scream freely and to beat with her gloved hands on the glass all round as the taxi, accelerating without mercy, made off with her into the hinterland of deserted streets.

Robert Penn Warren

(1905)

Robert Penn Warren was born in Guthrie, Kentucky, in 1905, was educated at Vanderbilt, California, and Oxford universities, and he is now a professor of English at Yale University. Once called the "pentathalon champion" of American literature, Warren has distinguished himself as a novelist, short story writer, poet, critic, and biographer. His *All the King's Men,* a penetrating study of moral courage and corrupt politics, won the Pulitzer Prize for fiction in 1947 and ten years later *Promises: Poems 1954–1956* won both a Pulitzer Prize and the National Book Award. "Blackberry Winter," a masterful story of a boy's initiation into the realities of life and the adult world, explores the common Warren theme of self-discovery.

Blackberry Winter

It was getting into June and past eight o'clock in the morning, but there was a fire—even if it wasn't a big fire, just a fire of chunks—on the hearth of the big stone fireplace in the living room. I was standing on the hearth, almost into the chimney, hunched over the fire, working my bare toes slowly on the warm stone. I relished the heat which made the skin of my bare legs warp and creep and tingle, even as I called to my mother, who was somewhere back in the dining room or kitchen, and said: "But it's June, I don't have to put them on!"

"You put them on if you are going out," she called.

I tried to assess the degree of authority and conviction in the tone, but at that distance it was hard to decide. I tried to analyze the tone, and then I thought what a fool I had been to start out the back door and let her see that I was barefoot. If I had gone out the front door or the side door she would never have known, not till dinner time anyway, and by then the day would have been half gone and I would have been all over the farm to see what the storm had done and down to the creek to see the flood. But it had never crossed my mind that they would try to stop you from going barefoot in June, no matter if there had been a gully-washer and a cold spell.

Nobody had ever tried to stop me in June as long as I could remember, and when you are nine years old, what you remember seems forever; for you remember everything and everything is important and stands big and full and fills up Time and is so solid that you can walk around and around it like a tree and look at it. You are aware that time passes, that there is a movement in time, but that is not what Time is. Time is not a movement, a flowing, a wind then, but is, rather, a kind of climate in which things are, and when a thing happens it begins to live and keeps on living and stands solid in Time like the tree that you can walk around. And if there is a movement, the movement is not Time itself, any more than a breeze is climate, and all the breeze does is to shake a little the leaves on the tree which is alive and solid. When you are nine, you know that there are things that you don't know, but you know that when you know something you know it. You know how a thing has been and you know that you can go barefoot in June. You do not understand that voice from back in the kitchen which says that you cannot go barefoot outdoors and run to see what has happened and rub your feet over the wet shivery grass and make the perfect mark of your foot in the smooth, creamy, red mud and then muse upon it as though you had suddenly come upon that single mark on the glistening auroral beach of the world. You have never seen a beach, but you have read the book and how the footprint was there.

The voice had said what it had said, and I looked savagely at the black stockings and the strong, scuffed brown shoes which I had brought from my closet as far as the hearth rug. I called once more. "But it's June," and waited.

"It's June," the voice replied from far away, "but it's blackberry winter."

I had lifted my head to reply to that, to make one more test of what was in that tone, when I happened to see the man.

The fireplace in the living room was at the end; for the stone chimney was built, as in so many of the farmhouses in Tennessee, at the end of a gable, and there was a window on each side of the chimney. Out of the window on the north side of the fireplace I could see the man. When I saw the man I did not call out what I had intended, but, engrossed by the strangeness of the sight, watched him, still far off, come along the path by the edge of the woods.

What was strange was that there should be a man there at all. That path went along the yard fence, between the fence and the woods which came right down to the yard, and then on back past the chicken runs and on by the woods until it was lost to sight where the woods bulged out and cut off the back field. There the path disappeared into the woods. It led on back, I knew, through the wood and to the swamps, skirted the swamp where the big trees gave way to sycamores and water oaks and willows and tangled cane, and then led on to the river. Nobody ever went back there except people who wanted to gig frogs in the swamp or to fish in the river or to hunt in the woods, and those people, if they didn't having a standing permission from my father, always stopped to ask permission to cross the farm. But the man whom I now saw wasn't, I could tell even at that distance, a sportsman. And what would a sportsman have been doing down there after a storm? Besides, he was coming from the river, and nobody had gone down there that morning. I knew that for a fact, because if anybody had passed, certainly if a stranger had passed, the dogs would have made a racket and would have been out on him. But this man was coming up from the river and had come up through the woods. I suddenly had a vision of him moving up the grassy paths in the woods, in the green twilight under the big trees, not making any sound on the path, while now and then, like drops off the eaves, a big drop of water would fall from a leaf or bough and strike a stiff oak leaf lower down with a small, hollow sound like a drop of water hitting tin. That sound, in the silence of the woods, would be very significant.

When you are a boy and stand in the stillness of woods, which can be so still that your heart almost stops beating and makes you want to stand there in the green twilight until you feel your very feet sinking into and clutching the earth like roots and your body breathing slow through its pores like the leaves—when you stand there and wait for the next drop to drop with its small, flat sound to a lower leaf, that sound seems to measure out something, to put an end to something, to begin something, and you cannot wait for it to happen and are afraid it will not happen, and then when it has happened, you are waiting again, almost afraid.

But the man whom I saw coming through the woods in my mind's eye did not pause and wait, growing into the ground and breathing with the enormous, soundless breathing of the leaves. Instead, I saw him moving in the green twilight inside my head as he was moving at the very moment along the path by the edge of the woods, coming toward the house. He was moving steadily, but not fast, with his shoulders hunched a little and his head thrust forward, like a man who has come a long way and has a long way to go. I shut my eyes for a couple of seconds, thinking that when I opened them he would not be there at all. There was no place for him to have come from, and there was no reason for him to come where he was coming, toward our house. But I opened my eyes, and there he was, and he was coming steadily along the side of the woods. He was not yet even with the back chicken yard.

"Mama," I called.

"You put them on," the voice said.

"There's a man coming," I called, "out back."

She did not reply to that, and I guessed that she had gone to the kitchen window to look. She would be looking at the man and wondering who he was and what he wanted, the way you always do in the country, and if I went back there now she would not notice right off whether or not I was barefoot. So I went back to the kitchen.

She was standing by the window. "I don't recognize him," she said, not looking around at me.

"Where could he be coming from?" I asked.

"I don't know," she said.

"What would he be doing down at the river? At night? In the storm?"

She studied the figure out the window, then said, "Oh, I reckon maybe he cut across from the Dunbar place."

That was, I realized, a perfectly rational explanation. He had not been down at the river in the storm, at night. He had come over this morning. You could cut across from the Dunbar place if you didn't mind breaking through a lot of elder and sassafras and blackberry bushes which had about taken over the old cross path, which nobody ever used any more. That satisfied me for a moment, but only for a moment. "Mama," I asked, "what would he be doing over at the Dunbar place last night?"

Then she looked at me, and I knew I had made a mistake, for she was looking at my bare feet. "You haven't got your shoes on," she said.

But I was saved by the dogs. That instant there was a bark which I recognized as Sam, the collie, and then a heavier, churning kind of bark which was Bully, and I saw a streak of white as Bully tore round the corner of the back porch and headed out for the man. Bully was a big, bone-white bull dog, the kind of dog that they used to call a farm bull dog but that you don't see any more, heavy chested and heavy headed, but with pretty long legs. He could take a fence as light as a hound. He had just cleared the white paling fence toward the woods when my mother ran out to the back porch and began calling, "Here you, Bully! Here you!"

Bully stopped in the path, waiting for the man, but he gave a few more of those deep, gargling savage barks that reminded you of something down a stone-lined well. The red clay mud, I saw, was splashed up over his white chest and looked exciting, like blood.

The man, however, had not stopped walking even when Bully took the fence and started at him. He had kept right on coming. All he had done was to switch a little paper parcel which he carried from the right to the left, and then reach into his pants pocket to get something. Then I saw the glitter and knew that he had a knife in his hand, probably the kind of mean knife just made for devilment and nothing else, with a blade as long as the blade of a frog-sticker, which will snap out ready when you press a button in the hand. That knife must have had a button in the handle, or else how could he have had the blade out glittering so quick and with just one hand?

Pulling his knife against the dogs was a funny thing to do, for Bully was a big, powerful brute and fast, and Sam was all right. If those dogs had meant business, they might have knocked him down and ripped him before he got a stroke in. He ought to have picked up a heavy stick, something to take a swipe at them with and something which they could see and respect when they came at him. But he apparently did not know much about dogs. He just held the knife blade close against the right leg, low down, and kept on moving down the path.

Then my mother had called, and Bully had stopped. So the man let the blade of the knife snap back into the handle, and dropped it into his pocket, and kept on coming. Many women would have been afraid with the strange man who they knew had that knife in his pocket. That is, if they were alone in the house with nobody but a nine-year-old boy. And my mother was alone, for my father had gone off, and Dellie, the cook, was down at her cabin because she wasn't feeling well. But my mother wasn't afraid. She wasn't a big woman, but she was clear and brisk about everything she did and looked everybody and everything right in the eye from her own blue eyes in her tanned face. She had been the first woman in the county to ride a horse astride (that was back when she was a girl and long before I was born), I have seen her snatch up a pump gun and go out and knock a chicken hawk out of the air like a busted skeet when he came over her chicken yard. She was a steady and self-reliant woman, and when I think of her now after all the years she has been dead, I think of her brown hands, not big, but somewhat square for a woman's hands, with square-cut nails. They looked, as a matter of fact, more like a young boy's hands than a grown woman's. But back then it never crossed my mind that she would ever be dead.

She stood on the back porch and watched the man enter the back gate, where the dogs (Bully had leaped back into the yard) were dancing and muttering and giving sidelong glances back to my mother to see if she meant what she had said. The man walked right by the dogs, almost brushing them, and didn't pay them any attention. I could see now that he wore old khaki pants, and a dark wool coat with stripes in it, and a gray felt hat. He had on a gray shirt with blue stripes in it, and no tie. But I could see a tie, blue and reddish, sticking in his side coat-pocket. Everything was wrong about what he wore. He ought to have been wearing blue jeans or overalls, and a straw hat or an old black felt hat, and the coat, granting that he might have been wearing a wool coat and not a jumper, ought not to have had those stripes. Those clothes, despite the fact that they were old enough and dirty enough for any tramp, didn't belong there in our back yard, coming down the path, in Middle Tennessee, miles away from any big town, and even a mile off the pike.

When he got almost to the steps, without having said anything, my mother, very matter-of-factly, said, "Good morning."

"Good morning," he said, and stopped and looked her over. He did not take off his hat, and under the brim you could see the perfectly unmemorable face, which wasn't old and wasn't young, or thick or thin. It was grayish and covered with about three days of stubble. The eyes were a kind of nondescript, muddy hazel, or something like that, rather bloodshot. His teeth, when he opened his mouth, showed yellow and uneven. A couple of them had been knocked out. You knew that they had been knocked out, because there was a scar, not very old, there on the lower lip just beneath the gap.

"Are you hunting work?" my mother asked him.

"Yes," he said—not "yes, mam"—and still did not take off his hat.

"I don't know about my husband, for he isn't here," she said, and didn't mind a bit telling the tramp, or whoever he was, with the mean knife in his pocket, that no man was around, "but I can give you a few things to do. The storm has drowned a lot of my chicks. Three coops of them. You can gather them up and bury them. Bury them deep so the dogs won't get at them. In the woods. And fix the coops the wind blew over. And down yonder beyond that pen by the edge of the woods are some drowned poults. They got out and I couldn't get them in. Even after it started to rain hard. Poults haven't got any sense."

"What are them things—poults?" he demanded, and spat on the brick walk. He rubbed his foot over the spot, and I saw that he wore a black, pointed-toe low shoe, all cracked and broken. It was a crazy kind of shoe to be wearing in the country.

"Oh, they're young turkeys," my mother was saying. "And they haven't got any sense. I oughn't to try to raise them around here with so many chickens, anyway. They don't thrive near chickens, even in separate pens. And I won't give up my chickens." Then she stopped herself and resumed briskly on the note of business. "When you finish that, you can fix my flower beds. A lot of trash and mud and gravel has washed down. Maybe you can save some of my flowers if you are careful."

"Flowers," the man said, in a low, impersonal voice which seemed to have a wealth of meaning, but a meaning which I could not fathom. As I think back on it, it probably was not pure contempt. Rather, it was a kind of impersonal and distant marveling that he should be on the verge of grubbing a flower bed. He said the word, and then looked off across the yard.

"Yes, flowers," my mother replied with some asperity, as though she would have nothing said or implied against flowers. "And they were very fine this year." Then she stopped and looked at the man. "Are you hungry?" she demanded.

"Yeah," he said.

"I'll fix you something," she said, "before you get started." She turned to me. "Show him where he can wash up," she commanded, and went into the house.

I took the man to the end of the porch where a pump was and where a couple of wash pans sat on a low shelf for people to use before they went into the house. I stood there while he laid down his little parcel wrapped in newspaper and took of his hat and looked around for a nail to hang it on. He poured the water and plunged his hands into it. They were big hands, and strong looking, but they did not have the creases and the earth-color of the hands of men who work outdoors. But they were dirty, with black dirt grounded into the skin and under the nails. After he had washed his hands, he poured another basin of water and washed his face. He dried his face, and with the towel still dangling in his grasp, stepped over to the mirror on the house wall. He rubbed one hand over the stubble on his face. Then he carefully inspected his face, turning first one side and then the other, and stepped back and settled his striped coat down on his shoulders. He had the movements of a man who had just dressed up to go to church or a party—the way he settled his coat and smoothed it and and scanned himself in the mirror.

Then he caught my glance on him. He glared at me for an instant out of the bloodshot eyes, then demanded in a low, harsh voice, "What you looking at?"

"Nothing," I managed to say, and stepped back a step from him.

He flung the towel down, crumpled, on the shelf, and went towards the kitchen door and entered without knocking.

My mother said something to him which I could not catch. I started to go in again, then thought about my bare feet, and decided to go back of the chicken yard, where the man would have to come to pick up the dead chicks. I hung around behind the chicken house until he came out.

He moved across the chicken yard with a fastidious, not quite finicking motion, looking down at the curdled mud flecked with bits of chicken-droppings. The mud curled up over the soles of his black shoes. I stood back from him some six feet and watched him pick up the first of the drowned chicks. He held it up by one foot and inspected it.

There is nothing deader looking than a drowned chick. The feet curl in that feeble, empty way which back when I was a boy, even if I was a country boy who did not mind hog-killing or frog-gigging, made me feel hollow in the stomach. Instead of looking plump and fluffy, the body is stringy and limp with the fluff plastered to it, and the neck is long and loose like a little string of rag. And the eyes have the bluish membrane over them which makes you think of a very old man who is sick about to die.

The man stood there and inspected the chick. Then he looked all around as though he didn't know what to do with it.

"There's a great big old basket in the shed," I said, and pointed to the shed attached to the chicken house.

He inspected me as though he had just discovered my presence, and moved toward the shed.

"There's a spade there, too," I added.

He got the basket and began to pick up the other chicks, picking each one up slowly by a foot and then flinging it into the basket with a nasty, snapping motion. Now and then he would look at me out of the blood-shot eyes. Every time he seemed on the verge of saying something, but he did not. Perhaps he was building up to say something to me, but I did not wait that long. His way of looking at me made me so uncomfortable that I left the chicken yard.

Besides, I had just remembered that the creek was in flood, over the bridge, and that people were down there watching it. So I cut across the farm toward the creek. When I got to the big tobacco field I saw that it had not suffered much. The land lay right and not many tobacco plants had washed out of the ground. But I knew that a lot of tobacco round the country had been washed right out. My father had said so at breakfast.

My father was down at the bridge. When I came out of the gap in the osage hedge into the road, I saw him sitting on his mare over the heads of the other men who were standing around, admiring the flood. The creek was big here, even in low water; for only a couple of miles away it ran into the river, and when a real flood came, the red water got over the pike where it dipped down to the bridge, which was an iron bridge, and high over the floor and even the side railings of the bridge. Only the upper iron work would show, with the water boiling and frothing red and white around it. That creek rose so fast and so heavy because a few miles back it came down out of the hills, where the gorges filled up with water in no time when a rain came. The creek ran in a deep bed with limestone bluffs along both sides until it got within three quarters of a mile of the bridge, and when it came out from between those bluffs in flood it was boiling and hissing and steaming like water from a fire hose.

Whenever there was a flood, people from half the county would come down to see the sight. After a gully-washer there would not be any work to do anyway. If it didn't ruin your crop, you couldn't plow and you felt like taking a holiday to celebrate. If it did ruin your crop, there wasn't anything to do except to try to take your mind off the mortgage, if you were rich enough to have a mortgage, and if you couldn't afford a mortgage you needed something to take your mind off how hungry you would be by

Christmas. So people would come down to the bridge and look at the flood. It made something different from the run of days.

There would not be much talking after the first few minutes of trying to guess how high the water was this time. The men and kids just stood around, or sat their horses or mules, as the case might be, or stood up in the wagon beds. They looked at the strangeness of the flood for an hour or two, and then somebody would say that he had better be getting on home to dinner and would start walking down the gray, puddled limestone pike, or would touch heel to his mount and start off. Everybody always knew what it would be like when he got down to the bridge, but people always came. It was like church or a funeral. They always came, that is, if it was summer and the floor unexpected. Nobody ever came down in winter to see high water.

When I came out of the gap in the bodock hedge, I saw the crowd, perhaps fifteen or twenty men and a lot of kids, and saw my father sitting his mare, Nellie Gray. He was a tall, limber man and carried himself well. I was always proud to see him sit a horse, he was so quiet and straight, and when I stepped through the gap of the hedge that morning, the first thing that happened was, I remember, the warm feeling I always had when I saw him up on a horse, just sitting. I did not go toward him, but skirted the crowd on the far side, to get a look at the creek. For one thing, I was not sure what he would say about the fact that I was barefoot. But the first thing I knew, I heard his voice calling, "Seth!"

I went toward him, moving apologetically past the men, who bent their large, red or thin, sallow faces above me. I knew some of the men, and knew their names, but because those I knew were there in a crowd, mixed with the strange faces, they seemed foreign to me, and not friendly. I did not look up at my father until I was almost within touching distance of his heel. Then I looked up and tried to read his face, to see if he was angry about my being barefoot. Before I could decide anything from that impassive, high-boned face, he had leaned over and reached a hand to me. "Grab on," he commanded.

I grabbed on and gave a little jump, and he said, "Up-see-daisy!" and whisked me, light as a feather, up to the pommel of his McClellan saddle.

"You can see better up here," he said, slid back on the cantle a little to make me more comfortable, and then, looking over my head at the swollen, tumbling water, seemed to forget all about me. But his right hand was laid on my side, just above my thigh, to steady me.

It was sitting there as quiet as I could, feeling the faint stir of my father's chest against my shoulders as it rose and fell with his breath, when I saw the cow. At first, looking up the creek, I thought it was just another big piece of driftwood steaming down the creek in the ruck of water, but all at once a pretty good-size boy who had climbed part way up a telephone pole by the pike so that he could see better yelled out, "Golly-damn, look at that-air cow!"

Everybody looked. It was a cow all right, but it might just as well have been driftwood; for it was dead as a chunk, rolling and roiling down the creek, appearing and disappearing, feet up or head up, it didn't matter which.

The cow started up the talk again. Somebody wondered whether it would hit one of the clear places under the top girder of the bridge and get through or whether it would get tangled in the drift and trash that had piled against the upright girders and braces. Somebody remembered how ten years before so much driftwood had piled up on the bridge that it was knocked of its foundations. Then the cow hit. It hit the edge of the drift against one of the girders, and hung there. For a few seconds it seemed as though it might tear loose, but then we saw that it was really caught. It bobbed and heaved on its side there in a slow, grinding, uneasy fashion. It had a yoke around its neck, the kind made out of a forked limb to keep a jumper behind fence.

"She shore jumped one fence," one of the men said.

And another: "Well, she done jumped her last one, fer a fack."

Then they began to wonder about whose cow it might be. They decided it must belong to Milt Alley. They said that he had a cow that was a jumper, and kept her in a fenced-in piece of ground up the creek. I had never seen Milt Alley, but I knew who he was. He was a squatter and lived up the hills a way, on a shirt-tail patch of set-on-edge land, in a cabin. He was pore white trash. He had lots of children. I had seen the children at school, when they came. They were thin-faced, with straight, sticky-looking, dough--colored hair, and they smelled something like old sour buttermilk, not because they drank so much buttermilk but because that is the sort of smell which children out of those cabins tend to have. The big Alley boy drew dirty pictures and showed them to the little boys at school.

That was Milt Alley's cow. It looked like the kind of cow he would have, a scrawny, old, sway-backed cow, with a yoke around her neck. I wondered if Milt Alley had another cow.

"Poppa," I said, "do you think Milt Alley has got another cow?"

"You say 'Mr. Alley,'" my father said quietly.

"Do you think he has?"

"No telling," my father said.

Then a big gangly boy, about fifteen, who was sitting on a scraggly little old mule with a piece of croker sack thrown across the saw-tooth spine, and who had been staring at the cow, suddenly said to nobody in particular, "Reckin anybody ever et drownt cow?"

He was the kind of boy who might just as well as not have been the son of Milt Alley, with his faded and patched overalls ragged at the bottom of the pants and the mud-stiff brogans hanging off his skinny, bare ankles at the level of the mule's belly. He had said what he did, and then looked embarrassed and sullen when all the eyes swung at him. He hadn't meant to say it, I am pretty sure now. He would have been too proud to say it, just as Milt Alley would have been too proud. He had just been thinking out loud, and the words had popped out.

There was an old man standing there on the pike, an old man with a white beard. "Son," he said to the embarrassed and sullen boy on the mule, "you live long enough and you'll find a man will eat anything when the time comes."

"Time gonna come fer some folks this year," another man said.

"Son," the old man said, "in my time I et things a man don't like to think on. I was a sojer and I rode with Gin'l Forrest, and them things we et when the time come. I tell you. I et meat what got up and run when you taken out yore knife to cut a slice to put on the fire. You had to knock it down with a carbeen butt, it was so active. That-air meat would jump like a bullfrog, it was so full of skippers."

But nobody was listening to the old man. The boy on the mule turned his sullen sharp face from him, dug a heel into the side of the mule and went off up the pike with a motion which made you think that any second you would hear mule bones clashing inside that lank and scrofulous hide.

"Cy Dundee's boy," a man said, and nodded toward the figure going up the pike on the mule.

"Reckin Cy Dundee's young-uns seen times they'd settle fer drownt cow," another man said.

The old man with the beard peered at them both from his weak, slow eyes, first at one and then at the other. "Live long enough," he said, "and a man will settle fer what he kin git."

Then there was silence again, and the people looking at the red, foam-flecked water.

My father lifted the bridle rein in his left hand, and the mare turned and walked around the group and up the pike. We rode on up to our big gate, where my father dismounted to open it and let me myself ride Nellie Gray through. When he got to the lane that led off from the drive about two hundred yards from our house, my father said, "Grab on." I grabbed on, and he let me down to the ground. "I'm going to ride down and look at my corn," he said. "You go on." He took the lane, and I stood there on the drive and watched him ride off. He was wearing cowhide boots and an old hunting coat, and I thought that that made him look very military, like a picture. That and the way he rode.

I did not go to the house. Instead, I went by the vegetable garden and crossed behind the stables, and headed down for Dellie's cabin. I wanted to go down and play with Jebb, who was Dellie's little boy about two years older than I was. Besides, I was cold. I shivered as I walked, and I had goose-flesh. The mud which crawled up between my toes with every step I took was like ice. Dellie would have a fire, but she wouldn't make me put on shoes and stockings.

Dellie's cabin was of logs, with one side, because it was on a slope, set on limestone chunks, with a little porch attached to it, and had a little whitewashed fence around it and a gate with plow-points on a wire to clink when somebody came in, and had two big white oaks in the yard and some flowers and a nice privy in the back with some honeysuckle growing over it. Dellie and Old Jebb, who was Jebb's father and who lived with Dellie and had lived with her for twenty-five years even if they never had got married, were careful to keep everything nice around their cabin. They had the name all over the community for being clean and clever Negroes. Dellie and Jebb were what they used to call "white-folks' niggers." There was a big difference between their cabin and the other two cabins farther down where the other tenants lived. My father kept the other cabins weather-proof, but he couldn't undertake to go down and pick up after the litter they strewed. They didn't take the trouble to have a vegetable patch like Dellie and Jebb or to make preserves from wild plum, and jelly from crab apple the way Dellie did. They were shiftless, and my father was always threatening to get shed of them. But he never did. When they finally left, they just up and left on their own, for no reason, to go and be shiftless somewhere else. Then some more came. But meanwhile they lived down there, Matt Rawson and his family, and Sid Turner and his, and I played with their children all over the farm when they weren't working. But when I wasn't around they were mean sometimes to Little Jebb. That was because the other tenants down there were jealous of Dellie and Jebb.

I was so cold that I ran the last fifty yards to Dellie's gate. As soon as I had entered the yard, I saw that the storm had been hard on Dellie's flowers. The yard was, as I have said, on a slight slope, and the water running across had gutted the flower beds and washed out all the good black woods-earth which Dellie had brought in. What little grass there was in the yard was plastered sparsely down on the ground, the way the drainage water had left it. It reminded me of the way the fluff was pastered down on the skin of the drowned chickens that the strange man had been picking up, up in my mother's chicken yard.

I took a few steps up the paths to the cabin, and then I saw that the drainage water had washed a lot of trash and filth out from under Dellie's house. Up toward the porch, the ground was not clean any more. Old pieces of rag, two or three rusted cans, pieces of rotten rope, some hunks of old dog dung, broken glass, old paper, and all sorts of things like that had washed out from under Dellie's house to foul her clean yard. It looked just as bad as the yards of the other cabins, or worse. It was worse, as a matter of fact, because it was a surprise. I had never thought of all that filth being under Dellie's house. It was not anything against Dellie that the stuff had been under the cabin. Trash will get under any house. But I did not think of that when I saw the foulness which had washed out on the ground which Dellie sometimes used to sweep with a twig broom to make nice and clean.

I picked my way past the filth, being careful not to get my bare feet on it, and mounted to Dellie's door. When I knocked, I heard her voice telling me to come in.

It was dark inside the cabin, after the daylight, but I could make out Dellie piled up in bed under a quilt, and Little Jebb crouched by the hearth, where a low fire simmered. "Howdy," I said to Dellie, "how you feeling?"

Her big eyes, the whites surprising and glaring in the black face, fixed on me as I stood there, but she did not reply. It did not look like Dellie, or act like Dellie, who would grumble and bustle around our kitchen, talking to herself, scolding me or Little Jebb, clanking pans, making all sorts of unnecessary noises and mutterings like an old-fashioned black steam thrasher engine when it has got up an extra head of steam and keeps popping the governor and rumbling and shaking on its wheels. But now Dellie just lay up there on the bed, under the patch-work quilt, and turned the black face, which I scarcely recognized, and the glaring white eyes to me.

"How you feeling?" I repeated.

"I'se sick," the voice said croakingly out of the strange black face which was not attached to Dellie's big, squat body, but stuck out from under a pile of tangled bedclothes. Then the voice added: "Mighty sick."

"I'm sorry," I managed to say.

The eyes remained fixed on me for a moment, then they left me and the head rolled back on the pillow. "Sorry," the voice said, in a flat way which wasn't question or statement of anything. It was just the empty word put into the air with no meaning or expression, to float off like a feather or a puff of smoke, while the big eyes, with the whites like the peeled white of hard-boiled eggs, stared at the ceiling.

"Dellie," I said after a minute, "there's a tramp up at the house. He's got a knife."

She was not listening. She closed her eyes.

I tiptoed over to the hearth where Jebb was and crouched beside him. We began to talk in low voices. I was asking him to get out his train and play train. Old Jebb had put spool wheels on three cigar boxes and put wire links between the boxes to make a train for Jebb. The box that was the locomotive had the top closed and a length of a broom stick for a smoke stack. Jebb didn't want to get the train out, but I told him I would go home if he didn't. So he got out the train, and the colored rocks, and fossils of crinoid stems, and other junk he used for the load, and we began to push it around, talking the way we thought trainmen talked, making a chuck-chucking sound under the breath for the noise of the locomotive and now and then uttering low, cautious toots for the whistle. We got so interested in playing train that the toots got louder. Then, before he thought, Jebb gave a good, loud *toot-toot,* blowing for a crossing.

"Come here," the voice said from the bed.

Jebb got up slow from his hands and knees, giving me a sudden, naked, inimical look.

"Come here!" the voice said.

Jebb went to the bed. Dellie propped herself weakly up on one arm, muttering, "Come closer."

Jebb stood closer.

"Last thing I do, I'm gonna do it," Dellie said. "Done tole you to be quiet."

Then she slapped him. It was an awful slap, more awful for the kind of weakness which it came from and brought to focus. I had seen her slap Jebb before, but the slapping had always been the kind of easy slap you would expect from a good-natured, grumbling Negro woman like Dellie. But this was different. It was awful. It was so awful that Jebb didn't make a sound. The tears just popped out and ran down his face, and his breath came sharp, like gasps.

Dellie fell back. "Cain't even be sick," she said to the ceiling. "Git sick and they won't even let you lay. They tromp all over you. Cain't even be sick." Then she closed her eyes.

I went out of the room. I almost ran getting to the door, and I did run across the porch and down the steps and across the yard, not caring whether or not I stepped on the filth which had washed out from under the cabin. I ran almost all the way home. Then I thought about my mother catching me with the bare feet. So I went down to the stables.

I heard a noise in the crib, and opened the door. There was Big Jebb, sitting on an old nail keg, shelling corn into a bushel basket. I went in, pulling the door shut behind me, and crouched on the floor near him. I crouched there for a couple of minutes before either of us spoke, and watched him shelling the corn.

He had very big hands, knotted and grayish at the joints, with calloused palms which seemed to be streaked with rust with the rust coming up between the fingers to show from the back. His hands were so strong and tough that he could take a big ear of corn and rip the grains right off the cob with the palm of his hand, all in one motion, like a machine. "Work long as me," he would say, "and the good Lawd'll give you a hand lak cass-ion won't nuthin' hurt." And his hands did look like cast iron, old cast iron streaked with rust.

He was an old man, up in his seventies, thirty years or more older than Dellie, but he was strong as a bull. He was a squat sort of man, heavy in the shoulders, with remarkably long arms, the kind of build they say the river natives have on the Congo from paddling so much in their boats.

He had a round bullet-head, set on powerful shoulders. His skin was very black, and the thin hair on his head was now grizzled like tufts of old cotton batting. He had small eyes and a flat nose, not big, and the kindest and wisest old face in the world, the blunt, sad, wise face of an old animal peering tolerantly out on the goings-on of the merely human creatures before him. He was a good man, and I loved him next to my mother and father. I crouched there on the floor of the crib and watched him shell corn with the rusty cast-iron hands, while he looked down at me out of the little eyes set in the blunt face.

"Dellie says she's might sick," I said.

"Yeah," he said.

"What's she sick from?"

"Woman-mizry," he said.

"What's woman-mizry?"

"Hit comes on 'em," he said. "Hit just comes on 'em when the time comes."

"What is it?"

"Hit is the change," he said. "Hit is the change of life and time."

"What changes?"

"You too young to know."

"Tell me."

"Time come and you find out everthing."

I knew that there was no use in asking him any more. When I asked him things and he said that, I always knew that he would not tell me. So I continued to crouch there and watch him. Now that I had sat there a little while, I was cold again.

"What you shiver fer?" he asked me.

"I'm cold. I'm cold because it's blackberry winter," I said.

"Maybe 'tis and maybe 'tain't," he said.

"My mother says it is."

"Ain't sayen Miss Sallie doan know and ain't sayen she do. But folks doan know everything."

"Why isn't it blackberry winter?"

"Too late fer blackberry winter. Blackberries done bloomed."

"She said it was."

"Blackberry winter just a leetle cold spell. Hit come and then hit go away, and hit is growed summer of a sudden lak a gunshot. Ain't no tellen hit will go way this time."

"It's June," I said.

"June," he replied with great contempt. "That what folks say. What June mean? Maybe hit is come cold to stay.

"Why?"

"Cause this-here old yearth is tahrd. Hit is tahrd and ain't gonna perduce. Lawd let hit come rain one time forty days and forty nights, 'cause

He wus tahard of sinful folks. Maybe this-here old yearth say to the Lawd, Lawd, I done plum tahrd, Lawd, lemme rest. And Lawd say, Yearth, you done yore best, you give 'em cawn and you give 'em taters, and all they think on is they gut, and, Yearth, you kin take a rest."

"What will happen?"

"Folks will eat up everything. The yearth won't perduce no more. Folks cut down all the trees and burn 'em cause they cold, and the yearth won't grow no more. I been tellen 'em. I been tellen folks. Sayen, maybe this year, hit is the time. But they doan listen to me, how the yearth is tahrd. Maybe this year they find out."

"Will everything die?"

"Everything and everybody, hit will be so."

"This year?"

"Ain't no tellen. Maybe this year."

"My mother said it is blackberry winter," I said confidently, and got up.

"Ain't sayen nuthin' agin Miss Sallie," he said.

I went to the door of the crib. I was really cold now. Running, I had got up a sweat and now I was worse.

I hung on the door, looking at Jebb, who was shelling corn again.

"There's a tramp came to the house," I said. I had almost forgotten the tramp.

"Yeah."

"He came by the back way. What was he doing down there in the storm?"

"They comes and they goes," he said, "and ain't no tellen."

"He had a mean knife."

"The good ones and the bad ones, they comes and they goes. Storm or sun, light or dark. They is folks and they comes and they goes lak folks."

I hung on the door, shivering.

He studied me a moment, then said, "You git on to the house. You ketch yore death. Then what yore mammy say?"

I hesitated.

"You git," he said.

When I came to the back yard, I saw that my father was standing by the back porch and the tramp was walking toward him. They began talking before I reached them, but I got there just as my father was saying, "I'm sorry, but I haven't got any work. I got all the hands on the place I need now. I won't need any extra until wheat thrashing."

The stranger made no reply, just looked at my father.

My father took out his leather coin purse, and got out a half-dollar. He held it toward the man. "This is for half a day," he said.

The man looked at the coin, and then at my father, making no motion to take the money. But that was the right amount. A dollar a day was what you paid them back in 1910. And the man hadn't even worked half a day.

Then the man reached out and took the coin. He dropped it into the right side pocket of his coat. Then he said, very slowly and without feeling: "I didn't want to work on your—farm."

He used the word which they would have frailed me to death for using.

I looked at my father's face and it was streaked white under the sunburn. Then he said, "Get off this place. Get off this place or I won't be responsible."

The man dropped his right hand into his pants pocket. It was the pocket where he kept the knife. I was just about to yell to my father about the knife when the hand came back out with nothing in it. The man gave a kind of twisted grin, showing where the teeth had been knocked out above the new scar. I thought that instant how maybe he had tried before to pull a knife on somebody else and had got his teeth knocked out.

So now he just gave that twisted, sickish grin out of the unmemorable, grayish face, and then spat on the brick path. The glob landed just about six inches from the toe of my father's right boot. My father looked down at it, and so did I. I thought that if the glob had hit my father's boot something would have happened. I looked down and saw the bright glob, and on one side of it my father's strong cowhide boots, with the brass eyelets and the leather thongs, heavy boots splashed with good red mud and set solid on the bricks, and on the other side the pointed-toe, broken, black shoes, on which the mud looked so sad and out of place. Then I saw one of the black shoes move a little, just a twitch first, then a real step backward.

The man moved in a quarter circle to the end of the porch, with my father's steady gaze upon him all the while. At the end of the porch, the man reached up to the shelf where the wash pans were to get his little newspaper-wrapped parcel. Then he disappeared around the corner of the house and my father mounted the porch and went into the kitchen without a word.

I followed around the house to see what the man would do. I wasn't afraid of him now, no matter if he did have the knife. When I got around in front, I saw him going out the yard gate and starting up the drive toward the pike. So I ran to catch up with him. He was sixty yards or so up the drive before I caught up.

I did not walk right up even with him at first, but trailed him, the way a kid will, about seven or eight feet behind, now and then running two or three steps in order to hold longer stride. When I first came up behind him, he turned to give me a look, just a meaningless look, and then fixed his eyes up the drive and kept on walking.

When we had got around the bend in the drive which cut the house from sight, and were going along by the edge of the woods, I decided to come up even with him. I ran a few steps, and was by his side, or almost, but some feet off to the right. I walked along in this position for a while, and he never noticed me. I walked along until we got within sight of the big gate that let on the pike.

Then I said: "Where did you come from?"

He looked at me then with a look which seemed almost surprised that I was there. Then he said, "It ain't none of yore business."

We went on another fifty feet.

Then I said, "Where are you going?"

He stopped, studied me dispassionately for a moment, then suddenly took a step toward me and leaned his face down at me. The lips jerked back, but not in any grin, to show where the teeth were knocked out and to make the scar on the lower lip come white with the tension.

He said: "Stop following me. You don't stop following me and I cut yore throat, you little son-of-a-bitch."

Then he went on to the gate, and up the pike.

That was thirty-five years ago. Since that time my father and mother have died. I was still a boy, but a big boy, when my father got cut on the blade of a mowing machine and died of lockjaw. My mother sold the place and went to town to live with her sister. But she never took hold after my father's death, and she died within three years, right in middle life. My aunt always said, "Sallie just died of a broken heart, she was so devoted." Dellie is dead, too, but she died, I heard, quite a long time after we sold the farm.

As for Little Jebb, he grew up to be a mean and ficey Negro. He killed another Negro in a fight and got sent to the penitentiary, where he is yet, the last I heard tell. He probably grew up to be mean and ficey from just being picked on so much by the children of the other tenants, who were jealous of Jebb and Dellie for being thrifty and clever and being white-folks' niggers.

Old Jebb lived forever. I saw him ten years ago and he was about a hundred then, and not looking much different. He was living in town then, on relief—that was back in the Depression—when I went to see him. He said to me: "Too strong to die. When I was a young feller just comen on and seen how things wuz, I prayed the Lawd. I said, Oh, Lawd, gimme strength and meke me strong fer to do and to in-dure. The Lawd hearkened to my prayer. He give me strength. I was in-duren proud fer being strong and me much man. The Lawd give me my prayer and my strength. But now He done gone off and fergot me and left me alone with my strength. A man doan know what to pray fer, and him mortal."

Jebb is probably living yet, as far as I know.

That is what has happened since the morning when the tramp leaned his face down at me and showed his teeth and said: "Stop following me. You don't stop following me and I cut yore throat, you little son-of-a-bitch." That was what he said, for me not to follow him. But I did follow him, all the years.

Contemporary Fiction

Jean-Paul Sartre

(1905)

Jean-Paul Sartre has been the focal point for atheistic existential philosophy since the end of World War II. Born in Paris in 1905, Sartre was reared as an only child by his widowed mother and grandparents in Alsace. "The death of [my father] was the big event of my life: it sent my mother back to her chains and gave me freedom," and freedom is the vital element in Sartre's thought. He was educated in philosophy and taught in French *lycées* until the war. In 1938 he published *Nausea,* an important, disquieting novel which investigates the inner life of a social dropout and his frightening perception of existence. (Incidentally, *Nausea* is, I believe, far more interesting and penetrating than most of the novels of Herman Hesse, that old Pied Piper of today's youth.) Captured by the Germans early in the war, Sartre escaped from a prison camp and returned to France to work in the *résistance.* His first night back in Paris, recalls his mistress Simone de Beauvoir, "he gave me yet another surprise. He had not come back to Paris to enjoy the sweets of freedom, he told me, but to *act.*" From that time until the present he has been politically and artistically committed to freedom, the concrete freedom of all men. Sartre has said, "Nothing can be better for us unless it is better for all," and as the editor of the highly intellectual French periodical *Les Temps Modernes,* he wrote, "We are with those who want to change both man's social condition and the conception which he has of himself." In his plays and novels Sartre, unlike most other artists, is concerned with moving his audience to action, with helping to change the world, and he unashamedly advocates the artist's social mission. "Through literature," Sartre has written, "the collectivity turns to reflection and meditation; it acquires an unhappy consciousness, an unstable image of itself which it forever seeks to modify and to improve." In "The Wall" Sartre dramatizes the tragic absurdity of the world and how extreme situations may reveal to what extent men are cut off from one another, trapped within their own bodies.

The Wall

They pushed us into a big white room and I began to blink because the light hurt my eyes. Then I saw a table and four men behind the table, civilians, looking over the papers. They had bunched another group of prisoners in the back and we had to cross the whole room to join them. There were several I knew and some others who must have been foreigners. The two in front of me were blond with round skulls; they looked alike. I supposed they were French. The smaller one kept hitching up his pants; nerves.

It lasted about three hours; I was dizzy and my head was empty; but the room was well heated and I found that pleasant enough: for the past 24 hours we hadn't stopped shivering. The guards brought the prisoners up to the table, one after the other. The four men asked each one his name and occupation. Most of the time they didn't go any further—or they would simply ask a question here and there: "Did you have anything to do with the sabotage of munitions?" Or "Where were you the morning of the 9th and what were you doing?" They didn't listen to the answers or at least didn't seem to. They were quiet for a moment and then looking straight in front of them began to write. They asked Tom if it were true he was in the International Brigade; Tom couldn't tell them otherwise because of the papers they found in his coat. They didn't ask Juan anything but they wrote for a long time after he told them his name.

"My brother José is the anarchist," Juan said, "you know he isn't here any more. I don't belong to any party, I never had anything to do with politics."

They didn't answer. Juan went on, "I haven't done anything. I don't want to pay for somebody else."

His lips trembled. A guard shut him up and took him away. It was my turn.

"Your name is Pablo Ibbieta?"

"Yes."

The man looked at the papers and asked me, "Where's Ramon Gris?"

"I don't know."

"You hid him in your house from the 6th to the 19th."

"No."

They wrote for a minute and then the guards took me out. In the corridor Tom and Juan were waiting between two guards. We started walking. Tom asked one of the guards, "So?"

"So what?" the guard said.

"Was that the cross-examination or the sentence?"

"Sentence," the guard said.

"What are they going to do with us?"

The guard answered dryly, "Sentence will be read in your cell."

As a matter of fact, our cell was one of the hospital cellars. It was terrifically cold there because of the drafts. We shivered all night and it wasn't much better during the day. I had spent the previous five days in a cell in a monastery, a sort of hole in the wall that must have dated from the middle ages: since there were a lot of prisoners and not much room, they locked us up anywhere. I didn't miss my cell; I hadn't suffered too much from the cold but I was alone; after a long time it gets irritating. In the cellar I had company. Juan hardly ever spoke: he was afraid and he was too young to have anything to say. But Tom was a good talker and he knew Spanish well.

There was a bench in the cellar and four mats. When they took us back we sat and waited in silence. After a long moment, Tom said, "We're screwed."

"I think so too," I said, "but I don't think they'll do anything to the kid."

"They don't have a thing against him," said Tom. "He's the brother of a militiaman and that's all."

I looked at Juan: he didn't seem to hear. Tom went on, "You know what they do in Saragossa? They lay the men down on the road and run over them with trucks. A Moroccan deserter told us that. They said it was to save ammunition."

"It doesn't save gas," I said.

I was annoyed at Tom: he shouldn't have said that.

"Then there's officers walking along the road," he went on, "supervising it all. They stick their hands in their pockets and smoke cigarettes. You think they finish off the guys? Hell no. They let them scream. Sometimes for an hour. The Moroccan said he damned near puked the first time."

"I don't believe they'll do that here," I said. "Unless they're really short on ammunition."

Day was coming in through four airholes and a round opening they had made in the ceiling on the left, and you could see the sky through it. Through this hole, usually closed by a trap, they unloaded coal into the cellar. Just below the hole there was a big pile of coal dust; it had been used to heat the hospital, but since the beginning of the war the patients were evacuated and the coal stayed there, unused; sometimes it even got rained on because they had forgotten to close the trap.

Tom began to shiver. "Good Jesus Christ, I'm cold," he said. "Here it goes again."

He got up and began to do exercises. At each movement his shirt opened on his chest, white and hairy. He lay on his back, raised his legs in the air and bicycled. I saw his great rump trembling. Tom was husky but he had too much fat. I thought how rifle bullets or the sharp points of bayonets would soon be sunk into this mass of tender flesh as in a lump of butter. It wouldn't have made me feel like that if he'd been thin.

I wasn't exactly cold, but I couldn't feel my arms and shoulders any more. Sometimes I had the impression I was missing something and began to look around for my coat and then suddenly remembered they hadn't given me a coat. It was rather uncomfortable. They took our clothes and gave them to their soldiers leaving us only our shirts—and those canvas pants that hospital patients wear in the middle of summer. After a while Tom got up and sat next to me, breathing heavily.

"Warmer?"

"Good Christ, no. But I'm out of wind."

Around eight o'clock in the evening a major came in with two *falangistas.* He had a sheet of paper in his hand. He asked the guard, "What are the names of those three?"

"Steinbock, Ibbieta and Mirbal," the guard said.

The major put on his eyeglasses and scanned the list: "Steinbock . . . Steinbock . . . Oh yes . . . You are sentenced to death. You will be shot tomorrow morning." He went on looking. "The other two as well."

"That's not possible," Juan said. "Not me."

The major looked at him amazed. "What's your name?"

"Juan Mirbal," he said.

"Well, your name is there," said the major. "You're sentenced."

"I didn't do anything," Juan said.

The major shrugged his shoulders and turned to Tom and me.

"You're Basque?"

"Nobody is Basque."

He looked annoyed. "They told me there were three Basques. I'm not going to waste my time running after them. Then naturally you don't want a priest?"

We didn't even answer.

He said, "A Belgian doctor is coming shortly. He is authorized to spend the night with you." He made a military salute and left.

"What did I tell you," Tom said. "We get it."

"Yes," I said, "it's a rotten deal for the kid."

I said that to be decent but I didn't like the kid. His face was too thin and fear and suffering had disfigured it, twisting all his features. Three days before he was a smart sort of kid, not too bad; but now he looked like an old fairy and I thought how he'd never be young again, even if they were to let him go. It wouldn't have been too hard to have a little pity for him but pity disgusts me, or rather it horrifies me. He hadn't said anything more but he had turned grey; his face and hands were both grey. He sat down again and looked at the ground with round eyes. Tom was good hearted, he wanted to take his arm, but the kid tore himself away violently and made a face.

"Let him alone," I said in a low voice, "you can see he's going to blubber."

Tom obeyed regretfully; he would have liked to comfort the kid, it would have passed his time and he wouldn't have been tempted to think about himself. But it annoyed me: I'd never thought about death because I never had any reason to, but now the reason was here and there was nothing to do but think about it.

Tom began to talk. "So you think you've knocked guys off, do you?" he asked me. I didn't answer. He began explaining to me that he had knocked off six since the beginning of August; he didn't realize the situation and I could tell he didn't *want* to realize it. I hadn't quite realized it myself, I wondered if it hurt much. I thought of bullets, I imagined their burning hail through my body. All that was beside the real question; but I was calm: we had all night to understand. After a while Tom stopped talking and I watched him out of the corner of my eye; I saw he too had turned grey and he looked rotten; I told myself "Now it starts." It was almost dark, a dim glow filtered through the airholes and the pile of coal and made a big stain beneath the spot of sky; I could already see a star through the hole in the ceiling: the night would be pure and icy.

The door opened and two guards came in, followed by a blonde man in a tan uniform. He saluted us. "I am the doctor," he said. "I have authorization to help you in these trying hours."

He had an agreeable and distinguished voice. I said, "What do you want here?"

"I am at your disposal. I shall do all I can to make your last moments less difficult."

"What did you come here for? There are others, the hospital's full of them."

"I was sent here," he answered with a vague look. "Ah! Would you like to smoke?" he added hurriedly, "I have cigarettes and even cigars."

He offered us English cigarettes and *puros,* but we refused. I looked him in the eyes and he seemed irritated. I said to him, "You aren't here on an errand of mercy. Besides, I know you. I saw you with the fascists in the barracks yard the day I was arrested."

I was going to continue, but something surprising suddenly happened to me; the presence of this doctor no longer interested me. Generally when I'm on somebody I don't let go. But the desire to talk left me completely; I shrugged and turned my eyes away. A little later I raised my head; he was watching me curiously. The guards were sitting on a mat. Pedro, the tall thin one, was twiddling his thumbs, the other shook his head from time to time to keep from falling asleep.

"Do you want a light?" Pedro suddenly asked the doctor. The other nodded "Yes": I think he was about as smart as a log, but he surely wasn't bad. Looking in his cold blue eyes it seemed to me that his only sin was lack of imagination. Pedro went out and came back with an oil lamp which he set on the corner of the bench. It gave a bad light but it was better than nothing: they had left us in the dark the night before. For a long time I watched the circle of light the lamp made on the ceiling. I was fascinated. Then suddenly I woke up, the circle of light disappeared and I felt myself crushed under an enormous weight. It was not the thought of death, or fear; it was nameless. My cheeks burned and my head ached.

I shook myself and looked at my two friends. Tom had hidden his face in his hands. I could only see the fat white nape of his neck. Little Juan was the worst, his mouth was open and nostrils trembled. The doctor went to him and put his hand on his shoulder to comfort him: but his eyes stayed cold. Then I saw the Belgian's hand drop stealthily along Juan's arm, down to the wrist. Juan paid no attention. The Belgian took his wrist between three fingers, distractedly, the same time drawing back a little and turning his back to me. But I leaned backward and saw him take a watch from his pocket and look at it for a moment, never letting go of the wrist. After a minute he let the hand fall inert and went and leaned his back against the wall, then, as if he suddenly remembered something very important which had to be jotted down on the spot, he took a notebook from his pocket and wrote a few lines. "Bastard," I thought angrily, "let him come and take my pulse. I'll shove my fist in his rotten face."

He didn't come but I felt him watching me. I raised my head and returned his look. Impersonally, he said to me, "Doesn't it seem cold to you here?" He looked cold, he was blue.

"I'm not cold," I told him.

He never took his hard eyes off me. Suddenly I understood and my hands went to my face: I was drenched in sweat. In this cellar, in the midst of winter, in the midst of drafts, I was sweating. I ran my hands through my hair, gummed together with perspiration; at the same time I saw my shirt was damp and sticking to my skin: I had been dripping for an hour and hadn't felt it. But that swine of a Belgian hadn't missed a thing; he had seen the drops rolling down my cheeks and thought: this is the manifestation of an almost pathological state of terror; and he had felt normal and proud of being alive because he was cold. I wanted to stand up and smash his face but no sooner had I made the slightest gesture than my rage and shame were wiped out; I fell back on the bench with indifference.

I satisfied myself by rubbing my neck with my handkerchief because now I felt the sweat dropping from my hair onto my neck and it was unpleasant. I soon gave up rubbing, it was useless; my handkerchief was already soaked and I was still sweating. My buttocks were sweating too and my damp trousers were glued to the bench.

Suddenly Juan spoke. "You're a doctor?"

"Yes," the Belgian said.

"Does it hurt . . . very long?"

"Huh? When . . . ? Oh, no," the Belgian said paternally. "Not at all. It's over quickly." He acted as though he was calming a cash customer.

"But I . . . they told me . . . sometimes they have to fire twice."

"Sometimes," the Belgian said, nodding. "It may happen that the first volley reaches no vital organs."

"Then they have to reload their rifles and aim all over again?" He thought for a moment and then added hoarsely, "That takes time!"

He had a terrible fear of suffering, it was all he thought about: it was his age. I never thought much about it and it wasn't fear of suffering that made me sweat.

I got up and walked to the pile of coal dust. Tom jumped up and threw me a hateful look: I had annoyed him because my shoes squeaked. I wondered if my face looked as frightened as his: I saw he was sweating too. The sky was superb, no light filtered into the dark corner and I had only to raise my head to see the Big Dipper. But it wasn't like it had been: the night before I could see a great piece of sky from my monastery cell and each hour of the day brought me a different memory. Morning, when the sky was a hard, light blue, I thought of beaches on the Atlantic; at noon I saw the sun and I remembered a bar in Seville where I drank *manzanilla* and ate olives and anchovies; afternoons I was in the shade and I thought of the deep shadow which spreads over half a bullring leaving the other half shimmering in sunlight; it was really hard to see the whole world reflected in the sky like that. But now I could watch the sky as much as I pleased, it no longer evoked anything in me. I liked that better. I came back and sat near Tom. A long moment passed.

Tom began speaking in a low voice. He had to talk, without that he wouldn't have been able to recognize himself in his own mind. I thought he was talking to me but he wasn't looking at me. He was undoubtedly afraid to see me as I was, grey and sweating: we were alike and worse than mirrors of each other. He watched the Belgian, the living.

"Do you understand?" he said. "I don't understand."

I began to speak in a low voice too. I watched the Belgian. "Why? What's the matter?"

"Something is going to happen to us that I can't understand."

There was a strange smell about Tom. It seemed to me I was more sensitive than usual to odors. I grinned. "You'll understand in a while."

"It isn't clear," he said obstinately. "I want to be brave but first I have to know . . . Listen, they're going to take us into the courtyard. Good. They're going to stand up in front of us. How many?"

"I don't know. Five or eight. Not more."

"All right. There'll be eight. Someone'll holler 'aim!' and I'll see eight rifles looking at me. I'll think how I'd like to get inside the wall, I'll push against it with my back . . . with every ounce of strength I have, but the wall will stay, like in a nightmare. I can imagine all that. If you only knew how well I can imagine it."

"All right, all right!" I said. "I can imagine it too."

"It must hurt like hell. You know, they aim at the eyes and the mouth to disfigure you," he added mechanically. "I can feel the wounds already; I've had pains in my head and in my neck for the past hour. Not real pains. Worse. This is what I'm going to feel tomorrow morning. And then what?"

I well understood what he meant but I didn't want to act as if I did. I had pains too, pains in my body like a crowd of tiny scars. I couldn't get used to it. But I was like him, I attached no importance to it. "After," I said, "you'll be pushing up daisies."

He began to talk to himself: he never stopped watching the Belgian. The Belgian didn't seem to be listening. I knew what he had come to do; he wasn't interested in what we thought; he came to watch our bodies, bodies dying in agony while yet alive.

"It's like a nightmare," Tom was saying. "You want to think something, you always have the impression that it's all right, that you're going to understand and then it slips, it escapes you and fades away. I tell myself there will be nothing afterwards. But I don't understand what it means. Sometimes I almost can . . . and then it fades away and I start thinking about the pains again, bullets, explosions. I'm a materialist, I swear it to you; I'm not going crazy. But something's the matter. I see my corpse; that's not hard but *I'm* the one who sees it, with *my* eyes. I've got to think . . . think that I won't see anything anymore and the world will go on for the others. We aren't made to think that, Pablo. Believe me: I've already stayed up a whole night waiting for something. But this isn't the same: this will creep up behind us, Pablo, and we won't be able to prepare for it."

"Shut up," I said, "Do you want me to call a priest?"

He didn't answer. I had already noticed he had the tendency to act like a prophet and call me Pablo, speaking in a toneless voice. I didn't like that: but it seems all the Irish are that way. I had the vague impression he smelled of urine. Fundamentally, I hadn't much sympathy for Tom and I didn't see why, under the pretext of dying together, I should have any more. It would have been different with some others. With Ramon Gris, for example. But I felt alone between Tom and Juan. I liked that better, anyhow: with Ramon I might have been more deeply moved. But I was terribly hard just then and I wanted to stay hard.

He kept on chewing his words, with something like distraction. He certainly talked to keep himself from thinking. He smelled of urine like an old prostate case. Naturally, I agreed with him, I could have said everything he said: it isn't *natural* to die. And since I was going to die, nothing seemed natural to me, not this pile of coal dust, or the bench, or Pedro's ugly face. Only it didn't please me to think the same things as Tom. And I knew that, all through the night, every five minutes, we would keep on thinking things at the same time. I looked at him sideways and for the first time he seemed strange to me: he wore death on his face. My pride was wounded: for the past 24 hours I had lived next to Tom, I had listened to him, I had spoken to him and I knew we had nothing in common. And now we looked as much alike as twin brothers, simply because we were going to die together. Tom took my hand without looking at me.

"Pablo, I wonder . . . I wonder if it's really true that everything ends."

I took my hand away and said, "Look between your feet, you pig."

There was a big puddle between his feet and drops fell from his pants-leg.

"What is it," he asked, frightened.

"You're pissing in your pants," I told him.

"It isn't true," he said furiously. "I'm not pissing. I don't feel anything."

The Belgian approached us. He asked with false solicitude, "Do you feel ill?"

Tom did not answer. The Belgian looked at the puddle and said nothing.

"I don't know what it is," Tom said ferociously. "But I'm not afraid. I swear I'm not afraid."

The Belgian did not answer. Tom got up and went to piss in a corner. He came back buttoning his fly, and sat down without a word. The Belgian was taking notes.

All three of us watched him because he was alive. He had the motions of a living human being, the cares of a living human being; he shivered in the cellar the way the living are supposed to shiver; he had an obedient, well-fed body. The rest of us hardly felt ours—not in the same way anyhow. I wanted to feel my pants between my legs but I didn't dare; I watched the Belgian, balancing on his legs, master of his muscles, someone who could think about tomorrow. There we were, three bloodless shadows; we watched him and we sucked his life like vampires.

Finally he went over to little Juan. Did he want to feel his neck for some professional motive or was he obeying an impulse of charity? If he was acting by charity it was the only time during the whole night.

He caressed Juan's head and neck. The kid let himself be handled, his eyes never leaving him, then suddenly, he seized the hand and looked at it strangely. He held the Belgian's hand between his own two hands and there was nothing pleasant about them, two grey pincers gripping this fat and reddish hand. I suspected what was going to happen and Tom must have suspected it too: but the Belgian didn't see a thing, he smiled paternally. After a moment the kid brought the fat red hand to his mouth and tried to bite it. The Belgian pulled away quickly and stumbled back against the wall. For a second he looked at us with horror, he must have suddenly understood that we were not men like him. I began to laugh and one of the guards jumped up. The other was asleep, his wide open eyes were blank.

I felt relaxed and over-excited at the same time. I didn't want to think any more about what would happen at dawn, at death. It made no sense. I only found words or emptiness. But as soon as I tried to think of anything else I saw rifle barrels pointing at me. Perhaps I lived through my execution twenty times; once I even thought it was for good: I must have slept a minute. They were dragging me to the wall and I was struggling; I was asking for mercy. I woke up with a start and looked at the Belgian: I was afraid I might have cried out in my sleep. But he was stroking his moustache, he hadn't noticed anything. If I had wanted to, I think I could have slept a while; I had been awake for 48 hours. I was at the end of my rope. But I didn't want to lose two hours of life: they would come to wake me up at dawn, I would follow them, stupefied with sleep and I would have croaked without so much as an "Oof!"; I didn't want that, I didn't want to die like an animal, I wanted to understand. Then I was afraid of having nightmares. I got up, walked back and forth, and, to change my ideas, I began to think about my past life. A crowd of memories came back to me pell-mell. There were good and bad ones—or at least I called them that *before.* There were faces and incidents. I saw the face of a little *novillero* who was gored in Valencia during the *Feria,* the face of one of my uncles, the face of Ramon Gris. I remembered my whole life: how I was out of work for three months in 1926, how I almost starved to death. I remembered a night I spent on a bench in Grenada: I hadn't eaten for three days. I was angry, I didn't want to die. That made me smile. How madly I ran after happiness, after women, after liberty. Why? I wanted to free Spain, I admired Pi y Margall, I joined the anarchist movement, I spoke in public meetings: I took everything as seriously as if I were immortal.

At that moment I felt that I had my whole life in front of me and I thought, "It's a damned lie." It was worth nothing because it was finished. I wondered how I'd been able to walk, to laugh with the girls: I wouldn't have moved so much as my little finger if I had only imagined I would die like this. My life was in front of me, shut, closed, like a bag and yet everything inside of it was unfinished. For an instant I tried to judge it. I wanted to tell myself, this is a beautiful life. But I couldn't pass judgment on it; it was only a sketch; I had spent my time counterfeiting eternity, I had understood nothing. I missed nothing: there were so many things I could have missed, the taste of *manzanilla* or the baths I took in summer in a little creek near Cadiz; but death had disenchanted everything.

The Belgian suddenly had a bright idea. "My friends," he told us, "I will undertake—if the military administration will allow it—to send a message for you, a souvenir to those who love you. . . ."

Tom mumbled, "I don't have anybody."

I said nothing. Tom waited an instant then looked at me with curiosity. "You don't have anything to say to Concha?"

"No."

I hated this tender complicity: it was my own fault, I had talked about Concha the night before, I should have controlled myself. I was with her for a year. Last night I would have given an arm to see her again for five minutes. That was why I talked about her, it was stronger than I was. Now I had no more desire to see her, I had nothing more to say to her. I would not even have wanted to hold her in my arms: my body filled me with horror because it was grey and sweating—and I wasn't sure that her body didn't fill me with horror. Concha would cry when she found out I was dead, she would have no taste for life for months afterward. But I was still the one who was going to die. I thought of her soft, beautiful eyes. When she looked at me something passed from her to me. But I knew it was over: if she looked at me *now* the look would stay in her eyes, it wouldn't reach me. I was alone.

Tom was alone too but not in the same way. Sitting cross-legged, he had begun to stare at the bench with a sort of smile, he looked amazed. He put out his hand and touched the wood cautiously as if he were afraid of breaking something, then drew back his hand quickly and shuddered. If I had been Tom I wouldn't have amused myself by touching the bench; this was some more Irish nonsense, but I too found that objects had a funny look: they were more obliterated, less dense than usual. It was enough for me to look at the bench, the lamp, the pile of coal dust, to feel that I was going to die. Naturally I couldn't think clearly about my death but I saw it everywhere, on things, in the way things fell back and kept their distance, discreetly, as people who speak quietly at the bedside of a dying man. It was *his* death which Tom had just touched on the bench.

In the state I was in, if someone had come and told me I could go home quietly, that they would leave me my life whole, it would have left me cold: several hours or several years of waiting is all the same when you have lost the illusion of being eternal. I clung to nothing, in a way I was calm. But it was a horrible calm—because of my body; my body, I saw with its eyes, I heard with its ears, but it was no longer me; it sweated and trembled by itself and I didn't recognize it any more. I had to touch it and look at it to find out what was happening, as if it were the body of someone else. At times I could still feel it, I felt sinkings, and fallings, as when you're in a plane taking a nosedive, or I felt my heart beating. But that didn't reassure me. Everything that came from my body was all cockeyed. Most of the time it was quiet and I felt no more than a sort of weight, a filthy presence against me; I had the impression of being tied to an enormous vermin. Once I felt my pants and I felt they were damp; I didn't know whether it was sweat or urine, but I went to piss on the coal pile as a precaution.

The Belgian took out his watch, looked at it. He said, "It is three-thirty."

Bastard! He must have done it on purpose. Tom jumped; we hadn't noticed time was running out; night surrounded us like a shapeless, somber mass, I couldn't even remember that it had begun.

Little Juan began to cry. He wrung his hands, pleaded, "I don't want to die. I don't want to die."

He ran across the whole cellar waving his arms in the air then fell sobbing on one of the mats. Tom watched him with mournful eyes, without the slightest desire to console him. Because it wasn't worth the trouble: the kid made more noise than we did, but he was less touched: he was like a sick man who defends himself against his illness by fever. It's much more serious when there isn't any fever.

He wept: I could clearly see he was pitying himself; he wasn't thinking about death. For one second, one single second, I wanted to weep myself, to weep with pity for myself. But the opposite happened: I glanced at the kid, I saw his thin sobbing shoulders and I felt inhuman: I could pity neither the others nor myself. I said to myself, "I want to die cleanly."

Tom had gotten up, he placed himself just under the round opening and began to watch for daylight. I was determined to die cleanly and I only thought of that. But ever since the doctor told us the time, I felt time flying, flowing away drop by drop.

It was still dark when I heard Tom's voice: "Do you hear them?"

Men were marching in the courtyard.

"Yes."

"What the hell are they doing? They can't shoot in the dark."

After a while we heard no more. I said to Tom, "It's day."

Pedro got up, yawning, and came to blow out the lamp. He said to his buddy, "Cold as hell."

The cellar was all grey. We heard shots in the distance.

"It's starting," I told Tom. "They must do it in the court in the rear."

Tom asked the doctor for a cigarette. I didn't want one; I didn't want cigarettes or alcohol. From that moment on they didn't stop firing.

"Do you realize what's happening," Tom said.

He wanted to add something but kept quiet, watching the door. The door opened and a lieutenant came in with four soldiers. Tom dropped his cigarette.

"Steinbock?"

Tom didn't answer. Pedro pointed him out.

"Juan Mirbal?"

"On the mat."

"Get up," the lieutenant said.

Juan did not move. Two soldiers took him under the arms and set him on his feet. But he fell as soon as they released him.

The soldiers hesitated.

"He's not the first sick one," said the lieutenant. "You two carry him; they'll fix it up down there."

He turned to Tom. "Let's go."

Tom went out between two soldiers. Two others followed, carrying the kid by the armpits. He hadn't fainted; his eyes were wide open and tears ran down his cheeks. When I wanted to go out the lieutenant stopped me.

"You Ibbieta?"

"Yes."

"You wait here; they'll come for you later."

They left. The Belgian and the two jailers left too, I was alone. I did not understand what was happening to me but I would have liked it better if they had gotten it over with right away. I heard shots at almost regular intervals; I shook with each one of them. I wanted to scream and tear out my hair. But I gritted my teeth and pushed my hands in my pockets because I wanted to stay clean.

After an hour they came to get me and led me to the first floor, to a small room that smelt of cigars and where the heat was stifling. There were two officers sitting smoking in the armchairs, papers on their knees.

"You're Ibbieta?"

"Yes."

"Where is Ramon Gris?"

"I don't know."

The one questioning me was short and fat. His eyes were hard behind his glasses. He said to me, "Come here."

I went to him. He got up and took my arms, staring at me with a look that should have pushed me into the earth. At the same time he pinched my biceps with all his might. It wasn't to hurt me, it was only a game: he wanted to dominate me. He also thought he had to blow his stinking breath square in my face. We stayed for a moment like that, and I almost felt like laughing. It takes a lot to intimidate a man who is going to die; it didn't work. He pushed me back violently and sat down again. He said, "It's his life against yours. You can have yours if you tell us where he is."

These men dolled up with their riding crops and boots were still going to die. A little later than I, but not too much. They busied themselves looking for names in their crumpled papers, they ran after other men to imprison or suppress them; they had opinions on the future of Spain and on other subjects. Their little activities seemed shocking and burlesqued to me; I couldn't put myself in their place, I thought they were insane. The little man was still looking at me, whipping his boots with the riding crop. All his gestures were calculated to give him the look of a live and ferocious beast.

"So? You understand?"

"I don't know where Gris is," I answered. "I thought he was in Madrid."

The other officer raised his pale hand indolently. This indolence was also calculated. I saw through all their little schemes and I was stupefied to find there were men who amused themselves that way.

"You have a quarter of an hour to think it over," he said slowly. "Take him to the laundry, bring him back in fifteen minutes. If he still refuses he will be executed on the spot."

They knew what they were doing: I had passed the night in waiting; then they had made me wait an hour in the cellar while they shot Tom and Juan and now they were locking me up in the laundry; they must have prepared their game the night before. They told themselves that nerves eventually wear out and they hoped to get me that way.

They were badly mistaken. In the laundry I sat on a stool because I felt very weak and I began to think. But not about their proposition. Of course I knew where Gris was; he was hiding with his cousins, four kilometers from the city. I also knew that I would not reveal his hiding place unless they tortured me (but they didn't seem to be thinking about that). All that was perfectly regulated, definite and in no way interested me. Only I would have liked to understand the reasons for my conduct. I would rather die than give up Gris. Why? I didn't like Ramon Gris any more. My friendship for him had died a little while before dawn at the same time as my love for Concha, at the same time as my desire to live. Undoubtedly I thought highly of him: he was tough. But it was not for this reason that I consented to die in his place; his life had no more value than mine; no life had value. They were going to slap a man up against a wall and shoot at him till he died, whether it was I or Gris or somebody else made no difference. I knew he was more useful than I to the cause of Spain but I thought to hell with Spain and anarchy; nothing was important. Yet I was there, I could save my skin and give up Gris and I refused to do it. I found that somehow comic; it was obstinacy. I thought, "I must be stubborn!" And a droll sort of gaiety spread over me.

They came for me and brought me back to the two officers. A rat ran out from under my feet and that amused me. I turned to one of the *falangistas* and said, "Did you see the rat?"

He didn't answer. He was very sober, he took himself seriously. I wanted to laugh but I held myself back because I was afraid that once I got started I wouldn't be able to stop. The *falangista* had a moustache. I said to him again, "You ought to shave off your moustache, idiot." I thought it funny that he would let the hairs of his living being invade his face. He kicked me without great conviction and I kept quiet.

"Well," said the fat officer, "have you thought about it?"

I looked at them with curiosity, as insects of a very rare species. I told them, "I know where he is. He is hidden in the cemetery. In a vault or in the gravediggers' shack."

It was a farce. I wanted to see them stand up, buckle their belts and give orders busily.

They jumped to their feet. "Let's go. Molés, go get fifteen men from Lieutenant Lopez. You," the fat man said, "I'll let you off if you're telling the truth, but it'll cost you plenty if you're making monkeys out of us."

They left in a great clatter and I waited peacefully under the guard of *falangistas.* From time to time I smiled, thinking about the spectacle they would make. I felt stunned and malicious. I imagined them lifting up tombstones, opening the doors of the vaults one by one. I represented this situation to myself as if I had been someone else: this prisoner obstinately playing the hero, these grim *falangistas* with their moustaches and their men in uniform running among the graves; it was irresistibly funny. After half an hour the little fat man came back alone. I thought he had come to give the orders to execute me. The others must have stayed in the cemetery.

The officer looked at me. He didn't look at all sheepish. "Take him into the big courtyard with the others," he said. "After the military operations a regular court will decide what happens to him."

"Then they're not . . . not going to shoot me? . . ."

"Not now, anyway. What happens afterwards is none of my business."

I still didn't understand. I asked, "But why . . . ?"

He shrugged his shoulders without answering and the soldiers took me away. In the big courtyard there were about a hundred prisoners, women, children and a few old men. I began walking around the central grass plot, I was stupefied. At noon they let us eat in the mess hall. Two or three people questioned me. I must have known them, but I didn't answer: I didn't even know where I was.

Around evening they pushed about ten new prisoners into the court. I recognized Garcia, the baker. He said, "What damned luck you have! I didn't think I'd see you alive."

"They sentenced me to death," I said, "and then they changed their minds. I don't know why."

"They arrested me at two o'clock," Garcia said.

"Why?" Garcia had nothing to do with politics.

"I don't know," he said. "They arrest everybody who doesn't think the way they do." He lowered his voice. "They got Gris."

I began to tremble. "When?"

"This morning. He messed it up. He left his cousin's on Tuesday because they had an argument. There were plenty of people to hide him but he didn't want to owe anything to anybody. He said, 'I'd go and hide in Ibbieta's place, but they got him, so I'll go hide in the cemetery.'"

"In the cemetery?"

"Yes. What a fool. Of course they went by there this morning, that was sure to happen. They found him in the gravediggers' shack. He shot at them and they got him."

"In the cemetery!"

Everything began to spin and I found myself sitting on the ground: I laughed so hard I cried.

James Baldwin

(1924)

James Baldwin, one of America's most gifted contemporary novelists and an articulate voice for blacks, was born in 1924, the oldest of nine children, in New York City. He was reared in Harlem, about which he has often written with compassion and anger. He lived in Paris for nearly ten years, where he wrote his first two novels, *Go Tell It on the Mountain* (1952) and *Giovanni's Room* (1956). In 1962 he published his third novel, *Another Country,* a violent, unforgettable story of hate and tension between individual blacks and whites in New York. Baldwin's *The Fire Next Time,* two open letters on the relationship of blacks and whites in America, became a best seller in 1963. An activist in the civil rights movement of the 1960's, he has often been severely critical of American society in his fiction and essays, but he has said, "I love America more than any other country in the world, and exactly for this reason, I insist on the right to criticize her perpetually."

Previous Condition

I woke up shaking, alone in my room. I was clammy cold with sweat; under me the sheet and the mattress were soaked. The sheet was gray and twisted like a rope. I breathed like I had been running.

I couldn't move for the longest while. I just lay on my back, spread-eagled, looking up at the ceiling, listening to the sounds of people getting up in other parts of the house, alarm clocks ringing and water splashing and doors opening and shutting and feet on the stairs. I could tell when people left for work: the hall doorway downstairs whined and shuffled as it opened and gave a funny kind of double slam as it closed. One thud and then a louder thud and then a little final click. While the door was open I could hear the street sounds too, horses' hoofs and delivery wagons and people in the streets and big trucks and motor cars screaming on the asphalt.

I had been dreaming. At night I dreamt and woke up in the morning trembling, but not remembering the dream, except that in the dream I had been running. I could not remember when the dream—or dreams—had started; it had been long ago. For long periods maybe, I would have no dreams at all. And then they would come back, every night, I would try not to go to bed, I would go to sleep frightened and wake up frightened and have another day to get through with the nightmare at my shoulder. Now I was back from Chicago, busted, living off my friends in a dirty furnished room downtown. The show I had been with had folded in Chicago. It hadn't been much of a part—or much of a show either, to tell the truth. I played a kind of intellectual Uncle Tom, a young college student working for his race. The playwright had wanted to prove he was a liberal, I guess. But, as I say, the show had folded and here I was, back in New York and hating it. I knew that I should be getting another job, making the rounds, pounding the pavement. But I didn't. I couldn't face it. It was summer. I seemed to be fagged out. And every day I hated myself more. Acting's a rough life, even if you're white. I'm not tall and I'm not good looking and I can't sing or dance and I'm not white; so even at the best of times I wasn't in much demand.

The room I lived in was heavy ceilinged, perfectly square, with walls the color of chipped dry blood. Jules Weissman, a Jewboy, had got the room for me. It's a room to sleep in, he said, or maybe to die in but God knows it wasn't meant to live in. Perhaps because the room was so hideous it had a fantastic array of light fixtures: one on the ceiling, one on the left wall, two on the right wall, and a lamp on the table beside my bed. My bed was in front of the window through which nothing ever blew but dust. It was a furnished room and they'd thrown enough stuff in it to furnish three rooms its size. Two easy chairs and a desk, the bed, the table, a straight-backed chair, a bookcase, a cardboard wardrobe; and my books and my suitcase, both unpacked; and my dirty clothes flung in a corner. It was the kind of room that defeated you. It had a fireplace, too, and a heavy marble mantelpiece and a great gray mirror above the mantelpiece. It was hard to see anything in the mirror very clearly—which was perhaps just as well—and it would have been worth your life to have started a fire in the fireplace.

"Well, you won't have to stay here long," Jules told me the night I came. Jules smuggled me in, sort of, after dark, when everyone had gone to bed.

"Christ, I hope not."

"I'll be moving to a big place soon," Jules said. "You can move in with me." He turned all the lights on. "Think it'll be all right for a while?" He sounded apologetic, as though he had designed the room himself.

"Oh, sure. D'you think I'll have any trouble?"

"I don't think so. The rent's paid. She can't put you out."

I didn't say anything to that.

"Sort of stay undercover," Jules said. "You know."

"Roger," I said.

I had been living there for three days, timing it so I left after everyone else had gone, coming back late at night when everyone else was asleep. But I knew it wouldn't work. A couple of the tenants had seen me on the stairs, a woman had surprised me coming out of the john. Every morning I waited for the landlady to come banging on the door. I didn't know what would happen. It might be all right. It might not be. But the waiting was getting me.

The sweat on my body was turning cold. Downstairs a radio was tuned in to the Breakfast Symphony. They were playing Beethoven. I sat up and lit a cigarette. "Peter," I said, "don't let them scare you to death. You're a man, too." I listened to Ludwig and I watched the smoke rise to the dirty ceiling. Under Ludwig's drums and horns I listened to hear footsteps on the stairs.

I'd done a lot of traveling in my time. I'd knocked about through St. Louis, Frisco, Seattle, Detroit, New Orleans, worked at just about everything. I'd run away from my old lady when I was about sixteen. She'd never been able to handle me. You'll never be nothin' *but* a bum, she'd say. We lived in an old shack in a town in New Jersey in the nigger part of town, the kind of houses colored people live in all over the U.S. I hated my mother for living there. I hated all the people in my neighborhood. They went to church and they got drunk. They were nice to the white people. When the landlord came around they paid him and took his crap.

The first time I was ever called nigger I was seven years old. It was a little white girl with long black curls. I used to leave the front of my house and go wandering by myself through town. This little girl was playing ball alone and as I passed her the ball rolled out of her hands into the gutter.

I threw it back to her.

"Let's play catch," I said.

But she held the ball and made a face at me.

"My mother don't let me play with niggers," she told me.

I did not know what the word meant. But my skin grew warm. I stuck my tongue out at her.

"I don't care. Keep your old ball." I started down the street.

She screamed after me: "Nigger, nigger, nigger!"

I screamed back: "Your mother was a nigger!"

I asked my mother what a nigger was.

"Who called you that?"

"I heard somebody say it."

"Who?"

"Just somebody."

"Go wash your face," she said. "You dirty as sin. Your supper's on the table."

I went to the bathroom and splashed water on my face and wiped my face and hands on the towel.

"You call that clean?" my mother cried. "Come here, boy!"

She dragged me back to the bathroom and began to soap my face and neck.

"You run around dirty like you do all the time, everybody'll call you a little nigger, you hear?" She rinsed my face and looked at my hands and dried me. "Now, go on and eat your supper."

I didn't say anything. I went to the kitchen and sat down at the table. I remember I wanted to cry. My mother sat down across from me.

"Mama," I said. She looked at me. I started to cry.

She came around to my side of the table and took me in her arms.

"Baby, don't fret. Next time somebody calls you nigger you tell them you'd rather be your color than be lowdown and nasty like some white folks is."

We formed gangs when I was older, my friends and I. We met white boys and their friends on the opposite sides of fences and we threw rocks and tin cans at each other.

I'd come home bleeding. My mother would slap me and scold me and cry.

"Boy, you wanna get killed? You wanna end up like your father?"

My father was a bum and I had never seen him. I was named for him: Peter.

I was always in trouble: truant officers, welfare workers, everybody else in town.

"You ain't never gonna be nothin' *but* a bum," my mother said.

By and by older kids I knew finished school and got jobs and got married and settled down. They were going to settle down and bring more black babies into the world and pay the same rents for the same old shacks and it would go on and on—

When I was sixteen I ran away. I left a note and told Mama not to worry, I'd come back one day and I'd be all right. But when I was twenty-two she died. I came back and put my mother in the ground. Everything was like it had been. Our house had not been painted and the porch floor sagged and there was somebody's raincoat stuffed in the broken window. Another family was moving in.

Their furniture was stacked along the walls and their children were running through the house and laughing and somebody was frying pork chops in the kitchen. The oldest boy was tacking up a mirror.

Last year Ida took me driving in her big car and we passed through a couple of towns upstate. We passed some crumbling houses on the left. The clothes on the line were flying in the wind.

"Are people living there?" asked Ida.

"Just darkies," I said.

Ida passed the car ahead, banging angrily on the horn. "D'you know you're becoming paranoiac, Peter?"

"All right. All right. I know a lot of white people are starving too."

"You're damn right they are. I know a little about poverty myself."

Ida had come from the kind of family called shanty Irish. She was raised in Boston. She's a very beautiful woman who married young and married for money—so now I can afford to support attractive young men, she'd giggle. Her husband was a ballet dancer who was forever on the road. Ida suspected that he went with boys. Not that I give a damn, she said, as long as he leaves me alone. When we met last year she was thirty and I was twenty-five. We had a pretty stormy relationship but we stuck. Whenever I got to town I called her; whenever I was stranded out of town I'd let her know. We never let it get too serious. She went her way and I went mine.

In all this running around I'd learned a few things. Like a prizefighter learns to take a blow or a dancer learns to fall, I'd learned how to get by. I'd learned never to be belligerent with policemen, for instance. No matter who was right, I was certain to be wrong. What might be accepted as just good old American independence in someone else would be insufferable arrogance in me. After the first few times I realized that I had to play smart, to act out the role I was expected to play. I only had one head and it was too easy to get it broken. When I faced a policeman I acted like I didn't know a thing. I let my jaw drop and I let my eyes get big. I didn't give him any smart answers, none of the crap about my rights. I figured out what answers he wanted and I gave them to him. I never let him think he wasn't king. If it was more than routine, if I was picked up on suspicion of robbery or murder in the neighborhood, I looked as humble as I could and kept my mouth shut and prayed. I took a couple of beatings but I stayed out of prison and I stayed off chain gangs. That was also due to luck, Ida pointed out once. "Maybe it would've been better for you if you'd been a little less lucky. Worse things have happened than chain gangs. Some of them have happened to you."

There was something in her voice. "What are you talking about?" I asked.

"Don't lose your temper. I said maybe."

"You mean you think I'm a coward?"

"I didn't say that, Peter."

"But you meant that. Didn't you?"

"No. I didn't mean that. I didn't mean anything. Let's not fight."

There are times and places when a Negro can use his color like a shield. He can trade on the subterranean Anglo-Saxon guilt and get what he wants that way; or some of what he wants. He can trade on his nuisance value, his value as forbidden fruit; he can use it like a knife, he can twist it and get his vengeance that way. I knew these things long before I realized that I knew them and in the beginning I used them, not knowing what I was doing. Then when I began to see it, I felt betrayed. I felt beaten as a person. I had no honest place to stand.

This was the year before I met Ida. I'd been acting in stock companies and little theaters; sometimes fairly good parts. People were nice to me. They told me I had talent. They said it sadly, as though they were thinking, What a pity, he'll never get anywhere. I had got to the point where I resented praise and I resented pity and I wondered what people were thinking when they shook my hand. In New York I met some pretty fine people; easygoing, hard-drinking, flotsam and jetsam; and they liked me; and I wondered if I trusted them; if I was able any longer to trust anybody. Not on top, where all the world could see, but underneath where everybody lives.

Soon I would have to get up. I listened to Ludwig. He shook the little room like the footsteps of a giant marching miles away. On summer evenings (and maybe we would go this summer) Jules and Ida and I would go up to the Stadium and sit beneath the pillars on the cold stone steps. There it seemed to me the sky was far away; and I was not myself, I was high and lifted up. We never talked, the three of us. We sat and watched the blue smoke curl in the air and watched the orange tips of cigarettes. Every once in a while the boys who sold popcorn and soda pop and ice cream climbed the steep steps chattering; and Ida shifted slightly and touched her blue-black hair; and Jules scowled. I sat with my knee up, watching the lighted half-moon below, the black-coated, straining conductor, the faceless men beneath him moving together in a rhythm like the sea. There were pauses in the music for the rushing, calling, halting piano. Everything would stop except the climbing soloist; he would reach a height and everything would join him, the violins first and then the horns; and then the deep blue bass and the flute and the bitter trampling drums; beating, beating and mounting together and stopping with a crash like daybreak. When I first heard the *Messiah* I was alone; my blood bubbled like fire and wine; I cried; like an infant crying for its mother's milk; or a sinner running to meet Jesus.

Now below the music I heard footsteps on the stairs. I put out my cigarette. My heart was beating so hard I thought it would tear my chest apart. Someone knocked on the door.

I thought: Don't answer. Maybe she'll go away.

But the knocking came again, harder this time.

Just a minute, I said. I sat on the edge of the bed and put on my bathrobe. I was trembling like a fool. For Christ's sake, Peter, you've been through this before. What's the worst thing that can happen? You won't have a room. The world's full of rooms.

When I opened the door the landlady stood there, red-and-whitefaced and hysterical.

"Who are you? I didn't rent this room to you."

My mouth was dry. I started to say something.

"I can't have no colored people here," she said. "All my tenants are complainin'. Women afraid to come home nights."

"They ain't gotta be afraid of me," I said. I couldn't get my voice up; it rasped and rattled in my throat; and I began to be angry. I wanted to kill her. "My friend rented this room for me," I said.

"Well, I'm sorry, he didn't have no right to do that, I don't have nothin' against you, but you gotta get out."

Her glasses blinked, opaque in the light on the landing. She was frightened to death. She was afraid of me but she was more afraid of losing her tenants. Her face was mottled with rage and fear, her breath came rushed and little bits of spittle gathered at the edges of her mouth; her breath smelled bad, like rotting hamburger on a July day.

"You can't put me out," I said. "This room was rented in my name." I started to close the door, as though the matter was finished: "I live here, see, this is my room, you can't put me out."

"You get outa my house!" she screamed. "I got the right to know who's in my house! The is a white neighborhood, I don't rent to colored people. Why don't you go on uptown, like you belong?"

"I can't stand niggers," I told her. I started to close the door again but she moved and stuck her foot in the way. I wanted to kill her, I watched her stupid, wrinkled frightened white face and I wanted to take a club, a hatchet, and bring it down with all my weight, splitting her skull down the middle where she parted her iron-grey hair.

"Get out of the door," I said. "I want to get dressed."

But I knew that she had won, that I was already on my way. We stared at each other. Neither of us moved. From her came an emanation of fear and fury and something else. You maggot-eaten bitch, I thought. I said evilly, "You wanna come in and watch me?" Her face didn't change, she didn't take her foot away. My skin prickled, tiny hot needles punctured my flesh. I was aware of my body under the bathrobe; and it was as though I had done something wrong, something monstrous, years ago, which no one had forgotten and for which I would be killed.

"If you don't get out," she said, "I'll get a policeman to put you out."

I grabbed the door to keep from touching her. "All right. All right. You can have the goddamn room. Now get out and let me dress."

She turned away. I slammed the door. I heard her going down the stairs. I threw stuff into my suitcase. I tried to take as long as possible but I cut myself while shaving because I was afraid she would come back upstairs with a policeman.

Jules was making coffee when I walked in.

"Good morning, good morning! What happened to you?"

"No room at the inn," I said. "Pour a cup of coffee for the notorious son of man." I sat down and dropped my suitcase on the floor.

Jules looked at me. "Oh. Well. Coffee coming up."

He got out the coffee cups. I lit a cigarette and sat there. I couldn't think of anything to say. I knew that Jules felt bad and I wanted to tell him that it wasn't his fault.

He pushed coffee in front of me and sugar and cream.

"Cheer up, baby. The world's wide and life—life, she is very long."

"Shut up. I don't want to hear any of your bad philosophy."

"Sorry."

"I mean, let's not talk about the good, the true, and the beautiful."

"All right. But don't sit there holding onto your table manners. Scream if you want to."

"Screaming won't do any good. Besides I'm a big boy now."

I stirred my coffee. "Did you give her a fight?" Jules asked.

I shook my head. "No."

"Why the hell not?"

I shrugged; a little ashamed now. I couldn't have won it. What the hell.

"You might have won it. You might have given her a couple of bad moments."

"Goddamit to hell, I'm sick of it. Can't I get a place to sleep without dragging it through the courts? I'm goddamn tired of battling every Tom, Dick, and Harry for what everybody else takes for granted. I'm tired, man, tired! Have you ever been sick to death of something? Well, I'm sick to death. And I'm scared. I've been fighting so goddamn long I'm not a person any more. I'm not Booker T. Washington. I've got no vision of emancipating anybody. I want to emancipate myself. If this goes on much longer, they'll send me to Bellevue, I'll blow my top, I'll break somebody's head. I'm not worried about that miserable little room. I'm worried about what's happening to me, *to me,* inside. I don't walk the streets, I crawl. I've never been like this before. Now when I go to a strange place I wonder what will happen, will I be accepted, if I'm accepted, can I accept?—"

"Take it easy," Jules said.

"Jules, I'm beaten."

"I don't think you are. Drink your coffee."

"Oh," I cried, "I know you think I'm making it dramatic, that I'm paranoiac and just inventing trouble! Maybe I think so sometimes, how can I tell? You get so used to being hit you find you're always waiting for it. Oh, I know, you're Jewish, you get kicked around, too, but you can walk into a bar and nobody *knows* you're Jewish and if you go looking for a job you'll get a better job than mine! How can I say what it feels like? I don't know. I know everybody's in trouble and nothing is easy, but how can I explain to you what it feels like to be black when I don't understand it and don't want to and spend all my time trying to forget it? I don't want to hate anybody—but now maybe, I can't love anybody either—are we friends? Can we be really friends?"

"We're friends," Jules said, "don't worry about it." He scowled. "If I wasn't Jewish I'd ask you why you don't live in Harlem." I looked at him. He raised his hand and smiled—"But I'm Jewish, so I didn't ask you. Ah Peter," he said, "I can't help you—take a walk, get drunk, we're all in this together."

I stood up. "I'll be around later. I'm sorry."

"Don't be sorry. I'll leave my door open. Bunk here for awhile."

"Thanks," I said.

I felt that I was drowning; that hatred had corrupted me like cancer in the bone.

I saw Ida for dinner. We met in a restaurant in the Village, an Italian place in a gloomy cellar with candles on the tables.

It was not a busy night, for which I was grateful. When I came in there were only two other couples on the other side of the room. No one looked at me. I sat down in a corner booth and ordered a Scotch old-fashioned. Ida was late and I had three of them before she came.

She was very fine in black, a high-necked dress with a pearl choker; and her hair was combed page-boy style, falling just below her ears.

"You look real sweet, baby."

"Thank you. It took fifteen extra minutes but I hoped it would be worth it."

"It was worth it. What're you drinking?"

"Oh—what're you drinking?"

"Old-fashioneds."

She sniffed and looked at me. "How many?"

I laughed. "Three."

"Well," she said, "I suppose you had to do something." The waiter came over. We decided on one Manhattan and one lasagna and one spaghetti with clam sauce and another old-fashioned for me.

"Did you have a constructive day, sweetheart? Find a job?"

"Not today," I said. I lit her cigarette. "Metro offered me a fortune to come to the coast and do the lead in *Native Son* but I turned it down. Type casting, you know. It's so difficult to find a decent part."

"Well, if they don't come up with a decent offer soon tell them you'll go back to Selznick. *He'll* find you a part with guts—the very *idea* of offering you *Native Son!* I wouldn't stand for it."

"You ain't gotta tell me. I told them if they didn't find me a decent script in two weeks I was through, that's all."

"Now that's talking, Peter my lad."

The drinks came and we sat in silence for a minute or two. I finished half of my drink at a swallow and played with the toothpicks on the table. I felt Ida watching me.

"Peter, you're going to be awfully drunk."

"Honeychile, the first thing a Southern gentleman learns is how to hold his liquor."

"That myth is older than the rock of ages. And anyway you come from Jersey."

I finished my drink and snarled at her: "That's just as good as the South."

Across the table from me I could see that she was readying herself for trouble: her mouth tightened slightly, setting her chin so that the faint cleft showed: "What happened to you today?"

I resented her concern; I resented my need. "Nothing worth talking about," I muttered, "just a mood."

And I tried to smile at her, to wipe away the bitterness.

"Now I know something's the matter. Please tell me."

It sounded trivial as hell: "You know the room Jules found for me? Well, the landlady kicked me out of it today."

"God save the American republic," Ida said. "D'you want to waste some of my husband's money? We can sue her."

"Forget it. I'll end up with lawsuits in every state in the union."

"Still, as a gesture—"

"The devil with the gesture. I'll get by."

The food came. I didn't want to eat. The first mouthful hit my belly like a gong. Ida began cutting up lasagna.

"Peter," she said, "try not to feel so badly. We're all in this together, the whole world. Don't let it throw you. What can't be helped you have to learn to live with."

"That's easy for you to say," I told her.

She looked at me quickly and looked away. "I'm not pretending that it's easy to do," she said.

I didn't believe that she could really understand it; and there was nothing I could say. I sat like a child being scolded, looking down at my plate, not eating, not saying anything. I wanted her to stop talking, to stop being intelligent about it, to stop being calm and grown-up about it; good Lord, none of us has ever grown up, we never will.

"It's no better anywhere else," she was saying. "In all of Europe there's famine and disease, in France and England they hate the Jews—nothing's going to change, baby, people are too empty-headed, too empty-hearted—it's always been like that, people always try to destroy what they don't understand—and they hate almost everything because they understand so little—"

I began to sweat in my side of the booth. I wanted to stop her voice. I wanted her to eat and be quiet and leave me alone. I looked around for the waiter so I could order another drink. But he was on the far side of the restaurant, waiting on some people who had just come in; a lot of people had come in since we had been sitting there.

"Peter," Ida said, "Peter please don't look like that."

I grinned: the painted grin of the professional clown. "Don't worry, baby, I'm all right. I know what I'm going to do. I'm gonna go back to my people where I belong and find me a nice, black nigger wench and raise me a flock of babies."

Ida had an old maternal trick; the grin tricked her into using it now. She raised her fork and rapped me with it across the knuckles. "Now, stop that. You're too old for that."

I screamed and stood up screaming and knocked the candle over: "Don't *do* that, you bitch, don't *ever* do that!"

She grabbed the candle and set it up and glared at me. Her face had turned perfectly white: "Sit down! Sit *down!*"

I fell back into my seat. My stomach felt like water. Everyone was looking at us. I turned cold, seeing what they were seeing: a black boy and a white woman, alone together. I knew it would take nothing to have them at my throat.

"I'm sorry," I muttered, "I'm sorry, I'm sorry."

The waiter was at my elbow. "Is everything all right, miss?"

"Yes, quite, thank you." She sounded like a princess dismissing a slave. I didn't look up. The shadow of the waiter moved away from me.

"Baby," Ida said, "forgive me, please forgive me."

I stared at the tablecloth. She put her hand on mine, brightness and blackness.

"Let's go," I said, "I'm terribly sorry."

She motioned for the check. When it came she handed the waiter a ten dollar bill without looking. She picked up her bag.

"Shall we go to a nightclub or a movie or something?"

"No, honey, not tonight." I looked at her. "I'm tired, I think I'll go on over to Jules's place. I'm gonna sleep on his floor for a while. Don't worry about me. I'm all right."

She looked at me steadily. She said: "I'll come see you tomorrow?"

"Yes, baby, please."

The waiter brought the change and she tipped him. We stood up; as we passed the tables (not looking at the people) the ground under me seemed falling, the doorway seemed impossibly far away. All my muscles tensed; I seemed ready to spring; I was waiting for the blow.

I put my hands in my pockets and we walked to the end of the block. The lights were green and red, the lights from the theater across the street exploded blue and yellow, off and on.

"Peter?"

"Yes?"

"I'll see you tomorrow?"

"Yeah. Come by Jules's. I'll wait for you."

"Goodnight, darling."

"Goodnight."

I started to walk away. I felt her eyes on my back. I kicked a bottle-top on the sidewalk.

God save the American republic.

I dropped into the subway and got on an uptown train, not knowing where it was going and not caring. Anonymous, islanded people surrounded me, behind newspapers, behind make-up, fat, fleshy masks and flat eyes. I watched the empty faces. (No one looked at me.) I looked at the ads, unreal women and pink-cheeked men selling cigarettes, candy, shaving cream, nightgowns, chewing gum, movies, sex; sex without organs, drier than sand and more secret than death. The train stopped. A white boy and a white girl got on. She was nice, short, svelte. Nice legs. She was hanging on his arm. He was the football type, blond, ruddy. They were dressed in summer clothes. The wind from the doors blew her print dress. She squealed, holding the dress at the knees and giggled and looked at him. He said something I didn't catch and she looked at me and the smile died. She stood so that she faced him and had her back to me. I looked back at the ads. Then I hated them. I wanted to do something to make them hurt, something that would crack the pink-cheeked mask. The white boy and I did not look at each other again. They got off at the next stop.

I wanted to keep on drinking. I got off in Harlem and went to a run-down bar on Seventh Avenue. My people, my people. Sharpies stood on the corner, waiting. Women in summer dresses pranced by on wavering heels. Click clack. Click clack. There were white mounted policemen in the streets. On every block there was another policeman on foot. I saw a black cop.

God save the American republic.

The juke box was letting loose with "Hamps' Boogie." The place was jumping, I walked over to the man.

"Rye," I said.

I was standing next to somebody's grandmother. "Hello, papa. What you puttin' down?"

"Baby, you can't pick it up," I told her. My rye came and I drank.

"Nigger," she said, "you must think you's somebody."

I didn't answer. She turned away, back to her beer, keeping time to the juke box, her face sullen and heavy and aggrieved. I watched her out of the side of my eye. She had been good looking once, pretty even, before she hit the bottle and started crawling into too many beds. She was flabby now, flesh heaved all over in her thin dress. I wondered what she'd be like in bed; then I realized that I was a little excited by her; I laughed and set my glass down.

"The same," I said. "And a beer chaser."

The juke box was playing something else now, something brassy and commercial which I didn't like. I kept on drinking, listening to the voices of my people, watching the faces of my people. (God pity us, the terrified republic.) Now I was sorry to have angered the woman who still sat next to me, now deep in conversation with another, younger woman. I longed for some opening, some sign, something to make me part of the life around me. But there was nothing except my color. A white outsider coming in would have seen a young Negro drinking in a Negro bar, perfectly in his element, in his place, as the saying goes. But the people here knew differently, as I did. I didn't seem to have a place.

So I kept on drinking by myself, saying to myself after each drink, Now I'll go. But I was afraid; I didn't want to sleep on Jules's floor; I didn't want to go to sleep. I kept on drinking and listening to the juke box. They were playing Ella Fitzgerald, "Cow-Cow Boogie."

"Let me buy you a drink," I said to the woman.

She looked at me, startled, suspicious, ready to blow her top.

"On the level," I said. I tried to smile. "Both of you."

"I'll take a beer," the young one said.

I was shaking like a baby. I finished my drink.

"Fine," I said. I turned to the bar.

"Baby," said the old one, "what's your story?"

The man put three beers on the counter.

"I got no story, Ma," I said.

Bernard Malamud

(1914)

Bernard Malamud, an American Jew concerned as a writer with the pathos and comedy of being Jewish, was born in Brooklyn in 1914. He attended the City College of New York and earned a master's degree in English at Columbia University. For several years he taught at Oregon State University—his experiences in the Pacific Northwest serving as a base for his hilarious novel *A New Life*—and he now teaches at Bennington College. Malamud received the National Book Award in 1958 for *The Magic Barrel,* a collection of short stories, and again in 1966 for *The Fixer,* an unforgettable novel of a solitary, courageous Jew persecuted in czarist Russia. Both in his stories and novels, Malamud is remarkably successful in creating individualized, believable characters no matter how strange they may seem. In contrast to other contemporary writers who appear to revel in the apparent absurdity of life and nihilism of the world, Malamud is a defender of traditional humanistic values. He has said, "My work, all of it, is an idea of dedication to the human. That's basic to every book. If you don't respect man, you cannot respect my work. I'm in defense of the human." Without undue *schmaltz,* that is, with restraint, Malamud dramatizes the injustice, misunderstanding, and grief that are part of life, but he also depicts the resiliency of the human spirit and man's ability to laugh in the face of destruction.

Black Is My Favorite Color

Charity Sweetness sits in the toilet eating her two hard-boiled eggs while I'm having my ham sandwich and coffee in the kitchen. That's how it goes only don't get the idea of ghettoes. If there's a ghetto I'm the one that's in it. She's my cleaning woman from Father Divine and comes in once a week to my small three-room apartment on my day off from the liquor store. "Peace," she says to me, "Father reached on down and took me right up in Heaven." She's a small person with a flat body, frizzy hair, and a quiet face that the light shines out of, and Mama had such eyes before she died. The first time Charity Sweetness came in to clean, a little more than a year and a half, I made the mistake to ask her to sit down at the kitchen table with me and eat her lunch. I was still feeling not so hot after Ornita left but I'm the kind of a man—Nat Lime, forty-four, a bachelor with a daily growing bald spot on the back of my head, and I could lose frankly fifteen pounds—who enjoys company so long as he has it. So she cooked up her two hard-boiled eggs and sat down and took a small bite out of one of them. But after a minute she stopped chewing and she got up and carried the eggs in a cup in the bathroom, and since then she eats there. I said to her more than once, "Okay, Charity Sweetness, so have it your way, eat the eggs in the kitchen by yourself and I'll eat when you're done," but she smiles absent-minded, and eats in the toilet. It's my fate with colored people.

Although black is still my favorite color you wouldn't know it from my luck except in short quantities even though I do all right in the liquor store business in Harlem, on Eighth Avenue between 110th and 111th. I speak with respect. A large part of my life I've had dealings with Negro people, most on a business basis but sometimes for friendly reasons with genuine feeling on both sides. I'm drawn to them. At this time of my life I should have one or two good colored friends but the fault isn't necessarily mine. If they knew what was in my heart towards them, but how can you tell that to anybody nowadays? I've tried more than once but the language of the heart either is a dead language or else nobody understands it the way you speak it. Very few. What I'm saying is, personally for me there's only one human color and that's the color of blood. I like a black person if not because he's black, then because I'm white. It comes to the same thing. If I wasn't white my first choice would be black. I'm satisfied to be white because I have no other choice. Anyway, I got an eye for color. I appreciate. Who wants everybody to be the same? Maybe it's like some kind of a talent. Nat Lime might be a liquor dealer in Harlem, but once in the jungle in New Guinea in the Second War, I got the idea when I shot at a running Jap and missed him, that I had some kind of a talent, though maybe it's the kind where you have a marvelous idea now and then but in the end what do they come to? After all, it's a strange world.

Where Charity Sweetness eats her eggs makes me think about Buster Wilson when we were both boys in the Williamsburg section of Brooklyn. There was this long block of run-down dirty frame houses in the middle of a not-so-hot white neighborhood full of pushcarts. The Negro houses looked to me like they had been born and died there, dead not long after the beginning of the world. I lived on the next street. My father was a cutter with arthritis in both hands, big red knuckles and swollen fingers so he didn't cut, and my mother was the one who went to work. She sold paper bags from a second-hand pushcart in Ellery Street. We didn't starve but nobody ate chicken unless we were sick or the chicken was. This was my first acquaintance with a lot of black people and I used to poke around on their poor block. I think I thought, brother, if there can be like this, what can't there be? I mean I caught an early idea what life was about. Anyway I met Buster Wilson there. He used to play marbles by himself. I sat on the curb across the street, watching him shoot one marble lefty and the other one righty. The hand that won picked up the marbles. It wasn't so much of a game but he didn't ask me to come over. My idea was to be friendly, only he never encouraged, he discouraged. Why did I pick him out for a friend? Maybe because I had no others then, we were new in the neighborhood, from Manhattan. Also I liked his type. Buster did everything alone. He was a skinny kid and his brothers' clothes hung on him like worn-out potato sacks. He was a beanpole boy, about twelve, and I was then ten. His arms and legs were burnt out matchsticks. He always wore a brown wool sweater, one arm half unraveled, the other went down to the wrist. His long and narrow head had a white part cut straight in the short woolly hair, maybe with a ruler there, by his father, a barber but too drunk to stay a barber. In those days though I had little myself I was old enough to know who was better off, and the whole block of colored houses made me feel bad in the daylight. But I went there as much as I could because the street was full of life. In the night it looked different, it's hard to tell a cripple in the dark. Sometimes I was afraid to walk by the houses when they were dark and quiet. I was afraid there were people looking at me that I couldn't see. I liked it better when they had parties at night and everybody had a good time. The musicians played their banjos and saxophones and the houses shook with the music and laughing. The young girls, with their pretty dresses and ribbons in their hair, caught me in my throat when I saw them through the windows.

But with the parties came drinking and fights. Sundays were bad days after the Saturday night parties. I remember once that Buster's father, also long and loose, always wearing a dirty gray Homburg hat, chased another black man in the street with a half-inch chisel. The other one, maybe five feet high, lost his shoe and when they wrestled on the ground he was already bleeding through his suit, a thick red blood smearing the sidewalk. I was frightened by the blood and wanted to pour it back in the man who was bleeding from the chisel. On another time Buster's father was playing in a crap game with two big bouncy red dice, in the back of an alley between two middle houses. Then about six men started fist-fighting there, and they ran out of the alley and hit each other in the street. The neighbors, including children, came out and watched, everybody afraid but nobody moving to do anything. I saw the same thing near my store in Harlem, years later, a big crowd watching two men in the street, their breaths hanging in the air on a winter night, murdering each other with switch knives, but nobody moved to call a cop. I didn't either. Anyway, I was just a young kid but I still remember how the cops drove up in a police paddy wagon and broke up the fight by hitting everybody they could hit with big nightsticks. This was in the days before LaGuardia. Most of the fighters were knocked out cold, only one or two got away. Buster's father started to run back in his house but a cop ran after him and cracked him on his Homburg hat with a club, right on the front porch. Then the Negro men were lifted up by the cops, one at the arms and the other at the feet, and they heaved them in the paddy wagon. Buster's father hit the back of the wagon and fell, with his nose spouting very red blood, on top of three other men. I personally couldn't stand it, I was scared of the human race so I ran home, but I remember Buster watching without any expression in his eyes. I stole an extra fifteen cents from my mother's pocketbook and I ran back and asked Buster if he wanted to go to the movies. I would pay. He said yes. This was the first time he talked to me.

So we went more than once to the movies. But we never got to be friends. Maybe because it was a one-way proposition—from me to him. Which includes my invitations to go with me, my (poor mother's) movie money, Hershey chocolate bars, watermelon slices, even my best Nick Carter and Merriwell books that I spent hours picking up in the junk shops, and that he never gave me back. Once he let me go in his house to get a match so we could smoke some butts we found, but it smelled so heavy, so impossible, I died till I got out of there. What I saw in the way of furniture I won't mention—the best was falling apart in pieces. Maybe we went to the movies all together five or six matinees that spring and in the summertime, but when the shows were over he usually walked home by himself.

"Why don't you wait for me, Buster?" I said. "We're both going in the same direction."

But he was walking ahead and didn't hear me. Anyway he didn't answer.

One day when I wasn't expecting it he hit me in the teeth. I felt like crying but not because of the pain. I spit blood and said, "What did you hit me for? What did I do to you?"

"Because you a Jew bastard. Take your Jew movies and your Jew candy and shove them up your Jew ass."

And he ran away.

I thought to myself how was I to know he didn't like the movies. When I was a man I thought, you can't force it.

Years later, in the prime of my life, I met Mrs. Ornita Harris. She was standing by herself under an open umbrella at the bus stop, crosstown 110th, and I picked up her green glove that she had dropped on the wet sidewalk. It was in the end of November. Before I could ask her was it hers, she grabbed the glove out of my hand, closed her umbrella, and stepped in the bus. I got on right after her.

I was annoyed so I said, "If you'll pardon me, Miss, there's no law that you have to say thanks, but at least don't make a criminal out of me."

"Well, I'm sorry," she said, "but I don't like white men trying to do me favors."

I tipped my hat and that was that. In ten minutes I got off the bus but she was already gone.

Who expected to see her again but I did. She came into my store about a week later for a bottle of Scotch.

"I would offer you a discount," I told her, "but I know you don't like a certain kind of a favor and I'm not looking for a slap in the face."

Then she recognized me and got a little embarrassed.

"I'm sorry I misunderstood you that day."

"So mistakes happen."

The result was she took the discount. I gave her a dollar off.

She used to come in about every two weeks for a fifth of Haig and Haig. Sometimes I waited on her, sometimes my helpers, Jimmy or Mason, also colored, but I said to give the discount. They both looked at me but I had nothing to be ashamed. In the spring when she came in we used to talk once in a while. She was a slim woman, dark but not the most dark, about thirty years I would say, also well built, with a combination nice legs and a good-size bosom that I like. Her face was pretty, with big eyes and high cheek bones, but lips a little thick and nose a little broad. Sometimes she didn't feel like talking, she paid for the bottle, less discount, and walked out. Her eyes were tired and she didn't look to me like a happy woman.

I found out her husband was once a window cleaner on the big buildings, but one day his safety belt broke and he fell fifteen stories. After the funeral she got a job as a manicurist in a Times Square barber shop. I told her I was a bachelor and lived with my mother in a small three-room apartment on West Eighty-third near Broadway. My mother had cancer, and Ornita said she was very sorry.

One night in July we went out together. How that happened I'm still not so sure. I guess I asked her and she didn't say no. Where do you go out with a Negro woman? We went to the Village. We had a good dinner and walked in Washington Square Park. It was a hot night. Nobody was surprised when they saw us, nobody looked at us like we were against the law. If they looked maybe they saw my new lightweight suit that I bought yesterday and my shiny bald spot when we walked under a lamp, also how pretty she was for a man of my type. We went in a movie on West Eighth Street. I didn't want to go in but she said she had heard about the picture. We went in like strangers and we came out like strangers. I wondered what was in her mind and I thought to myself, whatever is in there it's not a certain white man that I know. All night long we went together like we were chained. After the movie she wouldn't let me take her back to Harlem. When I put her in a taxi she asked me, "Why did we bother?"

For the steak, I wanted to say. Instead I said, "You're worth the bother."

"Thanks anyway."

Kiddo, I thought to myself after the taxi left, you just found out what's what, now the best thing is forget her.

It's easy to say. In August we went out the second time. That was the night she wore a purple dress and I thought to myself, my God, what colors. Who paints that picture paints a masterpiece. Everybody looked at us but I had pleasure. That night when she took off her dress it was in a furnished room I had the sense to rent a few days before. With my sick mother, I couldn't ask her to come to my apartment, and she didn't want me to go home with her where she lived with her brother's family on West 115th near Lenox Avenue. Under her purple dress she wore a black slip, and when she took that off she had white underwear. When she took off the white underwear she was black again. But I know where the next white was, if you want to call it white. And that was the night I think I fell in love with her, the first time in my life though I have liked one or two nice girls I used to go with when I was a boy. It was a serious proposition. I'm the kind of a man when I think of love I'm thinking of marriage. I guess that's why I am a bachelor.

That same week I had a holdup in my place, two big men—both black—with revolvers. One got excited when I rang open the cash register so he could take the money and he hit me over the ear with his gun. I stayed in the hospital a couple of weeks. Otherwise I was insured. Ornita came to see me. She sat on a chair without talking much. Finally I saw she was uncomfortable so I suggested she ought to go home.

"I'm sorry it happened," she said.

"Don't talk like it's your fault."

When I got out of the hospital my mother was dead. She was a wonderful person. My father died when I was thirteen and all by herself she kept the family alive and together. I sat shive for a week and remembered how she sold paper bags on her pushcart. I remembered her life and what she tried to teach me. Nathan, she said, if you ever forget you are a Jew a goy will remind you. Mama, I said, rest in peace on this subject. But if I do something you don't like, remember, on earth it's harder than where you are. Then when my week of mourning was finished, one night I said, "Ornita, let's get married. We're both honest people and if you love me like I love you it won't be such a bad time. If you don't like New York I'll sell out here and we'll move someplace else. Maybe to San Francisco where nobody knows us. I was there for a week in the Second War and I saw white and colored living together."

"Nat," she answered me, "I like you but I'd be afraid. My husband woulda killed me."

"Your husband is dead."

"Not in my memory."

"In that case I'll wait."

"Do you know what it'd be like—I mean the life we could expect?"

"Ornita," I said, "I'm the kind of a man, if he picks his own way of life he's satisfied."

"What about children? Were you looking forward to half-Jewish polka dots?"

"I was looking forward to children."

"I can't," she said.

Can't is can't. I saw she was afraid and the best thing was not to push. Sometimes when we met she was so nervous that whatever we did she couldn't enjoy it. At the same time I still thought I had a chance. We were together more and more. I got rid of my furnished room and she came to my apartment—I gave away Mama's bed and bought a new one. She stayed with me all day on Sundays. When she wasn't so nervous she was affectionate, and if I know what love is, I had it. We went out a couple of times a week, the same way—usually I met her in Times Square and sent her home in a taxi, but I talked more about marriage and she talked less against it. One night she told me she was still trying to convince herself but she was almost convinced. I took an inventory of my liquor stock so I could put the store up for sale.

Ornita knew what I was doing. One day she quit her job, the next day she took it back. She also went away a week to visit her sister in Philadelphia for a little rest. She came back tired but said maybe. Maybe is maybe so I'll wait. The way she said it it was closer to yes. That was the winter two years ago. When she was in Philadelphia I called up a friend of mine from the Army, now CPA, and told him I would appreciate an invitation for an evening. He knew why. His wife said yes right away. When Ornita came back we went there. The wife made a fine dinner. It wasn't a bad time and they told us to come again. Ornita had a few drinks. She looked relaxed, wonderful. Later, because of a twenty-four hour taxi strike I had to take her home on the subway. When we got to the 116th Street station she told me to stay on the train, and she would walk the couple of blocks to her house.

I didn't like a woman walking alone on the streets at that time of the night. She said she never had any trouble but I insisted nothing doing. I said I would walk to her stoop with her and when she went upstairs I would go back to the subway.

On the way there, on 115th in the middle of the block before Lenox, we were stopped by three men—maybe they were boys. One had a black hat with a half-inch brim, one a green cloth hat, and the third wore a black leather cap. The green hat was wearing a short coat and the other two had long ones. It was under a street light but the leather cap snapped a six-inch switchblade open in the light.

"What you doin' with this white son of a bitch?" he said to Ornita.

"I'm minding my own business," she answered him, "and I wish you would too."

"Boys," I said, "we're all brothers. I'm a reliable merchant in the neighborhood. This young lady is my dear friend. We don't want any trouble. Please let us pass."

"You talk like a Jew landlord," said the green hat. "Fifty a week for a single room."

"No charge fo' the rats," said the half-inch brim.

"Believe me, I'm no landlord. My store is 'Nathan's Liquors' between Hundred Tenth and Eleventh. I also have two colored clerks, Mason and Jimmy, and they will tell you I pay good wages as well as I give discounts to certain customers."

"Shut your mouth, Jewboy," said the leather cap, and he moved the knife back and forth in front of my coat button. "No more black pussy for you."

"Speak with respect about this lady, please."

I got slapped on my mouth.

"That ain't no lady," said the long face in the half-inch brim, "that's black pussy. She deserve to have evvy bit of her hair shave off. How you like to have evvy bit of your hair shave off, black pussy?"

"Please leave me and this gentleman alone or I'm gonna scream long and loud. That's my house three doors down."

They slapped her. I never heard such a scream. Like her husband was falling fifteen stories.

I hit the one that slapped her and the next I knew I was lying in the gutter with a pain in my head. I thought, goodbye, Nat, they'll stab me for sure, but all they did was take my wallet and run in three different directions.

Ornita walked back with me to the subway and she wouldn't let me go home with her again.

"Just get home safely."

She looked terrible. Her face was gray and I still remembered her scream. It was a terrible winter night, very cold February, and it took me an hour and ten minutes to get home. I felt bad for leaving her but what could I do?

We had a date downtown the next night but she didn't show up, the first time.

In the morning I called her in her place of business.

"For God's sake, Ornita, if we got married and moved away we wouldn't have that kind of trouble that we had. We wouldn't come in that neighborhood any more."

"Yes, we would. I have family there and don't want to move anyplace else. The truth of it is I can't marry you, Nat. I got troubles enough of my own."

"I coulda sworn you love me."

"Maybe I do but I can't marry you."

"For God's sake, why?"

"I got enough trouble of my own."

I went that night in a cab to her brother's house to see her. He was a quiet man with a thin mustache. "She gone," he said, "left for a long visit to some close relatives in the South. She said to tell you she appreciate your intentions but didn't think it will work out."

"Thank you kindly," I said.

Don't ask me how I got home.

Once on Eighth Avenue, a couple of blocks from my store, I saw a blind man with a white cane tapping on the sidewalk. I figured we were going in the same direction so I took his arm.

"I can tell you're white," he said.

A heavy colored woman with a full shopping bag rushed after us.

"Never mind," she said, "I know where he live."

She pushed me with her shoulder and I hurt my leg on the fire hydrant.

That's how it is. I give my heart and they kick me in my teeth.

"Charity Sweetness—you hear me?—come out of that goddamn toilet!"

Philip Roth

(1933)

Like Neil Klugman, the protagonist in *Goodbye, Columbus,* Philip Roth was born and reared in Newark, New Jersey. He attended Bucknell University and received his master's degree in English from the University of Chicago, where he taught for two years before returning to the East Coast. While still a graduate student he published a number of stories and film reviews, and a year after leaving Chicago his first published book, *Goodbye, Columbus and Five Short Stories,* won the National Book Award for "the most distinguished work of fiction published in 1959." Fellowships and grants followed, allowing Roth to write two novels, *Letting Go* (1962) and *When She Was Good* (1967). In 1969 his hilarious *Portnoy's Complaint* received both the critic's praise and the public's dollars (the novel remained on the New York *Times'* bestseller list for forty weeks). Like Malamud, Roth is essentially a Jewish writer with a marvelous comic sense and the ability to create striking characters. *Goodbye, Columbus,* is, among other things, the story of Neil Klugman's honest questioning of himself, his values, and his society. In some ways an unattractive character, Neil faces the cost and consequences of "making it" in the *nouveau riche* world of the Patimkins.

Goodbye, Columbus

"The heart is half a prophet." Yiddish proverb

The first time I saw Brenda she asked me to hold her glasses. Then she stepped out to the edge of the diving board and looked foggily into the pool; it could have been drained, myopic Brenda would never have known it. She dove beautifully, and a moment later she was swimming back to the side of the pool, her head of short-clipped auburn hair held up, straight ahead of her, as though it were a rose on a long stem. She glided to the edge and then was beside me. "Thank you," she said, her eyes watery though not from the water. She extended a hand for her glasses but did not put them on until she turned and headed away. I watched her move off. Her hands suddenly appeared behind her. She caught the bottom of her suit between thumb and index finger and flicked what flesh had been showing back where it belonged. My blood jumped.

That night, before dinner, I called her.

"Who are you calling?" my Aunt Gladys asked.

"Some girl I met today."

"Doris introduced you?"

"Doris wouldn't introduce me to the guy who drains the pool, Aunt Gladys."

"Don't criticize all the time. A cousin's a cousin. How did you meet her?"

"I didn't really meet her. I saw her."

"Who is she?"

"Her last name is Patimkin."

"Patimkin I don't know," Aunt Gladys said, as if she knew anybody who belonged to the Green Lane Country Club. "You're going to call her you don't know her?"

"Yes," I explained. "I'll introduce myself."

"Casanova," she said, and went back to preparing my uncle's dinner. None of us ate together: my Aunt Gladys ate at five o'clock, my cousin Susan at five-thirty, me at six, and my uncle at six-thirty. There is nothing to explain this beyond the fact that my aunt is crazy.

"Where's the suburban phone book?" I asked after pulling out all the books tucked under the telephone table.

"What?"

"The suburban phone book. I want to call Short Hills."

"That skinny book? What, I gotta clutter my house with that, I never use it?"

"Where is it?"

"Under the dresser where the leg came off."

"For God's sake," I said.

"Call information better. You'll go yanking around there, you'll mess up my drawers. Don't bother me, you see your uncle'll be home soon. I haven't even fed *you* yet."

"Aunt Gladys, suppose tonight we all eat together. It's hot, it'll be easier for you."

"Sure, I should serve four different meals at once. You eat pot roast, Susan with the cottage cheese, Max has steak. Friday night is his steak night, I wouldn't deny him. And I'm having a little cold chicken. I should jump up and down twenty different times? What am I, a workhorse?"

"Why don't we all have steak, or cold chicken—"

"Twenty years I'm running a house. Go call your girl friend."

But when I called, Brenda Patimkin wasn't home. She's having dinner at the club, a woman's voice told me. Will she be home after (my voice was two octaves higher than a choirboy's)? I don't know, the voice said, she may go driving golf balls. Who is this? I mumbled some words—nobody she wouldn't know I'll call back no message thank you sorry to bother . . . I hung up somewhere along in there. Then my aunt called me and I steeled myself for dinner.

She pushed the black whirring fan up to *High* and that way it managed to stir the cord that hung from the kitchen light.

"What kind of soda you want? I got ginger ale, plain seltzer, black raspberry, and a bottle cream soda I could open up."

"None, thank you."

"You want water?"

"I don't drink with my meals. Aunt Gladys, I've told you that every day for a year already—"

"Max could drink a whole case with his chopped liver only. He works hard all day. If you worked hard you'd drink more."

At the stove she heaped up a plate with pot roast, gravy, boiled potatoes, and peas and carrots. She put it in front of me and I could feel the heat of the food in my face. Then she cut two pieces of rye bread and put that next to me, on the table.

I forked a potato in half and ate it, while Aunt Gladys, who had seated herself across from me, watched. "You don't want bread," she said, "I wouldn't cut it it should go stale."

"I *want* bread," I said.

"You don't like with seeds, do you?"

I tore a piece of bread in half and ate it.

"How's the meat?" she said.

"Okay. Good."

"You'll fill yourself with potatoes and bread, the meat you'll leave over I'll have to throw it out."

Suddenly she leaped up from the chair. "Salt!" When she returned to the table she plunked a salt shaker down in front of me—pepper wasn't served in her home: she'd heard on Galen Drake that it was not absorbed by the body, and it was disturbing to Aunt Gladys to think that anything she served might pass through a gullet, stomach, and bowel just for the pleasure of the trip.

"You're going to pick the peas out is all? You tell me that, I wouldn't buy with the carrots."

"I love carrots," I said, "I love them." And to prove it, I dumped half of them down my throat and the other half onto my trousers.

"Pig," she said.

Though I am very fond of desserts, especially fruit, I chose not to have any. I wanted, this hot night, to avoid the conversation that revolved around my choosing fresh fruit over canned fruit, or canned fruit over fresh fruit; whichever I preferred, Aunt Gladys always had an abundance of the other jamming her refrigerator like stolen diamonds. "He wants canned peaches, I have a refrigerator full of grapes I have to get rid of . . ." Life was a throwing off for poor Aunt Gladys, her greatest joys were taking out the garbage, emptying her pantry, and making threadbare bundles for what she still referred to as the Poor Jews in Palestine. I only hope she dies with an empty refrigerator, otherwise she'll ruin eternity for everyone else, what with her Velveeta turning green, and her navel oranges growing fuzzy jackets down below.

My Uncle Max came home and while I dialed Brenda's number once again, I could hear soda bottles being popped open in the kitchen. The voice that answered this time was high, curt, and tired. "Hullo."

I launched into my speech. "Hello-Brenda-Brenda-you-don't-know-me-that-is-you-don't-know-my-name-but-I-held-your-glasses-for-you-this-afternoon-at-the-club . . . You-asked-me-to-I'm-not-a-member-my-cousin-Doris-is-Doris-Klugman-I-asked-who-you-were . . ." I breathed, gave her a chance to speak, and then went ahead and answered the silence on the other end. "Doris? She's the one who's always reading *War and Peace.* That's how I know it's the summer, when Doris is reading *War and Peace.*" Brenda didn't laugh; right from the start she was a practical girl.

"What's your name?" she said.

"Neil Klugman. I held your glasses at the board, remember?"

She answered me with a question of her own, one, I'm sure, that is an embarrassment to both the homely and the fair. "What do you look like?"

"I'm . . . dark."

"Are you a Negro?"

"No," I said.

"What *do* you look like?"

"May I come see you tonight and show you?"

"That's nice," she laughed. "I'm playing tennis tonight."

"I thought you were driving golf balls."

"I drove them already."

"How about after tennis?"

"I'll be sweaty after," Brenda said.

It was not to warn me to clothespin my nose and run in the opposite direction; it was a fact, it apparently didn't bother Brenda, but she wanted it recorded.

"I don't mind," I said, and hoped by my tone to earn a niche somewhere between the squeamish and the grubby. "Can I pick you up?"

She did not answer a minute; I heard her muttering, "Doris Klugman, Doris Klugman . . ." Then she said, "Yes, Briarpath Hills, eight-fifteen."

"I'll be driving a—" I hung back with the year, "a tan Plymouth. So you'll know me. How will I know you?" I said with a sly, awful laugh.

"I'll be sweating," she said and hung up.

Once I'd driven out of Newark, past Irvington and the packed-in tangle of railroad crossings, switchmen shacks, lumberyards, Dairy Queens, and used-car lots, the night grew cooler. It was, in fact, as though the hundred and eighty feet that the suburbs rose in altitude above Newark brought one closer to heaven, for the sun itself became bigger, lower, and rounder, and soon I was driving past long lawns which seemed to be twirling water on themselves, and past houses where no one sat on stoops, where lights were on but no windows open, for those inside, refusing to share the very texture of life with those of us outside, regulated with a dial the amounts of moisture that were allowed access to their skin. It was only eight o'clock, and I did not want to be early, so I drove up and down the streets whose names were those of eastern colleges, as though the township, years ago, when things were named, had planned the destinies of the sons of its citizens. I thought of my Aunt Gladys and Uncle Max sharing a Mounds bar in the cindery darkness of their alley, on beach chairs, each cool breeze sweet to them as the promise of afterlife, and after a while I rolled onto the gravel roads of the small park where Brenda was playing tennis. Inside my glove compartment it was as though the map of *The City Streets of Newark* had metamorphosed into crickets, for those mile-long tarry streets did not exist for me any longer, and the night noises sounded loud as the blood whacking at my temples.

I parked the car under the black-green canopy of three oaks, and walked towards the sound of the tennis balls. I heard an exasperated voice say, "Deuce *again.*" It was Brenda and she sounded as though she was sweating considerably. I crackled slowly up the gravel and heard Brenda once more. "My ad," and then just as I rounded the path, catching a cuff full of burrs, I heard, "Game!" Her racket went spinning up in the air and she caught it neatly as I came into sight.

"Hello," I called.

"Hello, Neil. One more game," she called. Brenda's words seemed to infuriate her opponent, a pretty brown-haired girl, not quite so tall as Brenda, who stopped searching for the ball that had been driven past her, and gave both Brenda and myself a dirty look. In a moment I learned the reason why: Brenda was ahead five games to four, and her cocksureness about there being just one game remaining aroused enough anger in her opponent for the two of us to share.

As it happened, Brenda finally won, though it took more games than she'd expected. The other girl, whose name sounded like Simp, seemed happy to end it at six all, but Brenda, shifting, running, up on her toes, would not stop, and finally all I could see moving in the darkness were her glasses, a glint of them, the clasp of her belt, her socks, her sneakers, and, on occasion, the ball. The darker it got the more savagely did Brenda rush the net, which seemed curious, for I had noticed that earlier, in the light, she had stayed back, and even when she had had to rush, after smashing back a lob, she didn't look entirely happy about being so close to her opponent's racket. Her passion for winning a point seemed outmatched by an even stronger passion for maintaining her beauty as it was. I suspected that the red print of a tennis ball on her cheek would pain her more than losing all the points in the world. Darkness pushed her in, however, and she stroked harder, and at last Simp seemed to be running on her ankles. When it was all over, Simp refused my offer of a ride home and indicated with a quality of speech borrowed from some old Katherine Hepburn movie that she could manage for herself; apparently her manor lay no further than the nearest briar patch. She did not like me and I her, though I worried it, I'm sure, more than she did.

"Who is *she?*"

"Laura Simpson Stolowitch."

"Why don't you call her Stolo?" I asked.

"Simp is her Bennington name. The ass."

"Is that where you go to school" I asked.

She was pushing her shirt up against her skin to dry the perspiration. "No. I go to school in Boston."

I disliked her for the answer. Whenever anyone asks me where I went to school I come right out with it: Newark Colleges of Rutgers University. I may say it a bit too ringingly, too fast, too up-in-the-air, but I say it. For an instant Brenda reminded me of the pug-nosed little bastards from Montclair who come down to the library during vacations, and while I stamp out their books, they stand around tugging their elephantine scarves until they hang to their ankles, hinting all the while at "Boston" and "New Haven."

"Boston University?" I asked, looking off at the trees.

"Radcliffe."

We were still standing on the court, bounded on all sides by white lines. Around the bushes back of the court, fireflies were cutting figure eights in the thorny-smelling air and then, as the night suddenly came all the way in, the leaves on the trees shone for an instant, as though they'd just been rained upon. Brenda walked off the court, with me a step behind her. Now I had grown accustomed to the dark, and as she ceased being merely a voice and turned into a sight again, some of my anger at her "Boston" remark floated off and I let myself appreciate her. Her hands did not twitch at her bottom, but the form revealed itself, covered or not, under the closeness of her khaki Bermudas. There were two wet triangles on the back of her tiny-collared white polo shirt, right where her wings would have been if she'd had a pair. She wore, to complete the picture, a tartan belt, white socks, and white tennis sneakers.

As she walked she zipped the cover on her racket.

"Are you anxious to get home?" I said.

"No."

"Let's sit here. It's pleasant."

"Okay."

We sat down on a bank of grass slanted enough for us to lean back without really leaning; from the angle it seemed as though we were preparing to watch some celestial event, the christening of a new star, the inflation to full size of a half-ballooned moon. Brenda zipped and unzipped the cover while she spoke; for the first time she seemed edgy. Her edginess coaxed mine back, and so we were ready now for what, magically, it seemed we might be able to get by without: a meeting.

"What does your cousin Doris look like?" she asked.

"She's dark—"

"Is she—"

"No," I said. "She has freckles and dark hair and she's very tall."

"Where does she go to school?"

"Northampton."

She did not answer and I don't know how much of what I meant she had understood.

"I guess I don't know her," she said after a moment. "Is she a new member?"

"I think so. They moved to Livingston only a couple of years ago."

"Oh."

No new star appeared, at least for the next five minutes.

"Did you remember me from holding your glasses?" I said.

"Now I do," she said. "Do you live in Livingston too?"

"No. Newark."

"We lived in Newark when I was a baby," she offered.

"Would you like to go home?" I was suddenly angry.

"No. Let's walk though."

Brenda kicked a stone and walked a step ahead of me.

"Why is it you rush the net only after dark?" I said.

She turned to me and smiled. "You noticed? Old Simp the Simpleton doesn't."

"Why do you?"

"I don't like to be up too close, unless I'm sure she won't return it."

"Why?"

"My nose."

"What?"

"I'm afraid of my nose. I had it bobbed."

"What?"

"I had my nose fixed."

"What was the matter with it?"

"It was bumpy."

"A lot?"

"No," she said, "I was pretty. Now I'm prettier. My brother's having his fixed in the fall."

"Does he want to be prettier?"

She didn't answer and walked ahead of me again.

"I don't mean to sound facetious. I mean why's he doing it?"

"He *wants* to . . . unless he becomes a gym teacher . . . but he won't," she said. "We all look like my father."

"Is he having his fixed?"

"Why are you so nasty?"

"I'm not. I'm sorry." My next question was prompted by a desire to sound interested and thereby regain civility; it didn't quite come out as I'd expected—I said it too loud. "How much does it cost?"

Brenda waited a moment but then she answered. "A thousand dollars. Unless you go to a butcher."

"Let me see if you got your money's worth."

She turned again; she stood next to a bench and put the racket down on it. "If I let you kiss me would you stop being nasty?"

We had to take about two too many steps to keep the approach from being awkward, but we pursued the impulse and kissed. I felt her hand on the back of my neck and so I tugged her towards me, too violently perhaps, and slid my own hands across the side of her body and around to her back. I felt the wet spots on her shoulder blades, and beneath them, I'm sure of it, a faint fluttering, as though something stirred so deep in her breasts, so far back it could make itself felt through her shirt. It was like the fluttering of wings, tiny wings no bigger than her breasts. The smallness of the wings did not bother me—it would not take an eagle to carry me up those lousy hundred and eighty feet that make summer nights so much cooler in Short Hills than they are in Newark.

2

The next day I held Brenda's glasses for her once again, this time not as momentary servant but as afternoon guest; or perhaps as both, which still was an improvement. She wore a black tank suit and went barefooted, and among the other women, with their Cuban heels and boned-up breasts, their knuckle-sized rings, their straw hats, which resembled immense wicker pizza plates and had been purchased, as I heard one deeply tanned woman rasp, "from the cutest little *shvartze* when we docked at Barbados,"

Brenda among them was elegantly simple, like a sailor's dream of a Polynesian maiden, albeit one with prescription sun glasses and the last name of Patimkin. She brought a little slurp of water with her when she crawled back towards the pool's edge, and at the edge she grabbed up with her hands and held my ankles, tightly and wet.

"Come in," she said up to me, squinting. "We'll play."

"Your glasses," I said.

"Oh break the goddam things. I hate them."

"Why don't you have your eyes fixed?"

"There you go again."

"I'm sorry," I said. "I'll give them to Doris."

Doris, in the surprise of the summer, had gotten past Prince Andrey's departure from his wife, and now sat brooding, not, it turned out, over the lonely fate of poor Princess Liza, but at the skin which she had lately discovered to be peeling off her shoulders.

"Would you watch Brenda's glasses?" I said.

"Yes." She fluffed little scales of translucent flesh into the air. "Damn it."

I handed her the glasses.

"Well, for God's sake," she said, "I'm not going to hold them. Put them down. *I'm* not her slave."

"You're a pain in the ass, you know that, Doris?" Sitting there, she looked like Laura Simpson Stolowitch, who was, in fact, walking somewhere off at the far end of the pool, avoiding Brenda and me because (I liked to think) of the defeat Brenda had handed her the night before; or maybe (I didn't like to think) because of the strangeness of my presence. Regardless, Doris had to bear the weight of my indictment of both Simp and herself.

"Thank you," she said. "After I invite you up for the day."

"That was yesterday."

"What about last year?"

"That's right, your mother told you last year too—invite Esther's boy so when he writes his parents they won't complain we don't look after him. Every summer I get my day."

"You should have gone with them. That's not our fault. You're not our charge," and when she said it, I could just tell it was something she'd heard at home, or received in a letter one Monday mail, after she'd returned to Northampton from Stowe, or Dartmouth, or perhaps from that weekend when she'd taken a shower with her boyfriend in Lowell House.

"Tell your father not to worry. Uncle Aaron, the sport. I'll take care of myself," and I ran on back to the pool, ran into a dive, in fact, and came up like a dolphin beside Brenda, whose legs I slid upon with my own.

"How's Doris?" she said.

"Peeling," I said. "She's going to have her skin fixed."

"Stop it," she said, and dove down beneath us till I felt her clamping her hands on the soles of my feet. I pulled back and then down too, and then, at the bottom, no more than six inches above the wiggling black lines that divided the pool into lanes for races, we bubbled a kiss into each other's lips. She was smiling there, at *me,* down at the bottom of the swimming pool of the Green Lane Country Club. Way above us, legs shimmied in the water and a pair of fins skimmed greenly by: my cousin Doris could peel away to nothing for all I cared, my Aunt Gladys have twenty feedings every night, my father and mother could roast away their asthma down in the furnace of Arizona, those penniless deserters—I didn't care for anything but Brenda. I went to pull her towards me just as she started fluttering up; my hand hooked on to the front of her suit and the cloth pulled away from her. Her breasts swam towards me like two pink-nosed fish and she let me hold them. Then, in a moment, it was the sun who kissed us both, and we were out of the water, too pleased with each other to smile. Brenda shook the wetness of her hair onto my face and with the drops that touched me I felt she had made a promise to me about the summer, and, I hoped, beyond.

"Do you want your sun glasses?"

"You're close enough to see," she said. We were under a big blue umbrella, side-by-side on two chaise longues, whose plastic covers sizzled against our suits and flesh; I turned my head to look at Brenda and smelled that pleasant little burning odor in the skin of my shoulders. I turned back up to the sun, as did she, and as we talked, and it grew hotter and brighter, the colors splintered under my closed eyelids.

"This is all very fast," she said.

"Nothing's happened," I said softly.

"No. I guess not. I sort of feel something has."

"In eighteen hours?"

"Yes. I feel . . . pursued," she said after a moment.

"*You* invited *me,* Brenda."

"Why do you always sound a little nasty to me?"

"Did I sound nasty? I don't mean to. Truly."

"You do! *You* invited *me,* Brenda. So what?" she said. "That isn't what I mean anyway."

"I'm sorry."

"Stop apologizing. You're so automatic about it, you don't even mean it."

"Now you're being nasty to me," I said.

"No. Just stating the facts. Let's not argue. I like you." She turned her head and looked as though she too paused a second to smell the summer on her own flesh. "I like the way you look." She saved it from embarrassing me with that factual tone of hers.

"Why?" I said.

"Where did you get those fine shoulders? Do you play something?"

"No," I said. "I just grew up and they came with me."

"I like your body. It's fine."

"I'm glad," I said.

"You like mine, don't you?"

"No," I said.

"Then it's denied you," she said.

I brushed her hair flat against her ear with the back of my hand and then we were silent a while.

"Brenda," I said, "You haven't asked me anything about me."

"How you feel? Do you want me to ask you how you feel?

"Yes," I said, accepting the back door she gave me, though probably not for the same reasons she had offered it.

"How *do* you feel?"

"I want to swim."

"Okay," she said.

We spent the rest of the afternoon in the water. There were eight of those long lines painted down the length of the pool and by the end of the day I think we had parked for a while in every lane, close enough to the dark stripes to reach out and touch them. We came back to the chairs now and then and sang hesitant, clever, nervous, gentle dithyrambs about how we were beginning to feel towards one another. Actually we did not have the feelings we said we had until we spoke them—at least I didn't; to phrase them was to invent them and own them. We whipped our strangeness and newness into a froth that resembled love, and we dared not play too long with it, talk too much of it, or it would flatten and fizzle away. So we moved back and forth from chairs to water, from talk to silence, and considering my unshakable edginess with Brenda, and the high walls of ego that rose, buttresses and all, between her and her knowledge of herself, we managed pretty well.

At about four o'clock, at the bottom of the pool, Brenda suddenly wrenched away from me and shot up to the surface. I shot up after her.

"What's the matter?" I said.

First she whipped the hair off her forehead. Then she pointed a hand down towards the base of the pool. "My brother," she said, coughing some water free inside her.

And suddenly, like a crew-cut Proteus rising from the sea, Ron Patimkin emerged from the lower depths we'd just inhabited and his immensity was before us.

"Hey, Bren," he said, and pushed a palm flat into the water so that a small hurricane beat up against Brenda and me.

"What are you so happy about?" she said.

"The Yankees took two."

"Are we going to have Mickey Mantle for dinner?" she said. "When the Yankees win," she said to me, treading so easily she seemed to have turned the chlorine to marble beneath her, "we set an extra place for Mickey Mantle."

"You want to race?" Ron asked.

"No, Ronald. Go race alone."

Nobody had as yet said a word about me. I treaded unobtrusively as I could, as a third party, unintroduced, will step back and say nothing, awaiting the amenities. I was tired, however, from the afternoon's sport, and wished to hell brother and sister would not tease and chat much longer. Fortunately Brenda introduced me. "Ronald, this is Neil Klugman. This is my brother, Ronald Patimkin."

Of all things there in the fifteen feet water, Ron reached out his hand to shake. I returned the shake, not quite as monumentally as he apparently expected; my chin slipped an inch into the water and all at once I was exhausted.

"Want to race?" Ron asked me good-naturedly.

"Go ahead, Neil, race with him. I want to call home and tell them you're coming to dinner."

"Am I? I'll have to call my aunt. You didn't say anything. My clothes—"

"We dine *au naturel.*"

"What?" Ronald said.

"Swim, baby," Brenda said to him and it ached me some when she kissed him on the face.

I begged out of the race, saying I had to make a phone call myself, and once upon the tiled blue border of the pool, looked back to see Ron taking the length in sleek, immense strokes. He gave one the feeling that after swimming the length of the pool a half dozen times he would have earned the right to drink its contents; I imagined he had, like my Uncle Max, a colossal thirst and a gigantic bladder.

Aunt Gladys did not seem relieved when I told her she'd have only three feedings to prepare that night. "Fancy-shmancy" was all she said to me on the phone.

We did not eat in the kitchen; rather, the six of us—Brenda, myself, Ron, Mr. and Mrs. Patimkin, and Brenda's little sister, Julie—sat around the dining room table, while the maid, Carlota, a Navaho-faced Negro who had little holes in her ears but no earrings, served us the meal. I was seated next to Brenda, who was dressed in what was *au naturel* for her: Bermudas, the close ones, white polo shirt, tennis sneakers and white socks. Across from me was Julie, ten, round-faced, bright, who before dinner, while the other little girls on the street had been playing with jacks and boys and each other, had been on the back lawn putting golf balls with her father. Mr. Patimkin reminded me of my father, except that when he spoke he did not surround each syllable with a wheeze. He was tall, strong, ungrammatical, and a ferocious eater. When he attacked his salad—after drenching it in bottled French dressing—the veins swelled under the heavy skin of his forearm. He ate three helpings of salad, Ron had four, Brenda and Julie had two, and only Mrs. Patimkin and I had one each. I did not like Mrs. Patimkin, though she was certainly the handsomest of all of us at the table. She was disastrously polite to me, and with her purple eyes, her dark hair, and large, persuasive frame, she gave me the feeling of some captive beauty, some wild princess, who has been tamed and made the servant to the king's daughter—who was Brenda.

Outside, through the wide picture window, I could see the back lawn with its twin oak trees. I say oaks, though fancifully, one might call them sporting-goods trees. Beneath their branches, like fruit dropped from their limbs, were two irons, a golf ball, a tennis can, a baseball bat, basketball, a first-baseman's glove, and what was apparently a riding crop. Further back, near the scrubs that bounded the Patimkin property and in front of the small basketball court, a square red blanket, with a white O stitched in the center, looked to be on fire against the green grass. A breeze must have blown outside, for the net on the basket moved; inside we ate in the steady coolness of air by Westinghouse. It was a pleasure, except that eating among those Brobdingnags, I felt for quite a while as though four inches had been clipped from my shoulders, three inches from my height, and for good measure, someone had removed my ribs and my chest had settled meekly in towards my back.

There was not much dinner conversation; eating was heavy and methodical and serious, and it would be just as well to record all that was said in one swoop, rather than indicate the sentences lost in the passing of food, the words gurgled into mouthfuls, the syntax chopped and forgotten in heapings, spillings, and gorgings.

TO RON: When's Harriet calling?

RON: Five o'clock.

JULIE: It *was* five o'clock.

RON: Their time.

JULIE: Why is it that it's earlier in Milwaukee? Suppose you took a plane back and forth all day. You'd never get older.

BRENDA: That's right, sweetheart.

MRS. P.: What do you give the child misinformation for? Is that why she goes to school?

BRENDA: I don't know why she goes to school.

MR. P. (*lovingly*): College girl.

RON: Where's Carlota? Carlota!

MRS. P.: Carlota, give Ronald more.

CARLOTA (*calling*): More what?

RON: Everything.

MR. P.: Me too.

MRS. P.: They'll have to *roll* you on the links.

MR. P. (*pulling his shirt up and slapping his black, curved belly*): What are you talking about? Look at that?

RON (*yanking his T-shirt up*): Look at *this.*

BRENDA: (*to me*) Would you care to bare your middle?

ME (the choir boy again): No.

MRS. P.: That's right, Neil.

ME: Yes. Thank you.

CARLOTA (*over my shoulder, like an unsummoned spirit*): Would *you* like more?

ME: No.

MR. P.: He eats like a bird.

JULIE: Certain birds eat a lot.

BRENDA: Which ones?

MRS. P.: Let's not talk about animals at the dinner table. Brenda, why do you encourage her?

RON: Where's Carlota, I gotta play tonight.

MR. P.: Tape your wrist, don't forget.

MRS P.: Where do you live, Bill?

BRENDA: Neil.

MRS. P.: Didn't I say Neil?

JULIE: You said "Where do you live, *Bill?*"

MRS. P.: I must have been thinking of something else.

RON: I hate tape. How the hell can I play in tape?

JULIE: Don't curse.

MRS. P.: That's right.

MR. P.: What is Mantle batting now?

JULIE: Three twenty-eight.

RON: Three twenty-five.

JULIE: Eight!

RON: Five, jerk! He got three for four in the second game.

JULIE: *Four* for four.

RON: That was an error, Minoso should have had it.

JULIE: I didn't think so.

BRENDA (*to me*): See?

MRS. P.: See what?

BRENDA: I was talking to Bill.

JULIE: Neil.

MR. P.: Shut up and eat.

MRS. P.: A little less talking, young lady.

JULIE: I didn't say anything.

BRENDA: She was talking to me, sweetie.

MR. P.: What's this *she* business. Is that how you call your mother? What's dessert?

The phone rings, and though we are awaiting dessert, the meal seems at a formal end, for Ron breaks for his room, Julie shouts "Harriet!" and Mr. Patimkin is not wholly successful in stifling a belch, though the failure even more than the effort ingratiates him to me. Mrs. Patimkin is directing Carlota not to mix the milk silverware and the meat silverware again, and Carlota is eating a peach while she listens; under the table I feel Brenda's fingers tease my calf. I am full.

We sat under the biggest of the oak trees while out on the basketball court Mr. Patimkin played five and two with Julie. In the driveway Ron was racing the motor of the Volkswagen. "Will somebody *please* move the Chrysler out from behind me?" he called angrily. "I'm late as it is."

"Excuse me," Brenda said, getting up.

"I think I'm behind the Chrysler," I said.

"Let's go," she said.

We backed the cars out so that Ron could hasten on to his game. Then we reparked them and went back to watching Mr. Patimkin and Julie.

"I like your sister," I said.

"So do I," she said. "I wonder what she'll turn out to be."

"Like you," I said.

"I don't know," she said. "Better probably." And then she added, "or maybe worse. How can you tell? My father's nice to her, but I'll give her another three years with my mother . . . Bill," she said, musingly.

"I didn't mind that," I said. "She's very beautiful, your mother."

"I can't even think of her as my mother. She hates me. Other girls, when they pack in September, at least their mothers help them. Not mine. She'll be busy sharpening pencils for Julie's pencil box while I'm carrying my trunk around upstairs. And it's so obvious why. It's practically a case study."

"Why?"

"She's jealous. It's so corny I'm ashamed to say it. Do you know my mother had the best back-hand in New Jersey? Really, she was the best tennis player in the state, man or woman. You ought to see the pictures of her when she was a girl. She was so healthy-looking. But not chubby or anything. She was soulful, truly. I love her in those pictures. Sometimes I say to her how beautiful the pictures are. I even asked to have one blown up so I could have it at school. 'We have other things to do with our money, young lady, than spend it on old photographs.' Money! My father's up to here with it, but whenever I buy a coat you should hear her. 'You don't have to go to Bonwit's, young lady, Ohrbach's has the strongest fabrics of any of them.' Who *wants* a strong fabric! Finally I get what I want, but not till she's had a chance to aggravate me. Money is a waste for her. She doesn't even know how to enjoy it. She still thinks we live in Newark."

"But you get what you want," I said.

"Yes. Him," and she pointed out to Mr. Patimkin who had just swished his third straight set shot through the basket to the disgruntlement, apparently, of Julie, who stamped so hard at the ground that she raised a little dust storm around her perfect young legs.

"He's not too smart but he's sweet at least. He doesn't treat my brother the way she treats me. Thank God, for that. Oh, I'm tired of talking about them. Since my freshman year I think every conversation I've ever had has always wound up about my parents and how awful it is. It's universal. The only trouble is they don't know it."

From the way Julie and Mr. Patimkin were laughing now, out on the court, no problem could ever have seemed less universal; but, of course, it was universal for Brenda, more than that, cosmic—it made every cashmere sweater a battle with her mother, and her life, which, I was certain, consisted to a large part of cornering the market on fabrics that felt soft to the skin, took on the quality of a Hundred Years' War . . .

I did not intend to allow myself such unfaithful thoughts, to line up with Mrs. Patimkin while I sat beside Brenda, but I could not shake from my elephant's brain that she-still-thinks-we-live-in-Newark remark. I did not speak, however, fearful that my tone would shatter our post-dinner ease and intimacy. It had been so simple to be intimate with water pounding and securing all our pores, and later, with the sun heating them and drugging our senses, but now, in the shade and the open, cool and clothed on her own grounds, I did not want to voice a word that would lift the cover and reveal that hideous emotion I always felt for her, and is the underside of love. It will not always *stay* the underside—but I am skipping ahead.

Suddenly, little Julie was upon us. "Want to play?" she said to me. "Daddy's tired."

"C'mon," Mr. Patimkin called. "Finish for me."

I hesitated—I hadn't held a basketball since high school—but Julie was dragging at my hand, and Brenda said, "Go ahead."

Mr. Patimkin tossed the ball towards me while I wasn't looking and it bounced off my chest, leaving a round dust spot, like the shadow of a moon, on my shirt. I laughed insanely.

"Can't you catch?" Julie said.

Like her sister, she seemed to have a knack for asking practical, infuriating questions.

"Yes."

"Your turn," she said. "Daddy's behind forty-seven to thirty-nine. Two hundred wins."

For an instant, as I placed my toes in the little groove that over the years had been nicked into a foul line, I had one of those instantaneous waking dreams that plague me from time to time, and send, my friends tell me, deadly cataracts over my eyes: the sun had sunk, crickets had come and gone, the leaves had blackened, and still Julie and I stood alone on the lawn, tossing the ball at the basket; "Five hundred wins," she called, and then when she beat me to five hundred she called, "Now *you* have to reach it," and I did, and the night lengthened, and she called, "*Eight* hundred wins," and we played on and then it was eleven hundred that won and we played on and it never was morning.

"Shoot," Mr. Patimkin said. "You're me."

That puzzled me, but I took my set shot and, of course, missed. With the Lord's blessing and a soft breeze, I made the lay-up.

"You have forty-one. I go," Julie said.

Mr. Patimkin sat on the grass at the far end of the court. He took his shirt off, and in his undershirt, and his whole day's growth of beard, looked like a trucker. Brenda's old nose fitted him well. There was a bump in it, all right; up at the bridge it seemed as though a small eight-sided diamond had been squeezed in under the skin. I knew Mr. Patimkin would never bother to have that stone cut from his face, and yet, with joy and pride, no doubt, had paid to have Brenda's diamond removed and dropped down some toilet in Fifth Avenue Hospital.

Julie missed her set shot, and I admit to a slight, gay, flutter of heart.

"Put a little spin on it," Mr. Patimkin told her.

"Can I take it again?" Julie asked me.

"Yes." What with paternal directions from the sidelines and my own grudging graciousness on the court, there did not seem much of a chance for me to catch up. And I wanted to, suddenly, I wanted to win, to run little Julie into the ground. Branda was back on one elbow, under the tree, chewing on a leaf, watching. And up in the house, at the kitchen window, I could see that the curtain had swished back—the sun too low now to glare off electrical appliances—and Mrs. Patimkin was looking steadily out at the game. And then Carlota appeared on the back steps, eating a peach and holding a pail of garbage in her free hand. She stopped to watch too.

It was my turn again. I missed the set shot and laughingly turned to Julie and said, "Can I take it again?"

"No!"

So I learned how the game was played. Over the years Mr. Patimkin had taught his daughters that free throws were theirs for the asking; he could afford to. However, with the strange eyes of Short Hills upon me, matrons, servants, and providers, I somehow felt I couldn't. But I had to and I did.

"Thanks a lot, Neil," Julie said when the game was ended—at 100—and the crickets had come.

"You're welcome."

Under the trees, Brenda smiled. "Did you let her win?"

"I think so," I said. "I'm not sure."

There was something in my voice that prompted Brenda to say, comfortingly, "Even Ron lets her win."

"It's all nice for Julie," I said.

3

The next morning I found a parking space on Washington Street directly across from the library. Since I was twenty minutes early I decided to stroll in the park rather than cross over to work; I didn't particularly care to join my colleagues, who I knew would be sipping early morning coffee in the binding room, smelling still of all the orange crush they'd drunk that weekend at Asbury Park. I sat on a bench and looked out towards Broad Street and the morning traffic. The Lackawanna Commuter trains were rumbling in a few blocks to the north and I could hear them, I thought—the sunny green cars, old and clean, with windows that opened all the way. Some mornings, with time to kill before work, I would walk down to the tracks and watch the open windows roll in, on their sills the elbows of tropical suits and the edges of briefcases, the properties of businessmen arriving in town from Maplewood, the Oranges, and the suburbs beyond.

The park, bordered by Washington Street on the west and Broad on the east, was empty and shady and smelled of trees, night, and dog leavings; and there was a faint damp smell too, indicating that the huge rhino of a water cleaner had passed by already, soaking and whisking the downtown streets. Down Washington Street, behind me, was the Newark Museum—I could see it without even looking: two oriental vases in front like spittoons for a rajah, and next to it the little annex to which we had traveled on special buses as schoolchildren. The annex was a brick building, old and vine-covered, and always reminded me of New Jersey's link with the beginning of the country, with George Washington, who had trained his scrappy army—a little bronze tablet informed us children—in the very park where I now sat. At the far end of the park, beyond the Museum, was the bank building where I had gone to college. It had been converted some years before into an extension of Rutgers University; in fact, in what once had been the bank president's waiting room I had taken a course called Contemporary Moral Issues. Though it was summer now, and I was out of college three years, it was not hard for me to remember the other students, my friends, who had worked evenings in Bamberger's and Kresge's and had used the commissions they'd earned pushing ladies' out-of-season shoes to pay their laboratory fees. And then I looked out to Broad Street again. Jammed between a grimy-windowed bookstore and a cheesy luncheonette was the marquee of a tiny art theater—how many years had passed since I'd stood beneath that marquee, lying about the year of my birth so as to see Hedy Lamarr swim naked in *Ecstasy;* and then, having slipped the ticket taker an extra quarter, what disappointment I had felt at the frugality of her Slavic charm . . . Sitting there in the park, I felt a deep knowledge of Newark, an attachment so rooted that it could not help but branch out into affection.

Suddenly it was nine o'clock and everything was scurrying. Wobblyheeled girls revolved through the doors of the telephone building across the way, traffic honked desperately, policeman barked, whistled, and waved motorists to and fro. Over at St. Vincent's Church the huge dark portals swung back and those bleary-eyes that had risen early for Mass now blinked at the light. Then the worshipers had stepped off the church steps and were racing down the streets towards desks, filing cabinets, secretaries, bosses, and—if the Lord has seen fit to remove a mite of harshness from their lives—to the comfort of air-conditioners pumping at their windows. I got up and crossed over to the library, wondering if Brenda was awake yet.

The pale cement lions stood unconvincing guard on the library steps, suffering their usual combination of elephantiasis and arteriosclerosis, and I was prepared to pay them as little attention as I had for the past eight months were it not for a small colored boy who stood in front of one of them. The lion had lost all of its toes the summer before to a safari of juvenile delinquents, and now a new tormentor stood before him, sagging a little in his knees, and growling. He would growl, low and long, drop back, wait, then growl again. Then he would straighten up, and, shaking his head, he would say to the lion, "Man, you's a coward . . ." Then, once again, he'd growl.

The day began the same as any other. From behind the desk on the main floor, I watched the hot high-breasted teen-age girls walk twitchingly up the wide flight of marble stairs that led to the main reading room. The stairs were an imitation of a staircase somewhere in Versailles, though in their toreador pants and sweaters these young daughters of Italian leatherworkers, Polish brewery hands, and Jewish furriers were hardly duchesses. They were not Brenda either, and any lust that sparked inside me through the dreary day was academic and time-passing. I looked at my watch occasionally, thought of Brenda, and waited for lunch and then for after lunch, when I would take over the Information Desk upstairs and John McKee, who was only twenty-one but wore elastic bands around his sleeves, would march starchily down the stairs to work assiduously at stamping books in and out. John McRubberbands was in his last year at Newark State Teachers College where he was studying at the Dewey Decimal System in preparation for his lifework. The library was not going to be my lifework, I knew it. Yet, there had been some talk—from Mr. Scapello, an old eunuch who had learned somehow to disguise his voice as a man's—that when I returned from my summer vacation I would be put in charge of the Reference Room, a position that had been empty ever since that morning when Martha Winney had fallen off a high stool in the Encyclopedia Room and shattered all those frail bones that come together to form what in a woman half her age we would call the hips.

I had strange fellows at the library and, in truth, there were many hours when I never quite knew how I'd gotten there or why I stayed. But

I did stay and after a while waited patiently for that day when I would go into the men's room on the main floor for a cigarette and, studying myself as I expelled smoke into the mirror, would see that at some moment during the morning I had gone pale, and that under my skin, as under McKee's and Scapello's and Miss Winney's, there was a thin cushion of air separating the blood from the flesh. Someone had pumped it there while I was stamping out a book, and so life from now on would be not a throwing off, as it was for Aunt Gladys, and not a gathering in, as it was for Brenda, but a bouncing off, a numbness. I began to fear this, and yet, in my muscleless devotion to my work, seemed edging towards it, silently, as Miss Winney used to edge up to the *Britannica.* Her stool was empty now and awaited me.

Just before lunch the lion tamer came wide-eyed into the library. He stood still for a moment, only his fingers moving, as though he were counting the number of marble stairs before him. Then he walked creepily about on the marble floor, snickering at the clink of his taps and the way his little noise swelled up to the vaulted ceiling. Otto, the guard at the door, told him to make less noise with his shoes, but that did not seem to bother the little boy. He clacked on his tiptoes, high, secretively, delighted at the opportunity Otto had given him to practice this posture. He tiptoed up to me.

"Hey," he said, "where's the heart section?"

"The what?" I said.

"The heart section. Ain't you got no heart section?"

He had the thickest sort of southern Negro dialect and the only word that came clear to me was the one that sounded like heart.

"How do you spell it?" I said.

"*Heart.* Man, pictures, Drawing books. Where you got them?"

"You meant art books? Reproductions?"

He took my polysyllabic word for it. "Yea, they's them."

"In a couple places," I told him. "Which artist are you interested in?"

The boy's eyes narrowed so that his whole face seemed black. He started backing away, as he had from the lion. "All of them . . ." he mumbled.

"That's okay," I said. "You go look at whichever ones you want. The next flight up. Follow the arrow to where it says Stack Three. You remember that? Stack Three. Ask somebody upstairs."

He did not move; he seemed to be taking my curiosity about his taste as a kind of poll-tax investigation. "Go ahead," I said, slashing my face with a smile, "right up there . . ."

And like a shot he was scuffling and tapping up towards the heart section.

After lunch I came back to the in-and-out desk and there was John McKee, waiting, in his pale blue slacks, his black shoes, his barber-cloth shirt with the elastic bands, and a great knit tie, green, wrapped into a

Windsor knot, that was huge and jumped when he talked. His breath smelled of hair oil and his hair of breath and when he spoke, spittle cobwebbed the corners of his mouth. I did not like him and at times had the urge to yank back on his armbands and slingshoot him out past Otto and the lions into the street.

"Has a little Negro boy passed the desk? With a thick accent? He's been hiding in the art books all morning. You know what those boys *do* in there."

"I saw him come in, John."

"So did I. Has he gone *out* though."

"I haven't noticed. I guess so."

"Those are *very* expensive books."

"Don't be so nervous, John. People are supposed to touch them."

"There is touching," John said sententiously, "and there is touching. Someone should check on him. I was afraid to leave the desk here. You know the way they treat the housing projects we give them."

"*You* give them?"

"The city. Have you seen what they do at Seth Boyden? They threw *beer* bottles, those big ones, on the *lawn.* They're taking over the city."

"Just the Negro sections."

"It's easy to laugh, you don't live near them. I'm going to call Mr. Scapello's office to check the Art Section. Where did he ever find out about art?"

"You'll give Mr. Scapello an ulcer, so soon after his egg-and-pepper sandwich. I'll check, I have to go upstairs anyway."

"You know what they do in there," John warned me.

"Don't worry, Johnny, *they're* the one's who'll get warts on their dirty little hands."

"Ha ha. Those books happen to cost—"

So that Mr. Scapello would not descend upon the boy with his chalky fingers, I walked up the three flights to Stack Three, past the receiving room where rheumy-eyed Jimmy Boylen, our fifty-one-year-old boy, unloaded books from a cart; past the reading room, where bums off Mulberry Street slept over *Popular Mechanics;* past the smoking corridor where damp-browed summer students from the law school relaxed, some smoking, others trying to rub the colored dye from their tort texts off their fingertips; and finally, past the periodical room, where a few ancient ladies who'd been motored down from Upper Montclair now huddled in their chairs, pince-nezing over yellowed, fraying society pages in old old copies of the Newark *News.* Up on Stack Three I found the boy. He was seated on the glass-brick floor holding an open book in his lap, a book, in fact, that was bigger than his lap and had to be propped up by his knees. By the light of the window behind him I could see the hundreds of spaces between the hundreds of tiny black corkscrews that were his hair. He was very black and shiny, and the flesh of his lips did not so much appear to be a different color as it looked to be unfinished and awaiting another coat. The lips were parted, the eyes wide, and even the ears seemed to have a heightened receptivity. He looked ecstatic—until he saw me, that is. For all he knew I was John McKee.

"That's okay," I said before he could even move, "I'm just passing through. You read."

"Ain't nothing *to* read. They's pictures."

"Fine." I fished around the lowest shelves a moment, playing at work.

"Hey, mister," the boy said after a minute, "where is this?"

"Where is what?"

"Where is these pictures? These people, man, they sure does look cool. They ain't no yelling or shouting here, you could just see it."

He lifted the book so I could see. It was an expensive large-sized edition of Gauguin reproductions. The page he had been looking at showed an 8½ × 11 print, in color, of three native women standing knee-high in a rose-colored stream. It *was* a silent picture, he was right.

"That's Tahiti. That's an island in the Pacific Ocean."

"That ain't no place you could go, is it? Like a ree-*sort?*"

"You could go there, I suppose. It's very far. People live there . . ."

"Hey, *look,* look here at this one." He flipped back to a page where a young brown-skinned maid was leaning forward on her knees, as though to dry her hair. "Man," the boy said, "that's the fuckin life." The euphoria of his diction would have earned him eternal banishment from the Newark Public Library and its branches had John or Mr. Scapello—or, God forbid, the hospitalized Miss Winney—come to investigate.

"Who took these pictures?" he asked me.

"Gauguin. He didn't take them, he painted them. Paul Gauguin. He was a Frenchman."

"Is he a white man or a colored man?"

"He's white."

"Man," the boy smiled, chuckled almost, "I knew that. He don't *take* pictures like no colored men would. He's a good picture taker . . . *Look, look,* look here at this one. Ain't that the fuckin *life?*"

I agreed it was and left.

Later I sent Jimmy Boylen hopping down the stairs to tell McKee that everything was all right. The rest of the day was uneventful. I sat at the Information Desk thinking about Brenda and reminding myself that that evening I would have to get gas before I started up to Short Hills, which I could see now, in my mind's eye, at dusk, rose-colored, like a Gauguin stream.

When I pulled up to the Patimkin house that night, everybody but Julie was waiting for me on the front porch: Mr. and Mrs., Ron, and Brenda, wearing a dress. I had not seen her in a dress before and for an instant she did not look like the same girl. But that was only half the surprise. So many of those Lincolnesque college girls turn out to be limbed for shorts alone. Not Brenda. She looked, in a dress, as though she'd gone through life so attired, as though she'd never worn shorts, or bathing suits, or pajamas, or anything but the pale linen dress. I walked rather bouncingly up the lawn, past the huge weeping willow, towards the waiting Patimkins, wishing all the while that I'd had my car washed. Before I'd even reached them, Ron stepped forward and shook my hand, vigorously, as though he hadn't seen me since the Diaspora. Mrs. Patimkin smiled and Mr. Patimkin grunted something and continued twitching his wrists before him, then raising an imaginary golf club and driving a ghost of a golf ball up and away towards the Orange Mountains, that are called Orange, I'm convinced, because in that various suburban light that's the *only* color they do not come dressed in.

"We'll be right back," Brenda said to me. "You have to sit with Julie. Carlota's off."

"Okay," I said.

"We're taking Ron to the airport."

"Okay."

"Julie doesn't want to go. She says Ron pushed her in the pool this afternoon. We've been waiting for you, so we don't miss Ron's plane. Okay?"

"Okay."

Mr. and Mrs. Patimkin and Ron moved off, and I flashed Brenda just the hint of a glare. She reached out and took my hand a moment.

"How do you like me?" she said.

"You're great to baby-sit for. Am I allowed all the milk and cake I want?"

"Don't be angry, baby. We'll be right back." Then she waited a moment, and when I failed to deflate the pout from my mouth, she gave *me* a glare, no hints about it. "I *meant* how do you like me in a dress!" Then she ran off towards the Chrysler, trotting in her high heels like a colt.

When I walked into the house, I slammed the screen door behind me.

"Close the other door too," a little voice shouted. "The air-conditioning."

I closed the other door, obediently.

"Neil?" Julie called.

"Yes."

"Hi. Want to play five and two?"

"No."

"Why not?"

I did not answer.

"I'm in the television room," she called.

"Good."

"Are you supposed to stay with me?"

"Yes."

She appeared unexpectedly through the dining room. "Want to read a book report I wrote?"

"Not now."

"What do you want to do?" she said.

"Nothing, honey. Why don't you watch TV?"

"All right," she said disgustedly, and kicked her way back to the television room.

For a while I remained in the hall, bitten with the urge to slide quietly out of the house, into my car, and back to Newark, where I might even sit in the alley and break candy with my own. I felt like Carlota; no, not even as comfortable as that. At last I left the hall and began to stroll in and out of rooms on the first floor. Next to the living room was the study, a small knotty-pine room jammed with cater-cornered leather chairs and a complete set of *Information Please Almanacs.* On the wall hung three colored photo-paintings; they were the kind which, regardless of the subjects, be they vital or infirm, old or youthful, are characterized by bud-cheeks, wet lips, pearly teeth, and shiny, metallized hair. The subjects in this case were Ron, Brenda, and Julie at about ages fourteen, thirteen, and two. Brenda had long auburn hair, her diamond-studded nose, and no glasses; all combined to make her look a regal thirteen-year-old who'd just gotten smoke in her eyes. Ron was rounder and his hairline was lower, but that love of spherical objects and lined courts twinkled in his boyish eyes. Poor little Julie was lost in the photo-painter's Platonic idea of childhood; her tiny humanity was smothered somewhere back of gobs of pink and white.

There were other pictures about, smaller ones, taken with a Brownie Reflex before photo-painting had become fashionable. There was a tiny picture of Brenda on a horse; another of Ron in bar mitzvah suit, *yamalkah,* and *tallas;* and two pictures framed together—one of a beautiful, faded woman, who must have been, from the eyes, Mrs. Patimkin's mother, and the other of Mrs. Patimkin herself, her hair in a halo, her eyes joyous and not those of a slowly aging mother with a quick and lovely daughter.

I walked through the archway into the dining room and stood a moment looking out at the sporting goods tree. From the television room that winged off the dining room, I could hear Julie listening to *This Is Your Life.* The kitchen, which winged off the other side, was empty, and apparently, with Carlota off, the Patimkins had had dinner at the club. Mr. and Mrs. Patimkin's bedroom was in the middle of the house, down the hall, next to Julie's, and for a moment I wanted to see what size bed those giants slept in —I imagined it wide and deep as a swimming pool—but I postponed my investigation while Julie was in the house, and instead opened the door in the kitchen that led down to the basement.

The basement had a different kind of coolness from the house, and it had a smell, which was something the upstairs was totally without. It felt cavernous down there, but in a comforting way, like the simulated caves children make for themselves on rainy days, in hall closets, under blankets, or in between the legs of dining room tables. I flipped on the light at the foot of the stairs and was not surprised at the pine paneling, the bamboo furniture, the ping-pong table, and the mirrored bar that was stocked with every kind and size of glass, ice bucket, decanter, mixer, swizzle stick, shot glass, pretzel bow—all the bacchanalian paraphernalia, plentiful, orderly, and untouched, as it can be only in the bar of a wealthy man who never entertains drinking people, who himself does not drink, who, in fact, gets a fishy look from his wife when every several months he takes a shot of schnapps before dinner. I went behind the bar where there was an aluminum sink that had not seen a dirty glass, I'm sure, since Ron's bar mitzvah party, and would not see another probably, until one of the Patimkin children was married or engaged. I would have poured myself a drink—just as a wicked wage for being forced into servantry—but I was uneasy about breaking the label on a bottle of whiskey. You had to break a label to get a drink. On the shelf back of the bar were two dozen bottles—twenty-three to be exact—of Jack Daniels, each with a little booklet tied to its collared neck informing patrons how patrician of them it was to drink the stuff. And over the Jack Daniels were more photos: there was a blown-up newspaper photo of Ron palming a basketball in one hand like a raisin; under the picture it said, "*Center,* Ronald Patimkin, Millburn High School, 6'4", 217 pounds." And there was another picture of Brenda on a horse, and next to that, a velvet mounting board with ribbons and medals clipped to it: Essex County Horse Show 1949, Union County Horse Show 1950, Garden State Fair 1952, Morristown Horse Show 1953, and so on—all for Brenda, for jumping and running or galloping or whatever else young girls receive ribbons for. In the entire house I hadn't seen one picture of Mr. Patimkin.

The rest of the basement, back of the wide pine-paneled room, was gray cement walls and linoleum floor and contained innumerable electrical appliances, including a freezer big enough to house a family of Eskimos. Beside the freezer, incongruously, was a tall old refrigerator; its ancient presence was a reminder to me of the Patimkin roots in Newark. This same refrigerator had once stood in the kitchen of an apartment in some four-family house, probably in the same neighborhood where I had lived all my life, first with my parents and then, when the two of them went wheezing off to Arizona, with my aunt and uncle. After Pearl Harbor the refrigerator had made the move up to Short Hills; Patimkin Kitchen and Bathroom Sinks had gone to war: no new barracks was complete until it had a squad of Patimkin sinks lined up in its latrine.

I opened the door of the old refrigerator; it was not empty. No longer did it hold butter, eggs, herring in cream sauce, ginger ale, tuna fish salad, an occasional corsage—rather it was heaped with fruit, shelves swelled with it, every color, every texture, and hidden within, every kind of pit. There were greengage plums, black plums, red plums, apricots, nectarines, peaches, long horns of grapes, black, yellow, red, and cherries, cherries flowing out of boxes and staining everything scarlet. And there were melons —cantaloupes and honeydews—and on the top shelf, half of a huge watermelon, a thin sheet of wax paper clinging to its bare red face like a wet lip. Oh Patimkin! Fruit grew in their refrigerator and sporting goods dropped from their trees!

I grabbed a handful of cherries and then a nectarine, and I bit right down to its pit.

"You better wash that or you'll get diarrhea."

Julie was standing behind me in the pine-paneled room. She was wearing *her* Bermudas and *her* white polo shirt which was unlike Brenda's only in that it had a little dietary history of its own.

"What?" I said.

"They're not washed yet," Julie said, and in such a way that it seemed to place the refrigerator itself out-of-bounds, if only for me.

"That's all right," I said, and devoured the nectarine and put the pit in my pocket and stepped out of the refrigerator room, all in one second. I still didn't know what to do with the cherries. "I was just looking around," I said.

Julie didn't answer.

"Where's Ron going?" I asked, dropping the cherries into my pocket, among my keys and change.

"Milwaukee."

"For long?"

"To see Harriet. They're in love."

We looked at each other for longer than I could bear. "Harriet?" I asked.

"Yes."

Julie was looking at me as though she were trying to look behind me, and then I realized that I was standing with my hands out of sight. I brought them around to the front, and, I swear it, she did peek to see if they were empty.

We confronted one another again; she seemed to have a threat in her face.

Then she spoke. "Want to play ping-pong?"

"God, yes," I said, and made for the table with two long, bounding steps. "You can serve."

Julie smiled and we began to play.

I have no excuses to offer for what happened next. I began to win and I liked it.

"Can I take that one over?" Julie said. "I hurt my finger yesterday and it just hurt when I served."

"No."

I continued to win.

"That wasn't fair, Neil. My shoelace came untied. Can I take it—"

"No."

We played, I ferociously.

"Neil, you leaned over the table. That's illegal—"

"I didn't lean and it's not illegal."

I felt the cherries hopping among my nickels and pennies.

"Neil, you gypped me out of a point. You have nineteen and I have eleven—"

"Twenty and *ten,*" I said. "Serve!"

She did and I smashed my return past her—it zoomed off the table and skittered into the refrigerator room.

"You're a cheater!" she screamed at me. "You cheat!" Her jaw was trembling as though she carried a weight on top of her pretty head. *"I hate* you!" And she threw her racket across the room and it clanged off the bar, just as, outside, I heard the Chrysler crushing gravel in the driveway.

"The game isn't over," I said to her.

"You cheat! And you were stealing fruit!" she said, and ran away before I had my chance to win.

Later that night, Brenda and I made love, our first time. We were sitting on the sofa in the television room and for some ten minutes had not spoken a word to each other. Julie had long since gone to a weepy bed, and though no one had said anything to me about her crying, I did not know if the child had mentioned my fistful of cherries, which, some time before, I had flushed down the toilet.

The television set was on and though the sound was off and the house quiet, the gray pictures still wiggled at the far end of the room. Brenda was quiet and her dress circled her legs, which were tucked back beneath her. We sat there for some while and did not speak. Then she went into the kitchen and when she came back she said that it sounded as though everyone was asleep. We sat a while longer, watching the soundless bodies on the screen eating a silent dinner in someone's silent restaurant. When I began to unbutton her dress she resisted me, and I like to think it was because she knew how lovely she looked in it. But she looked lovely, my Brenda, anyway, and we folded it carefully and held each other close and soon there we were, Brenda falling, slowly but with a smile, and me rising.

How can I describe loving Brenda? It was so sweet, as though I'd finally scored that twenty-first point.

When I got home I dialed Brenda's number, but not before my aunt heard and rose from her bed.

"Who are you calling at this hour? The doctor?"

"No."

"What kind phone calls, one o'clock at night?"

"Shh!" I said.

"He tells *me* shhh. Phone calls one o'clock at night, we haven't got a big enough bill," and then she dragged herself back into the bed, where with a martyr's heart and bleary eyes she had resisted the downward tug of sleep until she'd heard my key in the door.

Brenda answered the phone.

"Neil?" she said.

"Yes," I whispered. "You didn't get out of bed, did you?"

"No," she said, "the phone is next to the bed."

"Good. How is it in bed?"

"Good. Are you in bed?"

"Yes," I lied, and tried to right myself by dragging the phone by its cord as close as I could to my bedroom.

"I'm in bed with you," she said.

"That's right," I said, "and I'm with you."

"I have the shades down, so it's dark and I don't see you."

"I don't see you either."

"That was so nice, Neil."

"Yes. Go to sleep, sweet, I'm here," and we hung up without goodbyes. In the morning, as planned, I called again, but I could hardly hear Brenda or myself for that matter, for Aunt Gladys and Uncle Max were going on a Workmen's Circle picnic in the afternoon, and there was some trouble about grape juice that had dripped all night from a jug in the refrigerator and by morning had leaked out onto the floor. Brenda was still in bed and so could play our game with some success, but I had to pull down all the shades of my senses to imagine myself beside her. I could only pray our nights and mornings would come, and soon enough they did.

4

Over the next week and a half there seemed to be only two people in my life: Brenda and the little colored kid who liked Gauguin. Every morning before the library opened, the boy was waiting; sometimes he seated himself on the lion's back, sometimes under his belly, sometimes he just stood around throwing pebbles at his mane. Then he would come inside, tap around the main floor until Otto stared him up on tiptoes, and finally headed up the long marble stairs that led to Tahiti. He did not always stay to lunch time, but one very hot day he was there when I arrived in the morning and went through the door behind me when I left at night. The next morning, it was, that he did not show up, and as though in his place, a very old man appeared, white, smelling of Life Savers, his nose and jowls showing erupted veins beneath them. "Could you tell me where I'd find the art section?"

"Stack Three," I said.

In a few minutes, he returned with a big brown-covered book in his hand. He placed it on my desk, withdrew his card from a long moneyless billfold and waited for me to stamp out the book.

"Do you want to take this book *out?*" I said.

He smiled.

I took his card and jammed the metal edge into the machine; but I did not stamp down. "Just a minute," I said. I took a clipboard from under the desk and flipped through a few pages, upon which were games of battleship and tick-tack-toe that I'd been playing through the week with myself. "I'm afraid there's a hold on this book."

"A what?"

"A hold. Someone's called up and asked that we hold it for them. Can I take your name and address and drop a card when it's free . . ."

And so I was able, not without flushing once or twice, to get the book back in the stacks. When the colored kid showed up later in the day, it was just where he'd left it the afternoon before.

As for Brenda, I saw her every evening and when there was not a night game that kept Mr. Patimkin awake and in the TV room, or a Hadassah card party that sent Mrs. Patimkin out of the house and brought her in at unpredictable hours, we made love before the silent screen. One muggy, low-skied night Brenda took me swimming at the club. We were the only ones in the pool, and all the chairs, the cabañas, the lights, the diving boards, the very water seemed to exist only for our pleasure. She wore a blue suit that looked purple in the lights and down beneath the water it flashed sometimes green, sometimes black. Late in the evening a breeze came up off the golf course and we wrapped ourselves in one huge towel, pulled two chaise longues together, and despite the bartender, who was doing considerable pacing back and forth by the bar window, which overlooked the pool, we rested side by side on the chairs. Finally the bar light itself flipped off, and then, in a snap, the lights around the pool went down and out. My heart must have beat faster, or something, for Brenda seemed to guess my sudden doubt—*we should go,* I thought.

She said: "That's okay."

It was very dark, the sky was low and starless, and it took a while for me to see, once again, the diving board a shade lighter than the night, and to distinguish the water from the chairs that surrounded the far side of the pool.

I pushed the straps of her bathing suit down but she said no and rolled an inch away from me, and for the first time in the two weeks I'd known her she asked me a question about me.

"Where are your parents?" she said.

"Tucson," I said. "Why?"

"My mother asked me."

I could see the life guard's chair now, white almost.

"Why are you still here? Why aren't you with them?" she asked.

"I'm not a child any more, Brenda," I said, more sharply than I'd intended. "I just can't go wherever my parents are."

"But then why do you stay with your aunt and uncle?"

"They're not my parents."

"They're better?"

"No. Worse. I don't *know* why I stay with them."

"Why?" she said.

"Why don't I know?"

"Why do you stay? You do know, don't you?"

"My job, I suppose. It's convenient from there, and it's cheap, and it pleases my parents. My aunt's all right really . . . Do I really have to explain to your mother why I live where I do?"

"It's not for my mother. I want to know. I wondered why you weren't with your parents, that's all."

"Are you cold?" I asked.

"No."

"Do you want to go home?"

"No, not unless you do. Don't you feel well, Neil?"

"I feel all right," and to let her know that I was still me, I held her to me, though that moment I was without desire.

"Neil?"

"What?"

"What about the library?"

"Who wants to know that?"

"My father," she laughed.

"And you?"

She did not answer a moment. "And me," she said finally.

"Well, what about it? Do I like it? It's okay. I sold shoes once and like the library better. After the Army they tried me for a couple months at Uncle Aaron's real estate company—Doris' father—and I like the library better than that . . ."

"How did you get a job *there?*"

"I worked there for a little while when I was in college, then when I quit Uncle Aaron's, oh, I don't know . . ."

"What did you take in college?"

"At Newark Colleges of Rutgers University I majored in philosophy. I am twenty-three years old. I—"

"Why do you sound nasty again?"

"Do I?"

"Yes."

I didn't say I was sorry.

"Are you planning on making a career of the library?"

"Bren, I'm not planning anything. I haven't planned a thing in three years. At least for the year I've been out of the Army. In the Army I used to plan to go away weekends. I'm—I'm not a planner." After all the truth I'd suddenly given her, I shouldn't have ruined it for myself with that final lie. I added, "I'm a liver."

"I'm a pancreas," she said.

"I'm a—"

And she kissed the absurd game away; she wanted to be serious.

"Do you love me, Neil?"

I did not answer.

"I'll sleep with you whether you do or not, so tell me the truth."

"That was pretty crude."

"Don't be prissy," she said.

"No, I mean a crude thing to say about me."

"I don't understand," she said, and she didn't, and that she didn't pained me; I allowed myself the minor subterfuge, however, of forgiving Brenda her obtuseness. "Do you?" she said.

"No."

"I want you to."

"What about the library?"

"What about it?" she said.

Was it obtuseness again? I thought not—and it wasn't, for Brenda said, "When you love me, there'll be nothing to worry about."

"Then of course I'll love you." I smiled.

"I know you will," she said. "Why don't you go in the water, and I'll wait for you and close my eyes, and when you come back you'll surprise me with the wet. Go ahead."

"You like games, don't you?"

"Go ahead. I'll close my eyes."

I walked down to the edge of the pool and dove in. The water felt colder than it had earlier, and when I broke through and was headed blindly down I felt a touch of panic. At the top again, I started to swim the length of the pool and then turned at the end and started back, but suddenly I was sure that when I left the water Brenda would be gone. I'd be alone in this damn place. I started for the side and pulled myself up and ran to the chairs and Brenda was there and I kissed her.

"God," she shivered. "You didn't stay long."

"I know."

"My turn," she said, and then she was up and a second later I heard a little crack of water and then nothing. Nothing for quite a while.

"Bren," I called softly, "are you all right?" but no one answered.

I found her glasses on the chair beside me and held them in my hands. "Brenda?"

Nothing.

"Brenda?"

"No fair calling," she said and gave me her drenched self. "Your turn," she said.

This time I stayed below the water for a long while and when I surfaced again my lungs were ready to pop. I threw my head back for air and above me saw the sky, low like a hand pushing down, and I began to swim as though to move out from under its pressure. I wanted to get back to Brenda, for I worried once again—and there was no evidence, was there?—that if I stayed away too long she would not be there when I returned. I wished that I had carried her glasses away with me, so she would have to wait for me to lead her back home. I was having crazy thoughts, I knew, and yet they did not seem uncalled for in the darkness and strangeness of that place. Oh how I wanted to call out to her from the pool, but I knew she would not answer and I forced myself to swim the length a third time, and then a fourth, but midway through the fifth I felt a weird fright again, had momentary thoughts of my own extinction, and that time when I came back I held her tighter than either of us expected.

"Let go, let go," she laughed, "my turn—"

"But Brenda—"

But Brenda was gone and this time it seemed as though she'd never come back. I settled back and waited for the sun to dawn over the ninth hole, prayed it would if only for the comfort of its light, and when Brenda finally returned to me I would not let her go, and her cold wetness crept into me somehow and made me shiver. "That's it, Brenda. Please, no more games," I said, and then when I spoke again I held her so tightly I almost dug my body into hers, "I love you," I said, "I do."

So the summer went on. I saw Brenda every evening: we went swimming, we went for walks, we went for rides, up through the mountains so far and so long that by the time we started back the fog had begun to emerge from the trees and push out into the road, and I would tighten my hands on the wheel and Brenda would put on her glasses and watch the white line for me. And we would eat—a few nights after my discovery of the fruit refrigerator Brenda led me to it herself. We would fill huge soup bowls with cherries, and in serving dishes for roast beef we would heap slices of watermelon. Then we would go up and out the back doorway of the basement and onto the back lawn and sit under the sporting-goods tree, the light from the TV room the only brightness we had out there. All we would hear for a while were just the two of us spitting pits. "I wish they would take root overnight and in the morning there'd just be watermelons and cherries."

"If they took root in this yard, sweetie, they'd grow refrigerators and Westinghouse Preferred. I'm not being nasty," I'd add quickly, and Brenda would laugh, and say she felt like a greengage plum, and I would disappear down into the basement and the cherry bowl would now be a greengage plum bowl, and then a nectarine bowl, and then a peach bowl, until, I have to admit it, I cracked my frail bowel, and would have to spend the following night, sadly, on the wagon. And then too we went out for corned beef sandwiches, pizza, beer and shrimp, ice cream sodas, and hamburgers. We went to the Lions Club Fair one night and Brenda won a Lions Club ashtray by shooting three baskets in a row. And when Ron came home from Milwaukee we went from time to time to see him play basketball in the semi-pro summer league, and it was those evenings that I felt a stranger with Brenda, for she knew all the players' names, and though for the most part they were gawky-limbed and dull, there was one named Luther Ferrari who was neither, and whom Brenda had dated for a whole year in high school. He was Ron's closest friend and I remembered his name from the Newark *News:* he was one of the great Ferrari brothers, All State all of them in at least two sports. It was Ferrari who called Brenda Buck, a nickname which apparently went back to her ribbon-winning days. Like Ron, Ferrari was exceedingly polite, as though it were some affliction of those over six feet three; he was gentlemanly towards me and gentle towards Brenda, and after a while I balked when the suggestion was made that we go to see Ron play. And then one night we discovered that at eleven o'clock the cashier of the Hilltop Theatre went home and the manager disappeared into his office, and so that summer we saw the last quarter of at least fifteen movies, and then when we were driving home—driving Brenda home, that is—we would try to reconstruct the beginnings of the films. Our favorite last quarter of a movie was *Ma and Pa Kettle in the City,* our favorite fruit, greengage plums, and our favorite, our only, people, each other. Of course we ran into others from time to time, some of Brenda's friends, and occasionally, one or two of mine. One night in August we even went to a bar out on Route 6 with Laura Simpson Stolowitch and her fiancé, but it was a dreary evening. Brenda and I seemed untrained in talking to others, and so we danced a great deal, which we realized was one thing we'd never done before. Laura's boyfriend drank stingers pompously and Simp—Brenda wanted me to call her Stolo but I didn't—Simp drank a tepid combination of something like ginger ale and soda. Whenever we returned to the table, Simp would be talking about "the dance" and her fiancé about "the film," until finally Brenda asked him "Which film?" and then we danced till closing time. And when we went back to Brenda's we filled a bowl with cherries which we carried into the TV room and ate sloppily for a while; and later, on the sofa, we loved each other and when I moved from the darkened room to the bathroom I could always feel cherry pits against my bare soles. At home, undressing for the second time that night, I would find red marks on the undersides of my feet.

And how did her parents take all of this? Mrs. Patimkin continued to smile at me and Mr. Patimkin continued to think I ate like a bird. When invited to dinner I would, for his benefit, eat twice what I wanted, but the truth seemed to be that after he'd characterized my appetite that first time, he never really bothered to look again. I might have eaten ten times my normal amount, have finally killed myself with food, he would still have considered me not a man but a sparrow. No one seemed distressed by my presence, though Julie had cooled considerably; consequently, when Brenda suggested to her father that at the end of August I spend a week of my vacation at the Patimkin house, he pondered a moment, decided on the five iron, made his approach shot, and said yes. And when she passed on to her mother the decision of Patimkin Sink, there wasn't much Mrs. Patimkin could do. So, through Brenda's craftiness, I was invited.

On that Friday morning that was to be my last day of work, my Aunt Gladys saw me packing my bag and she asked where I was going. I told her. She did not answer and I thought I saw awe in those red-rimmed hysterical eyes—I had come a long way since that day she'd said to me on the phone, "Fancy-shmancy."

"How long you going, I should know how to shop I wouldn't buy too much. You'll leave me with a refrigerator full of milk it'll go bad it'll stink up the refrigerator—"

"A week," I said.

"A *week?*" she said. "They got room for a week?"

"Aunt Gladys, they don't live over the store."

"I lived over a store I wasn't ashamed. Thank God we always had a roof. We never went begging in the streets," she told me as I packed the Bermudas I'd just bought, "and your cousin Susan we'll put through college, Uncle Max should live and be well. We didn't send her away to camp for August, she doesn't have shoes when she wants them, sweaters she doesn't have a drawerful—"

"I didn't say anything, Aunt Gladys."

"You don't get enough to eat here? You leave over sometimes I show your Uncle Max your plate it's a shame. A child in Europe could make a four-course meal from what you leave over."

"Aunt Gladys." I went over to her. "I get everything I want here. I'm just taking a vacation. Don't I deserve a vacation?"

She held herself to me and I could feel her trembling. "I told your mother I would take care of her Neil she shouldn't worry. And now you go running—"

I put my arms around her and kissed her on the top of her head. "C'mon," I said, "you're being silly. I'm not running away. I'm just going away for a week, on a vacation."

"You'll leave their telephone number God forbid you should get sick."

"Okay."

"Millburn they live?"

"Short Hills. I'll leave the number."

"Since when do Jewish people live in Short Hills? They couldn't be real Jews believe me."

"They're real Jews," I said.

"I'll see it I'll believe it." She wiped her eyes with the corner of her apron, just as I was zipping up the sides of the suitcase. "Don't close the bag yet. I'll make a little package with some fruit in it, you'll take with you."

"Okay, Aunt Gladys," and on the way to work that morning I ate the orange and the two peaches that she'd put in a bag for me.

A few hours later Mr. Scapello informed me that when I returned from my vacation after Labor Day, I would be hoisted up onto Martha Winney's stool. He himself, he said, had made the same move some twelve years ago, and so it appeared that if I could manage to maintain my balance I might someday be Mr. Scapello. I would also get an eight-dollar increase in salary which was five dollars more than the increase Mr. Scapello had received years before. He shook my hand and then started back up the long flight of marble stairs, his behind barging against his suit jacket like a hoop. No sooner had he left my side then I smelled spearmint and looked up to see the old man with veiny nose and jowls.

"Hello, young man," he said pleasantly. "Is the book back?"

"What book?"

"The Gauguin. I was shopping and I thought I'd stop by to ask. I haven't gotten the card yet. It's two weeks already."

"No," I said, and as I spoke I saw that Mr. Scapello had stopped midway up the stairs and turned as though he'd forgotten to tell me something. "Look," I said to the old man, "it should be back any day." I said it with a finality that bordered on rudeness, and I alarmed myself, for suddenly I saw what would happen: the old man making a fuss, Mr. Scapello gliding down the stairs, Mr. Scapello scampering up to the stacks, Scapello scandalized, Scapello profuse, Scapello presiding at the ascension of John McKee to Miss Winney's stool. I turned to the old man, "Why don't you leave your phone number and I'll try to get a hold of it this afternoon—" but my attempt at concern and courtesy came too late, and the man growled some words about public servants, a letter to the Mayor, snotty kids, and left the library, thank God, only a second before Mr. Scapello returned to my desk to remind me that everyone was chipping in for a present for Miss Winney and that if I liked I should leave a half dollar on his desk during the day.

After lunch the colored kid came in. When he headed past the desk for the stairs, I called over to him. "Come here," I said. "Where are you going?"

"The heart section."

"What book are you reading?"

"That Mr. Go-again's book. Look, man, I ain't doing nothing wrong. I didn't do *no* writing in *any*thing. You could search me—"

"I know you didn't. Listen, if you like that book so much why don't you please take it home? Do you have a library card?"

"No, sir, I didn't take *nothing.*"

"No, a library card is what we give to you so you can take books home. Then you won't have to come down here every day. Do you go to school?"

"Yes, sir. Miller Street School. But this here's summertime. It's okay I'm not in school. I ain't *supposed* to be in school."

"I know. As long as you go to school you can *have* a library card. You could take the book home."

"What you keep telling me take that book home for? At home somebody dee-*stroy* it."

"You could hide it someplace, in a desk—"

"Man," he said, squinting at me, "why don't you want me to come round here?"

"I didn't say you shouldn't."

"I *likes* to come here. I likes them stairs."

"I like them too," I said. "But the trouble is that someday somebody's going to take that book out."

He smiled. "Don't you worry," he said to me. "Ain't nobody done that yet," and he tapped off to the stairs and Stack Three.

Did I perspire that day! It was the coolest of the summer, but when I left work in the evening my shirt was sticking to my back. In the car I opened my bag, and while the rush-hour traffic flowed down Washington Street, I huddled in the back and changed into a clean shirt so that when I reached Short Hills I'd look as though I was deserving of an interlude in the suburbs. But driving up Central Avenue I could not keep my mind on my vacation, or for that matter on my driving: to the distress of pedestrians and motorists, I ground gears, overshot crosswalks, hesitated at green and red lights alike. I kept thinking that while I was on vacation that jowly bastard would return to the library, that the colored kid's book would disappear, that my new job would be taken away from me, that, in fact my old job—but then why should I worry about that: the library wasn't going to be *my* life.

5

"Ron's getting married!" Julie screamed at me when I came through the door. "Ron's getting married!"

"Now?" I said.

"Labor Day! He's marrying Harriet, he's marrying Harriet." She began to sing it like a jump-rope song, nasal and rhythmic. "I'm going to be a sister-in-law!"

"Hi," Brenda said, "I'm going to be a sister-in-law."

"So I hear. When did it happen?"

"This afternoon he told us. They spoke long distance for forty minutes last night. She's flying here next week, and there's going to be a *huge* wedding. My parents are flittering all over the place. They've got to arrange everything in about a day or two. And my father's taking Ron in the business—but he's going to have to start at two hundred a week and then work himself up. That'll take till October."

"I thought he was going to be a gym teacher."

"He was. But now he has responsibilities . . ."

At the dinner Ron expanded on the subject of responsibilities and the future.

"We're going to have a boy," he said, to his mother's delight, "and when he's about six months old I'm going to sit him down with a basketball in front of him, and a football, and a baseball, and then whichever one he reaches for, that's the one we're going to concentrate on."

"Suppose he doesn't reach for any of them," Brenda said.

"Don't be funny, young lady," Mrs. Patimkin said.

"I'm going to be an aunt," Julie sang, and she stuck her tongue out at Brenda.

"When is Harriet coming?" Mr. Patimkin breathed through a mouthful of potatoes.

"A week from yesterday."

"Can she sleep in my room?" Julie cried. "*Can* she?"

"No, the guest room—" Mrs. Patimkin began, but then she remembered me—with a crushing side glance from those purple eyes, and said, "Of course."

Well, I did eat like a bird. After dinner my bag was carried—by me—up to the guest room which was across from Ron's room and right down the hall from Brenda. Brenda came along to show me the way.

"Let me see your bed, Bren."

"Later," she said.

"Can we? Up here?"

"I think so," she said. "Ron sleeps like a log."

"Can I stay the night?"

"I don't know."

"I could get up early and come back in here. We'll set the alarm."

"It'll wake everybody up."

"I'll remember to get up. I can do it."

"I better not stay up here with you too long," she said. "My mother'll have a fit. I think she's nervous about your being here."

"So am I. I hardly know them. Do you think I should really stay a whole week?"

"A whole week? Once Harriet gets here it'll be so chaotic you can probably stay two months."

"You think so?"

"Yes."

"Do you want me to?"

"Yes," she said, and went down the stairs so as to ease her mother's conscience.

I unpacked my bag and dropped my clothes into a drawer that was empty except for a packet of dress shields and a high school yearbook. In the middle of my unpacking, Ron came clunking up the stairs.

"Hi," he called into my room.

"Congratulations," I called back. I should have realized that any word of ceremony would provoke a handshake from Ron; he interrupted whatever it was he was about to do in his room, and came into mine.

"Thanks." He pumped me. "Thanks."

Then he sat down on my bed and watched me as I finished unpacking. I have one shirt with a Brooks Brothers label and I let it linger on the bed a while; the Arrows I heaped in the drawer. Ron sat there rubbing his forearm and grinning. After a while I was thoroughly unsettled by the silence.

"Well," I said, "that's something."

He agreed, to *what* I don't know.

"How does it feel?" I asked, after another longer silence.

"Better. Ferrari smacked it under the boards."

"Oh. Good," I said. "How does getting married feel?"

"Ah, okay, I guess."

I leaned against the bureau and counted stitches in the carpet.

Ron finally risked a journey into language. "Do you know anything about music?" he asked.

"Something, yes."

"You can listen to my phonograph if you want."

"Thanks, Ron. I didn't know you were interested in music."

"Sure. I got all the Andre Kostelanetz records ever made. You like Mantovani? I got all of him too. I like semiclassical a lot. You can hear my Columbus record if you want . . ." he dwindled off. Finally he shook my hand and left.

Downstairs I could hear Julie singing. "I'm going to be an a-a-aunt," and Mrs. Patimkin saying to her, "No, honey, you're going to be a sister-in-law. Sing that, sweetheart," but Julie continued to sing, "I'm going to be an a-a-aunt," and then I heard Brenda's voice joining hers, singing, "We're going to be an a-a-aunt," and then Julie joined that, and finally Mrs. Patimkin called to Mr. Patimkin, "Will you make her stop encouraging her . . ." and soon the duet ended.

And then I heard Mrs. Patimkin again. I couldn't make out the words but Brenda answered her. Their voices grew louder; finally I could hear perfectly. "I need a houseful of company at a time like this?" It was Mrs. Patimkin. "I asked you, Mother." "You asked your father. I'm the one you should have asked first. He doesn't know how much extra work this is for me . . ." "My God, Mother, you'd think we didn't have Carlota and Jenny." "Carlota and Jenny can't do everything. This is not the Salvation Army!" "What the hell does that mean?" "Watch your tongue, young lady. That may be very well for your college friends." "Oh, *stop* it, Mother!" "Don't raise your voice to me. When's the last time you lifted a finger to help around here!" "I'm not a slave . . . I'm a daughter." "You ought to learn what a day's work means." "Why?" Brenda said. *"Why!"* "Because you're lazy," Mrs. Patimkin answered, "and you think the world owes you a living." "Whoever said *that!"* "You ought to earn some money and buy your own clothes." "Why? Good God, Mother, Daddy could live off the stocks alone, for God's sake. What are you complaining about!" "When's the last time you washed the dishes!" "Jesus Christ!" Brenda flared, "Carlota washes the dishes!" "Don't Jesus Christ me!" "Oh, Mother!" and Brenda was crying. "Why the hell are you like this!" "That's it," Mrs. Patimkin said, "cry in front of your company . . ." "My *company* . . ." Brends wept, "why don't you go yell at him too . . . why is everyone so nasty to me . . ."

From across the hall I heard Andre Kostelanetz let several thousand singing violins loose on "Night and Day." Ron's door was open and I saw he was stretched out, colossal, on his bed; he was singing along with the record. The words belonged to Night and Day," but I didn't recognize Ron's tune. In a minute he picked up the phone and asked the operator for a Milwaukee number. While she connected him, he rolled over and turned up the volume on the record player, so that it would carry the nine hundred miles west.

I heard Julie downstairs. "Ha ha, Brenda's crying, ha ha, Brenda's crying."

And then Brenda was running up the stairs. "Your day'll come, you little bastard!" she called.

"Brenda!" Mrs. Patimkin called.

"Mommy!" Julie cried. "Brenda cursed at me!"

"What's going *on* here!" Mr. Patimkin shouted.

"You call *me,* Mrs. P?" Carlota shoulted.

And Ron, in the other room, said, "Hello, Har, I told them . . ."

I sat down on my Brooks Brothers shirt and pronounced my own name out loud.

"Goddam her!" Brenda said to me as she paced up and down my room.

"Bren, do you think I should go—"

"Shhh . . ." She went to the door of my room and listened. "They're going visiting, thank God."

"Brenda—"

"Shhh . . . They've gone."

"Julie too?"

"Yes," she said. "Is Ron in his room? His door is closed."

"He went out."

"You can't hear anybody move around here. They all creep around in *sneakers.* Oh Neil."

"Bren, I asked you, maybe I should just stay through tomorrow and then go."

"Oh, it isn't you she's angry about."

"I'm not helping any."

"It's Ron, really. That he's getting married just has her flipped. And me. Now with that goody-good Harriet around she'll just forget I ever exist."

"Isn't that okay with you?"

She walked off to the window and looked outside. It was dark and cool; the trees rustled and flapped as though they were sheets that had been hung out to dry. Everything outside hinted at September, and for the first time I realized how close we were to Brenda's departure for school.

"Is it, Bren?" but she was not listening to me.

She walked across the room to a door at the far end of the room. She opened it.

"I thought that was a closet," I said.

"Come here."

She held the door back and we leaned into the darkness and could hear the strange wind hissing in the eaves of the house.

"What's in here?" I said.

"Money."

Brenda went into the room. When the puny sixty-watt bulb was twisted on, I saw that the place was full of old furniture—two wing chairs with hair-oil lines at the back, a sofa with a paunch in its middle, a bridge table, two bridge chairs with their stuffing showing, a mirror whose backing had peeled off, shadeless lamps, lampless shades, a coffee table with a cracked glass top, and a pile of rolled up shades.

"What is this?" I said.

"A storeroom. Our old furniture."

"How old?"

"From Newark," she said. "Come here." She was on her hands and knees in front of the sofa and was holding up its paunch to peek beneath.

"Brenda, what the hell are we doing here? You're getting filthy."

"It's not here."

"*What?*"

"The money. I told you."

I sat down on a wing chair, raising some dust. It had begun to rain outside, and we could smell the fall dampness coming through the vent that was outlined at the far end of the storeroom. Brenda got up from the floor and sat down on the sofa. Her knees and Bermudas were dirty and when she pushed her hair back she dirtied her forehead. There among the disarrangement and dirt I had the strange experience of seeing us, *both* of us, placed among disarrangement and dirt: we looked like a young couple who had just moved into a new apartment; we had suddenly taken stock of our furniture, finances, and future, and all we could feel any pleasure about was the clean smell of outside, which reminded us we were alive, but which, in a pinch, would not feed us.

"What money?" I said again.

"The hundred-dollar bills. From when I was a little girl . . ." and she breathed deeply. "When I was little and we'd just moved from Newark, my father took me up here one day. He took me into this room and told me that if anything should ever happen to him, he wanted me to know where there was some money that I should have. He said it wasn't for anybody else but me, and that I should never tell anyone about it, not even Ron. Or my mother."

"How much was it?"

"Three hundred-dollar bills. I'd never seen them before. I was nine, around Julie's age. I don't think we'd been living here a month. I remember I used to come up here about once a week, when no one was home but Carlota, and crawl under the sofa and make sure it was still here. And it always was. He never mentioned it once again. Never."

"Where is it? Maybe someone stole it."

"I don't know, Neil. I suppose he took it back."

"When it was gone," I said, "my God, didn't you tell him? Maybe Carlota—"

"I never knew it was gone, until just now. I guess I stopped looking at one time or another . . . And then I forgot about it. Or just didn't think about it. I mean I always had enough, I didn't need this. I guess one day *he* figured I wouldn't need it."

Brenda paced up to the narrow, dust-covered window and drew her initials on it.

"Why did you want it now?" I said.

"I don't know . . ." she said and went over and twisted the bulb off.

I didn't move from the chair and Brenda, in her tight shorts and shirt, seemed naked standing there a few feet away. Then I saw her shoulders shaking. "I wanted to find it and tear it up in little pieces and put the goddam pieces in her purse! If it was there, I swear it, I would have done it."

"I wouldn't have let you, Bren."

"Wouldn't you have?"

"No."

"Make love to me, Neil. Right now."

"Where?"

"Do it! *Here.* On this cruddy cruddy cruddy sofa."

And I obeyed her.

The next morning Brenda made breakfast for the two of us. Ron had gone off to his first day of work—I'd heard him singing in the shower only an hour after I'd returned to my own room; in fact, I had still been awake when the Chrysler had pulled out of the garage, carrying boss and son down to the Patimkin works in Newark. Mrs. Patimkin wasn't home either; she had taken her car and had gone off to the Temple to talk to Rabbi Kranitz about the wedding. Julie was on the back lawn playing at helping Carlota hang the clothes.

"You know what I want to do this morning?" Brenda said. We were eating a grapefruit, sharing it rather sloppily, for Brenda couldn't find a paring knife, and so we'd decided to peel it down like an orange and eat the segments separately.

"What?" I said.

"Run," she said. "Do you ever run?"

"You mean on a track? God, yes. In high school we had to run a mile every month. So we wouldn't be Momma's boys. I think the bigger your lungs get the more you're supposed to hate your mother."

"I want to run," she said, "and I want you to run. Okay?"

"Oh, Brenda . . ."

But an hour later, after a breakfast that consisted of another grapefruit, which apparently is all a runner is supposed to eat in the morning, we had driven the Volkswagen over to the high school, behind which was a quarter-mile track. Some kids were playing with a dog out in the grassy center of the track, and at the far end, near the woods, a figure in white shorts with slits in the side, and no shirt, was twirling, twirling, and then flinging a shot put as far as he could. After it left his hand he did a little eagle-eyed tap dance while he watched it arch and bend and land in the distance.

"You know," Brenda said, "you look like me. Except bigger."

We were dressed similarly, sneakers, sweat socks, khaki Bermudas, and sweat shirts, but I had the feeling that Brenda was not talking about the accidents of our dress—if they were accidents. She meant, I was sure, that I was somehow beginning to look the way she wanted me to. Like herself.

"Let's see who's faster," she said, and then we started along the track. Within the first eighth of a mile the three little boys and their dog were following us. As we passed the corner where the shot putter was, he waved at us; Brenda called "Hi!" and I smiled, which, as you may or may not know, makes one engaged in serious running feel inordinately silly. At the quarter mile the kids dropped off and retired to the grass, the dog turned and started the other way, and I had a tiny knife in my side. Still I was abreast of Brenda, who as we started on the second lap, called "Hi!" once again to the lucky shot putter, who was reclining on the grass now, watching us, and rubbing his shot like a crystal ball. Ah, I thought, there's the sport.

"How about us throwing the shot put?" I panted.

"After," she said, and I saw beads of sweat clinging to the last strands of hair that shagged off her ear. When we approached the half mile Brenda suddenly swerved off the track onto the grass and tumbled down; her departure surprised me and I was still running.

"Hey, Bob Mathias," she called, "let's lie in the sun . . ."

But I acted as though I didn't hear her and though my heart pounded in my throat and my mouth was dry as a drought, I made my legs move, and swore I would not stop until I'd finished one more lap. As I passed the shot putter for the third time, I called "Hi!"

She was excited when I finally pulled up alongside of her. "You're good," she said. My hands were on my hips and I was looking at the ground and sucking air—rather, air was sucking me, I didn't have much to say about it.

"Uh-huh," I breathed.

"Let's do this every morning," she said. "We'll get up and have two grapefruit, and then you'll come out here and run. I'll time you. In two weeks you'll break four minutes, won't you, sweetie? I'll get Ron's stop watch." She was so excited—she'd slid over on the grass and was pushing my socks up against my wet ankles and calves. She bit my kneecap.

"Okay," I said.

"Then we'll go back and have a real breakfast."

"Okay."

"You drive back," she said, and suddenly she was up and running ahead of me, and then we were headed back in the car.

And the next morning, my mouth still edgy from the grapefruit segments, we were at the track. We had Ron's stop watch and a towel for me, for when I was finished.

"My legs are a little sore," I said.

"Do some exercises," Brenda said. I'll do them with you." She heaped the towel on the grass and together we did deep knee bends, and sit-ups, and push-ups, and some high-knee raising in place. I felt overwhelmingly happy.

"I'm just going to run a half today, Bren. We'll see what I do . . ." and I heard Brenda click the watch, and then when I was on the far side of the track, the clouds trailing above me like my own white, fleecy tail, I saw that Brenda was on the ground, hugging her knees, and alternately checking the watch and looking out at me. We were the only ones there, and it all reminded me of one of those scenes in race-horse movies, where an old trainer like Walter Brennan and a young handsome man clock the beautiful girl's horse in the early Kentucky morning, to see if it really is the fastest two-year-old alive. There were differences all right—one being simply that at the quarter mile Brenda shouted out to me, "A minute and fourteen seconds," but it was pleasant and exciting and clean and when I was finished Brenda was standing up and waiting for me. Instead of a tape to break I had Brenda's sweet flesh to meet, and I did, and it was the first time she said that she loved me.

We ran—I ran—every morning, and by the end of the week I was running a 7:02 mile, and always at the end there was the little click of the watch and Brenda's arms.

At night, I would read in my pajamas, while Brenda, in her room, read, and we would wait for Ron to go to sleep. Some nights we had to wait longer than others, and I would hear the leaves swishing outside, for it had grown cooler at the end of August, and the air-conditioning was turned off at night and we were all allowed to open our windows. Finally Ron would be ready for bed. He would stomp around his room and then he would come to the door in his shorts and T-shirt and go into the bathroom where he would urinate loudly and brush his teeth. After he brushed his teeth I would go in to brush mine. We would pass in the hall and I would give him a hearty and sincere "Good night." Once in the bathroom, I would spend a moment admiring my tan in the mirror; behind me I could see Ron's jock straps hanging out to dry on the Hot and Cold knobs of the shower. Nobody ever questioned their tastefulness as adornment, and after a few nights I didn't even notice them.

While Ron brushed his teeth and I waited in my bed for my turn, I could hear the record player going in his room. Generally, after coming in from basketball, he would call Harriet—who was now only a few days away from us—and then would lock himself up with *Sports Illustrated* and Mantovani; however, when he emerged from his room for his evening toilet, it was not a Mantovani record I would hear playing, but something else, apparently what he'd once referred to as his Columbus record. I *imagined* that was what I heard, for I could not tell much from the last moments of sound. All I heard were bells moaning evenly and soft patriotic music behind them, and riding over it all, a deep kind of Edward R. Murrow gloomy voice: "*And so goodbye, Columbus,*" the voice intoned, ". . . *goodbye, Columbus . . . goodbye . . .*" Then there would be silence and Ron would be back in his room; the light would switch off and in only a few minutes I would hear him rumbling down into that exhilarating, restorative, vitamin-packed sleep that I imagined athletes to enjoy.

One morning near sneaking-away time I had a dream and when I awakened from it, there was just enough dawn coming into the room for me to see the color of Brenda's hair. I touched her in her sleep, for the dream had unsettled me: it had taken place on a ship, an old sailing ship like those you see in pirate movies. With me on the ship was the little colored kid from the library—I was the captain and he my mate, and we were the only crew members. For a while it was a pleasant dream; we were anchored in the harbor of an island in the Pacific and it was very sunny. Up on the beach there were beautiful bare-skinned Negresses, and none of them moved;

but suddenly *we* were moving, our ship, out of the harbor, and the Negresses moved slowly down to the shore and began to throw leis at us and say "Goodbye, Columbus . . . goodbye, Columbus . . . goodbye . . ." and though we did not want to go, the little boy and I, the boat was moving and there was nothing we could do about it, and he shouted at me that it was my fault and I shouted it was his for not having a library card, but we were wasting our breath, for we were further and further from the island, and soon the natives were nothing at all. Space was all out of proportion in the dream, and things were sized and squared in no way I'd ever seen before, and I think it was that more than anything else that steered me into consciousness. I did not want to leave Brenda's side that morning, and for a while I played with the little point at the nape of her neck, where she'd had her hair cut. I stayed longer than I should have, and when finally I returned to my room I almost ran into Ron who was preparing for his day at Patimkin Kitchen and Bathroom Sinks.

6

That morning was supposed to have been my last at the Patimkin house; however, when I began to throw my things into my bag late in the day, Brenda told me I could unpack—somehow she'd managed to inveigle another week out of her parents, and I would be able to stay right through till Labor Day, when Ron would be married; then, the following morning Brenda would be off to school and I would go back to work. So we would be with each other until the summer's last moment.

This should have made me overjoyed, but as Brenda trotted back down the stairs to accompany her family to the airport—where they were to pick up Harriet—I was not joyful but disturbed, as I had been more and more with the thought that when Brenda went back to Radcliffe, that would be the end for me. I was convinced that even Miss Winney's stool was not high enough for me to see clear up to Boston. Nevertheless, I tossed my clothing back into the drawer and was able, finally, to tell myself that there'd been no hints of ending our affair from Brenda, and any suspicions I had, any uneasiness, was spawned in my own uncertain heart. Then I went into Ron's room to call my aunt.

"Hello?" she said.

"Aunt Gladys," I said, "how are you?"

"You're sick."

"No, I'm having a fine time. I wanted to call you, I'm going to stay another week."

"Why?"

"I told you. I'm having a good time. Mrs. Patimkin asked me to stay until Labor Day."

"You've got clean underwear?"

"I'm washing it at night. I'm okay, Aunt Gladys."

"By hand you can't get it clean."

"It's clean enough. Look, Aunt Gladys, I'm having a wonderful time."

"*Shmutz* he lives in and I shouldn't worry."

"How's Uncle Max?" I asked.

"What should he be? Uncle Max is Uncle Max. You, I don't like the way your voice sounds."

"Why? Do I sound like I've got on dirty underwear?"

"Smart guy. Someday you'll learn."

"What?"

"What do you mean *what*? You'll find out. You'll stay there too long you'll be too good for us."

"Never, sweetheart," I said.

"I'll see it I'll believe it."

"Is it cool in Newark, Aunt Gladys?"

"It's snowing," she said.

"Hasn't it been cool all week?"

"You sit around all day it's cool. For me it's not February, believe me."

"Okay, Aunt Gladys. Say hello to everybody."

"You got a letter from your mother."

"Good. I'll read it when I get home."

"You couldn't take a ride down you'll read it?"

"It'll wait. I'll drop them a note. Be a good girl," I said.

"What about your socks?"

"I go barefoot. Goodbye, honey." And I hung up.

Down in the kitchen Carlota was getting dinner ready. I was always amazed at how Carlota's work never seemed to get in the way of her life. She made household chores seem like illustrative gestures of whatever it was she was singing, even, if as now, it was "I Get a Kick out of You." She moved from the oven to the automatic dishwasher—she pushed buttons, turned dials, peeked in the glass-doored oven, and from time to time picked a big black grape out of a bunch that lay on the sink. She chewed and chewed, humming all the time, and then, with a deliberated casualness, shot the skin and the pit directly into the garbage disposal unit. I said hello to her as I went out the back door, and though she did not return the greeting, I felt a kinship with one who, like me, had been partially wooed and won on Patimkin fruit.

Out on the lawn I shot baskets for a while; then I picked up an iron and drove a cotton golf ball limply up into the sunlight; then I kicked a soccer ball towards the oak tree; then I tried shooting foul shots again. Nothing diverted me—I felt open-stomached, as though I hadn't eaten for months, and though I went back inside and came out with my own handful of grapes, the feeling continued, and I knew it had nothing to do with my caloric intake; it was only a rumor of the hollowness that would come when Brenda was away. The fact of her departure had, of course, been on my mind for a while, but overnight it had taken on a darker hue. Curiously, the darkness seemed to have something to do with Harriet, Ron's intended, and I thought for a time that it was simply the reality of Harriet's arrival that had dramatized the passing of time: we had been talking about it and now suddenly it was here—just as Brenda's departure would be here before we knew it.

But it was more than that: the union of Harriet and Ron reminded me that separation need not be a permanent state. People could marry each other, even if they were young! And yet Brenda and I had never mentioned marriage, except perhaps for that night at the pool when she'd said, "When you love me, everything will be all right." Well, I loved her, and she me, and things didn't seem all right at all. Or was I inventing troubles again? I supposed I should really have thought my lot improved considerably; yet, there on the lawn, the August sky seemed too beautiful and temporary to bear, and I wanted Brenda to marry me. Marriage, though, was not what I proposed to her when she drove the car up the driveway, along, some fifteen minutes later. That proposal would have taken a kind of courage that I did not think I had. I did not feel myself prepared for any answer but "Hallelujah!" Any other kind of yes wouldn't have satisfied me, and any kind of no, even one masked behind the words, "Let's wait, sweetheart," would have been my end. So I imagine that's why I proposed the surrogate, which turned out finally to be far more daring than I knew it to be at the time.

"Harriet's plane is late, so I drove home," Brenda called.

"Where's everyone else?"

"They're going to wait for her and have dinner at the airport. I have to tell Carlota," and she went inside.

In a few minutes she appeared on the porch. She wore a yellow dress that cut a wide-bottomed U across her shoulders and neck, and showed where the tanned flesh began above her breasts. On the lawn she stepped out of her heels and walked barefoot over to where I was sitting under the oak tree.

"Women who wear high heels all the time get tipped ovaries," she said.

"Who told you that?"

"I don't remember. I like to think everything's shipshape in there."

"Brenda, I want to ask you something . . ."

She yanked the blanket with the big O on it over to us and sat down. "What?" she said.

"I know this is out of the blue, though really it's not . . . I want you to buy a diaphragm. To go to a doctor and get one."

She smiled. "Don't worry, sweetie, we're careful. Everything is okay."

"But that's the safest."

"We're safe. It'd be a waste."

"Why take chances?"

"But we *aren't*. How many things do you need."

"Honey, it isn't bulk I'm interested in. It's not even safety," I added.

"You just want me to own one, is that it? Like a walking stick, or a pith helmet—"

"Brenda, I want you to own one for . . . for the sake of pleasure."

"Pleasure? Whose? The doctor's?"

"Mine," I said.

She did not answer me, but rubbed her fingers along the ridge of her collarbone to wipe away the tony globes of perspiration that had suddenly formed there.

"No, Neil, it's silly."

"Why?"

"Why? It just is."

"You know why it's silly, Brenda—because *I* asked you to do it?"

"That's sillier."

"If you asked *me* to buy a diaphragm we'd have to go straight to the Yellow Pages and find a gynecologist open on Saturday afternoon."

"I would never ask you to do that, baby."

"It's the truth," I said, though I was smiling. "It's the truth."

"It's not," she said, and got up and walked over to the basketball court, where she walked on the white lines that Mr. Patimkin had laid the day before.

"Come back here," I said.

"Neil, it's silly and I don't want to talk about it."

"Why are you being so selfish."

"Selfish? You're the one who's being selfish. It's your pleasure . . ."

"That's right. My pleasure. Why not!"

"Don't raise you voice. Carlota."

"Then get the hell over here," I said.

She walked over to me, leaving white footprints on the grass. "I didn't think you were such a creature of the flesh," she said.

"Didn't you?" I said. "I'll tell you something that you ought to know. It's not even the pleasures of the flesh I'm talking about."

"Then frankly, I don't know *what* you're talking about. Why you're even bothering. Isn't what we use sufficient?"

"I'm bothering just because I want you to go to a doctor and get a diaphragm. That's all. No explanation. Just do it. Do it because I asked you to."

"You're not being reasonable—"

"Goddamit, Brenda!"

"Goddamit youself!" she said and went up into the house.

I closed my eyes and leaned back and in fifteen minutes, or maybe less, I heard somebody stroking at the cotton golf ball. She had changed into shorts and a blouse and was still barefoot.

We didn't speak with each other, but I watched her bring the club back of her ear, and then swing through, her chin tilted up with the line of flight a regular golf ball would have taken.

"That's five hundred yards," I said.

She didn't answer but walked after the cotton ball and then readied for another swing.

"Brenda. Please come here."

She walked over, dragging the club over the grass.

"What?"

"I don't want to argue with you."

"Nor I with you," she said. "It was the first time."

"Was it such an awful thing for me to ask?"

She nodded.

"Bren, I know it was probably a surprise. It was for me. But we're not children."

"Neil, I just don't want to. It's not because you asked me to, either. I don't know where you get that from. That's not it."

"Then why is it?"

"Oh everything. I just don't feel *old* enough for all that equipment."

"What does age have to do with it?"

"I don't mean age. I just mean—well, *me.* I mean it's so conscious a thing to do."

"Of course it's conscious. That's exactly it. Don't you see? It would change us."

"It would change me."

"Us. Together."

"Neil, how do you think I'd feel lying to some doctor."

"You can go to Margaret Sanger, in New York. They don't ask any questions."

"You've done this before?"

"No," I said. "I just know. I read Mary McCarthy."

"That's exactly right. That's just what I'd feel like, somebody out of *her.*"

"Don't be dramatic," I said.

"You're the one who's being dramatic. You think there would be something affairish about it, then. Last summer I went with this whore who I sent out to buy—"

"Oh, Brenda, you're a selfish egotistical bitch! You're the one who's thinking about 'last summer,' about an end for us. In fact, that's the whole thing, isn't it—"

"That's right, I'm a bitch. I want this to end. That's why I ask you to stay another week, that's why I let you sleep with me in my own house. What's the *matter* with you! Why don't you and my mother take turns—one day she can plague me, the next you—"

"Stop it!"

"Go to hell, all of you!" Brenda said, and now she was crying and I knew when she ran off I would not see her, as I didn't, for the rest of the afternoon.

Harriet Ehrlich impressed me as a young lady singularly unconscious of a motive in others or herself. All was surfaces, and she seemed a perfect match for Ron, and too for the Patimkins. Mrs. Patimkin, in fact, did just as Brenda prophesied: Harriet appeared, and Brenda's mother lifted one wing and pulled the girl in towards the warm underpart of her body, where Brenda herself would have liked to nestle. Harriet was built like Brenda, although a little chestier, and she nodded her head insistently whenever anyone spoke. Sometimes she would even say the last few words of your sentence with you, though that was infrequent; for the most part she nodded and kept her hands folded. All evening, as the Patimkins planned where the newlyweds should live, what furniture they should buy, how soon they should have a baby—all through this I kept thinking that Harriet was wearing white gloves, but she wasn't.

Brenda and I did not exchange a word or a glance; we sat, listening, Brenda somewhat more impatient than me. Near the end Harriet began calling Mrs. Patimkin "Mother," and once, "Mother Patimkin," and that was when Brenda went to sleep. I stayed behind, mesmerized almost by the dissection, analysis, reconsideration, and finally, the embracing of the trivial. At last Mr. and Mrs. Patimkin tumbled off to bed, and Julie, who had fallen asleep on her chair, was carried into her room by Ron. That left us two non-Patimkins together.

"Ron tells me you have a very interesting job."

"I work in the library."

"I've always liked reading."

"That'll be nice, married to Ron."

"Ron likes music."

"Yes," I said. What had I *said?*

"You must get first crack at the best-sellers," she said.

"Sometimes." I said.

"Well," she said, flapping her hands on her knees, "I'm sure we'll all have a good time together. Ron and I hope you and Brenda will double with us soon."

"Not tonight." I smiled. "Soon. Will you excuse me?"

"Good night. I like Brenda very much."

"Thank you," I said as I started up the stairs.

I knocked gently on Brenda's door.

"I'm sleeping."

"Can I come in?" I asked.

Her door opened an inch and she said, "Ron will be up soon."

"We'll leave the door open. I only want to talk."

She let me in and I sat in the chair that faced the bed.

"How do you like your sister-in-law?"

"I've met her before."

"Brenda, you don't have to sound so damn terse."

She didn't answer and I just sat there yanking the string on the shade up and down.

"Are you still angry?" I asked at last.

"Yes."

"Don't be," I said. "You can forget about my suggestion. It's not worth it if this is what's going to happen."

"What did you expect to happen?"

"Nothing. I didn't think it would be so horrendous."

"That's because you can't understand my side."

"Perhaps."

"No perhaps about it."

"*Okay,*" I said. "I just wish you'd realize what it is you're getting angry about. It's not my suggestion, Brenda."

"No? What is it?"

"It's me."

"Oh don't start that again, will you? I can't win, no matter what I say."

"Yes, you can," I said. "You have."

I walked out of her room, closing the door behind me for the night.

When I got downstairs the following morning there was a great deal of activity. In the living room I heard Mrs. Patimkin reading a list to Harriet while Julie ran in and out of rooms in search of a skate key. Carlota was vacuuming the carpet; every appliance in the kitchen was bubbling, twisting, and shaking. Brenda greeted me with a perfectly pleasant smile and in the dining room, where I walked to look out at the back lawn and the weather, she kissed me on the shoulder.

"Hello," she said.

"Hello."

"I have to go with Harriet this morning," Brenda told me. "So we can't run. Unless you want to go alone."

"No. I'll read or something. Where are you going?"

"We're going to New York. Shopping. She's going to buy a wedding dress. For after the wedding. To go away in."

"What are *you* going to buy?"

"A dress to be maid of honor in. If I go with Harriet then I can go to Bergdorf's without all the Ohrbach's business with my mother."

"Get me something, will you?" I said.

"Oh, Neil, are you going to bring that up again!"

"I was only *fooling.* I wasn't even thinking about that."

"Then why did you say it?"

"Oh Jesus!" I said, and went outside and drove my car down into Millburn Center where I had some eggs and coffee.

When I came back, Brenda was gone, and there were only Carlota, Mrs. Patimkin, and myself in the house. I tried to stay out of whichever rooms they were in, but finally Mrs. Patimkin and I wound up sitting opposite each other in the TV room. She was checking off names on a long sheet of paper she held; next to her, on the table, were two thin phone books which she consulted from time to time.

"No rest for the weary," she said to me.

I smiled hugely, embracing the proverb as though Mrs. Patimkin had just then coined it. "Yes. Of course," I said. "Would you like some help? Maybe I could help you check something."

"Oh, no," she said with a little head-shaking dismissal, "it's for Hadassah."

"Oh," I said.

I sat and watched her until she asked, "Is your mother in Hadassah?"

"I don't know if she is now. She was in Newark."

"Was she an active member?"

"I guess so, she was always planting trees in Israel for someone."

"Really?" Mrs. Patimkin said. "What's her name?"

"Esther Klugman. She's in Arizona now. Do they have Hadassah there?"

"Wherever there are Jewish women."

"Then I guess she is. She's with my father. They went there for their asthma. I'm staying with my aunt in Newark. She's not in Hadassah. My Aunt Sylvia is, though. Do you know her, Aaron Klugman and Sylvia? They belong to your club. They have a daughter, my cousin Doris—" I couldn't stop myself "—They live in Livingston. Maybe it isn't Hadassah my Aunt Sylvia belongs to. I think it's some TB organization. Or cancer. Muscular dystrophy, maybe. I know she's interested in *some* disease."

"That's very nice," Mrs. Patimkin said.

"Oh yes."

"They do very good work."

"I know."

Mrs. Patimkin, I thought, had begun to warm to me; she let the purple eyes stop peering and just look out at the world for a while without judging. "Are you interested in B'nai Brith?" she asked me. "Ron is joining, you know, as soon as he gets married."

"I think I'll wait till then," I said.

Petulantly, Mrs. Patimkin went back to her lists, and I realized it had been foolish of me to risk lightheartedness with her about Jewish affairs. "You're active in the Temple, aren't you?" I asked with all the interest I could muster.

"Yes," she said.

"What Temple do *you* belong to?" she asked in a moment.

"We used to belong to Hudson Street Synagogue. Since my parents left, I haven't had much contact."

I didn't know whether Mrs. Patimkin caught a false tone in my voice. Personally I thought I had managed my rueful confession pretty well, especially when I recalled the decade of paganism prior to my parents' departure. Regardless, Mrs. Patimkin asked immediately—and strategically it seemed—"We're all going to Temple Friday night. Why don't you come with us? I mean, are you orthodox or conservative?"

I considered. "Well, I haven't gone in a long time . . . I sort of switch . . ." I smiled. "I'm just Jewish," I said well-meaningly, but that too sent Mrs. Patimkin back to her Hadassah work. Desperately I tried to think of something that would convince her I wasn't an infidel. Finally I asked: "Do you know Martin Buber's work?"

"Buber . . . Buber," she said, looking at her Hadassah list. "Is he orthodox or conservative?" she asked.

". . . He's a philosopher."

"Is he *reformed?*" she asked, piqued either at my evasiveness or at the possibility that Buber attended Friday night services without a hat, and Mrs. Buber had only one set of dishes in her kitchen.

"Orthodox," I said faintly.

"That's very nice," she said.

"Yes."

"Isn't Hudson Street Synagogue orthodox?" she asked.

"I don't know."

"I thought you belonged."

"I was bar-mitzvahed there."

"And you don't know that it's orthodox?"

"Yes. I do. It is."

"Then *you* must be."

"Oh, yes, I am," I said. "What are you?" I popped, blushing.

"Orthodox. My husband is conservative," which meant, I took it, that he didn't care. "Brenda is nothing, as you probably know."

"Oh?" I said. "No, I didn't know that."

"She was the best Hebrew student I've ever seen," Mrs. Patimkin said, "but then, of course, she got too big for her britches."

Mrs. Patimkin looked at me, and I wondered whether courtesy demanded that I agree. "Oh, I don't know," I said at last, "I'd say Brenda is conservative. Maybe a little reformed . . ."

The phone rang, rescuing me, and I spoke a silent orthodox prayer to the Lord.

"Hello," Mrs. Patimkin said. ". . . no . . . I can *not,* I have all the Hadassah calls to make . . ."

I acted as though I were listening to the birds outside, though the closed windows let no natural noises in.

"Have Ronald drive them up . . . But we can't wait, not if we want it on time . . ."

Mrs. Patimkin glanced up at me; then she put one hand over the mouthpiece. "Would you ride down to Newark for me?"

I stood. "Yes. Surely."

"Dear?" she said back into the phone, "Neil will come for it . . . No, *Neil,* Brenda's friend . . . Yes . . . Goodbye.

"Mr. Patimkin has some silver patterns I have to see. Would you drive down to his place and pick them up?"

"Of course."

"Do you know where the shop is?"

"Yes."

"Here," she said, handing a key ring to me, "take the Volkswagen."

"My car is right outside."

"Take these," she said.

Patimkin Kitchen and Bathroom Sinks was in the heart of the Negro section of Newark. Years ago, at the time of the great immigration, it had been the Jewish section, and still one could see the little fish stores, the kosher delicatessens, the Turkish baths, where my grandparents had shopped and bathed at the beginning of the century. Even the smells had lingered: whitefish, corned beef, sour tomatoes—but now, on top of these, was the grander greasier smell of auto wrecking shops, the sour stink of a brewery, the burning odor from a leather factory; and on the streets, instead of Yiddish, one heard the shouts of Negro children playing at Willie Mays with a broom handle and half a rubber ball. The neighborhood had changed: the old Jews like my grandparents had struggled and died, and their offspring had struggled and prospered, and moved further and further west, towards the edge of Newark, then out of it, and up the slope of the Orange Mountains, until they had reached the crest and started down the other side, pouring into Gentile territory as the Scotch-Irish had poured through the Cumberland Gap. Now, in fact, the Negroes were making the same migration, following the steps of the Jews, and those who remained in the Third Ward lived the most squalid of lives and dreamed in their fetid mattresses of the piny smell of Georgia nights.

I wondered, for an instant only, if I would see the colored kid from the library on the streets here. I didn't, of course, though I was sure he lived in one of the scabby, peeling buildings out of which dogs, children, and aproned women moved continually. On the top floors, windows were open, and the very old, who could no longer creak down the long stairs to the street, sat where they had been put, in the screenless windows, their elbows resting on fluffless pillows, and their heads tipping forward on their necks, watching the push of the young and the pregnant and the unemployed. Who would come after the Negroes? Who was left? No one, I thought, and someday these streets, where my grandmother drank hot tea from an old *jahrzeit* glass, would be empty and we would all of us have moved to the crest of the Orange Mountains, and wouldn't the dead stop kicking at the slats in their coffins then?

I pulled the Volkswagen up in front of a huge garage door that said across the front of it:

PATIMKIN KITCHEN AND BATHROOM SINKS
"Any Size—Any Shape"

Inside I could see a glass-enclosed office; it was in the center of an immense warehouse. Two trucks were being loaded in the rear, and Mr. Patimkin, when I saw him, had a cigar in his mouth and was shouting at someone. It was Ron, who was wearing a white T-shirt that said Ohio State Athletic Association across the front. Though he was taller than Mr. Patimkin, and almost as stout, his hands hung weakly at his sides like a small boy's; Mr. Patimkin's cigar locomoted in his mouth. Six Negroes were loading one of the trucks feverishly, tossing—my stomach dropped—sink bowls at one another.

Ron left Mr. Patimkin's side and went back to directing the men. He thrashed his arms about a good deal, and though on the whole he seemed rather confused, he didn't appear to be at all concerned about anybody dropping a sink. Suddenly I could see myself directing the Negroes—I would have an ulcer in an hour. I could almost hear the enamel surfaces shattering on the floor. And I could hear myself: "Watch it, you guys. Be careful, will you? *Whoops!* Oh, please be—*watch it!* Watch! Oh!" Suppose Mr. Patimkin should come up to me and say, "Okay, boy, you want to marry my daughter, let's see what you can do." Well, he would see: in a moment that floor would be a shattered mosaic, a crunchy path of enamel. "Klugman, what kind of worker are you? You work like you eat!" "That's right, that's right, I'm a sparrow, let me go." "Don't you even know how to load and unload?" "Mr. Patimkin, even breathing gives me trouble, sleep tires me out, let me go, let me go . . ."

Mr. Patimkin was headed back to the fish bowl to answer a ringing phone, and I wrenched myself free of my reverie and headed towards the office too. When I entered, Mr. Patimkin looked up from the phone with his eyes; the sticky cigar was in his free hand—he moved it at me, a greeting. From outside I heard Ron call in a high voice, "You can't all go to lunch at the same time. We haven't got all day!"

"Sit down," Mr. Patimkin shot at me, though when he went back to his conversation I saw there was only one chair in the office, his. People did not sit at Patimkin Sink—here you earned your money the hard way, standing up. I busied myself looking at the several calendars that hung from filing cabinets; they showed illustrations of women so dreamy, so fantastically thighed and uddered, that one could not think of them as pornographic. The artist who had drawn the calendar girls for "Lewis Construction Company," and "Earl's Truck and Auto Repair," and "Grossman and Son, Paper Box" had been painting some third sex I had never seen.

"Sure, sure, sure," Mr. Patimkin said into the phone. "Tomorrow, don't tell me tomorrow. Tomorrow the world could blow up."

At the other end someone spoke. Who was it? Lewis from the construction company? Earl from truck repair?

"I'm running a business, Grossman, not a charity."

So it was Grossman being browbeaten at the other end.

"Shit on that," Mr. Patimkin said. "You're not the only one in town, my good friend," and he winked at me.

Ah-ha, a conspiracy against Grossman. Me and Mr. Patimkin. I smiled as collusively as I knew how.

"All right then, we're here till five . . . No later."

He wrote something on a piece of paper. It was only a big X.

"My kid'll be here," he said. "Yea, he's in the business."

Whatever Grossman said on the other end, it made Mr. Patimkin laugh. Mr. Patimkin hung up without a goodbye.

He looked out the back to see how Ron was doing. "Four years in college he can't unload a truck."

I didn't know what to say but finally chose the truth. "I guess I couldn't either."

"You could learn. What am I, a genius? I learned. Hard work never killed anybody."

To that I agreed.

Mr. Patimkin looked at his cigar. "A man works hard he's got something. You don't get anywhere sitting on your behind, you know . . . The biggest men in the country worked hard, believe me. Even Rockefeller. Success don't come easy . . ." He did not say this so much as he mused it out while he surveyed his dominion. He was not a man enamored of words, and I had the feeling that what had tempted him into this barrage of universals was probably the combination of Ron's performance and my presence—me, the outsider who might one day be an insider. But did Mr. Patimkin even consider that possibility? I did not know; I only knew that these few words he did speak could hardly transmit all the satisfaction and surprise he felt about the life he had managed to build for himself and his family.

He looked out at Ron again. "Look at him, if he played basketball like that they'd throw him the hell off the court." But he was smiling when he said it.

He walked over to the door. "Ronald, let them go to lunch."

Ron shouted back, "I thought I'd let some go now, and some later."

"Why?"

"Then somebody'll always be—"

"No fancy deals here," Mr. Patimkin shouted. "We all go to lunch at once."

Ron turned back. "All right, boys, lunch!"

His father smiled at me. "Smart boy? Huh?" He tapped his head. "That took brains, huh? He ain't got the stomach for business. He's an idealist," and then I think Mr. Patimkin suddenly realized who *I* was, and eagerly corrected himself so as not to offend. "That's all right, you know, if you're a schoolteacher, or like you, you know, a student or something like that. Here you need a little of the *gonif* in you. You know what that means? *Gonif?*"

"Thief," I said.

"You know more than my own kids. They're *goyim,* my kids, that's how much they understand." He watched the Negro loading gang walk past the office and shouted out to them, "You guys know how long an hour is? All right, you'll be back in an hour!"

Ron came into the office and of course shook my hand.

"Do you have that stuff for Mrs. Patimkin?" I asked.

"Ronald, get him the silver patterns." Ron turned away and Mr. Patimkin said, "When I got married we had forks and knives from the five and ten. This kid needs gold to eat off," but there was no anger; far from it.

I drove to the mountains in my own car that afternoon, and stood for a while at the wire fence watching the deer lightly prance, coyly feed, under the protection of signs that read, DO NOT FEED THE DEER, *By Order of South Mountain Reservation.* Alongside me at the fence were dozens of kids; they giggled and screamed when the deer licked the popcorn from their hands, and then were sad when their own excitement sent the young loping away towards the far end of the field where their tawny-skinned mothers stood regally watching the traffic curl up the mountain road. Young white-skinned mothers, hardly older than I, and in many instances younger, chatted in their convertibles behind me, and looked down from time to time to see what their children were about. I had seen them before, when Brenda and I had gone out for a bite in the afternoon, or had driven up here for lunch: in clotches of three and four they sat in the rustic hamburger joints that dotted the Reservation area while their children gobbled hamburgers and malteds and were given dimes to feed the jukebox. Though none of the little ones were old enough to read the song titles, almost all of them could holler out the words, and they did, while the mothers, a few of whom I recognized as high school mates of mine, compared suntans, supermarkets, and vacations. They looked immortal sitting there. Their hair would always stay the color they desired, their clothes the right texture and shade; in their homes they would have simple Swedish modern when that was fashionable, and if huge, ugly baroque ever came back, out would go the long, midget-legged marble coffee table and in would come Louis Quatorze. These were the goddesses, and if I were Paris I could not have been able to choose among them, so microscopic were the differences. Their fates had collapsed them into one. Only Brenda shone. Money and comfort would not erase her singleness—they hadn't yet, or had they? What was I loving, I wondered, and since I am not one to stick scalpels into myself, I wiggled my hand in the fence and allowed a tiny-nosed buck to lick my thoughts away.

When I returned to the Patimkin house, Brenda was in the living room looking more beautiful than I had ever seen her. She was modeling her new dress for Harriet and her mother. Even Mrs. Patimkin seemed softened by the sight of her; it looked as though some sedative had been injected into her, and so relaxed the Brenda-hating muscles around her eyes and mouth.

Brenda, without glasses, modeled in place; when she looked at me it was a kind of groggy, half-waking look I got, and though others might have interpreted it as sleepiness it sounded in my veins as lust. Mrs. Patimkin told her finally that she'd bought a very nice dress and I told her she looked lovely and Harriet told her she was very beautiful and that *she* ought to be the bride, and then there was an uncomfortable silence while all of us wondered who ought to be the groom.

Then when Mrs. Patimkin had led Harriet out to the kitchen, Brenda came up to me and said, "I *ought* to be the bride."

"You ought, sweetheart." I kissed her, and suddenly she was crying.

"What is it, honey?" I said.

"Let's go outside."

On the lawn, Brenda was no longer crying but her voice sounded very tired.

"Neil, I called Margaret Sanger Clinic," she said. "When I was in New York."

I didn't answer.

"Neil, they *did* ask if I was married. God, the woman sounded like my mother . . ."

"What did you say?"

"I said *no.*"

"What did she say?"

"I don't know. I hung up." She walked away and around the oak tree. When she appeared again she'd stepped out of her shoes and held one hand on the tree, as though it were a Maypole she were circling.

"You can call them back," I said.

She shook her head. "No, I can't. I don't even know why I called in the first place. We were shopping and I just walked away, looked up the number, and called."

"Then you can go to a doctor."

She shook again.

"Look, Bren," I said, rushing to her, "we'll go together, to a doctor. In New York—"

"I don't want to go to some dirty little office—"

"We won't. We'll go to the most posh gynecologist in New York. One who gets *Harper's Bazaar* for the reception room. How does that sound?"

She bit her lower lip.

"You'll come with me?" she asked.

"I'll come with you."

"To the office?"

"Sweetie, your husband wouldn't come to the office."

"No?"

"He'd be working."

"But you're not," she said.

"I'm on vacation," I said, but I had answered the wrong question. "Bren, I'll wait and when you're all done we'll buy a drink. We'll go out to dinner."

"Neil, I shouldn't have called Margaret Sanger—it's not right."

"It is, Brenda. It's the most right thing we can do." She walked away and I was exhausted from pleading. Somehow I felt I could have convinced her had I been a bit more crafty; and yet I did not want it to be craftiness that changed her mind. I was silent when she came back, and perhaps it was just that, my *not* saying anything, that prompted her finally to say, "I'll ask Mother Patimkin if she wants us to take Harriet too . . ."

7

I shall never forget the heat and mugginess of that afternoon we drove into New York. It was four days after the day she'd called Margaret Sanger—she put it off and put it off, but finally on Friday, three days before Ron's wedding and four before her departure, we were heading through the Lincoln Tunnel, which seemed longer and fumier than ever, like Hell with tiled walls. Finally we were in New York and smothered again by the thick day. I pulled around the policeman who directed traffic in his shirt sleeves and up onto the Port Authority roof to park the car.

"Do you have cab fare?" I said.

"Aren't you going to come with me?"

"I thought I'd wait in the bar. Here, downstairs."

"You can wait in Central Park. His office is right across the street."

"Bren, what's the diff—" But when I saw the look that invaded her eyes I gave up the air-conditioned bar to accompany her across the city. There was a sudden shower while our cab went crosstown, and when the rain stopped the streets were sticky and shiny, and below the pavement was the rumble of the subways, and in all it was like entering the ear of a lion.

The doctor's office was in the Squibb Building, which is across from Bergdorf Goodman's and so was a perfect place for Brenda to add to her wardrobe. For some reason we had never once considered her going to a doctor in Newark, perhaps because it was too close to home and might allow for possibilities of discovery. When Brenda got to the revolving door she looked back at me; her eyes were very watery, even with her glasses, and I did not say a word, afraid what a word, any word, might do. I kissed her hair and motioned that I would be across the street by the Plaza fountain, and then I watched her revolve through the doors. Out on the street the traffic moved slowly as though the humidity were a wall holding everything back. Even the fountain seemed to be bubbling boiling water on the people who sat at its edge, and in an instant I decided against crossing the street, and turned south on Fifth and began to walk the steaming pavement towards St. Patrick's. On the north steps a crowd was gathered; everyone was watching a model being photographed. She was wearing a lemon-colored dress and had her feet pointed like a ballerina, and as I passed into the church I heard some lady say, "If I ate cottage cheese *ten* times a day, I couldn't be that skinny."

It wasn't much cooler inside the church, though the stillness and the flicker of the candles made me think it was. I took a seat at the rear and while I couldn't bring myself to kneel, I did lean forward onto the back of the bench before me, and held my hands together and closed my eyes. I wondered if I looked like a Catholic, and in my wonderment I began to make a speech to myself. Can I call the self-conscious words I spoke prayer? At any rate, I called my audience God. God, I said, I am twenty-three years old. I want to make the best of things. Now the doctor is about to wed Brenda to me, and I am not entirely certain this is all for the best. What is it I love, Lord? Why have I chosen? Who is Brenda? The race is to the swift. Should I have stopped to think?

I was getting no answers, but I went on. If we meet You at all, God, it's that we're carnal, and acquisitive, and thereby partake of You. I am carnal, and I know You approve, I just know it. But how carnal can I get? I am acquisitive. Where do I turn now in my acquisitiveness? Where do we meet? Which prize is You?

It was an ingenious meditation, and suddenly I felt ashamed. I got up and walked outside, and the noise of Fifth Avenue met me with an answer:

Which prize do you think, *schmuck?* Gold dinnerware, sporting-goods trees, nectarines, garbage disposals, bumpless noses, Patimkin Sink, Bonwit Teller—

But damn it, God, that *is* You!

And God only laughed, that clown.

On the steps around the fountain I sat in a small arc of a rainbow that the sun had shot through the spray of the water. And then I saw Brenda coming out of the Squibb Building. She carried nothing with her, like a woman who's only been window shopping, and for a moment I was glad that in the end she had disobeyed my desire.

As she crossed the street, though, that little levity passed, and then I was myself again.

She walked up before me and looked down at where I sat; when she inhaled she filled her entire body, and then let her breath out with a "Whew!"

"Where is it?" I said.

My answer, at first, was merely that victorious look of hers, the one she'd given Simp the night she'd beaten her, the one I'd gotten the morning I finished the third lap alone. At last she said, "I'm wearing it."

"Oh, Bren."

"He said shall I wrap it or will you take it with you?"

"Oh Brenda, I love you."

We slept together that night, and so nervous were we about our new toy that we performed like kindergartners, or (in the language of that country) like a lousy double-play combination. And then the next day we hardly saw one another at all, for with the last-minute wedding preparations came scurrying, telegramming, shouting, crying, rushing—in short, lunacy. Even the meals lost their Patimkin fullness, and were tortured out of Kraft cheese, stale onion rolls, dry salami, a little chopped liver, and fruit cocktail. It was hectic all weekend, and I tried as best I could to keep clear of the storm, at whose eye, Ron, clumsy and smiling, and Harriet, flittering and courteous, were being pulled closer and closer together. By Sunday night fatigue had arrested hysteria and all of the Patimkins, Brenda included, had gone off to an early sleep. When Ron went into the bathroom to brush his teeth I decided to go in and brush mine. While I stood over the sink he checked his supports for dampness; then he hung them on the shower knobs and asked me if I would like to listen to his records for a while. It was not out of boredom and loneliness that I accepted; rather a brief spark of lockerroom comradery had been struck there among the soap and the water and the tile, and I thought that perhaps Ron's invitation was prompted by a desire to spend his last moments as a Single Man with another Single Man. If I was right, then it was the first real attestation he'd given to my masculinity. How could I refuse?

I sat on the unused twin bed.

"You want to hear Mantovani?"

"Sure," I said.

"Who do you like better, him or Kostelanetz?"

"It's a toss-up."

Ron went to his cabinet. "Hey, how about the Columbus record? Brenda ever play it for you?"

"No. I don't think so."

He extracted a record from its case, and like a giant with a sea shell, placed it gingerly on the phonograph. Then he smiled at me and leaned back onto his bed. His arms were behind his head and his eyes fixed on the ceiling. "They give this to all the seniors. With the yearbook—" but he hushed as soon as the sound began. I watched Ron and listened to the record.

At first there was just a roll of drums, then silence, then another drum roll—and then softly, a marching song, the melody of which was very familiar. When the song ended, I heard the bells, soft, loud, then soft again. And finally there came a Voice, bowel-deep and historic, the kind one associates with documentaries about the rise of Facism.

"The year, 1956. The season, fall. The place, Ohio State University . . ."

Blitzkrieg! Judgment Day! The Lord had lowered his baton, and the Ohio State Glee Club were lining out the Alma Mater as if their souls depended on it. After one desperate chorus, they fell, still screaming, into bottomless oblivion, and the Voice resumed:

"The leaves had begun to turn and redden on the trees. Smoky fires line Fraternity Row, as pledges rake the leaves and turn them to a misty haze. Old faces greet new ones, new faces meet old, and another year has begun . . ."

Music. Glee Club in great comeback. Then the Voice: "The place, the banks of the Olentangy. The event, Homecoming Game, 1956. The opponent, the ever dangerous Illini . . ."

Roar of crowd. New voice—Bill Stern: "Illini over the ball. The snap. Linday fading to pass, he finds a receiver, he passes long *long* down field—and IT'S INTERCEPTED BY NUMBER 43, HERB CLARK OF OHIO STATE! Clark evades one tackler, he evades another as he comes up to midfield. Now he's picking up blockers, he's down to the 45, the 40, the 35—"

And as Bill Stern egged on Clark, and Clark, Bill Stern, Ron, on his bed, with just a little body-english, eased Herb Clark over the goal.

"And it's the buckeyes ahead now, 21 to 19. *What a game!*"

The Voice of History baritoned in again: "But the season was up and down, and by the time the first snow had covered the turf, it was the sound of dribbling and the cry *Up and In!* that echoed through the fieldhouse . . ."

Ron closed his eyes.

"The Minnesota game," a new, high voice announced, "and for some of our seniors, their last game for the red and white . . . The players are ready to come out on the floor and into the spotlight. There'll be a big hand of appreciation from this capacity crowd for some of the boys who won't be back next year. Here comes Larry Gardner, big Number 7, out onto the floor, Big Larry from Akron, Ohio . . ."

"Larry—" announced the P.A. system; "Larry," the crowd roared back.

"And here comes Ron Patimkin dribbling out. Ron, Number 11, from Short Hills, New Jersey. Big Ron's last game, and it'll be some time before Buckeye fans forget him . . ."

Big Ron tightened on his bed as the loudspeaker called his name; his ovation must have set the nets to trembling. Then the rest of the players were announced, and then basketball season was over, and it was Religious Emphasis Week, the Senior Prom (Billy May blaring at the gymnasium roof), Fraternity Skit Night, E. E. Cummings reading to students (verse, silence, applause); and then, finally commencement:

"The campus is hushed this day of days. For several thousand young men and women it is a joyous yet a solemn occasion. And for their parents a day of laughter and a day of tears. It is a bright green day, it is June the seventh of the year one-thousand nine hundred and fifty-seven and for these young Americans the most stirring day of their lives. For many this will be their last glimpse of the campus, of Columbus, for many many years. Life calls us, and anxiously if not nervously we walk out into the world and away from the pleasures of these ivied walls. But not from its memories. They will be concomitant, if not the fundament of our lives. We shall choose husbands and wives, we shall choose jobs and homes, we shall sire children and grandchildren, but we will not forget you, Ohio State. In the years ahead we will carry with us always memories of thee, Ohio State . . ."

Slowly, softly, the OSU band begins the Alma Mater, and then the bells chime that last hour. Soft, very soft, for it is spring.

There was goose flesh on Ron's veiny arms as the Voice continued. "We offer ourselves to you then, world, and come at you in search of Life. And to you, Ohio State, to you Columbus, we say thank you, thank you and goodbye. We will miss you, in the fall, in the winter, in the spring, but some day we shall return. Till then, goodbye, Ohio State, goodbye, red and white, goodbye, Columbus . . . goodbye, Columbus . . . goodbye . . ."

Ron's eyes were closed. The band was upending its last truckload of nostalgia, and I tiptoed from the room, in step with the 2163 members of the Class of '57.

I closed my door, but then opened it and looked back at Ron: he was still humming on his bed. Thee! I thought, my brother-in-law!

The wedding.

Let me begin with the relatives.

There was Mrs. Patimkin's side of the family: her sister Molly, a tiny buxom hen whose ankles swelled and ringed her shoes, and who would remember Ron's wedding if for no other reason than she'd martyred her feet in three-inch heels, and Molly's husband, the butter and egg man, Harry Grossbart, who had earned his fortune with barley and corn in the days of Prohibition. Now he was active in the Temple and whenever he saw Brenda he swatted her on the can; it was a kind of physical bootlegging that passed, I guess, for familial affection. Then there was Mrs. Patimkin's brother, Marty Kreiger, the Kosher Hot-Dog King, an immense man, as many stomachs as he had chins, and already, at fifty-five, with as many heart attacks as chins and stomachs combined. He had just come back from a health cure in the Catskills, where he said he'd eaten nothing but All-Bran and had won $1500 at gin rummy. When the photographer came by to take pictures, Marty put his hand on his wife's pancake breasts and said, "Hey, how about a picture of this!" His wife Sylvia, was a frail, spindly woman with bones like a bird's. She had cried throughout the ceremony, and sobbed openly, in fact, when the rabbi had pronounced Ron and Harriet "man and wife in the eyes of God and the State of New Jersey." Later, at dinner, she had hardened enough to slap her husband's hand as it reached out for a cigar. However, when he reached across to hold her breast she just looked aghast and said nothing.

Also there were Mrs. Patimkin's twin sisters, Rose and Pearl, who both had white hair, the color of Lincoln convertibles, and nasal voices, and husbands who followed after them but talked only to each other, as though, in fact, sister had married sister, and husband had married husband. The husbands, named Earl Klein and Manny Kartzman, sat next to each other during the ceremony, then at dinner, and once, in fact, while the band was playing between courses, they rose, Klein and Kartzman, as though to dance, but instead walked to the far end of the hall where together they paced off the width of the floor. Earl, I learned later, was in the carpet business, and apparently he was trying to figure how much money he would make if the Hotel Pierre favored him with a sale.

On Mr. Patimkin's side there was only Leo, his half-brother. Leo was married to a woman named Bea whom nobody seemed to talk to. Bea kept hopping up and down during the meal and running over to the kiddie table to see if her little girl, Sharon, was being taken care of. "I told her not to take the kid. Get a baby-sitter, I said." Leo told me this while Brenda danced with Ron's best man, Ferrari. "She says what are we, millionaires? No, for Christ sake, but my brother's kids gets married, I can have a little celebration. No, we gotta *shlep* the kid with us. Aah, it gives her something to do! . . ." He looked around the hall. Up on the stage Harry Winters (né Weinberg) was leading his band in a medley from *My Fair Lady;* on the floor, all ages, all sizes, all shapes were dancing. Mr. Patimkin was dancing with Julie, whose dress had slipped down from her shoulders to reveal her soft small back, and long neck, like Brenda's. He danced in little squares and was making considerable effort not to step on Julie's toes. Harriet, who was, as everyone said, a beautiful bride, was dancing with her father. Ron danced with Harriet's mother, Brenda with Ferrari, and I had sat down for a while in the empty chair beside Leo so as not to get maneuvered into dancing with Mrs. Patimikin, which seemed to be the direction towards which things were moving.

"You're Brenda's boy friend? Huh?" Leo said.

I nodded—earlier in the evening I'd stopped giving blushing explanations. "You gotta deal there, boy," Leo said, "you don't louse it up."

"She's very beautiful," I said.

Leo poured himself a glass of champagne, and then waited as though he expected a head to form on it; when one didn't, he filled the glass to the brim.

"Beautiful, not beautiful, what's the difference. I'm a practical man. I'm on the bottom, so I gotta be. You're Aly Khan you worry about marrying movie stars. I wasn't born yesterday . . . You know how old I was when I got married? Thirty-five years old. I don't know what the hell kind of hurry I was in." He drained his glass and refilled it. "I'll tell you something, one good thing happened to me in my whole life. Two maybe. Before I came back from overseas I got a letter from my wife—she wasn't my wife then. My mother-in-law found an apartment for us in Queens. Sixty-two fifty a month it cost. That's the last good thing that happened."

"What was the first?"

"What first?"

"You said *two* things," I said.

"I don't remember. I say two because my wife tells me I'm sarcastic and a cynic. That way maybe she won't think I'm such a wise guy."

I saw Brenda and Ferrari separate, and so excused myself and started for Brenda, but just then Mr. Patimkin separated from Julie and it looked as though the two men were going to switch partners. Instead the four of them stood on the dance floor and when I reached them they were laughing and Julie was saying, "What's so funny!" Ferrari said "Hi" to me and whisked Julie away, which sent her into peals of laughter.

Mr. Patimkin had one hand on Brenda's back and suddenly the other one was on mine. "You kids have a good time?" he said.

We were sort of swaying, the three of us, to "Get Me to the Church on Time."

Brenda kissed her father. "Yes," she said. "I'm so drunk my head doesn't even need my neck."

"It's a fine wedding, Mr. Patimkin."

"You want anything just ask me . . ." he said, a little drunken himself. "You're two good kids . . . How do you like that brother of yours getting married? . . . Huh? . . . Is that a girl or is that a girl?"

Brenda smiled, and though she apparently thought her father had spoken of her, I was sure he'd been referring to Harriet.

"You like weddings, Daddy?" Brenda said.

"I like my kids' weddings . . ." He slapped me on the back. "You two kids, you want anything? Go have a good time. Remember," he said to Brenda, "you're my honey . . ." Then he looked at me. "Whatever my Buck wants is good enough for me. There's no business too big it can't use another head."

I smiled, though not directly at him, and beyond I could see Leo sopping up champagne and watching the three of us; when he caught my eye he made a sign with his hand, a circle with his thumb and forefinger, indicating, "That a boy, that a boy!"

After Mr. Patimkin departed, Brenda and I danced closely, and we only sat down when the waiters began to circulate with the main course. The head table was noisy, particularly at our end where the men were almost all teammates of Ron's, in one sport or another; they ate a fantastic number of rolls. Tank Feldman, Ron's roommate, who had flown in from Toledo, kept sending the waiter back for rolls, for celery, for olives, and always to the squealing delight of Gloria Feldman, his wife, a nervous, undernourished girl who continually looked down the front of her gown as though there was some sort of construction project going on under her clothes. Gloria and Tank, in fact, seemed to be self-appointed precinct captains at our end. They proposed toasts, burst into wild song, and continually referred to Brenda and me as "love birds." Brenda smiled at this with her eyeteeth and I brought up a cheery look from some fraudulent auricle of my heart.

And the night continued: we ate, we drank, we danced—Rose and Pearl did the Charleston with one another (while their husbands examined woodwork and chandeliers), and then I did the Charleston with none other than Gloria Feldman, who made coy, hideous faces at me all the time we danced. Near the end of the evening, Brenda, who'd been drinking champagne like her Uncle Leo, did a Rita Hayworth tango with herself, and Julie fell asleep on some ferns she'd whisked off the head table and made into a mattress at the far end of the hall. I felt a numbness creep into my hard palate, and by three o'clock people were dancing in their coats, shoeless ladies were wrapping hunks of wedding cake in napkins for their children's lunch, and finally Gloria Feldman made her way over to our end of the table and said, freshly, "Well, our little Radcliffe smarty, what have *you* been doing all summer?"

"Growing a penis."

Gloria smiled and left as quickly as she'd come, and Brenda without another word headed shakily away for the ladies' room and the rewards of overindulgence. No sooner had she left than Leo was beside me, a glass in one hand, a new bottle of champagne in the other.

"No sign of the bride and groom?" he said, leering. He'd lost most of his consonants by this time and was doing the best he could with long, wet vowels. "Well, you're next, kid, I see it in the cards . . . You're nobody's sucker . . ." And he stabbed me in the side with the top of the bottle, spilling champagne onto the side of my rented tux. He straightened up, poured more onto his hand and glass, but then suddenly he stopped. He was looking into the lights which were hidden beneath a long bank of flowers that adorned the front of the table. He shook the bottle in his hand as though to make it fizz. "The son of a bitch who invented the fluorescent bulb should drop dead!" He set the bottle down and drank.

Up on the stage Harry Winters brought his musicians to a halt. The drummer stood up, stretched, and they all began to open up cases and put their instruments away. On the floor, relatives, friends, associates, were holding each other around the waists and the shoulders, and small children huddled around their parents' legs. A couple of kids ran in and out of the crowd, screaming at tag, until one was grabbed by an adult and slapped soundly on the behind. He began to cry, and couple by couple the floor emptied. Our table was a tangle of squashed everything: napkins, fruits, flowers; there were empty whiskey bottles, droopy ferns, and dishes puddled with unfinished cherry jubilee, gone sticky with the hours. At the end of the table Mr. Patimkin was sitting next to his wife, holding her hand. Opposite them, on two bridge chairs that had been pulled up, sat Mr. and Mrs. Ehrlich. They spoke quietly and evenly, as though they had known each other for years and years. Everything had slowed down now, and from time to time people would come up to the Patimkins and Ehrlichs, wish them *mazel tov,* and then drag themselves and their families out into the September night, which was cool and windy, someone said, and reminded me that soon would come winter and snow.

"They never wear out, those things, you know that." Leo was pointing to the fluorescent lights that shone through the flowers. "They last for years. They could make a car like that if they wanted, that could never wear out. It would run on water in the summer and snow in the winter. But they wouldn't do it, the big boys . . . Look at me," Leo said, splashing his suit front with champagne, "I sell a good bulb. You can't get the kind of bulb I sell in the drugstores. It's a quality bulb. But I'm the little guy. I don't even own a car. His brother, and I don't even own an automobile. I take a train wherever I go. I'm the only guy I know who wears out three pairs of rubbers every winter. Most guys get new ones when they lose the old ones. I wear them out, like shoes. Look," he said, leaning into me, "I could sell a crappy bulb, it wouldn't break my heart. But it's not good business."

The Ehrlichs and Patimkins scraped back their chairs and headed away, all except Mr. Patimkin who came down the table towards Leo and me.

He slapped Leo on the back. "Well, how you doing, *shtarke?*"

"All right, Ben. All right . . ."

"You have a good time?"

"You had a nice affair, Ben, it must've cost a pretty penny, believe me . . ."

Mr. Patimkin laughed. "When I make out my income tax I go to see Leo. He knows just how much money I spent . . . You need a ride home?" he asked me.

"No, thanks. I'm waiting for Brenda. We have my car."

"Good night," Mr. Patimkin said.

I watched him step down off the platform that held the head table, and then start towards the exit. Now the only people in the hall—the shambles of a hall—were myself, Leo, and his wife and child who slept, both of them, with their heads pillowed on a crumpled tablecloth at a table down on the floor before us. Brenda still wasn't around.

"When you got it," Leo said, rubbing his fingers together, "you can afford to talk like a big shot. Who needs a guy like me any more. Salesmen, you spit on them. You can go to the supermarket and buy anything. Where my wife shops you can buy sheets and pillowcases. Imagine, a grocery store! Me, I sell to gas stations, factories, small businesses, all up and down the east coast. Sure, you can sell a guy in a gas station a crappy bulb that'll burn out in a week. For inside the pumps I'm talking, it takes a certain kind of bulb. A utility bulb. All right, so you sell him a crappy bulb, and then a week later he puts in a new one, and while he's screwing it in he still remembers your name. Not me. I sell a quality bulb. It lasts a month, five weeks, before it even flickers, then it gives you another couple days, dim maybe, but so you shouldn't go blind. It hangs on, it's a quality bulb. Before it even burns out you notice it's getting darker, so you put a new one in. What people don't like is when one minute it's sunlight and the next dark. Let it glimmer a few days and they don't feel so bad. Nobody ever throws out my bulb—they figure they'll save them, can always use them in a pinch. Sometimes I say to a guy, you ever throw out a bulb you bought from Leo Patimkin? You gotta use psychology. That's why I'm sending my kid to college. You don't know a little psychology these days, you're licked . . ."

He lifted an arm and pointed out to his wife; then he slumped down in his seat. "Aaach!" he said, and drank off half a glass of champagne. "I'll tell you, I go as far as New London, Connecticut. That's as far as I'll go, and when I come home at night I stop first for a couple drinks. Martinis. Two I have, sometimes three. That seems fair, don't it. But to her a little sip or a bathtubful, it smells the same. She says it's bad for the kid if I come home smelling. The kid's a baby, for God's sake, she thinks that's the way I'm *supposed* to smell. A forty-eight-year-old man with a three-year-old kid! She'll give me a thrombosis that kid. My wife, she wants me to come home early and play with the kid before she goes to bed. Come home, she says, and *I'll* make you a drink. Hah! I spend all day sniffing gas, leaning under hoods with grimy *poilishehs* in New London, trying to force a lousy bulb into a socket—I'll screw it in myself, I tell them—and she thinks I want to come home and drink a martini from a jelly glass! How long are you going to stay in bars, she says. Till a Jewish girl is Miss Rheingold!

"Look," he went on after another drink, "I love my kid like Ben loves his Brenda. It's not that I don't want to play with her. But if I play with the kid and then at night get into bed with my wife, then she can't expect fancy things from me. It's one or the other. I'm no movie star."

Leo looked at his empty glass and put it on the table; he tilted the bottle up and drank the champagne like soda water. "How much do you think I make a week?" he said.

"I don't know."

"Take a guess."

"A hundred dollars."

"Sure, and tomorrow they're gonna let the lions out of the cage in Central Park. What do you think I make?"

"I can't tell.

"A cabdriver makes more than me. That's a fact. My wife's brother is a cabdriver, *he* lives in Kew Gardens. And he don't take no crap, no sir, not those cabbies. Last week it was raining one night and I said the hell with it, I'm taking a cab. I'd been all day in Newton, Mass. I don't usually go so far, but on the train in the morning I said to myself, stay on, go further, it'll be a change. And I know all the time I'm kidding myself. I wouldn't even make up the extra fare it cost me. But I stay on. And at night I still had a couple boxes with me, so when the guy pulls up at Grand Central there's like a genie inside me says get in. I even threw the bulbs in, not even caring if they broke. And this cabbie says, Whatya want to do, buddy, rip the leather? Those are brand new seats I got. No, I said. Jesus Christ, he says, some goddam people. I get in and give him a Queens address which ought to shut him up, but no, all the way up the Drive he was Jesus Christing me. It's hot in the cab, so I open a window and *then* he turns around and says, Whatya want to do, give me a cold in the neck? I just got over a goddam cold . . ." Leo looked at me, bleary-eyed. "This city is crazy! If I had a little money I'd get out of here in a minute. I'd go to California. They don't need bulbs out there it's so light. I went to New Guinea during the war from San Francisco. *There,*" he burst, "there is the other good thing that happened to me, that night in San Francisco with this Hannah Schreiber. That's the both of them, you asked me I'm telling you—the apartment my mother-in-law got us, this Hannah Schreiber. One night was all. I went to a B'nai Brith dance for servicemen in the basement of some big temple, and I met her. I wasn't married then, so don't make faces."

"I'm not."

"She had a nice little room by herself. She was going to school to be a teacher. Already I knew something was up because she let me feel inside her slip in the cab. Listen to me, I sound like I'm always in cabs. Maybe two other times in my life. To tell the truth I don't even enjoy it. All the time I'm riding I'm watching the meter. Even the pleasures I can't enjoy!"

"What about Hannah Schreiber?"

He smiled, flashing some gold in his mouth. "How do you like that name? She was only a girl, but she had an old lady's name. In the room she says to me she believes in oral love. I can still hear her: Leo Patimkin, I believe in oral love. I don't know what the hell she means. I figure she was one of those Christian Scientists or some cult or something. So I said, But what about for soldiers, guys going overseas who may get killed, God forbid." He shrugged his shoulders. "The smartest guy in the world I wasn't. But that's twenty years almost, I was still wet behind the ears. I'll tell you, every once in a while my wife—you know, she does for me what Hannah Schreiber did. I don't like to force her, she works hard. That to her is like a cab to me. I wouldn't force her. I can remember every time, I'll bet. Once after a Seder, my mother was still living, she should rest in peace. My wife was up to here with Mogen David. In fact, *twice* after Seders. Aachhh! Everything good in my life I can count on my fingers! God forbid someone should leave me a million dollars, I wouldn't even have to take off my shoes. I got a whole other hand yet."

He pointed to the fluorescent bulbs with the nearly empty champagne bottle. "You call that a light? That's a light to *read* by? It's purple, for God's sake! Half the blind men in the world ruined themselves by those damn things. You know who's behind them? The optometrists! I'll tell you, if I could get a couple hundred for all my stock and the territory, I'd sell tomorrow. That's right, Leo A. Patimkin, one semester accounting, City College nights, will sell equipment, territory, good name. I'll buy two inches in the *Times*. The territory is from here to everywhere. I go where I want, my own boss, no one tells me what to do. You know the Bible? 'Let there be light—and there's Leo Patimkin!' That's my trademark, I'll sell that too. I tell them that slogan, the *poilishehs*, they think I'm making it up. What good is it to be smart unless you're in on the ground floor! I got more brains in my pinky than Ben got in his whole *head*. Why is it he's on top and I'm on the bottom! *Why!* Believe me, if you're born lucky, you're lucky!" And then he exploded into silence.

I had the feeling that he was going to cry, so I leaned over and whispered to him, "You better go home." He agreed, but I had to raise him out of his seat and steer him by one arm down to his wife and child. The little girl could not be awakened, and Leo and Bea asked me to watch her while they went out into the lobby to get their coats. When they returned, Leo seemed to have dragged himself back to the level of human communication. He shook my hand with real feeling. I was very touched.

"You'll go far," he said to me. "You're a smart boy, you'll play it safe. Don't louse things up."

"I won't."

"Next time we see you it'll be *your* wedding," and he winked at me. Bea stood alongside, muttering goodbye all the while he spoke. He shook my hand again and then picked the child out of her seat, and turned towards the door. From the back, round-shouldered, burdened, child-carrying, they looked like people fleeing a captured city.

Brenda, I discovered, was asleep on a couch in the lobby. It was almost four o'clock and the two of us and the desk clerk were the only ones in the hotel lobby. At first I did not waken Brenda, for she was pale and wilted and I knew she had been sick. I sat beside her, smoothing her hair back off her ears. How would I ever come to know her, I wondered, for as she slept I felt I knew no more of her than what I could see in a photograph. I stirred her gently and in a half-sleep she walked beside me out to the car.

It was almost dawn when we came out of the Jersey side of the Lincoln Tunnel. I switched down to my parking lights, and drove on to the Turnpike, and there out before me I could see the swampy meadows that spread for miles and miles, watery, blotchy, smelly, like an oversight of God. I thought of that other oversight, Leo Patimkin, half-brother to Ben. In a few hours he would be on a train heading north, and as he passed Scarsdale and White Plains, he would belch and taste champagne and let the flavor linger in his mouth. Alongside him on the seat, like another passenger, would be cartons of bulbs. He would get off at New London, or maybe, inspired by the sight of his half-brother, he would stay on again, hoping for some new luck further north. For the world was Leo's territory, every city, every swamp, every road and highway. He could go on to Newfoundland if he wanted, Hudson Bay, and on up to Thule, and then slide down the other side of the globe and rap on frosted windows on the Russian steppes, if he wanted. But he wouldn't. Leo was forty-eight years old and he had learned. He pursued discomfort and sorrow, all right, but if you had a heartful by the time you reached New London, what new awfulness could you look forward to in Vladivostok?

The next day the wind was blowing the fall in and the branches of the weeping willow were fingering at the Patimkin front lawn. I drove Brenda to the train at noon, and she left me.

8

Autumn came quickly. It was cold and in Jersey the leaves turned and fell overnight. The following Saturday I took a ride up to see the deer, and did not even get out of the car, for it was too brisk to be standing at the wire fence, and so I watched the animals walk and run in the dimness of the late afternoon, and after a while everything, even the objects of nature, the trees, the clouds, the grass, the weeds, reminded me of Brenda, and I drove back down to Newark. Already we had sent our first letters and I had called her late one night, but in the mail and on the phone we had some difficulty discovering one another; we had not the style yet. That night I tried her again, and someone on her floor said she was out and would not be in till late.

Upon my return to the library I was questioned by Mr. Scapello about the Gauguin book. The jowly gentleman *had* sent a nasty letter about my discourtesy, and I was only able to extricate myself by offering a confused story in an indignant tone. In fact, I even managed to turn it around so that Mr. Scapello was apologizing to me as he led me up to my new post, there among the encyclopedias, the bibliographies, the indexes and guides. My bullying surprised me, and I wondered if some of it had not been learned from Mr. Patimkin that morning I'd heard him giving Grossman an earful on the phone. Perhaps I was more of a businessman that I thought. Maybe I could learn to become a Patimkin with ease . . .

Day's passed slowly; I never did see the colored kid again, and when, one noon, I looked in the stacks, Gauguin was gone, apparently charged out finally by the jowly man. I wondered what it had been like that day the colored kid had discovered the book was gone. Had he cried? For some reason I imagined that he had blamed it on me, but then I realized that I was confusing the dream I'd had with reality. Chances were he had discoverd someone else, Van Gogh, Vermeer . . . But no, they were not his kind of artists. What had probably happened was that he'd given up on the library and gone back to playing Willie Mays in the streets. He was better off, I thought. No sense carrying dreams of Tahiti in your head, if you can't afford the fare.

Let's see, what else did I do? I ate, I slept, I went to the movies, I sent broken-spined books to the bindery—I did everything I'd ever done before, but now each activity was surrounded by a fence, existed alone, and my life consisted of jumping from one fence to the next. There was no flow, for that had been Brenda.

And then Brenda wrote saying that she could be coming in for the Jewish holidays which were only a week away. I was so overjoyed I wanted to call Mr. and Mrs. Patimkin, just to tell them of my pleasure. However, when I got to the phone and had actually dialed the first two letters, I knew that at the other end there would be silence; if there was anything said, it would only be Mrs. Patimkin asking, "What is it you want?" Mr. Patimkin had probably forgotten my name.

That night, after dinner, I gave Aunt Gladys a kiss and told her she shouldn't work so hard.

"In less than a week it's Rosh Hashana and he thinks I should take a vacation. Ten people I'm having. Who do you think, a chicken clean itself? Thank God, the holidays come once a year, I'd be an old woman before my time."

But then it would only be nine people Aunt Gladys was having, for only two days after her letter Brenda called.

"Oy, Gut!" Aunt Gladys called. "Long *distance!*"

"Hello?" I said.

"Hello, sweetie?"

"Yes," I said.

"What *is* it?" Aunt Gladys tugged at my shirt. "What is it?"

"It's for me."

"Who?" Aunt Gladys said, pointing into the receiver.

"Brenda," I said.

"Yes?" Brenda said.

"Brenda?" Aunt Gladys said. "What does she call long distance, I almost had a heart attack."

"Because she's in Boston," I said. "Please, Aunt Gladys . . ."

And Aunt Gladys walked off, mumbling, "These kids . . ."

"Hello," I said again into the phone.

"Neil, how are you?"

"I love you."

"Neil, I have bad news. I can't come in this week."

"But, honey, it's the Jewish holidays."

"Sweet*heart,*" she laughed.

"Can't you say that, for an excuse?"

"I have a test Saturday, and a paper, and you know if I went home I wouldn't get anything done . . ."

"You would."

"Neil, I just *can't.* My mother'd make me go to Temple, and I wouldn't even have enough time to see *you.*"

"Oh God, Brenda."

"Sweetie?"

"Yes?"

"Can't you come up here?" she asked.

"I'm working."

"The Jewish holidays," she said.

"Honey, I can't. Last year I didn't take them off, I can't all—"

"You can say you had a conversion."

"Besides, my aunt's having all the family for dinner, and you know what with my parents—"

"Come up, Neil."

"I can't just take two days off, Bren. I just got promoted and a raise—"

"The hell with the raise."

"Baby, it's my job."

"Forever?" she said.

"No."

"Then come. I've got a hotel room."

"For me?"

"For us."

"Can you do that?"

"No and yes. People do it."

"Brenda, you tempt me."

"Be tempted."

"I could take a train Wednesday right from work."

"You could stay till Sunday night."

"Bren, I can't. I still have to be back to work on Saturday."

"Don't you ever get a day *off?*" she said.

"Tuesdays," I said glumly.

"God."

"And Sunday," I added.

Brenda said something but I did not hear her, for Aunt Gladys called, "You talk all day long distance?"

"Quiet!" I shouted back to her.

"Neil, will you?"

"Damn it, yes," I said.

"Are you angry?"

"I don't think so. I'm going to come up."

"Till Sunday."

"We'll see."

"Don't feel upset, Neil. You sound upset. It is the Jewish holidays. I mean you *should* be off."

"That's right," I said. "I'm an orthodox Jew, for God's sake, I ought to take advantage of it."

"That's right," she said.

"Is there a train around six?"

"Every hour, I think."

"Then I'll be on the one that leaves at six."

"I'll be at the station," she said. "How will I know you?"

"I'll be disguised as an orthodox Jew."

"Me too," she said.

"Good night, love," I said.

Aunt Gladys cried when I told her I was going away for Rosh Hashana.

"And I was preparing a big meal," she said.

"You can still prepare it."

"What will I tell your mother?"

"I'll tell her, Aunt Gladys. Please. You have no right to get upset . . ."

"Someday you'll have a family you'll know what it's like."

"I have a family now."

"What's a matter," she said, blowing her nose, "That girl couldn't come home to see her family it's the holidays?"

"She's in school, she just can't—"

"If she loved her family she'd find time. We don't live six hundred years."

"She does love her family."

"Then one day a year you could break your heart and pay a visit."

"Aunt Gladys, you don't understand."

"Sure," she said, "when I'm twenty-three years old I'll understand everything."

I went to kiss her and she said, "Go away from me, go run to Boston . . ."

The next morning I discovered that Mr. Scapello didn't want me to leave on Rosh Hashana either, but I unnerved him, I think, by hinting that his coldness about my taking the two days off might just be so much veiled anti-Semitism, so on the whole he was easier to manage. At lunch time I took a walk down to Penn Station and picked up a train schedule to Boston. That was my bedtime reading for the next three nights.

She did not look like Brenda, at least for the first minute. And probably to her I did not look like me. But we kissed and held each other, and it was strange to feel the thickness of our coats between us.

"I'm letting my hair grow," she said in the cab, and that in fact was all she said. Not until I helped her out of the cab did I notice the thin gold band shining on her left hand.

She hung back, strolling casually about the lobby while I signed the register "Mr. and Mrs. Neil Klugman," and then in the room we kissed again.

"Your heart's pounding," I said to her.

"I know," she said.

"Are you nervous?"

"No."

"Have you done this before?" I said.

"I read Mary McCarthy."

She took off her coat and instead of putting it in the closet, she tossed it across the chair. I sat down on the bed; she didn't.

"What's the matter?"

Brenda took a deep breath and walked over to the window, and I thought that perhaps it would be best for me to ask nothing—for us to get used to each other's presence in quiet. I hung her coat and mine in the empty closet, and left the suitcases—mine and hers—standing by the bed.

Brenda was kneeling backwards in the chair, looking out the window as though out the window was where she'd rather be. I came up behind her and put my hands around her body and held her breasts, and when I felt the cool draft that swept under the sill, I realized how long it had been since that first warm night when I had put my arms around her and felt the tiny wings beating in her back. And then I realized why I'd really come to Boston—it had been long enough. It was time to stop kidding about marriage.

"Is something the matter?" I said.

"Yes."

It wasn't the answer I'd expected; I wanted no answer really, only to soothe her nervousness with my concern.

But I asked, "What is it? Why didn't you mention it on the phone?"

"It only happened today."

"School?"

"Home. They found out about us."

I turned her face up to mine. "That's okay. I told my aunt I was coming here too. What's the difference?"

About the summer. About our sleeping together."

"Oh?"

"Yes."

". . . Ron?"

"No."

"That night, you mean, did Julie—"

"No," she said, "it wasn't *anybody.*"

"I don't get it."

Brenda got up and walked over to the bed where she sat down on the edge. I sat in the chair.

"My mother found the thing."

"The diaphragm?"

She nodded.

"When?" I asked.

"The other day, I guess." She walked to the bureau and opened her purse. "Here, you can read them in the order I got them." She tossed an envelope at me; it was dirty-edged and crumpled, as though it had been in and out of her pockets a good many times. "I got this one this morning," she said. "Special delivery."

I took out the letter and read:

PATIMKIN KITCHEN AND BATHROOM SINKS
"Any Size—Any Shape"

Dear Brenda—

Don't pay any Attention to your Mother's Letter when you get it. I love you honey if you want a coat I'll buy You a coat. You could always have anything you wanted. We have every faith in you so you won't be too upset by what your mother says in her Letter. Of course she is a little hysterical because of the shock and she has been Working so hard for Hadassah. She is a Woman and it is hard for her to understand some of the Shocks in life. Of course I can't say We weren't all surprised because from the beginning I was nice to him and Thought he would appreciate the nice vacation we supplied for him. Some People never turn out the way you hope and pray but I am willing to forgive and call Buy Gones, Buy Gones, You have always up till now been a good Buck and got good scholastic Grades and Ron has always been what we wanted a Good Boy, most important, and a Nice boy. This late in my life believe me I am not going to start hating my own flesh and blood. As for your mistake it takes Two to make a mistake and now that you will be away at school and from him and what you got involved in you will probably do all right I have every faith you will. You have to have faith in your children like in a Business or any serious undertaking and there is nothing that is so bad that we can't forgive especially when Our own flesh and blood is involved. We have a nice close nitt family and why not???? Have a nice Holiday and in Temple I will say a Prayer for you as I do every year. On Monday I want you to go into Boston and buy a coat. Whatever you need because I know how Cold it gets up where you are . . . Give my regards to Linda and remember to bring her home with you on Thanksgiving like last year. You two had such a nice time. I have always never said bad things about any of your friends or Rons and that this should happen is only the exception that proves the rule. Have a Happy Holiday.

Your Father

And then it was signed BEN PATIMKIN, but that was crossed out and written beneath "Your Father" were again, like an echo, the words, "Your Father."

"Who's Linda?" I asked.

"My roommate, last year." She tossed another envelope to me. "Here. I got this one in the afternoon. Air Mail."

The letter was from Brenda's mother. I started to read it and then put it down a moment. "You got this *after*?"

"Yes," she said. "When I got his I didn't know what was happening. Read hers."

I began again.

Dear Brenda:

I don't even know how to begin. I have been crying all morning and have had to skip my board meeting this afternoon because my eyes are so red. I never thought this would happen to a daughter of mine. I wonder if you know what I mean, if it is at least on your conscience, so I won't have to degrade either of us with a description. All I can say is that this morning when I was cleaning out the drawers and putting away your summer clothing I came upon something in your bottom drawer, *under* some sweaters which you probably remember leaving there. I cried the minute I saw it and I haven't stopped crying yet. Your father called a while ago and now he is driving home because he heard how upset I was on the phone.

I don't know what we ever did that you should reward us this way.

We gave you a nice home and all the love and respect a child needs. I always was proud when you were a little girl that you could take care of yourself so well. You took care of Julie so beautifully it was a treat to see, when you were only fourteen years old. But you drifted away from your family, even though we sent you to the best schools and gave you the best money could buy. Why you should reward us this way is a question I'll carry with me to the grave.

About your friend I have no words. He is his parents' responsibility and I cannot imagine what kind of home life he had that he could act that way. Certainly that was a fine way to repay us for the hospitality we were nice enough to show to him, a perfect stranger. That the two of you should be carrying on like that in our very house I will never in my life be able to understand. Times certainly have changed since I was a girl that this kind of thing could go on. I keep asking myself if at least you didn't think of us while you were doing that. If not for me, how could you do this to your father? God forbid Julie should ever learn of this.

God only knows what you have been doing all these years we put our trust in you.

You have broken your parents' hearts and you should know that. This is some thank you for all we gave you.

Mother

She only signed "Mother" once, and that was in an extraordinarily miniscule hand, like a whisper.

"Brenda," I said.

"What?"

"Are you starting to cry?"

"No. I cried already."

"Don't start again."

"I'm trying not to, for God's sake."

"Okay . . . Brenda, can I ask you one question?"

"What?"

"Why did you leave it home?"

"Because I didn't plan on using it here, that's why."

"Suppose I'd come up. I mean I have come up, what about that?"

"I thought I'd come down first."

"So then couldn't you have carried it down then? Like a toothbrush?"

"Are you trying to be funny?"

"No. I'm just asking you why you left it home."

"I told you," Brenda said. "I thought I'd come home."

"But, Brenda, that doesn't make any sense. Suppose you did come home, and then you came back again. Wouldn't you have taken it with you then?"

"I don't *know.*"

"Don't get angry," I said.

"You're the one who's angry."

"I'm upset, I'm not angry."

"I'm upset then too."

I did not answer but walked to the window and looked out. The stars and moon were out, silver and hard, and from the window I could see over to the Harvard campus where lights burned and then seemed to flicker when the trees blew across them.

"Brenda . . ."

"What?"

"Knowing how your mother feels about you, wasn't it silly to leave it home? Risky?"

"What does how she feels about me have to do with it?"

"You can't trust her."

"Why can't I?"

"Don't you see. You *can't.*"

"Neil, she was only cleaning out the drawers."

"Didn't you know she would?"

"She never did before. Or maybe she did. Neil, I couldn't think of everything. We slept together night after night and nobody heard or noticed—"

"Brenda, why the hell are you willfully confusing things?"

"I'm not!"

"Okay," I said softly. "All right."

"It's you who's confusing things," Brenda said. "You act as though I wanted her to find it."

I didn't answer.

"Do you believe *that?*" she said, after neither of us had spoken for a full minute.

"I don't know."

"Oh, Neil, you're *crazy.*"

"What was crazier than leaving that damn thing around?"

"It was an oversight."

"Now it's an oversight, before it was deliberate."

"It was an oversight about the drawer. It wasn't an oversight about leaving it," she said.

"Brenda, sweetheart, wouldn't the safest, smartest, easiest, simplest thing been to have taken it with you? Wouldn't it?"

"It didn't make any difference either way."

"Brenda, this is the most frustrating argument of my life!"

"You keep making it seem as though I *wanted* her to find it. Do you think I need this? Do you? I can't even go home any more."

"Is that so?"

"Yes!"

"No," I said. "You can go home—your father will be waiting with two coats and a half-dozen dresses."

"What about my mother?"

"It'll be the same with her."

"Don't be absurd. How can I face them!"

"Why can't you face them? Did you do anything wrong?"

"Neil, look at the reality of the thing, will you?"

"*Did* you do anything wrong?"

"Neil, *they* think it's wrong. They're my parents."

"But do you think it's wrong—"

"That doesn't *matter.*"

"It does to me, Brenda . . ."

"Neil, why are *you* confusing things? You keep accusing me of things."

"Damn it, Brenda, you're guilty of some things."

"*What?*"

"Of leaving that damn diaphragm there. How can you call it an oversight!"

"Oh, Neil, don't start any of that psychoanalytic crap!"

"Then why else did you do it? You wanted her to find it!"

"Why?"

"I don't know, Brenda, *why?*"

"Oh!" she said, and she picked up the pillow and threw it back on to the bed.

"What happens now, Bren?" I said.

"What does that mean?"

"Just that. What happens now?"

She rolled over on to the bed and buried her head in it.

"Don't start crying," I said.

"I'm *not.*"

I was still holding the letters and took Mr. Patimkin's from its envelope.

"Why does your father capitalize all these letters?"

She didn't answer.

"'As for your mistake,'" I read aloud to Brenda, "'it takes Two to make a mistake and now that you will be away at school and from him and what you got involved in you will probably do all right I have every faith you will. Your father. Your father.'"

She turned and looked at me; but silently.

"'I have always never said bad things about any of your friends or Rons and that this should happen is only the exception that proves the rule. Have a Happy Holiday.'" I stopped; in Brenda's face there was positively no threat of tears; she looked, suddenly, solid and decisive. "Well, what are you going to do?" I asked.

"Nothing."

"Who are you going to bring home Thanksgiving—Linda?" I said, "or me?"

"Who *can* I bring home, Neil?"

"I don't know, who can you?"

"Can I bring you home?"

"I don't know," I said, "can you?"

"Stop repeating the question!"

"I sure as hell can't give you the answer."

"Neil, be realistic. After this, can I bring you home? Can you see us all sitting around the table?"

"I can't if you can't, and I can if you can."

"Are you going to speak Zen, for God's sake!"

"Brenda, the choices aren't mine. You can bring Linda or me. You can go home or not go home. That's another choice. Then you don't even have to worry about choosing between me and Linda."

"Neil, you don't understand. They're still my parents. They did send me to the best schools, didn't they? They have given me everything I've wanted, haven't they?"

"Yes."

"Then how can I not go home? I *have* to go home."

"Why?"

"You don't understand. Your parents don't bother you any more. You're lucky."

"Oh, sure. I live with my crazy aunt, that's a real bargain."

"Families are different. You don't understand."

"Goddamit, I understand more than you think. I understand why the hell you left that thing lying around. Don't you? Can't you put two and two together?"

"Neil, what are you talking about! You're the one who doesn't understand. You're the one who from the very beginning was accusing me of things? Remember? Isn't it so? Why don't you have your eyes fixed? Why don't you have this fixed, that fixed? As if it were my fault that I *could* have them fixed. You kept acting as if I was going to run away from you every minute. And now you're doing it again, telling me I planted that thing on purpose."

"I loved you, Brenda, so I cared."

"I loved *you.* That's why I got that damn thing in the first place."

And then we heard the tense in which we'd spoken and we settled back into ourselves and silence.

A few minutes later I picked up my bag and put on my coat. I think Brenda was crying too when I went out the door.

Instead of grabbing a cab immediately, I walked down the street and out towards the Harvard Yard which I had never seen before. I entered one of the gates and then headed out along a path, under the tired autumn foliage and the dark sky. I wanted to be alone, in the dark; not because I wanted to think about anything, but rather because, for just a while, I wanted to think about nothing. I walked clear across the Yard and up a little hill and then I was standing in front of the Lamont Library, which, Brenda had once told me, had Patimkin Sinks in its rest rooms. From the light of the lamp on the path behind me I could see my reflection in the glass front of the building. Inside, it was dark and there were no students to be seen, no librarians. Suddenly, I wanted to set down my suitcase and pick up a rock and heave it right through the glass, but of course I didn't. I simply looked at myself in the mirror the light made of the window. I was only that substance, I thought, those limbs, that face that I saw in front of me. I looked, but the outside of me gave up little information about the inside of me. I wished I could scoot around to the other side of the window, faster than light or sound or Herb Clark on Homecoming Day, to get behind that image and catch whatever it was that looked through those eyes. What was it inside me that had turned pursuit and clutching into love, and then turned it inside out again? What was it that had turned winning into losing, and losing—who knows—into winning? I was sure I had loved Brenda, though standing there, I knew I couldn't any longer. And I knew it would be a long while before I made love to anyone the way I had made love to her. With anyone else, could I summon up such a passion? Whatever spawned my love for her, had that spawned such lust too? If she had only been slightly *not* Brenda . . . but then would I have loved her? I looked hard at the image of me, at that darkening of the glass, and then my gaze pushed through it, over the cool floor, to a broken wall of books, imperfectly shelved.

I did not look very much longer, but took a train that got me into Newark just as the sun was rising on the first day of the Jewish New Year. I was back in plenty of time for work.

Alain Robbe-Grillet

(1922)

"To tell a story has become strictly impossible," Alain Robbe-Grillet has said, meaning that some contemporary writers can no longer employ conventional plots because such devices presuppose a coherent, decipherable universe, something many of today's artists can no longer believe in. Another contemporary French writer, Nathalie Sarraute, has argued in her *The Age of Suspicion* that psychological analysis in fiction is obsolete for our time and is, in general, false because it distorts and oversimplifies psychological reality. Now it is true, as the student no doubt suspects by looking about him, that not all contemporary writers agree with Robbe-Grillet and Mme. Sarraute—plotted stories and novels of character continue to be written. But it is also true that more and more writers are sidling away from traditional themes and forms of fiction. Viewing the world as inscrutably complex, a meaningless but fascinating conundrum, Robbe-Grillet and writers like him have sought to apprehend a more accurate understanding of reality, the reality of the world in the sixth decade of the twentieth century in which man is aware that he is *not* the center of things but exists at the periphery of a massive extramental universe. Because he believes man has passed beyond the omnipotence of the individual to a radically less anthropocentric consciousness, Robbe-Grillet feels justified in focusing on things—the *thereness* of things—divested of all human associations. He is fascinated by this strange world of objects, but because it is unrelated to man, he objects to most metaphors as being misrepresentations of reality. His uncommon interest in the surface geometries of the physical world is surely related to his training as an agronomic engineer. Of course, Robbe-Grillet's stories (called snapshots in English) and novels are far more than the meticulous recording of objects and designs. He captures the baffling actions and emotions of human beings—but always from the outside, objectively, cinematically. (Incidentally, Robbe-Grillet is seriously interested in the creative possibilities of motion pictures and wrote the screenplay for *Last Year at Marienbad.*) Although deeply influenced by

Sartre, Robbe-Grillet is vigorously opposed to Sartre's idea of *littêrature engagée,* believing that imaginative literature should not serve social, political, or psychological ends. A work of art, he has written, should mean nothing outside of itself, being an irreducible aesthetic object.

The Way Back

Once beyond the line of rocks that had, until then, blocked our view, we saw the mainland again: the hill with the pine woods, the two small white houses, and the gradual slope down which we had walked. We had completed the circle of the island.

And yet, if we could easily recognize the landscape on the mainland, such was not the case for the narrow stretch of water that separated us from it or, even worse, for the shore where we now were. It took us several minutes, then, to realize fully that our way was cut off.

We should have known it at the first glance. The roadway, cut out of the hillside, went down parallel to the shoreline and, at the level of the coarse sand beach, made a sudden bend to the right, to join a sort of stone jetty, wide enough to allow a car to pass, and which permitted one to cross the strait on foot at low tide. At the bend was a high embankment supported by a retaining wall, straight toward which the road ran; seen from the spot where we were, this embankment hid from view the beginning of the jetty. At present, the rest of it was covered with water. It was the change of viewpoint that had puzzled us momentarily: now we were on the island, and then too, we had approached from the opposite direction, walking toward the north, while the end of the road lies toward the south.

From the top of the hill, just after rounding the turn marked by three or four pine trees standing apart from the little woods, one can see straight ahead down the road as far as the jetty, with the arm of the sea to the right, and the island, which is not yet entirely an island. The water, calm as the water in a pond, almost comes over the stone roadway, whose smooth brown surface has the same worn look as that of the nearby rocks. Delicate mossy algae, half bleached by the sun, stain the roadway with greenish spots—the proof that it is subjected to frequent, prolonged immersions. At the other end of the jetty, as on this side, the paved surface rises imperceptibly to meet the dirt road that cuts across the little island; but, on that shore, the road stays quite flat afterward, and meets the jetty at an almost insignificant angle. Although there is no embankment to justify its presence, a retaining wall—symmetrical to the one on this shore—nevertheless protects the left side of the road, from the beginning of the slope to the upper limit of the sand beach—where beach stones of various sizes give way to brush underwood. On the island the vegetation seems even more desiccated than the dusty, yellowed plants that lie about us here.

We go down the road cut out of the hillside, toward the jetty. Two fishermen's houses face the road on the left; the front of each is newly covered with rough plaster and freshly whitewashed; the only building stones still visible are those round the openings—a low doorway and one small, square window. Windows and doors are closed, and the glass panes masked by wooden shutters without slats, painted a dazzling blue.

Lower down, the edge of the road, cut out of the soil of the hillside, reveals a vertical wall of yellow clay, as high as a man, interrupted here and there by bands of shale rock bristling with sharp-edged broken protrusions; an irregular hedge of thorny brambles and whitethorn runs along the top, cutting off one's view in the direction of the moor and the pine woods. On our right, however, the roadway is bordered only by a narrow embankment, no higher than one or two steps of a stairway, so that one's glance clears it directly, falling upon the rocks of the beach, the motionless water of the strait, the stone jetty, and the little island.

The water almost reaches the level of the stone roadway. We shall have to act quickly. A few more strides and we have completed our descent.

The jetty makes a right angle with the road, which runs abruptly into a wall of yellow earth, triangular in shape, marking the end of the cut made into the side of the hill; its base is protected by a retaining wall that stretches to the right considerably beyond the point of the triangle, alongside the stone pavement, forming a kind of incipient parapet. But it comes to an end after several yards, just as the slope diminishes at the junction with the middle section of the jetty—horizontal and polished smooth by the sea.

Having reached this point, we hesitate to go farther. We look at the island, in front of us, trying to estimate how long it will take to circle it. Of course there is the dirt road that cuts across it, but to take that would scarcely be worth the trouble. We look at the island in front of us and, down by our feet, the stones of the roadway over the jetty, covered here and there by half-dried-up greenish algae. The water almost reaches the level of the algae spots. It is as calm as that of a pond. One cannot see it rising: but one feels that it is, because of the lines of dust that move slowly on its surface between the tufts of sea wrack.

"We won't be able to get back," says Franz.

The island, seen at close range and from the water's level, seems much higher than before—much larger, too. Again we look at the little gray lines that move forward with slow regularity, twisting into spirals among the clumps of seaweed. Legrand says:

"It's not rising so fast."

"All right then, let's hurry."

We set out walking rapidly. But as soon as we have crossed the strait, we leave the roadbed and climb down toward the right to the beach that forms the shore of the island, continuing along the seashore; there the uneven footing, strewn with rocks and holes, makes walking more difficult—and much slower than we had counted on.

Once having set out on this shoreline path, we are unwilling to go back. As we progress, however, the rocks become larger and more numerous. Several times we are obliged to climb over real barriers, stretching so far out into the sea that we cannot go around them. Elsewhere we have to cross relatively flat places that cause us to lose even more time, since the flat stones are covered with slippery algae. Franz repeats that we shall not be able to get back across the water. Actually it is impossible to know with certainty how fast the water is rising, because we haven't time to stop to observe any change in level. It may even be slack tide.

It is equally difficult to determine what fraction of the whole circuit of the island we have already covered, for outcroppings of land constantly block our view, and one indentation of the coast follows another without constituting the least landmark. Besides, our concern over not losing a single minute over this difficult terrain occupies our entire attention—and the wider landscape disappears, leaving us aware instead of intruding fragments: a water hole to be avoided, a series of loose rocks, a pile of kelp concealing almost any danger, a large rock that must be scaled, another hole surrounded by viscous algae, mud-colored sand which sinks deep beneath our feet—as if to hold them fast.

Finally, after a last line of rocks, which for some time had blocked our view, we saw the mainland again, the hill with the pine woods, the two small white houses and the gradual slope down which we had walked.

At first we did not realize where the jetty was. Between us and the mainland coastline stretched only an arm of the sea whose waters gushed wildly by, toward our right, swirling at various points in rapids and eddies. The shoreline of the island itself seemed changed: now it was a blackish strand, whose visibly horizontal surface shone with innumerable shallow pools of water, at most an inch or two in depth. Beside a short, wooden wharf a rowboat was moored.

The path that led down to the beach at this point did not resemble the dirt road that we remembered. We had not noticed, earlier, the presence of a rowboat. As for the wharf that served for boarding the boat, it had nothing in common with the stone jetty that we had taken on the way over.

It took us several minutes to discover, thirty yards farther on, the two retaining walls that formed, at each end of the passage over the jetty, an incipient parapet. The stone pavement in between had disappeared. The water rushed over it in a milky torrent. The tilted ramps at each end of the jetty no doubt still emerged from the water, but the two low walls were enough to hide these from view. Nor could we see the low point where the road made a right angle, behind the embankment, as it joined the stones of the roadbed over the jetty. Once again we look down at our feet and see the lines of dust rising with slow regularity and twisting into spirals among the clumps of seaweed.

But apart from this almost imperceptible movement on the surface, the water is as calm as that of a pond. Yet it has already come close to the level of the jetty, while on the other side it is still a foot below. It is true that the sea rises much faster in the indentation nearest the entrance of the gulf. When the obstacle interposed by the jetty is overcome, the sudden drop in the water level must produce a current strong enough to make any crossing immediately impossible.

"We won't be able to get back," says Franz.

It was Franz who spoke first.

"I told you we wouldn't be able to get back."

No one answered him. We had reached a point beyond the little jetty; it was obviously useless to jump over the low retaining wall to try to cross on the stone roadway—not because the water was already too deep there, but because the strength of the current would have knocked us over at once and washed us away. Up close, one could clearly see the drop in water level from one side of the jetty to the other: toward the sea, the water was smooth and looked quite motionless; then, at the jetty, it suddenly curved downward, between the two shores, in the form of a cylinder, with no more than an occasional ripple, in such a regular flow that in spite of its velocity it seemed to be without motion—as if caught in a fragile pause in its movement, at some instantaneous moment captured by a photograph, such as that showing a pebble about to break the quiet surface of a pool, frozen in its fall at a point an inch or two above the surface.

Only beyond the smooth cylinder appeared the beginning of the series of turbulent swells and whirlpools whose force was plainly revealed by the whitish color of the water. Yet even there the disturbance had a kind of fixed disorder, in which crests and low swirls remained constantly at the same places, retaining the same form, so that they seemed frozen solid. All this violence of water, in fact, was not so very different from the pattern—scarcely more deceitful—of the little gray lines among the tufts of seaweed, which our conversation, interrupted by pauses, attempts to drive away:

"We won't be able to get back."

"It's not rising so fast."

"All right then, let's hurry."

"What do you expect to find on the other side of the island?"

"Let's walk around it without stopping, it won't take long."

"We won't be able to get back to land."

"It's not rising so fast, we have time enough to walk around it."

As we turned around we saw the man, standing near the boat, on the little wharf. He was looking in our direction—almost, at any rate, since he seemed rather intent on something located a bit to our left, in the midst of the swirling foam.

We went back toward him, and before we had spoken one word to him, he said:

"You want to get across."

It was not a question; without waiting for an answer he got down into the boat. We took our places in it too, as best we could. There was barely enough room for the three of us and the man, who rowed facing forward. He should have sat facing us, but he had chosen to sit in the same direction as we had, facing the prow, which required him to row backwards, in a rather awkward fashion.

At this short distance from the jetty the swells were still strong. To fight against the current the man had to give to his efforts—and to his boat—a very oblique angle with respect to the line of movement over the water. In spite of his vigorous rowing, we were moving even so at no more than a ridiculous pace. It even seemed to us, after a time, that all his energy was being spent merely to keep us motionless at the same place.

Legrand said something well intentioned about the hard task that our imprudence had inflicted on this unfortunate man; there was no response. Thinking that the man had perhaps not heard, Franz leaned forward to ask if it were really no longer possible to ford the strait on foot. There was no response to this question, either. The sailor must be deaf. He continued to row with the regularity of a machine, smoothly and without changing his course by a single degree, as if he were trying to reach, instead of the wooden wharf on the opposite shore which matched the one from which we had left, some raging part of the sea more toward the north, near where the jetty began, at the spot where a great pile of rocks lay against the brush-covered embankment, beyond which lay the end of the gradually sloping road and its two little white houses, the abrupt bend protected by the low wall, the stone roadway of the jetty stained with mossy spots, the water as calm as that of a pond, with its tufts of seaweed protruding into the water here and there and its lines of gray dust, twisting imperceptibly into spirals.

Donald Barthelme

(1933)

Donald Barthelme was born in Philadelphia in 1933. He was reared in Houston, attended the University of Houston, and edited the school newspaper. After serving in the Army in Korea, Barthelme began writing stories for *The New Yorker, Harper's,* and other periodicals. These stories have been collected in three volumes, *Come Back, Dr. Caligari* (1964), *Unspeakable Practices, Unnatural Acts* (1968), and *City Life* (1970). "See the Moon?" is included in the 1968 volume. Barthelme's stories are satirical, surrealistic commentaries on the many insanities that characterize contemporary America. There is often a feeling of controlled hysteria in some of his stories, and "See the Moon?" is representative in this regard.

See the Moon?

I know you think I'm wasting my time. You've made that perfectly clear. But I'm conducting these very important lunar hostility studies. And it's not you who'll have to leave the warm safe capsule. And dip a toe into the threatening lunar surround.

I am still wearing my yellow flower which has lasted wonderfully.

My methods may seem a touch light-minded. Have to do chiefly with folded paper airplanes at present. But the paper must be folded *in the right way.* Lots of calculations and worrying about edges.

Show me a man who worries about edges and I'll show you a natural-born winner. Cardinal Y agrees. Columbus himself worried, the Admiral of the Ocean Sea. But he kept it quiet.

The sun so warm on this screened porch, it reminds me of my grandmother's place in Tampa. The same rusty creaky green glider and the same faded colored canvas cushions. And at night the moon graphed by the screen wire, if you squint. The Sea of Tranquillity occupying squares 47 through 108.

See the moon? It hates us.

My methods are homely but remember Newton and the apple. And when Rutherford started out he didn't even have a decently heated laboratory. And then there's the matter of my security check—I'm waiting for the government. Somebody told it I'm insecure. *That's true.*

I suffer from a frightful illness of the mind, light-mindedness. It's not catching. You needn't shrink.

You've noticed the wall? I pin things on it, souvenirs. There is the red hat, there the book of instructions for the Ant Farm. And this is a traffic ticket written on a saint's day (which saint? I don't remember) in 1954 just outside a fat little town (which town? I don't remember) in Ohio by a cop who asked me what I did. I said I wrote poppycock for the president of a university, true then.

You can see how far I've come. Lunar hostility studies aren't for everyone.

It's my hope that these . . . souvenirs . . . will someday merge, blur—cohere is the word, maybe—into something meaningful. A grand word, meaningful. What do I look for? A work of art, I'll not accept anything less. Yes I know it's shatteringly ingenuous but I wanted to be a painter. They get away with murder in my view; Mr. X on the *Times* agrees with me. You don't know how I envy them. They can pick up a Baby Ruth wrapper on the street, glue it to the canvas (in the *right place*, of course, there's that), and lo! people crowd about and cry, "A real Baby Ruth wrapper, by God, what could be realer than that!" Fantastic metaphysical advantage. You hate them, if you're ambitious.

The Ant Farm instructions are a souvenir of Sylvia. The red hat came from Cardinal Y. We're friends, in a way.

I wanted to be one, when I was young, a painter. But I couldn't stand stretching the canvas. Does things to the fingernails. And that's the first place people look.

Fragments are the only forms I trust.

Light-minded or no, I'm . . . riotous with mental health. I measure myself against the Russians, that's fair. I have here a clipping datelined Moscow, four young people apprehended strangling a swan. *That's* boredom. The swan's name, Borka. The sentences as follows: Tsarev, metalworker, served time previously for stealing public property, four years in a labor camp, strict regime. Roslavtsev, electrician, jailed previously for taking a car on a joyride, three years and four months in a labor camp, semi-strict regime. Tatyana Voblikova (only nineteen and a Komsomol member too), technician, one and a half years in a labor camp, degree of strictness unspecified. Anna G. Kirushina, technical worker, fine of twenty per cent of salary for one year. Anna objected to the strangulation, but softly: she helped stuff the carcass in a bag.

The clipping is tacked up on my wall. I inspect it from time to time, drawing the moral. Strangling swans is wrong.

My brother who is a very distinguished pianist . . . has no fingernails at all. Don't look it's horrible. He plays under another name. And tunes his piano peculiarly, some call it sour. And renders *ragas* he wrote himself. A night *raga* played at noon can cause darkness, did you know that? It's extraordinary.

He wanted to be an Untouchable, Paul did. That was his idea of a contemporary career. But then a girl walked up and touched him (slapped him, actually; it's a complicated story). And he joined us, here in the imbroglio.

My father on the other hand is perfectly comfortable, and that's not a criticism. He makes flags, banners, bunting (sometimes runs me up a shirt). There was never any question of letting my father drink from the public well. He was on the Well Committee, he decided who dipped and who didn't. That's not a criticism. Exercises his creativity, nowadays, courtesy the emerging nations. Green for the veldt that nourishes the gracile Grant's gazelle, white for the purity of our revolutionary aspirations. The red for blood is understood. That's not a criticism. It's what they all ask for.

A call tonight from Gregory, my son by my first wife. Seventeen and at M.I.T. already. Recently he's been asking questions. Suddenly he's conscious of himself as a being with a history.

The telephone rings. Then, without a greeting: *Why did I have to take those little pills?* What little pills? *Little white pills with a "W" on them.* Oh. Oh yes. You had some kind of a nervous disorder, for a while. *How old was I?* Eight. Eight or nine. *What was it? Was it epilepsy?* Good God no, nothing so fancy. We never found out what it was. It went away. *What did I do? Did I fall down?* No no. Your mouth trembled, that was all. You couldn't control it. *Oh. O.K. See you.*

The receiver clicks.

Or: *What did my great-grandfather do? For a living I mean?* He was a ballplayer, semi-pro ballplayer, for a while. Then went into the building business. *Who'd he play for?* A team called the St. Augustine Rowdies, I think it was. *Never heard of them.* Well . . . *Did he make any money? In the building business?* Quite a bit. *Did your father inherit it?* No, it was tied up in a lawsuit. When the suit was over there wasn't anything left. *Oh. What was the lawsuit?* Great-grandfather diddled a man in a land deal.

So the story goes. *Oh. When did he die?* Let's see, 1938 I think. *What of?* Heart attack. *Oh. O.K. See you.*

End of conversation.

Gregory, you didn't listen to my advice. I said try the Vernacular Isles. Where fish are two for a penny and women two for a fish. But you wanted M.I.T. and electron-spin-resonance spectroscopy. You didn't even crack a smile in your six-ply heather hopsacking.

Gregory, you're going to have a half brother now. You'll like that, won't you? Will you half like it?

We talked about the size of the baby, Ann and I. What could be deducted from the outside.

I said it doesn't look very big to me. She said it's big enough for *us.* I said we don't need such a great roaring big one after all. She said they cost the earth, those extra-large sizes. Our holdings in Johnson's Baby Powder to be considered too. We'd need acres and acres. I said we'll put it in a Skinner box maybe. She said no child of hers. Displayed under glass like a rump roast. I said you haven't wept lately. She said I keep getting bigger whether I laugh or cry.

Dear Ann. I don't think you've quite . . .

What you don't understand is, it's like somebody walks up to you and says, I have a battleship I can't use, would you like to have a battleship? And you say, yes yes, I've never had a battleship, I've always wanted one. And he says, it has four sixteen-inch guns forward, and a catapult for launching scout planes. And you say, I've always wanted to launch scout planes. And he says, *it's yours,* and then you have this battleship. And then you have to paint it, because it's rusting, and clean it, because it's dirty, and anchor it somewhere, because the Police Department wants you to get it off the streets. And the crew is crying, and there are silverfish in the chartroom and a funny knocking noise in Fire Control, water rising in the No. 2 hold, and the chaplain can't find the Palestrina tapes for the Sunday service. And you can't get anybody to sit with it. And finally you discover that what you have here is this great, big, pink-and-blue rockabye *battleship.*

Ann. I'm going to keep her ghostly. Just the odd bit of dialogue:

"What is little Gog doing."

"Kicking."

I don't want her bursting in on us with the freshness and originality of her observations. What we need here is *perspective.* She's good with Gregory though. I think he half likes her.

Don't go. The greased-pig chase and balloon launchings come next.

I was promising once. After the Elgar, a *summa cum laude.* The university was proud of me. It was a bright shy white new university on the Gulf Coast. Gulls and oleanders and quick howling hurricanes. The teachers brown burly men with power boats and beer cans. The president a retired admiral who'd done beautiful things in the Coral Sea.

"You will be a credit to us, George," the admiral said. That's not my name. I'm protecting my identity, what there is of it.

Applause from the stands filled with mothers and brothers. Then following the mace in a long line back to the field house to ungown. Ready to take my place at the top.

But a pause at Pusan, and the toy train to the Chorwon Valley. Walking down a road wearing green clothes. Korea green and black and silent. The truce had been signed. I had a carbine to carry. My buddy Bo Tagliabue the bonus baby, for whom the Yanks had paid thirty thousand. We whitewashed rocks to enhance our area. Colonels came crowding to feel Bo's hurling arm. Mine the whitest rocks.

I lunched with Thais from Thailand, hot curry from great galvanized washtubs. Engineers banging down the road in six-by-sixes raising red dust. My friend Gib Mandell calling Elko, Nevada, on his canvas-covered field telephone. "Operator I crave Elko, Nevada."

Then I was a sergeant with stripes, getting the troops out of the sun. Tagliabue a sergeant too. *Triste* in the Tennessee Tea Room in Tokyo, yakking it up in Yokohama. Then back to our little tent town on the side of a hill, boosting fifty-gallon drums of heating oil tentward in the snow.

Ozzie the jeep driver waking me in the middle of the night. "They got Julian in the Tango Tank." And up and alert as they taught us in Leadership School, over the hills to Tango, seventy miles away. Whizzing through Teapot, Tempest, Toreador, with the jeep's canvas top flapping. Pfc. Julian drunk and disorderly and beaten up. The M.P. sergeant held out a receipt book, I signed for the bawdy remains.

Back over the pearly Pacific in a great vessel decorated with oranges. A trail of orange peel on the plangent surface. Sitting in the bow fifty miles out of San Francisco, listening to the Stateside disc jockeys chattering cha cha cha. Ready to grab my spot at the top.

My clothes looked old and wrong. The city looked new with tall buildings raised while my back was turned. I rushed here and there visiting friends. They were burning beef in their back yards, brown burly men with beer cans. The beef black on the outside, red on the inside. My friend Horace had fidelity. "Listen to that bass. That's forty watts worth of bass, boy."

I spoke to my father. "How is business?" "If Alaska makes it," he said, "I can buy a Hasselblad. And we're keeping an eye on Hawaii." Then he photographed my veteran face, f.6 at 300. My father once a cheerleader at a great Eastern school. Jumping in the air and making fierce angry down-the-field gestures at the top of his leap.

That's not a criticism. We have to have cheerleaders.

I presented myself at the Placement Office. I was on file. My percentile was the percentile of choice.

"How come you were headman of only one student organization, George?" the Placement Officer asked. Many hats for top folk was the fashion then.

I said I was rounded, and showed him my slash. From the Fencing Club.

"But you served your country in an overseas post."

"And regard my career plan on neatly typed pages with wide margins."

"Exemplary," the Placement Officer said. "You seem married, mature, malleable, how would you like to affiliate yourself with us here at the old school? We have a spot for a poppycock man, to write the admiral's speeches. Have you ever done poppycock?"

I said no but maybe I could fake it.

"Excellent, excellent," the Placement Officer said. "I see you have grasp. And you can sup at the Faculty Club. And there is a ten-percent discount on tickets for all home games."

The admiral shook my hand. "You will be a credit to us, George," he said. I wrote poppycock, sometimes cockypap. At four o'clock the faculty hoisted the cocktail flag. We drank Daiquiris on each other's sterns. I had equipped myself—a fibre-glass runabout, someplace to think. In the stadia of friendly shy new universities we went down the field on Gulf Coast afternoons with gulls, or exciting nights under the tall toothpick lights. The crowd roared. Sylvia roared. Gregory grew.

There was no particular point at which I stopped being promising.

Moonstruck I was, after a fashion. Sitting on a bench by the practice field, where the jocks chanted secret signals in their underwear behind tall canvas blinds. Layabout babies loafing on blankets, some staked out on twelve-foot dog chains. Brown mothers squatting knee to knee in shifts of scarlet and green. I stared at the moon's pale daytime presence. It seemed . . . inimical.

Moonstruck.

We're playing Flinch. You flinched.

The simplest things are the most difficult to explain, all authorities agree. Say I was tired of p***yc**k, if that pleases you. It's true enough.

Sylvia went up in a puff of smoke. She didn't like unsalaried life. And couldn't bear a male acquaintance moon-staring in the light of day. Decent people look at night.

We had trouble with Gregory: who would get which part. She settled for three-fifths, and got I think the worst of it, the dreaming raffish Romany part that thinks science will save us. I get matter-of-fact midnight telephone calls: *My E.E. instructor shot me down.* What happened? *I don't know, he's an ass anyhow.* Well, that may be but still—*When's the baby due?* January, I told you. *Yeah, can I go to Mexico City for the holidays?* Ask your mother, you know she—*There's this guy, his old man has a villa. . . .* Well, we can talk about it. *Yeah, was grandmother a Communist?* Nothing so distinguished, she—*You said she was kicked out of Germany.* Her family was anti-Nazi. *Adler means eagle in German.* That's true. There was something called the Weimar Republic, her father—*I read about it.*

We had trouble with Gregory, we wanted to be scientific. Toys from Procreative Playthings of Princeton. O Gregory, that Princeton crowd got you coming and going. Procreative Playthings at one end and the Educational Testing Service at the other. And that serious-minded co-op nursery, that was a mistake. "A growing understanding between parent and child through shared group experience." I still remember poor Henry Harding III. Under "Sibs" on the membership roll they listed his, by age:

26
25
23
20
19
15
10
9
8
6

O Mrs. Harding, haven't you heard? They have these little Christmas-tree ornaments for the womb now, they work wonders.

Did we do "badly" by Gregory? Will we do "better" with Gog? Such questions curl the hair. It's wiser not to ask.

I mentioned Cardinal Y (the red hat). He's a friend, in a way. Or rather, the subject of one of my little projects.

I set out to study cardinals, about whom science knows nothing. It seemed to me that cardinals could be known in the same way we know fishes or roses, by classification and enumeration. A doomed project, perhaps, but who else has embraced this point of view? Difficult nowadays to find a point of view kinky enough to call one's own, with Sade himself being carried through the streets on the shoulders of sociologists, cheers and shouting, ticker tape unwinding from high windows . . .

The why of Cardinal Y. You're entitled to an explanation.

The Cardinal rushed from the Residence waving in the air his hands, gloved in yellow pigskin it appeared. I grasped a hand. "Yes, yellow pigskin!" the Cardinal cried. I wrote in my book, *yellow pigskin.*

Significant detail. The pectoral cross contains nine diamonds, the scarlet soutane is laundered right on the premises.

I asked the Cardinal questions, we had a conversation.

"I am thinking of a happy island more beautiful than can be imagined," I said.

"I am thinking of a golden mountain which does not exist," he said.

"Upon what does the world rest?" I asked.

"Upon an elephant," he said.

"Upon what does the elephant rest?"

"Upon a tortoise."

"Upon what does the tortoise rest?"

"Upon a red lawnmower."

I wrote in my book, *playful.*

"Is there any value that has value?" I asked.

"If there is any value that has value, then it must lie outside the whole sphere of what happens and is the case, for all that happens and is the case is accidental," he said. He was not serious. I wrote in my book, *knows the drill.*

(Oh I had heard reports, how he slunk about in the snow telling children he was Santa Claus, how he disbursed funds in unauthorized disbursements to unshaven men who came to the kitchen door, how his housekeeper pointedly rolled his red socks together and black socks together hinting red with red and black with black, the Cardinal patiently unrolling a red ball to get a red sock and a black ball to get a black sock, which he then wore together. . . .)

Cardinal Y. He's sly.

I was thorough. I popped the Cardinal on the patella with a little hammer, and looked into his eyes with a little light. I tested the Cardinal's stomach acidity using Universal Indicator Paper, a scale of one to ten, a spectrum of red to blue. The pH value was 1 indicating high acidity. I measured the Cardinal's ego strength using the Minnesota Multiphastic Muzzle Map, he had an M.M.M.M. of four over three. I sang to the Cardinal, the song was "Stella by Starlight." He did not react in any way. I calculated the number of gallons needed to fill the Cardinal's bath to a depth of ten inches (beyond which depth, the Cardinal said, he never ventured). I took the Cardinal to the ballet, the ballet was "The Conservatory." The Cardinal applauded at fifty-seven points. Afterward, backstage, the Cardinal danced with Plenosova, holding her at arm's length with a good will and an ill grace. The skirts of the scarlet soutane stood out to reveal high-button shoes, and the stagehands clapped.

I asked the Cardinal his views on the moon, he said they were the conventional ones, and that is how I know all I know about cardinals. Not enough perhaps to rear a science of cardinalogy upon, but enough perhaps to form a basis for the investigations of other investigators. My report is over there, in the blue binding, next to my copy of *La Géomancie et la Néomancie des Anciens* by the Seigneur of Salerno.

Cardinal Y. One can measure and measure and miss the most essential thing. I liked him. I still get the odd blessing in the mail now and then.

Too, maybe I was trying on the role. Not for myself. When a child is born, the locus of one's hopes . . . shifts, slightly. Not altogether, not all at once. But you feel it, this displacement. You speak up, strike attitudes, like the mother of a tiny Lollobrigida. Drunk with possibility once more.

I am still wearing my yellow flower which has lasted wonderfully.

"What is Gog doing."

"Sleeping."

You see, Gog of mine, Gog o' my heart, I'm just trying to give you a little briefing here. I don't want you unpleasantly surprised. I can't stand a startled look. Regard me as a sort of Distant Early Warning System. Here is the world and here are the knowledgeable knowers knowing. What can I tell you? What has been pieced together from the reports of travellers.

Fragments are the only forms I trust.

Look at my wall, it's all there. That's a leaf, Gog, stuck up with Scotch Tape. No no, the Scotch Tape is the shiny transparent stuff, the leaf the veined irregularly shaped . . .

There are several sides to this axe, Gog, consider the photostat, "Mr. W. B. Yeats Presenting Mr. George Moore to the Queen of the Fairies." That's a civilized gesture, I mean Beerbohm's. And when the sculptor Aristide Maillol went into the printing business he made the paper by *chewing the fibers himself.* That's dedication. And here is a Polaroid photo, shows your Aunt Sylvia and me putting an Ant Farm together. That's how close we were in those days. Just an Ant Farm apart.

See the moon? It hates us.

And now comes J. J. Sullivan's orange-and-blue Gulf Oil truck to throw kerosene into the space heater. Driver in green siren suit, red face, blond shaved head. The following rich verbal transaction:

"Beautiful day."

"Certainly is."

And now settling back in this green glider with a copy of *Man.* Dear Ann when I look at *Man* I don't want you. Unfolded Ursala Thigpen seems eversomuchmore desirable. A clean girl too and with interests, cooking, botany, pornographic novels. Someone new to show my slash to.

In another month Gog leaps fully armed from the womb. What can I do for him? I can get him into A.A., I have influence. And make sure no harsh moonlight falls on his new soft head.

Hello there Gog. We hope you'll be very happy here.

Appendix of Essays on Technique

The Reader of Fiction

Simon O. Lesser

The meager satisfaction that [man] can extract from reality leaves him starving.

Freud

In nostalgic moments we may tend to think of childhood as a time of almost unbroken happiness, free of the strivings, frustrations and complexities which make adult life so burdensome. But when we look more closely we discover that children, too, have their anxieties and discontents; they turn to reading as one way of dealing with these. The painful truth is that at each stage of our lives we are dissatisfied, unhappy and anxious a large part of the time. No matter how often we are reminded of this fact by philosophers and religious seers—or, more agonizingly, by events in our own lives—we only occasionally and momentarily accept its validity. We cannot, of course, deny that pain, dissatisfaction and disillusionment are inevitable aspects of human experience, but we can and do seek to minimize their significance. For example, we may attempt to treat painful aspects of experience as exceptional or even accidental. No matter what we have gone through, we tell ourselves with a stubbornness which has something magnificent about it that the next phase of our lives will fulfil more of our longings and give us less cause to feel wretched. Only exceptional men, or the rest of us in moments of exceptional honesty, face the possibility that there may be something about life itself which is inimical to our desire for happiness.

It is useless, and adolescent, to complain about the frustrating quality of much of our experience, and by and large man does not complain. Indeed, as we shall see in more detail when we analyze comedy and tragedy, the very works which call attention to the grimmest aspects of life pay tribute to the resiliency of the human spirit. *Candide* is at once the saddest and the gayest of books. These victories are achieved not only in literature, but in a sphere we hold more lightly despite the consolations it offers—the sphere of wit. Two old Jews were bemoaning the sadness of the world and the trials and tribulations of their own people. "Life is hard, hard," concluded one. "Better we should not have been born at all." "Yes, but who can have such luck," replied his companion. "Maybe one in a million." Many stories are like this, covertly counseling us to accept the human situation at the same time that they acknowledge its painfulness.

The joke reveals something else: the endeavor of human beings to wrest enjoyment from even the most unsatisfactory aspects of life. Man is an indefatigable seeker of pleasure. If human experience does not yield enough satisfaction—and, of course, it does not—then he will strive at least to protect himself from the pain it may give rise to and to create other worlds more in accord with his desires. With the first of these defenses, which include all the means men employ to keep the world from hurting them or to dull themselves to unavoidable suffering, we are not immediately concerned. Art, including fiction, is neither a means of avoiding pain nor of dulling oneself to it: neither a renunciation nor a narcotic. Like play, fantasy and wit, which are its close relations, it represents an attempt to augment the meager satisfactions offered by experience through the creation of a more harmonious world to which one can repair, however briefly, for refuge, solace and pleasure.

Character and Theme

Douglas A. Hughes

English novelist John Galsworthy wrote, "Character is plot," meaning that character determines the pattern of actions a fictional person will make in a narrative just as in life what one does and thinks depends, as we say, on a man's character. Character is an exceedingly important element in fiction, and the difference between a good and a great story often rests on the skill with which an author presents character. Although all the elements of narration (plot, point of view, etc.) are essential to the overall effect of any work, character is generally the most interesting, the ingredient which engages the reader's attention most intensely. And of course this is true for a very good reason. Most of us are interested in human nature, in people and why people act as they do, and narrative fiction, which frames reality and arrests time, permits us to appreciate and examine man in action and thought. Narrative fiction, especially in the twentieth century, is *primarily* about character.

Great writers are able to create characters out of their imaginations and then convince readers that these illusions are real, no mean task. By the subtlest means the novelist and, to a lesser extent, short-story writer must persuade readers that the fictional figures are real and alive and worth caring about, and the most distinguished writers succeed almost magically at this remarkable deception. Because we are often predisposed to understanding or identifying with characters who have problems much like our own, we lend ourselves to the psychological manipulation of the author and come to feel that we know some characters in novels better than our friends or members of our family. One reason for this feeling is that in fiction we are privileged to enter the private, hidden recesses of another self, whereas in life even our intimate friends remain relatively removed from us. In fact, this vicarious participation in the lives of other persons is one of the great pleasures of reading narrative fiction. In the final analysis, characters, if they are well done, are interesting, understandable, and convincing.

Since E. M. Forster's pronouncements on character in his often quoted *Aspects of the Novel* (1927), critics have distinguished between "flat" and "round" characters. Two-dimensional, static, predictable, flat characters tend to be types or representative figures who lack complexity and individuality. Most minor characters are flat and so are many major characters in the nineteenth-century novel. Flat, however, should not be equated with deficient, for flat characters are not necessarily less important than the more fully developed round ones. Everything depends on the author's overall design and how he wishes to use his characters. Uncomplicated characters may be used to focus on theme or plot, as in "The Birthmark," "The Three Strangers," "The Bride Comes to Yellow Sky." and "The Sin of Jesus." In contrast, round characters are complicated individuals who are capable of growth and change. The protagonist (central character) of a story or novel is generally round and therefore capable of self-discovery.

Characterization, the method or methods a writer employs to delineate his fictional persons, is commonly regarded as either expository or dramatic, though such a division is something of an oversimplification. In expository characterization the author presents his characters directly, explaining with an all-knowing power what they are. In the fifth paragraph of Maupassant's "Mademoiselle Fifi" one fines an example of the expository method. "The major was a giant with broad shoulders and a long, fair beard. . . . His whole solemn person suggested the idea of a military peacock, a peacock who was carrying his tail spread out onto his breast. He had cold, gentle blue eyes and the scar from a sword cut which he had received in the war with Austria; he was said to be an honorable man was well as a brave officer." Contemporary readers in general find the dramatic method more gratifying and twentieth-century writers have relied on it far more than their nineteenth-century counterparts. Indirect and subtle, dramatic characterization shows the person in action and encourages the reader to infer the kind of character from the actions and thoughts of the person. Dramatic characterization is achieved by means of action, dialogue, and listening to the character thinking, as in Joyce's "A Little Cloud" and Roth's *Goodbye, Columbus.* A particularly pleasing kind of dynamic characterization occurs when one person, the story's narrator, reveals his own character unintentionally while describing others, as in Malamud's "Black Is My Favorite Color."

Susan Sontag, a perceptive contemporary critic, has written, "A great work of art is never simply (or even mainly) a vehicle of ideas or of moral sentiments." This idea, which has been expressed by hundreds of artists since the middle of the nineteenth century, must again be stated for today's readers because many of them insist on reading narrative fiction as palatable philosophy or moral prescriptions. Fiction is an imaginative and emotional experience, but because it is concerned with men in action and conflict, it does express, indirectly or directly, ideas. Therefore, ideas and themes may play an important role in individual works, but their importance should not be exaggerated at the expense of the other elements of fiction. As the poet John Ciardi has said, "Literature . . . is never about ideas, but always and only about *the experience of ideas.*"[1]

The theme of a novel or story is the central idea which may be abstracted from the incidents in the narrative, but this is not to equate theme with *the* meaning of a work. The meaning of a work of narrative fiction is the work itself, i.e., everything the author has included, and presumably the meaning could not be expressed in any other way. The statement of theme formulates a major insight or idea that has emerged from the work, and although most stories have one or more themes, some have none, or at least not one that can be exactly expressed. The theme may be expressed briefly or in several sentences depending on the complexity of a work and the subtlety of its comments on life. A motif, which is related to theme, is an idea, one not central but subordinate, that is repeated several times in the course of the narrative for various effects.

[1] The student should keep in mind that class discussions of the themes and techniques of fiction, however interesting and informative they may be, are always peripheral to literature as art, as an organized imaginative experience.

Plot

E. M. Forster

"Character," says Aristotle, "gives us qualities, but it is in actions—what we do—that we are happy or the reverse." We have already decided that Aristotle is wrong and now we must face the consequences of disagreeing with him. "All human happiness and misery," says Aristotle, "take the form of action." We know better. We believe that happiness and misery exist in the secret life, which each of us leads privately and to which (in his characters) the novelist has access. And by the secret life we mean the life for which there is no external evidence, not, as is vulgarly supposed, that which is revealed by a chance word or a sigh. A chance word or sigh are just as much evidence as a speech or a murder: the life they reveal ceases to be secret and enters the realm of action.

There is, however, no occasion to be heard on Aristotle. He had read few novels and no modern ones—the *Odyssey* but not *Ulysses*—he was by temperament apathetic to secrecy, and indeed regarded the human mind as a sort of tub from which everything can finally be extracted; and when he wrote the words quoted above he had in view the drama, where no doubt they hold true. In the drama all human happiness and misery does and must take the form of action. Otherwise its existence remains unknown, and this is the great difference between the drama and the novel.

The speciality of the novel is that the writer can talk about his characters as well as through them or can arrange for us to listen when they talk to themselves. He has access to self-communings, and from that level he can descend even deeper and peer into the subconscious. A man does not talk to himself quite truly—not even to himself; the happiness or misery that he secretly feels proceed from causes that he cannot quite explain, because as soon as he raises them to the level of the explicable they lose their native quality. The novelist has a real pull here. He can show the subconscious short-circuiting straight into action (the dramatist can do this too); he can also show it in its relation to soliloquy. He commands all the secret life, and he must not be robbed of this privilege. "How did the writer know that?" it is sometimes said. "What's his standpoint? He is not being consistent, he's shifting his point of view from the limited to the omniscient, and now he's edging back again." Questions like these have too much the atmosphere of the law courts about them. All that matters to the reader is whether the shifting of attitude and the secret life are convincing, whether it is *πιταvov* in fact, and with his favourite word ringing in his ears Aristotle may retire.

However, he leaves us in some confusion, for what, with this enlargement of human nature, is going to become of the plot? In most literary works there are two elements: human individuals, whom we have recently discussed, and the element vaguely called art. Art we have also dallied with, but with a very low form of it: the story: the chopped-off length of the tapeworm of time. Now we arrive at a much higher aspect: the plot, and the plot, instead of finding human beings more or less cut to its requirements, as they are in the drama, finds them enormous, shadowy and intractable, and three-quarters hidden like an iceberg. In vain it points out to these unwieldy creatures the advantages of the triple process of complication, crisis, and solution so persuasively expounded by Aristotle. A few of them rise and comply, and a novel which ought to have been a play is the result. But there is no general response. They want to sit apart and brood or something, and the plot (whom I here visualize as a sort of higher government official) is concerned at their lack of public spirit: "This will not do," it seems to say. "Individualism is a most valuable quality; indeed my own position depends upon individuals; I have always admitted as much freely. Nevertheless there are certain limits, and those limits are being overstepped. Characters must not brood too long, they must not waste time running up and down ladders in their own insides, they must contribute, or higher interests will be jeopardised." How well one knows that phrase, "a contribution to the plot"! It is accorded, and of necessity, by the people in a drama: how necessary is it in a novel?

Let us define a plot. We have defined a story as a narrative of events arranged in their time-sequence. A plot is also a narrative of events, the emphasis falling on causality. "The king died and then the queen died," is a story. "The king died, and then the queen died of grief" is a plot. The time-sequence is preserved, but the sense of causality overshadows it. Or again: "The queen died, no one knew why, until it was discovered that it was through grief at the death of the king." This is a plot with a mystery in in it, a form capable of high development. It suspends the time-sequence, it moves so far away from the story as its limitations will allow. Consider the death of the queen. If it is in a story we say "and then?" If it is in a plot we ask "why?" That is the fundamental difference between these two aspects of the novel. A plot cannot be told to a gaping audience of cave men or to a tyrannical sultan or to their modern descendent the movie-public. They can only be kept awake by "and then—and then—." They can only supply curiosity. But a plot demands intelligence and memory also.

Curiosity is one of the lowest of the human faculties. You will have noticed in daily life what when people are inquisitive they nearly always have bad memories and are usually stupid at bottom. The man who begins by asking you how many brothers and sisters you have, is never a sympathetic character, and if you meet him in a year's time he will probably ask you how many brothers and sisters you have, his mouth again sagging open, his eyes still bulging from his head. It is difficult to be friends with such a man, and for two inquisitive people to be friends must be impossible. Curiosity by itself takes us a very little way, nor does it take us far into the novel—only as far as the story. If we could grasp the plot we must add intelligence and memory.

Intelligence first. The intelligent novel-reader, unlike the inquisitive one who just runs his eye over a new fact, mentally picks it up. He sees it from two points of view: isolated, and related to the other facts he has read on previous pages. Probably he does not understand it, but he does not expect to do so yet awhile. The facts in a highly organized novel (like *The Egoist)* are often of the nature of cross-correspondences and the ideal spectator cannot expect to view them properly until he is sitting up on a hill at the end. This element of surprise or mystery—the detective element as it is sometimes rather emptily called—is of great importance in a plot. It occurs through a suspension of the time-sequence; a mystery is a pocket in time, and it occurs crudely, as in "Why did the queen die?" and more subtly in half-explained gestures and words, the true meaning of which only dawns pages ahead. Mystery is essential to a plot, and cannot be appreciated without intelligence. To the curious it is just another "and then ——." To appreciate a mystery, part of the mind must be left behind, brooding, while the other part goes marching on.

That brings us to our second qualification: memory.

Memory and intelligence are closely connected, for unless we remember we cannot understand. If by the time the queen dies we have forgotten the existence of the king we shall never make out what killed her. The plotmaker expects us to remember, we expect him to leave no loose ends. Every action or word ought to count; it ought to be economical and spare; even when complicated it should be organic and free from dead matter. It may be difficult or easy, it may and should contain mysteries, but it ought not to mislead. And over it, as it unfolds, will hover the memory of the reader (that dull glow of the mind of which intelligence is the bright advancing edge) and will constantly rearrange and reconsider, seeing new clues, new chains of cause and effect, and the final sense (if the plot has been a fine one) will not be of clues or chains, but of something aesthetically compact, something which might have been shown by the novelist straight away, only if he had shown it straight away it would never have become beautiful. We come up against beauty here—for the first time in our enquiry: beauty at which a novelist should never aim, though he fails if he does not achieve it. I will conduct beauty to her proper place later on. Meanwhile please accept her as part of a completed plot. She looks a little surprised at being there, but beauty ought to look a little surprised: it is the emotion which best suits her face, as Botticelli knew when he painted her risen from the waves, between the winds and the flowers. The beauty who does not look surprised, who accepts her position as her due—she reminds us too much of a prima donna.

Point of View

Percy Lubbock

The whole intricate question of method, in the craft of fiction, I take to be governed by the question of the point of view—the question of the relation in which the narrator stands to the story. He tells it as *he* sees it, in the first place; the reader faces the story-teller and listens, and the story may be told so vivaciously that the presence of the minstrel is forgotten, and the scene becomes visible, peopled with the characters of the tale. It may be so, it very often is so for a time. But it is not so always, and the story-teller himself grows conscious of a misgiving. If the spell is weakened at any moment, the listener is recalled from the scene to the mere author before him, and the story rests only upon the author's direct assertion. Is it not possible, then, to introduce another point of view, to set up a fresh narrator to bear the brunt of the reader's scrutiny? If the story-teller is *in* the story himself, the author is dramatized; his assertions gain in weight, for they are backed by the presence of the narrator in the pictured scene. It is advantage scored; the author has shifted his responsibility, and it now falls where the reader can see and measure it; the arbitrary quality which may at any time be detected in the author's voice is disguised in the voice of his spokesman. Nothing is now imported into the story from without; it is self-contained, it has no associations with anyone beyond its circle.

Such is the first step toward dramatization, and in very many a story it may be enough. The spokesman is there, in recognizable relation with his matter; no question of his authority can arise. But now a difficulty may be started by the nature of the tale that he tells. If he has nothing to do but to relate what he has seen, what anyone might have seen in his position, his account will serve very well; there is no need for more. Let him unfold his chronicle as it appears in his memory. But if he is himself the subject of his own story, if the story involves a searching exploration of his own consciousness, an account in his own words, after the fact, is not by any means the best imaginable. Far better it would be to see him while he is actually at work in the agitation, whatever it may be, which is to make the book. The matter would then be objective and visible to the reader, instead of reaching him in the form of a report at second hand. But how to manage this without falling back upon the author and *his* report, which has already been tried and for good reasons, as it seemed, abandoned? It is managed by a kind of repetition of the same stroke, a further shift of the point of view. The spectator, the listener, the reader, is now himself to be placed at the angle of vision; not an account or a report, more or less convincing, is to be offered him, but a direct sight of the matter itself, while it is passing. Nobody expounds or explains; the story is enacted by its look and behavior at particular moments. By the first stroke the narrator was brought into the book and set before the reader; but the action appeared only in his narrative. Now the action is there, proceeding while the pages are turned; the narrator is forestalled, he is watched while the story is in the making. Such is the progress of the writer of fiction towards drama; such is his method of evading the drawbacks of a mere reporter and assuming the advantages, as far as possible of a dramatist. How far he may choose to push the process in his book—that is a matter to be decided by the subject; it entirely depends upon the kind of effect that the theme demands. It may respond to all the dramatization it can get, it may give all that it has to give for less. The subject dictates the method.

And now let the process be reversed, let us start with the purely dramatic subject, the story that will tell itself in perfect rightness, unaided, to the eye of the reader. This story never deviates from a strictly scenic form; one occasion or episode follows another, with no interruption for any reflective summary of events. Necessarily it must be so, for it is only while the episode is proceeding that no question of a narrator can arise; when the scene closes the play ceases till the opening of the next. To glance upon the story from a height and to give a general impression of its course—this is at once to remove the point of view from the reader and to set up a new one somewhere else; the method is no longer consistent, no longer purely dramatic. And the dramatic story is not only scenic, it is also limited to so much as the ear can hear and the eye see. In rigid drama of this kind there is naturally no admission of the reader into the private mind of any of the characters; their thoughts and motives are transmuted into action. A subject wrought to this pitch of objectivity is no doubt given weight and compactness and authority in the highest degree; it is like a piece of modelling, standing in clear space, casting its shadow. It is the most finished form that fiction can take.

But evidently it is not a form to which fiction can aspire in general. It implies many sacrifices, and these will easily seem to be more than the subject can usefully make. It is out of the question, of course, wherever the main burden of the story lies within some particular consciousness, in the study of a soul, the growth of a character, the changing history of a temperament; there the subject would be needlessly crossed and strangled by dramatization pushed to its limit. It is out of the question, again, wherever the story is too big, too comprehensive, too widely ranging, to be treated scenically, with no opportunity for general and panoramic survey; it has been discovered, indeed, that even a story of this kind *may* fall into a long succession of definite scenes, under some hands, but it has also appeared that in doing so it incurs unnecessary disabilities, and will likely suffer. These stories, therefore, which will not naturally accommodate themselves to the reader's point of view, and the reader's alone, we regard as rather pictorial than dramatic—meaning that they call for some narrator, somebody who *knows,* to contemplate the facts and create an impression of them. Whether it is the omniscient author or a man in the book, he must gather up his experience, compose a vision of it as it exists in his mind, and lay *that* before the reader. It is the reflection of an experience; and though there may be all imaginable diversity of treatment within the limits of the reflection, such is its essential character. In a pictorial book the principle of the structure involves a point of view which is not the reader's.

Types of Narration

Wayne C. Booth

We have seen that the author cannot choose to avoid rhetoric; he can choose only the kind of rhetoric he will employ. He cannot choose whether or not to affect his readers' evaluations by his choice of narrative manner; he can only choose whether to do it well or poorly. As dramatists have always known, even the purest of dramas is not purely dramatic in the sense of being entirely presented, entirely shown as taking place in the moment. There are always what Dryden called "relations" to be taken care of, and try as the author may to ignore the troublesome fact, "some parts of the action are more fit to be represented, some to be related."[1] But related by whom? The dramatist must decide, and the novelist's case is different only in that the choices open to him are more numerous.

If we think through the many narrative devices in the fiction we know, we soon come to a sense of the embarrassing inadequacy of our traditional classification of "point of view" into three or four kinds, variables only of the "person" and the degree of omniscience. If we name over three or four of the great narrators—say Cervantes' Cid Hamete Benengeli, Tristam Shandy, the "I" of *Middlemarch,* and Strether, through whose vision most of *The Ambassadors* comes to us, we realize that to describe any of them

Reprinted from *The Rhetoric of Fiction,* by Wayne C. Booth, pp. 140–155 by permission of The University of Chicago Press and Wayne C. Booth.

[1] *An Essay of Dramatic Poesy* (1668). Though this quotation comes from Lisideius, in his defense of French drama, and not from Neander, who seems to speak more nearly for Dryden, the position is taken for granted in Neander's reply; the only dispute is over *which* parts are more fit to be represented.

with terms like "first-person" and "omniscient" tells us nothing about how they differ from each other, or why they succeed while others described in the same terms fail.[2] It should be worth our while, then, to attempt a richer tabulation of the forms the author's voice can take, both as a summary of the preceding chapters and as a basis for Parts II and III.

Person

Perhaps the most overworked distinction is that of person. To say that a story is told in the first or the third person[3] will tell us nothing of importance unless we become more precise and describe how the particular qualities of the narrators relate to specific effects. It is true that choice of the first person is sometimes unduly limiting; if the "I" had inadequate access to necessary information, the author may be led into improbabilities. And there are other effects that may dictate a choice in some cases. But we can hardly expect to find useful criteria in a distinction that throws all fiction into two, or at the most three, heaps. In this pile we see *Henry Esmond,* "A Cask of Amontillado," *Gulliver's Travels,* and *Tristram Shandy.* In that, we have *Vanity Fair, Tom Jones, The Ambassadors,* and *Brave New World.* But in *Vanity Fair* and *Tom Jones* the commentary is in the first person, often resembling more the intimate effect of *Tristram Shandy* than that of many third-person works. And again, the effect of *The Ambassadors* is much closer to that of the great first-person novels, since Strether in large part "narrates" his own story, even though he is always referred to in the third person.

Further evidence that this distinction is less important than has often been claimed is seen in the fact that all of the following functional distinctions apply to both first- and third-person narration alike.

Dramatized and Undramatized Narrators

Perhaps the most inportant differences in narrative effect depend on whether the narrator is dramatized in his own right and on whether his beliefs and characteristics are shared by the author.

[2] There is no point in listing any of the conventional classifications here in order to reject them. They range from the simplest and least useful, in a clever popular essay by C. E. Montage ("'Sez 'e' or 'Thinks 'e,'" *A Writer's Notes on His Trade* [London, 1930; Pelican ed., 1952], pp. 34–35 to the valuable study by Norman Friedman ("Point of View," *PMLA*, LXX [December, 1955], 1160–84).

[3] Efforts to use the second person have never been very successful, but it is astonishing how little real difference even this choice makes. When I am told, at the beginning of a book, "You have put your left foot. . . . You slide through the narrow opening. . . . Your eyes are only half open . . . ," the radical unnaturalness is, it is true, distracting for a time. But in reading Michel Butor's *La Modification* (Paris, 1957), from which this opening comes, it is surprising how quickly one is absorbed into the illusory "present" of the story, identifying one's vision with the "vous" almost as fully as with the "I" and "he" in other stories.

The implied author (the author's "second self") Even the novel in which no narrator is dramatized creates an implicit picture of an author who stands behind the scenes, whether as stage manager, as puppeteer, or as an indifferent God, silently paring his fingernails. This implied author is always distinct from the "real man"—whatever we may take him to be—who creates a superior version of himself, a "second self," as he creates his work.[4]

In so far as a novel does not refer directly to this author, there will be no distinction between him and the implied, undramatized narrator; in Hemingway's "The Killers," for example, there is no narrator other than the implicit second self that Hemingway creates as he writes.

Undramatized narrators Stories are usually not so rigorously impersonal as "The Killers"; most tales are presented as passing through the consciousness of a teller, whether an "I" or a "he." Even in drama much of what we are given is narrated by someone, and we are often as much interested in the effect on the narrator's own mind and heart as we are in learning what *else* the author has to tell us. When Horatio tells of his first encounter with the ghost in *Hamlet,* his own character, though never mentioned, is important to us as we listen. In fiction, as soon as we encounter an "I," we are conscious of an experiencing mind whose views of the experience will come between us and the event. When there is no such "I," as in "The Killers," the inexperienced reader may make the mistake of thinking that the story comes to him unmediated. But no such mistake can be made from the moment that the author explicitly places a narrator into the tale, even if he is given no personal characteristics whatever.

Dramatized narrators In a sense even the most reticent narrator has been dramatized as soon as he refers to himself as "I," or, like Flaubert, tells us that "we" were in the classroom when Charles Bovary entered. But many novels dramatize their narrators with great fulness, making them into characters who are as vivid as those they tell us about *(Tristram Shandy, Remembrance of Things Past, Heart of Darkness, Dr. Faustus).* In such works the narrator is often radically different from the implied author who creates him. The range of human types that have been dramatized as narrators is almost as great as the range of other fictional characters—one must say "almost" because there are some characters who are not fully qualified to narrate or "reflect" a story (Faulkner can use the idiot for *part* of his novel only because the other three parts exist to set off and clarify the idiot's jumble).

We should remind ourselves that many dramatized narrators are never

[4] A fine account of the subtleties that underlie the seemingly simple relations between real authors and the selves they create as they write can be found in "Makers and Persons," by Patrick Cruttwell, *Hudson Review,* XII (Winter, 1959–60), 487–507.

explicitly labeled as narrators at all. In a sense, every speech, every gesture, narrates; most works contain disguised narrators who are used to tell the audience what it needs to know, while seeming to merely act out their roles.

Though disguised narrators of this kind are seldom labeled so explicitly as God in Job, they often speak with an authority as sure as God's. Messengers returning to tell what the oracle said, wives trying to convince their husbands that the business deal is unethical, old family retainers expostulating with wayward scions—these often have more effect on us than on their official auditors; the king goes ahead with his obstinate search, the husband carries out his deal, the hell-bound youth goes on toward hell as if nothing had been said, but *we* know what we know—and as surely as if the author himself or his official narrator had told us. "She's laughing at you to your face, brother," Cleante says to Orgon in *Tartuffe*, "and frankly, without meaning to anger you, I must say she's quite right. Has there ever been the like of such a whim? . . . You must be mad, brother, I swear"[5] And in tragedy there is usually a chorus, a friend, or even a forthright villian, to speak truth in contrast to the tragic mistakes of the hero.

The most important unacknowledged narrators in modern fiction are the third-person "centers of consciousness" through whom authors have filtered their narratives. Whether such "reflectors," as James sometimes called them, are highly polished mirrors reflecting complex mental experience, or the rather turbid, sense-bound "camera eyes" of much fiction since James, they fill precisely the function of avowed narrators—though they *can* add intensities of their own.

> Gabriel had not gone to the door with the others. He was in a dark part of the hall gazing up the staircase. A woman was standing near the top of the first flight, in the shadow also. He could not see her face but he could see the terracotta and salmon-pink panels of her skirt which the shadow made appear black and white. It was his wife. She was leaning on the banisters, listening to something. . . . He asked himself what is a woman standing on the stairs in the shadow, listening to distant music, a symbol of [Joyce's "The Dead"].

The very real advantages of this method, for some purposes, have provided a dominant theme in modern criticism. Indeed, so long as our attention is on such qualities as naturalness and vividness, the advantages seem overwhelming. Only as we break out of the fashionable assumption that all good fiction tries for the same kind of vivid illusion in the same way are we forced to recognize disadvantages. The third-person reflector is only one mode among many, suitable for some effects but cumbersome and even harmful when other effects are desired.

[5] From an unpublished translation by Marcel Gutwirth.

Observers and Narrator-Agents

Among dramatized narrators there are mere observers (the "I" of *Tom Jones, The Egoist, Troilus and Criseyde),* and there are narrator-agents, who produce some measurable effect on the course of events (ranging from the minor involvement of Nick in *The Great Gatsby,* through the extensive give-and-take of Marlow in *Heart of Darkness,*[6] to the central role of Tristram Shandy, Moll Flanders, Huckleberry Finn, and—in the third person—Paul Morel in *Sons and Lovers).* Clearly, any rules we might discover about observers may not apply to narrator-agents, yet the distinction is seldom made in talk about point of view.

Scene and Summary

All narrators and observers, whether first or third person, can relay their tales to us primarily as scene ("The Killers,"*The Awkward Age,* the works of Ivy Compton-Burnett and Henry Green), primarily as summary or what Lubbock called "picture" (Addison's almost completely non-scenic tales in *The Spectator),* or, most commonly, as a combination of the two.

Like Aristotle's distinction between dramatic and narrative manners, the somewhat different modern distinction between showing and telling does cover the ground. But the trouble is that it pays for broad coverage with gross imprecision. Narrators of all shapes and shades must either report dialogue alone or support it with "stage directions" and description of setting. But when we think of the radically different effect of a scene reported by Huck Finn and a scene reported by Poe's Montresor, we see that the quality of being "scenic" suggests very little about literary effect. And compare the delightful summary of twelve years given in two pages of *Tom Jones* (Book III, chap. i) with the tedious showing of even ten minutes of uncurtailed conversation in the hands of a Sartre when he allows his passion for "durational realism" to dictate a scene when summary is called for. The contrast between scene and summary, between showing and telling, is likely to be of little use until we specify the kind of narrator who is providing the scene or the summary.

Commentary

Narrators who allow themselves to tell as well as show vary greatly depending on the amount and kind of commentary allowed in addition to a direct

[6] For a careful interpretation of the development and functions of Marlow in Conrad's works, see W. Y. Tindall, "Apology for Marlow," in *From Jane Austen to Joseph Conrad,* ed. Robert C. Rathburn and Martin Steinmann, Jr. (Minneapolis, Minn., 1958), pp. 274–85. Though Marlow is often himself a victim of Conrad's ironies, he is generally a reliable reflector of the clarities and ambiguities of the implied author. A much fuller treatment, and a remarkable work for an undergraduate, is James L. Guetti, Jr., *The Rhetoric of Joseph Conrad* "Amherst College Honors Thesis," No. 2 [Amherst, Mass., 1960]).

relating of events in scene and summary. Such commentary can, of course, range over any aspect of human experience, and it can be related to the main business in innumerable ways and degrees. To treat it as a single device is to ignore important differences between commentary that is merely ornamental, commentary that serves a rhetorical purpose but is not part of the dramatic structure, and commentary that is integral to the dramatic structure, as in *Tristram Shandy.*

Self-conscious Narrators

Cutting across the distinction between observers and narrator-agents of all kinds is the distinction between *self-conscious narrators,* aware of themselves as writers *(Tom Jones, Tristram Shandy, Barchester Towers, The Catcher in the Rye, Remembrance of Things Past, Dr. Faustus),* and narrators or observers who rarely if ever discuss their writing chores *(Huckleberry Finn)* or who seem unaware that they are writing, thinking, speaking, or "reflecting" a literary work (Camus's *The Stranger,* Lardner's "Haircut," Bellow's *The Victim).*

Setting

Henry M. Beyle

Setting in narrative fiction may be defined as the backdrop (geographical location, historical moment, and general cultural environment) against which the action of a story or novel takes place. Like the background in a painting or photograph, setting is often unobtrusive or taken for granted, and yet it is one of the essential ingredients in a narrative. A story or novel must take place somewhere and at a particular time. Although it may function in many ways, the primary purpose of setting is to render fictional scenes vivid (i.e., visualizable) and clear and thus permit the reader to *feel* the world in which the characters are living. In fiction that is fundamentally realistic, a vaguely defined setting is almost always a weakness. The writer knows that the more a reader can visualize in a narrative, the more fully he may be able to participate in the story. Such stories as "Mademoiselle Fifi," "The Sire of Maletroit's Door," and "The Bride Comes to Yellow Sky" clearly require vivid settings, but there are stories in which a sense of place and time is incidental to the overall effect of the work. For example, setting is of only peripheral interest in "William Wilson" and "The Beast in the Jungle."

"There are . . . three ways only of writing a story," wrote Robert Louis Stevenson. "You may take a plot and fit characters to it, or you may take a character and choose incidents and situations to develop it, or lastly . . . you may take a certain atmosphere and get actions and persons to express and realize it.[1] In this third way of writing a story, the author employs set-

Printed here by permission of Henry M. Beyle.

[1] Here Stevenson uses "atmosphere" in the nineteenth-century sense to mean setting. Atmosphere is no longer regarded as synonymous with setting but is the emotional ambiance or mood that emerges from the various elements in a work, especially from setting. In Elizabeth Bowen's "The Demon Lover" the atmosphere of foreboding is dependent on the setting (World War Two, the empty house, the ominous weather).

ting as an active agent in the narrative, indicating its molding influence on the character or characters. We are all aware how in reality environment influences man's attitudes and behavior, how to some extent we are all products of where and when we live. For example, the man reared in Manhattan, accustomed to man-made canyons of glass and steel and inured to noises and overcrowding, will obviously view life differently from the man living in the quiet, windswept openness of Laramie, Wyoming. By description and focusing techniques a writer may choose to emphasize this characteristic of place or setting. In many novels characters come to express, in Stevenson's words, the setting of the American West, ghetto life, and so on. In extreme cases men become the playthings of their setting, and in such narratives setting may determine theme. In George Moore's "Home Sickness" the setting of a parochial, oppressive Ireland forces James Bryden to make a decision that will profoundly influence the course of his life. William Faulkner uses setting as an active force in "The Old People," showing the pervasive impact of the woods on Isaac McCaslin and other characters in the story.

By presenting it as an obstacle to be overcome, some writers rely on setting to precipitate a story's dramatic conflict. The author builds a tension between character and setting, as in those stories in which protagonist struggles against a hellish day in the desert, a Nebraska blizzard, or even the dispiriting environment of a slum. Jack London's well-known story "To Build a Fire" is a fine example of the clashing of character and setting in a dramatic situation.

In some stories the author may suffuse his narrative with descriptions of a singular place and time, creating a distinct flavor to the setting. Such local color writing emphasizes the unique quality of the region and its people and may indicate the indirect influence of setting on the characters. In Hardy's "The Three Strangers," for example, one appreciates a distinct, appealing flavor to the Wessex locale. However, Hardy—and many lesser local color writers—occasionally exaggerates his picturesque settings, indulging in description for its own sake.